THE MAGE-FIRE WAR

A Tom Doherty Associates Book

NEW YORK

This is a work of fiction. All of the characters, organizations, and events portrayed in this novel are either products of the author's imagination or are used fictitiously.

THE MAGE-FIRE WAR

Edited by Jen Gunnels

A Tor Book
Published by Tom Doherty Associates
120 Broadway
New York, NY 10271

www.tor-forge.com

Tor® is a registered trademark of Macmillan Publishing Group, LLC.

The Library of Congress Cataloging-in-Publication Data is available upon request.

ISBN 978-1-250-20782-1 (hardcover)
ISBN 978-1-250-20781-4 (ebook)

Our books may be purchased in bulk for promotional, educational, or business use. Please contact your local bookseller or the Macmillan Corporate and Premium Sales Department at 1-800-221-7945, extension 5442, or by email at MacmillanSpecialMarkets@macmillan.com.

First Edition: August 2019

Printed in the United States of America

0 9 8 7 6 5 4 3 2 1

For Cameron,

. . . and unexpected legacies

CHARACTERS

Beltur *Black mage and healer*
Jessyla *Healer*
Lhadoraak *Black mage*
Tulya *Consort of Lhadoraak*
Taelya *Beginning white mage, daughter of Lhadoraak and Tulya*
Korlyssa *Duchess of Montgren*
Korsaen *Protector of Montgren*
Maeyora *Trader and consort of Korsaen*
Margrena *Healer, mother of Jessyla*
Athaal *Black mage (deceased), partner of Meldryn*
Meldryn *Black mage, baker*
Barrynt *Merchant, Axalt (deceased)*
Johlana *Consort of Barrynt, sister of Jorhan*
Jorhan *Smith*
Massyngal *Duke of Hydlen*
Halacut *Duke of Lydiar*
Raelf *Captain, Montgren*
Cheld *Undercaptain, Montgren*

Northern
Candar
Gulf of Murr
Gulf of Candar
Recluce
Eastern Ocean
The WORLD
EMitchell 1995

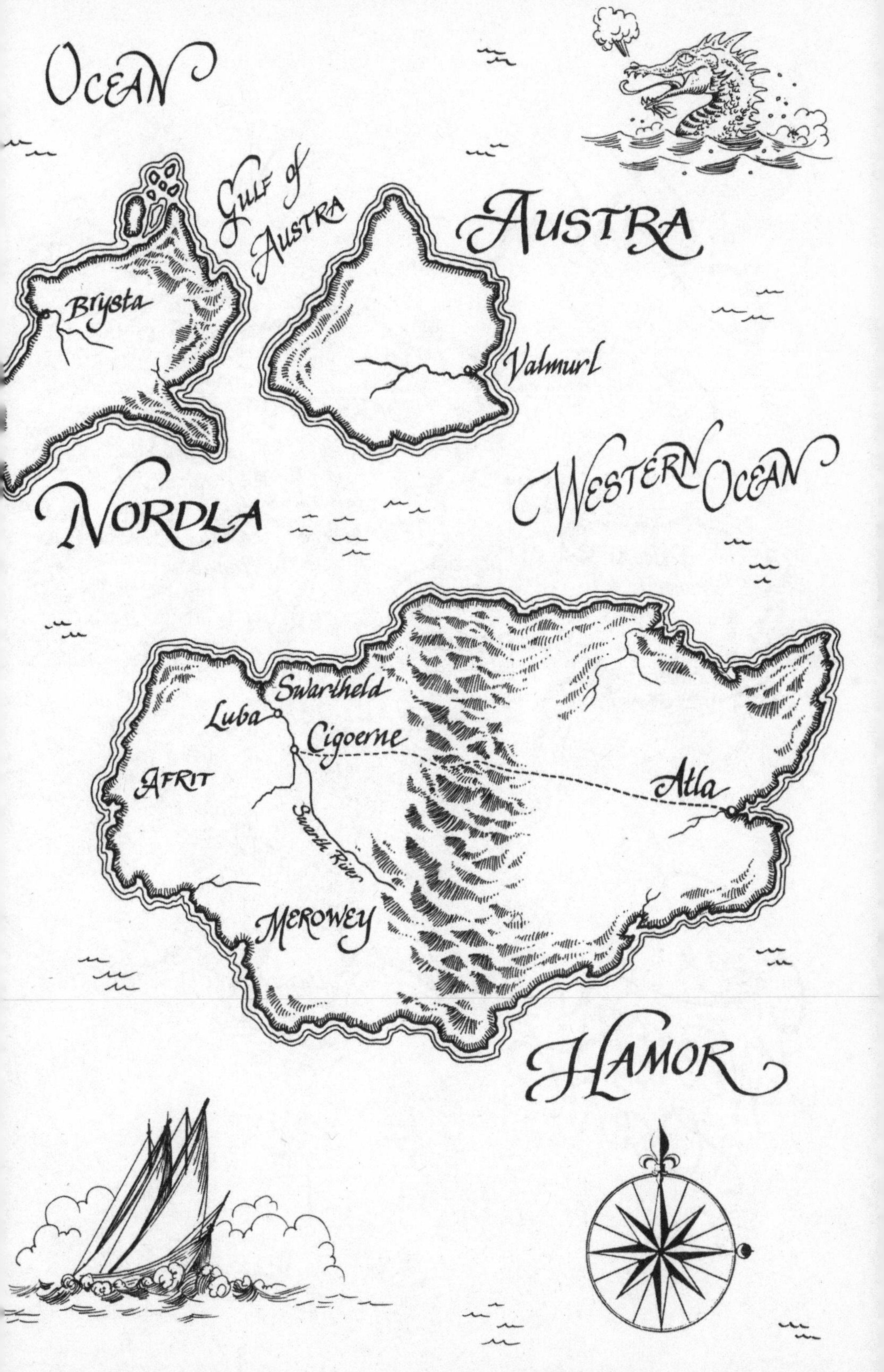

OCEAN

AUSTRA

GULF OF AUSTRA

Brysta

Valmurl

NORDLA

WESTERN OCEAN

Swartheld

Luba

Cigoerne

AFRIT

Atla

Swarth River

MEROWEY

HAMOR

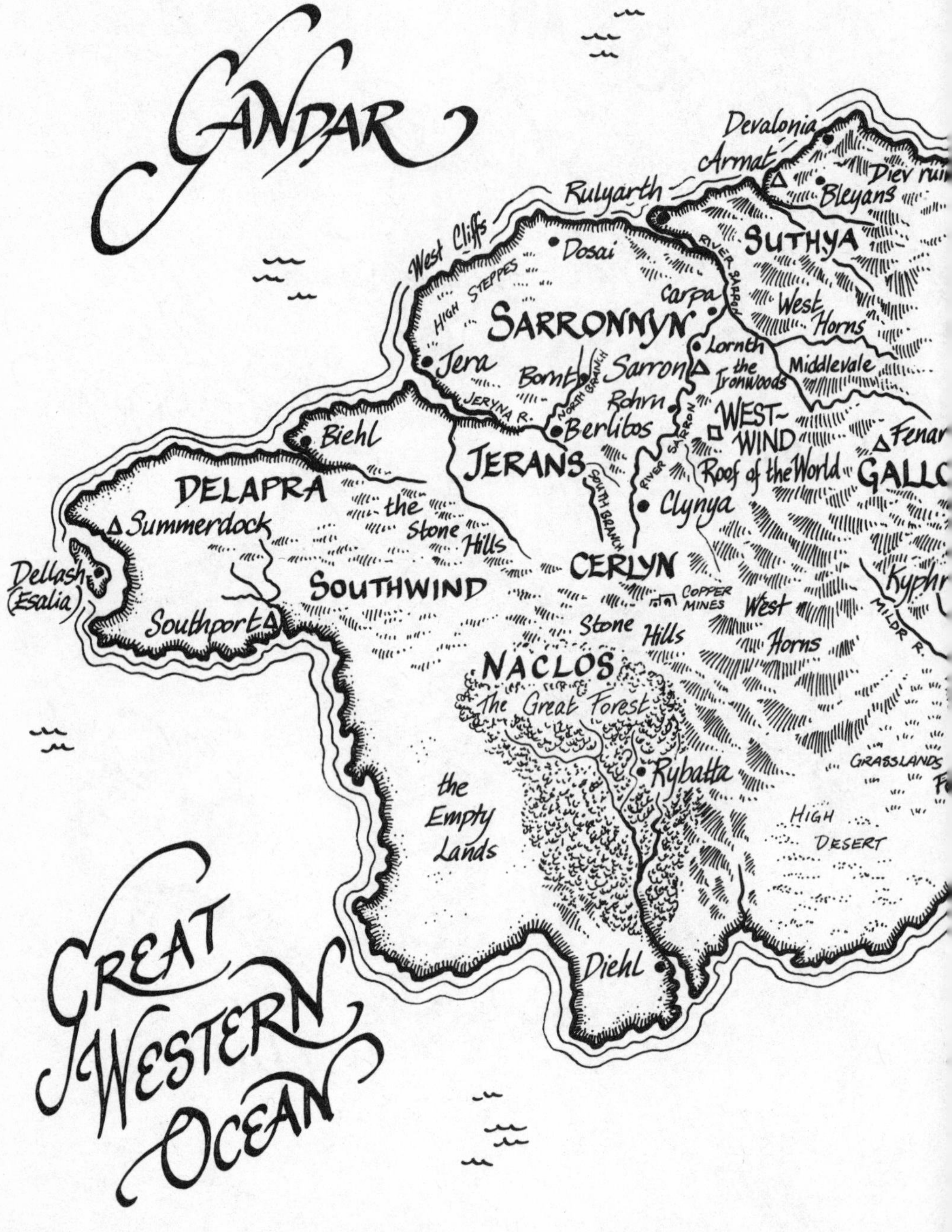

GANDAR

Devalonia
Armat
Diev ruin
Rulyarth
Bleyans
West Cliffs
SUTHYA
Dosai
RIVER SARRON
HIGH STEPPES
Carpa
West
Horns
SARRONNYN
Lornth
Jera
Bornt
NORTH BRANCH
Sarron
the
Ironwoods
Middlevale
Rohrn
JERYNA R.
WEST-
WIND
Biehl
Berlibos
RIVER SARRON
Fenard
JERANS
Roof of the World
GALLOS
DELAPRA
SOUTH BRANCH
Clynya
the
Summerdock
Stone
Hills
Dellash
(Esalia)
CERLYN
Kyphros
SOUTHWIND
COPPER
MINES
West
MILDR R.
Southport
Stone
Hills
Horns
NACLOS
The Great Forest
GRASSLANDS
Rybatta
the
Empty
Lands
HIGH
DESERT
Diehl

GREAT
WESTERN
OCEAN

Northern Ocean

Gulf of Murr
Land's End
Black Holding
Extina
Alberth
Reflin
Lydkler
Alaren
Feyn R.
Iron Works
Mattra
Feyn
Wandernaught
Clarion
Enstronn
Sigil
Nylan
Southpoint

Cape Devalin
Spidlaria
Spidlar
Quend
Kleth
East Horns
Elparta
Tyrhaven
Gulf of Candar
Sligo
Rytel
Lavah
Certis
Jellico
Montgren
Vergren
Great North Bay
Weevett
Fiven
Freetown
Tellura
Hydolar
Freetown (Lydiar)
Meltosia
Ohyde River
Renklaar
Kyphros
Hydlen
Dasir
Telsen
Asula
Arastia
Pyrdya
Sunta
Faklaar
Sturbal R.
High Desert
Fakla River
Ruzor
Worrak

Recluce

Eastern Ocean

C. Mitchell 1995

THE MAGE-FIRE WAR

I

For Beltur and Jessyla, eightday at Lord Korsaen's near-palatial dwelling was quiet, although the two spent some of the day talking and worrying, and some eating excellent fare, and Beltur spent some of it in Korsaen's library looking for anything that might shed light on Haven, the town where he, Jessyla, Lhadoraak, and Tulya would be councilors. He found nothing. He even scanned *The Wisdom of Relyn* to see if Relyn had written anything about Vergren or Haven. Relyn hadn't.

Oneday was much different. By eighth glass, Beltur and Lhadoraak were in the library sitting at a table looking at a stack of documents, as well as two slim volumes, one of which contained the code of laws of Montgren and the other of which set forth tariff procedures and schedules. Beltur started with the tariff volume and handed the legal book to Lhadoraak.

The fashion in which the duchy assessed tariffs was unlike anything Beltur had seen or heard of. The first surprise was that every building in Montgren paid a yearly tariff to the duchy and to the nearest town. The town got two parts in three; the duchy the other part. Likewise, every crafter and every shop or other business paid a tariff every season. Finally, every inn or public house paid an additional tariff based on the number of rooms and the amount of spirits consumed. One of the duties of a town council was to verify and keep track of both.

Beltur took a deep breath. He'd only read ten pages. He looked up at Lhadoraak. "I hope you're enjoying what you're learning more than I am."

"I was hoping the same," returned the blond black mage.

"Our consorts are going to have to read these as well," said Beltur.

"You can tell them both," said Lhadoraak, glancing toward the library door through which Jessyla and Tulya had just entered.

"Tell us what?" asked Tulya.

"That you're going to need to read what we're reading when we finish," said Beltur. "About tariffs and laws. Since we *are* the Council of Haven, or will be shortly . . ."

"Is there anything in these documents about whether there's a healing house?" asked Jessyla.

"I don't know," said Beltur. "Why don't you two read through the papers and see what you think is most important. Oh . . . and let me know if there are maps of the town, or the roads around it."

He struggled on with the tariff book, and for a time, there was silence in the library.

Abruptly, Tulya looked up. "I found a town map! It shows the square, a town hall, and lots of buildings, two inns with names, a rendering yard at the edge of town, and roads coming in and out."

"Is it recent?"

"It doesn't look that way. The paper is yellow." After several moments, Tulya added, "It says that it faithfully represents Haven in the fifth year of the rule of Duke Korlaan."

"If you'd keep looking for other maps . . ."

Tulya nodded.

After a time, Jessyla said, "There was a healing house, because there's an old letter here to a Duke Korslyn informing him that there are no healers in Haven and that the town can no longer afford to maintain the healing house."

Almost another glass passed before Korsaen entered the library. "I thought you'd like to know that Korwaen, Taelya, and Maenya are enjoying themselves together. I also thought you might like to take a break from your studies and have some refreshments."

"We'd appreciate that," said Beltur. "We do have a question. The only town map seems to be one made in the time of a Duke Korlaan. Do you know when that was?"

"Korlaan was Korlyssa's grandsire," replied Korsaen.

"I'm confused," said Jessyla, although Beltur doubted anything of the sort. "Korlyssa is the Duchess, and she's your aunt. You said that she was the only heir and had a daughter who would succeed her. That means either your father or mother was a brother or sister to the Duchess, and the Duchess-heiress is your cousin. Where do you fit in?"

"I said the Duchess was the only surviving heir. My mother was her younger sister. She died having me. My father was killed in a border skirmish with Lydian raiders when I was ten."

"I'm sorry," said Jessyla contritely.

"I should have made that clear to you. It's something everyone in Montgren knows. I sometimes forget that others don't."

"There's rather a lot we don't know," said Beltur wryly, gesturing to the pile of documents.

"Those are things you can learn. The skills you can't learn from papers and books are the reason why you're here. There's one other thing I might mention. Captain Raelf heads the post in Weevett. He's very good, and he understands both the Hydlenese and the Lydians." Korsaen offered a wryly amused smile. "He should. He served in both forces."

"Did he come here, or was he another one of your 'finds'?" asked Beltur.

Korsaen shook his head. "One of Maeyora's. Sometimes . . . let's just say that she sometimes knows how things should turn out."

"Druid foresight? Like that of Ryba?" asked Jessyla.

"How would we know?" replied Korsaen almost enigmatically.

Jessyla raised her eyebrows, but only said, "Oh, and one other question. Duke Korslyn?"

"He was Korlyssa's father and my grandfather." Korsaen looked quizzically at Jessyla.

"There was a letter to him about closing the healing house in Haven because there were no healers and not enough silvers to keep it open," she replied.

"I can see where that would concern you. Are you ready for some refreshments?"

All four smiled and rose.

As they left the library, Beltur glanced back. *You never thought . . .*

He shook his head. He could definitely use an ale.

II

By dinner on twoday, a light rain was falling, but it ended within a glass, and on threeday morning, Beltur and the others were up early, getting ready to ride to the gates of the palace to meet the armsmen who would escort them to Haven. Beltur took special care in seeing that the proclamations and documents were well-sealed in oilcloth. He also checked the other belt under his tunic, the one with the two hundred golds from the Duchess in it. His hidden wallet held his own personal golds, all twenty-one of them, while his belt wallet held silvers and coppers. He also checked to see that the load on the mule was securely in place.

Korsaen led his own mount out of the stable and joined the group as they were preparing to mount. "I'll ride over with you and introduce you to Captain Karch."

"Did you have any difficulty arranging for the armsmen?" asked Beltur.

"No. There's always one company ready to ride on a day's notice, and most towns are within a day's ride of a company. No town is more than two days' ride. That's one advantage of being a small land."

"Another being that, like Axalt, the effort to conquer you would never repay itself," said Beltur.

"Only because we maintain a very effective battalion of armsmen."

"Does your title mean Lord Commander?" asked Jessyla.

"No. I offer suggestions, but Commander Pastyn is in charge." With a smile, Korsaen swung himself up into the saddle.

Beltur and the others mounted, as did the two guards, who moved into position behind the others.

Once everyone was moving smoothly, with Beltur and Jessyla flanking Korsaen, Beltur said, "You know that settling down everything in Haven is going to take time."

"Most constructive things do. The Duchess is well aware of that. It took time to find the four—" Korsaen glanced back at Taelya. "—the five of you."

Beltur had to smile at the addition of Taelya, but didn't say more as they neared the avenue and then turned onto it.

As they rode north, Korsaen gestured ahead. "I see Captain Karch has everything in position."

The mounted troopers were in double files stretching back in the direction of the palace something like half a kay, including the two supply wagons and the four-horse teams. The captain and two scouts or outriders were drawn up even with the outer gates to the palace grounds.

As he rode closer, Beltur studied the captain, who looked to be about Beltur's size, if slightly heavier, and at least a good twenty years older, with gray hair streaked with white. He wore, as did all the troopers, a uniform of what looked to be almost faded blue, or light grayish blue, a color, Beltur realized, that would make a man far harder to see during the morning mists or twilight.

Korsaen reined up short of the captain, and the others reined up behind the lord.

"Captain, meet the new Council of Haven. Mage Beltur, Healer Jessyla, Mage Lhadoraak, Councilor Tulya. The younger woman is mage-apprentice Taelya." Korsaen gestured to each as he spoke. "I suggest that, for the ride through Vergren, the new council all ride with you at the head of the column. Beyond that, the deployment of your forces should be as you and Mage Beltur determine is necessary."

Karch inclined his head. "I accept this duty and mission, Lord Korsaen, in full knowledge of my obligations and duty to the duchy."

Korsaen eased his mount to the side of the avenue. "My best to all of you."

Karch gestured to the outriders and then guided his mount forward. "If you, Mage Beltur and Healer Jessyla, will flank me, and if the other councilors will follow us, then we will proceed."

In moments, the column was moving toward the center of Vergren.

"If it wouldn't discommode you, ser," said Karch to Beltur, "once we get through Vergren and are established in good order on the old south road, it might prove helpful for me to spend some time riding with each of you."

"Then I'd suggest you begin riding with Jessyla and me, and then when you think you have learned what you need to know, at least for now, you can let us know, and we'll switch positions."

"Thank you, ser."

Given that it was barely past sixth glass, there were few people on the main street that led to the square, but all those who were there definitely stopped and looked at the riders as they passed. Instead of continuing through the square to the road that had brought Beltur and the others to Vergren, the outriders turned left at the square and then followed that road out of the city. Roughly two kays later, as they passed the last of the cottages that were clearly in the city, Lhadoraak, Tulya, and Taelya dropped back to ride with the rearguard squad.

Karch wasted no time in looking to Beltur. "Lord Korsaen said you were an undercaptain and war mage in Spidlar."

"I was, during the invasion. So was Lhadoraak. Jessyla was one of the healers."

"I've never thought of black mages as warlike."

"We didn't have much choice."

"Might I ask how . . ."

"I was assigned first to a recon company. I discovered that Slowpoke, here, was strong enough that if I expanded my shields, we could smash through a line of troopers . . ." Beltur went on to explain how he'd used shields in battle, including blocking chaos bolts, and how iron arrows helped weaken white mages. ". . . and it turned out that when the whites couldn't use their chaos bolts, we could break their lines."

Karch nodded, then said, "Lord Korsaen mentioned your doing something to kill brigands."

"I can place a containment around a man tightly enough that he'll suffocate. But I have to hold it until he actually dies. It's rather time-consuming and takes effort."

"Then, might I ask how you killed white mages?"

"I had archers loose iron-headed arrows at them, and I put more order into the arrowheads. Usually, it took a number of arrows."

"Then you were close to the front?" Karch's words verged on the skeptical.

"Too many times, Captain," interjected Jessyla, almost acidly, "he *was* the front. He almost died twice. Five other blacks did die."

Karch stiffened in the saddle for a moment. "I see." His tone was placating, almost condescending.

"I don't think you do," said Jessyla coldly. "Without Beltur, Spidlar would have lost. The Council never appreciated what he did. In fact, they tried to kill him afterwards. I do hope you don't make that mistake."

"Healer . . . I was just trying to learn what you and the mages can do."

"I can do this." Jessyla abruptly threw a containment around Karch, holding it until he began to turn reddish before releasing. Beltur could tell that it had taken quite an effort on her part. Then she said, "I'm not just a healer, and Beltur is far more than just a mage."

Karch coughed several times, then managed a wry smile. "I apologize for any condescension you may have felt. I've never dealt with strong blacks before. I also suspect that the renegade traitors in Haven will be more surprised than I was."

Beltur could sense the truth behind the captain's words, as well as other feelings, one of which might have been consternation at Jessyla's words and actions. He also couldn't help but notice that Karch was not breathing as well as he had been, although he couldn't detect any wound chaos in the older captain's chest.

"I do have another question, one I ask out of ignorance. You mentioned shields. What if you should be taken unawares . . . ?"

"Lhadoraak, Jessyla, and I have some shields up all the time. Those don't take much effort. We don't shield many others for very long because the larger the shield the more strength it requires. So if someone loosed a shaft from a distance, we might not detect it fast enough to protect others." That wasn't completely true for a number of reasons, but Beltur didn't want to go into details.

"Then you don't require armsmen to shield you. What about the girl? Lord Korsaen said she was an apprentice mage."

"That was a courtesy. She has magely abilities, but not yet those of a full apprentice. She can raise very light shields for a short time. Enough to stop one or two shafts."

"That's more than some full-grown blacks."

"Taelya's had to learn more, earlier. She wasn't exactly welcome in either Elparta or Axalt. She showed magely abilities far earlier than most mages. That was considered less than propitious. That was why Lhadoraak and Tulya had to leave both."

"That's incredibly shortsighted. We've had to . . ." Karch broke off his words.

"Lord Korsaen has mentioned that. He was the one who let us know that we'd be welcome here."

"He and the Duchess and her daughter are the reason Montgren has not been conquered."

"We gathered that it might be something like that."

"Lord Korsaen also said," added Jessyla, "that you and your men are part of the best battalion of troopers in Candar."

Although her words flustered the captain, from the reaction of his natural order and chaos, Karch gave no outward sign, but said, "Lord Korsaen is kind."

"He's also very practical," said Beltur dryly. "That's why all of us are here."

Karch offered a hint of a smile. "Just so."

The rest of Karch's questions were more about how and why Beltur and Jessyla had ended up in Montgren.

Less than a glass later, Beltur and Jessyla dropped back to the rear guard and let the captain get better acquainted with Lhadoraak, Tulya, and Taelya.

Once there and riding alone at the head of Fifth Squad, Jessyla looked to Beltur and asked, "Did you notice that Karch struggled to breathe after I put that containment around him? There's no chaos there, but his lungs are weak. I think he might be even older than he looks."

"That might mean that Korsaen has trouble getting good officers."

Jessyla nodded. "I have another question. If we're successful and actually establish ourselves in some sort of position of power, what's to stop the Duchess from throwing us out?"

Beltur laughed softly. "Because they've obviously tried everything else, and she's not a fool. Even when we straighten things out, without us she can't afford to hold on to Haven. The fact that she's willing to give us the town is a desperate gamble on her part."

"Isn't it one on our part to try this?"

"Is it that much greater than what we did to leave Spidlar? Both of our interests lie in our success."

"I like it that you didn't say 'if we're successful.'"

So did Beltur. He just hoped he wasn't being unduly optimistic. But then, both Korsaen and the gambler had reminded him that everything in life was a gamble.

And what's worth gambling for more than the chance to direct our own lives from here on out?

III

Despite the early departure from Vergren, the white sun was low in the west when Karch pointed to the stone marker that listed Weevett as five kays ahead.

"We made good time, Mage."

"Good weather helps." Beltur wasn't about to mention that he didn't much care for the warm damp air with which much of Montgren seemed to be blessed.

"The post where we'll be staying is on the west edge of the town."

"Closer to the border with Certis," replied Beltur. "How many companies are posted there?"

"Just one. Quarters are tight when two companies are there."

"Have you had trouble with the Certans recently?"

"No. Their border guards are well-disciplined. They stay on their land, and we stay on ours."

"What about Hydlen?" asked Jessyla.

"I suspect that's why the Duchess wants you to put Haven right again. I don't see the Certans as a problem. The Gallosians, maybe, because they might support the Hydlenese."

While the size of the meadows and tilled fields around the cots flanking the road lessened somewhat as the group neared Weevett, all the cots were neat and well-tended, as were the flocks of sheep. The cottages at the edge of the town were of dusty yellow brick, and the roofs were of wooden shingles. The square in the center of the town still had vendors there, with others packing their carts, a good sign of a prosperous place given that few crops could possibly have been harvested besides early berries, and, of course, dairy products.

As they rode west from the square, the paved avenue soon gave way to a graveled but smooth road. Ahead, Beltur caught sight of yellow brick walls, set back no more than fifteen yards from the road, walls barely three yards high and not all that prepossessing. Nor were the iron-bound gates more than a few digits thick. The inner courtyard was brick-paved and spacious enough to contain a large quarters building, an equally large stable, and several other buildings.

Close to a glass later, after dealing with the horses, the mule, and other matters, Beltur and Jessyla stood in the small room for visiting officers, a space barely four yards by three with a narrow table with one pitcher and washbasin, wall pegs for clothes, and two narrow bunk beds. All the wood was the dark gold of aged oak.

Beltur looked at the two beds and shook his head.

"Four days in a lord's mansion, and you're already spoiled," offered Jessyla with a smile.

"I could hope, especially with what's waiting for us in Haven."

"Right now, I'm hoping for a decent hot meal."

After washing up, the two left the room and made their way toward the officers' mess. They'd only taken a few steps when Lhadoraak, Tulya, and Taelya joined them. When they reached the officers' mess, little more than a single table in a small room off the troopers' mess, Karch was already there, standing by the table and talking to another officer, also a captain from his collar insignia, but one who was balding and whose remaining hair was a pale gray, yet he was clearly younger than Karch. A much younger undercaptain stood a few paces back. All three officers looked up as the five approached.

"Ah . . . mages," said Karch. "This is Captain Raelf . . . and Undercaptain Cheld."

Raelf sat at one end of the table, with Beltur and Jessyla each sitting on a side next to him. Cheld was seated between Jessyla and Taelya, while Karch was at the other end of the table flanked by Lhadoraak and Tulya.

Once everyone was seated, two rankers immediately appeared with large bowls, baskets of bread, and pitchers. The bowls contained burhka and overfried sliced potatoes. The only beverage in the pitchers, Beltur soon discovered, was an amber lager, almost as bitter as the brews Beltur's uncle had preferred.

Beltur's first mouthful of the burhka told him that it was as highly spiced as any burhka he'd ever had, and the potatoes that followed were about as greasy as any he'd ever tasted. *At least it's all warm and cooked.*

After several moments, Raelf said pleasantly, "I understand you're the new councilors for Haven. I can't say that I envy you."

"Have you seen the town recently?" asked Jessyla.

"Two eightdays ago, I accompanied a squad there. There was almost no one there when we rode in, although it was obvious that there had been many people at what pass for inns there. They departed just before we arrived." Raelf shook his head. "It's been like that for over a year. Last summer, a squad stayed for an eightday. No travelers or traders appeared. I'm sure there were people there within glasses of the time the squad left."

"Has anyone considered posting a unit there permanently?" asked Beltur.

Raelf smiled gently. "I recommended that over a year ago. I've worried about Haven for some time."

"What was the reaction?" asked Jessyla.

"I was asked to send a proposal to the Duchess, detailing how many men it would require and what the costs would be for a permanent post there. I did. I was commended for my efforts and told the matter was under consideration."

"Can you tell us what the costs would be?"

"I reported it would take a minimum of two squads plus an undercaptain and a senior squad leader. Considering all the reasonable costs—I calculated that it would cost a minimum of ten golds an eightday, possibly even fifteen in the fall and winter. But then, costs tend to be more than you think."

Beltur almost choked on the bitter lager. *Between five hundred and seven hundred golds a year!* "I don't quite understand one thing," he said, knowing as he spoke that there was far more than one thing he didn't understand. "The Duchess doesn't tariff goods that come and go from Montgren. So why are there smugglers?"

"The Viscount does. So does the Duke of Lydiar. The Duke of Hydlen tariffs outlanders but not his own people. The smugglers, especially the Gallosians, use the old road because it's easier to avoid the Certan and Hydlenese tariff inspectors. They're all rather tough, and they want things their way."

"What would happen if we merely insisted that they behave?"

"They'd try to kill you or run you out." Raelf smiled wryly. "If . . . *if* you beat them and outlasted them, before too long, things would go back the way they were years ago. They'd put up with being orderly because they'd still make silvers, but they haven't had to for years."

"What's the worst thing we could do?" asked Beltur.

"Do nothing, but try to collect past-due tariffs," replied Raelf.

"If you had been sent with a company, what would you have done first?" asked Jessyla.

"Restore order. For small offenses, give the offender a warning. For the second offense, give them the maximum punishment under the duchy's laws. Don't try to do everything at once. Make the inns safe for everyone, first. Then do what you can. Those are my thoughts." Raelf grinned. "I'm just glad it's you and not me." The grin faded.

Beltur took another small swallow of the bitter lager.

Raelf cleared his throat and addressed Lhadoraak. "I understand that two of you were pressed into service as arms-mages against the Gallosians. He mentioned something I found interesting—you said that iron arrows could weaken white mages. What about strong white mages?"

Lhadoraak looked down the table. "Beltur had more experience with that."

Beltur set down his beaker. "Iron holds order naturally. That makes iron arrows dangerous to chaos mages. They can block the arrows, but each one that they block weakens them. I added a little order to some of the arrows. In one instance, there were enough arrows aimed at a mage that they killed him, and he exploded when the ordered iron pierced his shield. It can be hard on the archers shooting at a mage, though, unless they're shielded by a black."

"Still . . . that bears some thought," mused Raelf.

"Why do you say that?" asked Tulya.

"Montgren has few mages of any sort, and both Certis and Hydlen are known to have white mages that can accompany their troopers. Anything that could limit or weaken them might be useful."

Hydlen has whites that accompany their troopers? Beltur didn't recall that coming up before. He took another swallow of the ale. It was still bitter.

IV

Beltur and Jessyla rode at the head of the column, flanking Captain Karch, as they made their way out of Weevett at sixth glass on fourday morning. As before, Lhadoraak, Tulya, and Taelya rode with the rear guard, the mule with their own goods and provisions, and the two supply wagons.

Karch had been politely insistent after dinner the evening before, saying, "Ser, it would be best if we leave Weevett early so that we can arrive in Haven before midafternoon."

Beltur half smiled as he remembered the captain's less direct way of stating that it would be foolish to arrive late in the afternoon.

Once they were well clear of Weevett, heading south-southeast, Beltur said, "There don't seem to be many travelers."

"Just folks going to or from Hydolar. Almost no one goes to Haven anymore." The captain shrugged. "Anyone coming from Lydiar to Montgren or Jellico will take the shorter road that cuts off the Lydiar road east of Haven."

"Captain Raelf seems to have thought a great deal about Haven."

"He's thought a great deal about many things. He may be leaving Weevett before long. The word is that he'll be promoted to majer and become second to Commander Pastyn."

"Is he from somewhere in Montgren?"

"No, he's from Renklaar. He started there, and became a senior squad leader in the forces of the Duke of Hydlen, then went to Lydiar, where he was an undercaptain for five or six years. Then he came to Montgren."

Beltur shook his head. He should have remembered that Korsaen had said something like that, but it did explain why such an apparently capable officer was only a captain. "Did Lord Korsaen have anything to do with that?"

"I couldn't say, ser. I do know that Lord Korsaen respects ability, no matter where it comes from. All that Raelf has said was that the only ability rewarded in Hydlen was blind obedience, and the ability most rewarded in Lydiar was blind loyalty, and that was one reason why he came to Montgren. One of the unspoken rules is that we never ask where someone came from, only where they last served and in what capacity."

"Very practical," said Jessyla.

"The other rule is that we never share what another officer says about his past, except to the commander or Lord Korsaen. In your capacity, you and the others are considered officers."

"Thank you."

"The Duchess would have it no other way." Karch smiled pleasantly.

"I take it that there are few if any brigands plaguing the roads here."

"There have been no reports of anything—except on the road from

Haven to southern Certis and Gallos. Such reports are suspect, since they serve the interests of the Prefect or the Duke of Hydlen."

"Are town councils responsible for dealing with brigands near the town?"

"Only within the town proper." Karch paused, then added, "Or relatively nearby."

While Beltur doubted that any brigands were anywhere close, or that they'd stay around with a hundred mounted armsmen riding down the road, he still kept his senses out, as much to stay in practice knowing who and what was nearby—because he'd certainly need to know that for a long time to come. *Most likely for the rest of your life, one way or another.*

Slightly past midday, Karch cleared his throat. "According to the map and what I recall, Haven's less than ten kays away. We should be reaching a crossroads of sorts before long."

"A crossroads of sorts?"

"The road we're on joins the old road between Lydiar and Gallos that traders used to take to Jellico. West of that junction there's a newer road that forks off toward Hydolar. The border with Hydlen's only about five kays southwest of the crossroads . . . or what passes for one."

"I thought it was shorter to go through Weevett to Jellico."

"It is, now, ser. But before the grandsire of the Duchess built the road from Weevett through the hills and the shorter cutoff that goes from the Lydiar road to Weevett, the only way was through Haven. The shortest way from Hydolar to Lydiar is still through Haven."

"So the traders who've taken over Haven are likely from Hydolar?"

"Or they're smugglers who use the old roads to avoid the Viscount's and Duke's tariff inspectors." Before that long, Karch said, "You can see the old road just ahead."

"I do." Beltur could not only see the road about a kay ahead, but also sense a man on a slope above the junction, most likely in a tree, with a mount below, not that he could see either.

He had only ridden a few yards farther when he sensed that the man had mounted his horse. "Someone posted a watcher above the junction. He's riding toward Haven."

Karch snorted. "All the renegades will be gone by the time we reach the town. Majer Staarkyn said that would likely happen."

Beltur nodded. That was certainly what the Duchess had expected as well. "Is he the one that Captain Raelf might replace?"

"He is. He's the oldest majer ever in Montgren, and he asked to take a stipend beginning on the first day of summer."

Those words raised questions about the number of older officers, but questions that Beltur saw no point in voicing. He was more concerned with the fast-moving rider, but could only keep track of him for a time, because he was riding faster than Beltur and the others.

Just as Karch had said, the road from Weevett effectively ended—or made a sharp left turn to the east. The old road continued westward, but Beltur couldn't sense where the road to Hydolar branched off, and that meant it was more than two kays to the west. Farther to the southwest was a much taller hill, but the ground directly to the south had a definite slope to it, and the road heading toward Haven looked to have a gradual rise.

There were more than a few tracks on the road toward Haven, and not just those of the rider who had recently fled. The area around the junction seemed almost unsettled, with two ramshackle cots a half kay apart and some twenty yards back from the road. Trees, most of them less than fifteen years old, grew haphazardly on the slope to the northwest of the junction, as well as on the ground south of the road.

Beltur didn't see any sign of sheep, and realized that he hadn't for almost ten kays, definitely a departure from the usual in Montgren.

Roughly two kays later, Karch gestured to a stone marker ahead. "That's the kaystone for Haven." Then he leaned forward. "Someone's chiseled off the name."

Beltur looked more closely. There was a lighter-colored oblong where the name presumably had been, followed by a worn five and a "K." He looked to Karch. "I've never seen anyone do that before. Have you?"

The captain shook his head. "The stone where the name was looks newer, as if the old stone had been chiseled away. But I don't see any chisel marks. Whoever did it knows his craft. The name was here the last time that Raelf's men patrolled. He would have reported it otherwise."

That meant less than two eightdays ago. Beltur frowned. First, the rider galloping away toward Haven, and then the kaystone. "But why would they erase just the name?"

"It might be someone's idea of a prank, a way of saying that Haven no longer exists, but I don't see most pranksters wanting to put in that much work."

"What about Hydlenese troopers?"

"That doesn't make sense to me," replied the captain.

More than a few things weren't making sense to Beltur. He was just afraid that they'd make sense in a way he wouldn't like when he finally did figure them out.

Beltur kept riding and trying to sense what he couldn't see. What he did see was anything but encouraging. While many of the cots and cottages they passed were inhabited, and had likely once looked well-kept, even their yellow-gray brick walls now looked dingy. Most of the shutters were fastened tight, fitting for winter, but hardly the best practice in midspring—unless they were closed for protection against raiders or brigands, rather than the weather.

What he sensed was, for the most part, even less than he saw. Before long, they reached the edge of what once had been the town proper, marked by two brick posts, one on each side of the road. The square stone crown on the top of the right-hand post was only half there; the post on the left side had no top at all. Immediately beyond the right post was a house with an outbuilding reached by a narrow drive. The outbuilding looked like it had once been a smithy, but the door was boarded shut, as was the door of the house.

At that moment, Beltur sensed something near the middle of town, something unfamiliar . . . yet very familiar. *How could you not notice that?* Then he stiffened and immediately pulled full order and chaos shields around himself, so that the other mage couldn't sense him. He thought it likely that the other mage wouldn't notice, if he'd noticed anything. Also, before long, the other mage or mages would still sense Jessyla and Lhadoraak, if they hadn't already, and they shouldn't notice that Beltur couldn't be sensed. *You hope.*

Beltur turned in the saddle and said to Jessyla, "What do you sense ahead?"

She concentrated and then frowned. "I don't . . . oh . . . is that a white mage?"

"A very disordered one. Two in fact." *And one is surrounded by chaos.* More chaos than Beltur had ever sensed in one mage, but that could mean a strong disciplined mage or one not so strong and undisciplined, most likely younger, since strong undisciplined whites tended to die young.

"There are two white mages ahead?" asked Karch.

"So far, that's what we can sense."

"How far ahead?"

"About a kay."

"That's past the market square then," said the captain.

"The first inn. The Brass Bowl, that's on this side of the square, isn't it?"

"If you can call it an inn. It's two to three blocks this side of the square."

Closer to the square, there were more houses that were still occupied, but Beltur only saw a few people out, all of them older, and all of them working garden plots.

"There's hardly anyone living here," murmured Jessyla.

"It seems that way, but we need to find out more."

The Brass Bowl consisted of two connected yellow-brick buildings, one a square structure set on a corner with the public room clearly in front and the second a narrower structure extending rearward from the first, with two levels of rooms, and a stable at the far end. With smoke coming from the chimneys, the inn definitely looked as though it was actually catering to travelers and drinkers.

"Do you want to stop here?" asked Karch.

"I'd rather ride through the town, at least to the square, before we stop. Unless you think there's a better approach."

"We'll have to take over both inns for quarters," Karch reminded Beltur.

"Do you want to leave two squads and the supply wagons here, then?"

"If you think there's no danger of an attack."

"I don't know about the mages. They're still on the far side of the square. What if you just had the last two squads and the wagons pull up here and have them wait with Lhadoraak?"

"I don't have a problem with that."

"Then we should halt and make those arrangements before continuing."

Karch nodded.

While the captain briefed the two squad leaders, Beltur rode back and reined up short of Lhadoraak.

"What is it?" asked the older mage. "Is it about the mages ahead of us?"

"I need you to stay here with the last two squads and supplies. Jessyla and I are going to take three squads to deal with the whites. After we see about that, then we'll need to decide about what comes next."

"Are you sure you don't want us with you?"

"I worry about Taelya." Beltur didn't say what his worry was—that he didn't want Taelya seeing a white who possibly might throw chaos bolts, not at her age.

For a moment, Lhadoraak frowned, then abruptly nodded. "Thank you."

"We'll have to see why whites are even here." Whatever the reason, it couldn't be good.

"Better you than me. Besides, you're the head councilor."

"For all that means," said Beltur in words that were meant to be wry, but came out sardonic. He turned Slowpoke and urged him back toward the front of the company.

Since Karch hadn't returned, Beltur eased Slowpoke close to Jessyla. "I need to tell you something."

"That you're totally shielded? I realized that when you went to talk to Lhadoraak. Why?"

"That's the point. There are two whites. I don't think either can do that kind of shield. They will be able to sense you. They'll also sense Lhadoraak, and he's not that close. I want to see what they'll do."

"You have something in mind, don't you?"

"Only if they don't want to be cooperative. I'd be happy if they just want a place to live and would agree to help us put Haven back together. Five mages are stronger than three."

"If they agree."

"That's what we'll need to see." Beltur sensed Karch returning and turned. "Are we ready to continue?"

"We are." Raising his voice, he called out, "Company! Forward!"

A block later Beltur was studying the square as his force neared the western side, trying as he had since entering Haven to match what he saw with what was on the maps he'd studied. Since it was not yet midafternoon, the square should have held some vendors, selling something. The only person visible was a gray-haired man in faded brown clothes that looked closer to rags.

Beltur turned to Karch. "Just have the company halt here. I want to ride up and talk to the beggar."

"What about the mages?"

"They aren't moving. They can't sense me. If they're able to sense anyone, it would be Jessyla and Lhadoraak."

Karch frowned, but ordered, "Company! Halt!"

Beltur did not explain, but eased Slowpoke forward across the square in the midafternoon sun.

The gray-haired man did not look up initially, then finally raised his head. He sat on the chipped stone wall around the fountain from which no water flowed. He watched as Beltur rode closer and reined up. Then, as the beggar's eyes took in Beltur's blacks, he stiffened, as if he wanted to run, then decided against it.

"Where is everyone?" asked Beltur.

"Not here, ser mage."

"Is there another market square? Another place for people to buy and sell?"

"Not that I know of."

"Why isn't anyone selling?"

"It's not safe. No patrollers anymore. Not since the bravos killed the councilor. Not since the white ones came."

"When did they come?"

"Sometime after when the snow stopped falling. Not long ago. Maybe an eightday. Don't remember. Might have been a threeday."

"How do you know they were white ones?"

"They flame people."

Not exactly promising for cooperation. "Where would I find the white ones?"

"At the East Inn."

"Not the Brass Bowl?"

"That's where the bravos and traders are. When they're here. Most of them left a little while ago. The Duchess's armsmen are coming, you know? The traders all leave when the armsmen come. They come back when they leave. Been that way a while."

"How long is a while?"

"A while." The gray-haired man looked down at the cracked and uneven bricks that had once been the smooth surface of the square. He did not look up again.

Beltur turned Slowpoke and rode back to where Karch and the others waited.

"Did you learn anything?" Karch's tone was not quite dismissive.

"Enough. The white mages came an eightday ago, or so. They took over the East Inn. They flame people who don't obey them. The traders and bravos left when they learned we were coming, just as you thought."

"What do you plan now?"

"To go to the East Inn. I think one squad will be enough."

Again, Karch frowned.

"We need some armsmen behind us to prove that we represent the Duchess. It's easier for me to protect one squad than three. Also, if we leave two squads in the square it says something." Beltur hoped Karch didn't ask what, because Beltur couldn't have said. It just felt that way. He could sense that while the white mages had moved only slightly, to near the front of the building he thought was the East Inn, a number of others, likely armsmen of some sort, had assembled outside the building.

"What if the mages get around you?"

"So far, that's never happened. If it does, I'll know almost immediately, and I'll deal with it. The sooner we move with one squad to the East Inn, the less likely we are to have even more trouble."

"Even more?"

"Two white mages and a score of armsmen are trouble enough." Beltur was guessing at the exact number, but it had to be in that range. "Half the men in First Squad are archers, are they not?"

"Yes, ser."

"Have them ready their bows, and move them forward into a five-abreast formation."

"Might I ask why?"

"So that they will be in position to take out the armsmen waiting at the East Inn. You'd prefer to do it with shafts than blades, I presume."

"You think it will be necessary?"

"I hope not. I suspect it will be. There are two white mages there, not just one." Beltur could sense Karch's question and went on, "One white mage is an opportunist. Two and a squad of armsmen suggest organization and power."

Karch turned in the saddle. "First Squad! Archers forward. Five abreast. Ready bows!"

In moments, the squad was re-formed.

Once Beltur saw that, rather than say more, he urged Slowpoke forward, nodding to Jessyla.

"On the mage!" ordered Karch.

While the captain's voice was firm, Beltur had a good idea that Karch was less than pleased. But then, Beltur was less than pleased at the conditions that had been allowed to develop in Haven.

The East Inn was actually on the east side of the square, but its entry was on the main street that Beltur and his force had taken through the town. And, as Beltur had sensed, some fifteen armsmen, all wearing gray tunics, were waiting for them, formed up across the street, facing west as Beltur reined up some twenty yards away. Ten of them held bows at the ready. To one side, by the lane leading to the inn's stable yard, stood the two white mages. Both mages wore gray, if a lighter shade than the gray of the armsmen. The blond, slightly taller and more powerful, mage, around whom chaos swirled, declared, "You are all trespassing."

"Who are you, to block the road to the Council of Haven?" asked Beltur, directing his words to the mages.

"Haven no longer exists. Fairhold is this town's name," declared the white-blond mage. "We took it fairly, and we hold it."

"By what right?" asked Beltur, easing Slowpoke forward and to the side of the street closest to the inn, so that Karch's archers would have a clear line of fire, if necessary.

"The only right that matters. The ability to hold this town."

"Haven belongs to the Duchy of Montgren," replied Beltur. "You have not been chosen to govern Haven by the duchy. You have not paid the tariffs that all towns in Montgren pay. You're also defying the lawful authority of the duchy."

The white mage laughed. "You're young. Too young to understand that authority is only conferred by force. Our force is superior to yours. Your choice is simple. Go away or perish."

"What if I offered you a position as councilor of Haven?" asked Beltur.

Behind Beltur, Karch stiffened.

"You have that authority?"

"I do."

"Then I'd say that authority is worthless. Why should I share what I hold with a mere black stripling whose shade is barely enough to be termed black?"

That alone told Beltur that the mage could only sense Jessyla.

"You might consider survival as a good reason," replied Beltur.

The white laughed. "My men can take down all your armsmen before they could nock shafts."

"You seem rather certain of that," replied Beltur, still easing Slowpoke forward.

"Enough!" snapped the white. "You were warned." A fireball arced directly at Beltur, and the white ordered, "Loose shafts!"

Beltur extended shields, then captured the firebolt with a containment and hurled it straight back at the more powerful white. He also dropped his unnecessary order/chaos concealment.

The shafts from the gray-clad armsmen dropped short of First Squad . . . and kept dropping.

The returned chaos bolt splattered on the white's shields and flared away, and two more firebolts flew toward Beltur and Jessyla.

Beltur captured both and flung them back, focusing both on the lesser white. Then, before the stronger white could throw more chaos, he clamped a containment tight around the lesser white, reinforcing it with order.

The containment flared almost as bright as the sun for an instant, as a white-tinged black mist momentarily bathed Beltur. Beltur released the containment, and ashes and dust sifted to the ground.

The second white mage stood almost transfixed.

"Surrender, now!" snapped Beltur.

"Never! Keep loosing shafts!"

More shafts dropped to the ground as they struck Beltur's shields.

Beltur slammed an order-filled containment around the second mage.

There wasn't even time for a scream before a brief flash of light was followed by another black mist of death, a mist that only Beltur and Jessyla could likely sense.

The gray-clad armsmen kept loosing shafts.

Beltur's shields continued to block them.

Karch eased forward and reined up beside Beltur. "When do you want us to loose shafts?"

"Not until they stop shooting, or run out of shafts. The shield will block our shafts as well as theirs. If I drop the shield so your men can target them, some of their shafts will likely strike your men. I'd prefer that none of your men are injured." Then Beltur called out, "Hold your shafts if you want to live."

"Frig you, mage!" shouted one of the gray-clad armsmen.

Beltur sealed him in a containment. "Hold your shafts!"

Several of the armsmen dropped their bows and pulled out blades.

Beltur could see what was going to happen. "Tell your men to nock shafts. When I say 'Now!' have them loose shafts. One volley."

"Archers! Nock shafts!"

"Now." Beltur dropped the shield and the containment around the outspoken armsman.

"Loose shafts!"

As soon as the Montgren shafts flew past him, Beltur raised his shield again.

Six gray-clad armsmen dropped, staggered, or slumped.

"We'll do that once more," said Beltur.

"Archers! Nock shafts!"

"Now."

"Loose shafts!"

Although Beltur had his shields back up, there was little need. The remaining armsmen broke and began to run.

Beltur dropped his shields back around himself and Jessyla. "Pursue and take down any who resist. A captive or two would be useful."

"First Squad! Attack!"

As the armsmen swept past them, Beltur counted the gray-clad bodies. There were nine fallen. He'd sensed several black mists, but he hadn't kept track. Turning to Jessyla, he said, "Once they've dealt with the others," *one way or the other,* "we'll see if any survivors can be healed."

"They didn't listen . . . even after all you did." After a pause, she asked, "How did you know you'd prevail?"

"The white was powerful, but undisciplined. All that chaos around him just combined with the order I put inside the containment. I thought it would. All I had to do was get close enough so that I didn't have to strain. He couldn't even tell that the blackness he felt was you and not me." Beltur added sardonically, "Call it the advantage of good training."

After several moments, Jessyla said, "Beltur . . . two of them really need healing."

"Can you hold a shield while you check them?"

"I can."

"Then go ahead." Beltur glanced toward the gray-clad wounded. One of the men sat propped against the side of the building. Two lay flat, but seemed to be breathing. Another was clutching his shoulder, trying to stanch the blood seeping out around an arrow that still protruded.

Beltur took the reins to Jessyla's mount and led the mare to the hitching rail by the inn's door. There he dismounted and tied both horses to the rail, then walked to the door of the inn, which he opened.

A woman looked at him, taking in his mage's blacks, as if ready to flee.

"We need some clean cloths, and some spirits, for some of the wounded. Please bring them quickly."

The woman swallowed. "Yes, ser."

Beltur then walked back outside to where the two mages had stood. All that remained were two heaps of dust and ashes, and half-concealed within were various metal objects—and a pile of golds and silvers. One of the metal objects was all too familiar—a cupridium dagger. Beltur picked up what was left—the blade and tang. It wasn't one he and Jorhan had forged, and there was certainly no way to tell how old it might be. There was also a metal ring with two keys on it, which Beltur took. Then he scooped up the coins, nearly a score of golds, and seven or eight silvers, as well as a handful of coppers. All were still warm, almost hot. *Every coin will help.*

After dumping the coins into his belt wallet quickly, Beltur rejoined Jessyla, who had moved to the man with the protruding arrow.

The armsman looked toward Beltur in alarm.

"He's also a healer," said Jessyla quietly before turning to Beltur. "I'll need your knife. The arrowhead's wedged under the bone."

"I can use a containment to keep you from cutting more than you need to."

"That would help."

Between the two of them, they had the arrow out in moments, and Beltur was adding order around the wound's deepest point, while Jessyla was using some of the cloths that the woman from the inn had immediately brought.

By the time Karch and his squad returned, a quint or so later, Jessyla and Beltur had removed arrows from five armsmen and dressed their wounds. The other fallen had died, except for one who had fled as soon as Karch's men had begun to pursue the uninjured armsmen who had broken and fled.

"What will you do with them?" asked the still-mounted Karch, motioning toward the wounded, either sitting or lying on the front porch of the inn.

"Get them to recover and put them to work. There's a lot that needs to be rebuilt."

"Do you think . . ." Karch laughed harshly. "That would have been a stupid question."

"I think we need to talk to the innkeeper now," said Beltur. "I'd appreciate it if you'd accompany us. He should at least recognize the uniform. If you'd detail someone to inform Lhadoraak and the other squads what happened, and tell Lhadoraak, Tulya, and Taelya to join us here."

Karch nodded, then turned his mount and rode to the First Squad leader, returning shortly and dismounting.

The three entered the inn, which, at first sight, looked far better kept than anything Beltur had seen so far in Haven. Beltur could sense some residual and additional free chaos, but no sign of either concentrated order or chaos.

The young man wearing a maroon tunic standing in the front foyer immediately inclined his head. "Honored sers . . ."

Beltur heard the catch in his voice and could sense the man's worries from the swirl of natural order and chaos. "We'd like to see the innkeeper. Now."

"I don't know . . ."

"He's likely hiding someplace," replied Beltur. "Find him and tell him that he won't have an inn if he doesn't appear. We'll wait. For a very short time."

The young man hurried away, ducking into a side corridor that led to the steps to the upper level.

"You think that will work?" asked Karch.

"One way or another. I mean what I say."

"I've noticed that." Karch's tone verged on the sardonic. After a moment, he ventured, "I've never seen a mage do what you did."

"What do you mean?"

"Block arrows that way, and bind men so that they can't move. I thought blacks could only block chaos, not weapons."

Beltur frowned. "I couldn't say. I learned about containments in Elparta. After that, I just figured out more ways to use them."

Karch raised his eyebrows, but didn't say more.

Before that long, the young man and another emerged from the door that led to the staircase. The innkeeper was half a head shorter than Beltur, but broad-shouldered and beefy enough that his maroon tunic was bulging around his midriff. His eyes fixed on the three, but did not meet Beltur's steady gaze.

He stopped a yard short of Beltur and stammered, "Honored sers . . . I had nothing to do with it. The white mages insisted that I house them . . ." The innkeeper's entire figure shivered.

Beltur could sense that most of what the man said was true. Doubtless he was shading matters somewhat, but who wouldn't have with what Beltur had seen already in Haven? "I understand that, innkeeper. The Duchess has proclaimed a new council for Haven. That is why we were escorted here by a company of her troopers. I trust you will have no problem in housing a few squads—and the five of us who are the new council—until we can find other suitable housing and begin to restore order to Haven?"

"No, ser. I mean, that's not a problem . . . I mean, if it doesn't . . . ah . . ."

"You're saying that it costs you something to keep the inn going. Is that it?"

"Yes, ser."

"We'll talk about reimbursement later," said Beltur. "After we know more." *A great deal more.* He turned to Karch. "If you would make the necessary arrangements here and at the Brass Bowl . . . If you have *any* difficulty, please let me know. Oh . . . and we'd like to keep any arms and mounts left by the armsmen."

Karch frowned.

"We'll need them. You can always get more. I doubt we will."

"Yes, ser."

Beltur smiled warmly, trying to project that warmth as well. "I do appreciate all you've done. We should meet over dinner here and discuss what needs most to be done."

"I'll return here once the arrangements are made at the Brass Bowl." Karch inclined his head, then turned and departed.

"You said . . . something about the new Council of Haven, ser?"

"Yes. We're part of that council. There's another black mage as well. We have several documents from the Duchess. They're packed away for the moment." Beltur looked directly at the innkeeper. "But you really don't think the Duchess would have sent a full company of armsmen—"

"A full company?"

"Oh, we left two squads at the Brass Bowl and two squads in the main square. One or two of those squads will be joining the one here. Now, innkeeper, you can show us to the rooms used by the mages. And, no, we likely won't be staying in them. We'll need others. Please lead the way."

"He took the best rooms overlooking the square." The innkeeper turned and headed toward the staircase. Beltur and Jessyla followed.

Once he was on the second floor of the inn, Beltur could have made his way to the chambers taken by the white mages without any guidance, given the amount of residual free chaos that loomed from the pair of adjacent chambers on the west side of the inn.

Beltur sensed Jessyla's wince at the excessive chaos as she followed the innkeeper and Beltur to the larger chamber, which had clearly housed the stronger mage. The room was comparatively neat, with a single set of grayish whites hung on a wall peg and a set of clean smallclothes folded on the corner of the writing table. The shutters were drawn back and the pair of narrow windows did indeed offer a good view of the deserted square.

After scanning the room with both eyes and senses, Beltur discovered a box hidden in the bed frame, not only hidden, but dusted with chaos and a sort of concealment that made it hard even to look at. He concentrated enough free order on the chaos to reveal a small strongbox, which he removed and set on the writing table.

Then he went through the two leather kit bags, looking for any sign of documents or papers. He found nothing of that sort, nor anything that suggested the mage's origin, but under the folded smallclothes was an excellent map of Haven and the surrounding area.

Beltur studied the map, one that appeared far more recently drawn than any possessed by Korsaen, looking for any hint of from where it might have come. The only indication was a set of initials—"D H"—and the name "Hydolar" along the bottom right edge of the border.

"The map was drawn either in Hydolar or by someone from Hydolar," said Beltur as he pointed out the initials and name to Jessyla before turning to the innkeeper. "Did the mages or their men ever say where they came from?"

"The white in charge only said that where they came from didn't matter. I asked those in town, and all anyone could say was that they rode in from the west."

"What was his name?" asked Beltur.

"The chief white mage—he never said what his name was—he just said to call him 'Mage' or 'ser'—he said that things were going to change in Haven and that Fairhold would be the new name and that it would soon be an independent land, just like Montgren, except greater in time."

"That sounds like he was boasting," said Jessyla.

"No, Healer. He said he had visions of a great city rising here. He claimed to have seen it, with a great shining tower, and that mages would make it great."

Beltur and Jessyla exchanged glances.

Then Beltur asked, "What else can you tell us?"

"There is nothing else to tell, except he killed one server because she touched him with something iron. It burned his arm. He would not talk. He just kept saying that things would get better before long. He would not say why or how. After he killed Kaslena, I did not ask."

After several more questions, which elicited no more information, Beltur asked the innkeeper to show them the second mage's chamber. He brought the strongbox and handed the map to Jessyla. The second room had neither a strongbox nor any documentation.

When they finished looking over the second room, Beltur turned to the innkeeper. "Where are the best rooms on the other side?"

"I will show you."

In the end, Beltur and Jessyla settled on a room on the northeast corner of the inn that had windows on two sides, and the one adjacent for Lhadoraak and his family, after which they dealt with the horses and the mule, and moved their gear to their room, and took what else they thought would be useful from the mages' rooms, finishing just as the innkeeper was leading Lhadoraak and Tulya up to their room.

Once the innkeeper left, Beltur turned to the older mage. "Did you have any trouble?"

Lhadoraak shook his head. "The innkeeper at the other place is a sour sort, but he seemed almost relieved that we were here." After a moment, he asked, "What did you say to Karch?"

"I didn't say much of anything—"

"It wasn't what he said," Jessyla interjected. "It was what he did."

"He said two white mages threw firebolts and that you threw them back and turned them to ash. What else were you supposed to do?"

"I think the captain was surprised at the way Beltur took command," suggested Jessyla.

"I told Karch you had more battle experience than any mage in Spidlar," said Lhadoraak. "He shouldn't have been surprised."

"He was," affirmed Jessyla.

"We should probably wash up and get ready for dinner," said Beltur. "We're all meeting Karch in the public room. Think about what we need him and his men to do for the next eightday or so. Also about what are the first things we need to do."

"We can do that," said Tulya firmly.

Once Beltur and Jessyla returned to their room, Beltur took out the small strongbox and began to try the keys he'd found in the dust. The first was clearly too big. The second worked, but Beltur placed a shield between himself and the box, then lifted the hinged lid with the tip of his knife.

A small bolt of chaos flashed toward the shield, then flattened harmlessly.

"That could have killed someone," observed Jessyla.

"That was likely the intention." He glanced at the second key, wondering what it was for. Then he shrugged and set the ring and keys on the writing table.

There were close to a hundred golds in the chest. Beltur looked at each of them. Ninety of them showed an identical image he didn't recognize, meaning that they hadn't been minted in Gallos, Spidlar, or Axalt. He didn't think the image of the stone-walled citadel represented any place in Montgren, either. There were two other golds he didn't recognize, but he just put one of the golds like the ninety he didn't recognize in his pocket. After he replaced the golds, he placed a concealment and an order lock on the strongbox and slid it under the bed.

After washing up, they made their way down to the public room. The captain rose from the circular table where he'd been waiting. Beltur sat on Karch's left, and Jessyla on his right.

"They only have dark ale," said the captain. "That figures. To neither of our tastes. I told her to bring six."

"Thank you."

"Before the others arrive, I'd like to ask you a few things."

"Go ahead," replied Beltur.

"You offered the mages two chances. Did you know they'd refuse?"

"Anyone who flames people who disagree wasn't likely to want to share power, but I felt I had to offer."

"You knew you were more powerful, didn't you?"

"I was fairly certain."

"So they never had a chance?"

"I gave the mages the opportunity to join us. It would have allowed them to live, but they would have had to share in the work. They knew that, and they refused. I gave the armsmen the choice to surrender—after I'd destroyed both mages. They refused. What else was I to do that wouldn't have gotten your men killed needlessly?"

"You were more than a mere arms-mage, weren't you?"

"No. I was just an undercaptain arms-mage. I never commanded more than half a squad. We were always outnumbered. Any Gallosian who survived made it that much less likely that we'd live, let alone be able to drive the Gallosians out. I learned that quickly."

"Did you ever tell Lord Korsaen that?"

"He didn't ask. He did see me deal with a band of brigands."

"The Duchess will benefit enormously from what you do," said Karch slowly. "I'm not so sure her heirs will be quite so pleased."

"Why do you say that?"

"She's given you a free hand to rebuild Haven. You're as ruthless, in a kinder way, as any ruler in Candar. You're also committed to working with other mages to rebuild the town. The only other places where blacks have rebuilt lands are Axalt, Westwind, and Sarronnyn. None have been conquered. You're beginning with more mages than any of them, and as word gets out, I'd wager more will join you."

I certainly hope so. "It won't be that easy."

"That obviously hasn't stopped you so far."

"We've had to leave three different lands," Beltur pointed out.

"There's a difference between blind and senseless courage and wise withdrawal until you can prevail. All of you understand that." Karch's eyes flicked toward the archway.

Beltur gestured for Lhadoraak, Tulya, and Taelya to join them.

As soon as they did, the young man who had first met Beltur, Karch, and Jessyla reappeared with a tray holding six beakers of dark ale. "We only have a fowl pie tonight. It smells rather good, though."

"Then we'll take it," said Beltur cheerfully.

Once the server left, Beltur raised his beaker. "To rebuilding Haven."

"To rebuilding Haven."

After everyone took a swallow, Beltur said, "That was the easy part. We might have a few other difficulties." He extracted the gold from his pocket. "The white mage had a number of these in his wallet." He handed the gold from the strongbox to Karch. "Do you know where this was coined?"

Karch frowned. "That's a gold from Hydlen."

"The head white mage had a score of golds like it." For his own reasons, Beltur wasn't about to let Karch know the real total. "Most bore that image."

"That suggests he's from Hydlen."

"Or that someone from Hydlen gave him the golds," said Beltur. "I'd like you to keep that one and give it to Lord Korsaen when you return, and tell him about the white mages."

"You're keeping the rest?" Karch raised his eyebrows.

"If the Duke of Hydlen was behind those mages, we'll need every gold we can find. Just as we'll need whatever mounts and arms they had." Beltur paused, then asked, "Do you disagree?"

Karch's lips twisted. "I have the feeling that you're usually right. I also have the feeling that disagreeing with you, without good and solid reasons, is unwise. That one white mage should have known better." Karch looked to Taelya. "You're a white mage. What do you think?"

Taelya frowned. "Uncle Beltur knows best. That's why we're here."

"Exactly." Karch nodded. "Perhaps we should leave other arrangements until tomorrow when we're more rested and have had a chance to consider matters."

"An excellent idea," said Lhadoraak.

Neither Beltur nor Jessyla disagreed.

V

Much later that night, after a long and quiet dinner of a decent but not outstanding fowl pie, and a good glass after Beltur and Jessyla had returned to their room, Beltur stood before the open window, looking eastward along the street that became the Lydiar road outside Haven, the cool air of a spring night flowing slowly past him. He was all too conscious that he'd chosen a room that turned his back on the ruined square. *But going forward means turning your back on the mistakes and ruins of the past and moving forward, but not forgetting what led to those mistakes and ruins.*

The silence stretched out.

"Karch said he'd never seen a mage do what you did with shields and containments," Jessyla said quietly, "that other blacks could only stop chaos and not shafts or weapons."

"I think every mage must be a little different, maybe more than that."

She looked at him inquiringly.

"Everything in the world is made up of order and chaos," he finally replied. "So are shields and containments. It seemed logical to me."

She shook her head and laughed softly. "You see things others don't."

"That's because I was raised as a white."

"Perhaps, but that's not all." After another long pause, she went on, "The white mage said there would be a great city here, that he had visions. He died thinking that."

"Are you asking if he was wrong?"

"Wasn't he? He died."

Beltur shook his head. "It could be that his vision was true. I read something like that in *The Wisdom of Relyn* when we were in Axalt, in Barrynt and Johlana's parlor. I came across it again in the past eightday. Relyn was writing about Nylan. Nylan said that Ryba's visions were true, but the meaning she ascribed to them was often different from the truth of the vision. That's because all that we want to see is not always there in the truest of visions."

"You think the white mage saw the truth, or just what he wanted to see?"

"Why not both?" asked Beltur sardonically.

"Then we could be pursuing a vision that's only part true, as well."

"You're right. But nothing strong gets built without vision. We can build a strong town that will grow into a city . . . eventually. Well after our time. Cities don't grow overnight, and the city we hope for likely won't be quite what we envision. That's something we can't worry about."

"So you're saying his vision was true?"

Beltur smiled wryly. "How many lands have we traveled so far, just to find a place where we can be who we are?"

"I haven't counted," replied Jessyla almost playfully.

"Five. I don't argue with visions. I just try to do what I can. I know we can rebuild Haven. Changing the name would help."

"Not Fairhold." Jessyla's lips twisted in distaste.

"No."

"What, then?"

"Fairhaven. A fair haven for all, but especially for mages, black or white, and for healers, and others who will build and contribute, no matter where they come from. Like us . . . or Taelya."

"Fairhaven," repeated Jessyla. "I like that."

"But we should keep that name to ourselves until we've at least made a good start," said Beltur. "Once Haven no longer resembles a shambles of a town, then we can suggest a new name."

"With a few hints before that," added Jessyla.

"Of course," replied Beltur.

VI

Beltur and Jessyla awakened early, partly because the sun poured in through the cracks in the shutters of the east-facing room . . . and partly for other reasons. Even so, they thought they reached the public room fairly early, but found Captain Karch was already there. They'd barely seated themselves at the circular table when Lhadoraak, Tulya, and Taelya joined them.

"I had the kitchen feed the men," announced Karch. "They're used to early meals, and that will give them time to be ready for whatever you have in mind."

Beltur only had a general idea of what needed to be done, one he wasn't about to elaborate on without talking more to Karch and the others, but what was foremost in his mind was what the very sharp and very experienced Captain Raelf had said—that the first priority had to be to restore order. He just wished he'd asked Raelf more about Hydlen, and especially about the Duke.

"That's what we need to talk over," replied Beltur, "after we eat." He beckoned to the young man who had served them the night before.

"Yes, ser mage?"

"I never got your name or that of the innkeeper. Matters were a little confused last night."

"Ah . . . yes, ser. I'm Claerk, and the innkeeper is Bythalt."

"Thank you. I'm Beltur. The healer-mage is Jessyla, and we're consorted. The other black mage is Lhadoraak, and his consort is Tulya. Captain Karch commands the Duchess's company of troopers. Are you from Haven, Claerk?"

"Depends on what you mean, ser. Ma's the cook, and I grew up here. I wasn't born here."

"You're from Haven, at least compared to all of us. What's for breakfast?"

"We saved mutton strips and eggs and cheese for you mages, and warm bread. Ma's really good with a mutton and cheese scramble."

Beltur looked around the table, then said, "We'll try it. What is there to drink?"

"Ah . . . just the dark ale, ser."

"We'll have that, except water for the young woman."

"The water . . . would you like it boiled?"

"No. Just bring a pitcher. We'll take care of it. We'll have to see about that and a few other things in the future."

Karch tried not to frown.

"Adding a little chaos, and then a little order, will take care of most bad water," said Beltur. "I learned that when I accompanied my uncle to deal with the Analerian raiders."

In moments, Claerk returned with five beakers of ale and a pitcher and an empty tumbler.

"Taelya," said Beltur, "concentrate on what I'm doing."

"Yes, Uncle Beltur."

Beltur let his senses range over the water, which did contain a certain chaos, then eased order to the pitcher, after which he unsheathed his cupridium belt knife and stirred the water. Then he added a touch of pure chaos and stirred it again. He looked to Taelya. "Do you think you could do that?"

"I'd need to practice."

Beltur poured the clear water into the tumbler and eased it in front of her. "You'll have more than a few chances. We'll start at the next meal."

"What did you do?" asked Karch.

"Added order to the water to destroy the chaos, then added a touch of chaos to get rid of the excess order."

While Karch was thinking that over, Claerk returned with two baskets of bread. "It won't be long for the scramble."

The conglomeration of mutton, eggs, and cheese wasn't outstanding, but it was hot and more edible than many meals Beltur had eaten, and he was definitely hungry. The dark ale wasn't that bad, at least, not when drunk with the scramble and bread.

As Beltur finished his breakfast, Karch looked to him. "What do you need from us today?"

"My first thought was just to have them patrol the streets, but you know more about Haven than we do."

"It wouldn't hurt."

"What else would you suggest? For today?"

"That depends on what you have in mind."

Beltur couldn't fault Karch's caution. So he decided to change his approach. "How are city and town patrollers organized in Montgren?"

"However each town wants to organize them." Karch offered a humorous smile. "Some towns have patrollers, and some do not." After a pause, the captain added, "Most towns with a patrol have a captain appointed by the Council."

"We're going to need to set up some sort of town patrol," said Beltur, "but one of us will have to act as captain for a while." *Possibly a long while.*

Karch raised his eyebrows.

"Both Lhadoraak and I have some experience as patrol mages," Beltur replied to the unspoken question. "The Council in Elparta required mages to serve periodically as patrol mages."

Karch offered a wry smile. "Not that it's my purview, but what else have you done that you haven't mentioned?"

"Beltur's also a healer, and he's forged cupridium," replied Jessyla.

"More that I was the striker and mage while Jorhan forged it," corrected Beltur.

Karch frowned. "A black who is both a healer and an effective war mage . . . you killed two whites almost instantly . . . might I ask . . . ?"

"It's painful. Every death washes over me like a chill black mist."

"The odds are that Beltur has healed scores and killed thousands," said Lhadoraak quietly. "He's led charges and broken enemy lines and forces.

He's almost died several times. I'd appreciate it if you'd not fence with us. We know what we don't know. You likely do as well. Tell us what you think would work best. If you can't tell us that, tell us what you know from experience will not work."

Karch looked around the table. Then he shook his head ruefully. "I don't think the Duchess has any idea what she's unleashed. Or maybe she does, and she's figured that it's the only way to deal with Hydlen, Lydiar, and Certis." He cleared his throat. "The bravos that moved in here before the mage just waited us out. Now that the white mages are gone, they'll try and wait you out. If they can't do that, then they'll try to pick you off one at a time. If that doesn't work or they think you're too strong, then they'll start picking off townspeople so that no one will listen to you or only do what they absolutely have to do."

"So we need to be ready to pick them off while putting things back in order and letting the townspeople see that we're here to stay," replied Beltur.

"I can think of one way to start that off," said Jessyla. "We could open a healing house. They haven't had one in years."

"They won't likely come at first," said Karch.

"Unless they're desperate," said Jessyla. "There will be a few of those."

"There's another possibility," said Beltur. "We could just visit every dwelling in town. If anyone's there, we introduce ourselves and get their names. Then we'll have a record of who lives where, and they'll know we're serious. We'll also know which houses are vacant, and we could hire some local workers to repair and rebuild some of them for us . . . and one for a Council building, unless there already is one. If there is, it likely needs repairs."

"The first thing we likely should do," suggested Lhadoraak dryly, "is arrange to pay both innkeepers. Coins are much better than promises in reminding people that you keep your word."

Beltur couldn't help but grin. "A good practical start. Then, perhaps pay someone to clean up the town square and repair the fountain there, if possible." He turned to Karch. "What did you pay the innkeepers before?"

"Two coppers a man a day, and that was for the men sleeping in the stables."

More than two golds a day. That was just another confirmation of why Korlyssa had scarcely hesitated to agree to Beltur's terms. *We definitely should have asked for more.* "How many squads are billeted here?"

"Three."

"And two at the Brass Bowl?"

Karch nodded.

"How much did the Duchess send you with for your billeting?"

Karch hesitated, then nodded. "Enough for two eightdays."

"And a little more," said Lhadoraak.

"Ten golds extra for the unexpected." Karch paused, then asked, "Are all of you that good?"

"I'm not," said Tulya, "but the four of them are. Even Taelya."

"There's one other thing," said Beltur. "If you'd put all the weapons from the bravos in a safe place under guard."

"You don't seem to need weapons," said Karch mildly.

"But when we start a town patrol, we will, and finding or buying any here will be next to impossible." Beltur didn't mention the other reason, which was that the arms had value, a lesson he'd learned belatedly from his inability to profit from the arms captured from the Analerian raiders. "Now . . . we might as well talk to Bythalt." Beltur smiled as he saw the innkeeper approaching.

"How was your fare, Mages, Captain?"

"Adequate," replied Beltur.

Karch just nodded.

"Captain Karch will be paying you for billeting his men, and we will pay you for our lodging and food. Were you getting paid by the white mages?"

"Yes, ser mage. Not a lot. Two coppers a man, and that included food and rooms in the inn, not just the stable. We were losing coins that way, but"—Bythalt shrugged—"we couldn't argue."

"You weren't losing that much," declared Lhadoraak.

A despondent expression appeared on the innkeeper's face. "No, ser, but we never made that much."

"Putting Haven to rights," continued Lhadoraak, "is going to cost us dearly. We don't want you losing coins on lodging and feeding us, and you won't. But we're not here to allow you to recoup your losses from others. Is that clear?"

Some, but not all, of the despondency vanished from the innkeeper's face.

"You just keep the inn going, Bythalt, and we'll pay you," added Beltur, "and in time you'll likely do much better."

"Ser?"

"With us here, you not only won't lose coins on us, you also won't lose them to others, like the bravos and the sleazy traders."

"But there aren't any patrollers."

"There will be. For the moment, we'll take care of that. Both Lhadoraak and I have served as patrollers before."

"The traders and their bravos are tough. Maybe not on you . . ."

"Then we'll have to make sure that they're not tough on anyone in Haven," said Beltur. "Do you know if any of the houses near the square have been abandoned?"

"Some of them," replied the innkeeper cautiously.

"Do you know anyone who's a decent carpenter or a decent mason?"

"Gorlaak's good with wood, and so's his boy . . . if they're still around."

"There will be a few extra coins if you can find them and some others."

"I'll see what I can do. Might take a few days."

"That's fine. It'll take us a few days to decide where to start . . . beyond cleaning up the square and fixing the fountain. Now, we've been here one night, five of us for two meals. What's the standard for the inn, including dinner and lodging tonight?"

"Three coppers for each room. Three coppers each meal, with one ale."

"And a copper a day for each mount?"

"Ah . . . yes, ser."

"That's two silvers and seven coppers a day for the five of us." Beltur counted out three silvers. "The extra coppers are an advance on tomorrow. Try to find an ale that's not so bitter, if you can."

"Might be able to do that for you six. Can't for all the troopers."

"Here's a gold and two silvers for the troopers here," added Karch. "For last night. I'll pay every morning."

"We'll also need a few sheets of paper and two markers," added Beltur. "For lists. Can you have those ready in a quint or so?"

The innkeeper nodded. "Thank you, Mages, Captain." Bythalt definitely looked less morose as he inclined his head and turned toward the kitchen.

Lhadoraak said, "You didn't ask him who you should see."

"I thought about it, but I think Jessyla and I should start at one end of town and you three at the other end and introduce ourselves a house at a time."

"What if no one answers the door?" asked Jessyla. "That's more likely than not."

"That's why we should split up. A man and a woman . . . or a man and a woman and a child . . . that's not the same as a squad of troopers." Beltur turned to Karch. "How would you suggest your men patrol?"

"I've already dispatched two squads out to watch the roads, one to the east and one to the west. Another half squad should be enough to ride the streets."

"You'll let us know if your men see trouble coming?" Beltur's words weren't quite a question.

"I definitely will. I doubt it will be today. The sentries already saw a few men sneaking out of town, likely to report what happened."

Beltur nodded. "Before we start informing people, we need to make a stop at the Brass Bowl."

"I was there earlier. The innkeeper—his name is Phaelgren—he was a little concerned with what he heard you did."

"You think he's closer to the traders than Bythalt?"

"I wouldn't be surprised."

"I still don't understand some of this," interjected Tulya. "What do the traders get out of running down the town?"

"They can stop here for less than anywhere else. The tariff inspectors from Certis, Lydiar, and Hydlen don't dare come into the town without an armed force behind them, and none of those three rulers wants to lose troopers pacifying a town that the others don't want them to have. That means the traders can do what they want, because no one can stand up to them, and they can take anything that people can't hide or defend. You'll see. There aren't any young unattached women to speak of here. Not in town. There are likely some in the outlying steads. Most of the young men work in some way for the traders. Not many others have much in the way of coins. Most of the people are older . . . or a little strange. Sometimes both."

Beltur hadn't been expecting matters to be easy in Haven, but how were they supposed to rebuild a town that was short of able bodies? He didn't voice the thought.

As the six left the public room, Jessyla asked, "Where are the wounded bravos? We ought to take a look at them."

"In the stable tack room, under guard," replied Karch.

The tack room was at the end of the stable closest to the inn proper, and two troopers in the faded blue of Montgren stood outside.

As Jessyla stepped into the tack room, the five wounded men in gray looked at her, several with appreciative expressions that suggested they stood a good chance of recovering. Those expressions faded as Beltur appeared behind her.

"Let's take a look at that wound," said Jessyla, moving to the slightly older man who'd taken the arrow to the shoulder that had required both Beltur and Jessyla to remove.

Beltur followed, letting his senses touch the wound.

Jessyla looked to him. "There's still some chaos deep in there, just a tiny bit."

"Don't cut into me. You won't save me anyway."

Beltur smiled, easing a small bit of free order into the wound, and concentrating on making sure it touched both the tiny points of angry yellow-red wound chaos, both of which vanished. "That likely felt a little warm. I'll probably have to do that for a few more days, a deep wound like that."

"You sound like I'll be around that long."

"You will be, unless you do something stupid," replied Jessyla, moving from the older man to the younger one beside him, a youth barely more than a boy, propped up against the wall, his thigh heavily bound, his face sweaty, but his body shivering.

Beltur could sense the angry mass of chaos and tried not to wince. "There must have been something . . ."

"He was already hurt there. A burn from the white bastard," said the older man. "He was sitting behind the serving girl the white flamed."

"I didn't dare say anything," murmured the young man.

"Your leg is going to get very warm," declared Beltur, even as he doubted that he could remove all of the chaos. The only hope was to remove enough that he and Jessyla could eliminate more over the days ahead than the double wound created.

Bit by bit, Beltur targeted the nastiest segments of chaos, then stepped back and looked to Jessyla. "You do one or two."

"I'm not . . ."

"You are."

After Jessyla had inserted order bits into two areas, she turned to the young man. "Your leg is going to feel hot. I'll have them get you a small bucket or container of water and a cloth. Don't get the wound wet, but you can use the cloth to cool off other parts of your leg."

The other three were healing as expected, as least, as far as Beltur could tell.

When the two finished, Beltur looked around the tack room. "Once you're more healed, you'll have two choices. Work for us, and you'll be paid, or leave Haven. You've got a few days to think about it."

"What sort of work?" asked the older bravo.

"At first, whatever needs to be done. In time, we'll need some town patrollers, but some of you may not be suited to talking first and acting second."

"What do you know about it?"

"I was a mage patroller in Elparta before I was a war mage. So was Lhadoraak, the other black."

The older man laughed, a soft bitter sound.

Beltur gave him an inquiring look.

"Elshon said this'd be like taking biscuits from a baby."

"A year ago, he would have been right," replied Beltur. "But times change. You all can think about it. I wouldn't try to escape. First, you'd get hurt. Second, two of you will likely die if we don't keep treating you." Beltur didn't mention that they might anyway. "And third, if you don't want to stay once you're healed, we will let you go."

"Why?" asked the older man.

"We'll need men who'd like to earn an honest living, and we believe in second chances." He smiled. "And I know that Jessyla is an attractive woman. In addition to being a very good healer, she's also a mage and my consort. Those are three reasons why it's better to behave."

"Biscuits from a baby . . . ?" The older man shook his head.

After Beltur and Jessyla left the tack room, he checked the mule first, and then eased into Slowpoke's stall and checked the feed. "It's not the best, big fellow, but it will do."

Slowpoke swung his big head around and nuzzled Beltur, then whickered softly.

"I know. It's not as nice as Barrynt's or especially Korsaen's, but we'll have you out in a bit, and we won't be going that far." Just out of habit, Beltur checked all four hooves, although he would have sensed if there had been anything severely wrong.

After grooming and saddling the gelding, as well as continually talking to him, something that Slowpoke seemed to enjoy, Beltur led him out into the stable yard and over to where a boy was dumping stall refuse into a cart. "Where does that go?"

The boy looked up, then stiffened. "Ah . . . to grower Vortaan, ser. He pays a few coppers for it."

"Are you related to Claerk?"

"Yes, ser. He's my brother."

"What's your name?"

"Aaskar, ser."

"And your mother cooks here at the inn."

Aaskar nodded.

Given what Claerk had said, and Aaskar's much younger age than his brother, Beltur decided that further investigation of their familial or non-familial situation could wait. "Are you going to be an ostler?"

"Bythalt says I could do worse. The big warhorse is yours, isn't he?"

"He is."

"Do most mages have warhorses?"

"No. Most don't."

"Why do you?"

"Because I needed a horse, and he'd saved my life, and if I didn't buy him—except a friend bought him for me—then he would have been slaughtered."

"Why? He's a good horse."

"He doesn't like most other people to ride him." That was hardly the whole story, but Beltur didn't feel like telling it all.

Aaskar was still looking puzzled when Jessyla led her mount out of the stable and up beside Slowpoke.

"We can't waste time. Just staying here is costing us almost a gold a day," she said.

"That may be, but we need to find out more before we jump into something."

"This morning . . . it was a different—"

"It's not the same," Beltur said quickly, trying not to blush.

"Is that what most men say?"

"I didn't rush you. It was more than a year, and it was as much your idea as mine."

Jessyla grinned. "Sometimes, you're too serious."

Beltur just shook his head.

A little while later, after Aaskar had returned to the stable, Claerk appeared. "Bythalt said you needed paper and markers."

"We do, thank you."

"If you're heading to the Brass Bowl, be careful with Phaelgren. He can be nasty."

"That's kind of you to let us know," said Jessyla. "Is there anyone else who might be like that?"

"There's lots of folks who are gruff or who don't want to talk, but, except for Phaelgren and maybe Widow Taarbusk—everyone calls her Thornbush—they're not nasty and mean through and through. Anyone can be a little mean on a bad day."

Beltur smiled at that as he took the papers and crayons. "We appreciate it."

"I need to get back to work. I'm repairing some chairs that got broken. Maybe that won't happen so often now that you mages are here."

"People don't change overnight, but we'll see what we can do."

Claerk nodded and then headed back into the inn.

Once Lhadoraak, Tulya, and Taelya joined them, and Beltur gave Tulya some paper and a crayon, the five mounted and rode west on the main street past the still-empty square, which Beltur studied. Just a stone-paved area with a simple fountain ringed by the worn and chipped low stone wall. There was no sign of the older man who had been sitting there the day before. Beltur wondered how much work it would take to get water running to the fountain again.

The Brass Bowl was even more run-down than Beltur recalled, but then, he'd only taken a quick look at it on fourday. When he reined up outside the front door, there was no one around. So he dismounted and tied Slowpoke to the railing, as did the others with their mounts.

"Do you want us to come in?" asked Lhadoraak.

"Why don't you just stand in the doorway?" said Beltur. "That way you can watch the horses and still see what we're doing."

Beltur opened the door and walked into the small and dusty entry foyer, followed by Jessyla. He didn't sense any active chaos, but the inn had a certain lack of order, although it was superficially neat. Two men lounged on a bench in the corner, not even looking up.

"Looking for someone?" asked a figure emerging from a narrow doorway to a small room.

"We're looking for Phaelgren."

"You've found him, Mage. What do you want?" Unlike the short and beefy Bythalt, Phaelgren was taller, if still a digit or two shorter than Beltur, and thin, with a droopy brown mustache and hazel eyes that verged on yellow.

"Just to tell you that we've been sent as the new town council—"

"Begging your pardon, Mages, but what if some of us don't want a new town council. What if we like it better without a meddlesome council? What if we like things the way they are?"

"You're free to leave Haven," Beltur said mildly.

"You ride into town and tell me *I* can leave?"

"You don't have to leave," said Jessyla. "You can stay and follow the laws. We're not going to tariff traders. There's no reason for them not to come and stay at your inn, so long as they respect the people who live here."

"Healer . . . I was talking to the mage."

"I was talking to you," said Jessyla coldly. "And you will listen."

"Your mage friend is all that keeps me from putting you down good."

The two men in the corner snickered.

Jessyla concentrated.

Phaelgren opened his mouth, but no sound came out. Then, he yanked out a belt knife and lunged toward Jessyla, but the knife was wrenched from his hand as it struck her shields. With both fists, he pounded against the unseen barrier. His face began to turn red, and then redder . . .

Then, he took a gasping breath as Jessyla released whatever she had done.

Before he could speak, she did. "I did that. And if I'd held it a bit longer, you'd be dead. I'm more healer than mage, but I'm more than enough mage to kill a worthless arrogant bully like you."

Phaelgren's eyes went from Jessyla to Beltur, then toward the open front door, where Lhadoraak stood, and finally to Taelya.

"I wouldn't try it if I were you," said Beltur. "Taelya's shields are strong enough to protect her, and if you tried, then any one of us would happily kill you."

"Even her . . ." The innkeeper seemed to sink into himself. "You'll kill us all."

Beltur shook his head. "The town is our charge. We might end up killing a few bullying traders before they get the message."

"I thought . . . it was the troopers . . . killed the mages."

"Lhadoraak and Tulya were here protecting the squads we left. Jessyla and I dealt with the mages and their bravos. She even healed a few. We'll be putting them to work once they're able."

"They won't . . ." The innkeeper looked to Jessyla. "Maybe they will . . ."

"Oh . . . they will . . . if they want to stay," she said. "It's their choice."

Beltur smiled pleasantly but coolly at Phaelgren. "We just wanted you to know what was happening so that you wouldn't be surprised . . . or do anything foolish. Good day."

The two turned and walked out. Beltur kept his senses concentrated on the innkeeper, but Phaelgren didn't move until after Beltur closed the door.

"He's not trustworthy," said Jessyla as they untied their mounts.

"I worry more that he's stupid," commented Lhadoraak. "He didn't really understand that Jessyla could have killed him."

"In places like this," said Tulya, "men don't even think that a mere woman could do that."

"Why don't they?" asked Taelya.

"Because they don't think much of women," said Lhadoraak.

"Why not?" pressed the seven-year-old.

"You'd have to ask them," snorted Tulya, "and you don't get to do that until you're older and a much better mage. You saw what Jessyla had to do to get them to realize she was stronger than they were."

"That's a very good reason to keep working on your shields," added Beltur after swinging up into Slowpoke's saddle. "We'll head to the east end of town. Are you three ready to start at the west end of town?"

"We can do that," said Lhadoraak.

Beltur watched for a moment as the three turned their mounts westward, then eased Slowpoke back in the direction of the square.

"Phaelgren is still going to be a problem," said Jessyla.

"I know, but we'll just have to watch him." Beltur paused. "What exactly did you do to him? Put a confinement in his throat?"

"That doesn't take as much effort, and I've seen more than enough throats to know just where to place it."

"Good technique."

"I don't have your strength. I'll get stronger, but I'll never have the strength you do."

Beltur thought about disputing that, but realized that she was probably right, and only said, "You'll be strong enough to do what you need to do . . . or you'll figure out another way, just like you did with Phaelgren." As they neared the square again, he studied it more carefully, but it was exactly what it seemed to be—a stone-paved square with little more than a fountain, bordered by an almost tiny chandlery, certainly too small to be a factorage, several shops that looked as though they might be deserted, and several other buildings whose use he couldn't determine.

"Perhaps we should stop by the chandlery and the shops first. I should have thought about that."

"*We* should have thought about it. And, yes, we should. The chandlery first." Jessyla turned her mount toward the chandlery.

As they rode closer, Beltur still saw no one up and around, only a smoky gray cat sitting on the sunlit corner of the narrow front porch of the chandlery, its green eyes following the two as they dismounted and tied their horses to the railing. Beltur only sensed one person in the chandlery, but he still entered warily. Jessyla followed. The side walls held tools of various sorts, but spaced apart, as if there had been more at one time, and several of the tables held only a few items, although one table looked to have an assortment of dried fruits, nuts, and travel food.

The burly man who stepped out from the corner where he had been arranging something was half a head taller than Beltur, but as his eyes took in the blacks and Jessyla's greens, he seemed to relax . . . slightly. "I heard that some black mages got rid of that white . . . upstart . . . You'd have to be one of the blacks, wouldn't you? Blacks don't tend to be very numerous."

Beltur nodded and briefly explained what had happened and why they were in the chandlery.

"You're either young and real green, or you've seen more than it appears."

"How about young and forced to be an arms-mage, a city patroller, and a trader's road guard?"

"And a healer," added Jessyla. "He's a healer in addition to all that and a few other things."

"I'm Torkell. If you two are even half what you say, the next few seasons are going to be real interesting."

"So we've been told," replied Beltur.

"What have we missed?" asked Jessyla.

"Not much in the town works and hasn't for years. The last council never sent the Duchess her due in tariffs. Young women hide most of the time because they're not safe."

"That will stop," said Jessyla.

"You going to kill every brigand and bravo who grabs a girl?"

"If that's what it takes," replied Jessyla. "Haven hasn't had four mages before."

Torkell frowned. "Only heard tell there were four of you and a little girl."

More people had been watching than Beltur had guessed, then. He said, "Jessyla and the girl are mages as well. The girl knows enough to protect herself, and she'll get stronger as she gets older."

"Like I said, things'll be interesting."

"Do you live behind or over the chandlery?"

"Have to. If I weren't here, everything I have'd be gone in a day . . . maybe an eightday. Do a bit of smithing too, just because there's no one else."

"In time, we'll also have a patrol."

"Now what do you mages know about that?"

Beltur sighed. Loudly. "Both Lhadoraak and I served as patrol mages in Elparta."

"With all that, you just might make it work. Maybe. What do you want from me?"

"Just what you've already told us, and anything else that might help us get Haven back to where it's a prosperous town again."

"Some of the traders are bastards, and some are just greedy. The bastards you'll never straighten out. The greedy ones won't mess with you if you're fair and firm. Best of the greedy ones is Niklos. Comes from a little town north of Hydolar."

Before long, Beltur and Jessyla left the chandlery and looked at the adjoining buildings. No one was at the tiny shop that apparently was or had been that of a weaver and a seamstress. The potter's place looked recently used, but no one was there, and the cabinet maker's shop was just a shell that looked as if it hadn't been occupied in years.

From the square, Beltur and Jessyla rode past the East Inn, riding past one of Karch's patrols.

"Good morning, Mages!" called the squad leader. "Everything's quiet so far."

"Have you seen any of those graycoat bravos?"

"No, ser."

Once they were a block or so past the inn, the eastern part of Haven, or at least the dwellings on each side of the main road, didn't seem quite so run-down as the western end. Either that, or everything looked a little brighter in the midspring morning sunlight.

Just a hundred yards west of the worn brick gateposts indicating the east end of Haven stood a well-kept brick house, with a tended garden in the rear, and even several sets of grape trellises. Beltur gestured. "We could start there."

They rode up the narrow lane to the hitching rail, where they dismounted and tied the horses, then walked to the front door. Beltur knocked. Before long, he could sense someone approaching.

The door opened, held by a trim, gray-haired woman in a faded yellow tunic and brown trousers. She studied Beltur and then Jessyla. "A black mage and a healer by your garb. That or a talented pair of grifters. What would you be wanting?"

"Just to introduce ourselves and tell you why we're here in Haven."

"Most likely to relieve me of the few coppers I have."

"Duchess Korlyssa has chartered us, and two others, as the new town council of Haven. That's why the Montgren troopers accompanied us."

The woman laughed. "Likely story. You're as bad as that fellow in white." She started to close the door.

Beltur sighed, then eased a confinement around her, not a tight one. "It does happen to be true. We also destroyed the two whites, and killed or scattered their men."

As the woman realized that she was trapped, her eyes widened.

Beltur dropped the confinement. "That was just to get your attention. I'm Beltur, and my consort is Jessyla. She's a very good healer, and we will be opening a healing house. Until we do, if you need a healer, you can ask at the East Inn."

"You do have a way of getting a body's attention. What do you really want?"

"Only to tell you what we just did and to get your name so we know who lives in Haven. We're trying to reach as many people as we can."

The woman looked past the two toward the horses. "Good mounts. One looks like a warhorse." Her eyes went back to Jessyla. "You're a healer. Tell me what's wrong with me."

Beltur studied the woman with his senses, then looked to Jessyla and nodded.

"Not much of anything, except that you're not young. It feels like you broke your left arm when you were young. It could have been set better, but there's no weakness in the bone." Jessyla looked to Beltur. "Did I miss anything?"

"You've got a tiny bit of chaos in your left big toe. You might have scraped it or cut it, or just bruised it. Whatever it was, it's mostly healed."

For just an instant, the woman looked stunned. Then she frowned at Beltur. "Where in the world did the Duchess find you two?"

"She didn't. Lord Korsaen did. He and the Duchess said we could live here if we'd do our best to return Haven to prosperity."

"You say you got rid of those whites?"

"We did."

"That's a good start."

"You never did tell us your name," Jessyla said with a smile.

"Yamella. Zankar's my son. This is his house. I live in the cottage over there, but I watch the place while he's on the road."

"He's a trader?"

"A good one, too, not like those sleazy fellows from Hydlen . . ."

"Did he know about the whites?" asked Beltur.

Yamella shook her head. "He's been gone almost four eightdays. He goes first to Lydiar and then to Sligo. I have to say I worried when I heard about the mages, the white ones."

"Now you don't have to worry about them," affirmed Jessyla.

"I don't, do I." Yamella smiled, then took a step backward. "Thank you for coming by."

And she shut the door.

Jessyla frowned. "There's something . . ."

"There's something about everyone," said Beltur dryly.

After Jessyla wrote down the two names and the approximate location, they untied the horses and walked them across the main street to the house opposite Yamella's—or Zankar's—a two-story square structure with heavy wooden shutters on all the windows. The shutters on the ground-level windows were tightly fastened. They had to tie the horses to the branches of an ill-kept pearapple tree, since there was no hitching rail or fence.

"There's someone inside, several people," said Beltur as they approached the door. He knocked. No one responded. He knocked again.

Finally, the peephole in the middle of the heavy wooden door opened. "Who are you? What do you want?" The voice was likely that of an older man.

Beltur repeated what he'd said previously.

"That's all fine and good, but what do you want from us?"

"Nothing, except your name, and to tell you that."

"Name's Straetham. Good day." The peephole closed.

"Not exactly friendly," said Beltur.

"In this town, right now, would you be that friendly to strangers?" asked Jessyla.

No one was in the third house they approached.

The fourth house was little more than a cot, except it was built more like a fortress, with thick stone walls, small windows with heavy shutters, and a split slate roof. It also had a small outbuilding and was surrounded by gardens, all but one clearly devoted to vegetables. To Beltur's surprise, a woman of indeterminate age was weeding one of the beds on the west side of the house. She straightened as the two approached.

"You two must be part of the group that removed those nasty white mages. I'm Julli. Jullianya, really, but everyone calls me Julli." Her eyes went to Jessyla.

"I'm Jessyla, and this is Beltur. He's a black mage and my consort."

"I'd say you're both too young to do what everyone says, but Jaegyr saw it all, and he described you both pretty well, except he thought you were bigger than you are, Mage . . ."

"Beltur. Might I ask who Jaegyr is?"

"My consort. He's a woodworker, and he was at the East Inn repairing barrels for Bythalt when everything happened. If anyone else had told me, I wouldn't have believed it, but Jaegyr . . ." Julli shook her head.

Beltur nodded to Jessyla to do the talking.

"We're here just to get to meet people and to let them know that the Duchess sent the four of us to be the new town council . . ." Jessyla went on to elaborate somewhat, then waited.

"It's past time that someone did something," replied Julli, "but that's just my opinion, and I have too many of those, Jaegyr says."

"Have you had any trouble with the traders?"

"They're not so bad if you stay away from them, well, except for a few of them like Duurben. They don't bother us. It might be because there's no one else who can fix barrels and other things besides Jaegyr. Also, both Bythalt and Phaelgren want what comes from my gardens and root cellars for their public rooms."

"You also have a rather stout house," observed Beltur.

"Jaegyr's protective. There are inside iron shutters and the doors are iron-cored."

Beltur nodded. In Haven, that was sensible. Then he asked, "Is . . . Zankar . . . one of the decent traders?"

"Oh . . . you must have been talking to Yamella. You know, she's not quite right in the head."

"She seemed healthy enough."

"Healthy as a plow horse, but . . . she still thinks her son's going to come back."

"She said he was a trader."

"He was . . . until one of the Hydlenese traders carved him up."

"When did that happen?"

"A year ago. Might have been a little longer."

"Do you know which trader?"

"Wurtaan . . . Whartaan . . . something like that. Most of what I know about the traders comes from Jaegyr. I stay away from the inns. That's best unless you've got business there."

"How do most people even manage?" asked Jessyla.

"You just keep your head and stay away from trouble. Everyone knows who grows or makes what. We just trade among ourselves, or if we don't know, give it to Torkell. He makes sure you get a fair portion."

"What do you need from a council?" asked Beltur.

"Order and low tariffs. The rest we can handle."

"You don't have a healing house or healers," ventured Jessyla.

"We could use good healers, too, but good ones won't stay without order."

After another half quint of conversation, Beltur and Jessyla walked back toward their mounts.

"There are almost two towns here," said Beltur as he untied Slowpoke, "the one you see and the one you don't. I think it's going to be a very long day."

"Optimist," returned Jessyla. "It's going to be a very long eightday. And a longer year."

VII

By the time Beltur opened his eyes on threeday morning, he was more than ready to concede that Jessyla had been right. Over the previous five days, the five of them had covered the entire town. They had sheets of paper filled with names, and Tulya had drawn a copy of the map used by the whites. Then the four of them had painstakingly put names with houses and other structures—once Lhadoraak had pointed out that they had no records from which they could levy tariffs. They did have the instructions for how tariffs were levied, but before they could do that they'd have to create folders for each property indexed to the tariff ledgers they hadn't created.

They had located the old Council building, one of the narrow and empty structures on the nearly deserted square, and Jessyla had been pleased to learn that the adjoining structure had once been the healing house. Both needed a great deal of work, especially the former healing house, but that meant they wouldn't have to build either from scratch. Beltur had located the break in the fired-clay pipes that led to the fountain in the square, but hadn't had a chance to do more than that. Karch's troopers continued to patrol the streets and the roads leading into the town, and Haven remained disturbingly quiet, a quiet that the new council knew couldn't last. And, so far, the wounded bravos were all healing as well as could be expected, although Beltur had been required to remove more chaos than he'd anticipated from both the youngest and the oldest of the wounded.

With all those thoughts in his mind, Beltur stretched, sat up in the lumpy inn bed, and looked at Jessyla. "What should we do today, now that we've done what we can in learning about the town?"

"We need to find places to live, and we also need to find some carpenters, joiners, and masons, both for wherever we're going to live and to fix the Council building and the healing house. We also need to decide how we'll keep order when Karch and his company leave. Tomorrow will be the end of the first eightday."

"We'll likely need a gaol, too, except I suppose we could put that in the back of the Council building." Another thought struck Beltur. "We'll also need to write a letter to Johlana and Jorhan, telling them where we are. Karch can carry it back to Vergren to Korsaen or Essek so they can find someone headed to Axalt."

"If we're to do all that, you need to put on some clothes," suggested Jessyla, drawing the sheet around herself.

"And you don't?"

"You can wash up first."

Beltur tugged at the sheet and gave a mock-lecherous grin, although perhaps it wasn't totally false.

In return, Jessyla batted her eyes and glanced demurely down.

They both laughed.

Then Beltur hurriedly washed up and dressed, trying not to look too often in Jessyla's direction.

Lhadoraak, Tulya, and Taelya were already in the public room when Beltur and Jessyla arrived, but that was partly because Beltur and Jessyla had checked on the wounded men first. Even so, the three only had mugs of ale before them.

"Taelya woke up early and hungry," Lhadoraak explained. "I think she's growing again."

"That's good," declared Beltur, adding quickly, "For her, but maybe not for your sleep." He quickly let his senses run over Taelya, but was relieved that there were still no signs of the order binding that had almost killed her in Elparta. She was also keeping the free chaos around her separated by a thin line of order, the result being that she appeared far whiter to most mages than she actually was—and would live much longer if she maintained that disciplined approach to magery.

"Do you know what's for breakfast?"

"Egg toast, berry syrup, and mutton strips."

In moments, Claerk had appeared with two mugs of ale.

Belatedly, Beltur realized that Taelya had two mugs and a pitcher of water. One of the mugs was less than a third full of ale. The water in the pitcher had been order/chaos cleaned. "Did you clean the water, Taelya?"

"I did. Father watched, though."

"She did it perfectly."

Beltur took a sip of the ale, dark but not quite so bitter as the brew they'd had the first two days.

"What have you two been thinking about?" asked Lhadoraak, smiling slyly as he added, "If you had time for thinking."

Jessyla blushed slightly.

"We need to find a dwelling big enough for all of us . . . or two side by side," said Beltur quickly.

"I've marked the map," said Tulya. "We can go over it after we eat, or later. The houses without names are ones where no one is living, and no one's been for years, according to the neighbors. We could take any of them."

"Under the law?" asked Jessyla, her tone of voice dubious.

"I've been reading the laws Korsaen sent with us. Houses vacant for more than five years, where no previous inhabitant has made a statement of intent to return, and where no tariff has been paid during those times, can be claimed upon payment of back tariffs, or where no tariff is due, by restoring the house to a condition where a tariff can be levied. Once an effort at restoration has begun, a previous owner may not make a claim, unless the restoration is halted and the dwelling remains uninhabitable."

"That actually makes sense," said Beltur.

"So, among other things, we need to look at abandoned and run-down dwellings?" said Lhadoraak dryly.

"The sooner we find somewhere to live, the sooner we can stop paying Bythalt," replied Beltur. "It's likely going to take silvers and time to make any of those places livable."

"And some we'd have to practically rebuild," Tulya pointed out.

At that moment, Claerk reappeared carrying three platters and a basket of bread, setting them in front of the earlier arrivals. Then he looked to Beltur. "Just a few moments more."

"That will be fine. As I told you earlier, we're going to need some carpentry done. We'll pay. What about Gorlaak?"

"He sets timbers, floors, that sort of heavy work."

Beltur frowned. "Who does things like cabinets and trim?"

"Jaegyr's the only one Bythalt'll use."

"How good is he?"

"Seems like what he fixes stays fixed. Other than that, I wouldn't know."

"Does he do other woodwork?"

"He built a chest for pans and skillets in the kitchen."

"I'd like to look at it after breakfast."

"Can't do any harm, so long as you stay out of Ma's way." Claerk glanced toward the kitchen. "Best I see if yours is ready."

Before long, Beltur and Jessyla were served. As Beltur and Jessyla finished eating, Tulya left and returned shortly with the map, which she spread out on an adjoining table. Then the five moved to the table with the map.

Tulya began to explain. "These houses here are the closest to the square, but they're smaller. These will take more work . . ."

"We all ought to look at them together," suggested Lhadoraak.

At that moment, Captain Karch entered the public room.

"Good morning, Captain," offered Beltur. "What news do you have?"

"We haven't seen a sign of anyone like traders or bravos," replied Karch. "They'll just wait until we're gone."

Beltur understood the implied suggestion. "From what you said, we didn't expect any different. That's why we're working as fast as we can to find out what we need to know while you and your men are here. That gives us the time to get organized. We've located the old Council building and the healing house, and we're working on how to get started on housing, and building a small gaol in the back of the Council building . . . at least at some time."

"You've been busy on records . . ."

"There aren't any records of any sort. So we didn't know who lives where and what trades are still here. We have to know that in order to set up a tariff system. Doing all that also tells people we're here to stay."

"Talking with people also lets us know where there might be problems," added Jessyla.

"And what resources are here and what aren't," said Tulya.

"Have you and your men discovered anything we should know?"

"We've seen several mounted patrols from a distance. Their uniforms were bright green with yellow piping."

Beltur knew that brown uniforms with green trim were from Certis, and, of course, troopers from Gallos wore gray, except for the palace guards, who wore black. "I don't know those colors. Hydlen or Lydiar?"

"Green and yellow are Hydlen. Maroon is Lydiar."

Beltur should have guessed that the patrols had been from Hydlen, given the golds that the white mage had possessed. "Did they see your men?"

"I made certain that they did. I thought it might create a little consternation back in Hydolar."

That was probably true, Beltur reflected, but it also might create more problems for the four of them later. "No sign of smugglers or traders?"

"If they don't want to be seen, they're not, except by you mages." Karch paused, then asked, "Do you have any needs from my men?"

"Except for patrolling, not at the moment," said Beltur. "That's very necessary, because it allows us to work on getting ready without distraction. We appreciate it." While Beltur was repeating what he'd said earlier, he had the feeling it was necessary.

"Then we'll be getting on with it."

After Karch left, Beltur turned to the others. "If you'd get ready to ride so that we can see those houses, I'll meet you at the stable." Then he made his way to the kitchen, where he found Claerk and an older woman, presumably the young man's mother and the inn's cook.

"Thank you for breakfast," Beltur offered.

The woman inclined her head. "Ser mage."

"Which cabinet was the one Jaegyr made?" Beltur asked Claerk.

The young man walked to an open-faced oak cabinet some two yards high. "This one."

Beltur moved closer and studied the workmanship. The cabinet looked strong and solid. Although Beltur was no expert in woodworking, he could see that the finish was smooth, the joins and the mitered corners even. He nodded, then turned to Claerk. "That speaks well of Jaegyr. Where would we find Gorlaak?"

"His place is out the north lane off the square. Just keep going till you get to the stream. Then look right for the buildings beside it. That's his place. He won't be there today, though. He's out back. He came early to replace some timbers in the stable . . . now that Bythalt's got some coins to pay him."

"If you'd take me out and introduce me."

"Yes, ser."

Beltur followed Claerk out to the far end of the stables.

The man who wrestled a post into place was only slightly taller than Beltur but had shoulders seemingly twice as broad and arms twice as big as Beltur did.

Beltur just watched until he had the post in place, then stepped forward. "I'm Beltur, and Claerk here tells me that you do good work with floors and timbers."

"I might be the only one around here."

"We've got two buildings we need to put back in usable condition. Over on the square. I'd like you to take a look at them . . . if you're interested."

Gorlaak grinned. "You have the coins, I'll do the work. Likely be done in two glasses. Maybe a little sooner."

"We'll come back, and we'll go over to the square then."

"I'll be here."

Beltur nodded, then stepped away and headed to check the two mounts that the whites had used. They were in decent shape, and he'd groomed both the evening before. Then he saddled Slowpoke.

A quint later the five were riding south past the square.

"The first houses are a block past the Brass Bowl and two blocks south," Tulya said.

When Beltur reined up, he saw that there were actually three run-down houses in a row. All three had stone and brick walls and sagging rooftrees and shutters. The windows had either lost their glazing or had never been glazed. The space in front of the houses was partly bare ground and partly weeds, but the bare ground had more than a few shards of broken roof tiles scattered here and there. One of the houses had no door.

"Even if we repaired them, each one is smaller than the cot we had in Axalt," said Jessyla.

Beltur didn't dismount, but let his senses range over the small dwellings before nodding and saying, "I hope we can do better."

The next houses were a block farther south, across the narrow lane from each other, on opposing corners. They were each much larger than the first dwellings, but the roof at the end of one had caved in, and the other looked to have been gutted back to the brick walls, which appeared sturdy enough. The one that had been gutted also had a barn on the property, large enough, Beltur judged, to stable possibly as many as eight horses . . . and to store at least some hay in the loft.

"The walls are sound," said Lhadoraak. "The rest needs work. A little in some places, a lot in others."

The next three sets of dwellings were even worse than the ones they'd previously looked at, most likely because they were timber beam and post construction with plank walls.

Then the five turned north and rode past the square once more and looked at the five abandoned houses east of the East Inn. None were close to each other, and that bothered Beltur. Two would have been easier to repair, but each was quite small.

As they rode back toward the East Inn, Beltur cleared his throat. "The two brick-walled houses look to me like the best possibilities, but we ought to have Gorlaak look at them to see if they're reclaimable."

Once they reached the inn and stalled, but did not unsaddle, the horses, the five waited for almost a quint before Gorlaak appeared. Then they all walked over to the far side of the square where the old Council building still stood, a two-story structure some seven yards wide and close to ten deep. The door was locked or bolted from the inside, something Beltur had sensed earlier. The two narrow windows on each side of the door were also shuttered.

Beltur inspected each of the sets of shutters, then used a wedge of order to slide the bar behind one of the shutters enough that he could open them. The window behind had no locks, and he swung it open and stepped inside, where, after he took two steps, he began to sneeze from the dust raised by his boots. Despite the dust, the building didn't look that bad, although it appeared that all the furniture, if there had been any, had been removed. Beltur walked to the front door and after a struggle removed the heavy bar and opened the door. Then he sneezed again.

"It's dusty." Tulya wrinkled her nose as she stepped inside.

Beltur followed Gorlaak as he went from the front room, which extended the width of the building, but was only five yards deep, into the narrow hall flanked by two smaller chambers and then up a steep staircase. There were two rooms on the upper level. One of them held two table desks, scratched but seemingly sturdy, and two straight-backed chairs.

Gorlaak inspected the ceiling and the walls and then stood on one of the table desks to pry open the entrance to the attic above. After a time, he climbed down from the attic and looked at Beltur. "Roof's sound except for one corner. Wouldn't take much to fix it. Stairs are also sound. Looks like they just closed it up and left it after the traders killed Coront. He was the last councilor."

"Why did they kill him?"

"He collected tariffs and didn't do anything. Tried to order the traders around." Gorlaak shrugged. "You got another building to look at?"

"The old healing house next door and then two houses that need some hefty work."

"Healing house was shut down years and years ago."

"So we heard," replied Jessyla.

The three walked downstairs, and everyone but Beltur walked out to the square while he closed up the building. From there they went to the healing house, also shuttered, but the door was not barred or locked.

Jessyla opened it and stepped inside, followed by Beltur.

Unlike the Council House, there was a foyer, with two small rooms on each side, and an archway leading to a hallway. Two more small rooms were located on each side of the hall, and at the end of the hallway was a staircase to the upper level.

Gorlaak studied the rear staircase, then shook his head. "Need to replace the top timbers that hold the risers. See all that sawdust? Carpenter ants. Might need other timbers done, too."

"Can you get the timbers?" asked Beltur.

Gorlaak smiled. "I've got more seasoned timbers than you'll ever need. Figured someday someone would come and put Haven to rights." He shrugged. "Even if that didn't happen, people need timbers."

"Then you have a mill?"

"What passes for one in these parts. Got into replacing timbers and floors because not many folks were building."

"What do you think of Jaegyr's woodworking skills?"

"Better at cabinets and finishing than barrels."

"I'd think it would be the other way."

Gorlaak shook his head. "His father was a cabinetmaker. That was back in the day. Jaegyr ended up doing barrels and the simple carpentry because no one needed furniture. He's good at that, but . . . that's not where his heart is." The big man shrugged. "We all do what puts food on the table."

"Speaking of that," said Beltur, "what does a day of your work cost us?"

"Five coppers a day, in addition to the wood. Doesn't matter whether the day's long or short."

After a brief inspection of the healing house—with only one person on the staircase at a time—the four began to walk the five blocks to the two brick houses.

"I can still use the first floor of the healing house, once I get it cleaned up and can round up the supplies I need," said Jessyla.

"Supplies might be the hard part," suggested Beltur.

"I'm sure I can find herbs that will do. I could check with Julli. I thought I saw burnet and brinn there."

"She strikes me as someone who'd know where everything is," said Beltur wryly.

As they approached the two houses, Gorlaak cleared his throat. "I can remember when these were nice places. They just up and left, went to Lydiar, they said. Must have been a good ten years ago."

It took Gorlaak almost a glass to inspect both the houses. As he was walking back toward Beltur and Jessyla, she said, "My thought is that we need to get Gorlaak and Jaegyr to work on the houses first. We can clean the Council building or get someone to clean it and use it right now. I can use the lower floor of the healing house."

Beltur nodded. He'd had the same thought.

"Fixing both of them will take a fair amount of work," declared Gorlaak.

"How long would it take you and Jaegyr to make them livable?" asked Beltur.

"Just livable? The one that's gutted . . . two, maybe three eightdays. Walls are sound. So's the roof, mostly. Need to replace some tiles and repoint some of the bricks. Shutters mostly need to be replaced. Re-plank some of the inside walls."

"But there's nothing there," said Taelya.

"That means we don't have to tear out as much, little woman." Gorlaak smiled.

"We'll need them more than livable," declared Jessyla, "but we'll start there. When can you begin?"

The big man grinned. "Seeing as no one else is building and you're paying, how about tomorrow?"

"Does Jaegyr work for the same pay as you do?" asked Beltur.

"On something like this he will."

"Is there any way to get clean water anywhere close to the house?"

"There are some fired-clay water pipes that run from the north hill spring. Have to trace them."

"I can probably trace them," said Beltur, "if you can show me where they start. Can you do piping as well?"

"I could, but you'd do better with old Faastah. I'll have him come by and see you in the next day or so."

By the time Beltur had worked out arrangements with Gorlaak and the six had walked back to the East Inn, it was well past midafternoon, and Beltur was more than ready even for the passable ale offered by Bythalt.

VIII

By sixday afternoon, the Council House was clean, and the two table desks and chairs had been moved down to the front room of the first level. Tulya had managed to buy paper and even an old ledger from Torkell's chandlery and was busy creating the basis for a tariff ledger. Both Jaegyr and Gorlaak had begun work on the house with the sound roof, and Lhadoraak was helping them, since he'd been an apprentice cabinet maker for a short time before being discovered to have magely talents.

Jessyla had cleaned the healing house, but it was still empty. Beltur had traced out the main water pipes and gotten Faastah to repair the pipe to the fountain and the fountain basin. The fountain now offered water. Beltur had also hired two local youths to dig a trench from the nearest water pipe to the two houses under repair. Because Torkell had never even heard of a kitchen cistern, Beltur needed to figure out how to create the equivalent of the kitchen cistern that he and Jessyla had enjoyed in Axalt, since he didn't want either of them lugging water any farther than absolutely necessary.

At that moment, while Jessyla was at the chandlery trying to see what Torkell had that could be used as healing supplies, Beltur was standing beside the house under repair, waiting for Faastah, when Karch rode up.

Beltur turned and walked toward the captain. "Any more sightings of Hydlenese troopers?"

"Not this morning. Everything's quiet, just like I told you it would be." Karch paused. "Except we're seeing more folks than we usually do."

“That could just be that they’re taking advantage of what they think is the calm before the storm.”

“There’s that, too.” Karch frowned. “What are you going to do when the traders come back?”

“Not a thing so long as they behave themselves and pay the innkeepers and everyone else.”

“And if they don’t?”

“Take what they owe from them and send them on their way.”

“They’ll likely strike back at the townspeople.”

“That’s a good point. We’ll need to watch for that. If they do . . . then we’ll deal with it as well.” Beltur kept his voice pleasant.

“How much longer are you intending that we should stay in Haven?” asked Karch.

“Your presence has allowed us a good start on what we need to get done. The Duchess and Lord Korsaen had suggested two eightdays, I believe?”

“Somewhere in that neighborhood, give or take a few days.”

“That would be next fiveday morning. I think we should both plan on that, unless something changes drastically.”

Karch nodded. “That’s what we’ll plan for, but I think we should keep that to ourselves. That might give you a few more days of quiet.”

“That would be good.”

After the captain rode off, Beltur only had to wait a few moments more before Faastah appeared, suggesting that the mason had just stayed out of sight while Karch and Beltur were talking.

The white-haired mason ambled up to Beltur. “I saw you were talking to the captain. I haven’t seen that one before.”

“He’s posted out of Vergren, not Weevett.”

“That’s a long ride to do a patrol in Haven.”

“His company was escorting us.”

“They say all of you mages came a long way.”

“Two of us are originally from Gallos, and three are from Elparta in Spidlar. What about the pipes?”

“It’ll take me a couple of eightdays to fire enough pipe to run along that trench to your houses.”

While the distance was only a little over a hundred and fifty yards, Beltur could unfortunately understand the limitations of Faastah's comparatively small kiln. "I understand, but the sooner you can do it the better. There's something else . . . well, two something elses."

Faastah offered a snaggletoothed smile. "So long as you're paying and so long as it's something I can do."

"I'd like to put a stove in the hearth on the kitchen side. Do you have any ideas about how best to do that?"

"I'd need to be thinking about that, ser."

"The other thing is that I'd like you to build an indoor cistern in the corner of the kitchen."

Faastah frowned. "Out of what?"

"Brick and mortar."

"It'll leak, sooner or later. Make a terrible mess. You don't want that, ser. Also, it'd be too heavy for the floor."

"Not if we put a brick and stone foundation under it in that corner. It wouldn't take that much space out of the root cellar."

"It'd still leak."

"Even if it were glazed?"

"I can't glaze it in place, and if I glazed pieces and mortared them in place they'd come loose and it would still leak."

"Let's walk over and take a look at what might be possible."

Gorlaak looked up from where he was reinforcing the wall by replacing a timber, then nodded as Beltur led Faastah into the area that would be the kitchen.

Beltur pointed to the southeast corner of the room. "Couldn't you build two brick walls up from the cellar right there?"

"I could do that. I've got plenty of good brick from some of the old places. It won't match, but you don't care, I take it, since the only place you could see it would be in the root cellar?"

"That's right. Then Gorlaak could use two or three extra timbers across the top of the walls and under the floor planks, and you could begin with a stone base . . ." Beltur explained more what he had in mind.

"I could do that," Faastah said in response. "But before long it's still going to leak."

"What would happen if there happened to be several layers of glaze over the mortar lining the cistern?"

"Can't glaze it in place."

"Can you mix up some glaze, the kind that would line a pitcher or a cistern, and bring it here tomorrow?" Beltur grinned. "Before you start work on the support walls. You work on building the cistern, and we'll work on a way to glaze or seal the inside."

"You think you can glaze it with magery?"

"That's what I want to discover."

"What about getting the water out?"

"They have taps for kegs of lager and ale, don't they? You might have to fire and glaze a small length of pipe to go through the bricks and mortar."

"Iron or copper pipe might be better."

"Is there a coppersmith here?"

Faastah shook his head. "As for iron, I wouldn't trust Woffurd or Torkell to forge it, either. Poor excuses for a smith."

"Then we'll have to work with fired clay."

"You'll pay me each day?"

"If that's what you want." Beltur understood the mason's doubts—that the troopers and the mages might not be around long, one way or the other.

The two walked back out of the house, and Beltur watched as Faastah headed for the main street. Then he untied Slowpoke and mounted.

IX

After dinner, Beltur sat on the end of the lumpy inn mattress in the dim light reading, and occasionally paging through *The Wisdom of Relyn,* the volume given to him by the mage and councilor Naerkaal just before Beltur and Jessyla had left Axalt. Given all that they had been through, Beltur hadn't done much reading, but he was feeling more than a little discouraged. The more they did, the more it seemed that there was to do.

"Are you finding anything useful there?" asked Jessyla.

"Not exactly useful, but reading it reminds me that we're not the first to try to build something in a difficult place. At least we're not on the top of the Roof of the World where everything is frozen for a third of the year."

"The angels were lucky that it was hard for their enemies to get to them, and they had that black tower."

"They had to build it first, and they faced attacks all through the first year."

"Do you think Relyn could have been exaggerating?"

"It's possible, but I don't think so. Or not much. In one place, here, he asks, 'How could four exiles of Heaven—Ryba, Nylan, Saryn, and Ayrlyn—how could they and a handful of women, many of whom were penniless wretches who fled Gallos, how could they vanquish the armies that swarmed into the Westhorns bent on their destruction?'"

"That's a good question, but does he answer it?" asked Jessyla wryly.

"Here's the answer he gives." Beltur pointed to the lines that followed:

> It was not just their power that achieved victory, nor their vision. Rather it was the understanding that nothing else mattered. I watched Nylan labor over his forge long beyond the glasses anyone would deem possible. Saryn drilled and trained mere lasses, glass after glass, into warriors who could and did destroy men twice their size. Ryba watched over all, and let nothing lapse. Even Ayrlyn the singer went out and traded for any scrap, any item, that might prove useful . . .

"'The understanding that nothing else mattered . . .' That's frightening," said Jessyla. "Is that what we'll have to do?"

"What do you think?" countered Beltur.

For several moments, Jessyla did not reply. Finally, she said, "What else did he write about that?"

Beltur read the next section aloud.

> "Many have said that Tower Black and the other buildings that followed were what enabled the angels to survive and prosper, as if creating structures fostered that power. That was not so for Westwind nor has it ever been so. The great structures are the reflections and symbols of a great person or a great people.
>
> Such buildings last beyond the greatness of the people who built them. When this happens, those in that land, as well as in other lands, often come to believe that building great structures is the

way to eternal glory. They forget that the light of glory is fed by the deeds of the living and not by the cold stones and fired brick of massive structures.

Nor does building a structure to a deity or a cause create greatness in a people or a land. The most vital structures are those that serve a people, just as Nylan's cisterns and drains made it possible for the angels to survive and even prosper in winters that no other people could endure . . ."

He stopped and waited for Jessyla to say something.

"We haven't built much, and repairing things isn't building."

"We've only been here less than two eightdays. We've got the fountain working and before long the Council building and the healing house will be usable. We're paying people to do things, and that helps. If we do more things like that, maybe we can draw more people, the way the angels did."

"We aren't the angels," Jessyla pointed out.

"No . . . but we aren't on the Roof of the World, either, where everything freezes solid for a good part of the year."

She bent forward and kissed his cheek. "Optimist."

X

First thing on sevenday morning Beltur and Jessyla inspected the wounds of the five armsmen. After that, he brought Taelya with him to the house where they waited for Faastah. Gorlaak, Jaegyr, and Lhadoraak were already hard at work on reinforcing and replacing the weakened internal timbers.

"You said you'd explain why you wanted me here," prompted Taelya.

"I'm hoping that I can teach you how to use chaos carefully and precisely while also getting you ready to do something to help us prepare the houses. You remember the big kitchen cistern in the house in Axalt?"

Taelya nodded.

"Well . . . there aren't any cisterns anywhere around here, and none of us want to carry water all the way from the square, do we?"

"No." She also shook her head.

"Faastah can make a cistern out of bricks and mortar. It will have to have a well-fitted wooden top, but unless we glaze the inside of the cistern, after a short while it will leak. You and I are going to work on finding a way to use order and chaos to do that glazing."

"But he hasn't built the cistern yet."

"No, he hasn't. That will give us time to work out how to glaze it. We can practice on broken bricks."

Before long Faastah appeared with a cart loaded with bricks and wooden buckets. After tying the cart horse to the inset iron ring on the battered hitching post and lifting a small bucket out of the cart, he walked over to where Beltur and Taelya stood.

"This here's an ash glaze. Don't know if that's what you want. You brush it on, but the kiln's got to be really hot. Do you care what color the glaze is?"

Beltur shook his head. "Will it stick to brick and mortar?"

"It'll stick to hard-fired brick. I've never tried glazing mortar."

"Neither have we. That's why we need to see what it takes."

Faastah looked to Taelya.

"She's a beginning white mage. I thought she could learn with me."

"You're a black mage."

"I am, but I started out as a white mage before the Prefect chased me out of Gallos," replied Beltur. "It's a very long story. But it's also why I can teach Taelya."

"Times are changing, that's for sure." Faastah lifted the bucket.

Beltur took it. "Thank you. We'll see how we'll make this work."

"Best be getting to starting those walls for you . . . and doing repairs after Gorlaak gets done with the timbering and re-flooring." Faastah nodded and headed back to the cart.

Beltur smiled at Taelya. "I'm going to study the glaze a bit. Would you see if you can gather up any broken bricks or large pieces of brick?"

"I can do that."

As Taelya skipped up toward the house, Beltur wondered if he was being too optimistic, if mere repairs, and patrolling, would make any difference at all. *We have to start somewhere.*

He took a deep breath and let his senses range over the glaze, but he could discern neither excess order nor chaos. The question was whether a mixture of order and chaos, or chaos confined by order, could turn the paste into a solid glaze that would hold and not crack. *And that's going to be difficult to work out . . . if you can do it at all.* But if it would reduce water hauling . . .

Beltur stirred the glaze with the old brush in the bucket, thinking as he did.

When Taelya returned with several broken bricks, Beltur led the way to the heaped stone wall that presumably marked the property line between the house under repair and a stone-walled cottage that he knew was inhabited, although he couldn't remember the names of the older couple who lived there. Then he lined up the broken bricks on the uneven top of the wall and daubed the brick section on the far left with glaze. He stepped back and set the bucket on the ground well away from the wall.

"Taelya . . . I want you to make a point of chaos about the size of your fingertip and touch the glaze with it. Stand back from the wall a few steps."

As Taelya did that, Beltur extended his shields around her.

SPLATT! Glaze sprayed away from the chaos, which vanished instantly, and droplets struck the shields.

"Oh!!!" Taelya jumped back.

Beltur laughed softly. "I can see that this is going to take some work by both of us." He paused, then picked up the bucket and daubed the same brick again. "Do the same thing again, but this time, I'm going to use a shield around your chaos."

Taelya nodded and concentrated.

Beltur used a small shield to press Taelya's gathered free chaos against the surface of the brick.

Hsssttt . . . The glaze bubbled under the shield at the edges.

After several moments, Beltur eased the shield up from the brick. The glaze still looked liquid, but Beltur used the brush to remove most of the liquid, studying the surface of the brick with both his eyes and senses. He could sense the faintest amount of order loosely linked to the brick where there appeared to be a slight residue, but when he tapped it with the point of his belt knife, the small flake of glaze separated from the brick.

"Well . . . that's a little better, but we need to try again."

On the third try, Beltur applied more pressure with his shield . . . and the brick fragment split.

"Oops . . . you were too strong, Uncle Beltur."

"So it seems." Beltur studied the split fragment. In several places, there appeared to be the thinnest coating of a shiny brownish glaze. He was about to apply glaze to the side of the next broken brick when he sensed Lhadoraak walking toward the two of them. He turned and straightened. "Here comes your father. He's going to want to know what we're doing. Would you like to tell him?"

"I'll tell him."

"I thought I sensed chaos. What under the stars are you two doing?"

Taelya grinned. "You did. Uncle Beltur and I are trying to use order and chaos to make glaze stick to bricks."

Lhadoraak frowned and looked to Beltur. "What for?"

"So that we can have kitchen cisterns." Beltur quickly explained, then added, "I also thought that it would be a good controlled way for Taelya to learn to handle very small bits of chaos safely."

Lhadoraak shook his head. "I might have known you'd figure out something like that."

"We haven't worked it out yet," Beltur pointed out.

"You will. Somehow, you will." The older mage smiled and looked at his daughter. "Just don't do anything except what Uncle Beltur tells you."

"Yes, Father."

Lhadoraak turned and walked back toward the house.

Beltur daubed glaze on the next broken brick fragment.

XI

Since Gorlaak, Jaegyr, and Faastah professed not to mind working on eightday, so long as they were paid, all of them were at the house at seventh glass. Beltur suspected that all three feared that their pay would vanish once the Montgren troopers left, but he wasn't about to argue against that belief because he and Lhadoraak could help, at least to some degree, and that would be less possible once the two of them had to take over the task of keeping Haven safe and once the traders returned . . . and not to mention the possibility of armsmen, renegade or otherwise.

By eightday afternoon, when they quit for the day, Faastah had finished the short support walls for the kitchen cistern, and all the floor timbers had been reinforced or strengthened except for those that would underlie the cistern, and most of the windows had been reframed, those by Jaegyr and Lhadoraak, who was far better with wood than he'd ever let on to Beltur.

Beltur and Taelya were equally tired, but had far less to show for their efforts. After almost two full days of working on the idea of glazing the interior of the cistern, Beltur was about to give up, and would have said so, except the last few attempts of the day had produced a very thin but even glaze, and Beltur wanted to see if multiple layers of a thin glaze might work . . . assuming that they could overlap the applications without getting cracks or breaks. If that didn't work, they'd just have to deal with a leaky cistern . . . or tear it out.

The first glass working at the house on oneday morning was a repeat of eightday morning, except that Beltur and Taelya had finally discovered a way to make the glazing work when Beltur placed a "net" of order within the glaze and then let Taelya apply chaos while he pressed an order shield against the chaos-tinged glaze. That also allowed a heavier coating of glaze.

He wasn't sure why that had worked, as opposed to what else they had tried, but given two days of frustration, he was more than glad they'd found something that had finally worked.

Two days of experimenting isn't really that long, he thought. It just seemed that long, given everything that lay in front of them. He looked to Taelya. "How are you in small spaces?"

"Why, Uncle Beltur?"

"Someone's going to have to brush the glaze over all the bricks and mortar."

"And I'm smaller?"

"That's right. Then we'll lift you out and work on the order/chaos glazing together."

"I won't have to be inside when we do that?"

"No. We'll be outside looking into the cistern from the top. Let's go tell Faastah and your father that it looks like we can make the cistern work."

When they entered the house, Beltur noticed that Faastah was doing the brickwork in the large kitchen hearth for the stove and oven.

The mason grinned at Beltur. "Haven't done one of these in a long while. Your lady'll like it."

"I'll like it," returned Beltur. "I had a makeshift apprenticing with a baker." Then he announced, "I think Taelya and I have finally figured the glazing out."

"I thought you would," said Lhadoraak, from where he was helping Jaegyr.

"But it's going to take a while," Beltur announced. "A few days, anyway, and that's after the mortar's well set. It's only going to work if we apply the glaze bit by bit. And Taelya's absolutely necessary."

"Oh?" said Lhadoraak.

"It's not just the chaos. The glaze has to be applied from inside the cistern. All of us are too big to do that, unless we want to hang upside down and juggle a glaze bucket."

"You mages just might be starting something. Not only stoves, but inside cisterns, yet," offered the wiry Jaegyr as he blotted his forehead with the back of his hand. "Be good to have a healer, too. Your healer was talking to Julli when I left."

"She needs herbs."

"Julli's got 'em."

At the sound of hoofbeats, Beltur looked through the window to the lane and saw one of Karch's troopers reining up outside. "I think there's a problem. Taelya, stay with your father for the moment." Then he hurried outside and down the cracked paving stones of the walk to where the trooper had dismounted.

"Ser, the patrol thought you might like to know that some traders are riding into town. They asked where to find the new council. Squad leader told them to try the Council House first. Then he sent me to tell you."

"I appreciate it. My thanks, and please also convey them to the squad leader. How long before they get here?"

"They had a wagon. They were taking their time."

"Good. I need to get to the Council House, then. If you'd tell Lhadoraak—the other mage—what you told me and that I'm headed there, I'd appreciate it."

Since Beltur hadn't seen the need to bring Slowpoke just to have him stand around in the sun all day, he had to hurry, not quite at a run, back to the square and the Council House. He was definitely hot and breathing heavily when he hurried through the front door and into the large front chamber, but at least he'd beaten the traders.

"What is it?" asked Tulya, starting to stand from behind the table desk where she'd been working on setting up a tariff ledger.

"There are some traders headed here. They're looking for the new council. I'd like them to talk to you first, without them seeing me. I'll be right in the corner, and I'll have you shielded."

"Where's Taelya?"

"She's with Lhadoraak at the house. The troopers told the traders to come here."

"Does he know there are traders coming?"

"Yes. The only one who doesn't is Jessyla." Beltur eased past Tulya to stand behind her against the wall.

"What do you want me to say?"

"Offer to be helpful and tell the truth about everything except for the fact that I'm here protecting you. Try to draw them out."

"That might not be as easy as it sounds."

"If what we've heard about the traders is true, it won't be difficult. It also won't be pleasant. But perhaps we'll be surprised."

"If we're surprised pleasantly, that would be a change."

Beltur thought about saying that Korsaen had surprised them pleasantly, but he wasn't totally sure that Tulya would see it that way. "We'll have to see." He could both see and sense riders approaching and drew a concealment around himself. "Several men are riding toward the Council House. I'm concealed."

Tulya settled into the chair and waited.

Shortly, two men walked into the front room. Both were likely fifteen years older than Beltur, but the slightly shorter, red-bearded man was most likely a guard, given the long dirk and the sabre-length blades he wore at his wide leather belt. He positioned himself to cover the door, as though he expected someone might enter.

The taller man was clean-shaven and wore a dark gray jacket over a mostly white shirt. He stopped short of Tulya and the table. "Well . . . well . . . what have we here?"

"What are you looking for, Trader?" asked Tulya. "You are a trader, aren't you?"

"I'll ask the questions. What's this I hear about a new town council?"

"There is a new town council," replied Tulya evenly. "How might I be able to help you?"

"By telling this so-called council to leave. We don't need a council to collect tariffs for doing nothing."

"Traders in Montgren don't pay tariffs on goods transported through Montgren," replied Tulya evenly. "They do pay tariffs seasonally if their business is based in Montgren. That includes here in Haven."

"That's frigging robbery. Taking coins for doing nothing. There's not even a working fountain in the square."

"There is now," said Tulya.

"It won't stay that way."

"We'll have to see, won't we?" replied Tulya with a sweetness that masked irritation, Beltur sensed.

"Still say it's theft of a working trader's coins."

"That's true in any chartered town in Montgren."

"Haven's not chartered. It hasn't been for years."

"It *hadn't* been for years," corrected Tulya. "It is now."

"Whose charter?"

"The Duchess's."

"She going to keep those troopers here? Don't see any post or barracks being built. Otherwise, nothing's going to change."

Beltur decided it was time to put in an appearance. He dropped the concealment. "No. She decided it would be more effective to use mages. That's why we're the new council." He smiled pleasantly.

"Sort of young for that, aren't you?" sneered the trader.

"I suppose you'll have to find that out," replied Beltur. "By the way, I'm Beltur. Who might you be?"

"Duurben. And don't you forget it."

Duurben—one of those mentioned unfavorably by Julli. "Duurben—it's good to put a face to a name."

"Don't think that one mage is going to change anything."

"I wouldn't think of it, Duurben. Not at all. Neither did the Duchess. That's why she sent three and a healer."

Duurben paused, if just for an instant. "One or three . . . it makes no difference."

"You're absolutely right," replied Beltur with a smile. "Haven's returning to being an ordered town. You behave in an ordered way, and you'll have no problems at all."

There was another pause before Duurben said, "What did you promise that white to join you?"

"Oh . . . there were two whites. They decided not to join us. They departed in their own way."

"They'll be back."

Beltur shook his head. "No one returns from the ashes."

"You're a black."

"He was also the leading war mage for Spidlar," said Tulya. "The one who destroyed most of the white war mages of Gallos."

"So the Duchess hired the strongest black she could find." Duurben shook his head. "Even you can't change a town." He smiled. "But it will be interesting to watch." He half nodded. "We won't provide any trouble. We aren't based in Haven. So don't try to impose tariffs on us."

"We won't," replied Tulya. "Unless you store goods here for more than a season a year. Then you're a resident, according to the laws of Montgren."

"A woman clerk who knows the law . . . amazing!" Immediately, Duurben turned and departed, followed by his guard.

"I really don't like him," said Tulya.

"According to Julli, he's one of the worst." Beltur both saw and sensed that Duurben and his guard were riding across the square toward the East Inn.

"You didn't mention that I'm part of the Council," Tulya said.

"He didn't stay long enough for either of us to make that point . . . or to say anything about the Council. I'm going to the inn. For now, I don't think you'll have any trouble, but bar the door after I leave. If anyone comes and you stay out of sight, they'll likely think the building's empty."

"How long before we have to worry?"

"When Karch and the troopers leave, I'd guess. Excuse me, I need to follow the trader."

Before stepping out of the Council House, Beltur drew a concealment around himself. Then he walked swiftly across the square and into the inn through the rear door, making his way toward the front foyer where he suspected he would find Duurben and Bythalt. He wasn't mistaken. He eased closer, listening carefully.

"Bythalt . . . how long have I been coming here?"

"Years, ser. Years."

"How long has that mage been here? To the day?"

That question told Beltur that Duurben had a very good idea how long troopers had stayed in the past and was likely calculating when they would leave so that he and his men could return.

"One eightday and four days."

"Has he paid you? Or is it all promises?"

"He and the captain have paid . . . separately."

There was a momentary silence before Duurben spoke again. "How strong is that mage?"

"Which mage, ser? The younger one, the older black, or the healer?"

"There are two mages and a healer?"

"The younger mage is also a healer, and the healer is also a mage."

Beltur could sense a helpless shrug on Bythalt's part.

"You've seen this?"

"The younger mage and the healer destroyed the two whites and shielded the troopers while the troopers used arrows to kill or wound most of the whites' armsmen."

"What about the other mage?"

"He was also an arms-mage against the Gallosians. That is what I heard."

Abruptly, Duurben stepped back. "Do what you must, Bythalt. But remember . . . I will be back."

"You always come back, ser."

"Keep that very much in mind."

Beltur waited until Duurben left the inn before dropping the concealment. As he approached the innkeeper, he could see that Bythalt was agitated, but he simply said, "I take it that Trader Duurben made an appearance?"

Bythalt turned with a start. "You knew, and you did nothing?"

"He visited the Council building and then came in this direction. I didn't have my horse, and I didn't feel like running after him." All that was perfectly true.

"You should have killed him as you did the evil white mages."

"The white mages attacked us. Duurben has done nothing evil around us."

"He pays but a copper a night, and nothing for his food. His men are worse."

"Charge him what we pay."

"He will do awful things then."

Beltur offered a shrug he didn't feel. "We'll have to wait until he does."

"Then someone will be hurt or killed. That man is bad."

"We'll see what we can do before it gets that far." Beltur turned and headed toward the rear of the inn.

As soon as he was outside and heading to the stable he glanced across the square, but there was no sign of anyone near either the healing house or the Council building. He understood very well Bythalt's concerns, but while Julli and Bythalt had both said that Duurben was evil, Duurben hadn't offered any direct evidence to support that, even though Beltur hadn't the slightest doubts about the trader's past and likely present intentions.

Which means watching him closely until he does.

XII

A glass after sunset on oneday, heavy gray clouds marched through the sky over Haven, and rain began to fall, softly. Beltur checked with Karch, but from what the captain and his patrols knew, Trader Duurben had left Haven—at least for a time.

That same soft rain was still falling when Beltur and Jessyla went down to breakfast in the public room on twoday morning, and the clouds remained thick enough that the morning seemed more like twilight. Lhadoraak, Tulya, and Taelya joined them almost immediately, and Claerk had ale on the table quickly.

As they waited for breakfast, Lhadoraak said, "Faastah should be able to finish the cistern today and then move to the second house. He thinks that the mortar should dry for several days before you and Taelya try to glaze the cistern. That shouldn't be a problem so long as you only glaze the inside."

Beltur frowned. Why would they want to go to all the effort of glazing the outside as well?

"He said something about the mortar curing. He also said not to use the stove for two eightdays."

"Everything takes longer," said Beltur dryly. "Not that it matters because it's going to take more than two eightdays before even the first house is livable, and that's with us sleeping on the floor."

"Maybe not," said Jessyla. "I've been talking to Julli. Jaegyr has some pieces he never sold that they might be willing to part with. There are some tables and other odds and ends. They don't match exactly, she said, but they're solid."

"Why don't you look at them?" said Beltur.

"I thought we both should."

"What about that brigand trader Duurben?" asked Tulya. "Do you know if the troopers have seen any more of him?"

"He rode in from the west, and went back that way," replied Beltur. "Last night, Karch's men didn't see him again, but they did see another patrol wearing Hydlenese uniforms."

"Everyone's waiting for Karch and the troopers to leave," said Lhadoraak.

"Not everyone," countered Beltur, his voice light. "We haven't seen Lydians, Certans, or Gallosians. And not any pirates from Worrak, either."

"Just wait," said Tulya sardonically. "How long will you two have the troopers stay?"

Beltur managed not to wince. He'd meant to talk to Lhadoraak about that. "The Duchess suggested two eightdays, but the captain said that he had some extra golds, enough for another three or four days."

"We could use at least a few more days," suggested Lhadoraak. "I'd really like to get the roof repaired on the second house . . . or close to it."

"Three days would be eightday morning," said Beltur. "I'd prefer not to run him out of provisions . . . or have to pay for the troopers out of what we have."

"Eightday, then," said Lhadoraak.

At that moment, Claerk carried out three platters, and set them in front of Jessyla, Tulya, and Taelya. "I'll be back with the other platters and bread in a moment."

"Claerk," asked Beltur, "do you know where the trader Duurben hails from?"

"No, ser. He always approaches the inn from the west. He has coppers from Gallos, Certis, and Hydlen."

"Not from Lydiar or Montgren?"

"I haven't seen any of those. None of us get many. Bythalt might have." Claerk hurried back to the kitchen, then returned almost immediately with two more platters and a basket of bread.

"Thank you," said Beltur. "It sounds like Duurben never goes to Lydiar. Do most of the traders go in both directions?"

"Niklos and Whartaan do. The others, I couldn't say, ser."

"Are they from Hydlen?"

"Whartaan claims to be. Niklos talks like he's from Lydiar. Is there anything else you need, ser?"

"Not right now."

"Then I'll be heading back to the kitchen." Claerk hurried off.

Beltur immediately started eating the egg scramble, of which it seemed he'd already had too many.

Jessyla looked at her platter, hesitated, and then took a small bite, followed by an almost imperceptible sigh, and then another small bite.

When he neared eating the last scraps of the scramble, Beltur looked to Lhadoraak. "What are you going to do today?"

"The roof on the first house is solid. So Jaegyr and I can work on the interior walls. When the rain stops, Gorlaak will start on rebuilding the roof on the second house." Lhadoraak turned to Jessyla. "Which house do you like best?"

"Which one do you like best?" countered Jessyla, looking to Tulya.

"Whichever one you don't," returned Tulya.

Beltur and Lhadoraak exchanged glances.

Then Lhadoraak said, "Both houses are about the same size. Gorlaak said that they were built by brothers. We need to decide now. That way, if either of you two wants specific things we can do them while we're fixing them. That's if it's possible."

"As long as I get a kitchen cistern and a stove, and a tight roof and windows . . ." Tulya shrugged.

"Both houses will have those," Beltur said, "and we're working to finish them both about the same time."

"Then you and Jessyla should have the first one," said Tulya, "because, as a healer, before long she won't have that much time."

"As the recorder and justicer of the Council," replied Beltur, "you won't either."

"Me? As justicer?" Tulya looked appalled.

"You're the one who's read and knows all the laws," Beltur pointed out. "I was very impressed with what you said to Duurben."

"But I'm not a mage."

"All the more reason you should be justicer," said Jessyla. "You understand better than anyone how someone with no magery feels."

Tulya frowned. "I'm not certain that's a good reason."

"It's a very good reason," said Lhadoraak. "Considering who you'll be dispensing justice to."

There was a moment of silence.

"What are you going to do?" Jessyla asked Beltur.

"After we look at our walking wounded, I'm going to write a letter to Johlana and Jorhan. Then I'll go help Lhadoraak." He paused. "And you?"

"I'll have to see." She smiled enigmatically. "But I was thinking of visiting Julli again."

After breakfast, Beltur and Jessyla made their way from the public room to the stable tack room, where another pair of Montgren troopers stood guard.

"They're getting restless, Mages," offered the older guard.

Beltur had barely gotten into the tack room behind Jessyla when the oldest armsman cleared his throat.

"Mage, Healer . . . you did say we weren't prisoners . . ."

"Once you're healed," Beltur replied. "You're all getting close. Let's see how you're doing first."

Jessyla immediately moved to Therran, the youngest of the former bravos, the one who'd suffered a leg wound through a chaos burn.

Beltur followed, studying the leg with his senses. There wasn't any of the nasty orangish red in the leg, but there was still a certain amount of dull redness, which he diluted with free order, not wanting to do too much, given the heat they'd created in using order to keep the young man alive earlier.

Jessyla looked at him.

Beltur murmured, "Another few days."

Then they studied Gustaan, the older man who'd had the shoulder wound. There were lingering traces of wound chaos there, and Beltur smoothed away what was there, knowing that whatever remained in the healing wound likely would generate a little more. The other three showed no sign of wound chaos.

Beltur looked over the five, then gestured. "You three aren't fully healed, but if you don't hurt yourself again, you should be fine." His eyes went to the youngest. "It's going to take another eightday for you to get there, most likely, and that's if we keep treating you."

"They can go, and I can't?"

"You can go," said Jessyla coldly, "and you just might die."

"Therran," said Gustaan, almost wearily. "Without them, you'd be dead. Have some sense, man."

The older armsman had almost said "boy," Beltur felt. "Gustaan, you need a couple more days. There's still a little old and deep wound chaos." After a moment, Beltur went on. "I said you had two choices. Work for us, and you'll be paid, or leave Haven. If you decide to work for us, you'll have to promise that you won't steal, fight, or cause trouble." Beltur smiled. "If you don't think you can abide by that, don't promise you will. I'll know you're lying. So will Jessyla. We'll ask you for your choice tomorrow morning."

"Why not now?" asked Turlow, one of the three mostly-healed men.

"Because it's been raining all night, and it's still raining . . . and if you don't want to work for us and stay . . . or if you lie, I don't want you walking wherever you're going in the rain."

"What are we supposed to do, beg?" asked Ermylt.

"If you work for the Council, you'll be fed and can sleep here for a time, maybe a bit longer. If you don't, I'll give you five coppers and a warning not to hang around Haven. Considering you were part of a force that tried to kill us, I'd say I'm being more than generous."

Gustaan nodded.

"Why are you even bothering?" asked Dussef, a stocky red-bearded man.

"We need men to do things. You obviously need coins and a safe place."

"But we're armsmen, not crafters or growers."

"Before long Haven will need town patrollers. If you work hard and well, and we find we can trust you, then you'll have a permanent position. If it doesn't suit you, you'll be healthy and have a few coins in your wallet when you leave."

"You don't need to trust us," pointed out Dussef. "You know."

"That's true," replied Beltur. "But we need to know if the townspeople can trust you."

Surprisingly, to Beltur, Turlow nodded.

"Now," said Beltur dryly, "enjoy your quarters. We'll see you in the morning."

Once the two had left the tack room, Beltur turned to Jessyla. "What do you think?"

"Gustaan will likely stay. Maybe Dussef. Therran's just angry. Ermylt will go, and he'll likely try something as soon as he's out of sight. Turlow . . . I don't know."

"That's about what I think. Now . . . we need to get on with the day . . . and we'll see in the morning."

XIII

Threeday morning, Beltur hunted down Karch, finding him just outside the stable, looking at the thin gray clouds that appeared to be moving south.

"You look concerned," offered Beltur. "The weather or something else?"

"There's no point in fretting about the weather. It's going to do what it's going to do. I hope we don't get caught in a downpour on the ride back. No, you have to worry about people. I don't have a good feeling about that trader . . . or about the Hydlenese."

"Neither do I, but you can't stay forever. It's not as though you're leaving tomorrow. Your patrols seem to be discouraging the Hydlenese."

"Only until we leave."

That was likely true enough, but Beltur just nodded.

"I'd worried that the disagreements between the Prefect and the Viscount might make matters here worse, and from what we've seen it looks worse than I thought." Karch paused. "What about your captives?"

"This morning we'll give them the choice of working for us, or leaving Haven."

"You think some will stay?"

"We'll see."

"Good luck with that."

"I hope so, but you never know." With a smile, Beltur turned and walked back to the public room, once again checking his belt wallet to make sure he had enough actual coppers.

Jessyla was waiting for him at the archway. "Another tasty breakfast awaits us." She grimaced.

"At least someone else is cooking it."

"I'd rather do it myself." She shook her head. "I never thought I'd say that and mean it."

Beltur gestured, then followed her into the public room.

Claerk had just brought their ales and headed back to the kitchen when Lhadoraak, Tulya, and Taelya joined them.

"I'm glad it's not raining," announced Taelya.

"Did your head hurt yesterday?" asked Jessyla.

"No. I just don't like it when it's gray and rainy."

Beltur found it interesting, and possibly hopeful, that Taelya didn't seem to get headaches when it rained, given that so many whites did. *But maybe the headaches come when whites are older.*

At that moment, Claerk returned with platters for Beltur and Jessyla, and ales for the other three. Beltur started to eat. After a moment, so did Jessyla.

As they finished breakfast, Jessyla turned to Beltur. "Are you really going to let the five of them go this morning?"

"I said we'll make the offer, but we'll need to saddle our mounts first."

She raised her eyebrows.

"I don't trust Ermylt, and I want to be able to follow him. You need to be ready to follow any of the others." Beltur took a last swallow of the bitter ale, then stood, looking to Lhadoraak and Tulya. "We're giving the captives the option of working for us or leaving Haven this morning."

"Will any of them stay?" asked Tulya warily.

"Most will stay, at least for a time. They'll get a bed and fed, plus a copper a day, and we can use the extra hands in getting the houses repaired and ready to live in."

"We'll be watching them closely," added Jessyla.

"Good!" replied Tulya.

"Maybe not for them," said Lhadoraak.

Beltur and Jessyla hurried to the stable, where they groomed and saddled their mounts, after which they made their way to the tack room.

Once there, Beltur said to the guards, "We're letting them go. Some may stay, but they won't need guarding."

"Yes, ser. The captain said that might be happening. Do you want us to stay until you tell them?"

"No. One way or another, your duty's over." Beltur watched the pair leave, then opened the tack room door.

"How much longer are you going to keep us?" demanded Ermylt, even before Beltur and Jessyla had a chance to look over the wounds of the five.

"Let us look at each of you first," replied Beltur. "We can start with you." He let his senses range over Ermylt, then looked to Jessyla.

She nodded.

Dussef and Turlow were next, and almost before they finished, Turlow said, "I told you I'd be fine."

"You've told everyone more than they wanted to hear," said Gustaan dryly.

"That's because you never listen."

Beltur refrained from suggesting that might be because everyone already knew what the mouthy former trooper was going to say. He moved to Therran. "There's no wound chaos left, but you should be very careful with that leg."

"Don't know that I can do much else . . . ser."

That left Gustaan. While Beltur couldn't sense any wound chaos, there was still some dull redness of healing in the older man's shoulder. Beltur added a touch of free order. "You still need to be careful with that shoulder."

"It's tender enough I don't need much warning, ser."

"Are you going to let us go, now?" asked Ermylt.

"In a moment. First, how many of you want to stay and work for the Council?"

"Doing what?" asked Turlow.

"Fixing up houses and buildings. Carrying things. As I said the other day, later, we'll be looking for patrollers. In the meantime, if you work for the Council, you get fed, a place to sleep, and a copper a day."

Gustaan nodded slowly. "I've had better offers. Not any time recently, though. I'll stay."

"For now," said Turlow.

Dussef just nodded.

"I can't go anywhere yet," said Therran.

"Not me," said Ermylt. "The sooner I can leave this stinking town, the better. Five coppers, you said."

Beltur dug five coppers out of his wallet and handed them to the surly armsman. "That means you have a glass to leave Haven. You harm anyone here or remain longer, and your life is forfeit."

"Five stinking coppers." Ermylt shook his head. "You won't see me hanging around here any longer than I need to. Can I go?"

"In a moment," replied Beltur. "The other four of you . . . this will remain your bunk room, but there won't be any guards. You can have today to look around Haven, if you want. We'll go over what needs to be done first thing tomorrow. If you harm anyone, your life could be forfeit."

"You're awful touchy, Mage," said Ermylt.

"We're here to protect the people of Haven." Beltur nodded to Jessyla, who stepped out of the tack room. Beltur followed.

When they were outside, Beltur said quietly to her, "I'm getting Slowpoke. I'll follow Ermylt until I'm sure he's left Haven. You keep an eye on the other four."

"They'll likely just walk around, but I'll keep close."

Beltur hurried to the stable, where he unstalled Slowpoke and led him out into the stable yard. While he could sense Ermylt, the armsman was already almost to the main street and walking eastward. Although that made sense, since Ermylt shouldn't have wanted to go back to Hydlen, the purposefulness of the armsman's steps bothered Beltur.

After quickly mounting, Beltur turned Slowpoke toward the main street, then wrapped a concealment around the two of them, urging the big gelding into a fast walk. Even so, by the time Beltur and Slowpoke reached the street, Ermylt was a good fifty yards farther east, walking down the south side of the street, but he was easy to follow, since no one else was around east of the inn at the moment.

Over the next half kay, Beltur edged Slowpoke closer to the armsman, but then Ermylt angled across the street to the north side. Beltur couldn't help but notice that Jaegyr and Julli's small stone house was only a hundred yards or so ahead, and he eased Slowpoke to the north side as well and urged the gelding into a faster walk, trying to close the gap between him and the armsman, but not wanting to make any sound that might alert Ermylt.

After a quick glance over his shoulder, Ermylt turned from the street and sauntered toward the front garden where Julli was working with her plants, what kind Beltur couldn't tell from sensing, since he was reluctant to remove the concealment quite yet, although he was now only about twenty yards behind the armsman.

Julli straightened up, holding in her right hand a small garden spade.

"Hello, there, pretty woman by the tree," called Ermylt cheerfully. "Are you lonely like me?"

"I'm hardly lonely," replied Julli, stepping carefully out of the garden, but still holding the short spade. "I'm also not interested. You'd be better off with your smile and rhyming words at the inn."

"But you're here and not at the inn," said Ermylt. "That's such a shame." He continued to walk toward Julli.

"I told you the last time I wasn't interested."

"But I am."

Julli shifted her grip on the shovel. Beltur continued to shorten the distance between him and Ermylt.

Julli didn't move as the armsman stopped less than a yard from her. "You'd better be on your way. My consort wouldn't appreciate your being here, and neither would the councilors."

"But they're not here. It's just the two of us, and there's no point in your making such a fuss." With that, Ermylt lunged toward her.

Julli brought the butt end of the shovel up into Ermylt's gut, just as the armsman partly turned, lessening the impact of the shovel and ripping it out of Julli's hands.

Beltur dropped the concealment.

While the armsman staggered for a moment, he regained his balance, and, from somewhere, produced a dagger. "You're going to do what I want."

At that moment, Beltur placed a containment around the bravo and rode forward until he was only a few yards away. He looked down at the immobile armsman. "I told you that your life would be forfeit if you didn't leave Haven or if you harmed anyone."

"I didn't harm her. She hit me first," snapped Ermylt. "She and I were just going to have a little fun."

"With a knife?" Beltur's sarcasm was raw. "Tell me . . . tell me honestly that you weren't going to take her whether she wanted it or not."

"I was just looking for some fun."

Beltur almost sighed. "Let's try this one more time. Your life depends on your answer."

"I wasn't going to hurt her."

"That wasn't the question."

"You won't do anything, not if I don't lie. I'm not saying anything more." Ermylt offered an expression that was half triumphant smile, half smirk.

"That's an answer," said Beltur tiredly, as he snapped the containment tight around Ermylt's neck, feeling in moments the black mist of death. He released the containment and let the bravo's body drop to the ground. The knife fell separately.

Julli's eyes widened.

Beltur slowly dismounted and picked up the dagger, wondering just where Ermylt had gotten it and how he'd managed to keep it hidden. "I'm sorry he bothered you. He'd promised to leave Haven and not to harm anyone."

"You obviously didn't trust him. Why did you let him go at all?" Julli's voice was more curious than angry, although Beltur could sense some anger. She leaned forward and recovered the short gardening shovel, then straightened, her eyes on Beltur.

"As a councilor, I can't act against people for what I feel about them or what I think they *might* do. I can act against them for what they do, especially if they're trying to harm people. I warned him that failing to leave Haven or harming anyone would make his life forfeit. You heard what he said."

"He'd been threatened before and found those threats empty."

"I didn't threaten him," Beltur said quietly. "I told him what he could do and what he could not and what would happen to him if he harmed anyone."

"Would you have done anything if he'd walked out of Haven?"

"Not a thing . . . unless he later returned and did harm." Beltur bent and lifted the heavy form and eased it over the saddle. "I need to take his body back to his former comrades so that they can see what happened."

He took Slowpoke's reins and began the walk back to the inn. *How many men end up dying because they've gotten away with things for so long that they never believe that they'll ever pay for their acts?* The second thought that crossed his mind was darker. *How many do terrible things for which they never pay?*

He kept walking. Before long, he could see the East Inn clearly, and he glanced toward the square beyond, still empty, wondering if he'd judged the other four former bravos correctly. Their reaction to Ermylt's death might just tell him something.

He'd barely tied Slowpoke up outside the inn's stable when Gustaan appeared.

The older bravo's eyes narrowed.

Beltur handed him the dagger. "He walked to the house of a woman he'd seen before. He tried to force her. I stopped him. Then he lied to me. But then he was lying all along."

"You knew that, and you let him go?"

"He hadn't hurt anyone since we've been here. I told you all not to harm anyone. He not only tried to take a woman against her will—"

"How did you know that, ser?"

"I followed him under a concealment, like this." Beltur drew a concealment around himself, immediately sensing the other's involuntary steps away. After a moment, he removed the concealment and went on. "She was gardening. She told him she wasn't interested." From there Beltur explained what had happened.

Gustaan shook his head. "He never did listen. I told him that blacks didn't lie, and they meant what they said. He told me that they were people like anyone else."

"We are. That's why it's important that we keep our word," replied Beltur. "I'd appreciate it if you and the others would take care of the body. You can keep the dagger, and split his five coppers."

Gustaan looked levelly at Beltur. "I'll tell the others what happened, and we'll take care of the body."

"Thank you." Beltur paused, then added, "I wish it hadn't happened this way, but one of the reasons we're here is to protect the people of Haven." Beltur turned and lifted Ermylt's body off Slowpoke and laid it on the stone walk.

"Ser . . . you healed him and set him free. And you warned him what he couldn't do. He was ungrateful . . . and stupid. I knew he wasn't grateful. I didn't know he was that stupid. We'll take care of it."

"I appreciate it." Beltur nodded, then untied Slowpoke and mounted.

XIV

For the remainder of threeday morning, Beltur spent time with Jessyla setting up one of the small rooms at the front of the healing house as a study that also would hold supplies with a small table desk and chair that Torkell had located somewhere and an old open-faced cabinet with shelves that could be separated into cubes or rectangles for different supplies, not that Jessyla had been able to find many so far besides clean cloths—clean rags, actually—and a few lengths of canvas, and burnet and brinn from Julli, as well as several small bottles for spirits and salves yet to be formulated.

Then he returned to the houses and did what he could to help Lhadoraak. Still, by the end of the day, all the ruined interior and the damaged sections of the roof had been removed from the second house, and all the usable roof tiles saved and stored. Gorlaak promised to bring the beams and timbers on fourday to begin rebuilding the roof.

Beltur also arranged with Bythalt for the four remaining workers to continue to be fed the same fare as the troopers and to sleep in the tack room. He wasn't about to pay for actual rooms, not with all the expenses he saw ahead.

After grooming the two mounts that he—or the Council, properly—had acquired from the deceased mages, he finally joined the others, and Karch, in the public room for dinner.

Jessyla let him take a long swallow of the lighter ale—he couldn't call it pale—before she spoke seriously. "A woman brought her son in today."

"Broken bones?"

"Forearm. He fell out of a tree. There weren't any other bruises. There was some chaos. I thought I got it all, but I told her to come back on fiveday, or tomorrow if there was enough swelling to make it painful."

"How did you splint it?" It would have had to have been splinted since they had no plaster for a cast.

"Therran carved some of those pieces of wood for me, and we bound it with canvas strips."

"I'm glad he was of some help."

"How are you coming with the houses?" asked Karch, from where he sat between Beltur and Lhadoraak.

"Gorlaak says he'll have the roof back together by sevenday," replied Lhadoraak. "The tiles will take longer. He'll have to find more or have Faastah fire new ones."

"Given some of the abandoned houses, finding tiles might be easier," suggested the captain.

"Have any of the men working with you said anything about Ermylt?" asked Tulya.

"Dussef muttered something about the coppers he left were about the only good thing about him," replied Lhadoraak. "He was talking to Gustaan. Other than that . . ." He shook his head. "There still aren't too many people on the streets."

"There are a few coming to the fountain in the square," said Jessyla. "They look toward the healing house, but only the one woman has come in."

"It's a small town," Karch pointed out. "Not that many people need healers."

"Especially when the traders aren't around," added Beltur sardonically.

When Claerk brought the dinner platters, Beltur looked at the fare dubiously. So did Taelya.

"It's a red deer burhka over ale-boiled quilla. It tastes better than it looks."

"It couldn't taste any worse," murmured Karch.

Beltur cut a small slice of the meat and ate it. For a moment, the gravied reddish-brown sauce tasted mildly piquant. Then his mouth exploded with spiced fire, and he grabbed for a chunk of bread.

Karch, on the other hand, ate a larger mouthful and said, "It's not bad. A little hotter than I'd prefer, but not bad."

Not bad? Beltur wouldn't have described the burhka quite that way, but more like liquid flame that seared away any possible taste. As for the quilla, while it usually had a bitter taste, he didn't taste it at all, the bitterness either leached out by the ale or burned out by the peppers. He tried a second mouthful, quickly followed by a bite of bread. Perhaps because he'd lost most sense of taste, the burhka was palatable.

"Good, isn't it?" said Claerk.

"It's definitely better than it looks," Beltur replied.

Apparently satisfied, Claerk headed back to the kitchen.

"Your eyes are watering," said Jessyla, clearly amused.

"So are yours." Beltur looked to Taelya, who was eating in a fashion similar to Beltur, except she was taking a mouthful of bread first, followed by a little burhka, and then more bread.

"Are you still planning for us to leave on eightday morning?" asked Karch.

"We are. What do you think about it?"

Karch smiled wryly. "Whenever we leave will be too soon. It always is. But if we stay, you'll either have to pay the innkeepers or leave them with a very bad taste in their mouth."

Beltur nodded. "We've thought much the same. The extra three days will allow us to get more done without worrying about the traders or even armsmen from Hydlen. Beyond that, I don't see that much point in your staying too much longer. We're going to have to get along without your troopers sooner or later, and keeping you here will get expensive for us." What he wasn't saying was that, at twenty golds an eightday, the extra security that he and the others would have to pay for would eat through the golds the Duchess had provided all too quickly.

"How are the remaining armsmen doing? If you can call them that."

"So far, so good," replied Lhadoraak. "It's too early to tell, but it's been helpful to have them doing holding and carrying. Turlow's been able to help Faastah some. The other two working on the houses don't have much in the way of building skills, but their muscles really have helped with the roof work."

"What about the younger one?"

"He seems helpful," said Jessyla. "He's a bit doubtful."

"They all are," said Lhadoraak.

Beltur nodded. Until the traders returned, he and the others wouldn't know how the four would really turn out once they had a few more coppers and even more freedom. *And that means watching them closely.*

But, as Relyn wrote, you couldn't build anything without people, and Haven definitely needed more people.

XV

Fourday dawned warm and damp, but the light drizzle that was falling when Beltur woke ended before everyone finished breakfast and well before the time when he and Taelya walked the long blocks to the houses to begin glazing the first kitchen cistern. Beltur also carried three water bottles, two filled with ale, and one with water, as well as a loaf of bread. He had the feeling that he and Taelya would need them before they were done.

Faastah arrived while Beltur was still studying the circular brick cistern. The cistern itself stood on a solid timber base that rose a yard and a half from the wide planks of the kitchen floor. A four-step built-in ladder on one side allowed access to the top of the cistern. From what Beltur could sense, the structure was sound. He turned to Faastah.

"It's a handsome cistern, if I do say so myself," said the mason as he handed the bucket of glaze to Beltur. "It might not need glazing."

"It might not," agreed Beltur, "but a smooth inside surface will make cleaning it much easier."

Faastah nodded. "Make it last longer, too, I'd think."

If we can make the glaze even and bind it to the masonry. Beltur didn't voice those thoughts as he helped Taelya into the cistern. The top of her head was just below the rim for the cover. Then he handed her the smaller container and the brush.

"Put it on thinly," he said. "Start at the bottom of the sides."

"What about the bottom?"

"We'll have to do that last. If we do that first, you'll smudge it, and it won't glaze evenly."

By early midmorning the entire inside of the kitchen cistern in the first house was thin-coated with glaze, although Beltur had been required to tie the brush to a branch, pour the glaze onto the bottom of the cistern, and use the extended brush to finish applying the glaze. Still, a slightly thicker glaze on the bottom was probably better.

After taking a break, when Beltur had some of the ale and Taelya some water and bread, they returned to the cistern.

"Now comes the hard part," he said to Taelya.

She nodded solemnly.

Faastah offered a surprised look to Lhadoraak.

"Applying chaos and containing it with order takes physical strength," explained the older mage.

Beltur had Taelya stand on top of sections of plank stacked on the top step, while he stood on the slight edge of the platform across from her. Then he said, "Put a spot of chaos in the middle of the bottom. We'll work out from there."

Taelya concentrated.

Beltur immediately followed by surrounding the chaos with order, adding the order net, and compressing the order against the glaze until he could sense the heat and feel the change in the glaze. Then he added tiny order ties to the edges of the small segment of glaze as the finish vitrified under the heat of Taelya's chaos and the pressure of Beltur's order.

"Do it again, right next to the last one," Beltur said, using his shields to help Taelya guide her chaos into place.

After that, bit by bit, they extended the final glazing. With each section of glazing, the inside of the cistern got hotter.

Two quints later, with hot air swirling up out of the cistern, Beltur called a break and helped Taelya down.

"How do you feel?" Lhadoraak asked his daughter immediately.

"A little tired. It's getting easier each time."

"That's because your control is getting better," said Beltur. "But you need a break, and so do I." He could use the break, but Taelya definitely needed it.

Faastah climbed up the ladder and started to peer into the cistern, before moving his head back. "It's a mite bit warm in there."

"You said it took heat to finish the glaze," said Beltur, before taking a swallow of ale and blotting his forehead with the back of his sleeve. He broke off a chunk of bread and handed it to Taelya. "You need to drink some water, too."

"I am thirsty."

After a time, the two went back to glazing the cistern, and that was the pattern—working until heat and fatigue required a break, then returning and glazing, until they finally finished in midafternoon. By the time Beltur stepped away from the cistern, he had long since removed his tunic, and his shirt was soaked, and all three water bottles were empty. But the inside of the cistern was glazed, and Beltur had the feeling that between the embedded order net and the order ties he'd added, the glaze—and the cistern—would be solid indeed.

He wasn't looking forward to glazing the other cistern on sevenday, but he knew that was something that needed to be finished before Karch and his troopers left. He also knew it wouldn't be a good idea for him to be tied up once he and Lhadoraak needed to be acting as both councilors and town patrollers.

He turned to Taelya. "You did an excellent job, and it's something I really wouldn't have wanted to have done without your help."

Taelya frowned. "But you're so much stronger."

"Handling all that chaos would have been a strain on me. It's much easier for me to contain your chaos, than to muster chaos and then contain it as well. There are too many conflicts, and conflicts wear you out. You'd have a similar problem trying to handle lots of order." *Especially now, but much less so as you get more accomplished as a mage.* Still, Taelya had done marvelously for so young a mage, and it suggested that she might end up a very strong white.

Faastah climbed up the four steps of the ladder and looked inside. "Don't know how you two did that, but the glaze sure looks good."

"We did it because we didn't like hauling water far, especially in winter."

The mason glanced around the house. "Already a right sturdy dwelling. Both inside and outside shutters, too. Never saw those before."

"They have them in Axalt," replied Lhadoraak. "Keeps a house warm when it's really cold."

"Also give a housebreaker a second thought," said Faastah.

What he really meant, thought Beltur, was that it might dissuade unhappy brigandish traders. He just nodded, then turned to Lhadoraak. "Taelya and I have done all we can and should do for now. We'll head back to the Council House and the healing house." Then he looked to Faastah. "We'll need more glaze on sevenday morning. That's when we'll do the other cistern."

"I'll have it." The mason paused. "Think you'll need any more cisterns?"

"Not any time soon." Not if Beltur had anything to say about it. The last thing he wanted was to glaze the interior of a third cistern—ever.

XVI

After breakfast on fiveday, Beltur went, as usual, to find the innkeeper to pay him.

Bythalt was in the tiny study off the entry foyer of the inn. He looked up from the narrow table desk worriedly as Beltur tendered the silvers. "Thank you, Mage. You're a man of your word."

"You're looking troubled," said Beltur.

"I've heard that the troopers will be leaving soon."

"You didn't expect them to stay, did you?"

"No," replied Bythalt dolefully, "but this has been the best time in years, and pretty soon you and the other mages will be living in your own houses, and the troopers will be gone. Then the traders will come back. Then what will I do?"

"Charge them what's fair."

"They won't pay."

"Then send for the Civic Patrol."

Bythalt frowned. "There isn't one."

"The Council will act as the Civic Patrol until a Civic Patrol can be formed."

"You will?"

"That's one of the reasons we're here."

"Some of the traders won't come back, then."

Some of them may not leave, if what we've heard is true. "That's possible, but in time you'll get more paying customers." Beltur smiled. "And we will eat here occasionally."

"Still be hard for a while."

"Would you rather be dealing with that white wizard?"

"Demons, no! It's just . . . there won't be many silvers before long . . . maybe not many coppers."

"You'll still get a few from the men working for the Council. They'll need food and lodging for a while. That's a silver a day."

Bythalt brightened for a moment, then asked, "For how long?"

"I can't answer that. It depends on how long they want to stay and work for the Council." Beltur paused, then added, "From my calculations, you'll have gotten almost thirty golds from the Council and the captain by the time the troopers leave. Some of that should last you a while."

"A few eightdays, perhaps . . . because we did not get paid much . . . by the others."

Beltur wasn't about to mention that part of the problem was that no one in the town had either wanted or been able to stand up to the brigandish traders or the whites. "Matters will get better. They're already better, but it's going to take time. It took a while for them to get to where things were, and it will take a little time for what we're doing to work out."

"What if it doesn't?"

"You've got thirty golds you didn't have, and you don't have to worry about a white mage enslaving you."

"That's easy—"

"Bythalt," interrupted Beltur coldly, "you aren't risking anything near as much as every single member of the new council, and you've already benefitted more than you could have imagined. Stop complaining."

The innkeeper swallowed.

"We've fixed the fountain and repaired the water pipes. We've gotten rid of the white mages. We're rebuilding parts of the town square and two houses. You've got a healer and a healing house for the first time in a generation. Just what the frig do you expect in two eightdays?"

"Ser . . . you're right. But . . . once hope is offered . . . when there was none . . . I fear losing that hope . . ."

"We understand that more than you'd think," said Beltur sardonically. "That's why we have no intention of leaving. Now . . . stop worrying and get back to repairing the damage caused by the whites and others."

"What if . . . ?"

"I told you. If you can't handle it, let one of us know."

"But . . . what if they demand silvers?"

"If your life is in danger, give them what they ask for. Then come get us. We can tell who tells the truth and who doesn't." Beltur turned and headed for the stable to groom and check on Slowpoke.

Jessyla was already there, checking on her mount. "What took you so long?"

"Reassuring Bythalt. He's getting worried because he knows the troopers will be leaving before long. Once the traders start coming in, we're likely to be busy setting down the law."

"Maybe we should post some rules at both inns."

"Pay the innkeeper the posted tariff? No fighting, and leave the locals alone?"

"Perhaps something more general. Haven has a new council that expects law-abiding behavior. That gives you more leeway."

"That's a better idea."

"I do have them occasionally." Jessyla smiled mischievously. "Tulya has a beautiful hand. I'll ask her if she'll make up a notice for the East Inn. I don't think the Brass Bowl needs one."

Beltur shook his head and grinned, then said, "You won't have any problem with Taelya's spending the day with you and Tulya?"

"She's well-behaved, and she can shield herself for a short time."

"She can also focus a point of very hot chaos. That's what she did in the glazing."

"And?"

"I didn't even hint that could be a weapon . . . but it could be."

Jessyla nodded. "I'll keep that in mind . . . just in case, although I'd prefer for her not to think of it that way yet. I thought she and I could ride out to see Julli and that grower—Vortaan—just in case they might have something useful, like garlic. It smells awful, but you can use the juice to clean out wounds if there aren't any spirits."

"That's good to know. The way it smells, it makes sense, but I'd never heard that."

"It's something Mother picked up."

"That reminds me. I'll be writing that letter to send to Ryntaar. What about your mother?"

"I already started on one to her. I thought we could have Karch give them both to Essek to send."

"It could take only a few eightdays or as long as a season to reach her. It just depends on the traders and the weather, but it's likely to be quicker now that we're more than halfway through spring."

"That's hard to believe."

That wasn't hard for Beltur to believe. What was hard to believe was that, little more than a year before, the two of them had been in Gallos,

Beltur a struggling white mage and Jessyla a senior apprentice healer whom he'd never met.

Beltur was still mulling that over when he walked up onto the small stone stoop of the first house. After studying the solid door, freshly oiled, he opened it and stepped inside, not really a hall or a foyer but the left end of the large room that was the front parlor. To his right was a wall, behind which was the small bedroom. A two-sided hearth, flanked by a wall on each side, separated the front room from the kitchen. Beltur could see the back of the kitchen stove from where he stood.

The main bedroom was in the right rear corner of the house, with a small washroom between the small bedroom and the larger one. Directly opposite the front door was the door to the narrow staircase leading down to the root cellar, and farther back, in the back wall beside where the kitchen ended at the main bedroom wall, was the rear door.

The entire dwelling was a rectangle broader than deep, roughly eleven yards across the front and nine deep, making it comfortably larger than the cot that they had so briefly occupied in Axalt, and with a root cellar. The barn was also more than welcome. The house across the street was built the same way, except it didn't have a barn, only a small shed.

As Beltur was studying the house, Lhadoraak turned from where he and Jaegyr were resetting the door to the main bedroom. "Beltur . . . Jaegyr has a proposition for us." The older blond mage smiled.

Beltur walked across the end of the empty front room to where the two stood. "What is it?"

"Well, ser . . . once we finish fixing up the second house . . . there won't be that much work to do, and seeing as you don't have much in the way of furnishings . . ."

"And seeing as you're a cabinetmaker, you think you could remedy that?" asked Beltur with a smile.

"Mostly, ser. I've always made cabinets, but I could make bedsteads and tables and chairs. I've done those. Settees . . . haven't done any of those, but I could."

"It seems to me," said Beltur, "that bedsteads and good tables and chairs and a kitchen worktable and cabinet would be the first things we need."

"Tulya's located an old table and chairs," said Lhadoraak. "We could use those for a while."

"How much would this cost?" asked Beltur.

"Same as you're paying now. Five coppers a day, plus whatever Gorlaak charges for the wood."

"And just how long would it take?"

"Depends on how simple or ornate you want the furniture."

"Simple and clean," said Beltur. "And strong."

"I don't know exactly how long," confessed Jaegyr, "but let me craft two bedsteads for you, and then you can see whether you think it's worth it."

Beltur looked to Lhadoraak.

The older mage nodded.

"We'll start with two bedsteads—after the houses are done and livable."

"Yes, ser. Thank you. You won't regret it."

From what Beltur had seen of Jaegyr and his work, Beltur didn't think so, but then, how else were they likely to get furnishings in Haven?

XVII

Sixday brought more rain, something Beltur didn't find unexpected, given how warm and damp Montgren seemed to be most of the time—or at least damp, especially compared to Gallos, and even to Spidlar, although he understood that Montgren seldom received the windy lashing downpours like the northeasters of Spidlar, largely because the land was farther south and a greater distance from the Northern Ocean that spawned the violent storms.

Since both houses were roofed and the roof tiles finally replaced, if with a mix of tiles of different colors, and since the first house was finished, or at least as much as it could be, except for plastering the walls, all the work crews except Faastah and Therran moved to Lhadoraak and Tulya's house, while Faastah finished plastering Beltur and Jessyla's house. Beltur had the feeling that the house would feel more like a barracks for a while, but the sooner they could stop paying Bythalt, the better.

Beltur left the houses early and made his way through the rain to the main square and the healing house, where he sat down at the table desk and began to write while Jessyla prepared dressings and other supplies. When he finished, he beckoned to her. "Here's what I've written to Ryntaar and the others. Would you like to add anything?"

Jessyla took the sheets and began to read. When she finished, she looked at her consort. "You make it sound almost easy."

"I don't want them to worry too much."

"We did have to deal with brigands and bandits and those Certan officers in Corumtal and Bortaan. Then there was that trader in Rytel. The one who sounded like he had ties to the Viscount and his family."

"Factor Greshym," supplied Beltur. "But both Greshym and Jhotyl have ties to the Viscount of Certis."

"Greshym was nice enough to us, but only because he was afraid of you. He almost said that when he had us for dinner."

"It was a good dinner."

"You worried about the mushrooms . . ."

Beltur had to smile.

"Do you think you ought to mention that Haven doesn't have any coppersmiths?"

"So far as I know, there's not a real ironsmith around, either. Torkell does have a forge, but he admits that he only does that because no one else does. I'll add something like that, and that there aren't any cupridium blades around, but there also isn't anyone who could afford them, at least not until we clean up Haven and honest traders start traveling through again."

In the end, the letter was another page longer, with passing mentions of brigands and Certan officers and squad leaders, and that didn't include the two paragraphs that Jessyla added below Beltur's signature.

By then it was almost time for the evening meal.

The two of them closed up the healing house and stepped out into the rain.

Jessyla glanced back. "Someday, it will be what it should be."

"Longer than you'd like, but sooner than most will think possible," replied Beltur.

The dinner was unremarkable, mutton slices and potato slices covered with brown sauce, but at least it was hot and filling.

Beltur and Jessyla went to bed early to the sound of rain, but sevenday dawned sunny and bright. Even before Beltur and Taelya had crossed the square on the way to her house-to-be, Beltur was beginning to sweat. It didn't help that he was carrying two water bottles of ale, one of water, and a loaf of bread. He definitely had the feeling that by midsummer he was going to be very uncomfortable. Montgren was markedly warmer than either Elparta or Axalt, and the air was much moister than in Gallos, but . . .

This is where you can build something . . . If they could deal with everyone who either wanted Haven or didn't want the four of them to have it. And if they could gather more people with skills.

As the two neared the second house, Taelya turned to Beltur. "This really will be our house?"

"It is already. It's just not ready for you to move in."

Beltur followed Taelya through the front door and into the front room, where Jaegyr was already working on one window.

Taelya stopped and looked around. "It's all on one floor, but it's bigger than our house in Elparta."

"And you have a large root cellar, too, and a shed."

"I think I'll like it."

Beltur smiled. He had lived in bigger houses, first with his uncle and then with Athaal and Meldryn, but the house that was now his and Jessyla's was the first that was not someone else's, and certainly larger than the cot in Axalt had been. As he thought back on the house where Lhadoraak and Tulya had lived in Elparta, he realized that despite being on two levels, that house had indeed been smaller—and Lhadoraak and Tulya had only been able to rent it, not own it.

Beltur nodded toward the kitchen, then made his way to the cistern, Taelya beside him.

Faastah was already there with the bucket of glaze and the brush.

"We have to do this one the same way?" asked Taelya.

"We do." Beltur nodded. There might be a better or faster way, but since the first cistern had turned out well, and since he didn't plan on doing more, there wasn't any point in changing something that had worked.

"You sure you won't do more of these?" asked Faastah as he handed the bucket of glaze to Beltur.

"Not any time soon, I hope," replied Beltur. "You've seen how much work it is."

"Everything worth anything is work, ser."

"That's true, but . . ." Beltur let the silence draw out. ". . . once the Duchess's troopers leave, I'll be very surprised if we'll have the time to work solidly on something like this."

"Thought it might be something like that." Faastah grinned. "We'll still be willing to work."

"I imagine there will be more work. I just don't know what yet." Beltur turned to Taelya. "We'd better get started."

Before that long, Taelya was inside the cistern, with the smaller container of glaze and the brush.

Beltur had half hoped that the glazing process would go faster the second time around, but after little more than a glass it was clear that glazing would be just as tedious.

Late in midmorning, when Beltur and Taelya were taking a break, Karch arrived.

Beltur immediately left the house to meet him, knowing that the captain's arrival meant worry or trouble of some sort. "What have your men seen?"

Karch laughed. "You don't think I ever have good news?"

"After what you've told us about Haven?"

"In a way, it's likely good news . . . of a sort." Karch paused to clear his throat, then continued. "We spotted a Hydlenese patrol. We made sure they saw us, and they turned back toward the border. It's been five days since the last patrol, and the one before that was three days before that. I'd guess that means they won't be nosing around for at least a few days, maybe as many as five."

"Do you think that they'll actually come into town?"

"They haven't before, but the Duke of Hydlen hasn't paid a white mage to take over a town before, either. They may be prowling around to see how he's doing, or they may be ready to try to claim the town for the Duke on the pretext that it's ungoverned."

"Even with you here?"

Karch offered a wry expression and said, "Once we're gone they might try. They might think that the white mage absconded with whatever the Duke gave him."

"Lord Korsaen was of the opinion that others might contest the Duke taking over Haven."

"Something may have happened to change the situation. Something he didn't know about, possibly. Hydlenese troopers this close suggests something's different."

Beltur couldn't disagree with that. "Do you have any ideas about what may have changed?"

"Just before we left Montgren, Commander Pastyn said that the Certans and the Gallosians were skirmishing across their borders near the trade roads. It might be that the Duke of Hydlen sees an opportunity to grab a chunk of Montgren while Certis and Gallos are otherwise occupied."

"They've been exchanging heated words for over a year, and the Prefect increased tariffs considerably. But would the Duke want to distract them?"

"Do you think any of them care about a small town that doesn't have much trade these days?" asked Karch dryly.

Beltur smiled humorlessly. "Not unless it's to their advantage."

"That's the way I'd see it as well. You still want us to leave tomorrow?"

"Want?" Beltur shook his head. "But you can't stay as long as it would take to put Haven itself in a position to change things. One way or another, we're going to have to deal with it." *And I'd rather deal with it having more golds rather than less.* Especially since the more golds that went to people in Haven and not the Duchess's troopers, the more likely they'd support the new council.

"I thought you might see it that way."

"I'll see you later," said Beltur.

Karch nodded.

After the captain left, Beltur walked back to the house, thinking about what they could do if the Hydlenese tried to take over Haven.

As soon as he entered the kitchen area, Taelya spoke. "What did the captain want, Uncle Beltur?"

"He was telling me that there were armsmen to the west of town. He wasn't certain what they were doing, but they left when they saw the troopers."

"Will you and Father have to fight them?"

"It may not come to that. They may just be trying to find out what happened to the white mage who was here." Beltur hoped that the Hydlenese were just scouting out the situation. "We need to get back to glazing."

XVIII

Beltur was up early on eightday morning, not only from habit but because he also wanted to see Karch and the troopers off. While Jessyla was washing up, he made his way down to the stable area, where Karch stood watching as his men saddled their mounts and led them out.

The captain turned. "All the weapons are in the room next to yours, and the tack is above the stalls of the mounts the mages had. The early patrols this morning didn't see any sign of the Hydlenese."

"Thank you. We appreciate that. What you've done has allowed us to get more organized and to learn more about the people here." *Not as much as we need to know, but it's a start.*

"It will be interesting to see what Haven looks like a year from now," offered Karch.

"It should look better."

"It already does. You've cleaned up the square, and Bythalt's cleaned up the inn."

"That's because he doesn't have bravos destroying it, I suspect," replied Beltur.

"I do have to say that you made maintaining discipline here rather easy," said Karch.

"I can't believe you'd have much trouble with your men," replied Beltur.

"Usually not, but there wasn't even a hint of difficulty, especially after you took care of the bravo who tried to assault the local woman."

"I never mentioned it to your men."

"You didn't have to. One of the captives in your work group told the others that, if they wanted to collect their pay and keep their lives, they wouldn't try anything like that fellow did."

Beltur shook his head. "I couldn't let him terrify people, especially since he wouldn't ever change, but dead men don't spread the word."

"That might pose a problem," replied Karch. "From what I've heard, most of the men using Haven as a base weren't any better."

"We might have to stop some of them before they can do anything, perhaps ride some patrols."

"Most times, riders will show up in the afternoon, usually late afternoon."

Beltur nodded, then said, "Captain, if I might, I'd like to ask a small favor of you."

Karch tried not to frown.

Beltur handed him the two letters and a gold. "If you could talk to Factor Essek or someone who knows traders going to Axalt, we'd like to have this first letter delivered to a factor there. He and his parents took us in when we had nowhere to go in the midst of winter and made life much easier. The second is to Jessyla's mother. The gold should cover the costs to get them where they need to go."

"More than cover, I'd say." Karch looked down at the name on the front of the first letter.

Factor Ryntaar
Mountain Factorage
Axalt

"They wanted to know where we ended up and that we were safely here," added Beltur. "The second letter is to Jessyla's mother in Elparta. She's a healer there."

"The talent must run in the family."

"It does. Her aunt is also a healer."

Beltur sensed a strong black presence—Jessyla—and turned.

"I just wanted to thank you before you left, Captain," said Jessyla warmly. "We couldn't have done all we've done so far without you and your men."

"I'd thought we might need your healing touch, but you and your consort's magery meant that only the white bravos benefitted from it. I hope they appreciate it."

"We're hopeful those who are left will be appreciative enough to stay around and help." Beltur shrugged. "We'll just have to see."

"You do have a way of making your point," said Karch, who then mounted. From the saddle, he added, "We wish you all the best."

"Thank you."

Once the last of the troopers had ridden out of the stable yard, Beltur and Jessyla made their way to the public room, where they joined Lhadoraak, Tulya, and Taelya. In moments, Claerk had their beakers of ale on the table.

"We're on our own now," said Lhadoraak.

"We have been on our own most of the time since we left Elparta," said Tulya.

"Even before that," murmured Jessyla.

"I was talking to Karch before they left," said Beltur. "It might be a good idea if we took turns riding some sort of patrols around the town, for a while. He pointed out that most travelers arrive in the mid- to late afternoon. Greeting them just might get a certain message across."

"It might not, either," said Jessyla.

"That's true," replied Beltur, "but at least I'd feel better if I have to do something drastic after they've been warned. Also, that would convey to the townspeople that we're serious about protecting them and not just ourselves. I've also thought about wearing the uniform I got as an arms-mage."

"You brought that?" asked Tulya. "I thought Lhadoraak was the only one . . ." She shook her head.

Lhadoraak just smiled.

"I've never owned that many good garments," explained Beltur. "And the uniform might send a message."

"You already did that once," Tulya pointed out. "With that bravo."

"Often once is not enough," replied Beltur, trying not to shake his head when he realized what he'd said.

"I've heard that before," said Jessyla oh-so-sweetly.

Both Tulya and Lhadoraak tried—and failed—to stifle their laughter. Taelya merely looked puzzled.

Finally, Lhadoraak said, "How do you want to split it up?"

"I thought I'd ride out right after breakfast, just to get a better feel of the land immediately outside the town. I think we've got a good feel for the town itself, but we really left the scouting beyond the town to Karch and his men."

"Then I should take a patrol around midday," suggested Lhadoraak.

"That would be good. I thought I'd take another swing around late afternoon."

"What about me?" said Jessyla.

"Do you want to accompany me or Lhadoraak?"

"You after breakfast and Lhadoraak at noon."

A glass later, after Lhadoraak, Tulya, and Taelya left for the houses, Beltur and Jessyla were riding east from the inn, moving at a walk, and trying to take in everything. Beltur realized that he hadn't been on the east end of the town in days, in fact, not since he'd followed Ermylt to Jaegyr and Julli's small house. Before that long, they passed Julli's place, but she wasn't anywhere outside, although Beltur sensed someone inside, Julli most likely since Jaegyr was working with Lhadoraak.

Then they rode past Yamella's—or Zankar's—well-kept brick house. Beltur could see that the grapevines on the trellises had fully leafed out.

The gray-haired Yamella waved from her porch and called out, "It won't be long before Zankar is back."

Beltur just made a noncommittal gesture in return.

"Poor woman," murmured Jessyla.

"She's found happiness in her own way," said Beltur quietly.

"But she's living in a dream."

"Would living in Haven the way it is be any better for her? I'd like to make it a place where she doesn't have to live in dreams, but we aren't there. We won't be for a time." *And it could be a very long time.*

The open space between Yamella's house and the worn brick gateposts indicating the east end of Haven was a patchwork of low bushes and weeds. To the east of the town proper the road ran straight east for what looked to be a good kay, possibly almost two, before it angled south around a low rise topped with trees, below which grazed a small flock of sheep.

As Beltur and Jessyla rode farther, Beltur tried to sense if there were people beyond the curve around the hill, but all he could sense were two figures near the sheep. They turned out to be a youth who could have been either a girl or a boy and a large woolly white and gray dog.

"Do you sense anything besides the sheep, the shepherd, and the dog?" asked Beltur.

"Not near the road. There might be more sheep near the top of the hill."

When they neared the sheep, the young woman with the flock guided them farther uphill and away from the road. At that point, Beltur said, "We've gone far enough." He turned Slowpoke, and they headed back.

Yamella was gone from her porch, but Julli waved from her garden.

They didn't see anyone else until they reached the square, where two older women were filling buckets from the fountain.

When they neared the Brass Bowl, Beltur saw Phaelgren and another man unloading hay from the stable loft into a cart. *Unloading? Hay not used by the troopers that he's selling to someone else?*

Neither man glanced in the direction of the riders.

"He's trying to profit off what he charged Karch," said Jessyla. "Even Bythalt's not that brazen. Sneakier, maybe, but not brazen."

Beltur could agree with that.

They did see several people of various ages out and about near houses in the west end of town, but all of them quickly looked away, suggesting to Beltur that most of the inhabitants were anything but sure that the new council was in Haven to stay. After the ride, Beltur groomed and watered Slowpoke, and then walked to the houses to offer what help that he could, while Jessyla spent more time working at getting the healing house in better shape.

In late midafternoon, Beltur first rode out the west road, letting his senses reach as far as possible. Even when he reached the blank kaystone five kays west of town, he still couldn't sense anyone except a single cart and horse headed up the lane to a small stead. He rode back through town and made the same sweep on the east road that eventually led to Lydiar.

Then he turned Slowpoke back toward the East Inn, wondering how long before the traders began to return.

XIX

By oneday morning, the rain was coming down steadily once more, not quite in sheets, but enough that Beltur couldn't easily sense that far and that he spent the morning working inside on his and Jessyla's house. When the rain lightened in the early afternoon, he walked back to the healing house to see how Jessyla was doing.

"You're soaked." Those were her first words. "You should have stayed at the house."

"I did all I could with the tools I'd borrowed from Gorlaak. I smoothed down all the rough spots on the windows and doors and inside woodwork. Faastah finished the plastering, and it's drying . . . slowly. What are you working on?" He looked at the mortar and pestle on the table.

"I'm crushing the gypsum into a powder."

"So you have it to make casts?" Beltur had only done a handful of casts during his time as a healer in Axalt. The idea was simple. Wet the cloth strips thoroughly, then coat them with the powder and wrap them around the part of the arm or leg that was broken—after the bone had been reset, of course. He'd learned that the "simple" idea was harder in practice.

"I'd rather not have to make someone wait. Faastah brought me the gypsum."

Beltur was thinking about that when there was a hurried rap on the door of the healing house, and then a boy stepped inside.

For a moment, Beltur wondered who the child was; then he recognized him as the young stableboy. He mentally groped for the name, then asked, "Aaskar, what are you doing here?"

"Ser . . . the lady at the Council House said to come here. There's a man at the inn. He's got a big knife and a sword, and he's threatening everyone."

Beltur stood up. "What sort of man?"

"A big man with a sword." Aaskar gestured almost helplessly.

"Where? In the inn or the stable?"

"The inn."

"Was he the only one?"

"I didn't see any others."

"You stay here." Beltur didn't sigh, but he definitely felt like it. Just one day after the troopers left and there was already a renegade armsman at the inn causing trouble—and in the rain, no less. "I'll go take care of it."

Although Beltur hurried, his blacks were even wetter by the time he crossed the square and entered the inn. Claerk, standing well back from the foyer, just pointed.

Beltur kept walking until he reached the foyer, where he stopped a few yards from the intruder. The man in a wet and dirty gray tunic was definitely bigger and broader than Beltur, if not enormously so—perhaps half a head taller with broader and heavily muscled arms, as well as a slight paunch. While he had a blade in a scabbard, he held a long dirk and stood a yard from Bythalt, who was clearly discomfited.

Beltur wondered how he'd entered the town undetected, but that just might have been because of the rain. He cleared his throat. "You're looking for a mage?"

"I'm not looking for a black mage. I heard tell there was a white mage needed armsmen."

"Where did you hear this?"

"In Hydolar. What does it matter to you?"

"I just wondered. Are you interested in working for the new council?"

The bravo laughed. "Hardly. Where's the white mage?"

"He left," replied Beltur.

"Where'd he go?"

"There were two of them. They went to ashes."

"Don't play games with me, Mage. You do, and people'll get hurt."

"I don't play games," Beltur replied. "I told you the truth." He placed a shield around Bythalt just in case the bravo might try to use the innkeeper to make a point.

"You just did." The armsman turned, then slashed at Bythalt. The impact of the dirk on the shield ripped the weapon from his hand. He started to draw the blade from the scabbard, then stopped. He smiled broadly and insincerely. "Well . . . Mage, you do seem to have some talents. So do I. Perhaps we could work something out."

"Bythalt," said Beltur, "just how much did he threaten you? And please don't lie to me. You really don't want to do that."

The innkeeper swallowed. "Ser . . . he said that he'd stay where he pleased and that he'd pay nothing, and that he'd have any woman he wanted, and that I could agree with him or die."

Beltur nodded, then looked at the armsman. "Did you say that? Or words to the same effect?"

"You speak so well, Mage." The bravo smiled again.

"Answer the question."

"I don't have to answer you or anyone else."

"No . . . you don't, but you might have a chance to leave Haven alive if you do."

"No one threatens Mordosh."

"Are you going to answer the question?"

"Why should I?"

"To have at least a chance at staying alive."

"If you had the guts to kill me, you already would have."

Beltur clamped a containment around the bravo and tightened it. When Mordosh began to turn blue, he loosened the containment, then waited a moment before saying, "Did you threaten the innkeeper and insist that any woman was yours if you wanted her?"

"I'm not about to answer your questions or anyone else's. Kill me if you dare. If you can."

Beltur shook his head, then added a smaller containment around the bravo's throat, tightening it until Mordosh's throat was crushed. He didn't release either until the death mist passed over him.

Bythalt shivered.

"You told the truth," replied Beltur. "He didn't want to. If he'd told me that he'd threatened you, and he honestly promised to walk away from Haven, I would have let him. But I won't play games with lying bravos." Beltur smiled sadly as he walked forward. He bent and unfastened the sword belt. The man's wallet held but three coppers.

Beltur examined the sword belt. The hidden coin slots there were all empty. He shook his head and retrieved the dirk. He handed two of the coppers to the innkeeper. "You can take care of the body."

Beltur carried the dead man's weapons up to the chamber adjoining the one where he and Jessyla slept and left them there. Then he relocked the door, and replaced the order lock. He walked downstairs and then back to the Council House through the rain that had subsided to a drizzle.

When he stepped inside, Tulya looked up, as did Therran from where he stood by the rear archway.

"There was a bravo at the inn. He'd already threatened Bythalt. I had to kill him. If he'd left town without threatening or harming anyone, I'd have let him go." Beltur shrugged.

"How did he get to the inn without anyone seeing him . . . or sensing him?"

"How heavy was the rain?" asked Beltur. "There was just one man, walking through the rain, likely taking back streets . . . and at the time, Lhadoraak and I were at the houses, not here."

Tulya nodded, clearly thinking about how the rain hampered sensing. "How many more will show up, do you think?"

"More than I'd like. I keep hoping that some are halfway decent men just down on their luck. We could use more like the four of you." Beltur looked to Therran.

"You really would have let him walk away, ser?"

"I'd have followed him to make sure he did, but I would have."

"Could I go?"

"Your leg is almost healed deep inside. In another day or so, it will be enough that you could travel. You'd be sore, but you could, if you want."

"Why not until then?"

"Because the chaos in your leg could flare up. It might not, but it could, and, as a healer, I don't want to be responsible for letting you go until you're well enough to travel."

"I won't be telling anyone, ser. I won't."

"I wouldn't think so."

"No, ser. I won't." Therran was almost shivering.

"I added his weapons to those in the inn. We'll need somewhere to store them once we move."

"What about in the root cellars in the houses?"

"For a while, anyway." Beltur turned. "I need to tell Jessyla and let Aaskar know that it's safe to go back to the inn." Then he left the Council House.

As soon as he entered the healing house, he looked to Aaskar. "It's safe for you to go back to the inn now." Then he handed the single copper to the boy. "That's for being brave and coming to tell us."

"Yes, ser. Thank you, ser."

In moments, Aaskar was gone.

"I take it that it was a bravo and that he had no intention of being reasonable," said Jessyla.

"Less so than any of the others. I left his weapons in the inn. Tulya suggested we store them in the house cellars. I agreed with that—once we move in."

"I'd agree. When will that be, do you think?"

"If we want to sleep on the floor, possibly an eightday. Jaegyr will craft us bedsteads once he's done what he can on the houses."

"You mentioned that already."

"I have been known to repeat myself . . . more than once." Beltur offered a crooked smile. "We also need to worry about mattresses or pallets . . . or something other than boards in the bedsteads."

"I've talked to Julli about that. She has some older women who are working on stitching heavy mattress covers. A few silvers should cover all three covers. Then they can be stuffed with wool."

"When were you going to tell me?"

"I meant to last night. You had other . . . matters on your mind."

Beltur smiled ruefully, even as he shook his head.

XX

While the rain ended late on oneday and twoday was clear, the air was still heavy with moisture. Whether as a result of the rain or for other reasons, neither armsmen nor traders showed up on twoday, but when Beltur left the inn for a midday patrol on threeday, he had no doubt that either free-lance armsmen or traders, if not both, would be entering Haven before all that long. That was another one of the reasons he'd decided to wear the blue uniform, with the black-banded sleeves and visored cap of a Spidlarian arms-mage, a uniform he'd carried across four countries, largely because he'd been reluctant to discard such costly apparel.

With sweat oozing from under the visor cap, he guided Slowpoke out the east road first, where he saw more sheep and young shepherds, each with the same type of white woolly dog he and Jessyla had seen earlier, except this one was more massive, almost a yard high at the top of its shoulders. As before, the young shepherds were wary of him, or of the strange uniform.

Short of the curve in the road, he turned Slowpoke and headed back toward Haven.

When he neared Julli's cot, she raised an arm to hail him and then walked from the garden to the edge of the street. "Whose uniform is that?"

"Mine. From when I was an arms-mage in Spidlar. Lhadoraak has his as well. We thought it might be better if we wore them while patrolling."

"That's a good idea. It'll remind people that there's at least some order coming back to town."

"More than some." *We hope.*

"Jaegyr can't wait to get started on those bedsteads. It's been so long since there's been real work for him."

"There's likely to be more, but it may take a while."

"Even gardens take time and work." She nodded. "I won't keep you."

Beltur took a more circuitous route through town, just so people wouldn't get the idea that he only patrolled the main street, but he did swing past the Brass Bowl, which seemed to be quiet. He also rode to the houses, where he saw Gustaan lugging a bucket of water toward the house.

The former bravo set down the bucket and walked toward Beltur, then stopped and looked at him. "Some sort of Spidlarian officer's uniform, ser?"

"It's mine. Spidlarian arms-mage. I thought wearing it when I'm patrolling might help remind people."

"It might make you a target, too."

"It might . . . but that will show me who's a problem."

"Are you really going to have a Civic Patrol?"

"Once we deal with the initial problems. Are you interested?"

"I just might be. Some of the others might, too. Haven could be better than a lot of places I've seen."

Beltur smiled. "That's the idea."

"I heard that there was a problem at the inn the other afternoon."

"Not for long."

"I heard that, too." Gustaan nodded. "If you'll excuse me, ser, the mason needs this water."

Beltur watched until Gustaan entered the second house, then turned Slowpoke toward the main street. From there he studied each of the dwellings he passed. He thought that fewer of them had closed shutters, but whether that was his imagination, or even the warmer weather, he couldn't say.

Beyond the west end of town, the ground was rugged and rocky, with far fewer grassy stretches and more stands of trees that appeared to have grown almost haphazardly. At one point, Beltur saw two men working a crosscut saw to bring down what looked to be a dead or dying tree. Neither gave him more than a passing glance.

When Beltur was within a kay or so of the defaced kaystone, he saw a cart moving toward Haven, drawn by a single horse led by a man. He extended his senses as far as he could, but he couldn't sense anyone else to the west or south of the traveler.

Beltur's first thought was that the cart might be carrying produce, but as he rode closer he could see that oiled canvas covered objects of various sizes and shapes. The man leading the cart horse could have been thirty or fifty, with a weathered and tanned face and a brown beard that was roughly trimmed.

"Never seen a uniform like that before," offered the peddler, bringing the cart horse to a halt as Beltur reined up in the middle of the road.

"It was the uniform of a Spidlarian arms-mage. Now, it's the temporary uniform of a Haven town patrol mage."

"That you?"

Beltur nodded. "I'm one of several."

"I heard that there was a new council there. Been a long while since I've been in Haven. It was run-down a fair bit. Changed much?"

"The Council House is open. There's a healer in the healing house. The fountain in the square is flowing again. There haven't been any honest traders returning yet."

"Some of them will take a look."

"What about you?" Beltur gestured toward the cart.

"I'm no trader, just a tinker and a knife-sharpener. I sell a few things, pots, skillets, knives, a blade or two."

Thinking of the tinker he'd seen in Analeria—just about a year ago, but a time that almost seemed like another life—Beltur asked, "Are you thinking of staying in Haven for a time, or do you just travel from town to town?"

"I travel. Stay only as long as folks need me. Maybe a bit longer if I feel welcome." The tinker chuckled. "Have to say that doesn't happen that often."

"I understand that."

"Mages are like tinkers that way. Folks don't like us around once they don't need us."

"Haven will be different. Most of the new councilors are mages or healers."

"How'd that ever happen?"

"That was the price the Duchess had to pay to get us to clean up Haven." Beltur smiled pleasantly. "Did you happen to see anyone else headed this way?"

"Can't say as I did. I don't travel all that fast, though, and no one passed me going either way."

"Thank you. I imagine I'll be seeing more of you." With that, Beltur turned Slowpoke back toward the town, hoping that he'd see more like the tinker than like Duurben, who was bound to show up again before very long.

XXI

Fourday morning after breakfast, Beltur went to find Aaskar, who might be able to help him with a particular problem. He found the boy removing straw and manure from a stall with a rake taller than he was.

Aaskar looked up dolefully at Beltur.

"Aaskar," said Beltur, "how would you like to earn some extra coppers?"

"What'd I have to do for them?"

"Just come over to the Council House or the healing house and tell someone if a new trader or bravo has come to town. Or tell me if I'm closer. I'll pay you a copper a day for the next eightday, and we'll see how it works out."

"A real copper? Like last time. Every time?"

Beltur shook his head. "One copper every day. You get the copper even if no one comes. You get one copper even if two traders come." He paused. "But if you don't want the coppers, I could find—"

"No, ser! I'll do it." The boy looked inquiringly at Beltur.

"You get paid every morning for the day before . . . after the work's done."

Aaskar sighed. "Yes, ser."

Beltur managed not to laugh at the obvious acting. "Tomorrow morning. Now . . . keep your eyes and ears open."

After leaving the stable Beltur straightened the blue uniform, because he and Lhadoraak had agreed it made more sense for Beltur to do all the patrolling until the two houses were both livable, since Lhadoraak had some skills in woodworking and Beltur did not. Then he walked to the market square adjoining the inn, heading to where the tinker had set up his cart not all that far from the fountain. Several yards away was another cart that Beltur had never seen, its wooden sides bare, the donkey that had pulled it drinking from a wooden pail while a stocky, dark-haired woman in faded brown watched both the donkey and the cart. Her lined face suggested she was at least fifteen years older than Beltur.

Beltur stopped and looked at the array of vegetables laid out on the extended tailgate of the cart. Some of the leafy greens he didn't recognize, but he definitely could pick out the bunches of carrots and radishes.

"You one of the mages that fixed the fountain?"

Beltur turned. "I'm one of the mage-councilors who paid Faastah and some others to fix it."

"You're wearing a uniform today."

Even though Beltur had never seen the woman, she'd obviously seen him. "The uniform is for when we act as town patrollers."

She barked a laugh. "Do you intend to do everything?"

"We'll do what needs to be done. In time, we'll have a regular patrol."

"That might be a mite difficult. There aren't many young men left here."

"Not at the moment," agreed Beltur. "That will change."

"You seem sure of that, Mage. Others might not be."

"You're here in the square. So's the tinker. That's a change, isn't it?"

"If it stays that way. Would you like some fresh vegetables?"

"Not today," Beltur replied with a smile. "We don't have everything in the house yet."

"The ones you've got Jaegyr and Gorlaak working on?"

Beltur nodded.

"Those houses aren't that large. Not for mages who are councilors."

"They're big enough for us." *At least for now.* "Especially since we didn't bring much with us."

"You can afford to stay in the inn."

"Only for a time, and only because the Duchess is paying for it."

"Perhaps you should have insisted she pay more."

"We're all she could afford. Montgren has far more sheep than people."

"What's in it for you, then?"

"A town where we've got some control of our lives and a chance to make things better. Isn't that what most people want?"

"Some of the traders that frequent the inns want more than that."

"They can have it . . . if they behave and don't hurt or beggar people."

"Keeping them from doing that might be a challenge even for mages."

"We didn't think it would be easy," replied Beltur genially.

"Also a few local folk who like it the way it is."

"Such as?"

"The ones who make coins. Who else?"

"Phaelgren, you mean?"

"He's one."

"Bythalt?"

The woman shook her head. "He gets by. Too honest to cheat enough. And too scared to stand up to the traders. I'll leave it for you to discover the others. Phaelgren's the worst, though."

"My name's Beltur, by the way."

"I've heard. Ennalee. You won't have heard of me. My consort is Vortaan."

"He's a grower, I've heard. Or are you the grower, and he has the land?"

"I like the land." Ennalee smiled faintly.

That was enough of an answer for Beltur.

"I imagine we'll be seeing you around," said Ennalee, easing the bucket away from the donkey.

"Most likely." Beltur turned and walked to the tinker, who was setting up a small foot-powered sharpening wheel. "Greetings . . . again."

"Greetings, Mage."

"Do you think you'll have customers?"

"I will. How many . . . who knows?"

Beltur studied the items laid out for sale on the tailboard—several knives, used but sharp and in decent condition; one sabre, with a plain leather scabbard; three copper skillets of different sizes; two copper cookpots; and a small kettle. "Do you buy as well as sell?"

"More likely trade, but I do all three."

"Where are you from, originally?"

"Worrak. That was a long time ago. Haven't been back. Won't be."

Beltur looked at the large skillet. "What might something like that skillet go for?"

"Whatever I can get that's more than what it cost me."

Beltur nodded, guessing that such a skillet might well cost several silvers, possibly more. "Have you had any trouble?"

"Not yet. I probably won't."

"Because you're from Worrak?" That was an allusion to the fact that so many pirate vessels used the natural harbors around Worrak.

"It doesn't hurt."

From the square, Beltur made his way to the Council House, where Tulya was seated at the table desk, working on the town tariff ledger.

"I sent Therran to help with the houses. Jessyla said it wouldn't hurt him, and she's keeping an eye on the square in case anyone should head this way."

"I'm paying Aaskar to report any traders or bravos. If he can't find me immediately, he'll come here. I thought it might be best if we knew some of those coming into town. If you'd also write down the trader's name or anything Aaskar knows."

"That also might help keep track of traders who should be paying tariffs and aren't." Tulya smiled sardonically. "But I'd wager more of those will stay at the Brass Bowl."

Beltur suspected that as well.

After leaving the Council House, he stopped at the healing house and told Jessyla about Aaskar, then returned to the East Inn, where he groomed and saddled Slowpoke. After that, he rode out to the east, and then to the west.

When he neared the defaced kaystone, he sensed some ten riders farther to the southwest, likely on the road to Hydolar, but they were already moving away from Haven. *Ten riders . . . half a squad . . . more than a recon.*

Beltur waited for a time, but the riders kept moving until he could no longer sense them, and since he could also sense no mages, he turned Slowpoke back toward the town, making his way along the side streets until he came to the houses. There, he reined up, studying them for several long moments before proceeding.

The rest of the day, including the patrols, was uneventful, and when he finished the last ride out to the west and rode into the stable, he barely had dismounted when Aaskar appeared.

"Ser! Trader Duurben rode up to the front door. He is arguing with Master Bythalt."

Beltur frowned. He'd seen no sign of anyone on the west road. "Do you know where he came from?"

"He came from the east."

Had the trader been watching from a distance and waiting until Beltur headed to the west side of town and out to the kaystone? And then used back lanes to come in from the east? It really didn't matter in one sense, but it did point out the shortcomings of just one patroller.

Beltur immediately stalled Slowpoke, leaving the unsaddling and grooming for later, which he hated to do, but he needed to deal with Duurben. "You stay here, Aaskar."

"Yes, ser."

Then Beltur hurried from the stable into the inn, wrapping a concealment around himself as he did, making his way to the front foyer. As he neared it, he could not only sense the trader, but a wagon drawn by two horses outside the front of the inn, with a driver as well.

Duurben stood in the doorway to Bythalt's small study.

Beltur eased closer as quietly as he could, trying to hear what was being said.

". . . you say I *must* pay three coppers a night and pay for my horses and wagon as well. That's not very hospitable, Bythalt, not very hospitable at all."

"Honored trader . . . I cannot be hospitable when I lose coins."

"That's your problem, not mine. You must be paying your help too much . . . or perhaps yourself."

"They cannot work for less."

"Then find cheaper help. It's not as though there are many places they can find work in Haven."

"I cannot . . ."

"Cannot . . . or will not?"

"I . . . cannot . . ."

"Then I'll have to change your mind, Bythalt. That would be very unpleasant for you . . . and for others . . ."

Shaking his head, Beltur dropped the concealment and stepped forward. "Not nearly so unpleasant for him as it would be for you, Duurben."

The trader turned, his mouth momentarily open. After a silence, he finally said, "So is this new council setting the prices for inns and everything else?"

"No. We're letting the inns charge what they think is fair."

"What recourse do I have if I think the charges are unfair, as is the case of this hovel of an inn?"

"You can go to another inn, or you can choose not to stay here. You can even ask the innkeeper to lower the charge. You can't threaten him with physical harm. You can't threaten anyone else with harm, either."

"That's not how business works. I'm the one paying for the room. I should be able to bargain for the best price."

"I didn't say you couldn't bargain. I said you couldn't threaten with harm. You can certainly threaten that you won't stay here if Bythalt charges what you think is too much."

"That's not business."

"No, Trader. Using force to get your way is not a fair way to do business. If you want to stay here, you pay what you can bargain for without using force or the threat of force. And if you threaten the innkeeper, you'll end up confined and paying a penalty."

"You can't do that."

"If you can threaten an innkeeper, and you believe that's the way business works, then the Council has the right to work in the same fashion. If you prefer not to pay the East Inn, then you might try the Brass Bowl."

Duurben scowled. "I'll bring the matter before the Duchess."

"Be our guest."

"I'll also bring it before the Duke of Hydolar."

"You're certainly welcome to do that as well," replied Beltur.

"You don't seem willing to make Haven hospitable." Duurben sneered.

"If being hospitable means allowing people to be threatened and beggared, then we'd prefer not to offer that particular kind of hospitality."

"You'll ruin this town."

"It seems to me that you've already done your best to do that."

"This place was ruined long before I came here," replied Duurben with another sneer.

From the documents Beltur had read, he had to admit that the trader was likely correct. "That may be, but have you done anything to make it better?"

"That's not business, and especially not my business."

"Then it appears it's the Council's business, and since what you've been doing isn't making things better, it's time for a change." Beltur managed to keep his voice even, difficult as it was.

"You can't change things just by insisting on unrealistic prices."

"Most inns across Candar charge three coppers a night, some even more."

"And you'd know, Mage?" Duurben's tone was scornful.

"I've stayed in inns in Gallos, Spidlar, Certis, and Montgren."

"Not as bad as this one."

"My inn is better than many!" insisted Bythalt.

"Worse than any," snapped Duurben.

"Are you going to pay what the innkeeper asked? Or are you just going to keep insulting people?" asked Beltur.

"You'll see where this high-handedness gets you. Both of you." Duurben turned and stalked out.

Beltur let the trader take several paces before he drew a concealment around himself and followed the trader.

Once outside, Duurben walked to the teamster, still in the wagon seat, and said, "We'll drive on, Baarys. A pox on this place."

"There's nowhere else to stay, ser. Except . . . that . . . other place."

"I didn't say how far we're going."

Beltur stopped and watched until Duurben mounted his horse and the teamster urged the two-horse team forward. Then he hurried back to the stable, where he immediately took Slowpoke from the stall and rode out to the main street. He could still sense the trader and the wagon, seemingly pulling up in front of the Brass Bowl. Still under a concealment, he guided the gelding past the square and to the Brass Bowl, where he reined up in the street, but close enough that he'd be able to hear anything the two said when Duurben returned from the inn, presumably after meeting with Phaelgren.

Duurben came out shortly. "He's not much better, but we'll stay here tonight."

Beltur followed the two and waited in the stable yard, still under a concealment, until he was certain that they were settling in for the night. Then he eased Slowpoke away from the inn and rode back to the East Inn, shedding the concealment when he neared the square and he didn't think anyone was watching.

He didn't trust Duurben in the slightest, but he didn't see the point in watching the Brass Bowl all night.

He was also hungry and tired.

XXII

"Fire!"

Beltur bolted awake, yanking on his trousers and boots and throwing open the shutters. He couldn't see any fire, but he could sense chaos—fire chaos—coming from the stable. He didn't wait to see what Jessyla was doing, except to see she was also throwing on clothes, before he sprinted down the stairs and to the back of the inn, where he saw flames rising from the corner of the stable, the corner nearest where Slowpoke was stalled. The fire only looked to be a few yards wide.

Maybe you can stop it from growing . . .

He kept running until he was within yards of the flames before, almost without thinking, he threw a containment around the flames, immediately trying to squeeze it tight . . . and realizing that the fire was larger than he'd thought. Immediately, he could feel heat welling up around him, even as he kept tightening the containment. His forehead felt as though it was on fire, and his trousers and smallclothes began to smolder.

More order . . . and make the containment smaller.

Good as that idea seemed, Beltur could barely hold the containment, let alone squeeze it, but after what seemed a glass, but could only have been a fraction of a quint, if that, the fire began to die down. For a moment Beltur wondered why, but then he realized that, just like a forge fire dying down when he stopped pumping the bellows, the stable fire was dying down. While the effort to hold the containment was less, he could tell that if he released the containment immediately, the fire would rekindle itself with the inflow of air.

"Can you keep holding that?" asked Jessyla from beside him.

So concerned with the fire had Beltur been that he'd scarcely been aware of her presence. "It's getting easier, but there's a lot of heat behind the containment shields."

"What if we cooled your shields with water?" she asked.

"Try it with just a little. I worry about the cold order against the hot order of the containment."

"I can help with that," added Lhadoraak as he hurried up beside Beltur, and added shields at the edge of Beltur's.

"Is Taelya all right?" asked Beltur.

"She's fine. I told her to protect her mother." Lhadoraak paused, then said, "I just hope she doesn't have to."

"That makes two of us," replied Beltur, turning his full attention back to continuing to contain the fire.

Shortly, Jessyla reappeared with a bucket of water, then threw perhaps a third of a bucketful at the shield holding the fire.

Beltur winced as the first bucket of water spayed across the containment and a cloud of steam formed, but said, "You can throw more water than that."

Each bucket hurt, but less so with each one. After a time, Beltur could compress the containment. More than a glass passed before he released the containment, while Claerk and others soaked the charred wooden wall of the stable. Beltur could feel that his legs were a little shaky, but as soon as the fire was clearly dowsed and out, he made his way into the stable.

Slowpoke was agitated, but not uncontrollable, possibly because he'd been through battles with chaos-fire, and he began to settle down as soon as Beltur began to talk to him. "Quite a fire there, big fellow. Looks like you're all right. This wasn't near as bad as that last battle in Elparta . . ." He patted the big gelding and kept talking for a time before he walked from Slowpoke's stall to the others, which he checked one at a time, also talking quietly to the other mounts.

Jessyla was waiting. "Your face is red, and you're going to have a blister or two."

"I couldn't think of anything else that would have worked fast enough."

"You need some ale and more." She looked to Lhadoraak. "You, too." Then she guided Beltur toward the inn door, where Bythalt stood.

"You saved the inn . . . I can't tell you . . ."

"They need ale," declared Jessyla.

"It had to be Duurben," insisted Bythalt, seemingly ignoring what Jessyla had told him. "I said you should have killed him. He is evil."

Beltur knew the innkeeper was right—logically. But it hadn't felt right at the time. Now . . .

"What did you do to stop the fire?" asked Bythalt.

"Used order to contain the chaos of the fire." *Nothing compared to what I'm going to do to someone.* "Now . . . I need to deal with—"

"Not yet," said Jessyla firmly. "You're in no shape to go anywhere. Neither are you, Lhadoraak." She glared at the innkeeper. "Get them both large ales, Bythalt. Right now. The good ale. We'll meet you in the public room."

"Yes, lady mage. Right away."

Beltur's legs felt a little less shaky as he walked into the inn and made his way to the dark public room, where the three sat down at a side table.

Bythalt appeared with three large ales almost immediately. "I thought you might need one as well, lady mage."

"Thank you," replied Jessyla.

Beltur took a long and slow swallow of the ale. How good the brew tasted told him how much he needed it, since he usually found it barely passable.

After about a quint, he looked to Lhadoraak. "We need to visit the Brass Bowl. Now."

"Duurben might not be there."

"He may not, but if he is, we can do something about him."

Jessyla looked sharply at Beltur.

He smiled. "You aren't coming. That's because someone who's a mage needs to watch the inn, just in case. We will try not to be seen, but I'd rather not spend strength on a concealment."

She frowned, then nodded. "You're right, but I don't have to like it."

"I don't like it, either." *Most likely for a very different reason.* Beltur stood. "If Duurben or any other would-be malefactor shows up, keep your distance and don't be gentle."

"After this? I'm not feeling charitable or gentle."

"Good." Beltur turned to Lhadoraak. "We should walk. It's not that far."

The older mage nodded.

Once the two were outside and walking west through the misty air past the square, Lhadoraak said, "What do you think this will accomplish? Duurben isn't foolish enough to stay around after setting a fire . . . or if he didn't do it, after someone else did."

"It will give us a much better feel of the situation." *So I won't feel quite so guilty when the inevitable happens.*

The street was quiet and empty, except for the muted sounds of insects Beltur didn't recognize, and the air was still and heavy.

Beltur wasn't surprised in the least when they arrived at the Brass Bowl to find a wall lamp lit in the front foyer and Phaelgren waiting.

"Where's Duurben?" asked Beltur, his voice cold.

Phaelgren looked from Beltur to Lhadoraak and back to Beltur, then smiled. "I'm afraid you . . . councilors . . . missed him. He and his man and their wagon left the inn more than a quint ago."

Beltur could sense that the innkeeper was telling the truth . . . and was also pleased. "Did he say where he was headed?"

"He did not. In fact, I didn't speak to him at all. The sound of the horses and the wagon woke me. They did turn west on the main street."

"Did you put him up to it . . . or suggest it?"

Beltur could sense a certain amount of chaos swirling around Phaelgren immediately following his question.

"Put him up to what? I have no idea what you mean."

That was definitely a lie, but Beltur just said, "Thank you, innkeeper. That's all I needed to know."

"Good evening, then," replied Phaelgren.

Beltur nodded and turned to Lhadoraak. "We'll leave the innkeeper to his business."

When they were well away from the Brass Bowl, walking back to the East Inn, Lhadoraak said, "He had something to do with the fire."

"He likely suggested it. If we couldn't control it, Phaelgren would have the only inn in Haven."

"Too bad we couldn't do away with Phaelgren."

"With no proof and with what I've already done?" replied Beltur. "To make matters worse, even now, Duurben's delivered a message."

"That he'll move against the townspeople? That's what Karch predicted. What can we do about that?"

"Whatever's necessary to protect them." Beltur laughed raggedly. "But don't ask me what that will be."

"You're not going after Duurben then?"

"In the middle of the night, the way we feel?" Beltur gave a shrug he didn't really feel. "He'll be back. One way or another."

The two kept walking.

Beltur just hoped he could get some sleep . . . and wondered how many uneasy nights lay ahead.

XXIII

Despite Beltur's worries, fiveday and sixday passed without significant incidents, except for several women who brought children to the healing house. Sevenday and eightday were equally uneventful, and that worried Beltur, because he knew Duurben would be back sooner or later, in some fashion, and he might not be alone. The trader would likely try to work through threats to townspeople, and Beltur worried that some of them wouldn't come to the Council.

He was also concerned about the patrols from Hydlen that always turned away and rode back across the border if they caught sight of him on his own patrols. None of the Hydlenese troopers had stayed long in Montgren territory, but that they seemed to know what he was bothered him.

Even so, by late on eightday, both houses were at least livable, and Julli had promised to deliver three mattresses by oneday afternoon. Jaegyr had said that the first bedstead would be ready in less than an eightday. Beltur had paid for wood for the stoves, as well as feed and hay for the horses, both already delivered. Jessyla had arranged for cookware for both houses from Torkell. Each house had some tables and chairs, and Beltur had commissioned Jaegyr to provide more furniture as he could after the bedsteads.

As the five sat at the round table in the public room in the East Inn, Beltur said, "This is likely the last breakfast we'll be eating here."

"Not the last meal?" asked Tulya.

"That all depends on your cooking," said Lhadoraak.

Tulya mock-slapped her consort.

Lhadoraak grinned, then asked Beltur, "What are you going to tell Gustaan and the others?"

"They can stay here under the same arrangement for a while. I asked about that vacant building that once had a cabinet maker. It's close to the Council House. The man who owned it died years ago, and relatives took everything and left Haven. No one knows where. It'll take work to turn it into rooms for those working for the Council. It should be suitable for single town patrollers as well."

"Gorlaak and Jaegyr would like the work."

"Just Gorlaak. We need Jaegyr to craft furniture. Besides, he's better at that. You'd mentioned that Turlow had a feel for wood and building. Do you think he'd be interested?"

Lhadoraak shrugged. "We can ask him."

Beltur turned to Jessyla. "What about Therran?"

"He's been dependable, but he doesn't really have the talent for healing. He borrowed some tools from Torkell and shored up that staircase."

"In other words, he's handy, but was that because he was trying to look good or because he likes that sort of work?"

"He doesn't know what he likes, like too many men," said Jessyla, adding quickly, "unlike you two."

"Thank you for that quick recovery," said Beltur, smiling. "What do you suggest we do with him?"

"Ask him, just like the others."

Beltur turned to Lhadoraak. "What do you think about Gustaan as a patroller?"

"He keeps his temper, so far as I can see. He was a squad leader once. Whether he'll want to stay . . . who can say? Are you going to ask him?"

"Not yet. I thought I'd put him more in charge with the fixing-up of the old cabinetmaker's shop . . . the one that I'd thought might have been Jaegyr's and wasn't."

Lhadoraak frowned. "I thought . . ."

"You're in control, but . . . I don't think things are going to stay quiet much longer. They've been too quiet for too long, and I'm still seeing and sensing Hydlenese patrols."

"You said that they avoided you."

"They do, but they're not going away. It's as if they're waiting for reinforcements . . . or something."

"Couldn't they just be checking to see if we're going to leave?" asked Tulya. "Montgren forces have always left before."

"That's possible," conceded Beltur, "but it doesn't feel that way."

"Is that why you're wearing the patrol uniform? I don't like it when you get those feelings," said Lhadoraak almost dourly. "You're too often right."

"Would it help if I said I don't have any bad feelings about moving into the houses?"

"Some." Lhadoraak smiled.

After breakfast, Beltur walked to the small study and paid Bythalt. "We'll be leaving. We're moving into our houses today."

"That is good for you." The innkeeper's words were delivered in a doleful tone.

"You know where the Council House is . . . and if we're not there, where we live. Send Aaskar for us if you see trouble coming. If Duurben or someone else gives you trouble, just agree with them, but as little as possible and then let us know."

The innkeeper nodded. "And the workers, the ones who were prisoners?"

"We agreed on keeping the arrangement," Beltur pointed out. "You're getting eight coppers a day for them."

"How will I pay for everything?"

"You've gotten more than twenty golds from me, and close to twenty-five from the captain."

"Twenty-three and eight," said Bythalt mournfully.

"Almost fifty golds. Those should last you for a while. I doubt any of the traders paid you anything like that." Beltur looked hard at the innkeeper. "Did they?"

"No, ser. But I owed everyone, because what they paid was not enough."

"I can't help that. We've paid more than our share, and you'll be able to charge enough to cover your costs."

"No one will stay here."

"You think Phaelgren is going to lose silvers when he doesn't have to?"

For a moment, there was hope on the innkeeper's face. Then he sighed. "He will ask for less."

"If you want to ask less, be my guest," said Beltur dryly. He was more than a little tired of Bythalt's moroseness.

"What will be, will be, and order and chaos will decide."

"We'll have to see, won't we?" Beltur eased out of the study and went to join Lhadoraak, who had remained in the back hall, waiting for Beltur.

From there, the two made their way to the tack room.

They'd barely stepped inside when Gustaan stepped forward. "The houses are finished. Are we done? Are you sending us off, or is there more work?"

"There's more work, if you want it," replied Beltur. "We'd like to rebuild an old shop into rooms for single men who work for the Council."

"At the same pay?"

"Until the rooms are finished. Then you'd get a room and slightly more pay, but we wouldn't feed you."

"For now . . . just for now, that's fine with me."

Turlow and Dussef nodded.

Therran frowned.

"What do you want to do, Therran?" asked Beltur.

"I don't know. Can I work with them for a while?"

"If you'll listen to Gustaan," said Lhadoraak. "He'll be in charge when I'm out on patrol or not there."

"I can do that."

"Good." Beltur cleared his throat. "You have the morning off, with pay. Meet us at the Council House at noon."

Gustaan nodded once more.

From the tack room, Beltur headed up to the chamber where he and Jessyla had slept for the past eightdays to help with packing up the last items.

A glass later, all the mounts and the mule were ready, with the captured arms and tack on the two horses taken from the mages. The five set out for the houses. With so little to move, comparatively, Beltur and Jessyla were finished within a glass, and the weapons were in the dry root cellar, with the tack in the barn.

The two stood in the kitchen, before the wide hearth that held the stove. Beltur studied the kitchen cistern that he and Jessyla had filled the day before, using order to make sure that the water contained no chaos and that there were no leaks—which there weren't.

"We don't have the furnishings we did in Axalt," said Jessyla, "but it's ours."

"We'll have good furniture before that long. And it will match." *That's going to be the least of our problems.* "There's one other thing I need to take care of." Beltur gestured to the small metal strongbox he'd earlier set on the slightly warped, if sturdy, main kitchen table, the unidentified wood a grayish brown.

"Where?"

"In the bedroom." Beltur picked up the box and headed into the bedroom, where he concealed it in a hidden space in the wall between their bedroom and the washroom and jakes, using a light order concealment on the box, before sliding the plastered panel that looked like all the others back into place. The box held the majority of the remaining golds from his own small stash, those from the Duchess, and those he'd claimed from the renegade white. He worried about what had seemed to be an all-too-rapid spending, but they still had more than three hundred golds remaining. *Three hundred and forty-one and some silvers.* But over a hundred of those had been taken from the white mage, and that meant they'd already spent almost a fifth of what Korlyssa had provided, in less than half a season.

"You're worried about the golds, aren't you?" said Jessyla from where she stood looking down at the new mattress, one that Beltur had paid extra for to have it stuffed with wool, rather than straw or hay, although it hadn't cost as much as it would have in Gallos or Spidlar, most likely because of the number of sheep in Montgren.

"We've done well, when you think about it. We have two solid houses, with stoves and kitchen cisterns. What worries me the most is paying people. Just the four men cost almost two silvers a day, for their lodging, food, and pay. That would amount to almost a hundred golds a year. Jaegyr and Gorlaak cost more than the other four together, and we'll likely need them for several more eightdays."

"But we're already two seasons into the year," replied Jessyla. "Tariffs are due after harvest and before winter. So we only have to cover two seasons, twenty eightdays. That's less than forty golds."

"*Only* forty? Do you remember what Tulya calculated for tariffs due the Council?"

"Between thirty and fifty golds for all the houses, maybe another twenty to thirty for the inns and shops, depending . . . well . . . on a lot of things . . ."

"That means we can't keep all of the workers, especially when we start paying more, not if we're going to pay them for the entire year."

"Once you have that shop turned into a barracks, won't that help?"

"We can give them lodging, but they'll have to buy their own food. That means we'll need to pay them a little more."

"We should have asked the Duchess for more."

"We should have, but we're not exactly experienced in running a town and collecting tariffs. We may be able to increase the tariffs in the future if we can make Haven more prosperous."

"From your calculations, we have to."

"That's a worry I'll put off for now. If need be, we can use some of the golds we took from the white. After Lhadoraak and I and the men look at the shop, I'll need to do a patrol. I worry about both traders and troopers. What are you going to do?" Beltur turned and motioned for her to precede him from the bedroom.

"Go shopping for food and some herbs. Julli has some vegetables and gave me ideas of where I could find a few other things. After I come back here and store what I get in the cold cellar, except for what I need at the healing house, I'll go there. I may stop by the square. While I'm making up some ointments, I can keep an eye on the Council House in case Tulya and Taelya need any help."

"That's why you're shopping first?"

"Trouble's more likely to arrive in the afternoon." Jessyla looked down at the mattress, smiled, then turned and left the bedroom. Beltur followed.

The locks on the doors weren't all that good, but Beltur added a second lock on each door, one made out of order, showing Jessyla what he'd done and how she could undo the order lock. Then he handed her an iron key to the physical lock. "If you work at it, you'll be able to use order rather than the key to unlock the doors."

"Is that a challenge?"

He grinned, but didn't answer.

"For that, I'm going to have to come up with a healing puzzle."

"That's fair." He paused, then said, "You and Taelya need to learn concealments next. We really should have started on those earlier." Except there didn't seem to be enough time to do everything.

"I wondered about that."

"I'm sorry. It's just . . ."

"Don't apologize. There's been so much to do." Jessyla smiled. "I've been watching you. I think I might be able to do one with a little help from you."

"Good." Beltur certainly hoped so.

After giving both mounts some water, they rode back to the square together. From there Jessyla kept riding in the direction of Julli's house, while Beltur rode to the Council House, where he tied Slowpoke.

Lhadoraak came outside. "I sent them over to the cabinet shop with Gorlaak. They all want to stay and work . . . at least for now."

"They need the coins."

"Don't we all?"

Beltur laughed softly, then said, "You still have the golds and silvers you earned on the trip, don't you?"

"No." Lhadoraak smiled wryly. "Tulya does."

"I have the twenty-five golds that the Duchess provided for your first year's pay. Do you want me to keep them for now? Or would you like some at the beginning of each season?"

"I'll wait until we need them. Where do we stand on the golds for the houses?"

"I used twenty-five of them to pay for everything at the inn, and another fifteen or so for the workers and the materials to repair the houses. That leaves sixty. We'll need to pay Jaegyr for the furnishings out of that. That's likely to take another ten golds, maybe more."

"Tulya was wondering."

"I've kept track."

"We'd better see what Gorlaak and the others have discovered," said Lhadoraak, stepping away from the Council House door.

When the two mages reached the building that had held the cabinet maker, Gorlaak and the others were standing in the large open room that took up the front half of the building, a space roughly possibly eight yards wide and almost as deep. A square archway in the left end of the rear wall of the chamber showed a narrow staircase leading to the upper level. In the middle of the rear wall was an open door to a hallway that seemed to lead straight to the back of the building.

Beltur looked to Gorlaak. "What do you know about the building?"

"This was Bartolyn's place, years back," said Gorlaak.

"How many years back?" asked Turlow. "Before Westwind . . . or before Cyador?"

"Maybe just before there were sheep in Montgren," suggested Dussef.

Gustaan gave the smallest of headshakes, but did not speak.

"When I was still running errands for Torkell's father," replied Gorlaak good-naturedly. "Bartolyn just dropped dead as he was working his pedal lathe. Never consorted. His brother stripped the shop, sold what he could, and moved to a town somewhere in Hydlen. Been empty ever since."

"Can it be repaired without rebuilding everything?" asked Beltur.

"Walls are mostly solid, except around the back door," offered Gorlaak. "Some planks upstairs could use replacing. Most of the windows need tightening."

"How many rooms could we have up there?" asked Beltur. "Just big enough for one man and his bunk, and a wall table and chair, maybe a narrow cabinet for clothes."

"A fellow might go cooped-in-crazy like that," said Dussef.

"I'd thought we'd have a common parlor down here, washroom in back with a separate jakes."

"Five, maybe six," replied Gorlaak.

"How long would it take to get it ready?"

"Be ready before you'd get mattresses and beds for here."

"That doesn't tell me much," said Beltur dryly.

"There's not enough hemp left here in Haven to make the cording for mattress ticking. Julli got the last of it for your mattresses. Take a while to get it. It has to come from Lydiar or Renklaar."

Gorlaak's comments reminded Beltur that Haven seemed to be one of those small towns where nothing remained secret for long, except possibly what occurred behind closed bedroom doors . . . and he wasn't sure even about that. "Can't we just use woolens?"

"The mattresses won't last as long."

"How long to repair the building and change the upstairs to rooms?"

"Two, three eightdays, depending on what we find under the floors. Could be longer."

"What about your son?" asked Beltur. "I heard he worked with you sometimes."

"He'll be busy for a while. Bythalt hired him to repair the burned part of the inn stable."

Beltur nodded. He'd almost forgotten about the damage. He'd been more concerned about Duurben.

"When can you start?" asked Lhadoraak.

"Tomorrow morning. The same terms?"

Lhadoraak looked to Beltur. Beltur nodded.

"I'll be here. With some timbers."

After Gorlaak left, Lhadoraak turned to Gustaan and the others. "We need to clean out all the rubbish and start getting rid of anything that's broken or rotten." Then he looked to Beltur. "You're going on patrol?"

"I'd thought to."

"Then I'll see you later."

In short, you're not much use here, and you're more valuable patrolling. Beltur didn't disagree. "I'll let you know what I find out."

When he left the empty shop, he glanced up at the clear green-blue sky, then out into the square where the tinker had once more set up near the fountain, not too far from Ennalee and her cart, and another cart, a dull gray, beside which stood an older man. He decided to begin with the tinker, making his way there. "Seeing as this is the third time I've seen you and you look to be staying for at least a bit, might I ask your name? Mine's Beltur."

"Ennalee told me. I'm Worrfan. Leastwise, that's the name I've used for the last twenty years."

"Since you left Worrak?"

"A bit after that."

"How are you finding Haven?"

"Pleasant enough town right now. Might be a tad warm for me by midsummer. Might even get hot in other ways."

"What have you heard that makes you think that?"

"Haven't heard anything. But when a ruler gives a town to a bunch of mages, it just might worry other rulers."

"Even a poor and struggling town?"

"Three or four mages might change that, and a strong town here . . . well . . . that might worry some."

Beltur frowned. "I'd be curious as to your thoughts on why. We're not raising a fighting force. We're not collecting trade tariffs. We're not blocking the road."

"You might make it . . . more difficult for certain ambitious rulers."

"Which ones?"

Worrfan shrugged. "The dukes of Lydiar aren't what they were in the time of Heldry. Renklaar isn't the port that Lydiar is."

"Have you been to Jellico or Hydolar recently?"

"No tinker in his right mind enters Certis. The Viscount isn't fond of those he can't control." Worrfan smiled innocently. "Gossip and maps only suggest."

"How long have they been suggesting?" asked Beltur dryly.

"Might be a year. Might be less. Time's different for a tinker."

"All that's suggestive, but what have you heard that would confirm that?"

"Nothing," admitted the tinker. "It's all feelings. You've been around as long as I have, and you get feelings about people and places, even lands."

"Do you really think the Viscount would let the Duke of Hydlen take Lydiar?"

"Not if he could help it, but the Prefect of Gallos is massing an army in Passera, it's said."

Frig! Beltur just nodded. "That's very interesting. And why might you be telling me?"

Worrfan laughed. "I'm selfish. Lydiar and Montgren don't bother me. They let me travel where I want so long as I hold to the laws. Hydlen's getting dangerous, and I told you about Certis. I can't make a living just in Montgren. You mages just might be the only thing that gives the Duke of Hydlen pause."

"Three mages against an entire land?"

The tinker shrugged again. "I can hope. In the old times, two mages brought down Cyador . . . or so it's said. Lydiar doesn't have many more armsmen than Montgren, and they're not very good, except to back up the tariff inspectors at the port." He looked past Beltur toward a woman who approached with a basket. "Are those the shears and knives you said needed sharpening?"

The young woman, scarcely more than a girl, Beltur thought, only nodded, starting to circle around Beltur.

Beltur smiled at her. "We're here to protect you, not scare you." Then he looked to Worrfan. "Thank you. We'll talk more later . . . if you decide to stay."

"I'll be here for at least a few more days."

Easing away from the tinker and his customer, Beltur thought over what Worrfan had said, and the fact that there hadn't been the slightest hint of chaos or deception. Trying not to shake his head, he walked over to the produce cart. "Good afternoon, Ennalee."

"Good afternoon, Mage. Your consort was already here."

"I'm not surprised. Have you heard anything I should know?"

"Not anything of interest to a mage or the new council. Heersyn's old mare had a late foal, but the mare and filly are doing well."

"You see any travelers?"

"We live south of town, out the old south road that peters out at the base of the hills. We're not that far out, maybe two kays, but the road goes on for another two kays. There aren't any other steads out there now, except for Samwyth, and no one travels there."

"I imagine you get around."

"Some, but I haven't seen any travelers lately except Worrfan. I heard that no-good Duurben was in town. Also heard he didn't stay long and left just before you stopped the fire at Bythalt's place. I imagine he had a reason for leaving in the middle of the night."

"So do I," returned Beltur good-naturedly. "If he returns, his reception might be a bit different."

"You like to give people a chance to be better, don't you?"

"More that I warn them, and give them the chance to behave and stay within the law."

"Some folks ignore warnings."

"Some do. The problem is that most people listen to warnings. And how does a patroller or a councilor justify hurting or killing someone because of what others have said?"

"You're a black. What if you know that what others tell you is true?"

Because Beltur had thought about that—more than once—he had an answer. "I can tell when people tell me what they believe to be true. That does not mean that it is true, only that they firmly believe it is true. With most people, what they believe they saw is what happened. But it is not always. And sometimes, what they saw is not the whole story. It's another thing when someone is caught in the act . . . or after it."

"That makes it hard on the ones they hurt."

"It does. That's always been a problem. But it's worse when a ruler or a mage decides to act on just feelings. I've seen that. It's much worse."

Ennalee shivered slightly. "When you talk like that, you look fifteen years older, and I'm not sure I'd want to see what you've seen."

Beltur's smile was coldly sardonic. "I didn't want to see much of what I saw."

"So you will be mage, councilor, patroller, and justicer?"

"I'll be the first three for a time, until we can find and train patrollers. The councilor who is not a mage is the justicer."

Ennalee frowned. "Why her?"

"Because she is the one who has studied the laws of Montgren. And she's older."

Surprisingly, at least to Beltur, Ennalee nodded. Then she said, "It might be better if we had a regular market day when you or the other mage could be nearby."

"What day would you suggest?"

"Threeday . . . and sevenday afternoon."

"We could try that."

"Starting this threeday?"

Beltur nodded.

"Then we'll be here, and I'll see if I can persuade a few others."

"That would be helpful. Now . . . if you'll excuse me."

"Go. I've taken enough of your time."

Beltur turned and walked toward the older man.

"So you're a councilor, a mage, and a patroller, all in one." The older man's voice was raspy, but Beltur didn't sense anger or chaos. "Do you intend to tariff us to death?"

"No. There will be tariffs. They'll be based on the methods used in other towns in Montgren, due at the end of autumn. If you live in town, you'll get a notice."

"Tariffs shouldn't be much. New council or not, you haven't done much for the town."

"Not yet. Except for removing white wizards and bravos and fixing the fountain, that is. I'm Beltur, by the way."

"I've heard. Samwyth. I'd ask if you need potatoes, but Ennalee told me that the young healer who bought some was your consort."

"She is. She's also a very good healer."

"We could use one, now and again. You need more potatoes or onions, our place is the closest one to Vortaan and Ennalee."

"Thank you."

Samwyth nodded, a gesture that signified that he was done.

Beltur turned and walked back to the Council House. Once there, he untied Slowpoke and walked him to the watering trough fed by the fountain, where he let him drink some, before he mounted and headed west on the main street.

On the way through town, he saw more people out and about, although he didn't recognize any of them. He did notice that none of them turned away and that, after a quick glance in his direction, those who did look continued whatever they were doing. *At least, that's an improvement.*

As he rode past the brick posts marking the west end of Haven, he saw that someone had repaired both posts. *Faastah?*

He looked back, but there was no one nearby. He also sensed no one near the road for the next two kays. With all his patrolling, he had discovered that he was able to sense even farther than he had when he'd been an arms-mage. He rode almost two kays before sensing a pair of riders on a slope to the south of the road, just at the edge of his ability to discern them. He raised a concealment and kept riding.

Even when he approached the defaced kaystone, the two riders had not moved. After riding another two hundred yards, Beltur came to an abandoned or neglected lane angling south-southwest from the main road. He turned Slowpoke onto it and continued, narrowing the distance between him and the two mounted men.

Before long the lane began to slope upward, and Beltur could sense that he was coming to a point where even the scattered trees were thinning, giving way to a rugged pasture. He eased Slowpoke close to one of the trees and dropped the concealment. Both riders wore the bright green uniforms of Hydlen. Neither seemed to have seen him, possibly because they appeared to be looking in the direction of the junction with the road heading north to Weevett.

Why there? Because they're worried about Montgren troopers?

Beltur watched the two for a short time, then raised the concealment, turned Slowpoke, and headed back toward Haven. After returning to the square, he let Slowpoke drink some water while he finished his water bottle, wishing he'd made provisions for a keg of decent ale at the house.

Then he mounted and rode east.

Julli waved from her garden as he rode past, but he didn't see Yamella as he passed her son's house, wondering if she'd ever accept that Zankar was dead.

Even before he was much more than half a kay from the edge of Haven, Beltur could sense a wagon and riders nearing. He eased Slowpoke under the shade of what he thought was a linden and waited, out of the bright white light of afternoon.

Two riders preceded the wagon, one of whom was a guard armed with a pair of sabres. The other was an older man in brown trousers and tunic. The wagon body was high-walled and brass-bound with a solid roof. A guard sat on the bench seat beside the teamster, one hand on the long spear whose base was set in a brass holder. Suspended from a bracket over his right shoulder was a small crossbow.

Beltur eased Slowpoke out onto the road, reined up, and again waited.

When the riders were a good twenty yards from Beltur, the merchant or trader in brown gestured, and the wagon slowed to a halt. The two riders continued until they were several yards from Beltur, then reined up.

"Welcome to Haven," offered Beltur.

"Is that a welcome or the beginning of an attempt to insist on some form of extortion?" asked the man in brown.

"It's just a welcome," replied Beltur. "I was patrolling and thought it might be alarming if I just turned and rode back into town."

"Haven's never had patrols before."

"Not in recent years," agreed Beltur.

"What's that uniform?"

"This is my patrol uniform." Beltur smiled wryly. "It was the uniform that the other black and I wore when we were Spidlarian arms-mages."

The trader looked to the guard, who nodded, then said, "We heard that a white mage was bringing the town under control."

"He wanted to set up his own land. The Duchess, obviously, wasn't about to agree to that. That's why we're here." Beltur's words weren't strictly accurate, but they were certainly true to the situation, and he didn't feel like giving yet another long explanation.

"You're planning on staying?"

"We wouldn't have rebuilt houses for our families if we thought otherwise."

"Is the East Inn still there?"

"It was a quint ago." Beltur smiled.

"Would you mind riding into town with us, ser?" asked the guard.

"I'd be happy to. My name is Beltur."

"Maunsel," offered the trader.

"Raastyl," added the guard. "Your mount's a warhorse, isn't he?"

"He is. He was mine, and I managed to buy him after my service."

"I didn't know blacks rode into battle."

"Most don't. We didn't have much choice." Beltur eased Slowpoke into a walk, turning him back west.

Once they were all headed toward town, Beltur was the first to speak. "Might I ask where you're headed after Haven? And what you trade."

"We trade largely in spices. They're moderately valuable, and they're not heavy, and everyone needs them. As for our destination, we could only be going to Hydolar," replied Maunsel. "It's far faster to take the north road through Weevett to reach anywhere in Certis. The old road could also take us to Gallos, but I'm not interested in paying the Prefect's tariffs." Before Beltur could ask another question, the trader went on. "The last time we were here, the square was empty. Is it used now?"

"We got the fountain working, and there are a few who sell there now. Market days are threeday and sevenday afternoon."

"Only wait one day . . ." mused the trader.

Beltur said little more on the rest of the ride to the side yard of the East Inn. There he reined up and turned to Maunsel. "I need to continue my rounds. Both the Council House and the healing house are on the square." Beltur smiled, then turned Slowpoke toward the square. He could sense their eyes on his back for several moments, but he didn't turn in the saddle.

XXIV

Oneday evening, both families ate crowded around the table in Lhadoraak and Tulya's "new" house, since Jessyla and Tulya had agreed that, for the immediate future, dinner would be the main meal and that they would alternate fixing it. Dinner was a mutton stew that contained, Beltur thought, an excessive amount of carrots and turnips. Because there hadn't been time to bake, Beltur had fixed skillet bread that hadn't quite gotten done in the middle in places, but was still a welcome change from the fare at the East Inn. He would have liked to try to have captured a local yeast, but that would have to wait. *Perhaps for quite some time.*

Tulya smiled broadly. "I can't believe we actually own this."

"You've more than paid for it," replied Jessyla.

"I've never had a house with water in the kitchen."

"Except for the cottage in Axalt, neither have I," replied Jessyla. "And I don't want to do without it again."

Beltur kept his smile to himself, glad that he'd come up with the way to do it. "It wouldn't have been possible without Taelya."

Taelya smiled. "It took both of us, Uncle Beltur."

"It did indeed." Beltur took another bite of the skillet bread, then a drink of water. He definitely needed to find a way to get a keg of ale. "We need to talk over a few things." He looked to Lhadoraak. "How are the repairs on the quarters building coming?"

"We have the building stripped down to what's solid. Gorlaak will be bringing in more timbers and planks tomorrow. I'll need silvers to pay him . . . and to pay the men."

"Does our treasury owe you anything besides the silver and three coppers for today?"

Lhadoraak shook his head.

"I'll have silvers and coppers for you in the morning for yesterday, today, and tomorrow. Are there any other problems with the building?"

"We'll likely find out that in the next day or so."

Beltur turned to Tulya. "I've kept track of what we're spending, but we really need a ledger of some sort because, sooner or later, I will lose track."

"I can find or make something."

"Thank you." Then Beltur looked at Jessyla. "Did anyone come to the healing house today?"

"A woman with child. She's worried because she had some pains. There's no chaos there, but . . ."

"But?" asked Tulya.

"She can start into having a child before it's ready without any signs of chaos. In those cases, the chaos comes with the birth." Jessyla paused, then turned to Beltur. "It might be that the chaos is so tiny that I can't sense it."

"That didn't happen when I was in the healing house in Axalt, but you've much more experience than I do." After a moment, he added, "You have a feeling there might be something you can't sense."

Jessyla nodded.

"Try and find me if she comes back."

"I can do that."

"There are a few other things," Beltur continued. "I met a trader and accompanied him and his wagon to the East Inn. He's named Maunsel, and he seems as honest as most traders."

"What does he trade?" asked Tulya before Beltur could finish what he wanted to say.

"Spices, he said. He has two armed guards and a solid wagon."

"We could use spices, quite a few," Tulya pointed out.

"He's headed to Hydolar. He said that no trader in his right mind would go to Gallos. But he said he *might* stay a day for market day."

"Market day?" questioned Lhadoraak.

"That was another thing that came up. I went around and talked to people in the square today. Ennalee wants threeday and sevenday afternoon to be market days at the square. I think, at least in the beginning, one of us should be patrolling there."

"Do you really think it would encourage more people to come?" asked Tulya.

"I think people will feel safer if we patrol," replied Beltur. "We can't do it all day every day, but one and a half days for now . . . it's worth a try. I'll do most of it, but, Lhadoraak, you'll have to be there when I ride patrols."

"The quarters are close enough that Gustaan can come and get me if they need me for a decision or a problem."

"How is he doing?"

"He's in control in a quiet way, but Dussef and Turlow are better with the wood."

"There's also something else," offered Beltur. "Have any of you talked to Worrfan?"

For a moment, no one said anything. Then Tulya spoke up. "Is that the tinker with the cart?"

"That's Worrfan. Did you talk to him?"

"No, not really," replied Tulya. "I said good morning to him. He seemed pleasant enough. Why do you ask?"

"He suggested that the Hydlenese troopers might be watching Haven and waiting until war breaks out between Gallos and Certis so that they can take over Haven and use the east road as a corridor to invade Lydiar. However he found out, he seems certain that war, or some sort of open fighting between the Prefect and the Viscount, is going to happen. Karch felt the same way."

"What if the white mage was part of that plan?" asked Jessyla. "He had some fresh-minted golds from Hydlen."

"You think that the mage was supposed to unsettle things so that the Duke of Hydlen could move troops in on the grounds that no one else was truly governing Haven?"

"He could claim that his traders were being hurt," said Lhadoraak. "The Duchess might not want to risk an all-out war."

"Maybe the Duchess has been worried about that all along," countered Jessyla. "Maybe that's one of the reasons we're here."

Beltur had a very sinking feeling that Jessyla's surmise was most likely accurate. He shook his head and looked at Lhadoraak and then Tulya. "I think Jessyla's right . . . and, if she is, I'm very sorry to have gotten you two into this."

"Well," said Lhadoraak dryly, "we're here, and no one else wants us. So we'll have to figure out a way to hold on to Haven."

"Just how?" asked Tulya sardonically.

"I don't know," replied Lhadoraak, with a grin that seemed slightly forced, "but Beltur's much better at that sort of thing than I am. I'm sure he'll think of something."

Frig! "Then I think I'd better do a lot more scouting over the next few days." He had another thought, one that was obvious in retrospect. "And I think I'd better have a serious talk with Gustaan tomorrow. There is the question of where the white mage managed to come up with a squad of armsmen."

Lhadoraak nodded slowly. "You think some of the wounded . . . ?"

"I have no idea, but we need to find out, and now it's something that we can't put off." Even though he had already put it off in trying to settle things as quickly as possible.

For the rest of dinner, Beltur kept thinking over how blithely he'd taken too much at face value . . . and how ill-equipped he was in dealing with politics, governing, and schemes he hadn't even considered, except in a very general way. *The only problem is that it looks like there's no one else anywhere around Haven better than the four of us.* And that made him very uneasy.

After dinner, Beltur took Taelya and Jessyla into the front room. "We're going to work on concealments."

"So we can disappear like you?" asked Taelya.

"I don't really disappear, and neither will you. A concealment is just a way of making it so that others can't see you. This might be a little harder for you, Taelya, because it requires order almost entirely, but you can put chaos between you and the order so that it doesn't make you uncomfortable."

Taelya frowned. "Why does it take more order?"

"Because you'll be using a shield against light, and the shield has to make the light flow around you as if you weren't there. Now . . . if you can find a way to do that with less order, and in a way that doesn't reveal you, then I'd be very happy. Now . . . both of you sense what I'm doing with my shield." Beltur strengthened his shield slightly, then shifted it so that the edges all were what he could only call "downhill" and "smooth."

"He's gone, but he's here," said Taelya.

"Now . . . I'm going to do a concealment from even sensing."

"He's really gone."

"No . . . I'm here. People can still hear you or smell you or walk right into you." Beltur shifted his shield back to just visual concealment. "Study how my shield feels. In a moment, you're going to try that." After a few moments, he dropped the concealment. "Now Taelya, I'm going to put a concealment around you. Everything will turn black, blacker than the darkest night. The first thing you need to do is to sense where I am and where Jessyla is. Can you do that?"

"I'll try, Uncle Beltur."

Although Beltur spent half a glass with both of them, Jessyla could only hold a concealment for a few moments, as if her shields wanted to revert. Taelya couldn't manage anything.

"That's hard." The girl's voice trembled, as if she wanted to cry.

"Taelya," Beltur said, "it's really hard. Some whites never manage it. You can do more with chaos and order than most whites twice your age. I'm sure you'll be able to do it, but it will take time. That's why we're starting now. Jessyla's much older and stronger than you are, and she could only hold a concealment for a few moments."

"I couldn't do anything you're doing when I was your age," said Jessyla.

"Neither could I," said Beltur.

"You're both telling the truth," said Taelya. She sighed. "Maybe I can find another way."

"You can try to do that," said Beltur, "but also try what I was showing you. Even if it doesn't work right now, it will make you a stronger mage."

"I will. I will." Taelya yawned.

"And I think it's time for bed for you, Taelya," said Lhadoraak as he entered the front room.

"I'm learning concealments, Father."

"I heard. Tell Uncle Beltur and Aunt Jessyla good night."

"Good night."

After Beltur and Jessyla left the house in early evening and started to walk across the street to their own house, Jessyla said quietly, "You're really worried, aren't you?"

Beltur laughed softly, not quite bitterly. "I can't think of a single reason not to be."

"The Duke can't possibly know what you and Lhadoraak can do."

"We did all of that with armsmen to protect us when we were doing it. Now . . . it's just the four of us."

"We'll work it out." Jessyla stopped short of the front stoop. "It's pleasant at this time of evening, and there aren't that many bugs out yet, either."

In short, you can't do anything tonight. Beltur let his senses range, but he felt no untoward chaos. *Not for the moment.* That was good, even if it was unlikely to last. "It is pleasant."

She took his hand and said again, "We'll work it out." After a moment, she added, with a smile, "And our mattress is a lot better than the one in the inn."

XXV

When Beltur woke on twoday he immediately looked over at Jessyla, who was already awake and looking at him. Managing not to yawn, he said, "You're right. Our mattress is much better. Even on the floor."

"You weren't thinking about the mattress last night," she replied with a fond smile.

"Neither were you."

They both laughed.

Then they hurried to get ready for the day. Breakfast was little more than oat porridge and leftover skillet bread.

Knowing he'd be doing patrols, Beltur groomed and saddled one of the "new" horses, because they needed riding, but then led the mare as he and Jessyla walked to the healing house. There he tied the horse and walked to the cabinet shop, noticing that Gorlaak's wagon, laden with assorted planks and timbers, already stood outside, and that the four workers were unloading it.

Gorlaak and Lhadoraak were directing them, but Lhadoraak left to join Beltur, with an inquiring glance.

"Once they're done unloading the wood, I'll talk to Gustaan."

"He's good at getting the others to work."

Beltur understood what Lhadoraak wasn't saying—that they could use Gustaan and that he'd be an asset. "I've seen that, and we need all the help we can get. How does Tulya like the house?"

"She's pleased. We never would have owned anything in Elparta. She really likes the stove and cistern." Lhadoraak frowned. "What if the glazing cracks?"

"It shouldn't, with all the order I put into it, but you and Taelya could reglaze parts of it."

The older mage shook his head. "You two could. I can't exert the order force you used. I wouldn't be surprised if you could focus order into a point that would penetrate iron plate."

"I wouldn't want to try. Glazing the cisterns was really hard work. Taelya got so she could narrow chaos into a point."

"That worries me."

"She'll have that power, regardless. All we can do is make sure she knows how and when to use it . . . and when not."

"I'll be interested to see how you feel when you have a child." Lhadoraak's tone was humorous.

"Probably the same way you do now. But we'll have to see."

"I just might enjoy that." Lhadoraak grinned.

"Don't laugh too hard."

When Turlow and Dussef carried the last plank into the building, Lhadoraak beckoned to Gustaan.

"Yes, ser."

"Beltur needs to talk to you. When you're finished, just rejoin us inside."

Gustaan nodded, then turned to Beltur. "Ser?"

"I've been talking to a few people, and I've learned some things that may prove troublesome for us here in Haven. You said you had been a squad leader. Where was that?"

Gustaan looked stolidly ahead. "I'd rather not say."

"It might be best if you did."

"I'd rather not say, ser."

"In Hydlen, perhaps?"

Gustaan did not speak.

Beltur could sense the chaotic discomfort and said, "You had some difficulties, possibly, and it was suggested that, if you accompanied the white mage, Elshon, was it?" That was a guess.

"It was more than difficulties, ser. The captain was green. He was little more than . . . a boy. He was the son of a noted factor. He shouldn't have been even an undercaptain. I tried to keep him from making too many mistakes. He wouldn't listen. We lost half a company in a border skirmish with Certis near Chaitel. Half a company because he wouldn't listen. He didn't survive."

Beltur unfortunately understood exactly what Gustaan meant. "And his father was very well-placed?"

"Yes, ser. The overcaptain was demoted and transferred, to the army east of Passera, and the majer felt that I and the rest of my squad . . . that . . . detached duty . . ."

"So the Duke was covertly supporting Elshon?"

"Yes, ser." Gustaan's voice was resigned.

"Is that why there are Hydlenese patrols just beyond the border . . . and sometimes even closer?"

Gustaan said nothing.

"Were you the one who was supposed to send reports to them?"

"No, ser. Lankyl was."

"Who is Lankyl?"

"He was the lesser white mage. He could conceal himself . . . the way they say you can. That way no one would see him."

"What were your duties?"

"Just to take charge if anything happened to the mages." Gustaan snorted. "When it did, I couldn't do anything. I certainly can't go back to Hydlen. None of us can."

"All of you were Hydlenese troopers?"

"We were. We were held responsible for the little prick's death, even if no one could prove it."

"Which you were," said Beltur. "I do understand. I've seen it happen."

"Begging your pardon, ser . . ."

"In the short war between Gallos and Spidlar, there was an undercaptain who met a similar fate during a battle along the river, except the officer in command was far better in dealing with it. No, I wasn't that officer. I was an undercaptain, and I was in a different part of the field when it happened . . . but I was with the squad that had to reinforce his after that." Beltur didn't even like thinking about Zandyr, much less what had happened, but Zandyr had brought it on himself through arrogance that seemed to run in too many powerful families, compounded by his own stupidity. "What was it that your captain didn't listen about?"

"He ordered two charges against two Gallosian companies. One was a company of archers dug in behind earthworks, supported by a company of heavy infantry with a white mage."

"How many Hydlenese companies were there?"

"Just one, ser, two squads of light cavalry, and two of foot. We were on patrol. We could have withdrawn and reported the incursion. But no . . . he insisted."

"The Certan heavy infantry—spears or pikes?"

"The Certans use spears shorter than a pike."

"What happened?"

"The undercaptain insisted the cavalry squads charge the heavy infantry. What the spears didn't get, the archers mostly did. Then, when the Certan heavy infantry advanced, he insisted we hold our ground." Gustaan shrugged. "After they broke through, I had what was left of my squad withdraw. We lost some there, too."

Beltur wasn't totally surprised, except by the fact that there wasn't a trace of deception in Gustaan's recounting. "How long after that were you . . . persuaded to accompany Elshon?"

"Two eightdays." Gustaan looked directly at Beltur. "What are you going to do with us?"

"Offer you jobs as patrollers. You didn't lie to me. The Duke of Hydlen used the situation to force you into an impossible situation." Beltur smiled wryly. "Being a patroller here might not be much better than where you've been, but it's the best I can offer. You can also leave, if you want. If you choose to become patrollers, I will want a promise that you'll stay." Before Gustaan could say another word, he went on. "I don't want an answer now. Think about it and talk it over among yourselves. After you finish refinishing the building, we'll talk. One other thing—are any of the others supposed to report to Hydlenese forces?"

Gustaan shook his head. "I wasn't told about that. The majer told me that none of the men should try to leave Haven until matters were settled."

"What did he mean by that?"

"I asked. He said that I'd know."

That also made sense to Beltur . . . unfortunately. "When did you think matters would be settled?"

"When Hydlen took over Haven and this part of Montgren."

"What were they going to do about Elshon?"

"Let him run the town mostly as he pleased so long as he didn't cause problems. No one told me that, but it made sense."

"How big an army is the Duke gathering to invade Lydiar?"

"They're recruiting everywhere, even in Worrak. They'll use the gutter rats for archer fodder."

"How soon?"

"Not that soon. They'd just started when they sent us off. Sometime in late summer, I'd say. Not early, though."

Beltur shook his head.

The picture he was getting wasn't pleasant. Elshon was supposed to take over Haven and create a mess, most likely take on and possibly slaughter the next group of Montgren troopers who visited Haven. That would have forced the Duchess either to give up the town or send more troops and one of her few mages. If she sent more troops, and Elshon prevailed, the Duke would wait to see what Korlyssa did. If she did nothing, he'd claim that she'd lost control and move in large numbers of troopers. If she attacked and destroyed Elshon, he'd likely claim that she breached the borders—or find some excuse to attack a weakened Montgren.

"Ser?" asked Gustaan, interrupting Beltur's thoughts.

"Oh . . . I was thinking about what happens next. You can go back to work. Talk it over with the others, and we'll get together in a few days."

"That's all . . . ser?"

"You did what you had to. You didn't lie. The question now is what you intend to do next. So long as you don't hurt or betray anyone, the choice is yours."

"Yes, ser. Thank you, ser."

Beltur had the definite feeling that Gustaan either didn't believe him or didn't know what to make of the situation. *Possibly both.*

He walked back to the healing house, where he untied the second mare and mounted, riding across the square, still empty of even the small number of vendors that had been present on oneday, but that might have been because of Ennalee's efforts to make threeday a market day. Turning east and riding at a walk, he studied the buildings he passed, with both eyes and senses. He had the impression that some looked like they'd had a bit more care, but that just might have been what he wanted to see.

What exactly could he, Lhadoraak, and Jessyla do if several companies of Hydlenese troopers rode or marched into Haven? A conflict would likely just ignite the very war that Beltur wanted to avoid . . . or put off for at least as long as possible. Yet the last thing any of them wanted was to be under the rule of the Duke of Hydlen.

He took a deep breath and straightened in the saddle.

XXVI

Beltur was at the square by eighth glass on threeday morning, wearing his "patrol" uniform. He brought Slowpoke, but left the gelding tied in front of the healing house, where Jessyla could keep an eye on him. Seeing as the square was largely empty, with the only vendor present early being Worrfan, Beltur walked to the cabinet shop that was being converted into patroller quarters. There Gustaan and the other three were unloading planks.

The former squad leader paused, then said, "These quarters won't be bad."

"Even with pallet beds and thin wool-stuffed mattresses," replied Beltur amiably.

"That's better than squad leaders get in Hydlen."

"Shouldn't the quarters be better? We'll be asking more of patrollers."

"More?"

"Patrollers have to be civil and polite, and using weapons should be the last resort."

At Gustaan's skeptical look, Beltur laughed and added, "After we settle things down. That's another reason why Lhadoraak and I are handling the patrolling for now. Also, that will establish the fact that any of you who choose to become patrollers can always suggest that those who are thinking about causing trouble would much rather deal with you than us."

After a moment, Gustaan nodded. "I can see that."

Beltur turned and walked toward the fountain.

By two quints after eighth glass, Ennalee and Samwyth had arrived with their carts, and there was a handcart pushed by a woman that held what looked to be an assortment of linen garments. Then the spice merchant arrived with his brass-bound wagon.

His first customer was Tulya, and the second was Jessyla. While Tulya smiled at Beltur, she didn't stop to talk to him. Jessyla did.

"What did you get?" asked Beltur.

"Pepper, of course, and hot paprika . . ."

"You're not going to make that hot burhka . . ."

"Not as hot as some, but even the milder version won't taste right without a little paprika. He also had cinnamon, nutmeg, kerdan, cloves, and cardamom . . ."

"Dare I ask what it all cost?"

"You'll feel better if you don't. Tulya bought more than I did, but she's a better cook."

"Did you have to—"

"Only what we can't get here. We can get mustard seed, dill, garlic, muhart seeds, oregano, chives . . . in time I can grow them and quite a few others." With a smile and her bag full of small spice bags, Jessyla hurried back to the healing house.

Beltur turned to see Bythalt talking with Maunsel. After Bythalt came a woman Beltur didn't recognize, but who left the square walking in the direction of the Brass Bowl. He wondered if she happened to be the cook there. *But would Phaelgren even pay for costly spices?*

Clearly, the spice merchant had spread the word that he'd be in the square, because more than a score of individuals appeared over the next glass.

Just after midday, Beltur walked to the unfinished quarters to find Lhadoraak. One aspect of wearing the blue uniform was that it was cooler than blacks, especially in the sun.

The older mage was coming down the narrow stairs. "I thought I sensed you heading this way, but it's getting hard to tell you and Jessyla apart from a distance. You're stronger up close, but she's getting stronger."

"So is Taelya," replied Beltur as he turned back toward the open front door. "When I worked with her last night, she could change her shield some. Not enough for a concealment, but she'll get it before long."

The two walked out of the building before Lhadoraak replied. "Taelya appears stronger than she is."

"No . . . she's that strong," said Beltur. "Jessyla is working with her, during the day."

"Won't that confuse Taelya?"

Beltur shook his head. "Remember, Jessyla's the one who got me on the right path. She can sense order and chaos far better than many blacks. It's the handling of it that she had to learn in a different way."

"It doesn't seem that much different from what I can sense."

"It's not, but we had to work more through feelings than just thought. That helps with Taelya."

Lhadoraak pursed his lips. "Do you think more healers could be mages if they approached it that way?"

"Some might, but I think she was always a mage. Because she could sense order and chaos, Margrena likely just thought of her as a healer, since healing runs in the family."

"It's something to keep in mind."

"It is. I'll let you know when I'm back. I'll head west first to see if those Hydlenese patrols are still close to the border."

"They'll be close. Just how close is the question."

As he rode past the Brass Bowl, Beltur looked and sensed carefully. He didn't see any signs of recent arrivals, but it was early in the day for travelers to appear.

Just after he passed the repaired brick posts flanking the road at the west end of town, Beltur sensed people or figures on the road several kays ahead, but as he rode closer, he realized that he'd sensed two shepherdesses moving a flock of sheep across the road to the north side. To him, the grazing looked better on the south side. So he rode closer to the shepherdesses, neither of whom was likely even a young woman yet. Each did have a massive white and gray dog, and both dogs positioned themselves between the girls and Slowpoke when he reined up.

"Shepherdesses, I'm one of the new town patrollers. I noticed you moving the sheep from the grass on the other side of the road. Yet it looks better to the south. Are there raiders or rustlers over there?"

"There were armsmen in green uniforms there early this morning," said the taller girl, dark-haired and blue-eyed. "Last eightday we lost two ewes. Mother said to move them when we saw anyone. There was just one, and he was riding west."

"You decided it would be safer on this side, then?"

"They haven't crossed the road so far," said the shorter girl.

"Thank you very much. I wish you a good day." He started to turn Slowpoke, then said, "In case you didn't know, there is now a healer at the old healing house on the square in town."

"She's not old and gray, is she?" asked the shorter girl.

"She's about my age and red-haired. She's very pleasant." With a smile, Beltur finished turning Slowpoke and made his way back to the road and continued westward. He didn't know quite what to make of the fact that the Hydlenese hadn't crossed the road, unless the Duke had decided the road would be the "new" border between Montgren and Hydlen.

Even when he neared the defaced kaystone, he could sense no mounted men likely to be troopers. There were others out and about, but all close to fields and steads. When he had reined up beside the kaystone, he blotted his forehead again. The stillness of the air made the day feel warmer than it was, and with summer less than two eightdays away, the air was more than pleasantly warm. He eased Slowpoke into the shade of a tree and blotted his brow again.

Then he concentrated on trying to sense possible troopers, but could discern nothing. After taking a long swallow from his water bottle, he turned Slowpoke back toward Haven.

The ride back to the square was uneventful. Once there, he watered Slowpoke, let him rest in the shade of the Council building for a quint, then mounted and rode out the east road. He saw and sensed only scattered locals, and he had the feeling that nothing untoward was likely to happen for the remainder of threeday.

And that worried him as well.

XXVII

Fourday morning dawned hot and hazy, and when he went out to the barn to feed and water the horses, and, also, to clean the stalls, Beltur couldn't help but wonder if summer would be even hotter and damper. The house was definitely cooler than the air outside, possibly because of the heavy brick walls and the fired-clay roof tiles. Slowpoke seemed happier in the barn than he had been in the inn stable, but that might have been Beltur hoping it was so, perhaps because the big gelding seemed pleased to see him every morning.

After dealing with the horses, eating, and washing up, Beltur donned the blue patrol uniform, and, as before, he saddled Slowpoke and then led him to the square, walking beside Jessyla. When they reached the square, it was definitely empty, except for Gorlaak and his wagon in front of the quarters building. Most likely Maunsel had left early on his way to Hydolar.

Since no one was in the square, Beltur left Jessyla at the healing house, mounted Slowpoke, and then rode west on the main street. When he reached the kaystone west of Haven, there was no doubt that he was being watched. He could sense a half squad of troopers to the southwest, and other riders farther away, but none of them were moving. Still, after watching and sensing for more than a quint, with nothing happening, Beltur decided not to immediately ride to the east side of town, but to ride back and wait at the square, since he could sense more riders even farther west, but not clearly enough to discern how many there were or whether they were approaching or moving away from Haven.

Once he returned to the square, he tied Slowpoke outside the healing house and stepped inside.

"What is it?" asked Jessyla.

"There's a half squad of Hydlenese troopers southwest of here. They're waiting for something."

"What are you going to do?"

"Wait and see. They're on their side of the border, or close enough, but I am going to tell Lhadoraak. Then I'll be back." Beltur turned and left the healing house, heading across the square.

Lhadoraak must have sensed Beltur coming, because he stepped out of the building onto the narrow covered porch. "You have that determined walk."

"There's a half squad of Hydlenese troopers southwest of here. I'm waiting to see what they do. If it's only half a squad, we can handle them."

"What if they're just the van for a larger force?"

"Then we might have to disappear and rethink matters, but I don't think they'll just attack or ride in and try to take over the town."

"Earlier you suggested that they might," Lhadoraak pointed out.

"They need a reason. They also need to be sure that the Certans won't send forces against them."

"Aren't we supplying a reason?"

Beltur offered a short and harsh laugh. "You have a point there, and before it's all over we'll probably give them even more reason."

"Are you going to go out and meet them if they ride this way?"

"No. I'd rather let them find out what we can do later. Much later. Also, going out to meet them lets them know how well we can watch them. I'd rather be able to claim that they acted without provocation and without any good reason."

"That won't help as far as fighting or a battle goes."

"No . . . but it will later." Beltur grinned ruefully. "I'm still an optimist at heart."

"Someone has to be," replied Lhadoraak. "I'd say it's easier when you're younger, except your life's been anything but easy. Let me know if you need me to do anything."

"I can do that."

Beltur walked back to the healing house, where Jessyla stood in the front room, clearly impatient.

"Well . . . ?"

"The Hydlenese haven't moved. Yet."

"What should we do if they ride into Haven? What can we do?"

"If they don't attack anyone or anything, we ask why they're here."

"What if they say that they're claiming Haven?"

"We ask on what grounds."

"And if they persist?"

"That depends on the situation."

"Does that mean you don't know what you'll do?" Jessyla pressed.

Beltur offered a lopsided grin. "That's exactly what it means. I really don't want to reveal what we can do if we don't have to."

Jessyla nodded. "I can see that. Surprise and magery are all we have."

"We also need time."

Jessyla frowned. "How much time can we afford? With each eightday we have fewer golds, and we aren't creating armsmen or gathering that much support."

Beltur shrugged helplessly. "I don't know. What I do know is that one of the weaknesses Haven had was that it had no Council. If we can improve Haven and continue as a council, that makes it harder to claim."

"I don't think that will matter much to Hydlenese officers or to their Duke."

"Not now, but the longer we can put off acting while governing Haven, the more we can tilt things in our favor."

"Optimist." Jessyla shook her head.

"Lhadoraak said the same thing."

"I'd have to agree."

"Also," added Beltur, the silence dragging out after the single word.

"Also . . . what?"

"I can't think of anything else," he finally admitted, "but I thought I could."

Jessyla smiled, then said, "My questions really don't matter. We can't let Haven become part of Hydlen, or of Certis, if it comes to that. We'll have to think of something."

Beltur nodded, although he wasn't so sure that he could think of anything more. It was one thing to be a black protecting armsmen who were doing most of the violence. It was another matter to try to find a way to stop an army with just a few mages—even a small army or a few companies. He could only hope that the Hydlenese didn't ride into Haven with several companies.

Almost a glass passed before Beltur sensed any measurable movement, and what he sensed felt like roughly a half squad of riders was escorting a wagon drawn by two horses and followed by two other riders.

"They're coming," he told Jessyla, "about a half squad and a wagon."

"That doesn't sound like an invasion."

"It might be an announcement that Haven now belongs to Hydlen."

"What good would that do?"

"If no one protests, the Duke has an easy conquest, and he can build a fort here and install a garrison. If we do protest and resist, he could claim that Haven was disruptive and needed order to be imposed—by sending an army."

"It's likely to be more gradual," suggested Jessyla.

"We'll see very soon. I need to tell Lhadoraak, and then we might as well go next door and wait at the Council House."

Jessyla nodded. "I'll wait outside."

Beltur hurried across the square.

As was often the case, Lhadoraak must have sensed him coming and stepped outside onto the porch just before Beltur reached the quarters building. "Now what?"

"Before long, you'll be sensing Hydlenese troopers—half a squad. They're headed into town, escorting a wagon."

"You didn't go out to meet them? Or you'd rather not let them know from how far you can sense them?"

Beltur nodded. "The less they know about what we can do, at least right now, the better. That might give us more time to get Haven working the way a town should. I hope so, anyway."

"It also might make them even angrier when they find out."

"If they want to take over Haven, we'll end up making them angry sooner or later." *If we're successful, and if we're not, it won't matter.*

"Do you want me with you at the Council House?"

"I'd rather you just kept an eye—and senses—out."

"I can do that."

"How is work on the quarters coming?"

"We ran into a problem. We're replacing a whole section of the upper wall on the north side. Between carpenter ants and rot . . ." Lhadoraak shook his head. "We're fortunate the rot didn't get any farther. I'll need more silvers for timber."

"Let me know how much you need, and I'll give it to you at dinner. Jessyla and I are cooking tonight."

"Assuming you don't have a long session with the Hydlenese."

"I doubt it will be too long . . . but I could be wrong. I need to go. They're only a few blocks away."

"More than that. I can just barely sense them. I'll watch what happens from here, discreetly."

Beltur turned and hurried back across the square to where Jessyla waited.

"He's not joining us?"

Beltur shook his head. "He'll watch, but I think it's better that all of us don't meet them. That's as much a feeling as anything."

When they stepped inside the Council House, Tulya looked up. "I got a small ledger from Torkell. Do you want to keep the account of the Duchess's golds . . . or have me do it?"

"I'd prefer you do it. I'll give you a list of what I've spent so far tomorrow . . . or as soon as I can. There's a half squad of Hydlenese troopers riding into Haven from the west right now. We think they'll come here. I've already told Lhadoraak. He'll keep an eye out from where he is."

"Hydlenese armsmen? Lhadoraak thought they might show up before long. What do you want me to do?"

"Just stay here, with Jessyla. I think they only deserve to talk to a single councilor." Beltur paused, then said, "Unless you think one of you should be with me."

The two women exchanged glances.

Then Jessyla said, "Not this time."

Tulya nodded.

Beltur understood exactly what they meant. He managed to keep from smiling ruefully as he stepped outside to wait for the troopers.

Less than a third of a quint later, the half squad of Hydlenese troopers reined up in front of the Council House, where Beltur stood waiting on the narrow plank stoop outside the door. The leading trooper held the pole bearing a square flag split diagonally into two triangles—one white, the other black, a design that suggested a parley ensign, given that Hydlen's colors were green and yellow. Reined up beside the ensign bearer was a captain, and behind the squad a wagon was drawn up. As Beltur watched, another rider moved forward and reined up beside the officer.

That rider was Duurben, and he was smiling at Beltur, but he did not speak.

The captain said nothing.

"Might I ask what brings Hydlenese troopers into Montgren?" asked Beltur evenly and politely.

"Who are you even to ask?" countered the captain, arrogance in every word.

"I'm one of the new councilors of Haven appointed by Duchess Korlyssa. My name is Beltur. Now . . . why are you here?"

"Councilor, I am here only to assure that traders, especially traders from Hydlen, are being received fairly. Trader Duurben believes that you intend him harm. The Duke would be most displeased if Hydlenese traders were ill-treated. I'm certain you understand that could create ill will . . . and certain . . . difficulties . . ." Behind the polite phrases lay impatience.

"I can certainly understand that, Captain, but you have escorted Trader Duurben back under a misapprehension. While I am most certain that you have responsibilities, those responsibilities are limited to what happens in Hydlen, unless we are at war, which I don't believe we are. Surely you must also understand that traders, from wherever they hail, must obey the laws of Montgren. Trader Duurben threatened an innkeeper twice with physical violence and set fire to the stable of that innkeeper. When I finished dealing with that fire, he had fled Haven."

"Those are all lies. Lies," replied Duurben smoothly.

Beltur looked coldly at the trader. "Black mages don't lie. These were not the first times you've abused people here." Then he turned to the captain. "I realize that the trader's falsehoods and your responsibilities leave you in a difficult position, but Duurben is not welcome here. Given his history of violence and abuse, the Council of Haven cannot be responsible for his life or safety. Other traders, however, are welcome so long as they do not abuse citizens and so long as they obey the laws."

"The Duke must insist—" The captain's voice rose, but remained cold.

"Haven is in Montgren. The Duchess rules here, not the Duke."

"The Duke will not be pleased, and you may regret this."

"Captain, Duurben harmed and threatened our people. That doesn't count the evils he did before we arrived." Despite the other's obvious anger, Beltur smiled pleasantly. "For your sake, Captain, it might be best if you didn't press the case of an evil man."

"He is a citizen of Hydlen, and the Duke stands behind him."

"The Duke may stand behind him in Hydlen. That is his prerogative. But a trader who has repeatedly broken the laws and assaulted people is not welcome here. How the Duke treats such a trader in Hydlen is up to the Duke. How the trader is treated in Montgren is up to those carrying out the wishes of the Duchess."

"I do not see any armsmen here," observed the captain, almost ironically.

"I'd appreciate it if you'd avoid threats, veiled or otherwise."

"It's said you're a black mage. Blacks are not known for their warlike skills."

"I'm glad you phrased it that way. We aren't, but that doesn't mean we don't have such skills. You might ask what remains of the army that the Prefect of Gallos sent against Spidlar. And yes, I am wearing the uniform of an arms-mage of Spidlar." Beltur smiled, despite his own growing anger with the arrogance of the captain.

"Words can be empty, and uniforms can be bought or stolen."

"That's very true," replied Beltur. "So I will provide some proof, but remember, you asked for such." He slipped a shield around the captain, and slowly tightened it, watching as the captain began to turn red.

The ensign bearer looked at the captain in alarm.

"If I wanted to kill him, he'd be dead," said Beltur as he released the containment.

"You—"

Before the captain could say more, Beltur applied a small shield across the man's mouth. "I could easily kill you. Not a one of your men could touch me. I do not wish to kill anyone. We merely wish to be left alone. Traders who obey the laws are welcome. Those who do not are not." He removed the small containment.

"That's little more than a magely parlor trick," said the captain.

"Are you asking to be killed?" replied Beltur. "I'd rather not, not because you're worth saving, but because of all the others from Hydlen who will die if I do. So . . ." Beltur let his voice take on a tired tone . . . "I'd appreciate it if you'd just escort back to Hydlen this trader whose only real use to you is to try to create chaos so that you can justify trying to take over Haven."

"You haven't shown any skills that are truly arms skills."

Beltur's voice turned cold. "I've killed more men than are likely in your entire army, and I've felt the black mists of death of every one. Are you really asking me to kill you to prove that I can?" His eyes bored into the captain.

The captain looked away, if for a moment, then said, "This is only the beginning."

Beltur could feel the almost palpable anger. "For your sake, Captain . . . I hope not. I truly do."

Duurben glared at Beltur.

"Duurben . . . don't tempt me," Beltur said quietly. "You're here on my sufferance." Then he stood and watched as the captain gestured, and the Hydlenese—and Duurben and his wagon—turned.

He walked to the healing house, where he untied Slowpoke and mounted. Then he followed the riders and the wagon, some hundred yards back, until they were outside Haven. He reined up Slowpoke and continued to follow them with his senses until he lost them, somewhere close to the border.

It's just the beginning . . . And it was definitely going to get ugly, because the captain had clearly been under orders to provoke Beltur . . . and, in the process of not killing the captain, Beltur had humiliated him in front of his men. *But what else could you do?*

If he'd let Duurben stay, he would have ended up imprisoning, if not killing, the trader, and once that became known, and it would have, then the Duke would have had a pretext to attack Haven. At present, that sort of reason didn't exist, but one furious and vengeful captain did.

He'd also have to explain it all to Lhadoraak and Tulya at dinner and see what they thought.

XXVIII

When he woke on fiveday morning, Beltur was still worrying about how the Hydlenese captain might retaliate. While both Lhadoraak and Tulya had agreed with Beltur's actions when they had discussed the problem at supper, the four adults hadn't come to a consensus on what the Hydlenese might do next.

Beltur shook his head in the gray light of dawn, trying to sort out the possibilities. "The only way they can undermine the Council is to injure townspeople in order to prove that we can't protect them. Then . . . if we stop that, they'll insist we attacked their troopers who were only doing reconnaissance to make certain that we weren't mistreating traders."

"You think that will happen?" asked Jessyla from beside him on the mattress.

Beltur started. He hadn't realized that he'd spoken aloud. "Uh . . . I don't know. That was just one possibility."

"Couldn't they just attack and claim that you refused to treat their traders fairly? Or even killed someone?"

"That's another possibility, but we've never seen that many troopers." He paused, then added, "But he was a captain, and that suggests at least a company."

"What's to keep them from just riding in and taking over the town?"

"Besides the five of us, you mean?"

"How could we . . . ?"

"Simply enough," Beltur said with a sigh. "Let them ride in. Then we start killing them, beginning with the captain and the squad leaders. We could do it, but I don't think that would be a good way to start. Some of them would escape, and those who did would likely take it out on the townspeople. If they do try to invade, I could put a shield across the road and conceal it, and then watch as the first few riders went down. Then I could reveal myself and suggest they go back to Hydlen."

"I like that better."

"They just might charge me, and I'd have to kill some of them . . . and then we'd be back to the others wanting revenge, even though they started it all."

"At least, you'd be giving them a choice."

Beltur shook his head, then sat up. "If the Duke has decided he wants Haven and this part of Montgren, those troopers will be sent against us until either we or they can't fight. Warning them the next time might—just might—make what we do acceptable to the Duchess and justifiable to the Prefect and the Viscount. That is, if we prevail. If we don't, it doesn't matter."

"I'd feel better if we gave them a chance." Jessyla sat up quickly.

"They might not do that at all," he replied. "The captain might have his men raid our growers for forage, possibly with several groups at once."

"Whatever they do, we'd better get up. You don't want to face troopers in your smallclothes."

At that thought, Beltur quickly extended his senses to the main street and road, but could sense no groups or riders.

They dressed and ate quickly, then saddled Slowpoke and another of the mounts they had gained from Elshon, and rode to the square. As they reined up outside the healing house, Beltur said, "Either you or Lhadoraak may need a mount in a hurry, but, if I'm gone for long, please don't forget to water him."

After tying the second mount, Beltur rode Slowpoke over to the quarters building while letting his senses range across Haven, finding individuals, animals, occasionally couples, but nothing that felt like troopers or raiders.

Lhadoraak, again, was waiting for Beltur, who decided not to dismount.

"Have you heard or sensed anything?" asked Lhadoraak.

"Have you?"

The older mage shook his head. "You can sense farther than I can."

"Have you any new thoughts about what the Hydlenese will do?"

"No. Not besides causing some sort of trouble that will try to destroy people's belief in our ability to keep them safe."

"That's my thought as well. If they wanted to ride in and take over the town, I think they'd bring in more troopers and possibly some mages . . . if the Duke has any."

"Doesn't every ruler or council have a few? Even not counting us, the Duchess has a handful of mages."

Beltur felt a little stupid at his thoughtless remark, but only said, "You're right. Since the Hydlenese are somewhere to the southwest, I thought I'd ride out and see if I can see anything. Also, I brought one of the spare mounts. He's tied up at the healing house, in case you need a horse in a hurry."

"That was a good idea. I just hope I don't need him."

"If you don't, Jessyla will watch him and water him. I thought you'd have your hands full here."

"It's looking that way." Lhadoraak nodded, then said, "Don't go too far west. They might stay well south of the main road and ride along the front edge of the hills south of town."

"That looks like rough ground."

"It does, but there might be a growers' road there that we don't know about, and it is close to five kays from the south edge of Haven to the hills."

Beltur nodded at the gentle reminder that there was a certain distance between how far he could sense and where the really rugged slopes of the hills began—a distance that neither of them had explored but only observed from several kays away, and, incidentally, he recalled, where growers like Vortaan, Ennalee, and Samwyth had their lands. "That's a good point. If they decide to forage-raid, the steads to the south and southwest would be the easiest for them to reach."

"It's also the quickest way into and out of Montgren."

That might not save them if they do too much violence or damage. But that was a thought Beltur wasn't about to voice. If it came to that, he'd just have to see how matters played out. As the gambler in Axalt had pointed out, life itself was a gamble, and you had to know when not taking a chance was the greatest gamble of all. "I'd better start riding now. They'll either be on their way here . . . or it will be another day or so."

"Let's hope they take their time," said the older mage.

So did Beltur, but he wasn't about to count on it.

He didn't ride through the back lanes and streets on his way to the west end of Haven. He could do that on his way back, assuming he didn't run into troopers or other difficulties.

Even when he and Slowpoke neared the repaired brick pillars, Beltur didn't see or sense any sign of troopers or other riders, not that he expected any so early in the day. And, early as it was, the air was warm and damp, and the sky a clear and brilliant green-blue, definite indications that summer was almost upon Haven.

Should you ride on a little farther? Not too much farther, he decided, but he continued for about another kay. He still couldn't sense any troopers or groups of riders, even after reining up and concentrating.

After about a third of a quint he headed back into Haven, seeing more people outside and working than he thought he had before. One older woman he didn't remember before actually waved. Beltur inclined his head in return.

As he neared the square, he recalled what Lhadoraak had said about the possibility of the Hydlenese troopers trying to circle around and attack from the south. So he turned Slowpoke onto the old south road mentioned by Ennalee. Perhaps a kay or so south of the last houses of Haven, he caught sight of three steads ahead, just about two kays from the town, which likely meant that two of those belonged Vortaan and Samwyth. The nearest holding looked almost abandoned, with a small cot, an unpainted and weathered barn, and a tiny shed or outhouse. New-growth weeds sprouted near the sagging poles of what had been a corral.

Farther south, the next two holdings, one on each side of the narrow and dusty road, looked far better kept, suggesting that they were the steads held by Vortaan and Samwyth, although Beltur didn't see or sense anyone outside whose presence might confirm that. He sensed sheep, a horse or two, but no riders or troopers, even after reining up and waiting awhile. So he turned Slowpoke back toward the center of Haven, wondering when and what the next move by the Hydlenese captain might be.

A quint or so later, as he neared the healing house, he could sense a certain formless chaos, an unpleasant chaos. He immediately rode to the hitching rail, dismounted, tied Slowpoke, and hurried inside. There was no one in the front room, but he could sense Jessyla and two others in one of the rear chambers. Jessyla seemed fine, but one of the others . . . "Jessyla?"

"I'm in back. I could use your help. Wash up first. There's clean water and spirits on the side table in the supply room."

Beltur immediately followed her directions, then slipped into the rear chamber.

"This is Beltur," Jessyla explained to the woman lying on the table, also nodding to the gray-haired woman standing in the corner. "He's a mage who's also a healer."

Beltur took the moments while Jessyla explained to use his senses on the woman on the table, her large and extended, and very bruised, abdomen, suggesting that she was very much with child even before he sensed the problem . . . and the chaos surrounding that still figure within the mother. He managed to keep a pleasant expression on his face, but it was clear to him that the child she carried and was trying to deliver was already dead. He looked to Jessyla, who gave the slightest of nods.

"Have you felt any movement in the past days?" Jessyla asked the woman. "Except for the pain that comes with the contractions?"

Tears began to seep from the corners of the woman's eyes. "No, Healer. Not after . . ." She winced. "That's why my mother . . ."

"Why she had you come here?"

The woman nodded slowly.

"You've been injured more than you know," said Jessyla gently. "We'll do everything we can . . . both of us."

The older woman, standing in the corner behind her daughter, mouthed, "Just save her."

Jessyla offered a nod that was acknowledgment, but not necessarily assent, and turned to Beltur. "If you'd do what you can about the chaos . . ."

In turn, Beltur nodded. Much of the chaos around the dead unborn child would likely be expelled by her labor, but that which remained could easily kill her. He'd seen that once in Axalt and been lectured on it by Herrara during his time at the healing house in Axalt more than a few times.

"Oh . . . !"

Beltur sensed the pain of the contraction, and concentrated on working slowly on eliminating the chaos that most needed to be eliminated.

Two long glasses later, after Jessyla had removed the stillborn child, and the two had done what they could for the exhausted mother, who lay on the table, half-covered by an old but clean blanket, the older woman looked to Jessyla.

"Thank you, Healers. How . . . ?"

"She should heal . . . if she is careful," said Jessyla. "Beltur removed the worst of the wound chaos. She needs rest."

"She will be with me. Now."

"If she gets very hot, bring her here," said Jessyla.

"I will, but I do not think that will be necessary."

Nearly another glass passed before the two left.

When Beltur and Jessyla were alone, they were still finishing the cleaning up, which included bundling up the soiled clothes and blanket that needed to be washed—as did her greens.

"We need help so that women like her can stay longer," said Jessyla.

"You mean that we need a full-time healing house like in Axalt? It's going to be a while before we can do that." *Like all too many things that Haven—or the Fairhaven to come—needs.*

"I know . . . but it's hard."

"It's better than before you came," he pointed out.

"It's not as good as we could make it . . ."

"If we had more golds and healers to train? That's going to take a while." Before Jessyla could say more, Beltur quickly asked, "Was she the one who came to you the other day?"

"She was. I was worried, but she wasn't bruised then."

"Why . . . ?"

"The man she lives with . . . he was angry that she came here."

"But you're a healer. Why wouldn't she come?"

"He works for Phaelgren. Phaelgren told him to stay away from us or he'd lose his position."

"Even for healing?"

Jessyla shrugged wearily.

Beltur picked up the bundle of things that needed washing and started toward the front door.

Neither mentioned that they were going to be late for dinner, but then, Beltur wasn't sure he really wanted any more than a beaker of ale.

XXIX

By midmorning on sixday, Beltur was even more worried, since he'd neither sensed nor seen any sign of Hydlenese troopers, and he was beginning to wonder what their captain was planning or whether he was just waiting for massive reinforcements. Beltur strongly doubted that, after at least five eightdays of scouting Haven, the Hydlenese were simply going to ride away, especially after Beltur's encounter with the captain on fourday.

But even after two patrols, Beltur could detect no sign of anything untoward until, in midafternoon, he sensed four riders nearing Haven from the west.

Again, he decided not to meet them, but to return to the Council House, where he could keep Slowpoke ready and continue sensing the riders as they proceeded. After going to the healing house and informing Jessyla, he returned to the Council House to wait.

"Just four riders?" asked Tulya. "That seems strange."

"I'd guess that it's another message. Possibly some sort of demand." Beltur couldn't imagine what else could be conveyed by four riders.

Not surprisingly, the four proceeded to the square, where they stopped for a short time before turning and heading for the Council House.

When Beltur stepped outside to wait for them, he was initially surprised to discover the four wore the pale blue uniforms of Montgren troopers, rather than the green of Hydlen.

"Ser . . ." The lead courier looked slightly puzzled as he studied Beltur.

"I'm Beltur, one of the councilors. I wear the blue uniform when I'm patrolling. It's actually what I wore when I served as a Spidlarian arms-mage."

"Ser . . . might I ask you who was second-in-command at the last post you visited?"

"Captain Raelf was in command." Beltur had to struggle. "Captain Karch made introductions. As I recall, it was Undercaptain Chald . . . or maybe Cheld. Cheld."

The trooper dismounted and stepped forward, handing Beltur a sealed envelope as well as a leather pouch, also sealed with a large amount of pale blue wax. "These are for you, ser, from Lord Korsaen. We're here to be at the service of the Council of Haven. The dispatch will explain."

Four troopers showing up and declaring they were sent to serve the Council? What could four troopers do? Beltur didn't know, but there wasn't the slightest hint of chaos or deception in any of the four.

"Would you like to come into the Council House? One councilor is already there. I'd like to get another from the healing house." Beltur turned and opened the door. "Tulya, the riders are troopers from Lord Korsaen. They'll be coming in. I'm going to get Jessyla."

Jessyla and Beltur made it back to the Council House before the four had finished tying their mounts. Beltur noticed that each rider had a small duffel fastened behind the saddle of his mount.

Once everyone was in the Council House, Beltur said, "The healer is Councilor Jessyla, and she and I are also consorted. She's also a mage. Tulya is another councilor and our acting justicer. Lhadoraak is a black mage and the fourth councilor, but he's in charge of rebuilding the quarters for future patrollers." He looked to the blocky and square-faced trooper who had handed him the envelope and pouch. "If you'd introduce yourselves?"

"Waerdyn. I'm the lead scout."

The sole redhead announced himself as Ruell, while the lean angular trooper was Chestyn, and the swarthy one was Taasn. Waerdyn looked pointedly at Beltur, who smiled and broke the seal on the envelope, extracting the single sheet, which he read immediately.

> This dispatch is to inform the councilors of Haven about certain developments in the increasingly bitter situation developing between Certis and Gallos. These may affect both the Council and people of Haven and possibly all of Montgren. Both Gallos and Certis are massing forces, and the Viscount has moved a large army through the Easthorns to a point within ten kays of Passera. The Prefect has invested Passera with a large force. Reliable estimates of the size of the two armies are not available, but it is unlikely that either force consists of less than three thousand troopers.
>
> Some Certan forces have been removed from the southern border of Certis, but where they have been sent is not known. This removal may well encourage the Duke of Hydlen to become more adventurous, since he earlier had proposed the consorting of his son with the daughter of the Duke of Lydiar, who has no sons and is known to be ailing . . .

That would have been nice to know, thought Beltur, except it really wouldn't have made that much difference.

> We would request that you immediately inform Captain Raelf in Weevett if you see solid indications of a large Hydlenese force nearing Haven or any part of the land of Montgren. To this end, I have dispatched four couriers to remain in Haven to allow rapid communication with Weevett. The sealed pouch should contain ten golds, enough to pay for their lodging at the East Inn for almost a season. The couriers are troopers as well and are under the Council's command while they are in Haven.

The signature and seal were those of Korsaen.

Without a word, Beltur handed the document to Tulya, who read it, and then passed it to Jessyla.

While they were reading, Beltur broke the seal on the pouch and inspected the contents—ten golds. Then he retied the pouch, slipped it inside his tunic, and said, "The golds mentioned in the dispatch were there. You don't have to worry about them now. When we're finished here, I'll go with you to the inn and explain to the innkeeper. According to the dispatch, you're under the orders of the Council and may be assigned duties suitable for troopers. Is that also your understanding?"

"Yes, ser," replied Waerdyn.

"You've had a long ride today, and you made good time. That means your mounts need rest, feed, and water. You'll meet all the councilors, including Mage-Councilor Lhadoraak, here tomorrow morning at seventh glass, and we'll discuss how you can be helpful in line with your capabilities as troopers. Don't saddle your mounts in the morning until after we meet." Beltur turned to Jessyla and Tulya. "Would either of you like to add anything?"

"Not at the moment," said Tulya.

Jessyla merely nodded and said, "Tomorrow."

"Then we'll head to the inn." Beltur gestured toward the door, then followed the four out into the very warm, but not-quite-hot afternoon sunlight.

"Did you say that the healer was a mage, ser?" asked Waerdyn, once the door to the Council House was shut.

"I did. She is. For what it's worth, I'm also a healer."

"That's sort of rare, isn't it?"

"There have been a handful of black mages who have also been healers. I'm not aware of a healer ever also becoming a black mage."

"If you don't mind my asking, ser, have there been troopers from Hydlen around?"

"Unfortunately, yes. On fourday, a Hydlenese captain rode into town under a parley flag escorting one of their traders. He told me that the Duke didn't want us mistreating traders . . ." Beltur quickly told the rest of the story.

"That doesn't sound good," offered the lead scout worriedly.

"It isn't. We've been watching to see what they'll do next."

"You were expecting us, weren't you?"

"I knew riders had entered the town. I didn't know who you were, though." Beltur mounted Slowpoke and waited for Waerdyn to do the same. Then he eased Slowpoke forward.

While Waerdyn moved his mount up beside Slowpoke, the other three followed.

Beltur thought he heard a few murmured words from the rider behind him along the lines of a "mage riding a warhorse," but he didn't reply to them.

When they reached the inn, Beltur tied Slowpoke outside, then led Waerdyn inside to Bythalt's small study, where the innkeeper looked up in surprise . . . and with a wary expression.

Before Bythalt could jump to the wrong conclusion, Beltur immediately announced, "I have some good news for you. Waerdyn here is the lead scout of four Montgren troopers who will be your paying guests in rooms for several eightdays. You'll charge them the same as you charged us, and I'll be the one handing you the coins. Lord Korsaen—or the Duchess—is supplying those coins."

"That is welcome news," admitted the innkeeper, "but—"

"No more comments about how matters could be better," interjected Beltur. "They always could be better, and they often could be worse. I told you matters would eventually get better . . . and they will . . . if you don't get too impatient." He managed a warm smile. "I need to get back to patrolling, but either I or Councilor Tulya will pay you, the same way as before."

Bythalt rose. "Unlike some, your word has always been good." He nodded to Waerdyn. "Welcome to the East Inn."

After making sure that the four troopers were taken care of, Beltur rode back to the quarters building to find Lhadoraak. The older mage was working with the others on the upper level, but walked down the staircase to meet Beltur.

"I saw you and the four troopers."

"They're here for courier duty and our use." Beltur went on to explain.

Even before Beltur had finished Lhadoraak was frowning, but he didn't speak until the younger mage finished. "The tinker was right, then. We're likely to face some sort of attack, sooner or later."

"But we can count on some support from Raelf, it sounds like."

"That's only one company."

"According to Korsaen, every Montgren company is very, very good. So far, everything he's said has been accurate."

"That's true," mused Lhadoraak, "but that company is a day away."

"I think that means I need to do some scouting. On the other side of the border." Once more, Beltur wished he'd asked Raelf about Hydlen. "That might give us more time. We could have the troopers ride the streets, in pairs, alternating, when I'm scouting. They could report to you if there's a problem."

"They're scouts . . ."

"They can't do concealments," Beltur pointed out. "And I did spend most of my time against the Gallosians with a recon company."

Lhadoraak nodded. "I'd forgotten that."

"How are you coming with the rooms upstairs?"

"We've finished with the repairs to the roof, and we're framing the inside walls. Less than two eightdays, I'd say. That's if we don't end up in a war before then."

"Have you heard anything about whether any of them want to stay?"

The older mage smiled wryly. "No one's talking about leaving. Therran did say something about how it would be nice to have even a small room to himself."

"Encouraging, but not exactly any sort of commitment. What about Gustaan?"

"He'd be better as a patroller than a woodworker. He's good at organizing the men, though."

After leaving the quarters building, Beltur stopped by the healing house to see Jessyla, and the Council House to tell Tulya that he was headed out on another patrol round and to arrange for her to pay Bythalt regularly. That was something that she should do anyway, since she was keeping the records.

This time he started out taking the old south road out as far as Vortaan's stead and then took a side lane that was little more than a track heading west. After little more than half a kay, the track ended near the ruins of a tumbledown cot, beyond which was a forest with a thick undergrowth, thick enough that a mounted force would have found it impassable. He took the track back several hundred yards to another path, not even a trail, heading north and bordering the woods, which eventually led him back to

Haven several blocks south and slightly west of his and Jessyla's house. From there, he followed the northern edge of the thick forest almost a kay westward before it gave way to rough, rocky, and uneven pastureland. Roughly a half kay to the southwest, a modest stone dwelling squatted on a low rise. From the dwelling, a narrow lane ran northeast, presumably to join one of the streets of Haven.

Beltur decided he could check that later. Instead, he studied the western edge of the thick forest that seemed to run almost due south farther than he could see or sense. He still couldn't tell if it ran into the hills farther to the south. He thought it might, but there could be space for a road between the southern edge of the forest and the rocky hills.

He took a deep breath and turned Slowpoke south, guiding the gelding along the rocky pasture less than a few yards from where the forest ended and where a line of jumbled rocks that once might have been a wall marked the separation between pasture and woods. Although the grass had recently been grazed, Beltur neither saw nor sensed sheep or even cattle. Nor did he sense any large forms of life within the forest.

He rode for what he judged to be a good three kays and then came over a low rise from the top of which he could clearly see the rocky hills rising out of the rocky grasslands about another two kays to the south. He looked to the southeast and nodded as he saw that there was a narrow gap between the forest and the hills, and the hint of what might have been an old road running through that gap. Although there were no signs of troopers anywhere near, it was clear that the Hydlenese had two possible ways to approach Haven, three, in fact, if they wanted to ride over the uneven ground that Beltur had just traversed.

Feeling that he might have spent too much time away from the town, especially since he hadn't told anyone what he'd done, he turned Slowpoke and headed back toward Haven.

Rather than retrace his outbound route, once he reached the spot where he'd turned south along the wall, he angled northwest and rode to the lane that apparently extended from the stone dwelling to Haven. He followed the lane, only to discover that it joined one of the back streets on the southwest corner of Haven just slightly east of the brick road posts marking the west end of the town. From what he could see of the few tracks in the road and what he could sense, no large group of riders had entered Haven while he had been scouting.

When he reached the square and the healing house, Jessyla practically bolted outside.

"I was worried. You've never taken that long to do a patrol. Did you run into trouble?"

"Not exactly. I did discover another way that the Hydlenese could attack Haven. Has there been any trouble here?"

"Not that I know of. I did have a woman come to the healing house. She had a terrible boil. I cleaned it out and added a little free order. There wasn't any wound chaos away from the boil, but I told her to come back in a few days just to make sure."

"She might not if it seems to be healing."

"That's fine, too. I'm headed home. It's dinner at our house tonight."

"I'll be there in a bit. I want to stop by the inn."

"Don't be too long."

"I won't."

Despite Beltur's concerns, there were no problems at the inn . . . and also no new arrivals, and for that reason, after talking briefly with Claerk, Beltur left and rode home. Once there, he quickly unsaddled, groomed, fed, and watered Slowpoke, and then made his way to the house, where he smelled what seemed to be mutton.

"Is that a stew?" he asked as he stepped into the kitchen through the back door.

"It's a mutton ragout, thank you. Would you check the bread? I used the dough you set out. I hope it will be all right."

"So do I. I've been trying to develop a decent yeast." Beltur looked into the small bread oven, sniffing as he did; the loaf was a light brown and at least smelled like bread, but it was clear that the dough hadn't risen as much as it should have. He just hoped it tasted as good as it smelled.

In less than a quint Lhadoraak and his family arrived.

"That smells wonderful," were Lhadoraak's first words.

"It smells like mutton," said Taelya, almost under her breath.

Beltur couldn't help smiling at her words.

"The bread smells good," added Tulya.

"We'll see," replied Beltur. "I'm still working on yeasts."

"Everyone sit down," declared Jessyla, her words almost but not quite an order.

In a fraction of a quint, everyone was seated, with the stew-like dish that Jessyla called a ragout in a large and stout but chipped clay pot in the middle of the table and a basket of the bread Beltur felt was too heavy beside it. The only beverage remained water, if water that was cool and order-treated. Beltur really would have preferred ale, and he kept forgetting to ask Bythalt about obtaining a keg of the somewhat better brew. Even that would be preferable to plain water.

"Did you see any sign of the Hydlenese when you were patrolling?" asked Lhadoraak after everyone was served and had started eating, all but Taelya, who looked sourly at her platter and held her spoon more like a standard of rebellion.

"Not a sign, but I also discovered that you were right. There is an old road at the base of the hills to the south of Haven, some four or five kays south. There's also a forest that would block mounted troopers . . ." Beltur went on to describe what he had discovered.

"In a way," mused Lhadoraak after Beltur finished, "it doesn't make that much difference. It would if we had an army, but it would be easier for them just to take the main road into Haven. We certainly couldn't stop an entire army. So why would they circle around?"

"They might if the Duchess sent forces," suggested Tulya, who then turned to her daughter and said, "That's all there is, and no more bread until you eat some of the mutton and vegetables."

"Mother . . ."

"You can go hungry, then."

Beltur watched as Taelya took a tiny spoonful of the mutton and vegetables, more like a chunk of carrot covered in sauce, and grimacing, put it in her mouth.

"That's only a start," said Tulya.

Beltur glanced at Tulya's platter. "Are you all right? You've hardly eaten anything."

"I'm fine. I just don't feel like eating," Tulya said.

"You're sure?" pressed Beltur.

Jessyla's boot connected firmly but quietly with Beltur's calf, even as she said, "Every woman has times when she doesn't feel like eating."

Beltur managed not to wince, but managed to say, "I'm sorry. I wasn't thinking."

Tulya smiled wanly. "I understand. You two haven't been consorted that long."

As he continued to eat, Beltur let his senses range over Tulya. He managed not to look at either Jessyla or Tulya for several moments, but reached for another chunk of bread.

"The bread's tasty, Beltur," said Lhadoraak, "but . . ."

"It's a little heavy," replied the younger mage. "I'm still working on finding a better yeast. I learned some things from Meldryn, but not nearly enough, it's clear."

"It's fresh, and it tastes good," said Tulya.

Beltur realized as she spoke that the bread was about all that Tulya had eaten, unlike Lhadoraak, who'd had two helpings of the ragout.

Taelya took another small mouthful, and a sip of water, then gave her father a questioning look.

"Your mother doesn't feel well," Lhadoraak said to Taelya. "You feel fine. Keep eating."

Taelya took another mouthful, not looking at either parent, or even at Beltur.

Before that long, Lhadoraak, Tulya, and Taelya left.

Then Jessyla looked hard at Beltur.

"I'm sorry. I just saw that Tulya wasn't eating."

"You made it harder for them with Taelya."

Beltur understood that, but didn't want to dwell on it. "It isn't really her time to be out of sorts, is it?"

"Why do you say that? Besides trying to change the subject?"

"She's with child, I think. There's a tiny knot of order—"

"Beltur . . . how could you?"

"How could I what? I only used my senses. After you kicked me, I was worried that she was really ill . . . especially after what happened yesterday."

Jessyla sighed. Loudly. "There's a difference."

Beltur waited.

"You aren't to tell Lhadoraak. Is that clear?"

"What if he asks me?"

"Tell him that you're not trained in women's problems and that he should ask me."

"I can do that."

"You can also clean up the kitchen. I'll check the barn."

Beltur managed not to shake his head until Jessyla had shut the door behind her as she left the house.

XXX

After he left the house on sevenday morning, well before seventh glass, Beltur's first stop was at the East Inn. After tying Slowpoke outside, he entered, looking for Claerk, whom he found in the kitchen. He drew the young man aside.

"Where does Bythalt get the better ale?"

"Ah . . . ser . . ."

"I just want to get a keg for our house. I'm not in trade, but I don't want to pay both Bythalt and the brewmaster."

"Ah . . . yes, ser. Well . . . he's never said . . ."

"Claerk," said Beltur firmly.

"He gets the barrels at night."

"He's trying to keep it secret, you're saying."

"Yes, ser."

"Why would I tell anyone? I just want something close to decent to drink."

"There's a barn on the south side of Widow Taarbusk's stead . . ."

"Which is where?"

"On the other side of the creek from Gorlaak's place. He gets it from there. I don't know who brews it. Might be her hired man. Might be one of her sons. Might be someone I don't know."

"Thank you. Has anyone else been here who's tried to threaten Bythalt?"

"Not that I know, ser."

With that, Beltur left the inn and headed to the Council House, arriving there half a quint before seventh glass. Lhadoraak, Tulya, Taelya, and Jessyla were all there, but not any of the four troopers.

"My thought is that I should spend much of the day scouting the Hydlenese," said Beltur. "What does each of you think?"

"What about protecting Haven?" asked Tulya.

"Today is market day," replied Beltur. "This afternoon, anyway. Two of the troopers could patrol the streets this morning, and the other two could just watch the square this afternoon. If anything happens that they can't handle, they can summon Lhadoraak and Jessyla."

"Just me, at first, anyway," suggested Lhadoraak. "Gorlaak and Dussef are doing most of the real building. Therran's learning. Turlow's good with what metalwork there is. Gustaan and I just supply muscle."

"And a little woodworking and magery," added Beltur.

"Some," admitted Lhadoraak.

"How long will your scouting take?" asked Jessyla.

"I don't know, but likely all day . . . or most of it, unless I discover that they're riding toward Haven. Then my scouting will be rather quick."

"Do you think they'll attack today?" asked Tulya.

Beltur shrugged. "Who knows? I doubt that they have a large enough force close by, but that could change any time now. That's why I want to see just how many troopers they have, and if they have any mages."

"If they have mages . . . ?" said Jessyla.

"I'll be very careful. If there's any hint of mages, I'll use full shielding."

"Good."

"Here come the troopers," said Lhadoraak. "They're walking across the square."

"I told them not to saddle any mounts until after they met with us," replied Beltur. "I had the feeling that we'd only be using two at a time."

"Feeling?" asked Tulya dryly.

"They rode all day yesterday. Their mounts shouldn't be ridden heavily today. We might need to send two of them back to Weevett sooner than we'd like." Beltur walked to the door and opened it, waiting for the troopers, and then ushering them into the large front chamber.

Once the four were inside, he gestured to the older mage. "This is Councilor Lhadoraak. He's been in charge of rebuilding the Council House, the healing house, and now the quarters building for patrollers and others who might work for the Council in the future."

"What are you in charge of, ser?" asked Waerdyn.

"He's in charge of everything," replied Lhadoraak, a touch of humor in his voice, "especially dealing with troublemakers."

"Oh . . . then you're the one who . . . took care of the white mages?"

Beltur nodded. "With Jessyla's help, while Lhadoraak was handling the rear guard."

Ruell looked at Taelya. "What do you do, little woman?"

Taelya looked to Beltur.

"You can put a shield around him, if you like, just for a moment." Beltur doubted that Taelya could hold a shield around the trooper for long, but Ruell didn't have to know that.

The trooper froze for several moments, a panicked expression on his face, before Taelya released the shield and said, "That's what I can do, ser."

Ruell swallowed.

Waerdyn offered a rueful smile. "You *did* ask."

"She's . . . a mage, too?"

"She's a beginning white," said Beltur. "She can shield herself and stop others"—*if only for a few moments*—"and do a few other things. Now, let's talk about what you'll be doing today. Two of you will just ride the streets of Haven, from now until noon, no farther than the eastern road posts or the western posts. Then you'll be off duty, but I expect you to remain either in the East Inn or somewhere around the square. The other two will simply walk around the square, keeping order, from noon to fourth glass. That's because those glasses are when market day is—and all day on threeday. If you run into difficulty, you can immediately find Lhadoraak in the quarters building. I'm having you do that so that I can go scout what the Hydlenese company is doing."

"Ser . . ." offered Waerdyn, "I am a scout."

Beltur drew a concealment around himself, then said, "So was I." Then he dropped the concealment. "You likely know more about scouting than I do, but since I cannot be seen, the Hydlenese cannot complain about Montgren troopers crossing the border into Hydlen. There are also a few other talents that may prove useful."

"But . . . why . . . ?"

"Why do we need you?" replied Beltur. "Because there are only five of us. By patrolling the town, you allow us to do other things. We'd hoped to have time to build a small force of town patrollers and do more than we have, but the apparent war—or standoff—between Certis and Gallos has changed matters."

Waerdyn nodded.

"Now . . . which two of you will be riding patrols this morning?"

"Ruell and I will do that. Chestyn and Taasn can act as town patrollers this afternoon."

Less than a quint later Beltur mounted Slowpoke and rode away from the Council House. He had already decided not to ride out the main road west, but to take the back streets to the lane that led to the stone dwelling in the middle of the rocky grassland. Where he went from there would depend partly on what he sensed when he reached the edge of the heavy woods.

Even before he reached the edge of the forest, he could sense riders, if barely, near the steads of Vortaan and Samwyth and he urged Slowpoke into a fast walk.

Once he was past the eastern edge of the small but thickly grown forest, Beltur could definitely sense riders moving around Samwyth's lands, especially near the corral that held a small flock of sheep. He didn't sense any sign of a mage, but because he and Slowpoke could move more quickly when not under a concealment, he waited until he was almost to where he could be seen before he concealed himself and Slowpoke.

He was within fifty yards of the small cottage and the outbuildings behind it when he sensed a figure lying on the walk in front of the dwelling, a figure with so little natural order and chaos that death was imminent. Slowpoke hadn't taken more than a dozen steps more before the black death mist drifted across Beltur.

Samwyth . . . or his consort? Since Beltur didn't sense anyone else near or inside the cot, he eased Slowpoke past the cottage.

One rider, most likely a trooper in green, walked into the corral that held a small flock, then lifted a lamb, then carried it to the edge of the corral where another hoisted it so that the third rider had it in front of him. The two selected another lamb for the fourth rider.

"Get moving! Two's enough," said the man who'd carried the lambs. "You let that woman get away. She gets to town, and that mage'll be out here before you know it."

"You don't know that, Vaertyr."

"You want to be fried or strangled . . . be my guest. We're getting out of here. Now that you've got the lambs, just open the corral. Let the frigging sheep wander where they will. I'll take Brembal and his mount."

Beltur hadn't noticed the fifth mount, but he could sense something laid over the saddle, something that looked like a dead trooper. *How did Samwyth . . . or whoever . . . kill the man?*

He reined up and waited.

The two troopers on foot untied their mounts from the corral posts and quickly mounted, and the four riders turned south along the narrow trail heading toward the rocky hills that marked roughly the border between Montgren and Hydlen.

Beltur could have killed all four of the troopers, but that wouldn't have made much difference, and he could sense three others farther south. More important, he also wanted to follow the group to see where they went and just what he and the others faced, especially whether there happened to be more than a single company posted just beyond the border . . . or possibly even inside the border, although Beltur strongly doubted that.

As carefully as he could under a concealment, he followed the Hydlenese back along the lane that was little more than a dirt track until it joined the path that threaded its way between the steep and rocky hills and the thickly wooded and overgrown forest. None of the troopers seemed to look back, or if they did not a one noticed anything that alarmed them. Following wasn't that hard, because two of the seven had lambs across the front of their saddles, and one was leading another mount with the body of the slain trooper.

A kay or so later the forest ended, and to Beltur's right was the rocky grassland that presumably stretched north to the low stone house just south of Haven proper. On the south side of the path the hills continued. The seven troopers kept riding.

Beltur thought they had covered another two kays or so when the troopers reached a point where the hills seemed lower. Before long they turned onto a somewhat wider track that headed not quite due south through a low patch of ground between the hills and across an unrailed bridge over the small creek that Beltur *thought* marked the border between Montgren and Hydlen. Even though the concealment kept direct sunlight off Beltur, he was still sweating in the heavy muggy air, and he had to keep blotting his forehead and adjusting his visor cap in the darkness of the concealment.

Around a kay later, the riders neared what Beltur sensed was a modest stead. He also could sense more troopers, possibly a company's worth, but certainly not a battalion, and likely not even two companies. The riders continued toward the stead house, as did Beltur, still under his concealment. The troopers reined up short of the narrow covered porch.

Beltur sensed two figures standing there and eased Slowpoke forward and to the side of the porch away from the riders before bringing the gelding to a halt.

"Captain, ser!" called out one of the troopers.

"Report!"

"Captain, Undercaptain . . . mission accomplished. We struck one stead, and scattered the sheep."

At least, that was what Beltur thought the squad leader said, given the odd accent and cadence of the trooper's speech. Odd at least from Beltur's point of view.

"How did you let a man get killed?" The officer gestured toward the mount carrying the body.

Again, Beltur had to concentrate on the words.

"The local got him with a crossbow. We took him down before he could use it again. Nasty old bastard. Told us we'd pay."

"You should have killed everyone on the stead for that."

"There wasn't anyone else there, ser."

Beltur could sense the untruth.

The captain obviously didn't, because he immediately replied, "Then you should have gone to the next stead and slaughtered everyone. They need to learn who's in charge."

"Yes, ser."

"They'll all learn. Sooner or later." After a pause, the officer added, "At least, you brought fresh lamb back. Better than mutton. Take the lambs to the cooks."

"Yes, ser."

As the troopers rode toward one of the larger outbuildings, Beltur waited, listening.

"You shouldn't have to tell them everything, ser," said one, presumably an undercaptain by his address of the other.

"They're too soft. The only way to deal with that arrogant mage is to show the locals that he can't protect them. You weren't there to hear how insufferable he was. As if he were the equal of the Duke." After a pause, the captain said, "Skallyt? Do you hear a horse, somewhere near?"

Beltur didn't wait any longer. He put containments around the necks of both officers, tightening them brutally and swiftly, crushing the men's throats and windpipes. Before that long the captain and undercaptain pitched forward and off the low porch, followed by the rising of the cold black mists that drifted across Beltur.

Then he turned Slowpoke back toward the lane away from the stead house and in the direction of Haven. He was almost a hundred yards from the stead house before he heard the first shout, doubtless as someone found the two dead officers.

That might slow down the Hydlenese efforts against Haven. Then again, when those efforts were resumed, the Hydlenese might be even more vicious. He kept riding, but could sense no one following him. Slowpoke had doubtless left some tracks in the dust of the paths and trails, but with all the other riders who had traveled the same way, Beltur doubted that anyone would be able to tell much.

Once he was well away from the Hydlenese encampment, he dropped the concealment, which allowed Slowpoke to walk more swiftly, but for several moments, after glasses in darkness, Beltur was blinded by the light. He also felt even warmer with the late spring sunlight pouring down on him directly.

Despite Slowpoke's faster pace without the hindrance of the concealment, it was more than a glass later, and well past midday, before he reached Samwyth's stead. There, Lhadoraak and two of the Montgren troopers stood by the cottage porch. Beltur glanced around. From what he could tell, the sheep, or most of them, were back in the fenced area.

As Beltur reined up, Lhadoraak looked to him. "You followed them?"

"I did. There's a company encampment a kay or two across the border, I'd guess some five kays to the southwest. I had to ride some of it under a concealment."

A gray-haired woman appeared on the porch. She looked at Beltur. "You just followed them? Why didn't you stop them before they killed Samwyth?"

"I didn't get to your stead until after they killed him. They were picking out two lambs when I got there."

"And you let them?" Her tone was accusing.

"I did. Then I followed them back to their encampment to learn what I could. The captain had ordered his men to raid your stead and Vortaan's, but both Vortaan and Ennalee had both left for the square, it seemed."

"All you did was follow the raiders?"

"I didn't say that was all I did. I killed the captain and the undercaptain who'd ordered the troopers to raid your stead. Then I scouted around a little more and rode back here."

"You a powerful mage, and that's all you did?" The woman's voice was bitter. "They'll just come again, and they'll do worse."

"They'll come anyway, but they might hesitate a day or two after losing both their officers, especially since there's only one company near Haven at the moment." Beltur was very much aware that that would change before long. *Especially after what you did.* Except, he knew, that some sort of attacks would have occurred regardless. "The troopers were doing what they were ordered to do. I killed the men who gave the orders. And I'll try to keep doing that. We'll see how long officers will give orders like that, if they risk their own death by attacking Haven and its people." Beltur could see Lhadoraak wince.

But what other tactic do you have? You're not strong enough to kill a hundred men at once or even in a short time. Not unless a white mage showed up and conveniently started throwing chaos . . . or a thunderstorm miraculously appeared.

"Why didn't you just kill them all?"

"Black magery doesn't work well that way," Beltur said. "We're doing the best we can."

"You need to do better." The woman looked away.

Beltur glanced to Lhadoraak. "Was there anything else?"

The older mage shook his head.

"Then I'm heading back to the Council House."

"All of you . . . just go," said the woman, not looking at either mage. "You've done enough."

Beltur didn't even try to reply. He just waited for Lhadoraak to mount, and then turned Slowpoke and urged him toward the road leading back to the square. Lhadoraak eased up beside Beltur, while the two troopers fell in behind.

After several long moments, Lhadoraak asked, "What do we do now?"

"We wait, and I keep scouting. The moment we discover a larger force headed for Haven, we send two of the troopers to Weevett to report that."

"What about the Hydlenese still here?"

"If they do nothing and stay on their side of the border, we do nothing. If they try any more raids, then I'll do what I can to discourage them." Beltur turned slightly in the saddle to look at the older mage. "Unless you have a better suggestion."

Lhadoraak shook his head, then offered a smile that was sad, rueful, and wry, all at once. "I don't. Neither does Tulya or Jessyla. We talked for a moment after Frydika rode to the Council House for help."

"Frydika? Samwyth's consort?" Beltur realized that he'd never even known her name.

The older mage nodded. "It's all going to depend on who's stronger. Usually, that means who can destroy more of the other side. You're better at that than any of us."

That was the last thing Beltur wanted to hear, but he just nodded and kept riding. After a time, he asked, "How far can you sense?"

"Not nearly as far as you. Between half a kay and a kay, and that's if it's not raining or snowing."

Even Jessyla can sense farther than that. And that meant that Beltur was the only one who could provide an early warning when the Hydlenese did finally attack . . . unless patrollers that Haven didn't yet have were posted well away from the town—and mounted as well. Beltur managed not to sigh.

When he and Lhadoraak rode into the square, the two troopers separated and rode toward Waerdyn and Ruell, who stood close to the fountain, surveying the handful of vendors—more than Beltur had ever seen in the square—as well as the ten or so possible customers surveying produce and wares. Several stood by a wagon talking with Ennalee and a man, presumably her consort, Vortaan.

"I'd best tell Ennalee and Vortaan," said Beltur, "before someone else does."

"We both should," suggested Lhadoraak.

Even before the two of them neared the small crowd, Ennalee's eyes fixed on Beltur.

He reined up several yards from the wagon's tailgate, on which rested samples of various root vegetables.

"The two of you have that same look," said Ennalee. "Did the Hydlenese attack our stead?"

"No. They raided Samwyth's before I got there." Beltur then went on to explain what had happened.

"Samwyth just should have let them take the lambs." Ennalee shook her head.

"Always was a stubborn cuss," added Vortaan.

"There's stubborn, and there's stupid," replied Ennalee, a disgusted tone to her words.

"You going to let them walk in here?" asked Vortaan.

"No," replied Beltur.

"How are you going to stop them?"

"However I can."

"What about the Duchess?" asked Ennalee. "Where are her troopers?" She gestured to the four by the fountain. "Not a few."

"The Duchess has said that she'll send troopers if the Hydlenese bring more than a company of their troopers to attack Haven." That wasn't quite what Korsaen had written, but it was close enough. "That's why those four are here."

"Feel a lot safer if those troopers were here now," pointed out Vortaan.

"They're not, and they won't be unless the mages here can hold off the Hydlenese for a time." Ennalee looked directly at Beltur. "Isn't that so?"

"Most likely," Beltur agreed, knowing that he and the others on the fledgling Council were going to have to be very creative in dealing with the likely invaders. "Now . . . if you'll excuse us . . ." He inclined his head, then turned Slowpoke in the direction of the Council House.

XXXI

After Beltur and Jessyla finished breakfast on eightday, he announced, "I'm going to patrol out west first, then stop by the Widow Taarbusk's place on the way back."

"Just because of the ale?" asked Jessyla, with a hint of a smile.

"Just because?" Beltur shook his head. "I'm tired of drinking just water. So are you. She's the only one around who brews a decent ale. That's what Claerk said, anyway, and I don't want to fight battles drinking only water."

"And what do you expect me to do?"

"Would you rather get the ale?"

"No. I'm not about to try to carry a keg back here, and I doubt the widow delivers kegs, at least not on eightday."

"Good. I'd like you to ride out to Vortaan and Ennalee's stead, just to sense if there are any Hydlenese around. If there are, find me."

"I can do that. Tulya and I thought you might be thinking like that.

She's fixing dinner for all of us. Half past fourth glass. That's if the Hydlenese don't raid or attack."

The two walked to the barn, where Beltur saddled Slowpoke and Jessyla saddled one of the former Council horses. Once they had led the horses out and Beltur had secured the barn, he mounted Slowpoke and turned to Jessyla, already in the saddle. "I thought I'd head out west from here. I don't sense anyone in the square, and there's no point riding there, and then back."

She nodded and said, "Why don't I ride out east and then to the south?"

"That would be good."

"And don't spend too much time with the widow," she added.

Beltur frowned. "Why would I do that?"

"So you won't get stuck. I imagine there's a reason why they all call her 'the Widow Thornbush.'" Jessyla grinned at him.

"I just want some decent ale," declared Beltur.

"I'd enjoy that as well."

"I thought I'd get some for Lhadoraak and Tulya as well."

"They'd enjoy that. Now . . . after I scout out the steads to the south," added Jessyla, "I'll stop by the healing house for a bit, and then I'll be at Tulya's helping her fix dinner. Lhadoraak is working on the quarters building until the second glass of the afternoon."

"He'd said he would be. He wants to finish that as soon as he can."

Once they reached the main street, Beltur turned west, and Jessyla east.

As he rode past the brick posts at the west end of Haven, Beltur tried to sense anyone or anything that might be out of place, but he found nothing. When he reached the side lane where he'd once sensed Hydlenese troopers, he followed it for almost a kay, but neither saw nor sensed any riders. He couldn't help wondering where they might be and when the next attack might come . . . and what form it might take.

Since there was little point in waiting for what might not come for glasses or even days, he turned Slowpoke back toward Haven, and less than half a glass later, he was reining up in front of the weathered stone and timber dwelling that he hoped was that of the widow. After tying Slowpoke to a somewhat battered but seemingly sturdy wooden post, he walked to the front porch and knocked on the door.

A youth opened it. His eyes widened as he took in Beltur in his patrol uniform. "Yes, ser."

"I'm here to see the Widow Taarbusk."

"Yes, ser." The boy turned and called, "It's one of the mages for you, Ma." Then he stepped back.

The woman who appeared at the door wasn't at all what Beltur expected. Not only was she much younger, most likely only ten years or so older than Beltur, but she was broad-shouldered and only a few digits shorter than Beltur. While her face had a definite angular hardness to it and her eyes were a cold green, and her hair a short-cut whitish blond, the figure beneath, even in a long-sleeved shirt, worn brown leather vest, and brown trousers, was definitely feminine. The dirk at her waist was in a worn sheath. "Why might you be here, Mage?"

"I understand you brew the best ale around."

"We brew the only ale for sale."

"I was referring to the better brew that Bythalt offers. Do you have some of that, or something better?"

"How much do you want?"

"Two kegs, if you have them."

"The regular is four silvers, and two extra for the keg. You bring back the keg, and the next keg is four. The best is five silvers."

"I'd be interested in the best. Two kegs."

"A gold and four silvers."

Beltur managed not to wince, but he reminded himself that he was buying eightdays' worth of ale, at far less than it would have cost at the inn. "That would be fine. About carrying them . . . ?"

"I don't do that. I can lend you a leather keg sling that will hold two kegs—if your horse will carry it—and you're willing to walk him back to town. Otherwise, you'll have to hire a wagon."

"What does each keg weigh?"

"Six stone full, or thereabouts."

That meant the two kegs weighed almost a stone more than Beltur, but Slowpoke could carry that. "I'll borrow the sling."

"Since you're a mage, I won't ask for surety for the sling. I'd appreciate having it back within the next few days."

The word "surety" struck Beltur as odd. "Are you originally from Haven?"

"No more than you, Mage. My late consort's father was a brewmaster in Renklaar. So was my consort."

"Might I ask how you came to Haven?"

"You can ask, but all I prefer to say is that Haven suited us better. Now . . . if you'll lead your horse to the brew house—that's the second and larger building at the base of the small hill."

Beltur didn't press, and by the time he walked Slowpoke back to the second structure, the widow was waiting for him with two kegs and a sling-like leather harness set on a wooden platform in front of the door. She'd obviously lifted the kegs herself. He handed over the gold and the silvers.

"Thank you." She nodded. "I'll hold the harness in place, while you center the first keg. Then, I'll come round and hold that keg in place while you center the second."

Beltur lifted the first keg—and it was definitely a solid six stones—and managed to get it centered in the harness without scraping or bumping Slowpoke. Then he repeated the process with the second keg.

"Your mount is well-behaved, Mage."

"We get along well. We've been through a lot together."

She just nodded.

"I'll bring the harnesses back before too long."

"We'd appreciate that."

She remained in front of the brew house, watching as he led Slowpoke back out to the lane and began the kay-long walk back to Haven.

Three quints later, he led Slowpoke up to the back door of Lhadoraak's house, glad that he hadn't sensed any raiders or troopers.

After he tied Slowpoke, but before he could knock, Tulya opened the door. "Beltur! What are you doing here?"

"Delivering a keg of ale. I got tired of just drinking water, and I thought you three might have felt the same way as well."

"Beltur . . . we can't let you—"

"We're all going to need this ale if we get into battle after battle. It's the only way to keep going when you're fighting from the saddle. Besides, you both deserve it." He lifted the heavy keg, watching the sling harness, but it didn't move. Then he carried the keg into the kitchen and set it beside the kitchen cistern, belatedly realizing that neither house had a stand in which to place the keg for easy use of the spout. "For now, Lhadoraak will have to tie the keg in place on top of the cistern, maybe anchor it with an order link."

Tulya looked at him. "Thank you. We appreciate it."

"I got you all into this mess. The least I can do is come up with some ale."

"I had a part in it, too. I hated the cold in Axalt. Here, at least, things seem . . . more real. And I can do things besides cook and clean and watch Taelya."

"You've made everything much easier. I appreciate your taking care of the ledgers and paying Bythalt."

"Beltur . . . do you think we can . . . ?"

"I think so." *I just don't know how many people will die for how long. Or whether anyone besides the five of us will think it worth the price.* He offered a cynical smile. "We might have to kill a lot of troopers whose only fault is that they serve the Duke of Hydlen."

She looked at him evenly. "It won't be the first time."

"No. Unfortunately." He paused. "I need to get the other keg put away and then get back to scouting . . . just in case."

"Can I do anything?"

"Besides what you're doing? No."

After leaving Tulya, Beltur then led Slowpoke back across the street to his and Jessyla's house, holding on to one side of the sling. Once there, he tied Slowpoke to the rear hitching post and then lugged the second keg into the kitchen, setting it beside the cistern and shaking his head at the thought that he'd never considered the need for a stand or small table.

Then he left the house, locking it behind him, and removed the sling harness before mounting Slowpoke. Since he didn't sense anyone to the west, he rode back to the widow's place. He didn't even have to dismount, since he saw her outside the brew house and rode there.

"Thank you for the sling." He handed it down to her.

"Thank you for buying the ale. Few want to pay extra for the better brew."

"Does Phaelgren ever buy it?"

Beltur's question drew a barked laugh. "He brews his own. It's worse than swill. Bythalt knows better."

"You must sell to others, then."

"It's a living. You've got better things to do than talk with me, Mage."

"Beltur."

"You've got better things to do, Beltur."

"Knowing about the people in town is one of those better things," he replied. "Until next time." He offered a friendly smile before turning Slowpoke back toward the road.

Because he could sense Jessyla's presence at the healing house, that was his next stop, since he wanted to know what, if anything, she had seen or sensed.

When he entered the healing house, he found Jessyla busy with her mortar and pestle.

She looked up and said, "I stopped by Julli's and picked up some knitbone. That's not what I'm working on. I'm powdering more gypsum so that I can do casts."

"Did you find out anything?"

"It's quiet out to the south. I stopped and asked Ennalee if they'd seen anyone. They haven't. Not so far. I also talked to some shepherd girls out east. No one they didn't know has been on the road this morning. What about you?"

"No sign of anything. There's a keg of the widow's better ale in our house and in Lhadoraak and Taelya's. The widow's not very talkative. I didn't learn much from her, except that she and her consort and consort's father came from Renklaar . . . and that Phaelgren makes his own brews, and they're terrible."

"How did you carry two kegs?"

"I borrowed a sling harness from her and Slowpoke carried them. I walked him. Then I returned the harness and came to see how you'd fared."

"What will you do now?"

"More scouting to the south and west. I need to know which ways the Hydlenese are most likely to take if they decide to bring a larger force here."

Jessyla frowned. "I thought you had worked that out."

He shook his head. "There are several ways for mounted troopers, but if they bring a larger force, they'll have wagons. Wagons need better roads. Also, the better the road, the faster they can advance."

"Try to get back by third glass."

"If I can't, we'll likely all not be worrying about dinner."

"I'd rather worry about dinner."

Beltur definitely shared that sentiment. He walked around the table, bent down, and kissed Jessyla on the cheek. "I'll see you later."

When he left the healing house, he rode by the quarters building. Although he didn't see anyone, he could sense a number of people working on the upper level, including Lhadoraak. Two women were filling buckets at the fountain. Neither looked at him.

As he rode westward on the main street, he saw a few people outside in the warm and muggy air. One woman, whom he didn't recognize, waved, and he nodded in return. The rest of the ride through the west side of Haven was similar. Beyond the brick posts, since there were fewer dwellings, he saw only a handful of people.

As he neared the kaystone five kays west of town, Beltur studied the side lanes intently. All but the one that he'd explored earlier in scouting the two Hydlenese troopers ended within less than a kay of the main road. Even when he passed the kaystone and reached the junction with the road north to Weevett, he sensed no travelers. So he kept riding west.

Beltur reined up two quints later, slightly more than two kays farther west, just past a hill on the south side of the road that extended into a long ridge running toward the southwest, an unusual direction, Beltur thought, given that all the other hills in the area seemed to run largely east-west. He studied the junction ahead where another road branched off, angling to the southwest. The southwest road had clearly seen more travelers recently, but since there hadn't been that much rain, it was almost impossible to tell when the latest travelers had passed by.

From what he could sense, there were no travelers on either road . . . except . . . he thought he could sense a single figure on horseback farther west, on a low rise between the road to Hydolar and the road to Jellico. *Most likely a Hydlenese scout.*

Beltur kept watching and sensing, but the rider didn't move.

Finally, a quint later, Beltur turned Slowpoke back toward Haven . . . and saw a wall of dark thick clouds to the northeast, clouds that were definitely moving toward the town.

If that brings a good solid rain, it just might slow down whatever the Hydlenese might have in mind. And if you don't keep riding, you and Slowpoke just might get caught in the rain.

The first few drops began to fall as Beltur dismounted outside the barn, and a light rain was falling by the time he'd groomed and watered Slowpoke and was walking up to the house to wash up. After doing that, he had to dash through a heavy rain to Lhadoraak and Tulya's house.

"I'm glad you're here," said Jessyla as he stepped inside. "I was afraid you might get caught in the storm."

"I tried some of that ale you brought," said Lhadoraak, his voice level.

Beltur tried not to wince. "Is it all right?"

The older mage grinned. "It's actually much better than decent, and far better than Bythalt's best."

Beltur took a deep breath. "Good."

"What do we owe you?"

"You don't. Ale's a necessary supply, and I'm afraid it's going to be more necessary. We need to get in the habit of carrying at least one water bottle full anytime we're patrolling."

"Did you see any signs of the Hydlenese?"

"Just one scout some four kays west of the kaystone."

"You went that far beyond the junction with the road north to Weevett?"

"I wanted to see where the road to Hydlen turned off. Karch mentioned it, but I'd never seen it." Beltur explained briefly, including the fact that a large force would likely take the road.

"Then why did they take back roads and attack from the south?" asked Tulya.

"I'm only guessing," replied Beltur, "but I didn't see much along that road, just sparse grasslands and lots of low rocky hills. The company I followed had taken over a stead. It might be one of the few in that corner of Hydlen. Also, they didn't have any wagons."

"Then maybe it would be worth it to post the troopers out west, during the day, anyway," said Lhadoraak, "where they can see any large force approaching. The smaller forces can't do that much damage, and we can whittle them down if they keep attacking."

"Any damage that they do will be considered as significant by those who suffer," pointed out Tulya.

"If we prevail in the end, we can put things back together," said Beltur. "If we don't, it doesn't matter."

"Putting things back together, as you put it," replied Jessyla, "could take years, and we can't undo death."

"You're both right," admitted Beltur. "What do you suggest that would be better?"

"Isn't there any way you could do that whittling before the Hydlenese attack steads?" asked Tulya.

"We could try, but it would be a guess," said Beltur. "It's unlikely that they'll attack steads north and east of the town. There's no easy way to get east of town, and there really aren't many steads to the north and west. But that still leaves a large area."

"I could patrol the road to the west," declared Jessyla. "Not too far out. If you could watch the south . . . and each of us had a courier with us . . . then the courier could ride to tell the others."

"Shouldn't I be doing that?" asked Lhadoraak.

Jessyla shook her head. "Your shields are stronger, I think, but I can sense farther than you can. That means that you need to be able to come to help whoever senses the raiders. I can't hold them off as well, but I can give you more time."

Lhadoraak looked to Beltur, with an expression both questioning and rueful.

"She can sense farther, and your shields are stronger." *But not by much and probably not for long.*

"Then that makes sense," declared Lhadoraak.

"Also," interjected Tulya, "that just might allow you to finish working on the quarters building, and that might mean that some of those workers might just be willing to serve as patrollers or armsmen."

Lhadoraak shook his head, then smiled. "I can't argue about any of that . . . and I'm getting very hungry."

XXXII

At one point during the night, rain pounded the roof so violently that hammering impacts woke Beltur, tired as he was. Even after getting back to sleep, when he woke up in the deep gray before dawn, he had a slight headache, of the sort he had usually experienced during a northeaster . . . although the rain had subsided to a drizzle, at least from what he sensed and heard.

He sat up slowly, then massaged his forehead.

Jessyla turned. "My head aches, too."

"Congratulations. That's one of the benefits of magery. You get headaches during severe rainstorms. I've heard it's even worse for whites."

Jessyla slowly sat up on the mattress, then yawned. Finally, she said, "Do you think Taelya has a headache?"

"She might. I've never heard anything about whether young mages get headaches from storms."

"I'll ask Tulya if I see her before you do." She glanced toward the window. "After all that rain, I'd be surprised if the Hydlenese would choose to ride out and attack anyone today."

"I'd think not, but you never know. They might do it because they think no one would be expecting it."

"I'd wager they don't."

Beltur smiled. "I won't wager against you."

Before that long, the two of them were sitting at the old, sturdy, and slightly warped kitchen table. Beltur sipped the ale he definitely appreciated and slowly ate the oat porridge he liked a great deal less. The ale and the porridge seemed to help in lifting the headache.

After a time, Jessyla said, "Before dinner last night, I had this feeling you left something out when you said that Lhadoraak had stronger shields. What didn't you say?"

"He has stronger shields for now. If you keep working, yours will be stronger."

She frowned. "You aren't just saying that, are you?"

Beltur shook his head. "Your technique is better than his."

"That's because you taught me." She paused, then asked, "Why doesn't he see what you do and follow it? He's seen how much you've taught Taelya, and he's listened to how you've explained things."

"He's older than I am, and I'm not about to force him. Besides, he may have tried some of what I've explained and found it doesn't work for him. Magery doesn't work the same for all mages. There are abilities mentioned in both *The Wisdom of Relyn* and *The Book of Ayrlyn* that I couldn't figure out, but they definitely happened, and Karch was definitely surprised by the way I used containments . . . as if he'd never seen that before."

"If he said he hadn't, then he hadn't."

Beltur didn't doubt that. The captain wasn't the deceptive type.

"When we get more mages," added Jessyla, "you should be the one teaching them."

"If they're willing to listen," he replied wryly, finishing the last of the ale and looking at the empty and slightly chipped beaker, then toward the window, its glazed surface beaded with rain. "I'm really glad I got the ale yesterday."

"Do you think we should patrol today . . . the way we planned last night?"

"I thought we'd wait just a little. I really need to clean out the barn, and I'm hoping that the rain will let up a little more. Even if the Hydlenese are planning an attack, they won't be near Haven for a little while, not with the roads as muddy as they're bound to be."

"Then I'll go to the healing house . . . and you'll meet me there, say, in a glass?"

Beltur nodded. "But don't forget to fill your water bottle with ale."

"Thank you. I almost forgot that we have ale."

Less than a glass later, Beltur rode east along the side street from the house to the square. He carried two full water bottles of ale, just in case. While the rain had stopped falling, patches of fog had appeared here and there, largely above places where hail had fallen, Beltur thought, since he could see a thin layer of white. That suggested that the storm he'd largely slept through had been more violent than he'd thought, and likely explained his earlier headache.

Too bad you can't call up a thunderstorm when you need one—like when the Hydlenese attack with a battalion or more.

When he reached the Council House, he tied Slowpoke there, beside the mounts of the two troopers, and walked next door to the healing house.

As soon as he walked into the front room, Jessyla called out, "Beltur . . . would you help me here?"

He immediately hurried into the second room, where a woman supported a child, sitting on the edge of the table.

The woman stiffened.

"He's also a healer and mage," Jessyla explained. "With him helping, it will be easier on your son." Her head turned to Beltur. "He was attacked by a pig. We need to clean out the wounds and stitch the worst of the slashes. I've cleaned off his arm around the bites." The cloth in her hand showed blood, dirt, and other substances before she dropped it into the basket beside the table. "If you can hold his arm still . . ."

Beltur understood. She didn't want the child squirming and threshing while she cleaned the wounds properly and then did what stitching was absolutely necessary. He tried not to wince when he sensed the bites on the child's forearm, one or two almost to the bones. Just cleaning and stitching was going to be more than a little painful for the boy, who was likely younger than Taelya.

"I do have some clear spirits. I got them from Julli and used order on them as well." Then she looked to the mother and the boy. "This will hurt some. Beltur is going to do something so that you don't move, either yourself or your arm. That will go away once your arm is bound up. It's only to keep you from being hurt more."

Beltur eased a containment around the arm, leaving an open area around the wounds. He also linked the containment to the floor.

Jessyla took another cloth, but as soon as she touched the first wound, even gently and deftly, the boy screamed. The mother winced, but kept her arm around her son as Jessyla continued to clean and debride the wounds.

More than a quint passed before the wounds were cleaned, dressed, stitched where necessary, and the arm bound. Then Beltur used free order to remove the worst of the wound chaos.

By then, the boy had stopped crying.

"You'll need to bring him back on threeday," Jessyla told the mother. "I'll need to check the wounds. I might need to change the dressings."

"Will his arm work when he heals?"

"He has a good chance . . . if you bring him back on threeday. What Beltur did will have to be repeated."

The mother looked at Jessyla questioningly.

"It didn't look as though he did anything, but he took away some of the chaos that the pig's bite put in your son's arm. That's something that only a mage-healer can do."

"Thank you, Healers." The woman inclined her head. "I would pay anything to see him well. I have nothing."

"Just bring him back on threeday."

Once the two had left, Beltur asked, "Do you still want to ride west this morning?"

"Of course. And you'll go to where that forest is and see what you can sense."

The two left the healing house and walked next door to the Council House, where Waerdyn and Ruell were waiting in the front room.

Before either could speak, Beltur said, "There aren't any strange riders within a kay of Haven. We needed to heal a boy. Waerdyn, you'll accompany Jessyla, and Ruell will ride with me. If she senses any Hydlenese, you ride back and get Lhadoraak to help her. If they're coming from the south, I'll send Ruell to let Lhadoraak and you two know." He paused. "I don't think it's likely after all the rain, but they might try an attack because it is unlikely."

Waerdyn nodded.

Beltur gestured toward the mounts tied outside the Council House, then followed the others outside, closing the door firmly. Once everyone was mounted, he watched as Jessyla headed out with Waerdyn beside her, then turned to Ruell. "We're headed through the back streets of Haven."

"To that stead they attacked before, ser?"

"Not exactly. To a place where I can sense whether they might be headed there . . . or to a number of other places along the south side of town."

As Beltur and Ruell rode through the intermittent fog and cooler damp air along the back lane that angled from the southwest side of Haven to the stone dwelling in the middle of the stony grasslands, the trooper cleared his throat, then said, "Beggin' your pardon, ser . . . but . . . how did two Spidlarian arms-mages end up in Montgren? If you don't mind my asking?"

"The black mages of Elparta didn't like me, and they didn't like the fact that Lhadoraak's daughter is a beginning white mage. Neither did the Council of Axalt. Lord Korsaen was looking for mages with our talents. So we're here."

"Seems like you went from one war to another."

"We didn't plan it that way. Neither did the Duchess or Lord Korsaen."

"You know that, ser?"

"I can usually tell when people lie to me. We did know we'd have trouble." Beltur laughed softly. "Just not as much trouble as it looks like."

"Why did you kill the Hydlenese officers, and not the troopers?"

"They gave the orders. Troopers have to carry them out. Samwyth killed one of the troopers. They killed him. I can't blame them for that."

"Some would . . . beggin' your pardon, ser."

"Would you?" asked Beltur.

"I can't say as I would, ser, but I'm a trooper." After another pause, Ruell went on, "They say blacks don't use magery to kill."

"And you've heard that I've killed more than a few?"

"Yes, ser."

"Most black magery isn't suited to attacking. It's better used for defending. I'm better at defending, but I've found ways to attack as well. Killing bothers almost all blacks. I guess, after what I've seen, it bothers me a lot less."

"You said you'd been a scout."

Beltur decided to give a short answer that he hoped would foreclose more questions. "When Gallos invaded Spidlar, I was assigned to a mounted recon company as an undercaptain. I was with the company until the last battle, when I was assigned to support the attack on the Gallosians. I ended up protecting companies attacking the enemy. Sometimes I ended up leading the attack." He smiled pleasantly. "Does that answer your concerns?"

Ruell swallowed. "Yes, ser. Mostly."

"And?"

"Do you know any other mages who did that?"

"Not in Spidlar, Gallos, or Axalt. I have no idea what other black mages do in other lands."

"Thank you, ser."

When they reached the northwestern edge of the overgrown forest, Beltur reined up and concentrated on sensing. There was a small flock of sheep less than half a kay south of the stone dwelling, and, with the flock, one figure, most likely a grown man, and a large dog. No one was outside in the gray mist near either Samwyth's or Vortaan's stead. Nor could he sense any riders anywhere.

For the rest of the morning and early afternoon, he and Ruell moved more to the southwest, but never caught sight of any troopers. At second glass, he sent Ruell to Waerdyn, with instructions for them to stop patrolling and rest their mounts and for Jessyla to return to the healing house.

Then he rode along the south side of Haven halfway to the kaystone, but still found no signs of travelers or troopers. So he headed back toward the center of Haven, but decided to stop by the house on the way, possibly for an ale, since, over the course of the day, he'd gone through the ale he'd brought.

But when he neared the house, he was surprised to see a wagon pulled up close to the rear door and Jessyla's mount tied to the hitching post next to the dray horse. As he rode closer to the door, she hurried out, followed by Jaegyr.

Jessyla was smiling broadly. "Jaegyr came by the healing house. He brought our bedstead. Well, he brought two, one for us and one for Lhadoraak and Tulya. He already delivered and set up theirs."

Jaegyr looked up to Beltur, who was still mounted. "I would have brought them earlier, but it was still too damp, and I don't have enough oilcloth to cover them," explained the cabinet maker.

"Come in and take a look!" Jessyla smiled again.

Beltur dismounted, tied Slowpoke, and walked to the front porch, where he carefully wiped and brushed off his boots before following her inside and to the bedroom.

The golden oak bedstead was set between the two narrow and high windows on the east wall of the house. The broad headboard featured but a single adornment—a hexagon carved into the wood just below the middle of the gentle arch that formed the top. The lines were strong, graceful, and simple, far better than Beltur had expected. "It's beautiful."

"It's an oil finish, and you'll have to rub it down every so often for a while. I left some oil in the kitchen," declared Jaegyr. "I had to put something on the headboard, and the hexagon's the old-time symbol for order. Seemed fitting to me."

"He also brought a wash table. I put it in the washroom," added Jessyla.

"Thought you could use that as well."

"We owe you a good amount then, for both of them."

"Ten days' work, and two silvers for the wood."

"That's all?"

Jaegyr nodded.

Beltur took out his belt wallet, then handed the cabinet maker the seven silvers. "What would you suggest next?"

"I could do a padded bench for the front parlor with two wooden armchairs—same set for each of you. That'll take a little longer."

Beltur looked to Jessyla.

She nodded.

"Go ahead."

Jaegyr smiled. "Good to have real work again. Julli'll do the pad for the bench." He looked to Jessyla. "You tell her what you want. She can do cushions for the chairs, too, but that's extra, and you need to work that out with her."

"I can do that."

After a clearly happy Jaegyr left, Beltur looked to Jessyla. "We might even have a properly furnished house by the end of summer."

"Maybe even before that."

As they took their mounts to the barn, neither one mentioned the Hydlenese.

XXXIII

Twoday dawned cloudless, if misty with patches of fog, but the bright white sun above the mist promised a hot and muggy day once the mist and fog burned off. Beltur and Jessyla were dressed and out of the house early, just after sixth glass, riding toward the square and the Council House to meet with the four troopers.

"You should be the one to check on the southern steads today," said Beltur as they neared the square.

"Why do you think that?"

"I couldn't say . . . not exactly, except . . . well . . . it rained a lot yesterday, and the back roads and paths would be muddier."

Jessyla smiled. "I'll accept your feelings more than your words. You sound like you're trying to find a reason for something that you feel."

"I probably am," he admitted.

"Probably?"

"I definitely am."

"We'll go with your feelings," said Jessyla.

"Because you feel the same way?"

"I was going to suggest it, if you didn't."

"Feelings . . . or reasons?" he asked, gently teasing.

"Both. If they're trying to make people fear them or make people want to get rid of us, it doesn't benefit them to attack the same place again. They'll want to strike lots of different places to get the idea across that we can't stop them."

Beltur nodded. "That makes sense." And it was a better reason than any he had thought of, not that he really wanted to admit that out loud.

It was still before seventh glass when they reached the square and turned their mounts toward the Council House, although the exact time was a judgment based on the sun and feeling, since Haven didn't have a bell ringer, let alone a bell tower, unlike all the other places in which Beltur had lived.

Just before they reached the Council House, Beltur sensed the approach of two riders from the direction of the East Inn. Glancing back over his shoulder, he saw that the two were Taasn and Chestyn. "Do you have any preference for whether Taasn or Chestyn rides with you?"

"Chestyn. Waerdyn said he was the better archer."

"You asked Waerdyn?"

"Not in so many words. I just . . . guided what he said."

That was something Beltur likely needed to be better at or Jessyla wouldn't have said it that way. He smiled wryly.

Less than a quint later, he was riding west out of Haven, accompanied by Taasn, trying to listen carefully as the trooper continued his reply to Beltur's question as to how Taasn had ended up as a Montgren trooper.

". . . something about hay and sheep . . . sneezing and coughing . . . my eyes were watering and burning by midday every day . . . my da said I'd grow out of it . . . I never did. One day I just walked away. I thought I could ride a little. I was tired of walking up and down over the same hills . . . I walked to the nearest trooper post . . . two towns over . . . The captain laughed. He said I was undersized, but he'd give me a try . . . worked hard . . . never wanted to go back to sheep . . . that was six years ago . . ."

"Are you as good as Chestyn with the bow?"

Taasn shook his head. "Not many are." Then he grinned. "But he can't match me with a blade . . . any blade. And he's almost a head taller." The trooper frowned. "How did you know he was good with a bow?"

"I didn't. My consort found out." Beltur tried to sense if there were any riders on the road ahead, but he couldn't discern any, at least not within more than two kays, possibly nearly three.

"Never heard of a healer who was also a mage."

"Neither had I until I met her."

"Never heard of a mage who was also a healer."

"There are some, and there always have been."

"Begging your pardon, ser, but were any of them war mages . . . like you?"

"I don't know. I only heard of the mage-healers. There have been black mages who were true war mages, like Nylan and Saryn of the black blades."

"Saryn . . . like in Sarronnyn?"

"She was the one who founded Sarronnyn. Any of the old lords of Lornth who opposed her ended up dead."

Taasn actually shuddered at Beltur's words. "Don't know as I'd ever want to meet a woman like that."

"There have been men like that."

"Wouldn't want to meet them, either, but a woman . . ." The trooper shook his head.

Beltur smiled faintly, then returned the wave of a woman standing on the porch of a cot on the south side of the street. He had no idea who she was, although he was sure he had met her when he was knocking on doors. Several hundred yards ahead were the repaired brick posts that marked the western edge of Haven. Another hundred yards beyond that, on the right side of the road, Beltur saw a large vulcrow, perched on a sagging fence post.

As the two rode closer, the vulcrow spread its wide wings and took off, headed west-northwest. Beltur frowned. He'd only seen a handful of vulcrows in his entire life, and always in the hills or mountains. Yet the bird hadn't looked ill or hurt.

"Don't like that," murmured Taasn. "Usually means something large died somewhere near."

"You think the Hydlenese have already raided another stead?" Beltur didn't like that possibility, but it could mean that they'd attacked an outlying stead beyond his ability to sense.

"That or some herder's lost an animal. They don't scavenge cats or squirrels . . . nothing small."

Beltur was still thinking about the vulcrow a quint later when the two reached a side lane about a kay outside of Haven. He had the feeling that there were riders or troopers farther away, but whether the feeling was based on his senses or his fears that there might be, he couldn't tell. Because of that feeling and because he also wanted to see if there were recent traces of riders on the Hydolar road or the road to Gallos, he kept riding past the west kaystone.

Then, when they were about a kay from where the road to Weevett branched off, Beltur definitely sensed riders—except they were to the northwest and they weren't heading toward Haven but almost due north from the road that eventually led to Gallos.

Beltur turned to Taasn. "I've just sensed riders northwest of us. They're riding north on a back lane or trail. More than a squad of them. Do you know if there's a hamlet northwest of here? Or maybe a back road that circles to come into Haven from the north?"

"No, ser. I'm from Grenylt."

"Where's that?"

"The northwest corner of Montgren. Lavah's the nearest real town."

Beltur frowned. Someone had mentioned Lavah, but not where it was.

"Lavah's across the Rugged Hills in Sligo," explained Taasn, clearly in response to Beltur's puzzled expression. "Grenylt's on the old trade road from Rytel to Lavah. Not many traders go that way anymore."

"There must be something north on that back lane," said Beltur. "That many riders wouldn't be there otherwise." *And that means some stead is going to get raided.* He urged Slowpoke into a faster walk. "We need to get closer so that I can find out more before I send you back to Lhadoraak and Jessyla."

The Hydlenese troopers seemed to be proceeding slowly, so that, by the time Beltur and Taasn reached the side lane that the troopers had taken, as evidenced by the fresh hoofprints in the damp clay of the road, Beltur estimated that they were only a kay or so ahead. While he could sense them, the low rolling hills, the intermittent stands of trees on the hilltops, and the winding nature of the lane kept him from actually seeing the troopers.

What was worse was that Beltur sensed a hamlet perhaps half a kay from the Hydlenese. "All right, Taasn. There's a hamlet ahead. The chances are that the Hydlenese are going to raid there. You can't do much to help me. So head back and tell Lhadoraak what's happening and that I'll be doing what I can. Also tell him that they might attack somewhere closer on the south side of Haven this afternoon and for him and Jessyla to be aware of that. It's just a guess, but I suspect that they plan to set fires and scatter people, hoping we'll come out here to see what happened, and then attack Haven."

And if they don't, and this is just a raid, another mage can't get here fast enough to make any difference.

"You're sure, ser?"

"Very sure. It's important that Lhadoraak and Jessyla know. I'll be fine." *Whether I can do enough that the people in the hamlet will be the same is another question.* "Now, go!"

Once the trooper was headed back to Haven, Beltur returned his full concentration to the troopers ahead. Before long he was less than a thousand yards behind the two men acting as rear guards, and he had raised a concealment, because at times, when the road was straight, he could have been seen. It was clear that the troopers knew exactly where they were going, since there were no delays or hesitations at two of the places where another lane forked off. That meant that someone had scouted the area earlier.

After another quint had passed and Beltur was within a few hundred yards, the narrow dirt road, flanked mostly by the rocky grasslands, scrub bushes, and occasional trees, straightened as it entered a broad and gentle vale. Given the fields to the north and an ordered grouping of trees that Beltur sensed and that had to be an orchard of some sort, there had to be a spring or a stream somewhere, although Beltur had not yet discerned any watercourse. He did make out what appeared to be five dwellings larger than mere cots, but smaller than most stead dwellings, and a number of low outbuildings, as well as several flocks of sheep on the hillsides east of the vale. As he rode, Beltur took several long swallows of the ale in one of his water bottles.

The troopers abruptly came to a halt, but Beltur, still under a concealment, kept moving closer to the troopers, what appeared to be a full squad of twenty. Although someone, likely the squad leader, was giving orders, Beltur was too far back to hear what those orders might be. Several of the troopers near the front of the squad appeared to string bows. The others unsheathed blades.

Then the troopers resumed their advance, walking their mounts toward the center of the hamlet.

Beltur could sense people in the hamlet running, presumably into cots or other places where they felt safe. Having no idea exactly how the troopers were going to proceed, Beltur moved up to within a few yards of the last troopers, who in turn had moved up so there was no longer a gap between them and the bulk of the squad.

When the squad reached the center of the hamlet, an open space roughly in the middle of the dwellings, the troopers reined up. Then the squad leader called out, "The Duke of Hydlen has claimed these lands. If you don't open your doors to his forces and pay tribute, we will break down those doors and take anything and anyone we desire."

Beltur did not sense any doors opening, and, still under a concealment, he eased Slowpoke off the road and forward along the left side of the riders, if several yards from the nearest.

"I'm warning you!" bellowed the squad leader. "This is your last chance."

Beltur released the concealment as he neared the front rank of the squad and called out, "Aren't you being a little hasty?"

The squad leader turned toward Beltur, momentarily frowning, before replying, "Who are you to deny the Duke?"

"I'm just a representative of the Duchess, and she won't take kindly to anyone claiming lands in Montgren, especially a mere squad leader."

"You're not wearing a Montgren uniform. How can you claim that?"

"It's actually a uniform of a Haven patroller, although I did dispatch a Montgren trooper back to Haven to send a report to the Duchess about your incursion."

"You're no patroller. Strike him down!" The squad leader gestured to the front rank.

Beltur just expanded his shields slightly and anchored them to the ground, waiting.

The two leading troopers rode toward Beltur, flanking him on each side. Both riders and their mounts rebounded from the shields even before they could strike with their blades.

Beltur held his ground, then fastened a containment around the squad leader's neck, tightening and twisting it. The squad leader stiffened, grasping futilely at his neck. More troopers swarmed toward Beltur, pressing against the shields.

Before that long, the squad leader slumped forward in his saddle, and a black mist followed.

Another trooper called out, "He can't get us all! Go for the cots! Take what you can! Keep moving!"

The moment the troopers broke away from Beltur, he released the anchors from his shields, widened them and angled them like the prow of a boat, and then urged Slowpoke into a charge at the nearest group.

The combination of the big gelding's weight and power and the angled shields scattered the four horses through which Slowpoke burst, unhorsing at least one of the troopers. Beltur turned the gelding toward another group of troopers farther away and urged Slowpoke into a gallop across the flat ground in the middle of the hamlet. That charge scattered more troopers and unhorsed a pair.

A trooper turned and slashed at Beltur, so hard that when his blade struck the shields, it flew from his hand, and he turned his mount away so quickly that he and another trooper collided. Beltur turned Slowpoke back across the level common toward another group of four troopers in front of a cot. Because they were so close to the dwelling, he angled Slowpoke to one side and extended his shields on that side. The impact unhorsed another rider and caused two others to slam into each other.

Abruptly, the remaining troopers turned their mounts and fled.

Beltur saw, to his dismay, that the most distant group had actually forced their way into a cot and had seized a woman and were riding off with her. Shaking his head, he reined up, since there was no way to catch them and he still needed to deal with the unhorsed troopers and their mounts.

He glanced around, and seeing a trooper about to remount, rode toward him, throwing a containment around the man, freezing him in place, holding the reins to his mount. But while Beltur was doing that, another trooper reclaimed his mount and galloped off, far enough from Beltur that he couldn't use a third containment, especially after what the effort of using his shields as a weapon had cost him.

Beltur turned Slowpoke back toward the center of the hamlet, only to see that men and women had hurried from several of the cots, and with axes and clubs, immediately killed the other three fallen troopers—again, before Beltur could have done much, even if he'd been so minded, which he decided he wasn't.

He rode slowly toward the remaining trooper, caught in the containment, which had also protected the man from the growing crowd, clearly frustrated by their inability to attack him. Several of the locals pressed toward him, but then, rebuffed by Beltur's shields, backed off and watched warily as Beltur reined up beside the captive trooper.

The trooper's eyes went from Beltur to the crowd and back again.

"You'll be far better off riding back to Haven with me, you know," Beltur said conversationally.

"He deserves to die!" shouted someone from the back of the crowd.

A tall bearded man was running toward Beltur from the direction of the southernmost cot, the one from which the troopers had seized a young woman. The others in the crowd looked toward him as he stopped short of Beltur and Slowpoke.

"Why didn't you flame them with chaos before they took my daughter?" demanded the tall bearded man.

"I can't. I'm a black mage, not a white. I did all that I could. You might have seen—"

"You're a mage. You should have done more!" shouted the man.

"I kept them from taking more and from killing any of you."

"You should have done more. A lot more. The bastards'll be back again when you aren't around."

Beltur knew that was certainly possible. "They'll likely look for easier pickings. It's more likely they'll attack Haven than here."

"What the frig do we care about Haven?" called out another man. "It's a worthless excuse for a town. The innkeepers'd rob us blind, and there's not even a decent market square anymore."

"We've been working on that."

". . . heard that before . . ."

Beltur nodded. "I'm sure you have, but I did what I could here, and I need to get back there to deal with whatever else the Hydlenese may be doing."

"If you mages hadn't come to Haven, the greencoats wouldn't be here. They wouldn't have taken my daughter."

"They were already here when we arrived. We didn't bring them," replied Beltur evenly. "And if I hadn't been here, you'd have lost a lot more." He turned to the Hydlenese trooper. "I'm going to loosen the containment enough to let you mount. You try anything else, and I'll yank you off your mount and leave you here. Do you understand?"

"Yes, ser." The trooper swallowed.

"You're letting him go free? After what they did?"

"He's my prisoner," replied Beltur, "and he's coming back to Haven with me." He loosened the containment and watched as the trooper mounted. "Now, you ride in front of me, back the way you came."

"Much good you are, Mage," snapped one of the men.

Beltur turned and looked at him. "Then perhaps I shouldn't have come at all."

"Ser mage!" called out a woman. "Don't listen to him! We're thankful you did what you could."

Beltur inclined his head in her direction, wondering, as he often had in the last year, why so often women had more common sense than men. "Thank you." Then he said to the prisoner, "Start riding."

Only after the two were well away from the hamlet and Beltur could sense that none of the troopers who had fled were nearby did Beltur ease Slowpoke alongside the trooper. "What's your name?"

"Graalur, ser."

"Why was your squad attacking the hamlet?"

Graalur didn't answer.

"Someone had to have ordered the attack." Beltur placed a small containment around the trooper's neck. Not too tight, but enough to remind the man that it was there.

"That was Squad Leader Waaren. You killed him. Why? He was just following orders."

"Whose orders?"

"They must have come from headquarters."

"Why did you start attacking steads and hamlets?"

"The captain said we had to show that no one was in charge in Haven."

"So where is the captain? Why wasn't he leading some of the attacks?"

"He died. So did the undercaptain. We got a new undercaptain from the other company. He ordered the squad leaders to continue the attacks. They were afraid that they'd be executed if they didn't. The Duke kills officers who don't follow orders."

The other company? That confirmed that there were two, and that was anything but good.

"Even stupid orders?"

"Any orders, ser."

Beltur winced. That suggested that the only way to win against Hydolar was to kill a huge number of the Duke's troopers. *Unless* . . . "What about the Duke's family? Do they have to follow orders?"

Again, Graalur was silent.

This time, Beltur waited and kept riding. He took several swallows of ale, and waited some more.

Finally, the trooper spoke. "He has three sons and some daughters. He used to have four sons. The second son was beheaded for not obeying the Duke. No one knows what he failed to do."

That told Beltur plenty. Whether or not that was strictly true didn't matter, he realized. All that mattered was that troopers and their officers believed it was true. "Where did you grow up?"

"In Telsen."

Beltur had never heard of the town. "Where is that?"

"It's south of Hydolar, an eightday ride, just east of the mountains."

"How did you end up being a trooper?"

"What else could I do? My father was a tinsmith. I was the fifth son."

Beltur kept asking questions and listening to Graalur's answers, even while he kept trying to sense the Hydlenese troopers. When they neared the road to Gallos, he could finally sense them, and from what he could tell, the squad had left the Gallos road and was continuing southwest along the Hydolar road, although Beltur suspected they'd eventually turn in the direction of the encampment he had scouted earlier. Given that, Beltur didn't see much sense in following them, especially since he worried about what might be happening south of Haven.

"We're turning east."

"Yes, ser."

The two rode past the junction with the road that led to Hydolar and then almost another kay when Beltur saw a vulcrow briefly circle, then drop behind a low hill about half a kay ahead, in turn less than a few hundred yards from the road heading north to Weevett. From what he recalled, the area behind the hill and bordering the Weevett road was uneven ground with a mixture of scrub, grass, and trees, marginally suitable for sheep.

By the time they reached the hill, which turned out to be a long low rise, Beltur could sense several large birds on the ground on the far side. *Vulcrows.* As Taasn had pointed out earlier, vulcrows only scavenged large animals. After a deep breath, Beltur announced, "We're going to ride through that land to the left up through the bushes to see what's on the other side."

"Ser?"

"Vulcrows are scavenging something. I'd like to know what." Beltur turned off the road and guided Slowpoke and Graalur and his mount between the bushes and up the gentle slope, avoiding the scattered trees.

"Can all mages see through hills?"

"I can't see through hills. I can sense what's beyond them for a short distance. Some mages can. Others can't. All of the mages in Haven can sense for some distance." *Even if Taelya can only sense a hundred yards or so.*

"You knew we were headed to that hamlet?"

"I knew you were headed north on that side road. I thought you had to be heading for a stead or hamlet. There wasn't any other reason for you to be on a back track, otherwise."

At the top of the rise, Beltur looked north. It took him several moments to locate the vulcrows because there were three clustered beyond several low bushes at the base of the rise. After a moment, Beltur swallowed because he made out a pale blue cloth between two of the vulcrows. He turned to Graalur. "Did your squad come this way today or earlier?"

"No, ser. I don't think any squads from our company went north of the east-west road until this morning."

From what Beltur could determine, the trooper was telling the truth, and that meant more trouble. As he headed down the slope, the vulcrows took wing. He kept riding until he could see what was left of a figure in the torn pale blue uniform and the tracks around it.

Then he reined up and looked to the captive trooper.

"Ser . . . we didn't do it."

"I got that feeling, but, if you didn't, who did?"

"I don't know, ser. It might have been the other company. When we left the camp this morning, everyone else in our squads was still there."

And that meant that the other Hydlenese company was likely the one that had killed the trooper lying there. The dead trooper couldn't have been Taasn, Beltur realized as he saw the scroll collar pin on the uniform, and the single dark blue embroidered rank slash on the sleeve.

"He was a courier, ser. That's what the scroll on the collar means. At least, it does for us."

Beltur studied the ground around the body.

The single set of hoofprints to and from the east meant that someone had carried the dead trooper from the Weevett road and then returned to the road, and had done so at least several glasses earlier, because of the damage to the body, confirming that it couldn't have been Taasn.

"Graalur, dismount and search the body. See if there's anything left in his uniform."

Beltur watched as the trooper did so, gingerly but carefully.

Graalur finally straightened. "There's nothing, ser. They cut away his wallet and took his sabre and scabbard. Likely his riding jacket as well. There's nothing to say who he was, except for the pin on his collar."

"Remove the pin. Hand it to me and mount up."

Beltur had to momentarily remove the containment around Graalur, but did so smoothly enough that the trooper apparently didn't even notice.

After slipping the pin into his belt wallet, and still trying to sense whether there might be other troopers around, Beltur, with Graalur riding just behind him, followed the hoofprints back to the Weevett road. Just before they reached the road, Beltur saw that the tracks vanished. Rather, they had been removed or smoothed over, presumably by a pine branch lying beside a scraggly scrub oak.

Beltur again reined up and studied the road and the traces of hoofprints. From what he could tell, there were a number heading in both directions, but the most recent headed back north toward Weevett. After a time, Beltur turned Slowpoke south toward the junction with the old road, which lay only a few hundred yards away. At the junction, he studied the road once more, but the mass of hoofprints all ended there, as if the riders had just turned around and headed back north.

But who would ride south, kill a courier, ride to the junction, then turn and ride back north? And where did they come from?

And what message had the dispatch rider been carrying . . . and to whom? Most likely, it had been sent to the Council of Haven, but that wasn't certain. Even if it had, had it been a warning? An announcement that a force would be arriving, or a statement not to expect such a force?

"Are you sure that there weren't any more troopers coming from Hydlen?"

"Ser, the captain said that more companies would be coming. That was before he died. He said he didn't know when. Well . . . that was what the squad leader said. No other companies had arrived when we left camp this morning."

Beltur definitely didn't like what he heard. He immediately turned Slowpoke toward Haven. He kept asking questions, but it was clear that Graalur didn't know much more than what he'd already said.

Even before Beltur reached the main square, he could sense, if but faintly, riders and the chaos of fire on the east side of Haven. He could also sense two sets of order shields, shields that had to be those of Jessyla and Lhadoraak.

Now what the frig do you do? Beltur was going to need every last bit of order he could muster, including what he was presently using to hold Graalur. *You could bluff . . . or wait and see.* He urged Slowpoke into a fast walk and tried to sense more clearly what was happening. He didn't think that the burning house was that of Jaegyr and Julli, because it felt as though it happened to be on the south side of the main road, and theirs was on the north side. He pulled out his water bottle and drank some more ale, hoping that would help maintain his strength for what likely lay ahead.

Before long he sensed more clearly that there had to be a full company attacking various dwellings on the east end of town, and he immediately urged Slowpoke into a canter, then turned and said, not quite conversationally, "There's some fighting going on up ahead. If you want to come out of it alive, just stick by me and don't lift a weapon."

"Who's fighting?" asked Graalur.

"I don't know, but I'd wager that it's your other company from Hydlen."

"And I'm not supposed to fight?"

Beltur shrugged. "If you do, I'll have to treat you like the others. It's your choice."

"Some choice."

"Only if we lose," replied Beltur, releasing the containment around Graalur.

When Beltur neared the east end of Haven and caught sight of the attackers, he was so startled that he almost froze in the saddle. Instead of the green of Hydlen, all the attacking troopers wore maroon uniforms. *Maroon?* Why would troopers from Lydiar be attacking Haven?

Abruptly, it made a strange sort of sense. Beltur immediately put Slowpoke into a full charge down the main street, aiming the big gelding right toward the center of the mass of troopers who had formed a line across the main street while, behind the main body, several squads were raiding dwellings and had actually set fire to two. The line of troopers was little more than two deep, and behind them, perhaps fifty yards back, was a smaller group of riders. Among those riders, Beltur wagered, was the captain. He could also sense Jessyla, who was mounted and positioned close to Jaegyr and Julli's cottage, as was Lhadoraak.

With Graalur hanging close, Beltur continued past Jessyla, straight toward the troopers. Although he didn't hear the order, the captain or whoever was in command must have called out to archers, because a good score of shafts rebounded from his shields.

Then someone shouted, "It's a mage!"

A horn blared out a signal, and all of the troopers in maroon turned and departed at a good pace, at least a canter, if not a gallop. Seeing that he wasn't going to catch any of the withdrawing troopers, Beltur eased Slowpoke to a stop at roughly the point where the troopers in maroon had been holding the line. Ahead and to his right, the trim house that had belonged to the trader Zankar—or his mother—was engulfed in flame, as was another house to the south of it . . . and another even farther south.

Since the troopers in maroon kept riding along the road to Lydiar, clearly not intending to stop any time soon, Beltur turned, only to see Graalur grasping his left arm, from which protruded one of the shafts meant for Beltur.

"Jessyla!" Even before the words were out of his mouth, Beltur could sense that she was riding toward him.

After several moments, Lhadoraak followed.

When Jessyla reined up, Beltur gestured to the wounded man. "This is Graalur. I took him prisoner and made him follow me. If you wouldn't mind dealing with that wound . . . I don't think it's that serious, and we do need to talk to him more." He added to Graalur, "She's a healer."

The Hydlenese inclined his head.

"You'll need to dismount," said Jessyla, dismounting and handing the reins of her horse to Beltur.

Lhadoraak reined up beside Jessyla.

Beltur looked to Lhadoraak. "If you'd hold his horse for a moment."

Lhadoraak looked quizzically at Beltur but took the reins from Graalur.

Beltur looked around. The east end of Haven looked deserted, except for the four riders and the three burning houses, all three of which were clearly beyond any hope of saving. He shook his head, then asked Lhadoraak, "What happened?"

"You were right. There was an attack on Vortaan's stead around eighth glass, just a squad or two of the greencoats. Jessyla was holding them off. She'd already killed several when I got there, and when they saw me and Waerdyn and Ruell, they decided they'd had enough, and they turned and headed off. We were just heading back when Chestyn rode up and said that a company of Lydian troopers was raiding the east end of town. That was a glass ago . . . something like that, I think. We couldn't deal with that many so we decided to try to save Jaegyr and Julli's place. All I could do was use shields to keep them away."

"We have three more mounts," declared Jessyla, not looking away from where she worked on Graalur's arm. "Julli tied them up behind her cot."

"Small containments?" asked Beltur, knowing what killing did to her and trying not to wince.

"Yes. I hated it, but they would have torched Julli's place. I couldn't let that happen to them, and we couldn't have saved anyone else by then." Jessyla returned her attention to Graalur. "Don't move. This will hurt."

The captive said nothing.

"There," added Jessyla. "This will feel hot for several moments, but it will cool before long."

Beltur didn't see what she used to bind the wound, but as she finished, he returned his attention to Lhadoraak. "Then what?"

"After Jessyla . . . did what she did . . . they sort of avoided us. Then you showed up, and they just turned and rode off. The Lydian must have thought you were bringing more troopers or something."

"I don't think they were Lydians."

"They wore maroon uniforms," Lhadoraak pointed out. "Who else does?"

"I think that's what everyone is supposed to think. You said that Jessyla killed some of them. Where are their bodies?"

"Over by Jaegyr's cottage."

"Are you finished with Graalur's arm?" asked Beltur.

"For now. I did the best I could here. You'll need to check it in the morning." To Graalur's questioning expression, Jessyla replied, "Beltur's better at finding and removing deep wound chaos."

"Then we need to go over and take a look at the bodies." Beltur turned and looked down at Graalur. "Why don't you hand over your sabre? It'll be safer for everyone that way, including you. I also need it to check something."

The captive trooper frowned, but unfastened the sabre belt awkwardly and handed it up to Beltur.

"Do all troopers have the same kind of sabre?"

"Yes, ser. So far as I know. There might be small differences, but they all look pretty much alike."

"Thank you."

"Might I mount?"

"You can, but I wouldn't try riding off."

"No, ser. I won't."

Once everyone was mounted, Beltur turned Slowpoke toward Julli's cottage and eased the gelding forward. Then he halted Slowpoke short of the nearest body and dismounted, handing the reins to Jessyla. He knelt by the dead trooper, comparing the sabres. He stood and walked to the second body, where he made another comparison. He did the same with the third body before walking back to the others. "The sabres are the same as Graalur's."

The captive's mouth opened, then closed, but he said nothing.

"Also, look at the three uniforms. They're almost new, all three."

Jessyla nodded.

"They were Hydlenese troopers dressed as Lydians?" asked Lhadoraak. "But why?"

"I'd like to say that it's because we've proved difficult," replied Beltur dryly, "but this had to have been planned well before we arrived. You can't come up with a hundred Lydian uniforms and get a company of troopers from Hydolar to Haven in an eightday, or even two."

"You suspected this?" asked Lhadoraak.

"No. Not until I saw them. There were tracks of a company on the Weevett road. They stopped there, and then went back north. I didn't follow them, but I suspect they went far enough east and then came down the road as though they'd come all the way from Lydiar. We found the body of a Montgren courier hidden off the road. Rather, the vulcrows found it . . ." Beltur quickly explained what had happened with him and the Hydlenese squad.

"We need to get back to the Council House and tell Tulya," said Lhadoraak.

Beltur looked to Jessyla. "Can you have Julli strip the bodies and keep the valuables and uniforms? We may need them as proof of some sort. We'd better take the sabres, though. We'll send troopers for the horses as soon as we can."

In less than half a quint, the four were riding back toward the town square and the Council House, with all the sword belts slung over the front of Beltur's saddle. Beltur felt slightly guilty in leaving the ruins of the houses that were barely flaming, but mostly smoldering heaps, yet there really wasn't much he and the others could do that others couldn't do as well, if not better. "Where did you post Waerdyn and the others?"

"At the Council House," replied Jessyla. "We couldn't protect them the way you can. They'd only have gotten killed, but between the four of them and Taelya, we thought Tulya would be protected as well as possible."

"I'd agree with that," said Beltur. "If the raiders had gotten that far, they'd have picked an easier target."

"Why did they leave when they did?" asked Lhadoraak. "They didn't even see what you could do—except shield yourself against arrows."

"And you and Jessyla did that already?"

"That's right." Lhadoraak's tone was between puzzled and annoyed.

"I'm just guessing, but I think they were already getting ready to leave. I also think they didn't want us to capture anyone who might reveal that they were really Hydlenese."

"But you proved that already," said Jessyla.

"The fact that three dead men all wore newish uniforms and had the same kind of blades as troopers of Hydlen is thin proof, especially when everyone saw them ride to and from the east and when they killed several people and burned three dwellings." Beltur snorted. "The fact that both the Lydians and the Hydlenese could attack Haven will be seen as proof that Montgren can't really control the area."

"So what can we do?" Jessyla asked.

"Find some way to change that image."

"How?" said Lhadoraak.

"We'll have to think about that. All of us." Beltur wished he could talk to Raelf. With the captain's experience as a Lydian undercaptain, he might have been able to offer some additional insight. After a silence, Beltur said, "I saw that the false Lydians fired Zankar's house."

"They killed his mother," said Jessyla. "I saw her body in the yard before we turned to save Julli's place."

Beltur turned in the saddle and looked at Graalur. "Did you know anything about troopers dressing like Lydians?"

"No, ser! I never heard anything like that. The captain did say we might have trouble with Lydians. He said they were prowling around . . ." Graalur stopped, his words trailing off.

"You never scouted to the east, did you?" asked Beltur.

"No, ser."

"I wonder how the captain knew that you might have trouble with Lydians," said Beltur, his voice slightly sardonic.

"He . . . he didn't say, ser."

"Rather interesting, don't you think?" continued Beltur. "Did anyone else mention the Lydians?"

"Just the squad leader."

"When did he mention the Lydians?"

"An eightday or so ago . . . I think."

Before all that long the four were riding across the square.

Tulya burst out of the Council House even before they reined up. She glared directly at Beltur. "Where were you when everyone attacked?"

Beltur could hear the anger in her voice, but immediately replied, "Dealing with a squad of Hydlenese troopers attacking steads a bit northwest of the west crossroads. I came back as soon as I could and joined Jessyla and Lhadoraak."

Tulya's eyes took in Graalur. "Why's he here?"

"I captured him when the Hydlenese attacked a hamlet south of Haven. I managed to chase them off, but not before they took a young woman captive. Some of the locals there were mad that I hadn't done more."

"Everyone's unhappy that we can't do more. What do they expect out of four people?"

"The impossible," answered Lhadoraak dryly. "And that's what we'll have to do . . . sooner or later."

Waerdyn and the other three troopers appeared on the porch.

"Who was attacking?"

"What happened?"

Beltur held up a hand. "Let us dismount and meet in the front room. We can each tell what we know . . . including Graalur, here."

More than a quint later, after everyone had spoken, although Graalur hadn't said much more than he'd already told Beltur, Waerdyn cleared his throat, then said, "Ser, why did you think the trooper in blue was a dispatch rider?"

Beltur reached into his belt wallet, extracted the scroll pin, and handed it to the scout.

"That's a courier pin, all right. But you said you only found one Montgren trooper, didn't you?"

"That's right."

"Couriers and dispatch riders always ride in pairs. What happened to the other rider?"

"There wasn't any sign of another rider, and the vulcrows weren't circling anywhere else. He might have gotten away." Beltur paused, musing, "Although it seems unlikely that they'd catch one and not the other, especially with a whole company."

"Unless they wanted one of them to escape," suggested Waerdyn. "All the troopers in the company were wearing Lydian uniforms, weren't they?"

"Frig . . . frig . . . frig . . ." muttered Beltur. "The surviving courier rides back to Weevett and tells the captain there that Lydians are attacking . . . and not Hydlenese . . ." He straightened. "I think we need to send two of you back to Weevett with a full description of what's going on. I'll ride with you as far as the crossroads to make sure that the false Lydians aren't around."

"Taasn and Chestyn are the best courier riders," said Waerdyn.

"Then get them ready to ride."

"Lhadoraak . . . what do you think we should do with Graalur, here?"

"Make him Waerdyn's charge for now. Ruell can watch him for the moment."

Beltur nodded.

While Waerdyn helped the two troopers prepare themselves, Beltur sat down at the table and began to write as complete and as succinct a report about what had happened as he could manage.

Jessyla stood at his shoulder.

Every so often he looked up and asked, "Should I say more?"

Three times, she said, "No." Once she said, "You need to make it clearer that the Hydlenese wanted the false Lydians seen west of Haven . . . but never south." The last time, she said, "You might add that the false Lydians avoided having any troopers captured."

Finally, he asked, "Have I left anything out?"

"Nothing that they'll understand, and that's for the best."

"All of us should sign it."

When the four had all signed it, Waerdyn rolled the sheets and then eased them into the leather dispatch tube. He looked to Beltur. "It should be sealed, ser."

In turn, Beltur looked to Tulya.

"Just a moment." Tulya produced the seal provided by Korsaen and cut a piece of blue sealing wax from one of the sticks also provided, then laid it on the closed top of the tube. "Taelya?"

Taelya stepped forward and concentrated. The tiniest bit of chaos appeared above the wax, which softened.

Warden's eyes widened.

Tulya pressed the seal in place, then removed it. "We've practiced that. It's much easier than using a flame, and it takes less wax."

The scout looked at the seven-year-old and then at Beltur.

"I told you she was a beginning mage." Beltur smiled and turned to the door. "We need to head out."

The ride from the square to the kaystone, and from there to the junction with the Weevett road, was uneventful. Beltur sensed no riders or groups of men. He even rode another three kays north on the Weevett road, but could sense no one but a shepherd and several scattered people working outside.

At that point, he reined up. "The road's clear for another two kays. Beyond that, I can't tell."

"Thank you, ser," replied Taasn, who carried the dispatch tube. He nodded and urged his mount forward, as did Chestyn.

Beltur watched the pair for a time, still sensing no other troopers. Then, as he turned Slowpoke back toward Haven, he realized that it was barely past the second glass of the afternoon. It seemed much later than that . . . much later.

XXXIV

When Beltur finally rode back to the square, Lhadoraak stepped out from the quarters building before Beltur reached the Council House, gesturing to the younger mage. Beltur turned Slowpoke and brought him to a halt several yards short of Lhadoraak.

"I take it that the couriers got away all right?"

"There weren't any troopers anywhere close. I'd be surprised if the Hydlenese, even those posing as Lydians, would go that much farther north on the Weevett road." Beltur snorted. "But then, I didn't expect a whole company in Lydian uniforms. Did you get the bodies and the mounts from Julli?"

"She and Jaegyr had them here less than a quint after you started out with the couriers. Tulya, Taelya, and Jessyla left after that. They took all the weapons to put in the armory under your house. They're at our house, likely fixing supper."

"What about the mounts?"

"Since the couriers took their horses, Bythalt had space in his stables. I made the arrangements."

"And Graalur?"

"Waerdyn and Chestyn are taking care of him right now," replied Lhadoraak, "with a little help from Gustaan and his men." Lhadoraak grinned. "I took care of one of your other obligations, too."

Other obligations? Beltur frowned. What other obligation had he forgotten?

"Aaskar. The stableboy?"

"Oh . . . frig!" Beltur shook his head. With everything that had happened, he'd totally forgotten the coppers he'd promised.

"He said you'd promised a copper a day."

"I did."

"I gave him a silver and said you'd make up any difference in the next day or so."

"Thank you." Beltur's appreciation was heartfelt.

"I told him you'd had a lot to do in the last eightday. I think he actually understood. He said things were better since we came."

"There are times when even I wonder," said Beltur dourly. "People weren't getting killed and having their homes burned."

"Beltur. People were getting killed. That young trader—Zantaak . . ."

"Zankar," Beltur corrected almost involuntarily.

"The serving girl at the inn . . . and lots of others." Lhadoraak paused, then added, "The burnings would have happened whether we were here or not. You were the one who pointed that out. They were planned before the Hydlenese even knew we were coming."

"Still . . . it's hard." Beltur managed a rueful smile. "How are the quarters coming?"

"We're almost done. I decided just to have them build in platforms for mattresses or pallets. That will cost less over time and be sturdier."

"That's a very good idea."

"It's also looking like the men in the work crew want to stay. Gustaan's asked some good questions about what patrollers here should do. He even asked if a patroller who got consorted could be paid a little extra instead of getting lodging. I told him that we could work something out, but we'd need to talk about it."

"We'll have to do something." Beltur smiled. "Does he have his eye on anyone?"

"I don't think so. He's just thinking ahead. Why don't you head home?

Gorlaak and Therran are almost finished for the day here. I'll be along shortly."

"Are you sure?"

"I'm certain. Besides, Slowpoke needs feed, water, and rest, even if you don't think you do."

Beltur had to grin at Lhadoraak's sardonic declaration. "I hear and obey, sage and elder mage."

"Elder, perhaps, but not sage. If I were truly sage, I'd have figured out an even better destination for all of us." Before Beltur could reply, he added quickly, "And don't ask what, where, or how that might be."

Or if Haven is the best we could ever do. Beltur didn't voice that. "I'll see you before long." With that he turned Slowpoke and started home.

He was hungry . . . and more tired than he really wanted to admit.

By the time he had rubbed down Slowpoke, groomed, fed, and watered him, as well as watering and feeding the other horses in the barn, and then washed up and walked over to the other house, Lhadoraak was already there. Everyone was gathered in the kitchen with Tulya at the stove and Jessyla at the side table, slicing something.

The older mage immediately handed Beltur a beaker of ale. "You need this."

Beltur took the beaker, gratefully.

"Supper won't be ready for almost another glass," Tulya announced. "I can't imagine why."

Taelya looked askance at her mother.

"Not a word, Taelya," said Tulya, before smiling. "Everyone knows why."

"But I—"

"Haven't we all been busy?" asked Tulya gently, cutting off her daughter's words. "That's why. Sometimes we just say what everyone knows, rather than why they do. You'll understand in time."

"Like I'll understand more about order and chaos?"

"Exactly," said Beltur.

"Those Hydlenese in Lydian uniforms," said Tulya. "How does the Duke think he can get away with something like that?"

"He'll ignore what Beltur and the Duchess will say, and he'll claim that the Lydian attack proves that Montgren can't protect Haven and the traders coming to Hydolar as well as those on the way to Certis and Gallos. He'll also send protests to all the other rulers complaining, including one to the Duke of Lydiar," replied Lhadoraak. "By the time Beltur's information gets anywhere, the Prefect and the Viscount will be happy to have an excuse to look the other way."

"I thought that they didn't want anyone else to take over Haven and this part of Montgren."

"They likely don't," replied Lhadoraak, "but they have more immediate problems, and they'll leave it to Lydiar, Montgren, and Hydlen—and us—to sort it out."

"Fight it out, you mean," snapped Jessyla.

"If that's what it comes to," admitted the oldest mage.

"How do we win against Hydlen, then?"

"By making it too costly for them to continue," said Beltur.

"How do we do that?" pressed Tulya. "We don't even have a company of troopers, let alone an army."

"We've already started, I think," replied Jessyla, turning to Beltur and asking, "Isn't that why you killed the officers? You didn't say, not exactly, but didn't you also kill the squad leader who led the attack against that hamlet?"

Beltur nodded. "I did. We can't kill all the troopers who come against us. Besides, they're just following orders. If officers or leaders who give the orders are the ones to suffer, before long, just how many officers are going to want to fight?" *Even with the Duke's orders.* But that opened another possibility . . . especially for troopers bright enough to see what was happening. *Maybe . . . just maybe . . .*

"But how many people here will have to die?" asked Tulya.

"Unhappily," said Lhadoraak slowly, "many of them would die or suffer even if we did nothing. Just . . . not quite as many."

"Not necessarily the same people, either," said Tulya.

"Since we might be among the ones who'd suffer if we do nothing," said Jessyla dryly, "I prefer Beltur's approach."

Beltur said nothing, but took a last swallow from the beaker.

"You look like you need another ale," said Lhadoraak.

Among other things. "Yes, please."

"Did you tell Lhadoraak and Tulya about the benches?" asked Jessyla.

Beltur understood that there would be no more talk about fighting for the evening, especially if he wanted to avoid another sort of conflict.

"Benches?" asked Lhadoraak, from where he stood by the kitchen cistern, on top of which was tied the keg of ale from which he was refilling Beltur's beaker.

Tulya merely smiled, suggesting to Beltur that Jessyla had already told her.

"I arranged for Jaegyr to craft a padded backed bench with two wooden armchairs as well. That's for each of us," said Beltur. "That way we can actually sit in the front parlor."

"And Julli will sew the padding and cushions," added Jessyla. "Tulya can arrange exactly what you two want."

"What Tulya wants," replied Lhadoraak genially, as he walked back to Beltur and handed him the refilled beaker.

"What about me?" asked Taelya.

"You can decide when we get to your furnishings," said Tulya.

"You promise?"

"We promise," replied Lhadoraak solemnly.

Beltur and Jessyla smiled.

XXXV

Beltur and Jessyla woke early on threeday, well before dawn, and found themselves looking at each other in the deep gray light.

"You were restless last night," Beltur ventured. "More than a little."

"Nightmares. What about you?"

"I kept dreaming that the couriers were ambushed, and that we were facing scores of battalions of Hydlenese troopers . . . and no one anywhere else in Montgren even knew what was happening."

"Isn't that what's already happened?" asked Jessyla.

"Except for the scores of battalions of troopers," he admitted.

"So what do we do?"

"I only see two choices. We either do what we planned to do . . . or we pack up and leave Haven."

"And if we leave Haven . . . then what?"

Beltur shrugged. "I don't know."

"You said that you believed in the vision of that white mage."

"I did. I do. He had a vision of a great city with a white tower. We might be the ones to start building that city. We might not. He thought he would be the one to do that. He wasn't. Are we making the same mistake?" Beltur took a long deep breath. "I don't know. I knew this wouldn't be easy, but I'd hoped I was done with killing scores and scores of men whose only fault was that they served someone who wanted to kill me and those with me."

"There's always a price," she said quietly. "We want to build a place where both whites and blacks can live. If we leave here . . . will we get another chance? Exactly where? And if we do, do you think the price will be any less? From what I've seen already, the prices just get higher."

"You mean . . ." Beltur didn't know how to phrase what he wanted to say without it sounding condescending or cruel.

"I'm still a healer. I'm also becoming a mage. Part of that price is that I'm having to kill just to protect other people. I don't want to have to go somewhere else and do the same thing all over again."

Do you think I do?

"I don't want to travel all over Candar," Jessyla continued, "or the rest of the world, thinking that there might be a better place that will accept us. We've been forced out of three countries. That doesn't count Certis, where healers and mages are little better than servants. Or Westwind, where the Marshal doesn't want men who are strong and mages. Or Sarronnyn, which isn't much of an improvement. Just where would be any better?"

Beltur laughed, softly and ironically. "You've just answered my questions and your nightmares." He reached over, took her hand, then bent and kissed it. "We'd better get started."

By two quints before seventh glass, they were in the Council House, meeting with Lhadoraak, Waerdyn, and Ruell. Their mounts were tied outside, and each had two water bottles filled with ale, as well as a half loaf of bread.

Beltur was direct. "You and Ruell each have a simple task—to let Lhadoraak and Jessyla know if either the false Lydians or the Hydlenese are moving toward Haven. They'll be here near the Council House so that they can go in any direction. One of you will take up a post two kays west of the edge of Haven on the main road. The other will do the same two kays east of Haven."

"You can sense farther than we can see, ser," Waerdyn pointed out.

"That's true," Beltur agreed, "but I can't be in three places at once. Neither can Jessyla or Lhadoraak, and they'll need to work together. If I'm in the west I can't sense as far as a courier posted in the east can see. The same is true if I'm in the south. I'm going southwest to see if I can find out more about what they're doing, but we don't know if the false Lydians withdrew to the southeast or due south . . . or even southwest." He knew that his recon mission would likely end up being more than that, at least if he ran into Hydlenese forces, but he wasn't about to say that.

"There are only three of you mages," Waerdyn said.

"We've restrained ourselves so far," said Jessyla coldly, looking directly at the scout. "This mage is through with that."

Waerdyn dropped his eyes.

Even Lhadoraak stiffened slightly.

"Do you have any other questions?" asked Beltur.

"No, ser."

"Then I'll be heading out to see what I can discover. I hope to get where I'm going before they've made much progress." He nodded to Waerdyn, then looked to Jessyla. "I intend to follow your advice."

"Good."

Once outside, Beltur wasted no time in mounting and leaving the square, riding south between the Council House and the healing house. He had already decided not to ride under a concealment, at least not in the beginning. He and Slowpoke could move more quickly if they could see clearly, and since the Hydlenese were already crossing the border all the time the Hydlenese couldn't claim he was the invader. He smiled tightly at that thought. *They'll claim whatever they think will serve the Duke's purposes.* Given how the current situation had developed, all that mattered any longer was who won—*whatever that means*—and who controlled Haven and the lands around the town when the fighting was over, one way or another.

As he took the back lane leading to the stone house west of the overgrown forest and Vortaan's stead, he kept sensing for any hint of riders. He found none, even when he crossed the rocky grasslands and reached the back path that paralleled the hills and led to the encampment where he'd been before. There were no hoofprints on the path, suggesting that the Hydlenese had moved. When he turned onto the second narrow road, he still could sense no one at the old stead. Not only was the stead empty, but it looked as though the buildings had been stripped of anything of any value well before the attack on twoday.

Beltur decided to follow the lane that led farther westward from the stead. He'd only ridden a few hundred yards from the wooden posts marking the entry when the narrow dirt track joined a wider road, a road which bore a myriad of recent hoofprints. Beltur followed the tracks along a wide curve that circled a hill bearing largely neglected pearapple trees and an abandoned cot with a caved-in roof. On the far side of the hill the road straightened, heading west-northwest toward, Beltur thought, the main road to Hydolar.

Early as it was in the day, Beltur was already blotting his forehead where the sweat oozed from under his visor cap. That wasn't exactly a surprise, given that the beginning of summer was only six days away.

Less than a kay from the now-abandoned stead, he began to get the feeling of more men and horses gathered together, most likely two kays ahead. He also sensed scouts posted on the hills overlooking the road less than a kay from him, suggesting that he was nearing a larger encampment. *Or that whoever's in command wants to avoid a surprise attack.*

Reluctantly, he created a concealment around himself and Slowpoke. Because the road was fairly level, Slowpoke could maintain the same steady walk, a pace that didn't raise dust behind him, especially since the ground hadn't dried out that much since the rain. As he neared the first of the lookouts on the hills, he began to sense riders coming toward the encampment from the southwest, possibly from the Hydolar road. He could also tell that, once again, the Hydlenese had taken over a stead, but one larger and with more outbuildings than the one that they had abandoned and stripped.

A hundred yards or so short of the wooden posts that marked the beginning of the lane to the buildings of the stead, Beltur eased Slowpoke to the shoulder of the road so that he could study the stead and where buildings, mounts, and troopers were . . . as well as try to determine just how many troopers there might be. Given how long he'd ridden and how hot he was, he took out one of his water bottles and uncorked it, then slowly and carefully took several long swallows before replacing it in its leather holder.

He sensed a squad or so of troopers approaching the lane and the pair of mounted sentries posted there and kept track of the squad from there until the troopers reined up short of a large building, most likely a barn that had been turned into a stable.

What can you do that they won't expect? He needed to do something that would disrupt the encampment, and that would allow him to target at least an officer or two, since there was no way for him to determine, not by sensing, which trooper might be an officer or a squad leader—except when they were in formation, and no one in the encampment was in formation at the moment.

Then he nodded and guided Slowpoke along the road toward the sentries until he found a break in the low stone wall. He had to dismount to lead the gelding through the opening, but the ground beyond was level enough that he could mount, which he did. It took him more than a quint to cover the more than a hundred yards necessary to get close enough to the barn for what he had in mind.

When he was only about fifteen yards from the east side of the barn—the side away from the other buildings in the stead—Beltur reined up. That wall was also just planked, with no doors, except a narrow one near the south end. He began to draw free chaos together, very carefully, always keeping it separated from him with order. He didn't want to use a chaos bolt, although he could have managed a small one, painful as it would have been, but he needed chaos strong enough that the wood would catch fire instantly and strongly.

He eased the chaos into position in two places separated by more than five yards, then removed the order. In instants, the old wood burst into flame, and in moments the two fires were more than respectable. Setting fire to a barn with horses inside was one of the last things Beltur wanted to do, but sometimes, fire was necessary to fight fire.

Even using that small amount of chaos made him uneasy, although he didn't have a headache. *Not yet, anyway.*

Then he moved Slowpoke back another ten yards before moving westward some, so that he'd be closer to any officers or squad leaders who might come from the stead house to take charge of the firefighting or the evacuation of the horses.

Almost a fifth of a quint passed before the smoke and flames caught someone's attention.

"Fire! Fire in the barn!"

"Get the horses out!"

From seemingly everywhere, troopers began to run toward the barn, but Beltur concentrated on the stead house. Several figures moved from the side porch, and one gestured to the other. Beltur couldn't make out what was said, but he had the feeling that the one receiving the gestures was a junior officer. Beltur also sensed another figure still standing on the porch, but only watching. He smiled under the concealment and eased Slowpoke closer to the porch, close enough to place a containment around the neck of the man standing there, and twist and close it fast enough to crush his windpipe.

Should you do more?

Beltur shifted his attention, but, by then, he couldn't tell which of the figures around the barn and the fire were troopers and which officers. *You should have taken out the one giving orders first, and then the one on the porch.*

He still didn't want to start killing rank-and-file troopers—except in an actual fight. *Not yet, anyway.* So he turned Slowpoke away from the fire and milling troopers, noting that it seemed as though the troopers were getting the horses away from the fire in a mostly orderly fashion.

By the time he had retraced his path to where he was able to drop the concealment, he definitely had a headache, but finishing off the first bottle of ale reduced the throbbing feeling to more like a faint ache. He frowned as he considered. He'd done much more, and often, without getting a headache. Had gathering that comparatively small amount of chaos made the difference? He'd definitely have to watch that. He'd need all the strength he could muster against the Hydlenese.

When he finally reached the square and reined up at the healing house, after stopping briefly at the fountain to water Slowpoke, it was almost a glass past midday.

Jessyla hurried out to meet him. "I've been worried. You don't usually take that long."

"I went almost ten kays out. The Hydlenese have more troopers and have taken over another stead, closer to the road to Hydolar." Beltur dismounted and stretched. "There haven't been any more raids here, have there?"

She shook her head. "It's been quiet. Too quiet . . . well, except for the boy that the pig bit. There was more wound chaos, but I got rid of everything I could sense. I think he'll be all right."

"It may not be quiet around here tomorrow. I'll tell you why, and then I'd better tell Lhadoraak. I made things a little warmer for the

Hydlenese . . ." He continued to explain as he followed Jessyla into the shade of the healing house, trying to explain quickly because he didn't want to leave Slowpoke tied up for long. The gelding needed food . . . and rest. So did Beltur, but he could wait.

XXXVI

Threeday's damp heat gave way to a much cooler fourday, with a drizzling rain that intermittently paused and then resumed. On fiveday, the drizzle turned into a steady downpour. Since rain reduced Beltur's abilities with magery, if not nearly so much as it would have if he'd remained a white, he decided against any lengthy recon rides, and certainly not any attempts at ambushing Hydlenese officers.

Sixday was cloudy without rain, and Beltur and Lhadoraak posted Ruell and Waerdyn as scouts, Waerdyn to the west, Ruell to the east. Neither saw any signs of riders, nor did Beltur sense anyone on the roads or near them except people who were clearly from Haven or nearby. Since Gustaan and Turlow weren't needed to deal with the finishing touches on the quarters building, they'd taken over guarding Graalur, not that the captive had shown much interest in escaping, even though his wound appeared to be healing without untoward wound chaos, at least from what Beltur could tell.

Late on sixday afternoon, the four councilors and Taelya gathered in the front room of the Council House.

"Do you think they'll attack tomorrow?" asked Tulya.

"The back roads are still sloppy," said Lhadoraak. "They might raid a stead, but I'd be surprised if they attacked with a full company. Eightday's more likely, but I'd wager on oneday."

"They might try eightday, thinking we wouldn't expect it," suggested Jessyla.

"That's possible," said Beltur. "I'd like to know what their reaction was to the fire and to my killing one of their officers."

"You have to ask?" replied Lhadoraak. "They're angry. Some of the more perceptive officers might be afraid, but they can't admit that. Graalur made it clear that disobedience is as good as death, and that includes officers. They'll want reinforcements, possibly mages, but they can't actually ask for them, not when they're attacking a small town that doesn't even have regular troopers."

"So they'll keep attacking until we kill too many of them for the Duke or his commanders to ignore, and then they'll send an army?"

"They might send another company or two first," suggested Lhadoraak. "We really haven't caused them huge losses. What . . . three officers, a squad leader or two, and a handful or two of troopers out of two companies."

"When you put it that way," said Beltur dryly, "it sounds like we haven't done much at all."

"Well . . ." Lhadoraak drew out the word. ". . . we have kept them from taking over Haven, and if you count the squad with the white . . . then the casualties we've—you and Jessyla—inflicted are definitely significant. It depends on how they look at it."

"They'll ignore the loss of the whites and Gustaan's squad," declared Jessyla. "Most men would, because they don't think of outcasts as part of 'their' army, even when they didn't do anything wrong. I don't think the Hydlenese are any different."

"Sometimes, it's even worse when the outcasts happen to be right," said Beltur in a deadpan voice. "That has been known to happen."

"I wonder where," said Jessyla ironically.

"As for tomorrow," Beltur went on, "I think we should do the same thing as we did today."

"It is market day in the afternoon," Tulya pointed out.

"I doubt that the Hydlenese know that or care," answered Jessyla.

"Most likely not," agreed Lhadoraak. "We do need to think about what we'll do when they make an actual attack."

"That depends on the attack," replied Beltur. "What is there to attack? It's not as though we have a company to stand up to them. If they ride in and do nothing, what do we do? If we start killing them . . ."

"What do you suggest?"

"Telling them that they're not welcome, and that if they stay around they'll find it very uncomfortable."

"And if they insist that they're staying, then what?"

"If an officer delivers the ultimatum, ask if he's an officer, just to make sure. If he is, tell him that if he doesn't withdraw on the spot, he'll be killed. If he refuses, kill him."

Lhadoraak swallowed.

"They have to get the point that we're serious," replied Beltur. "I don't like killing troopers. They haven't much choice. I realize that the officers don't either, but killing officers has a greater impact, and I'm hoping the total number of troopers killed will be lower. Also, an officer does have a choice. He can remove the troopers. He may face death later, or he can desert, but he has more choices."

"Not many," replied Lhadoraak.

"Neither do we, and I'm tired of accommodating to other people's choices, especially when they're trying to take over land that isn't theirs in the first place. We accepted the lawful proposal of the lawful ruler. We should have the right to protect ourselves and the town however we can."

"They won't see something like that as fair. Wars aren't fought that way."

"No . . . the way they're fought means hundreds or thousands of men will die because of the wishes of a ruler. How is that fair?" countered Beltur.

Lhadoraak looked to Tulya.

"I'm afraid he has a point," she replied. "There might be a very high cost to making that point, however. They might try to burn the entire town in revenge." She turned to Beltur. "Are you willing to risk that?"

Would they really do that? He almost nodded in reply to his own question, but stopped, because the nod might have been taken as an answer to Tulya's question. "I honestly don't know. I do know that I'm tired of us getting pushed around. I also doubt that killing one officer would result in that kind of action. The second or third time . . . then it might well do so."

"Can you be sure of that?" asked Tulya.

"No. But I think it might point out to the Hydlenese the cost of their wanting to take over part of Montgren."

"We should think this over," said Jessyla quickly. "At least get some dinner and sleep on it. We've discussed the possibilities, and each of us can think about it."

Lhadoraak nodded. "That's better. We'll have at least until tomorrow. Maybe longer."

Tulya nodded quickly.

Taelya frowned, but said nothing.

As the five left the healing house, they saw a wagon outside, and Jaegyr standing there, smiling. "I've got two benches with pads here, Mages. Thought you'd like to have them soon as you could. Be another eightday or so before the chairs and cushions are ready. If you're headed home, I'll follow you."

"Even if we weren't," said Tulya, "we would be now. The three of us are walking. So why don't you deliver the one to Beltur and Jessyla first."

"I can do that."

Jessyla was in the saddle before Beltur, but he refrained from showing the grin he felt—both in relief and in amusement at her reaction to Jaegyr's appearance.

Once they were far enough in front of the wagon, Beltur said quietly, "Thank you for suggesting we think things over."

"It won't change the problem."

"I know."

"No. I meant the problem with Lhadoraak. He's the same as many blacks. He feels that there's something wrong if a black does anything but defend. Your suggestion of attacking first bothers him."

"Except we're not attacking first. They've attacked first several times."

"Beltur . . . he doesn't see it that way. He also has a problem with your idea of attacking officers."

"Officers shouldn't be responsible for the orders they carry out?"

"Most people think that they should only be responsible to higher officers."

"Then maybe I should find a way to kill the Duke of Hydlen," replied Beltur sarcastically.

"It might have to come to that, you know . . . if nothing else works. But I wouldn't mention it to Lhadoraak or Tulya."

"You really think so?"

"If what Graalur said is true . . . how else can you change things?"

"The majers and commanders might persuade the Duke that taking Haven isn't that good an idea."

"They might. Anything's possible." Jessyla didn't sound terribly convinced. "You don't have to decide that now. Besides, I want to see how the bench looks in the house."

So did Beltur, and he definitely wanted time to think over Jessyla's words.

XXXVII

Eightday dawned misty, even if there was no actual rain. Since Beltur felt that the most likely attack would be early, he rode out to the southwest before seventh glass, and after a time, when he found no sign that the Hydlenese were leaving their encampment, he returned to the healing house, where Jessyla wanted him to take another look at Graalur, as much, Beltur suspected, because she worried that no one would have the time on oneday.

"The arm doesn't hurt that much," Graalur declared as he entered the healing house, escorted by both Gustaan and Ruell.

"That's good," said Jessyla, "but that doesn't mean there isn't some chaos deeper in the wound."

Graalur looked to Jessyla. "You said the other day—"

"Beltur can sense smaller bits of chaos than I can. That's why I wanted him to look at it."

Graalur shivered. "It feels fine."

"They healed all of us when we likely would have died," said Gustaan.

"For what?" asked the Hydlenese morosely. "We're likely to get killed anyway."

"I've thought that several times in the last season," replied Gustaan, "but we're still here and healthy, a lot healthier than we'd be if we'd stayed with the Duke."

"For now."

"That's right," said Gustaan amiably, "but now is all we have, and the mages seem to have a way with things that I'm not certain I'd wager against. If they hadn't healed me, I'd have died half a season ago. It's been a good five eightdays."

Beltur moved closer to Graalur. "Would you rather that I'd left you in that hamlet?"

"No, ser. It's just . . ." The captive shook his head. "You don't know the Duke. He's terrible when he's angered."

"That's good to know," said Jessyla.

Graalur frowned. "How can that be good to know?"

"Because it's easier to fight an evil man than one who's merely misguided," replied Jessyla. "Beltur?"

"There's a tiny bit of wound chaos near the bone," Beltur said. "It might go away by itself, but I'd feel better dealing with it now."

"Dealing with it?" Graalur seemed to draw into himself.

"You'll likely feel a point of heat," replied Beltur. "It will fade over the next glass, possibly sooner." With that, he eased several small bits of free order into the captive trooper's upper arm, guiding them to the wound chaos, bright red, but not the nasty yellowish red. The red faded to gray. "There."

"My arm feels like it's fevered. Nothing else, just my arm."

"You're fortunate," said Gustaan dryly.

"Very fortunate," added Ruell. "Don't complain."

Graalur opened his mouth, then shut it without speaking.

"Ruell, why don't you show Graalur the quarters building?" Gustaan's words weren't really a question.

Ruell looked to Beltur as if to get an agreement.

Beltur nodded. He had the feeling Gustaan had something to say that he didn't want Graalur to hear.

"Yes, ser. We can do that."

"And Graalur . . . don't even think about trying to escape," added Gustaan. "If we don't kill you first, the mages will. Besides, you have a better chance of staying alive here than you ever would if you returned to Hydlen."

Once the two left the healing house, Gustaan cleared his throat, then said, "Poor fellow, it's clear he never had a decent squad leader or captain."

"Could you straighten him out?" asked Beltur.

"If he's willing to make an effort."

Beltur nodded, then asked, "How long were you a squad leader?"

"Six years or so."

"Did you ever think about becoming an undercaptain?"

"That doesn't happen in Hydlen . . . unless you can pay for the commission. I couldn't." Gustaan shrugged. "Might have been for the best. Half the majers are idiots. Most of the rest are toadies." He paused for a moment. "It's said you were an undercaptain in Spidlar. What was that like?"

Beltur smiled. "Are you asking if the officers there were that bad? Most weren't. Some were very good. The captain of the recon company I was assigned to was very good. Most of the captains were good."

"And the majers?" pressed Gustaan.

"I can't say I really saw that many majers. The two I did observe were very competent."

"That, by itself, does much to explain why the Gallosian invasion failed."

Jessyla opened her mouth, then shut it as Beltur threw a sharp glance at her.

"I also suspect," added Gustaan, "that the Spidlarian mages were more effective than those of Gallos."

"Not so much more individually effective as used to better effect," replied Beltur. *If not always for the right reasons.* But Gustaan didn't have to know that.

"That suggests better officers."

"You don't seem to have a high opinion of Hydlenese officers," observed Beltur. "When we talked a while ago, you mentioned that you had trouble with an undercaptain. It sounded like the merchants have quite a bit of influence with the Duke . . ."

"I wouldn't know. I've heard that the Duke doesn't pay much attention to most of them. We were unfortunate to be saddled with the incompetent son of one of the few to whom he does listen, and the captain worried about his family."

Beltur offered a quizzical look.

"The captain was too trusting . . . let Undercaptain Herraat know about his family and where they lived."

"Herraat threatened him?"

"Not in so many words, but . . . it was clear enough."

"Do you know what happened to his family?"

Gustaan shook his head. "I wouldn't be surprised if the captain no longer has a family. He never said anything before we were . . . volunteered, but I saw he was worried."

"Is everyone in Hydlen that vindictive?" asked Jessyla.

"Only those who have coins or power," replied Gustaan. "Isn't it that way everywhere? Or most places?"

"I've seen those with coins who've been fair and generous," said Beltur, "and some who've been vicious and petty. I don't think power and wealth make people mean. I think power and wealth allow people to be what they are at heart."

"You see life as fairer than I do, Mage."

"I don't see life as fair or unfair, Gustaan. Life just is. How it turns out is how people make it turn out. Some people have choices. Some don't. How fair it turns out depends on how those with real choices make those choices."

"I agree there," replied the former squad leader. "I just think there are more selfish folks than good ones."

"Maybe that depends on the ruler," suggested Jessyla. "The Duchess of Montgren seems to be fair . . . and so do most of the people we've met in Montgren. You've said that the Duke of Hydlen is cruel, vicious, self-centered, and vindictive, and you also feel that more people in Hydlen are selfish."

"Is it the ruler . . . or the people, lady mage?" asked Gustaan.

"With a vicious and self-centered ruler, how much choice do the people have?" countered Jessyla.

Gustaan chuckled and looked at Beltur. "She thinks . . . and speaks her mind."

"If she didn't and hadn't, I'd likely be long dead," replied Beltur.

"No," said Jessyla, with an amused smile, "you're here not because I spoke, but because you listened. Too many men don't listen, even to other men, and certainly not to women."

"If we all survive the summer," said Gustaan, glancing toward the quarters building, "it will be interesting to see what Haven will be like. Likely be a better place to live than anywhere I've been."

Beltur understood what Gustaan wasn't saying, that he wanted the Council to succeed, but wouldn't say so outright. "If we do, it will be."

"I'd better catch up with Ruell." Gustaan nodded. "Appreciated talking with you both."

He turned and left the healing house.

Once the door closed behind Gustaan, Beltur looked to Jessyla.

"He hopes we'll prevail, but he's doubtful."

"If I were him, I'd be doubtful, too."

"From what he just told us," said Jessyla, "the officers in Hydlen don't have much more choice than the troopers."

"They have some leeway. I heard one order his men to kill everyone at a neighboring stead just because people resisted having their lambs taken. That sort of killing wasn't required by his superiors. That was his choice."

"Do you think he felt he had a choice?"

"He should have thought he did."

"That's not the same thing."

Beltur sighed. "I know."

"What are you going to do if the Hydlenese ride in tomorrow and ask us to turn the town over to the Duke?"

"We can't do that."

"Even if scores of people here will die?"

"You heard what Graalur said . . . and what Gustaan said. Do you want to live under that sort of ruler? Do we want to turn over the town and the people to that kind of ruler?"

"Of course not. That's not the question. The question is whether we're willing to impose all the deaths that resisting those troopers will cause. It's not as though we can actually ask the people." Jessyla snorted. "If we did, they'd say something like, 'Protect us, but keep each of us safe.' And if we told them the truth, they'd say that maybe we'd just better leave."

Beltur nodded. "They probably would. Those who are left aren't the fighting kind. They'll try to survive quietly under the worst of rulers. They deserve better."

"And we're the ones to decide that?"

"Who else? Besides, even if we rode away, there will likely still be a war. Even if the Duchess surrenders Haven, Hydlen will try to invade Lydiar and hundreds or thousands will die. If we stop Hydlen here, more people may die here, but that just might stop a much bigger war."

"Do we know that?"

"It's very likely."

"Is that enough?"

"I think . . ." Beltur paused. "I think believing that will have to do." He looked to her. "What do you think?"

"I agree. And I don't like it at all."

XXXVIII

Beltur woke uneasy and early on oneday morning. The fact that it was the first day of summer did nothing to cheer him, either, as he wondered what tack the Hydlenese would take . . . and when. Except he had a feeling that something would happen before the day was out and that, whatever it was, he wouldn't be pleased.

As he sat up and swung his legs over the side of the bed, he took a deep breath.

"I know," said Jessyla from behind him. "I feel the same way. Something will happen today."

"Do you have any feel for what it will be?"

"They'll propose something we can't accept. That way, they'll feel justified in attacking. Or they'll be deceptive from the start."

Beltur nodded. "I wouldn't be surprised."

After washing up and dressing, the two ate barely warm porridge and bread, washed down with ale, then filled two water bottles apiece with ale and walked to the barn. Beltur didn't sense any troopers near, but he had no doubt that would change before that long.

By seventh glass, Waerdyn and Ruell were posted, with Waerdyn to the west and Ruell to the east, and by two quints past seven, Beltur could sense both a small number of troopers advancing eastward on the road from the defaced kaystone and Waerdyn riding quickly down the main road toward the square.

"It looks like a small group of troopers riding toward us, and Waerdyn's hurrying to warn us," Beltur announced. "You tell Tulya and Taelya, and I'll let Lhadoraak know and the work crew know, although he may already have sensed them."

In less than a fifth of a quint, everyone was back at the Council House, including the four from the work group and Graalur, but not the two Montgren troopers posted as sentries.

Beltur summarized what he knew, adding, "There are only five troopers coming in at the moment, and it looks as though they'll be making a demand of some sort. Waerdyn should be here in a moment. He might be able to tell us more."

When the lead scout arrived, he dismounted, hurriedly tied his mount beside Slowpoke, and rushed through the door held open by Beltur into the front room of the Council House.

"There are five of them," he announced. "Four troopers and an undercaptain. They're riding under a parley ensign."

"It looks like they'll demand something like our departure or our turning the town over to the Duke," Beltur said. "Or something that amounts to the same thing."

"How do you think we should respond?" asked Tulya evenly.

"It all depends on what they say and how they present it."

"You're not going to give up the town, are you?" asked Gustaan.

"No," replied Beltur, "but we'll be better off knowing what they're proposing before we decide how to fight them."

Lhadoraak frowned, but said nothing.

"Should we all be outside when they arrive?" asked Tulya.

"No," said Jessyla. "Only those of us with shields, just in case. That doesn't include Taelya."

Lhadoraak looked at his consort and nodded firmly.

"What do you want the rest of us to do?" asked Gustaan.

"Nothing . . . right at the moment. If it looks like they're going to attack the town, I'd like all of you to move to Lhadoraak's dwelling. Jessyla will get the arms from our storeroom, and you can defend Tulya and Taelya. That house has stone walls, and I trust you made the shutters strong." Beltur grinned.

"We did," affirmed Dussef. "The inside door bars are strong, too."

"Now . . . let's just wait and see how the Duke's men want to take Haven," said Beltur. "The three of us should probably wait outside."

Less than half a quint later, five riders in green uniforms with yellow piping reined up short of the hitching rail outside the Council House, with the trooper carrying the parley ensign at one end and the undercaptain at the other.

"Let them speak first," murmured Beltur.

The undercaptain edged his mount forward, his eyes moving from one mage to another. Finally, he said, "Who might you be?"

"Besides being mages and healers," replied Beltur, "we are also councilors of the town of Haven, chartered and appointed by Korlyssa, Duchess of Montgren. And who might you be?"

"An undercaptain of the Duke of Hydlen. I've been charged with conveying a message." The undercaptain lifted a sheet of paper and began to read. "'The Duke of Hydlen understands that a council now claims to govern Haven'—"

"The Duchess of Montgren appointed the Council," interjected Beltur. "That is not a claim. Now . . . you were saying?"

The undercaptain did not reply for a moment, glancing down at the sheet of paper again. Finally, he continued. "'That council has proved to be inadequate in stopping the incursions of renegade Lydian troopers and has failed to appreciate the rights of the traders of Hydlen. Therefore, as a representative of the Duke, Majer Smalkyn suggests that this . . . so-called council meet with him to discuss the peaceful transfer of the nonfunctioning governing of Haven to the Duchy of Hydlen.'" The undercaptain cleared his throat.

"Undercaptain . . ." Beltur managed a smile. "The Council does not have the power to surrender any lands now held by the Duchy of Montgren to another duchy, regardless of what the majer says or believes. Or what the Duke contends. That is a matter that lies between the Duke of Hydlen and the Duchess of Montgren, not between the Council of Haven and the majer."

The undercaptain shook his head, as if he could not believe what he had heard. "You refuse to meet with the majer?"

"I didn't say that," replied Beltur. "I said that the Council has no authority to turn over lands of Montgren to Hydlen, regardless of what the majer thinks or proposes. I would be more than happy to accompany you to explain this to the majer."

"He said 'the Council.'"

"In this, I can speak for the Council."

"But . . ."

"Undercaptain," said Beltur gently, "you can have me accompany you, or you can go back and report that you could get no one to meet with the majer. That is your choice."

"I must insist," declared the undercaptain.

"If you take that position . . . how well do you think the five of you would fare against three mages? Is getting yourself killed so that the majer can start a war how you'd like to be remembered?" Beltur surveyed the troopers. "Or how the rest of you would like to die?"

The undercaptain stiffened in the saddle.

Beltur waited.

"You other councilors," the undercaptain finally said, "do you agree that he speaks for your council?"

"We do," said Lhadoraak and Jessyla, not quite simultaneously.

"Then we can proceed," declared the undercaptain.

"In just a moment," replied Beltur, motioning Jessyla and Lhadoraak closer to him, and then murmuring, "What I want you two to do is wait until we leave the square, then follow us, under a concealment, if necessary. Wait for me a few hundred yards west of the brick posts at the end of town. I suspect that the majer has something less than honorable in mind, but we'll see. If they attack, don't just defend yourselves. Kill the officers and squad leaders." Ignoring how Lhadoraak stiffened, he stepped forward and untied Slowpoke.

The ensign bearer looked to the big gelding, then to Beltur, and tried not to frown.

Beltur smiled and mounted, moving Slowpoke up beside the undercaptain as the officer turned his own mount. It didn't escape Beltur's attention that, for the first time in eightdays, there wasn't a single person in sight anywhere in or around the square.

"How long did it take you to get here from Hydolar?" asked Beltur conversationally, checking his shields.

"That would be up to the majer to say."

"Whose idea was it to attack the steads wearing Lydian uniforms?"

"That's why we're here, to keep the Lydians from taking over Haven." The undercaptain's voice was measured, as if he'd practiced the words.

Beltur caught the touches of chaos underlying the words, but went on, "Funny thing about those so-called Lydians, they all wore new uniforms, and they carried Hydlenese sabres."

"What the Lydians wear and carry isn't something with which we're concerned."

"Of course not," replied Beltur. "But it did seem strange. So what happens after I meet with the majer?"

"You'll be free to return."

That was the first fully false statement the undercaptain had made.

Beltur glanced toward the Brass Bowl as they rode by. He couldn't help but notice Phaelgren standing in the main entry, watching. "Are you attached to the battalion command or detached from a company for this mission?"

"That's not your business to know, Mage."

"You must be from a merchanting family. What . . . a third or fourth son?"

The undercaptain did not reply, but Beltur sensed the chaos his question had apparently roiled.

"Where are we meeting the majer?"

"Outside of town. I'd appreciate it if you refrained from any more questions."

"Why? Because you don't like to lie or be deceptive?"

That question generated more chaotic consternation, and Beltur could see and sense the tightness in the officer, a man likely only a year or two older than Beltur himself, but the undercaptain said nothing.

After they rode another hundred yards or so, Beltur spoke again. "Nothing that relies on lies and untruths generally ever turns out well. The question then is who survives and in what condition."

"Spare me the homilies, Mage."

"It wasn't a homily, Undercaptain. It was a warning."

"You seem to forget who has the army."

"I know full well who has the army."

Again, the undercaptain refrained from replying, and Beltur decided not to press conversation. He knew he was riding into a trap, and he had to trust that he could create enough consternation to escape . . . after he did what was necessary.

As they neared the west end of Haven, Beltur could sense the troopers little more than a kay ahead, a far greater number than he'd sensed or seen in one place since the invasion of Spidlar. He judged that there was a full battalion of mounted infantry ahead, one company on each side of the road, and three in the middle, each company formed up four horses abreast. The companies in the middle would likely advance more quickly and then peel off to one side or the other to accomplish whatever destruction and devastation the majer had already ordered.

The lead Hydlen company formed a semicircle on the road. In the middle waited the majer, mounted, flanked by two mounted troopers holding shields and sabres. Beltur immediately noted that the troopers in the middle of the road, but not on the sides, carried riding bows, strung, but over their shoulders. Their quivers were full of shafts.

As much for Lhadoraak's sake as anything, Beltur decided to go through with what had to be a charade, even though he knew he could do more damage, at least initially, if he attacked first. *But that would give them a way to rationalize what they intend to do anyway.* Besides, going through with the charade might get him closer, and that might be for the best.

Even before the undercaptain slowed and gestured for Beltur to approach the waiting officer, Beltur was studying the formation he neared.

"Are you really Majer Smalkyn?" he asked, reining up well short of the man in the majer's uniform.

"Of course. Who else would I be?"

Beltur immediately detected the lie. He couldn't say he was surprised, after what he'd already done.

"And who are you?" the Hydlenese continued. "I requested the entire Council of Haven."

Beltur smiled politely, looking with eyes and senses to those men mounted closest to the archers, figuring that the real majer wanted to be close, but not where any stray arrows might fly.

"As I told the undercaptain . . . the Council has no authority to surrender or to convey any lands in Montgren to anyone. He didn't seem able to comprehend that. So I volunteered to come and explain it myself." Even as he talked Beltur kept searching, finally deciding on a wiry and slightly older man—as evidenced by a lower order/chaos level and a certain feel. He just hoped he was correct, but in what was going to be a bloody mess, there would be mistakes. *You just hope you aren't the one making too many of them.*

"You and this Council will leave Haven, or you will die in Haven."

Beltur shrugged, positioning the two containments. "Whether we leave or not, the lands still belong to the Duchess. You are invading lands that do not belong to you."

The man Beltur thought was the real majer made a small gesture, and the false majer flattened himself in the saddle, while the archers nocked and fired shafts.

Beltur felt the impact on his shields like a blow, but he not only threw a concealment around himself, he twisted the two containments viciously, while turning Slowpoke to the right side of the formation, having already determined that there was more open land beyond the road there than on the left side. In instants, the blows on his shields ceased, just before the big gelding pushed those shields between two troopers, knocking one mount aside and unhorsing the other trooper.

"Overcaptain . . . !" yelled someone, suggesting that Beltur had found the actual majer.

That would only buy a little time, while the battalion re-formed itself and began the actual attack. While that was happening, Beltur guided Slowpoke along the side of the road, then returned to the road once he was well clear of the troopers. He retained the concealment until he neared the brick posts and could sense Lhadoraak and Jessyla and their mounts.

Jessyla urged her horse toward, him, reining up, followed by Lhadoraak. "What happened?"

"They demanded we abandon Haven, then decided to try to assassinate me when I told them that regardless of what we did, we couldn't turn over Montgren lands to Hydlen. They had a half score archers ready to fire at the majer's command. They did. He's dead. They were calling for the overcaptain to take charge. They've got a full battalion coming."

"And we're supposed to stop them?" asked Lhadoraak.

"It's not a massed battle," said Beltur. "They'll have to attack house by house. We can take out the squad leaders of each squad."

"You can," said Lhadoraak. "All I can do is knock troopers off their horses without them seeing me."

"Then you do that . . . and do it around our houses. Jessyla and I will do what we can in that area, but farther away."

"You're sure?" asked the older mage.

"We're sure," declared Jessyla. "Go!"

Once Lhadoraak rode off, she looked to Beltur. "Where do we start?"

"Right past the brick posts. I think they'll come charging down the main road. At least, I hope they do. If they do, I'm going to put a low containment across the road, anchored to the rock below, just long enough to bring down the lead horses and riders. Then I'll use neck containments on whoever seems to be in charge and as many as we can take out. We just keep withdrawing and taking out whoever we can. I'll stay on the south side, you on the north. There's more space on the north. If you get tired, draw back, have a swallow of ale, and take a moment. This is going to take all day. If we lose touch with each other, you join Lhadoraak."

"A battalion is five hundred troopers, Beltur, isn't it?"

"There aren't quite that many anymore. Say four hundred eighty after their losses."

"Quibbler."

"That's why it will take all day." Beltur laughed harshly.

"You mean it, don't you?"

"I do."

"Order and chaos help us . . ." Jessyla shook her head, then guided her mount to the north side of the main street, seemingly disappearing as she concealed herself.

Beltur didn't move Slowpoke that far off the road and, concealing himself, waited for the onslaught. As he'd predicted, the lead company moved quickly toward Haven, but the flanking companies had dropped back, apparently realizing that there was not enough space and too much overgrown vegetation beside the road. Beltur thought that was to his advantage, but that remained to be seen. The horses neared, not at a gallop or a canter, but something almost like a fast trot. He'd hoped for a faster pace, but the horses were still fairly close together, with the following companies bunched closer than Beltur would have put them.

Just before the first rank passed the brick posts, Beltur set the low containment and anchored it. All five horses went down, and Beltur felt as though he'd been pummeled all over. He immediately released the containment and studied the following ranks as best he could with his senses, finally finding a trooper, possibly an undercaptain or a squad leader, yelling something that could not be made out over the screams of injured horses and the shouts and curses of troopers. With savage quickness, Beltur used a neck containment to kill the man who was likely a squad leader, then another, and another. Beltur didn't even wince at the black mists of death. A man—clearly an officer—rode along the shoulder of the road toward the pile of mounts and men.

Beltur took him out as well.

In a fraction of a quint more than fifteen men were dead from Beltur's containments. He had a vague sense of other death mists as well.

"Circle round the area! There's a mage here!"

Amid the chaotic pileup and milling mounts, Beltur couldn't tell who issued the order, only that other squads or companies were threading their way away from the congested mess. He turned Slowpoke east, randomly taking out any trooper who seemed on the verge of taking control of the scattered forces.

Ahead, in the open space where a lane and a side street intersected, an officer was trying to re-form a company. Beltur used a small containment to break his neck . . . and that of the squad leader who then tried to take control. Three houses farther on, troopers had dismounted and smashed into a house, setting it afire. Beltur forced himself to ignore the flames, and the screams. He killed two more troopers and moved on.

Still under a concealment, but feeling light-headed, he eased Slowpoke next to a shed, pulled out a water bottle, and took several very long swallows. He'd barely corked it and replaced it when a Hydlenese trooper rammed into his shield.

"He's here—"

Beltur cut off the shout and the trooper's life.

He could sense that at least one company was moving close to Lhadoraak's and his dwelling, and he threaded Slowpoke through the back of two houses to a dwelling some three west of Lhadoraak's. From what he could sense, Lhadoraak was north of his own house trying to block troopers riding south from the main street.

Beltur turned his attention to the dwelling in front of him, where two troopers were using a length of log in trying to batter through the door. Beltur killed both, and the squad leader supervising them. The remaining squad members turned farther south. Beltur followed them, then killed the first trooper who tried to batter into the next house, followed by the squad leader, and another trooper. The squad lost interest in that house.

The remainder of the squad moved to another house.

Beltur picked off three more troopers, and the Hydlenese moved on.

Beltur reined up. His head was slowly spinning, or felt as though it was, and he could barely stay in the saddle.

After drinking more ale, he felt the dizziness abate, but only slightly. *You're going to have to rest for a bit.* He forced himself to wait, reduced his shields to the minimum, and when no one else seemed to be around, dropped the concealment.

After a time, he eased Slowpoke toward where Lhadoraak and now Jessyla were fending off a handful of troopers less than a block from their houses. He drank a bit more ale while he rode.

As he guided Slowpoke around the corner, he saw yet another squad of troopers riding toward the houses west of where Jessyla and Lhadoraak were using their shields to push away another set of troopers. Both of them had dropped concealments, and Beltur realized that he should have done the same earlier. Then he sensed another death mist from the troopers facing Jessyla, but that didn't seem to stop the Hydlenese, almost as if they recognized that she couldn't kill that many of them—or that they were so enraged that they didn't care.

Half of the second squad of troopers moved into a wedge formation, apparently preparing to charge Lhadoraak and Jessyla from the rear. The other ten troopers rode toward the nearest dwelling—less than half a block from Beltur's house.

Beltur didn't bother with a concealment. He just urged Slowpoke into a full gallop and extended his shields, but the extension began only at Slowpoke's shoulder height. What Beltur hoped for was merely to sweep the troopers off their mounts, so that he and his shields didn't take quite a beating.

He and Slowpoke burst through the center of the five-man front, and most of the troopers in both ranks were yanked from their mounts, the impact being strong enough that Slowpoke was barely moving when Beltur reined him up.

One trooper at the end of the five abreast in the second rank stayed mounted . . . but blood gushed from his shoulder—and his arm was missing. Then he slumped in the saddle. *How . . . ?*

Beltur swallowed. The edge of the shield must have cut like a sword or knife.

The survivors of Beltur's impromptu attack fled—those who could—as did the five troopers who had been trying to beat their way past Lhadoraak and Jessyla's shields.

Beltur once more turned the big gelding and let him walk slowly toward the other two mages.

"Now what?" asked Lhadoraak, looking toward the retreating troopers.

"What did you do to that one trooper?" asked Jessyla, gesturing to the one-armed form sprawled on the trampled clay of the street.

"I think I just discovered a nastier way to use shields."

"Does it take less effort?" asked Jessyla. "I got too tired to hold shields and use containments very often. If I only had to hold shields . . ."

Trying not to breathe hard, Beltur explained. As he finished, he saw the horrified expression on Lhadoraak's face and added, "It's not that much different from a sabre or a lance."

"The way you can use it . . ." Lhadoraak shook his head.

Beltur wasn't about to dispute the older mage. "We need to rest, get something to eat . . . and then I'm going to see if I can find any more officers."

"What about the townspeople?"

"Right now, the best thing we can do is get rid of as many Hydlenese as possible."

"You're sounding like them," said Lhadoraak.

"Forbearance doesn't win battles . . . or wars," said Beltur tiredly. "Destroying the enemy does. Besides, they're the ones who started it."

"You're white," declared Jessyla.

"So are you."

"You need to eat and rest. Until you do that, you can't do any more."

"More people will die . . ."

"Your dying won't help them . . . or us."

"She's right," added Lhadoraak.

Beltur couldn't argue with that.

"This way . . ." Jessyla gestured.

Beltur didn't look back at the bodies as the three of them rode to Lhadoraak and Tulya's house. Immediately Gustaan and Waerdyn hurried outside.

"Are you all right?" demanded Gustaan.

"Nothing that something to eat, drink, and a little rest won't fix," replied Beltur. *Mostly, anyway.*

"Where did the Hydlenese go?" asked Waerdyn.

"Nowhere far. They're attacking and plundering the eastern half of Haven." Beltur realized he was hoarse, but he had no idea why. He hadn't been shouting or yelling. He didn't think so, anyway, but the morning was turning into a blur . . . except that when he glanced in the direction of the white sun blazing through the clear green-blue sky, he realized it was slightly past midday.

"We'll take care of the horses while you eat and rest," said Gustaan.

"And gather up weapons and spoils," added Waerdyn, "while none of the green-asses are nearby."

Gustaan frowned at that.

"The way they're acting," said Waerdyn, "they're green-asses. Trying to kill everyone they can because the town doesn't want them." He shook his head.

"That's the Duke, not the men."

"That's why I tried to take out the officers," Beltur said as he dismounted. He knew he was in worse shape than he thought when his boots hit the ground, because his legs were shaky, and he was again light-headed. He walked into the house, slowly and carefully . . . and said nothing until Gustaan eased him into a chair at the warped kitchen table. "At some point . . . ought to have Jaegyr make us both good tables."

"That will have to wait," said Tulya, setting a bowl of burhka in front of him, accompanied by a half loaf of warm bread.

"You . . . didn't have to do this," Beltur half protested. "You really didn't."

"I had to do something, or I'd have worried myself to death. Anyway, I knew you three would need something hot and solid sooner or later."

Beltur took a mouthful of burhka, then another, before realizing that Jessyla and Lhadoraak were at the table with him . . . and that neither had spoken. All three were just eating, not talking.

He kept eating and suddenly the bowl was empty. He wasn't hungry any longer, and the light-headedness had left him. He also hadn't even been aware of whether the burhka had been too spicy-hot. He was about to take another swallow of ale when he realized his beaker was empty. For a moment, he just looked at it.

Tulya immediately said, "Taelya . . . would you refill Uncle Beltur's beaker? Not quite to the top, please."

"Yes, Mother."

When Taelya handed the beaker back to Beltur, he said, "Thank you. I needed that."

"Your order and chaos were swirling, Uncle Beltur. They're better now."

"I hope so."

Beltur forced himself to drink the second beaker of ale slowly, knowing he needed some time, even as he also knew that houses were burning and people dying . . . or at best, losing everything. Finally, he set down the empty beaker and stood. "It's time to go and do what else we can to run them off."

"I'm coming with you," declared Jessyla. "I can protect myself, and someone needs to make sure you don't do too much."

Beltur almost asked "too much what," but was afraid she just might tell him what he already feared. *Yet what else can you do? What else will work?*

Jessyla looked to Lhadoraak. "You need to stay close to here, just in case some of the Hydlenese circle back."

"I should go, too."

Beltur caught the expression of alarm on Tulya's face and immediately said, "That won't work. We'll be too far east to get back here in time if they turn and attack here."

"You're sure?"

"Absolutely!" declared Beltur, realizing that Jessyla was saying the same word nearly simultaneously.

"You're outvoted, dear," said Tulya quietly. "After what those uniformed brigands tried to do to the other houses down the way, it's better you stay."

"I hope this doesn't take long," declared Beltur, knowing as he spoke how unlikely that hope was. He headed for the front door.

As he stepped outside into the summer sunlight weakened by haze and acrid smoke, Gustaan edged closer, holding Slowpoke's reins. He tendered them to Beltur, saying quietly, "Ser, do what you can, but make sure you come back. You're the only one . . . Just be careful. We refilled your water bottles with ale."

"Thank you." Since Beltur really didn't know what else he could say, he just nodded and took the gelding's reins. He frowned at the fact that he hadn't even noticed that Gustaan had refilled the bottles. Next, for a brief moment, he looked closely at Slowpoke, with both eyes and senses. The gelding seemed to be in better shape than Beltur felt. He patted Slowpoke's neck and said, "We've got a lot to do yet, big fellow." Then he mounted.

Since Beltur sensed no one near the houses, he turned Slowpoke north, toward the main street, where he sensed several handfuls of troopers in various places, but all east of him and Jessyla, as if the attackers had realized that the pickings were easier away from where the mages had been. That made Beltur feel slightly guilty. *But don't you have the right to protect those close to you?* "They're all east of here."

"Does that really surprise you?" asked Jessyla, with just a tinge of irony in her voice.

"I suppose not."

"What are you planning?"

"To ride east on the main street, under a concealment until I get close, then charge them with shields extended like narrow blades just above the withers of most horses."

"That's going to be hard on the horses."

"What else can I do?" *What else will inflict enough death and injury on the Hydlenese to drive them off without killing myself?*

"I didn't say you had a choice."

"They have a choice. They could have not attacked. They could have attacked and left. They haven't done either."

"You killed their commander and squad leaders and some officers, not to mention a lot of troopers. They're angry."

And that means a lot more are going to be dead.

As they turned east on the main street, Beltur could see thin columns of smoke above and between the scattered trees in yards and gardens ahead, but no actual flames nearby, suggesting that nothing had recently been put to the torch. He could also make out the sickly sweet stench that was likely that of burning flesh, either animal or human, if not both. As they neared the main square, Beltur saw that, while the Brass Bowl was shuttered tight, it bore no signs of attack or destruction.

Ahead was a line of mounted troopers across the street just east of the inn. "They're cordoning off where they're having their fun." His voice was bitter, partly because he'd caused the situation and partly because he'd had to stop and rest. If either had been different . . . He shook his head. "I don't think I'll bother with the concealment."

"I don't see any archers."

"Stay well behind me."

"I can do that."

Beltur said nothing more as he rode toward the squad blocking the street.

"Halt!" called out one of the troopers as Beltur neared a point less than fifty yards from the troopers, some of whom had dark splotches on their uniforms.

Blood, and not theirs, most likely. Beltur kept riding.

"Ready arms!"

Beltur almost laughed bitingly. Because he had used a concealment at the beginning of the battle for Haven, the poor bastards in front of him had no idea who—*or what*—he was. Instead, he extended the thin, bladed, and invisible shields and urged Slowpoke into a gallop.

"Charge!" ordered the squad leader . . . or acting squad leader.

Not wanting to bear the direct impact on his shields of hitting another horse, Beltur aimed Slowpoke at a gap between two mounts. The big gelding swept through the line of riders, and there were almost no screams or yells. Beltur didn't look back at the heaped bodies of men and mounts, but he still had to swallow the bile that rose in his throat. *You didn't start this. They did.*

He eased Slowpoke back to a walk by the time they were passing the vacant square. A quick glance showed that both the Council House and the healing house were charred and still-smoldering heaps.

"They didn't have to burn the healing house," said Jessyla.

"We repaired it. That means they have to destroy it, to prove that nothing we've done will last." *Death lasts, though.* He had a fleeting desire to laugh maniacally. He did not, but kept riding.

Four troopers rode out from a lane across from the shuttered and so-far-untouched East Inn and immediately turned toward Beltur and Jessyla.

"There's a woman!"

"She's mine."

"I saw her first!"

"Take care of the patroller or whatever first."

The four raised blades and urged their horses forward.

Beltur extended his narrow deadly shields and brought Slowpoke into almost a gallop before crossing the thirty or so yards between them. He again angled for a point between riders. He barely felt the impact and glanced back, only to see four downed mounts and four bodies. He quickly looked around for Jessyla.

She said nothing as she eased on his right side.

Beltur momentarily pondered the fact that both inns were untouched, then realized that the Hydlenese wanted them intact for their own use. Pushing that thought away, he extended his senses once more, discovering a larger group of troopers ahead on the north side of the main street, as well as a number of other, and smaller, groups, scattered around on the south side. He decided to deal with the larger group before he got too tired.

Before long, he saw what he had feared with that larger group. More than a squad of riders milled around Jaegyr and Julli's small but sturdy stone-walled and slate-roofed home. What remained of the outbuilding that had been Jaegyr's workshop was still partly in flames, and the gardens in front had been trampled flat. So far the troopers had not found a way to break into the house, but two were pushing Jaegyr's wagon toward the door, and a log had been fastened to the wagon bed, protruding far enough so that it could be used as a battering ram.

No one seemed to notice Beltur and Jessyla as they approached. Beltur did not hurry Slowpoke, but studied how the Hydlenese squad was scattered around the dwelling—scattered, and certainly not deployed, suggesting that, at least to some degree, Beltur's efforts to destroy the command structure had been effective.

He turned in the saddle. "Just stay close to that tree, and if some of them escape, conceal yourself." Then he turned Slowpoke and raised a concealment, since it would take more than one run to strike the majority of those around the dwelling and since he didn't want the unsuspecting troopers to have even a hint of what was in store for them, at least at first.

He eased the gelding almost due north from the road until he was parallel to the bulk of the troopers, then turned Slowpoke directly toward them and brought him up to as fast a pace as he dared. The shouts and yells came not from those he felled, but from those on the east side of the dwelling when they saw the carnage inflicted on their comrades. Some of the survivors were trying to flee when Beltur came back for a second run alongside the east side of the house, dropping the concealment in an effort to save as much strength as he could.

The two men who had been pushing the wagon looked up in horror before Beltur used two containments, one after the other, to crush their necks. After that, Beltur turned back toward the road, but two troopers he'd missed were spurring their mounts eastward on the main road, clearly fleeing for all they were worth. Not wanting to spend his energy or that of Slowpoke in chasing the two, Beltur walked Slowpoke back to where Jessyla waited. He looked down at the trooper lying at the edge of the road, then at Jessyla.

"I couldn't let him escape, not . . . with all the blood on his uniform."

Blood that had to have come from an innocent, given that the way Beltur had dealt with the attackers earlier hadn't spilled blood. He nodded. "We need to move on."

Neither spoke as he turned Slowpoke south and headed across the main road to the lane on the other side, a lane that would lead to another dwelling surrounded by troopers.

The door to the once-neat one-story dwelling had been smashed in, as had one of the front windows, where a shutter hung askew. Three troopers sat on their mounts watching the lane . . . and likely the three riderless horses tied to the porch railing. All three looked almost bored as Beltur rode toward them . . . until they caught sight of him.

One yelled something, and two other troopers hurried out of the dwelling. Beltur waited, letting them mount. Then, once they were on the lane, he and Slowpoke charged them. The narrow, razor-edged shields, propelled by the considerable force of a hundred-stone horse, cut them all down.

Without speaking Beltur turned Slowpoke back to the house. By the time he reached it, the remaining trooper, eyes wide, stood on the porch, glanced toward his mount, then started to turn when Beltur threw the containment around his neck. In moments, his still figure lay on the wide planks next to another figure, that of a man in brown clothing sprawled facedown there.

A woman peered from the door, clutching torn garments to herself, looking down at the dead in brown and then to Beltur. "Where . . . were . . . you?!!!" Each word was punctuated with sobs.

Beltur looked directly at her. "Fighting my way here. I'm sorry."

"Sorry? Is that . . . all you can say?"

Beltur just looked at her sadly. "What else could I say?"

He turned Slowpoke toward the next house.

After that, what he did turned into a blur, one house, one group of troopers after the other . . .

. . . until he found himself riding . . . somewhere . . .

"Beltur . . . Beltur!"

Belatedly . . . and through a haze, and the harsh and acrid smoke of still-burning wood, he realized that Jessyla was the one calling to him. He reined up Slowpoke and looked around, realizing that he was a good half kay east of the edge of Haven. He also could feel that Slowpoke was breathing hard. *Did you run him that hard . . . or was it the effort of pushing those shields?*

He was too tired to shake his head. And if he did, the slow spinning feeling might turn into a whirl with the entire world swirling around him. He didn't realize that Jessyla had caught up and her mount was right beside Slowpoke until she spoke.

"Beltur . . . we can go back to the house now."

"Not if there are any Hydlenese around." The last thing he wanted to do was to wake up tomorrow and do what he'd just done.

"They're all gone. Every last one of them . . . the ones who are still alive, that is. There can't be more than a few left. If that."

"You're sure?"

"Beltur . . . you've done enough."

For now. Even that thought was difficult for Beltur.

"We need to walk slowly. You asked a lot of Slowpoke."

"I should walk."

"Just let him carry you. He's in better shape than you are."

How long the walk back took, Beltur wasn't sure, but it seemed that suddenly Slowpoke had come to a stop.

"Beltur . . . we're home."

"Home?"

"That's right. Gustaan is going to help you dismount."

". . . don't need . . . help . . ."

"Just in case."

Beltur felt an arm guiding him, and then heard some words.

". . . frigging . . . dark angels . . ."

Then he didn't hear anything at all.

XXXIX

When Beltur woke up, the room was dim. Was it night, or dawn, or twilight? Then he coughed. Almost immediately, the bedroom door opened, and light flooded in. The glare was so bright that Beltur had to close his eyes. Then he felt constricted, closed in, and he realized that he could sense absolutely nothing. Nothing at all.

Jessyla hurried in. "Beltur . . . are you there?" She closed the door, and the glare subsided as she walked toward him.

"What . . . do you mean . . . am I here?" He opened his eyes again . . . slowly, sitting up slowly in the bed as he spoke. His voice was rough and hoarse, and it hurt to talk.

"You're here." The relief in her voice was palpable. "You're really here."

"Where else would I be?"

"You haven't been you. You've been threshing and raving for the past two days—"

"Two days? What day is it?" Beltur stiffened, and a jolt of pain shot through his head. He massaged his forehead, then asked, "What happened?"

"It's fourday. Midmorning. We got you to drink some ale, but nothing you said made any sense at all. Then you'd fall asleep. Sometimes, you'd talk. The words were all jumbled. I was so worried. We all were." Standing by the bed, she reached down and took his hand, gently squeezing it. "It's so good to know you're back to being you." Again, very gently, she released his hand.

"What about the Hydlenese? Have they attacked again?"

"No. Lhadoraak doesn't think they can. Not until they get reinforcements, and that's likely to take more than an eightday, possibly two if they have to come from Hydolar."

"But they still must outnumber us," Beltur protested.

"You didn't leave that many survivors. Gustaan doesn't think any of those who fled would ever want to fight here again."

"I . . . I thought more of them fled."

"The time we took to eat and rest convinced them that we couldn't do any more. You took most of them by surprise." Jessyla swallowed. "I couldn't stop you at the end, not until you almost collapsed. By then . . ." She swallowed again. "There was so much blood . . . so many bodies. And I had so little strength left . . . even if they had survived . . ."

"How many?" Beltur asked. *Surely there couldn't have been that many . . . except you made so many charges . . . so many . . . and you were so tired . . .*

"More than four hundred . . . Gustaan thought."

Four hundred . . . that . . . that couldn't be.

"Some . . . a few," continued Jessyla, "were killed by townspeople when the troopers fled you. There were bodies and blades everywhere. Gustaan and Waerdyn gathered up close to three hundred eighty sabres."

Four hundred . . . that . . . it couldn't be . . . you couldn't have . . . Finally, Beltur blurted out, "Slowpoke? How is he?"

"He's been sluggish, but he was better this morning. I've been feeding him and talking to him."

"He likes that. What about everyone else?"

"Taelya's been worried about you. She kept saying that your order and chaos weren't right."

"Was she right? Am I still . . . that way?"

"You'll be fine."

"I'm not fine! I can feel it. I can't sense anything. Not anything. I couldn't raise a shield if . . ."

"Dear . . ." Jessyla swallowed again. "You came even closer to dying this time, closer than even in Elparta. I wasn't certain . . ."

"But . . . no one touched me . . ." He paused. "I used everything, didn't I? Everything."

"Not quite. If you had, you wouldn't be alive. Your natural order is still low. You have barely enough natural chaos . . . even now."

"You . . . you gave me some . . . didn't you?"

"Just a little. Just enough."

All you could, most likely. Beltur shuddered, and he could feel dull aches throughout his entire body. "Will it come back . . . what I could do?"

"I don't see why not. Right now, you barely have enough order/chaos strength to hold yourself together. That's why you need to get up . . . slowly . . . and have a little to eat. Just a little."

Beltur looked down and realized he was wearing only smallclothes . . . and that purple streaks ran across the top of his thighs . . . and his forearms. "I'm bruised all over . . . aren't I?"

"Not all over . . . but in lots of places. Your shields took a beating, and so did you." She held out a hand. "You're going to be unsteady, I think."

Beltur started to rise, but as his legs started to shake, he took her hand, and then found her easing him into a standing position. "Is anyone else here?"

"In our house? Not at the moment. You can take your time."

Beltur couldn't help but feel relieved that no one else would see him almost as helpless as an infant as he leaned partly on Jessyla and tottered toward the kitchen. It was a relief to sit down, except that when he leaned back the pressure of the chair on his shoulders hurt enough that he winced involuntarily and immediately straightened. That hurt as well.

"There's some warm bread and a fowl soup that Julli brought."

"They're both all right?"

"Thanks to you and to their house." Jessyla ladled out soup from the pot on the stove into a battered bowl and set it before Beltur. "Small mouthfuls, please, and little bites of the bread at first."

"What about the townspeople?" asked Beltur.

"Waerdyn asked around. He thinks about fifteen were killed."

"So few?" Beltur found that hard to believe, given that an entire battalion had swarmed over the town.

"Most houses here only have a few people in them, and the Hydlenese had to break into each one. People here have been worried about brigands for years. Most houses are strongly shuttered and barred. We . . . you . . .

didn't give them that much time." Jessyla paused. "Some of the women . . . they survived only because you killed the troopers before . . ."

"They finished having their way with the women?"

Jessyla nodded.

Abruptly, Beltur recalled the sobbing woman, asking where he'd been. He swallowed, except there was nothing to swallow, so dry was his mouth.

"Now eat. Slowly."

Beltur followed her instructions, sipping the soup and interspersing it with small bites of bread. He didn't quite finish the small bowlful before he felt full . . . and tired.

"You need more rest."

"All . . ." Beltur yawned. ". . . I've done is rest."

"Healing takes a lot out of you, especially when you're wounded the way you were." She moved beside the chair and helped him back to the bedroom.

Beltur felt that he wasn't quite so unsteady on the way back.

XL

By the time he woke up on fiveday morning, after dozing and eating and dozing and eating throughout fourday, and getting a largely uninterrupted sleep that night, Beltur could again sense objects, if only within a few hundred yards, and he could create light shields, which he was going to try to hold for as long as he could.

He washed up after breakfast and donned his oldest blacks, then took a carrot from the kitchen before walking down to the barn to see Slowpoke.

The big horse turned his head immediately and nickered.

"I'm glad to see you, too." Beltur eased up beside Slowpoke and stroked his neck. "I wouldn't have made it without you."

Slowpoke nuzzled him, both seeming happy to see Beltur and likely also looking for the carrot.

"Here it is, big fellow."

Beltur just brushed Slowpoke and talked to him. After recalling what he had done on oneday, and knowing that he didn't recall even half of the deaths he'd caused, he wasn't certain he even wanted to talk to anyone besides Jessyla, although he knew he'd have to, sooner or later.

He was finishing up when Jessyla appeared at the barn door. "How are you feeling?"

"I just wanted to see how Slowpoke was."

She smiled, an expression with a hint of sadness. "I don't think you answered my question."

"You must have some idea how I feel . . ."

"You need to say it, if only to me."

"I . . . I can tell myself . . . that I did what I had to . . . but . . . what . . . I did . . . was terrible. What they did would have . . . been worse for the townspeople. I feel . . . I've been asking myself if I could have done something else. Would it have been better for the people? It would have been . . . at least for now . . . if we'd just walked away. But . . . why should we always be the ones to leave? We left Gallos. We left Elparta. We left Axalt . . . because other people didn't like who we are . . . or what we did. I did terrible things on oneday. I did them because . . . partly, anyway, I was tired of always being the one to walk away . . . and now . . . even more people will die because I don't want to walk away any more."

"Neither do I," replied Jessyla.

"But it's a terrible price to pay."

"It is. You're willing to pay it. So am I, even if I can't do all that you can. We've made that choice. We have to finish this . . . and live with it. Otherwise, it will have been for nothing."

She stepped forward and put her arms around him.

We have to live with it . . . as best we can. For a long time, Beltur just hung on to her.

Finally, he straightened and stepped back. "I need to talk to Lhadoraak."

"We both need to talk to Tulya and Lhadoraak." She pulled a small object from somewhere within her tunic. "First, there's something you need to see."

"That? What is it?"

"It's a mirror. You don't need to see it. You need to look at yourself in it."

Beltur took the small brass mirror gingerly, absently wishing he'd taken the time to make a special mirror for her. *Another thing you should have done.* Then he turned the mirror, and looked at the reflected image of himself.

He half expected the bruises on his cheeks, and along his jawline, bruises that were showing deep purple in spots, as were those he had on his arms and legs, and even his chest, and the redness of his eyes was certainly understandable. What he didn't expect was the purple-black band that covered his forehead from a digit above his eyebrows and that appeared to cover his entire skull, even under his hairline.

"How . . . what?"

"I don't know," replied Jessyla. She moistened her lips. "I think . . . I'm afraid . . . it might not go away, the black on your forehead and skull."

"But . . . how . . . ?" repeated Beltur.

"It was there when we got you off Slowpoke. I don't think people really noticed. You were in such bad shape. I just wanted to get some ale into you and make sure you didn't have any broken bones that weren't immediately obvious. No one but me has seen you since then. It might be a shock to them . . . and to you, because we don't have any mirrors in the house."

"I wanted to make one for you, like we did for Halhana, but . . . there was never time. There's never been enough time."

She smiled. "I know. You talked about it once in your sleep. I can wait."

Beltur couldn't help but think that he still should have insisted, but, as in so many things, regrets were a waste of time—except as a warning not to put off the little things that were more important than he realized. *Except you didn't understand that it was important.*

"Shall we walk over to see Tulya and Lhadoraak?"

Beltur smiled at the gentle reminder. He did realize that he was reluctant to see Lhadoraak. He could still remember the stunned expression on the face of the older mage when Beltur had told Lhadoraak of the need to kill as many officers as possible. He also knew how difficult Lhadoraak found even using shields to disable troopers.

The two walked from the barn across the narrow street and up to the front door.

Beltur knocked, then heard footsteps, not the light ones of Taelya, but Lhadoraak's boots.

The door opened.

Lhadoraak stared, if only for an instant. "Are you sure you're all right?"

"Jessyla would have stopped me from coming if I weren't all right to see you. I'm not all right for any more battles at the moment."

"I don't think any of us are." Lhadoraak stepped back, opening the door wide and gesturing toward the hearth.

Beltur glanced around the front parlor, where the kitchen chairs had been brought in and arranged facing the backed bench Jaegyr had delivered earlier. Besides Tulya, Waerdyn and Gustaan were there.

"Since the Hydlenese burned down the Council House, we've been using our front room to meet," explained Lhadoraak. "That made sense, especially since your house has become the armory."

Beltur hadn't noticed that, but then he hadn't been in shape to notice much of anything.

"You sit here. I'll get the stool," said Tulya, rising from one of the chairs and heading for the kitchen.

"Thank you." Beltur eased himself into the chair, very carefully. He was more than aware of the covert scrutiny of his appearance.

Jessyla moved to stand behind him, and Tulya reappeared carrying the stool. She gestured for Jessyla to take the only vacant chair. Jessyla shook her head.

"How bad are things in Haven?" asked Beltur. "Obviously, I've been in no condition to ride around."

Lhadoraak seated himself and gestured to Waerdyn. "They've been riding patrols and reporting."

The lead scout cleared his throat. "It's not as bad as it would have been . . . without what you did. We counted eleven houses that burned. Also some sheds."

Gustaan added, "Most of those inside the burned houses died. There's no sign of the Hydlenese. There weren't many wounded. There were a lot of dead troopers. More than I ever saw in a battle. Some had their necks crushed. A lot . . . most of them were slashed in half."

Lhadoraak looked to Beltur. "If you'd explain . . ."

"I turned my shields into invisible blades. Slowpoke supplied the muscle." Beltur's voice was flat. "They would have slaughtered everyone they could. It was the only thing I could do. I just kept riding until I couldn't find any more."

"They're gone," Lhadoraak said tiredly. "At least, there's no trace of any of them. Waerdyn, Gustaan, and the others have gathered up some of the horses that . . . survived."

"How many?" asked Beltur warily.

"A little more than a score," said Lhadoraak.

Beltur couldn't help but wince.

"You did what you had to, ser," said Gustaan. "We've got some mounts in the East Inn and some in a barn at that widow's place. She said that was the least she could do, seeing as you'd pretty much saved Haven."

Saved it by slaughtering hundreds, and most of them never really saw it coming . . . or knew why. "They'll be back," Beltur said bleakly. "With an army."

"Do you really think so?" asked Tulya. "After all they lost?"

Beltur turned to Gustaan. "What do you think? You might have a better idea."

"The Duke hates it when things don't go his way. Losing most of a battalion will just anger him more. A battalion means nothing to him. Like the mage said, he'll muster a large force, and this time he'll send white mages as well."

"Does he have many?" asked Jessyla. "How many?"

Gustaan shrugged. "I don't know. He has some. The officers said he saved them for when it counted. They used them against a pirate base near Pyrdya a few years ago. Burned most of the pirate ships with chaos bolts."

Beltur looked to Waerdyn. "Have we heard anything from Weevett or from the Duchess or Korsaen?"

"Nothing."

Lhadoraak cleared his throat. "On twoday, I wrote a report and sent it with Ruell and Therran to Weevett. I hope you don't mind, but we didn't know . . ."

"I'm glad you did," Beltur said quickly. "Therran?"

"He volunteered," interjected Gustaan. "He and Ruell get along."

"I thought we ought to have at least one Montgren trooper here," added Lhadoraak. "I can't believe they won't send someone after an attack like this."

"We'll have to see," replied Beltur. "More than a few times, people haven't seen things the way we have."

"It's in the interests of both Lydiar and Montgren to put a stop to this," pointed out Jessyla, "and if they don't support us, it will be much worse in the future."

"Unless they're willing just to let Hydlen have Haven," said Tulya.

"We can't do anything more than we've done, can we?" asked Beltur, looking around the parlor.

All the others shook their heads.

Beltur managed a wry smile. "Bad as it was, it could have been worse." *And it will be, especially if the Duchess doesn't send her own troopers.*

XLI

After a solid night's sleep on fiveday, Beltur woke up on sixday feeling better and slightly reassured, since he could sense people almost half a kay away and hold decent, if not strong, shields. Still, compared to what he had been able to do, he worried about whether he would regain those abilities . . . and how long it might take. The purpled bruises on his body were turning yellowish in places. Jessyla assured him that was normal. Normal or not, they still hurt, and hurt more if something touched them, which was difficult to avoid since it felt like every place on his body had a bruise. The purplish blackness that covered the skin on his forehead and higher wasn't turning yellow, but appeared to be shifting to solid black.

As he finished his beaker of ale at breakfast, Beltur looked to Jessyla. "Do you have any idea why the skin on my forehead is turning even blacker?"

"I don't. I've never heard of anything like that."

"I can't sense any difference in the natural order and chaos there."

"Well . . . there isn't any difference between people who have lighter or darker skins. That might mean that what's happened is . . . natural . . . in a way."

"Half the skin on my head being black is natural?"

"As far as order and chaos are concerned. That's what I meant."

"Could it change again?"

"I suppose it's possible."

"You don't sound very convincing," said Beltur dryly.

"I told you. I've never heard of anything like it." She paused. "I also never heard of a mage who could do what you did on oneday."

"You think the two are connected?"

"Beltur . . . how could they not be?"

He took a deep breath. "I look . . . deformed."

"You still have the same shape and physical build."

"After what I did . . . this will convince everyone that I'm some kind of monster." He swallowed. "And maybe I am. I just knew . . . if I did anything else . . . we wouldn't have a chance."

"You wear your visor cap when you ride anyway. Most people won't see the difference."

"They will when they meet me."

"I know who you are. That hasn't changed."

Beltur could sense she meant every word . . . but that she was more worried than she let on. "Maybe Lhadoraak . . ."

"Absolutely not," declared Jessyla. "He's a nice, sweet, caring man, but he's not strong enough to do what needs to be done. Especially not in a war with Hydlen. Even Tulya knows that."

"Has she said anything?"

"Not in words, but she doesn't have to."

Beltur stretched, very carefully . . . and very gingerly. "I'd like to take a ride this morning."

"I'll come with you."

Beltur smiled. "You're not letting me go off on my own?"

"Not any time soon. You're bruised all over. You need to recover your full strength, and I don't want you getting any ideas about riding off to see what the Hydlenese might be doing. Even if there were any around, killing a few wouldn't change anything." She paused, just for an instant. "I'm glad you're wearing your blacks, though."

"I'm glad something I'm doing meets your approval," Beltur replied with a sheepish grin. He'd chosen to wear blacks, rather than the patroller/Spidlarian blues, although Jessyla had washed them, most likely to remove blood and worse, because he certainly wasn't in shape to be a patroller, and the black-banded healer greens certainly didn't feel appropriate at the moment.

"Most of what you do meets with my approval . . . except when you do too much and almost kill yourself."

"Then we should take our ride together." He stood, and after finding his visor cap, and a carrot, he and Jessyla walked down to the small barn. When Beltur entered Slowpoke's stall, the gelding immediately nuzzled him.

"Is that for me . . . or for the carrot?" asked Beltur, scarcely hesitating to hand over the treat.

He took his time readying the gelding and trying not to wince when he lifted the saddle, although he knew Jessyla must have sensed from the adjoining stall where she readied her own horse.

Once mounted, he headed west on the side street to see if there was any real damage to the houses from which he'd effectively herded the Hydlenese. He didn't see any. Then he turned Slowpoke north toward the main street and headed west. Once he and Jessyla reached the brick posts, they turned back east. There were a handful of people outside, but none of them looked that obviously at the two riders.

Because they're preoccupied . . . angry and don't want to show it . . . reluctantly convinced we did what we could . . . Beltur had no idea, and with his still limited senses, he wasn't close enough to get a hint.

Again, outside of trampled bushes and gardens, there wasn't that much damage west of the main square. Beltur wasn't looking forward to what he was certain he was going to see east of the square. As they rode past the Brass Bowl, he saw that most of the first-floor shutters remained closed. The square was empty, except for two women filling buckets at the fountain. All that remained of the Council House and healing house was charred heaps, but the quarters building and the chandlery appeared undamaged, as was the East Inn.

Two blocks farther on, they passed the first burned dwelling. Beltur didn't remember what the house had looked like, except that the siding had been whitewashed and it had always been neatly kept. There was no sign that anyone had been near the place since it had burned.

Fifty yards later, they rode past a still-shuttered house that looked untouched, but a shed or barn on the property had been burned down. Someone had been working there, because all the charred material had been gathered into a pile and the stone and mortar foundation was being restored. Beltur didn't see the restorer.

Before that long, the two neared the east end of town.

Julli was working in the front garden, clearly trying to salvage what she could. When she saw the two riders, she gestured and then immediately hurried toward them, not quite at a run.

Glancing around and not seeing anyone else close, Beltur reined up and waited, as did Jessyla.

"I heard that you'd been wounded," said Julli. "How are you feeling?"

"Better. It was an order-chaos wound." Beltur didn't know how else to describe what happened in any other succinct fashion. "It will be a while before I'm fully recovered." *If ever.* But he wasn't about to say that, for a number of reasons, including the fact that it might not be true.

"He almost died," said Jessyla. "We're fortunate he's still here."

"Why did they want to destroy Haven? We haven't done anything."

"We rejected the Duke's offer to take over Haven," said Beltur. "The Duke doesn't like to be rebuffed. His officers won't cross him. So they attacked."

"Why would we ever want to be a part of Hydlen? The Duke is as bad as the Viscount. Some say he's worse."

"As Beltur said, the Duke's used to getting his own way," replied Jessyla.

"Is the Duchess going to send you some help?"

"We've reported the situation. We haven't heard yet," said Beltur. "By the way, thank you for earlier helping with the horses and weapons. How is Jaegyr? I saw that his workshop . . . was destroyed."

"He's working with Gorlaak to plan a better one. He's sorry he'll be late in doing those chairs for you."

"We're just glad you two are all right," Jessyla said quickly.

"Do you think the Duke's men will be back?"

"Those men won't, but the Duke may send a larger force," replied Beltur.

Julli's face fell. "We thought . . . maybe . . ."

"Duke . . . Massyngal . . ." Beltur struggled to remember the Duke's name. ". . . doesn't like to be thwarted. He also wants to take over this part of Montgren so that he can more easily conquer Lydiar."

"Oh . . . What will you do?"

"That depends on what everyone else does," said Beltur. "We'll do what we can."

"We're riding through town to see the damage," added Jessyla. "Beltur didn't have a chance earlier. Did the other gardens fare as badly as the one in front?"

"The one on the east side was partly destroyed. The ones on the west and back are mostly fine."

"We're glad to hear it." Jessyla smiled, then nodded to Beltur, and eased her horse forward.

"Until later," Beltur said pleasantly before urging Slowpoke after Jessyla.

After leaving Julli, Beltur turned south on a side street, past the burned-out ruins of both houses owned by the late trader Zankar, then past a smaller house that appeared undamaged before coming to another property where a larger barn, a shed, and the main house had all been burned. There was no sign that anyone had been near the charred heaps.

From there, Beltur turned toward the house where he'd been too late to save the consort of the woman who'd been raped by the troopers. The house was there, and the door had been repaired. Beltur saw no one. He did not slow or stop.

The two followed back streets on the south side of town, where they passed only three more burned-out dwellings, before they reached the lane that led south to Vortaan and Ennalee's holding. Beltur expected the worst there, but neither holding appeared to have suffered damage.

Based on what Lhadoraak and Gustaan had reported, Beltur and Jessyla had missed seeing several other burned-out houses, but he felt he had a better understanding of what had been damaged and what had not.

When they neared their own house, Gustaan hurried toward them.

"Sers! Ruell, Therran, and Taasn just returned with a dispatch from Captain Raelf."

"We'll be right there after we stable the horses," replied Beltur. A fraction of a quint—or even a full quint—wasn't going to make much difference, and Beltur saw no point in leaving Slowpoke out in the summer sun.

Still, he hurried through unsaddling Slowpoke and made sure the gelding had water before he left the barn and walked with Jessyla back across to the other house.

Inside were Lhadoraak, Tulya, Waerdyn, and Gustaan, as well as Taelya and the three recent arrivals. Once Beltur closed the door, he took off the visor cap, but no one looked terribly surprised.

Lhadoraak stepped forward and handed the single sheet to Beltur. "I took the liberty of opening it, since we didn't know when you two would be back."

"Thank you. That's what you should have done." Beltur quickly read the words.

Your reports regarding the unprovoked attacks on Haven and your response have been forwarded to the Duchess and Lord Korsaen.

Your ability to defend and repulse such attacks speaks highly of your resourcefulness.

We have requested additional troopers to help repulse Hydlenese assaults. We anticipate a rapid response from Vergren, but cannot say exactly what that will be or when you can expect to know. Some reinforcements from Weevett should arrive within the next few days.

Beltur handed the dispatch to Jessyla, who read it and handed it back.

"That doesn't offer much support," said Tulya, her tone of voice verging on outrage.

"What he's saying is that he's sending what he can as soon as he can," replied Lhadoraak, "but to stop the Hydlenese will take more men than he has."

"That's pretty much what the captain told us when we left," said Taasn.

Both Ruell and Therran nodded.

Almost absently, Beltur noted that Therran wore Montgren blues, if without any insignia or emblems.

"How many companies are at Weevett?" asked Beltur. "Just one?"

"Yes, ser," replied Ruell.

"Does anyone know what the message we didn't get might have said?" Beltur looked to Taasn, then Ruell.

"It was to warn you that the Hydlenese might attack wearing Lydian or Certan uniforms. According to the captain, Lord Korsaen found out something about that."

"That would have helped," said Tulya reproachfully.

"The messenger was captured and killed only a day before the attack," said Beltur. "I'm not sure that would have changed matters much. Speaking of uniforms . . . did we scavenge any Hydlenese uniforms? Besides Graalur's?"

"Maybe three or four," offered Gustaan. "Most of the rest of them . . . either . . . well . . ."

"Those killed early were stripped by townspeople, and the uniforms of those killed later were . . . rather mangled?" suggested Beltur.

"Something like that."

"The fighting between us and Hydlen could go on for a time. We might find a use for captured uniforms. If you'd keep an eye out . . ."

"Yes, ser," Gustaan and Waerdyn replied almost together.

"What about Graalur?" asked Beltur.

"His arm is better," replied Gustaan. "He's asked to stay here." The former squad leader's tone turned sardonic. "It occurred to him that he might not be exactly welcome in Hydlen."

Beltur nodded. If anyone could convey that to Graalur, it would be Gustaan.

"We were talking about setting up a more formal civic patrol," said Tulya.

Beltur could see and sense that Tulya's words surprised Lhadoraak, but he said, "We'd talked about that earlier. Are there enough men to make it workable?"

"You shouldn't be riding patrols that others could do," said Lhadoraak. "We'd talked about Gustaan acting as head patroller."

"Is that agreeable to you?" Beltur asked the former squad leader.

"Yes, ser. Dussef, Therran, and Turlow all would like to be patrollers . . . and even Graalur. With all the captured mounts and weapons, we'd have enough equipment. Except for uniforms."

"Gustaan and I have been working on that," said Jessyla. "Julli says she can do something with the captured uniforms, dyeing and bleaching them into a blue close to the Spidlarian uniforms you and Lhadoraak wear."

"You do know that there's still a chance that you'll be patrollers for a very short time?" Beltur said.

"If we're being honest, ser," Gustaan continued, "we stand a better chance of surviving as Haven patrollers no matter what happens. And a better chance if people see us as patrollers soon."

Beltur laughed softly. "You're likely right."

"But, ser," Gustaan went on, "after what we've seen, we think that it's more likely we'll prevail against Hydlen than not."

From what Beltur could tell, Gustaan actually believed what he said. While Beltur appreciated Gustaan's faith in him, what could he say when dealing with just a single battalion had almost killed him? "We might have an easier time if the Duchess sends some troopers."

"If I know Captain Raelf, he'll send everything he can," declared Waerdyn.

Which won't likely be enough, and Raelf's smart enough to know it. Beltur just said, "The captain's a good man, and I've heard he's an excellent commander. It's a good thing we've got a little time before the Duke can muster another assault."

"What about the real Lydians?" asked Jessyla.

"They've got every reason to support us," said Waerdyn, "but I've heard that they take a long time before they make the wrong decision."

Tulya winced.

Gustaan smiled sardonically.

"Let's hope they make the right decision quickly this time," said Lhadoraak cheerfully. "Now . . . how soon will we have uniforms?"

"I've already got Julli working on redoing the uniforms," said Jessyla. "They ought to be ready by oneday, if it doesn't rain."

"I can have a patrol schedule and procedures written up by then," said Gustaan, "if you can help me, Councilor Tulya."

"I can do that."

Lhadoraak cleared his throat and looked to Beltur. "We will need some coins."

"Let me know how many." Beltur paused. "Do we still have records and ledgers?"

Tulya nodded. "I thought it likely they might fire the Council House. So I brought all the ledgers and records—those we have—here for safekeeping."

Almost a glass passed before Jessyla said, "If that's all, as chief healer, I need to see that Beltur gets some rest."

"Would you like me to bring over some burhka later?" asked Tulya.

"That would be wonderful. I did bake some bread this morning. Would you like a loaf?"

"Please."

As Beltur got up to leave, Taelya hurried into the parlor from the small bedroom, hers, in fact. "Uncle Beltur! Are you feeling better?"

"Much better than a few days ago."

"That black bruise on your forehead isn't going away, is it?"

"It doesn't look that way, Taelya."

"Then everyone will know you're a black mage."

Beltur smiled. "That's certainly one way of looking at it. Thank you."

By the time Beltur got back to their house, his legs were unsteady, and he immediately sat down on the padded bench in the front room. Then he decided that he'd turn sideways and put up his legs, and just close his eyes for a moment.

It was past midafternoon when he woke, and Jessyla immediately appeared with a beaker of ale. "I'm glad you took a nap."

Beltur sat up and stretched. "I'm a little sore. That pad isn't as soft as the bed."

"I was going to suggest the bed, but you were already asleep."

Beltur took a swallow of the ale. "This tastes good."

"It's the same as always." Jessyla sat down beside him. "Your natural order/chaos level is better."

"The way you put that makes me worry."

"It's not where it should be, but there's a great improvement over yesterday."

"But?"

"I worry that the Hydlenese will show up before you're recovered."

"I've thought about that, but there's not a lot we can do about it."

"Don't try anything stupid if they come soon."

"Like using shields as blades?"

"Anything."

"At the moment, I don't feel up to anything that strenuous."

"Good." She handed him a black leather-bound book. "Why don't you read this for a little bit? I'd like to go over and help Tulya. She's feeding everyone."

Beltur took the volume—the copy of *The Wisdom of Relyn* that Naerkaal had given him just before they had left Axalt, a time that seemed far longer than just a season ago. "You think this will help?"

"Didn't Naerkaal tell you that you were a lot like Relyn?"

"Besides," replied Beltur, "reading will keep me quiet."

"There is that," she replied with a smile.

"I promise. I'll just read . . . and perhaps get myself another ale."

"Good." She rose from the bench.

Beltur took another slow swallow from the beaker, then set it down and began to read, skimming through the first part to refresh his memory, then settling into the next section, the one he hadn't really read thoroughly, he realized, but must have just leafed through, because he kept coming across passages he didn't remember reading.

One such passage struck him immediately.

There are those who say that no good can come from killing and that all killing is evil. From what I have seen, there is both a grain of truth in that saying and often a great many grains of untruth. Whether men will admit it or not, weapons and the killing they enable are tools, and how those tools are used determines how evil the death they cause might be . . . or if that death or those deaths are evil at all. Is the death of an evil man evil? While it is regrettable that an evil man must be killed, at times there is no other way to put an end to his evil. The danger lies not in the killing of those evil, but whether someone who is different is called evil in order to justify his killing. Many of the lords of Lornth called the angels evil, because they were different, possibly also because women held power among them. The angels were not evil, only different, and they did not attempt to take lands of the lords but to live in the cold heights. Yet when they killed those who tried to kill them, all Lornth was told they were evil.

In turn, when the Emperor of Light, who had also decreed that women must be chained, heard that Lornth had been weakened by the angels, he determined to conquer Lornth, as his forebears once had, although they had since lost those lands. The angels not only destroyed his armies, but caused a great cataclysm that leveled all the cities of Cyador and unleashed the Great Forest. Was it evil for the angels to slaughter an army and level a land? Or was the greater evil the attempt to seize lands that did not wish to be part of Cyador?

I must confess that I was not without evil, for as I have written, I also attempted to gain lands through conquest and killing . . .

Beltur lowered the book, thinking.

XLII

By the time he finished breakfast on sevenday, Beltur was feeling stronger, and he could sense farther, more than a kay, which reassured him somewhat.

"You're looking very serious," said Jessyla as she sat across the kitchen table from him.

"I'm doing better, but I worry whether I'm getting better fast enough."

Jessyla took a deep breath and shook her head, then said, "It takes a good two days to get from Vergren to Haven. Hydolar is something like three times as far away. That means that most likely the Duke hasn't even heard about what happened here on oneday, and there are more hills between here and Hydolar than here and Vergren. Very few of the Hydlen troopers survived. Even fewer would want to report such a disaster. Even if they did, the Duke couldn't put together an army overnight. He has to gather men, mounts, and supplies. It's likely to be at least another eightday before we see any more Hydlen troopers. It might be two eightdays, or even longer."

"I know . . . but I still worry."

"Just what are you worrying about? That you can't save Haven single-handedly again? If the Duchess doesn't send a lot of troopers, you're not going to lose your life over Haven. Is that clear?"

"After all we've done . . ." Beltur shook his head.

"I don't like walking away, either. But we're young. We can find some place . . . somewhere . . ."

"Maybe we were too impatient," said Beltur. "Maybe we should have stayed in Axalt."

"We didn't. None of us felt all that comfortable there." Jessyla stood. "You and I need to take a ride. Except for yesterday, Slowpoke hasn't been out for days. Besides, everyone needs to see that you're out and about."

Beltur looked at his consort and shook his head. "Besides, as you aren't saying, you don't want me moping around and feeling sorry for myself."

"Besides, as you say I'm not saying," replied Jessyla, "if we stay here complaining, I might get even more worried, and that won't help anything."

Beltur got up from the table. "You're right about that."

Two quints later, after dealing with all the horses, and then saddling up their mounts, Beltur and Jessyla rode toward the square under clear green-blue skies and a white sun whose heat announced that it was definitely summer. Rather than take the main street, they rode along the back streets south of the main road.

"They didn't fire any houses here," he said.

"We chased them away from this part of town, remember?"

Beltur was about to say something to the effect that they might not be able to do that a second time when a woman called out "Thank you!" from where she was beating a carpet hung on a rope between two sturdy posts.

Beltur tipped his visor cap in return.

Jessyla waved, then said to Beltur in a low voice, "More of them than you'd think want us to stay. They're just afraid we won't, and they'll be abandoned again."

"What you're saying is totally the opposite of what you said a glass ago, you know," replied Beltur in an amused tone.

"I'm a woman. I reserve the right to have two views on the same matter." After a brief pause, she asked, "Don't you? Or won't men admit it?"

Beltur laughed softly and ruefully. "You know that I do." The problem was that Haven had been neglected and ignored, but the cost of saving was already high and getting higher, and there was no certainty that they could in fact save Haven, especially without essentially destroying it. "We'll just have to see."

When the two rode into the square, Beltur was more than surprised—in fact he was shocked—to see Worrfan and his wagon set up near the fountain. So he rode closer, then waited until the tinker finished using his pedal grindstone to finish sharpening several knives for a dark-haired older woman that Beltur had seen from a distance several times, but whom he had actually never met. Once she left, he moved Slowpoke closer and reined up.

"Greetings, Mage."

"The same to you, Worrfan. I didn't realize you'd stayed here in Haven."

"I didn't. I repaired to a safe distance, offered my prayers to Kaorda, and was pleased to see that they were granted, or that you and the other mages were empowered to grant them, and then I returned."

Kaorda? The goddess/god of order and chaos? Beltur had heard of Kaordists, but he hadn't realized that there were any believers anywhere in

Candar. "I think you're the first Kaordist I've met . . . well, that I knew was a Kaordist."

Worrfan laughed. "Whether you know it or not, all you mages are practicing Kaordists. You apply both order and chaos. You believe it works, and the goddess/god makes sure that it does."

"I can't say that I ever thought of it that way," replied Beltur as tactfully as he could, not wanting to offend the tinker.

"It doesn't matter whether you think of it that way or not. Chaos and order are. They are opposites that can never be completely separated in life, only in death."

"That's indisputable," agreed Beltur cheerfully. "Are there many Kaordists in Worrak?"

"More than a few. Most are pirates. The ones who don't acknowledge their beliefs are the wealthy whose ancestors were pirates."

"So everyone is a Kaordist? It's just that some just don't know it or acknowledge it?"

"Exactly."

"How long do you plan to remain in Haven this time?" asked Jessyla.

"As long as I can." Worrfan shrugged. "Who knows? It may be a few days . . . or the rest of my life. But then, life is uncertain, and a few days could be the rest of my life."

"You're rather cheerful about it," said Beltur.

"There's no point in weeping, except in brief grief. Prolonging sadness is just self-punishment."

The tinker turned as another woman approached, this one gray-haired and lugging a heavy wicker basket.

Beltur nodded, then turned Slowpoke toward the main street.

"Mages as Kaordists?" murmured Jessyla.

"I think we've been called a great deal worse," said Beltur, "especially in Gallos and Spidlar."

"You don't really believe in a goddess/god of order and chaos, do you?"

"No, but what Worrfan believes isn't vicious or harmful. So there's not much point in getting upset about it." *Especially not at the moment.*

When they reached the main street, the two turned east. Beltur was pleased to see that the East Inn had its shutters open. Recalling what he'd promised, or what Lhadoraak had promised for him, he turned Slowpoke in toward the stables.

"Why are you—"

"Keeping a promise. I never had a chance to pay the rest of what I owed Aaskar."

Jessyla started to say something, then nodded. "A promise is a promise."

Beltur managed to keep from smiling when he reined up outside the stable. He didn't even have to ask for the stableboy, because Aaskar appeared immediately.

"Ser mage?"

"Aaskar, I believe I owe you a bit more than Mage Lhadoraak paid you on my behalf." Beltur extracted two silvers, more than was due, bent over and handed them to the stableboy. "There's some extra there because, now that the Council House has been burned, there's no way for you to report to Councilor Tulya, and there may not be for some time."

"Thank you, ser mage." Aaskar looked slightly downcast, and not all of that was pretense.

"Once matters are decided with the Hydlenese, we'll see what you might be able to do for the Council."

The boy brightened slightly.

"Thank you, again, Aaskar." Beltur nodded and urged Slowpoke back to the street.

"He's a good actor," observed Jessyla.

"He is, but I did promise, and people don't forget when you don't keep promises, even to children."

"Especially to children."

"Have I forgotten something I promised to Taelya?"

Jessyla laughed. "Not that I know of."

"Good."

The ride from the inn to the eastern edge of Haven was uneventful, but as they passed Julli, who waved from where she labored in the east garden, Beltur noticed neat stacks of bricks and stones next to where Jaegyr's shed workshop had been, an area now cleared with trenches in place for a foundation, it appeared. "I think Jaegyr's decided to rebuild his workshop in stone and brick."

"That makes sense."

Neither mentioned the fact that it only made sense if, one way or another, Haven survived the attack likely to come.

On a line in the sunshine hung quite a few uniforms that looked, to Beltur, as though they were Spidlarian blue.

"Thank you for taking care of the patroller uniforms."

"It was something I could do, and it needed to be done."

"I can still appreciate it and thank you."

The words brought a brief smile to Jessyla's face.

The gentle and circuitous ride through the town took more than two glasses, and dealing with the horses and the barn when they returned took another glass before Beltur and Jessyla walked back into their house and sat down at the kitchen table to enjoy an ale.

"We're running low on the ale," Beltur observed.

"Jaegyr is bringing kegs from the widow for both houses tomorrow."

"On an eightday?"

"He said he'd be happy to do it. Of course, I paid him a few coppers."

"You arranged for it? You didn't have to do that."

"It was one thing you didn't need to worry about. Besides, I wanted to meet her."

"And?"

"I didn't need to, but I'm glad I did. We had a very nice talk."

"Thank you for taking care of that, as well." Beltur nodded, deciding the less said, the better.

While Beltur didn't take a nap, he did spend the next few glasses resting and reading more of *The Wisdom of Relyn.* He also found himself marking several passages.

Then, around third glass he sensed and then heard a rider galloping up the street toward the houses. When he looked out, he saw that it was Ruell. He immediately stepped out and waited outside the front door.

Ruell reined up and announced, "Ser! There's half a company from Montgren coming. I thought you should know. You might have sensed them and thought they were from Hydlen. I told them to come here, but I'll head back and guide them."

"Thank you. I'll tell Lhadoraak."

"Thank you, ser." With that, Ruell turned his mount and headed back toward the main street, but this time at a walk.

Beltur turned to tell Jessyla, only to find her standing behind him.

"It's about time."

Beltur just nodded. "We should tell Lhadoraak and Tulya."

Jessyla stepped forward and shut the door behind her.

The two walked across the street, where Beltur knocked on the door.

Taelya opened it.

Beltur nodded as he sensed the separation of natural order and chaos. "You're doing well with separating order and chaos. We need to talk to your father and mother."

"We're in the kitchen, Beltur," Lhadoraak called out.

Beltur and Jessyla followed Taelya to the kitchen.

"What did Ruell tell you?" asked Tulya. "I saw him talking to you."

"He said that half a company of troopers from Montgren was on the outskirts of town. He's going to escort them here."

"I hope more than that are coming," replied Tulya tartly.

"I imagine the half company is to reassure us," said Lhadoraak. "Also, it makes sense for them to come first and arrange things, not that there's all that much to arrange."

"One other thing. Did Jessyla tell you that Jaegyr will be delivering more ale from the widow tomorrow? She arranged it."

"Excellent!" declared Lhadoraak. "We're running low."

Tulya merely smiled knowingly at Jessyla.

"Can I show you how much better I can do shields, Uncle Beltur?"

"In the front room, please, Taelya," said Tulya. "When you showed me . . . it got a little . . . tight in here."

"I didn't know you were going to walk in when I was showing Father."

"Her shields almost shoved Tulya into the stove," said Lhadoraak.

"The front room, definitely," agreed Beltur.

Beltur, Lhadoraak, and Taelya moved to the front room.

Taelya stood next to the backed padded bench. "I can put a shield around me and the bench."

"Go ahead," said Beltur.

Without hesitation Taelya built a shield as large as she'd promised.

"I'm going to poke at it with order," said Beltur, immediately doing so.

"I can feel that," replied Taelya, "but it doesn't hurt."

Beltur pressed harder, and a bit harder, then just maintained the pressure, pleasantly surprised that Taelya was holding a comparatively large shield against order pressure. "I'm going to keep pressing like this to see how long you can hold it."

"I can hold it," declared Taelya.

After half a quint, she was still holding the shield.

Beltur found himself grinning, and released the pressure. He could see and sense that Taelya was still holding the shield. "You can release it now."

"I can hold it longer."

"I can sense that, but the troopers are coming up the street now, and we have to talk to them," replied Beltur.

Taelya released the shield and took a deep breath. "I've been working hard. Father said my shield had to be strong enough to protect Mother and me."

"It's strong enough to stop blades," said Beltur. "But you might need to hold it for a half glass or longer."

"I can already hold it a quint."

Beltur looked to Lhadoraak, who nodded.

"You're better than I was when I was twice your age," Beltur admitted, then said, "I hear horses. We might as well go out and greet them."

Ruell reined up in front of the column of Montgren troopers. He looked to the squad leader beside him and gestured toward the five just outside the house. "Those are the four councilors. The taller blond mage is Lhadoraak, the darker one Beltur, and he's a healer, too. The healer is Jessyla, and she's a mage as well, and the blond woman is Tulya, and she's the justicer." The courier grinned, adding, "And the young woman there is Taelya, and she's a beginning mage."

The squad leader inclined his head. "I'm Senior Squad Leader Tallud, and I'm in charge of these two squads, at least until Undercaptain Cheld gets here tomorrow with two more squads and all the supply wagons. The captain had to wait with the last squad for the Lydian companies. For some reason the Duke of Lydiar insisted that they be escorted by a senior officer." Tallud grinned. "So the captain's now Majer Raelf. He deserved it a long time ago."

"How long will it be before the majer and the Lydians arrive?" asked Beltur. "Do you have any idea?"

"They're coming through Hrisbarg, we heard." Tallud shook his head. "That's the long way, and it doesn't make sense to me. But that means it might be close to an eightday."

Beltur was afraid he knew exactly why the Lydians were taking the long way, and that was because the shorter way might have exposed them to a Hydlenese attack, given that Hydlenese forces had already shown up east of Haven on that very road that led to Lydiar. That also suggested the quality of the Lydian companies. He smiled politely. "Let's just hope the Duke of Hydlen is having as much difficulty mustering his forces."

"Never heard of an army that moved fast, ser. The bigger it is, the slower it moves."

"There's enough space for two squads, maybe more, at the East Inn," said Beltur. "We'll have to see what else we can work out."

"The supply wagons have some tents, ser, and one's a camp kitchen . . ."

Beltur nodded as Tallud went on. Someone, likely either Raelf or Korsaen, if not both, had thought out some aspects of the campaign to come. The only question was how much thought and magery could compensate for a lack of troopers.

XLIII

Beltur woke up with a start in the darkness before dawn. Had he heard the sounds of horses? The shouts of riders? Immediately, he sat up and cast out his senses, trying to determine what had awakened him so abruptly.

Horses! Riders! Scores of them were sweeping toward Haven, coming in from the south, the east, and the west. The closest group was already past the brick posts on the west end of town.

"Jessyla! They're attacking from everywhere!" Beltur bolted from his bed, already sweating in the heat of a too-hot summer night, and yanked on trousers, tunic, and boots, then sprinted from the bedroom out through the back door and straight for the barn, hoping he could get there and get Slowpoke saddled and out on the streets before the seemingly endless stream of riders reached the house.

At least, he could protect the small area around the houses.

Somehow, mostly using his senses, he found the saddle and other tack and managed to get the big gelding saddled and out of the barn into the steamy night. He'd barely mounted when a squad of troopers carrying flaring torches and bare blades glittering in the torchlight galloped toward the house.

Beltur widened his shields into the killing blades and charged toward the oncoming riders, scything through one line of riders, then another . . . and another. He had to expand his shields to get enough room to turn Slowpoke to get clear of the mass of equine and human bodies he'd created by his first charge. Yet he had to get back closer to the house because another column was riding up the side street from the south.

He'd also lost Jessyla. There were so many troopers and mounts that he couldn't make out any one person.

Then to the south, he saw flames flaring into the sky, as if the houses fired by the night attack had been helped by oils—and by chaos, he realized, as he sensed chaos bolts slamming into houses and turning them into fiery infernos, one after the other, the chaos flames marching toward him, backlighting the masses of mounted men that thronged everywhere Beltur could see.

He urged Slowpoke forward, once again through rank after rank of troopers whose faces were lost in the gloom and all too briefly illuminated by the torches they carried—and lost—as Beltur and Slowpoke cut through them and blood flowed everywhere.

But even as he cut down a score of troopers, more replaced them, and the flames from yet more and more burning houses drew closer and closer . . . and then from somewhere in the sky, a blade, or scythe, brighter than the sun itself, swept toward Beltur, past a white tower he didn't recall that sagged like a melting candle, then burning and searing everything around him . . . and then him, so hot that he screamed—

"Beltur! Wake up! It's all right . . . It's all right!"

The brilliant burning light was gone, and Beltur was half-sitting in the bed, drenched in sweat, with Jessyla's arms tight around him.

"You're all right. It's only a nightmare."

Only a nightmare . . . "Only . . . a nightmare?" Despite the sweat that poured from him, Beltur's throat was so dry that even those few words were hard to utter.

"You were shouting and flailing, as if you were fighting."

"I was. It was awful . . . so real."

"Let's go to the kitchen. You need an ale. You can barely talk. You also need to sit up to cool off and dry out a little."

Beltur's legs were still shaking as he walked to the kitchen beside Jessyla. "It was so real . . . thousands of troopers . . . chaos and torches . . . and then it was like the sun itself burned and melted everything . . ."

"Sit down. I'll get us each an ale. You can tell me all about it after you drink a little and cool your throat. I never heard a scream like that before."

"I was being . . . burned alive . . . and the worst was that I lost you. I couldn't sense you anywhere . . . and there were so many of them . . . and chaos bolts everywhere . . ."

"Here." Jessyla handed him a beaker of ale. "Just take a swallow while I get a beaker for myself."

In fact, Beltur took several swallows, and his shudders subsided. Finally, he said, "I've never had a nightmare that real. It was like I was really there . . ." He went on to describe what he'd seen and felt, ending with, "And that fire from the sky was so real, as if everything, even stones and bricks, caught fire or instantly melted."

"Well . . . it obviously didn't," she pointed out. "I can hear the crickets chirping outside, and there's no sign of flames. I don't sense anyone on the streets. Do you?"

Beltur had been so upset, and the nightmare so real, that he hadn't even tried to sense anything beyond the house. He took another small swallow of ale and concentrated. At last, he said, "There's no one out, not for close to two kays, anyway."

"Dear . . . even the Duke of Hydlen doesn't have that many troopers, and he certainly couldn't have gotten them here by tonight."

While what Jessyla said made sense, it was hard to ignore what he'd felt. "But it was so real. I just hope . . ." He shook his head.

"You're worried, really worried about what might happen."

"Now that we have more troopers, we should post sentries or scouts farther out, even at night."

"Do you really think they'd attack at night?"

"If they thought it would work. If they know we're watching, they might not take the risk." He paused. "I can't tell you how real it all felt."

Jessyla paused, then quietly asked, "Do you think it wasn't just a dream, but a vision? Maybe not even what will happen any time soon, but like the white mage's vision of a white shining city?"

"If it was a vision of what might happen in the future, it was a mixed-up vision, because I was definitely in this house and I definitely went out to fight the Duke's troopers. But I don't know any way that someone could make the sun burn up an entire town in an instant." Beltur paused. "I do recall, just for a moment, an image of a tower melting." He shook his head.

"No . . . it has to have been a nightmare. I've been worrying about how the Hydlenese might attack, and it just got to me."

"What about the white tower melting?"

"That's probably because of what the white mage said about a white city. We're certainly not going to be building towers, especially white ones. We'll be fortunate just to keep Haven close to what it is." Beltur took a last sip from the beaker. "I'm almost ready to go back to bed. Almost."

"You don't have to hurry, dear. Just sit there and cool off some more."

Beltur took a deep breath, trying to concentrate on the quiet of the evening . . . and even the crickets.

XLIV

Most likely because of the nightmare, Beltur didn't sleep all that well for the rest of the night and woke up with both images of dying and dead troopers and questions swirling through his head.

Was it all just about power? From all reports, Duke Massyngal killed people who challenged his authority. *But didn't you make a war inevitable when you killed officers and troopers who insisted on carrying out Massyngal's orders?*

No, Beltur decided, the war was already in progress, even if he and the other councilors didn't know it. What his actions meant was that what would have been a relatively bloodless takeover of one small town by the Hydlenese had much more quickly become a bloody conflict that would kill hundreds more, if not more than that. *But wouldn't such a takeover still have led to a bloody war, just later?*

It would have led to more fighting, but likely not to as much bloodshed as would now happen. At least, that was how Beltur saw it. *Isn't it likely that any place you want to settle down and have some control over your lives will result in bloodshed? Or is that just a way of rationalizing it? Are you any different from the Duke?*

Definitely a rationalization. Except every place you've been there's been bloodshed because other people wanted to use you for their ends. And Haven wasn't an exception. *The cost is just higher.*

As for the comparison to the Duke . . . he wanted everything his way and killed anyone who disobeyed. *We just want to live without being harassed and taken unfair advantage of, and that's different.*

Different enough to stay put in Haven, for better or worse, and pay the price?

The price was already high. All the dead Hydlenese troopers, the burned houses and dead townspeople—and his nightmare was suggestive of just how much higher it might well get. *But if you leave and walk away, won't the same thing happen again?*

Only if you insist on being free.

And that was the problem, because there was a price for everything, especially freedom and control of their own lives.

He didn't even bother to sigh as he got out of bed.

"Are you all right?" asked Jessyla.

"As right as I can be under the circumstances. I'm not quite as sore. I think I can sense farther . . . and it's not raining."

"After last night . . ." she ventured.

"In some ways, last night and the last eightday have made some things much clearer."

"Clearer."

He pulled on his trousers, then laughed, harshly. "We might as well pay the price now. I don't see the costs getting any less."

"I think you're right about that." After a moment, she added, "But that means others will pay dearly as well."

"They'll have to. Otherwise, we'll just be the ones paying." He pulled on the older black tunic. "When is Jaegyr going to deliver the ale?"

"Between midmorning and noon."

"Then I'll clean the barn and deal with the horses right after we get something to eat. I don't see the next squads arriving until midafternoon, maybe later if they have a lot of wagons."

"I'll feel happier when Raelf arrives," replied Jessyla. "You'd do a better job of leading than Cheld."

"I don't know about that."

"You've been in a real war as a junior officer. He hasn't. He felt arrogant to me, and he doesn't like women."

Beltur almost asked how she knew, but choked off the question before uttering a word. She would have felt what he scarcely noticed.

Beltur had just finished a thorough cleaning of the barn, including grooming all the horses, when he saw Jaegyr's wagon approaching the house. He walked up to meet the cabinet maker.

Jaegyr's eyes widened slightly as he looked at Beltur.

"The black is what looks to be a permanent bruise as a result of the last encounter with the Hydlenese troopers." Beltur offered the words conversationally.

"Julli said you'd been bruised, but . . ." Jaegyr shook his head, then quickly added, "The widow said that she'd like back the empty keg when you have time."

"We're not quite done yet. It might be a day or so."

"I don't think she's in any hurry. It's not as though you're going anywhere."

"How do you think people feel about the Council and the Hydlenese attack?"

"Most are angry at the Duke. A few blame the Duchess for ignoring Haven for so long. Most think you mages did the best you could. Mages or not, there's only three of you, and one being as much healer as mage. Some feel better now that there are more Montgren troopers here." Jaegyr lowered the wagon tailboard and hoisted the keg. "In the kitchen?"

"That's right. Next to the kitchen cistern." Beltur led the way, opening the rear door and stepping aside as Jaegyr carried the keg in and set it beside the cistern. Jessyla watched from beside the stove.

"Julli heard about this." Jaegyr pointed to the cistern. "She said she'd like to have one."

"It makes life and cooking much easier," said Jessyla.

"This one's sort of makeshift," admitted Beltur. "Gorlaak might have told you. We had to reinforce the floor to carry the weight. The good ones are all glazed and fired clay, but no one around here has a kiln big enough for that."

"Might be worth thinking about. Well, better get the other keg over there."

"How's the foundation coming for your new shop?"

"Haven't had a chance to crush and fire the limestone to make the mortar yet."

Once Jaegyr had left, Beltur turned to Jessyla and said humorously, "Now we have enough ale for another battle."

"You can't do what you did again," said Jessyla. "It will kill you."

The cold certainty of her words chilled Beltur.

"You'll have to let the Montgren and Lydian troopers take the brunt of any attack. This is really their fight. If they'd supported Haven more, Duke Massyngal wouldn't even be thinking about starting a war over it."

"Probably not, but we wouldn't be here either, most likely."

"It's never simple, is it?"

Beltur shook his head. "Not where we're concerned. Oh . . . and that reminds me. I need to get out more silvers for Tulya to pay Bythalt for feeding the horses stabled at the inn. I'm glad she's keeping track of all that."

"So am I. It's something we don't have to do, and she's good at it."

After going to the bedroom and undoing the order locks on the metal box, Beltur extracted six golds and ten silvers, then replaced the box in its hidden and shielded recess before returning to the kitchen. "How is Tulya doing?"

"She's fine. Why do you ask?"

"You know very well. She is with child, early as it is. And you know a great deal more about that than I do."

"So far as I can tell, she's fine."

"Has she talked to you about it?"

"Not yet. I'm sure she will when she feels like it. She lost two, you know, early. That's another reason why she probably doesn't want to talk about it, especially to Lhadoraak. That's why . . ."

"You didn't want me to even hint at it."

"He likely knows, but he wouldn't want to say anything until he believes things will work out."

That, unfortunately, also made sense to Beltur. "Do you want to go over with me?"

"Of course. There might be something I could help Tulya with."

"Along with keeping me from committing myself to more than I should?"

"That has happened occasionally," Jessyla replied cheerfully.

The two walked across the street. Before they even reached the door, Taelya had it open and was announcing, "Uncle Beltur and Aunt Jessyla are here."

Lhadoraak immediately appeared. "Is something wrong?"

"No," replied Beltur. "I just realized that I needed to give Tulya more coins to pay people, and since it's actually quiet for the moment, it seemed like a good time."

"I came to see if she needed any help in fixing supper," added Jessyla.

"She's in the kitchen."

"I was showing Father how I could aim little points of chaos," declared Taelya, "while I was still holding a shield. You always hold shields when you use order and chaos, don't you, Uncle Beltur?"

"I do. It's a very good habit to get into holding shields as much as you can." Beltur looked to Lhadoraak. "I take it you encouraged her."

The older mage nodded.

"Thank you. I should have started her on that."

"You've had your hands full." Lhadoraak headed toward the kitchen.

Tulya looked up from the small side table. "What brings everyone to the kitchen? Making a shepherd's pie doesn't require a Council meeting."

"It'll be good," said Jessyla.

"I hope so," replied Tulya. "More root vegetables than meat, but there's enough, and meals have been irregular." She glanced to Beltur inquiringly.

"As I was telling Lhadoraak, I wanted to bring you some golds and silvers so you'd have enough to pay everyone. Is six golds and ten silvers enough for now, or did I lose track of something?"

"That should be enough through the end of next eightday. We're paying more for feed for the extra horses, both to Bythalt and the widow, and for the four couriers. Well, we were, but now they're billeted with the rest of the troopers."

"And missing comfortable beds, no doubt," said Lhadoraak.

"We'd just about run through what Raelf sent us, hadn't we?" asked Beltur.

"I'd have to look at the ledgers, but I'd say it was close." After a moment, Tulya asked, "What about the ale?"

"We're paying for that," replied Jessyla. "It doesn't come from the golds for the Council."

"You're sure?"

"Very sure," declared Beltur. *Ale is little enough, especially after what I've gotten us all into.* While Tulya talked, Beltur had been studying her with his senses, but from all he could determine, Tulya and her barely conceived child both seemed to be fine, and that was a definite relief, especially after what Jessyla had told him.

"Can I do anything?" asked Jessyla.

"I'm sure I can find something for you to do, after you shoo our consorts and Taelya back into the parlor to work with Taelya some more."

Lhadoraak chuckled. "We don't need to be pushed out. We're going."

The three withdrew from the kitchen and moved to the open space in front of the hearth.

"Taelya," said Beltur, "show me what you were doing just before we arrived."

She nodded and immediately created a shield around herself, then gathered chaos into a point half a yard beyond the shield, almost touching the stones of the chimney that framed the hearth.

"That's good, Taelya. Now, I'd like you to try something else. Can you use tiny bits of order to form the chaos into a point, like a triangle?"

The girl frowned.

Beltur didn't sigh. Instead he went to the firebox and picked up a split chunk of wood and set it in the middle of the hearth. "Aim the chaos the way you were at the wood. Right in the middle."

Taelya concentrated. A point of chaos flared into a brief flame, then died away, leaving a charred circle roughly two digits across.

"Now, I'm going to do the same things, with the same amount of order and chaos, except with the chaos ordered into a point." Beltur concentrated. The chaos flared into a flame, slightly larger than Taelya's, but the flame didn't die away. After a moment, it started to grow. Beltur snuffed it out with order. "Do you see the difference?"

"Yes, Uncle Beltur." The girl's tone was resigned.

"Taelya," said Lhadoraak in an edged tone of warning.

"I'm sorry, Uncle Beltur. It's harder that way."

"It works better that way. I wouldn't be asking you to do it otherwise."

Lhadoraak looked sidelong at Beltur, but said nothing as Taelya began to concentrate.

On the first attempt, Taelya's shield collapsed as she struggled with the triangular structure of ordered chaos. The second time, the triangular form of chaos sagged into a momentary bright flame before even coming close to the log on the hearth.

"Watch what I do, with your eyes and your senses," said Beltur gently. Very carefully and slowly he created a shield much like Taelya's, then formed the triangular structure and moved it to touch the log. This time, he let it burn for a while, to show Taelya that the fire created by chaos persisted long after the chaos had dispersed. Then he snuffed out the flame with order. "You try it now."

It took Taelya three more tries before she could do what Beltur had requested. By then she was sweating, and trembling when she finally released the shield.

"Excellent!" Beltur smiled broadly. "You did well."

"Father . . ."

"She needs something to eat," Beltur said.

"Tulya, Taelya's headed into the kitchen. She needs something to eat."

"I worked her hard," added Beltur.

Once Taelya had left the front room. Lhadoraak moved closer to Beltur and said in a low voice, "You're teaching her how to throw chaos bolts without her realizing it."

"With far better control than most whites ever have," replied Beltur. "She'd have that ability in any case. This way, she'll have control." *Also, if worse comes to worst, she'll have a chance at defending herself and her mother.*

Less than a glass later, Beltur was back at his house, reading more in *The Wisdom of Relyn,* while Taelya was resting, although Beltur had the feeling that Taelya had fallen asleep even before he'd left. He'd read more than twenty pages, carefully, when he sensed Jessyla approaching the house.

She opened the door, stepped inside, closed it, and walked over to the bench. "So . . . what do you think about Tulya?"

"She looks fine."

"Beltur . . . you know very well what I meant. And don't tell me that you didn't sense her."

"As far as I can tell, she and the child are healthy. I couldn't sense any non-natural chaos anywhere. There aren't any order or chaos ties or blocks."

"Good." Jessyla sat down on the other end of the bench facing him. "What about you?"

"I can almost sense as far as I could. I'm holding normal shields. They wouldn't last very long in a fight or against a strong white mage." Beltur paused, then asked, "What about the black band around my head?"

"It's more like a black skullcap, and it hasn't changed color. You can tell as well as I can that your natural order/chaos is balanced there as well as anywhere."

"You're telling me that it's not going away."

"Not so far."

"There's nothing about anything like it in Relyn's book."

"Did you think there would be?"

"No . . . but I could hope." Beltur frowned. "There's a rider headed this way. The scouts have either sighted the squads from Weevett or some troopers from Hydlen."

"Montgren."

Beltur smiled. "Do you *know* that? In the way that you sometimes do?"

"No. This time, it's a considered guess."

Considered guess or not, the scout who reported to Beltur was Taasn, and Jessyla's guess was correct. Two quints later, Undercaptain Cheld was in the front parlor of Lhadoraak's house, along with Waerdyn, while his squad leaders were on their way with the troopers—and five heavily loaded supply wagons—to the Brass Bowl and the East Inn.

"It's rather strange to be meeting in . . . a house," said Cheld, his eyes lingering on Beltur's forehead before taking in the sparse furnishings and mismatched chairs. "What happened to the Council House?"

"The Hydlenese battalion burned it before we could stop them," replied Beltur.

"I thought you were mages." Cheld's tone was not quite scornful.

"We are. We were more interested in saving townspeople and their homes, and in killing the attackers, than worrying about the Council House."

"How did you fare in saving local houses?" The question was perfunctory, almost uninterested.

Lhadoraak offered a withering look before saying, "Beltur saved quite a few dwellings. He also killed at least four hundred troopers."

"I find that difficult—"

"Begging your pardon, ser," interjected Waerdyn, "but I counted the sabres we collected from the dead. There were something like three hundred and eighty. We figure the townspeople grabbed a score before we got to them. Now, if you don't like my count, you can go over to the armory in the mage's cellar and count for yourself. They're piled head-high. And, ser, seven of them are officers' sabres."

Cheld looked hard at the senior scout.

Waerdyn looked back levelly.

"I see." Cheld's tone became much less edged. "I don't understand how they fired any houses at all if you killed so many."

"It's very simple, unfortunately," said Beltur. "There are three of us. There were five hundred of them. We're blacks. We can't throw massive chaos bolts. We had to chase down and kill each trooper one at a time. While we were doing that, they did fire eleven or twelve houses and some outbuildings." It hadn't been exactly like that, but it was essentially true to Beltur's limitations.

Cheld looked to Waerdyn.

"Yes, ser. It took the mages most of a day. It took us days to collect the gear and weapons, and burn the bodies."

"Also," added Jessyla, "none of us could do any magery for several days after."

"Considering we did destroy and rout a full battalion with three black mages and five armsmen, it wasn't too shabby a performance," added Lhadoraak.

"So far as we could determine," Beltur continued, "we killed the majer in command and most of the officers."

"That didn't count the company we drove off an eightday earlier," added Tulya. "They lost almost a score of armsmen then as well."

"Given what we did, especially to his officers, it's likely that Duke Massyngal will send a considerably larger force before that long," said Beltur. "Most likely with mages. That will require us to deal with the other mages, and for you and whatever forces arrive with Majer Raelf to deal with the Hydlenese troopers."

Cheld moistened his lips. "I can see why the Duke might not be pleased. To lose almost an entire battalion to a town supposedly undefended or defended only by black mages . . . and all the officers . . . that . . . that isn't often done. He is reputed to be rather intemperate."

"So we've heard," said Jessyla.

"That's why we requested the squad leaders of the squads already here post scouts some distance out from Haven along the possible approaches to the town," said Beltur, knowing full well that he'd more than "requested" such postings.

"I'm sure you can see," added Jessyla, firmly but pleasantly, "why we decided that spending any effort to save the Council House wasn't a high priority."

"Ah . . . I can see that. I'm certain that Majer Raelf will also. Is there anything else I should know?"

"I assume that the majer briefed you about the Hydlenese who attacked wearing Lydian uniforms."

"There was a report about that."

"We can show you the uniforms, all rather new, and all with Hydlenese sabres," said Beltur.

"That won't be necessary. The Lydian majer might wish to see them when he arrives, though."

Lhadoraak smiled pleasantly. "We shouldn't keep you longer, Undercaptain. I imagine you'll have a great deal to do."

"But you might remind your men that the local women have suffered enough already," said Jessyla, "and if they suffer from Montgren troopers, they won't be pleased, and neither will we. Remember, we're black mages, and we can tell who lies and who doesn't."

Cheld managed not to swallow. "I will definitely make certain that word is passed. Now . . . if there's nothing more."

"Thank you for coming, Undercaptain," said Tulya pleasantly. "We do appreciate it. You understand, I trust, that the last several eightdays have been trying here in Haven."

"I can see that. We will do our best." He smiled, if not entirely happily, then turned and made his way out. Waerdyn turned, just before leaving, and nodded.

Once the door was closed, Lhadoraak said, "Do you think we were too hard on him? He's only an undercaptain."

"He needed to hear it," replied Tulya. "Waerdyn definitely thought so."

"The older rankers, like Waerdyn," said Beltur, "usually know more than undercaptains. That's why I listened, especially to the older squad leaders."

"That's another reason why you're still alive," said Lhadoraak. "What do we do now?"

"Prepare, as best we can," said Beltur, "and watch . . . and wait."

XLV

Oneday dawned cloudy, and by seventh glass, the rain was falling steadily. Since there was no thunder or lightning, Beltur didn't have a headache, although the rain did keep him from sensing more than about a kay.

"This rain is definitely going to slow down Raelf," observed Beltur, standing in the kitchen, debating what he should do for the day.

"If the Duke sends white mages, the rain will slow his army just as much, maybe more," replied Jessyla.

"It might slow his army, but not because his white mages are impaired by the rain. The Duke doesn't seem to care much for anyone except himself."

"I've never understood how unpleasant and unpopular rulers hang on to power."

"Some don't," Beltur pointed out. "But the smart ones make sure that those close to them will suffer even more if something happens to the ruler. That's one reason why some of the nastiest deeds are delegated to subordinates. That way, if something happens to the ruler, something bad is likely to happen to those subordinates. That gives them an incentive to support the ruler, or least support him while they're scheming to replace him. And those subordinates repeat the process with those beholden to them."

"You're talking about Gallos, aren't you?"

"That's what I saw there, but Cohndar was starting to do the same thing in Elparta."

"Don't you think some of that was Waensyn's doing?"

"Certainly. He also did the unpleasant tasks to ingratiate himself with Cohndar."

"What do you think will happen now in Elparta?"

Beltur shrugged. "I couldn't say. If Osarus stands up to Caradyn, things might get better. If not, they'll get worse. I hope Osarus does, because if he doesn't it won't be good for Meldryn."

"That wouldn't be good for anyone." After a long pause, Jessyla asked, "Do you think Mother will have my letter by now?"

"There's no telling for certain, but I'd think so. It's been three eight-days, and it is summer. That's when there are more traders traveling."

"I just hope she and Auntie are all right."

"Even if it gets nasty for Meldryn, mages usually leave healers alone."

"Unless a healer has a mind of her own," Jessyla pointed out.

"I know where you got it from," Beltur replied. "Your mother does have a mind of her own, even if she's not quite so quick to decide as you are."

"I might not have decided any differently from her if I'd been in her boots." Jessyla shook her head. "She'd love to hear me say that. But I do miss her. A lot. I don't say it much, but she was always there for me."

"I miss my father . . . and my uncle," Beltur admitted. "They both cared for me. They never said much, but they did. Uncle . . ." He shook his head, realizing his eyes were burning. "Sometimes . . . we don't realize . . . until it's too late. He was stern . . . but he was never cruel."

"He loved you in his own way. He had to."

Beltur swallowed, then nodded.

"You don't mention your mother much. Is that because you were so young when she died?"

"I don't know why I don't remember much about her."

"You've never said much about her, besides her having long blond hair and singing to you. Can you tell me any more about her?"

"Her hair was silver-blond. That's how I remember it. Her voice was beautiful. At least, it sounded that way to me, and she always looked at me when she sang. She sang to me even when I wasn't a baby."

"Why do you think that?"

"I remember fragments of songs. There was one about catching a falling fire and holding it to the skies, and another about horses that spoke in the darks."

"In the dark, you mean?"

"No, she sang about 'the darks.' That might be why I remember it."

"Do you remember more than a phrase from any of those songs?"

"There's one. She must have sung it often."

"Tell me the words. You don't have to sing it."

"I don't know . . . it sounds . . . strange. I'm not sure I remember it correctly."

"Beltur," said Jessyla gently . . . but firmly.

"The words . . . the ones I remember, they went like this . . .

"Oh, my dear, my dear little child,
What can we do in a place so wild,
Where the sky is so green and so deep,
And who will rock you to sleep . . .
When your mother's not here to sing
And neither the bells nor the words will ring?
But when the stars shine over the western sky
Try to remember we all say goodbye . . ."

Beltur stopped. "That's all . . . That's all I recall."

"It almost sounds as if . . ."

"As if she knew she wouldn't see me grow up," Beltur finished.

"You come from a family of mages . . . and some of them . . . they can see . . ."

"You think she was like Ryba or Ayrlyn?"

"Do you know anything about her parents?"

"No. Uncle Kaerylt said that they died young, and it was better that way. He never would say more."

"And you didn't ask more?"

"When Uncle said he wouldn't say more, he never did. I asked twice. The second time, he told me not to ask again. I think he must have promised my mother he wouldn't say anything. They were very close."

"That's so sad. You don't remember any more?"

"Once she said that some of the songs had been written for a lutar."

"I've never seen a lutar."

"Neither have I. I wouldn't know what it looked like."

A silence fell across the kitchen.

Finally, Jessyla spoke. "There's always been something . . . different . . . about you. It had to have come from your mother. You don't know anything more about her . . . where she came from, where her parents came from?"

Beltur shook his head. "I've never said much because I never knew much. Because my father was an orphan child of two strangers no one in Fenard knew, I had no family to speak of, especially after he died."

"You have me now." She smiled and took his hand.

"I do . . . and I'm very glad." *More than I can possibly tell you.*

XLVI

The rains continued, on and off, through all of oneday and most of twoday. Even so, Julli delivered the patroller uniforms late on twoday, and Lhadoraak took them over to the quarters building, along with four sabres, since Graalur wasn't totally recovered, although he'd asked Lhadoraak to be considered as a patroller.

Threeday dawned clear and sunny, and when Beltur went down to the barn to deal with the horses and cleaning up the stalls, even at sixth glass he could tell that the day was going to be hot and damp, most likely hotter and damper than he'd ever seen, given that while Gallos got very hot, it was generally dry, and while Spidlar and Axalt were often damp, they weren't as hot as Montgren had proved to be—and it was still well before midsummer.

Since neither he nor Lhadoraak had seen Cheld by seventh glass, Beltur walked over to Lhadoraak's and knocked on the door. When the older mage opened it, Beltur said, "We need to see what Cheld is doing. We ought to saddle up and ride to the inn, just in case."

"Just the two of us?"

"For now. After that," Beltur added, "we can see how Gustaan and the others are doing."

"I told those not patrolling the square to stay close to the quarters, except for breakfast."

"Good idea."

In little more than a quint, the two mages were riding along the main street toward the East Inn.

They didn't have far to look for Cheld. He was in the public room of the East Inn, seated around the large circular table with his squad leaders. Beltur didn't recognize any of the squad leaders. He also didn't see Waerdyn or any of the troopers with whom he and Lhadoraak had worked.

"Mages . . . how good of you to come," said Cheld in a tone more perfunctory than welcoming.

"We thought we should see how you're settled in," replied Beltur, "and whether your men have discovered any signs of Hydlenese troopers."

"The scouts haven't seen any signs, none at all," said Cheld. "Isn't it possible that the Duke doesn't think Haven is worth the trouble?"

"That's always possible," said Lhadoraak amiably, "but it's a bit early to tell that. The battle that destroyed the Hydlenese battalion happened just ten days ago. It would take any survivors a good five days to get to Hydolar, and that would be without rain. Even if they ran into other troopers, after what happened, they'd likely hold off on mounting an attack until hearing from the Duke or whoever is the commander."

"The Duke has a marshal in command of his armies," said Cheld.

"Even if the marshal wanted to attack as soon as possible and left Hydolar the next day after a report, it's unlikely that an army could reach Haven much before next oneday."

"That's likely why Majer Raelf isn't pushing to arrive any sooner," said Beltur. "I'd think he wouldn't want his main force worn down by travel. Did he give you specific orders about dealing with the Hydlenese?"

Cheld looked as though he didn't want to answer before finally speaking. "He said to avoid any pitched battles, if at all possible, and to make our presence visible at a distance."

"To give the impression of greater strength," replied Beltur. "The majer struck us all as a very perceptive officer."

"He is that. Is there anything else?"

"Just one thing . . . at the moment." Beltur paused. "We would appreciate learning at the earliest possible time if you do detect any Hydlenese presence. That way, we will be able to determine the best ways to use magery in support of your forces." Beltur smiled pleasantly.

"You can be sure that you will know almost as soon as I do."

"Thank you, Undercaptain. We do appreciate you and your men being here." Beltur inclined his head.

Lhadoraak did as well.

"Then we will keep you informed, Mages." Cheld barely nodded.

After they left the public room and walked to the stable where they had left their mounts, Lhadoraak looked to Beltur. "I think I'll be much happier when Raelf arrives . . . or I would be, were it not for the fact that the Duke's army will likely arrive soon after that."

"I have to say that I'd expected a bit more . . . something," Beltur finished, not really sure what words would describe his expectations.

"He's still rather skeptical."

"I don't think he's fought in anything really bloody," suggested Beltur. "Either that, or he's never worked with war mages. I wasn't about to ask whether he had, though."

Lhadoraak stopped at the hitching rail where the horses were tied. "What should we do now . . . besides wait?"

"We need to think about ways to use what we can do to the advantage of the Montgren and Lydian forces in ways that tariff us as little as possible."

"That's an excellent idea, but, at the moment, I'm not sure I can think of any. Can you give me an example?"

Beltur almost frowned, but realized that, even in the battles for Elparta, Lhadoraak had basically been deployed to protect senior commanders. "How large a concealment can you create?"

"I don't know. I've never tried a large one."

"Do you remember when I threw a concealment over the brigands who were chasing us? What happened?"

Lhadoraak nodded slowly. "They couldn't see."

"What if we concealed the elements of a charge? Wouldn't that disrupt matters? Both for the commander and for the troopers who couldn't see?"

"That might help."

"We could also conceal a company somewhere on the enemy's flank so that they could mount a rear attack after the Hydlenese advanced."

"You'd have to brief Raelf on what his men would see, or not be able to see, and how to take advantage of it."

"We'll have to brief *him* on anything we might do. Why don't you think about possibilities? Ask Tulya. She might have a good idea, and I'll ask Jessyla." Beltur untied Slowpoke. "I'll ride over to the quarters building with you."

As the two rode across the square, Beltur saw that Turlow was now in a patroller uniform, standing near the fountain, while Dussef was also in uniform and posted to the west, in front of the chandlery. Worrfan was already set up with his wagon and grindstone, as was Ennalee with her cart and produce. He also saw the brass-trimmed wagon of the spice merchant, whose name he struggled to remember. Then he belatedly realized that, as a threeday, it was market day, which was why Jessyla had earlier told him that she'd be going to the square.

He shook his head. Clearly, his thoughts had been elsewhere.

"Beltur!"

At the woman's voice, Beltur turned in the saddle to see Julli leading a horse and cart. "You managed to save some from your gardens?"

"More than I'd hoped. Will your consort be here later?"

"She said she would be. I don't know when."

"Tulya will definitely be here," said Lhadoraak. "I imagine they'll come together. They usually do."

Beltur grinned and said to Julli, "That's about the best we can do."

She smiled back. "I'll save some things for them."

"Thank you."

"She's a good woman," said Lhadoraak after they had ridden several yards. "They've made our lives much easier. I'm glad you were able to save her and Jaegyr."

"So am I, but I couldn't have done it if they hadn't reinforced their house." Beltur couldn't help thinking about the houses that had burned, and those who had been killed, but he also knew that, because so many had left Haven over the years, the number of deaths had been lower than would have otherwise been the case. *So far.*

When he dismounted outside the quarters building, Beltur sensed as far as he could, but the only riders he could detect were clearly the sentries posted by Cheld.

Gustaan and Therran—and Graalur—were all in the main-floor common room of the quarters building when Lhadoraak and Beltur entered. Even from the doorway, Beltur could sense that Graalur's arm was well on the way to healing. Graalur was wearing nondescript grays, rather than the Hydlen-green uniform in which he'd been captured, or the blue patroller uniform, possibly because he wanted to save it for when he was on duty.

"What did you do with your green uniform, Graalur?"

"Ser?"

"I was hoping you didn't destroy it."

"Ser," interjected Gustaan, "we've stored a number of Lydian and Hydlenese uniforms in the armory under your house next to the captured weapons."

Beltur smiled. "Excellent. There's always the possibility that we might need them. I hope not, but you never can tell." Beltur wasn't about to say that he thought the likelihood was almost a certainty, one way or another. "Turlow and Dussef look good in their uniforms. The square's actually getting to look like a real market square."

"That's because it is," said Lhadoraak. "Now all we have to do is fight off the Hydlenese to keep it that way. So far, the Montgren troopers are behaving themselves."

"I've told the patrollers," said Gustaan, "not to get into fights with the troopers, just to ask them if they want to deal with the mages who are the town councilors. I figured that might work better."

Lhadoraak nodded. So did Beltur.

"You've dealt with officers from Hydlen," began Beltur. "How long do you think it will be before the Duke's forces show up?"

"It'd just be a guess, ser."

"Your guess will likely be more accurate than either of our most considered judgments," returned Lhadoraak cheerfully.

"I'd be very surprised if it wouldn't be at least another eightday. The road here from Hydolar's not bad, but it's narrow. That will slow down a large force, and if the Duke sends a force, it will be a large one."

"Do you think he'll ignore Haven?" asked Beltur skeptically.

"No, ser. From everything I overheard, he doesn't like being denied at all. That's another reason why he won't rush. He'll want to make certain he sends a force strong enough to crush us."

Beltur looked to Therran. "What do you think?"

"We lost half the men in the squad because of a stupid officer, but they sent us to Haven with a crazy mage. They'll attack, just to prove they're right."

Even before Beltur could look at Graalur, the former captive said, "They'll try to kill everyone so that there's no one left alive to tell what really happened."

"You'll have to beat them thoroughly, sers," said Gustaan. "Otherwise, they'll send another army."

Beltur had the feeling that the Duke might anyway, even if he lost an entire army, although Beltur hadn't the faintest idea how he, Lhadoraak, Jessyla, and perhaps a battalion of Montgren and Lydian troopers would be able to accomplish something like that. "We'll do the best we can."

"Are your patrollers splitting the day?" Lhadoraak asked Gustaan.

"Yes, ser. Therran and me'll relieve Dussef and Turlow at noon."

"Good."

"We'll let you know if we find out anything more," added Beltur.

"Thank you, sers."

Once he and Lhadoraak were outside again, Beltur turned to the older mage. "I'm going to talk to the spice merchant. After that, I think I'll pay Phaelgren a visit. Maybe you could stop in and say a few words to Bythalt?"

Lhadoraak's smile was amused. "I can do that, especially if you're going to take on Phaelgren. What do you think you'll get from him?"

"Nothing. I just want to remind him that I haven't forgotten about him."

"Do you think he needs reminding?"

"His kind always does."

Rather than ride Slowpoke the comparatively short distance to the spice wagon, Beltur just untied the gelding and led him. As he walked, he kept thinking, and finally dredged up the merchant's name from somewhere in the recesses of his mind.

The trader spoke first. "Greetings, Mage."

"The same to you, Trader Maunsel. I didn't expect to see you again so soon."

"I can't say I expected to see you quite so soon again, either. You're in mage blacks today."

Beltur gestured toward Dussef, the nearer of the patrollers. "I don't have to be a patroller as well as a councilor. At least, not often."

Maunsel looked hard at Beltur. "That black band across your forehead . . . ?"

"It's the result of the last battle with a Hydlenese battalion."

"Is it true that you mages killed almost an entire battalion?"

"It cost us thirteen houses and those in them, and another score, from what we could tell."

"The Duke won't take kindly to that, you know?"

"He might not," replied Beltur. "Is that part of the reason you're here? Heading to Vergren or Lydiar?"

"Some of my regular clients in Hydolar said that the Duke was upset over how you treated traders from Hydlen. Any truth to that?"

"We turned away a trader who threatened an innkeeper and tried to burn down the inn. A Hydlenese captain insisted we allow him to cross Montgren on his own terms. We said he'd have to pay for what he did. The captain wasn't happy. So they started attacking steads. We put a stop to the raids. Also to the captain and his squad leaders." Beltur shrugged. "So the Duke sent a battalion demanding that we turn over Haven to Hydlen. We pointed out that a town council couldn't do that. They tried to kill me and attacked the town. We did what was necessary."

Maunsel shook his head. "How do you think you can possibly win? How does the Duchess believe she can stop Duke Massyngal?"

Since Beltur didn't have an answer, at least, not a good one, he asked, "What did you hear about what the Duke might do?"

"No specifics. Several said that they didn't want to be anywhere around Haven this summer, not when the Duke was that angry." Maunsel paused, then added, "That was before he found out about what happened to that battalion. I can't imagine what he feels now."

"And that's why you headed to where there's going to be a battle, if not a war?"

"The last place a merchant wants to be is in the middle of a war, especially one that involves angry rulers and mages. I told everyone I was headed to Certis . . . I don't know as they believed me . . . but I wasn't about to tell them where I was headed. They might have tried to seize everything and claimed I was trading with the Duke's enemies. I had to take the north river road for more than a day, and then some miserable side roads to get on the old road to Haven."

"You're headed to Lydiar, then?"

"Where else? If it looks like Massyngal is going to conquer Lydiar, I'll take a ship, either to Nordla or Austra. If Lydiar falls and Montgren's under the Duke's fat thumb, I'll soon starve, anyway." Maunsel offered a falsely cheerful smile. "But I can offer some good prices on rare spices, since I'll be needing silvers more than spices."

"My consort will be here later. I'm sure she'll be interested." Beltur inclined his head. "Thank you for the information."

"I doubt it will help you much. I do wish you the best, though."

Beltur readjusted his visor cap, then eased Slowpoke away from the wagon and mounted, guiding the gelding toward the main street and then east to the Brass Bowl.

After he dismounted outside the front entrance to the inn, he patted Slowpoke. "I really don't want to do this, big fellow." Then he tied the gelding to the hitching post, strengthening the reins with order, before turning and entering the building.

He'd barely set one boot on the worn wooden flooring inside the door before a young man scurried away. Beltur kept walking toward the empty table desk on the far side of the empty foyer. He hadn't quite reached it when the thin-faced Phaelgren stepped out of the narrow hallway presumably leading to the public room and other chambers.

"What might you want, Mage?" The innkeeper's hazel-yellow eyes did not quite meet Beltur's.

"I thought I'd stop and see how you were doing."

"We're surviving, no thanks to you. Your stubbornness will turn Haven into a charred pile of rubble."

"You seem rather certain of that," replied Beltur mildly.

"Haven't you made a good start? First, two houses burned, then a half score more. The next time, the Duke's men will likely burn everything."

"Perhaps, except that there are more troopers coming, not only from Montgren, but also from Lydiar."

"So . . . in order for you to rule one small town, you're going to plunge three lands into a bloody war? Congratulations, Mage." Sardonic scorn dripped from Phaelgren's every word.

"That would have happened in any event," returned Beltur evenly. "The odds just might be a bit better this way."

"I beg to differ, Mage. The Duke will bring not only troopers but mages. The carnage will be mighty, and you will change nothing."

"How do you know that?"

"Because all you have done thus far is to get people killed and buildings burned. You will doubtless get even more people killed and more buildings burned. It will change nothing. Now . . . if you will excuse me . . ."

"Of course." Beltur inclined his head, then turned and left the inn.

Once outside, he paused, realizing that Phaelgren had seemingly not even noticed the black band across Beltur's forehead. *Because he's so into his own concerns, or because he already knew?*

Then again, Beltur had to admit that there was a certain truth to what the innkeeper had said, no matter how despicable Beltur thought Phaelgren happened to be.

So what can you do to make sure all the killing does in fact change things?

Beltur had to admit that he had no real idea. *Only hope that you can come up with something.*

In the meantime, he needed to ride out west and see where they might be able to place forces in spots from where they could position archers to reduce the numbers of the attackers.

XLVII

Fourday dawned even warmer than threeday. By seventh glass, Beltur had ridden past the Brass Bowl, with all of its windows unshuttered, which Beltur found most interesting, and possibly informative, although Phaelgren might be relying on the same sort of calculation as Beltur himself was, and had tied Slowpoke outside the stables at the East Inn.

Aaskar appeared immediately. "Ser?"

"I don't have any tasks for you today. Is Bythalt in the inn or somewhere else?"

The boy's face fell. "He's inside, ser."

Despite his being able to sense that the boy's disappointment was largely feigned, Beltur still felt slightly guilty, but not guilty enough to part with any coins. "Thank you. I did say it would be a while, Aaskar." He smiled sympathetically, then turned and entered the inn, making his way toward the small study off the entry foyer. As he passed the archway to the public room, he could see it was empty, except for Claerk and several servers who were cleaning the tables.

Bythalt turned and stood when Beltur reached the study door. "Ser mage, what can I do for you?"

"I just thought I should spend a few moments with you. You know what's likely to happen, don't you?"

"The Duke of Hydlen will attack, and if you and the troopers from Montgren and those possibly from Lydiar do not defeat them, we will all likely perish." Bythalt's voice was even more gloomy than usual.

"That's a fair assessment."

"Why did you mages ever come here?"

"Because we were offered a place to make better, and because the Duchess did not know that Duke Massyngal had decided to seize Haven and the lands around it."

"Did not know, or neglected to tell you?"

"Did not know," replied Beltur. "Any of us could have sensed if she had been lying."

"So . . . we are caught between the ignorance of a Duchess and the greed of a Duke, and all that can save us is if three mages and a little girl who is barely a mage can hold off and destroy a mighty army?"

"Three mages and possibly a battalion of troopers."

"Do the troopers even matter?"

"Very much so," replied Beltur. "Rather than our having to fight hand-to-hand, we can help the troopers be much more effective. That was how the Spidlarians defeated a much larger army of the Prefect of Gallos."

"And you can do this?"

Beltur laughed ironically. "That is our intent, but how battles come out depends on what happens in the field. No outcome is absolutely foreordained." *Although any sensible individual would wager on the Duke's forces.* "I notice that the spice merchant is no longer in Haven. Do you know when he left?"

"Merchant Maunsel left just before dawn, barely early enough to see the road. He asked for and paid for an early breakfast, even before the troopers ate."

"Did he say anything?"

"He only said that all of us were fools to remain in Haven."

"Nothing more?" Beltur looked hard at the innkeeper.

"He did say . . ."

Beltur waited.

". . . that if by some improbable magery you mages did win it would change Candar beyond recognition. He thought it unlikely, but would not say it was impossible."

"That sounds rather excessive. We're only looking for a place where we can't be ordered around."

"Mage . . . if rulers cannot order four mages around, that will change everything. Even I, humble innkeeper that I am, can see that."

"I still suspect that he was excessive in his assessment of what we could do."

"I must hope that he was correct," replied Bythalt sourly. "Being alive in a changed world is to be preferred over being dead in an unchanged world."

"I would agree with you," said Beltur with a smile, "but there are those who would die rather than accept change." *And I very much suspect much of Hydlen feels that way . . . especially the Duke.*

"The more fools they." Bythalt shook his head. "With life, there's always hope. Might be faint, but it's possible." After a pause, he asked, "Anything else you need to know?"

"How are the troopers treating your people?"

"They're behaving themselves." Bythalt grinned, if momentarily. "Might be because Claerk told a few of them about what you did to that bravo who wanted to force himself on the girls. The undercaptain asked me if it was true. I told him it was. Also told him what happened to the other one who tried to force himself on Julli—except I didn't use her name. He thanked me. Didn't seem pleased, more like he'd have to deal with it."

"So long as he does."

"He will." After another pause, the innkeeper added, "Things like that . . . maybe some changes in the world wouldn't be so bad."

"We'll have to see. Thank you."

Bythalt nodded brusquely, almost as if he'd regretted saying too much.

"We'll try to let you know what's happening. I don't expect anything for at least a few more days."

"That's what the undercaptain said, too."

"Until later."

Bythalt nodded again, and Beltur eased out of the study, and headed back toward the stable and the post to which he'd tied Slowpoke.

Two troopers stood by the pump outside the stable. Both avoided looking at Beltur as he untied the gelding and then mounted, but he could hear their murmurs.

". . . he's the one . . ."

". . . one what?"

". . . killed four hundred greenies by himself . . . hand-to-hand . . . him and that horse . . ."

". . . think the horse is maged?"

Beltur turned and smiled. "He's not, but he's very strong . . . and very determined."

Then he turned Slowpoke and rode out of the stable yard toward and then onto the main street, heading east. Even when he reached the eastern end of town, he couldn't sense any riders except those who had to be sentries posted by Cheld. On the way back, he saw that Jaegyr looked to be close to finishing the stone foundation for his new workshop. There were piles of stone and bricks, most of which were likely scavenged, seeming ready to be used. *If we can hold off* . . .

He shook his head. Holding off wouldn't be sufficient. That would just lead to another battle. The problem was that he still didn't have a good plan for dealing with what was certain to be an overwhelming number of greencoat troopers. Not to mention mages.

With a wry smile, he kept riding west, although he doubted that he'd sense anything there, either. *Not yet.*

He wanted to take a better and closer look at the low hills that bordered the road from Hydolar on the east, just a kay or so from where that road joined the east-west road from Haven that eventually led to Certis and then to Jellico. The farther from Haven that the Montgren forces could first engage the Duke's forces, the better. Besides which, most of Haven was flat and afforded few heights from which to loose shafts downward and to force an attacker to come uphill.

XLVIII

Fiveday was hotter than fourday, and sixday still warmer, but Beltur spent most of both days scouting for possible points of ambush. Two offered particular possibilities, depending on how the Hydlenese decided to attack Haven. One was the back road some two kays south of Vortaan's stead study, along the kay-long stretch between the rugged hills on the south side of the road and the forest with the thick undergrowth on the north side. The other was the long hilly ridge bordering the road from Hydolar that he'd earlier scouted.

A lesser possibility was the half-forested hill to the northwest of the junction of the road from Weevett with the east-west road west of the defaced kaystone. There were other possibilities, but those seemed the best to Beltur.

By noon on sevenday, he and Lhadoraak rode back toward the East Inn after doing more study of the terrain between the west end of Haven and the junction with the Weevett road.

"Do you think you could conceal a full company on the east side of that hill by the Weevett road?" Beltur asked.

"That shouldn't be too hard." Lhadoraak paused. "You're trying to put me where I only have to conceal and protect, aren't you?"

"That's what you do best, isn't it?"

"I'd say that wasn't really an answer," replied Lhadoraak wryly.

"The answer is that if we each don't do what we do best, we may not be able to defeat the Hydlenese."

"We may not even if we do."

"That's true, but we have a better chance. Also, the fewer troopers we lose, the better our chances. That means the more you can protect . . ."

"Beltur . . . I understand. I also understand that you understand what I can do and what I can't. I appreciate that."

"I'm sorry. I didn't mean to be condescending or anything like that."

"No. You were trying not to hurt my feelings. I just can't . . . kill the way you can. I know it takes a toll on you, but you can do it. I can't."

"I know," replied Beltur, "but protecting troopers is also vital. I want you to understand that I know that."

Lhadoraak laughed warmly. "We're clear on that. Now . . . what do you think that courier we saw heading into Haven is going to tell Cheld?"

"Something that Cheld won't tell us unless we ask. Which we will."

When Lhadoraak and Beltur reined up their mounts outside the stables of the East Inn, Beltur couldn't really tell how much hotter the day was than sixday had been, only that it was. He also knew that for the past days he'd been sweating almost from sunrise to well past sunset, and that his ale consumption was more than it should have been.

"Do you think Cheld will actually tell us?" asked Lhadoraak as the two entered the inn, only slightly cooler than the stable yard.

"If we press. He won't like it, though. Otherwise, he'll tell us when he feels like it, and we should know as soon as he does. I don't think the undercaptain really understands that the more we know, and the sooner we know it, the better his chances for surviving are." Beltur's smile was almost amused. "We need to make certain the good undercaptain understands that and a few other things."

"He won't like that."

"He probably won't."

"Beltur . . ."

"It's one thing to be surprised by our enemies. It's another to be surprised by those supposedly on our side."

Beltur could sense Lhadoraak's discomfort, but he felt he had to go on his instincts in the matter. Besides, Cheld reminded him all too much of Zandyr. *And while Cheld might be as arrogant . . . he likely isn't as stupid.* Beltur could certainly hope so.

As Beltur had suspected, Cheld was at the circular table in the public room, with three of the four squad leaders. None of them looked anywhere near the two mages who appeared in the archway.

"What was the news?" asked Beltur.

Cheld looked up from the table, an expression between annoyance and resignation on his face. He did not speak immediately.

Beltur just fixed his eyes on the undercaptain and waited.

"It was a dispatch from Majer Raelf."

"It might be useful for us to know what the majer had to say."

"It's a military dispatch."

"I'm sure it is," replied Beltur, walking toward the table. "And what it deals with affects not only you and your men, but the town. I assume the Duchess and the majer are expecting that we will lend our efforts to the defense of Haven. Is that not so?"

"What does that have to . . ." Cheld broke off his words. "You're not suggesting that you're just going to leave . . . after all you've done to create this mess?"

"Demons, no," replied Beltur, stopping short of the table. "But first, we didn't create it. The neglect by the Duchess and her predecessors did. We were brought in to repair that neglect. Second, no one knew, or bothered to tell us, that we would be facing an attempt at an armed takeover of part of Montgren by Hydlen. Third, no one informed us that the Duke of Hydlen apparently turns into a hog-headed madman whenever he's thwarted. Under those circumstances, I trust you understand why we might be a little concerned about not being immediately informed." Beltur smiled pleasantly. "Especially since we've been putting our lives on the line for the last three eightdays." He thought that was correct. He hadn't actually counted, and it was close enough.

"Ah . . . I can see . . ."

"So what did the majer, Lord Korsaen, or the Duchess have to say?" asked Beltur pleasantly, smiling after he spoke.

"You won't tell anyone else?"

"Only the other two councilors. They've also put their lives on the line."

Cheld took a deep breath, then picked up the sheet before him and handed it to Beltur. "It might be best if you read it yourselves."

Beltur took the sheet and began to read. After the honorifics and cautions, the basic information and instructions were succinct.

> Majer Raelf will arrive in Haven on oneday, with the last squad from the Weevett garrison, along with two other companies, one from Woolsey, under the command of Captain Reynaard, and one from Northfeld, under the command of Captain Knutwyl. In addition, three companies of heavy mounted troopers from Lydiar, under the command of Lydian Majer Rojak, will accompany this force.
>
> Majer Raelf is the overall commander, but until his arrival, take all possible steps to avoid provoking an all-out attack by the Hydlenese, should they arrive prior to Majer Raelf.
>
> In addition, bear in mind that, in the interim and throughout all evolutions, considerable deference must be employed in coordinating with the mage-councilors of Haven, in consideration of the fact that the overall success of the mission will likely depend on their ability to significantly reduce the effectiveness of the Hydlenese forces.

Below the flowery closing that ended the dispatch, the signature and seal were those of Raelf.

For a moment, Beltur wondered at that, but then decided that either Raelf had wanted it impersonal, or that the impersonal style was a military custom. He had no idea which might be the case, because the dispatch was the first Montgren dispatch—in fact, the first military dispatch of any sort—that he'd actually seen.

He did manage not to smile. Clearly, Raelf had some concerns about Cheld as well. He handed the sheet to Lhadoraak and said to the undercaptain, "It's a perceptive dispatch, and I can assure you that we have no interest in provoking the Hydlenese, at least not until Majer Raelf arrives and we have all consulted on what he believes to be the best strategy and tactics to use against the Hydlenese."

Lhadoraak nodded and returned the sheet to Cheld. "I take it that your sentries have not yet seen any sign of Hydlenese forces?"

"Not so far."

"Have you ever worked with Lydian forces before?" asked Beltur.

"I asked the majer that, and he told me that it hasn't been done at any time since he's been an officer. Possibly not ever. I'd judge that the Lydians are worried."

They should be, but sending just three companies suggests they're not worried nearly enough.

"From what Lord Korsaen said," said Lhadoraak, "I gained the impression that your troopers are considered . . . more capable than those of Lydiar."

"More capable than those of Hydlen as well."

Left unsaid was the fact that capability only went so far if an enemy had vastly greater numbers.

Beltur inclined his head to Cheld. "Thank you very much for your openness. We are working on ways to conceal your men so that they can attack from more advantageous positions. Specific tactics will depend on how the Hydlenese deploy their troopers and what the majer and you think will be the most effective use of your men."

"You can conceal large groups?"

"For a limited time, yes. It also depends on whether they have mages, and what kind."

Cheld frowned.

"Black mages can usually see through concealments." That wasn't precisely true, Beltur knew, but the reality was more complex. "White mages seldom can discern concealments at any distance, but so far as we know, in recent years, only Elparta has used black mages in battle."

"In recent years?"

"Nylan and Saryn of the black blades were both black war mages. There hasn't been a black mage that effective in hundreds of years," replied Beltur.

"Beltur is a bit modest," said Lhadoraak. "He's likely almost as effective as Saryn was, but besides him, there haven't been any others. The rest of us blacks, with the possible exception of Jessyla, are restricted to protecting and concealing."

"The healer . . . she can kill with magery?"

"She can," Beltur admitted. "But only one trooper at a time." *So far.*

"Should you learn anything that bears on the possible battle to come," said Lhadoraak smoothly, "we would appreciate your letting us know immediately."

"And thank you for sharing the dispatch," added Beltur. "We do appreciate it. We won't take any more of your time at present."

"I will certainly make sure you know anything of import, Mages."

Beltur was debating whether to challenge that when Lhadoraak spoke. "We appreciate that. Good day, Undercaptain."

Beltur just nodded before he and Lhadoraak turned and walked back toward the stable.

They'd covered a few yards before the older mage said, "He wants to feel in control, and arguing with him will gain nothing."

"You sound like Meldryn," replied Beltur, thinking of the older mage who, with his partner, had taken him in when he'd arrived in Elparta with nowhere to stay. "He has good sense about people. I still worry about him."

"Well . . . if we do the impossible, you can always invite him here," replied Lhadoraak.

"First, we have to do that."

"You'll manage."

"Aren't you the optimist."

"There's no point in being anything else now," replied Lhadoraak.

And that . . . Beltur realized as he stepped back outside into the steaming and sweltering heat . . . was absolutely true.

XLIX

Despite the heat, Beltur and Jessyla did sleep slightly later on eightday. After breakfast, he turned to her and said, "We need to take a ride."

"I can't. Well . . . not until after eighth glass. Vartella is coming, and I need to look at the burn on her arm."

"She's the one . . ."

"Who barely escaped the fire in her cot that was set by the Hydlenese," Jessyla said.

Left unsaid was the fact that the woman had been raped and left for dead.

Another victim of our limited abilities to deal with large numbers of troopers. Yet Beltur still hadn't been able to figure out what else he could have done any sooner than he had. No matter what he learned about magery, it seemed as though the more he learned, the more there was to learn. *And whatever you do is never enough.* But then, perhaps what anyone could do was never enough—except that thought could rationalize failure.

"Why do we need to take a ride?" asked Jessyla.

"So that I can show you the places I've scouted out, tell you what I think might work, and see what you think. You need to know all that because we're likely going to need to be in different places at the same time."

"What about Lhadoraak? Doesn't he need to know?"

"I've shown him some of the places, those where he's likely to be most useful. That's what we did yesterday."

"The ones where he only has to conceal and protect?" asked Jessyla.

Beltur nodded.

"Does he know that?"

"He does. I think he's relieved that I'm not asking him to use magery to kill people, directly, that is."

"That's an odd way to put it."

"We both know that if he protects troopers, there are more of them left to kill Hydlenese. I don't see much difference between enabling killing and killing."

"You didn't tell him that, did you?"

"No, I didn't. We need him too much. Is it that wrong to let him deceive himself?"

"He's not deceiving himself. He'd prefer being able to kill people who threaten Tulya and Taelya. He just *can't* do it. So he'll do what he can."

With Jessyla's words, Beltur felt almost petty. He said nothing for several moments. "You're right. That makes him braver—"

"Stop frigging comparing!" snapped Jessyla. "You're both brave. You both will do all you can to protect Haven and those you care for. What you can do is different. We're all different. Leave it at that."

Beltur felt even worse. "I didn't mean . . ."

"I can feel that . . . but how do you think Lhadoraak feels? He knows that all he can do likely won't be enough to protect Tulya and his children. Think about that."

Thinking about that didn't make Beltur feel any better.

"And no, there's nothing you can do about it. Neither the world, nor chance, nor order and chaos are fair. You had the unfairness to lose your entire family and the fortune to have the raw talent to become a supremely talented mage, but you worked at it. I had the fortune to meet you, because I'd never have found anyone who cared enough for me and who could teach me to be a mage—and I had to leave my mother to keep you . . . and now we're in a position that could kill both of us. Poor Lhadoraak did nothing wrong. You saved his daughter, and she became a white mage, and they threw him and his whole family out of Spidlar. They say there's a balance, but I don't see it. I see lumps of fortune and misfortune thrown out as if by chance, and we're left to sort it all out the best we can."

"There is a balance there," replied Beltur. "Every time you get something good, you pay more for it."

"That's not balance. It's the world taking revenge for the fact that you got some fortune."

At that moment, Beltur sensed Vartella coming to the front door, and he turned to Jessyla. "I'm going to saddle the horses so that we can leave as soon as you're finished with Vartella."

"You don't have to hide in the barn. You aren't the one who attacked her, and you couldn't have done any more than you did. Just come back up when you're finished."

Beltur understood that her words weren't exactly a request. "I'll do that." He nodded, turned, and left the house by the kitchen door.

While he didn't dawdle in readying the horses, he didn't exactly rush. Even so, when he walked back to the house he could tell that Vartella was still there, but that the two appeared to be in the kitchen. So he entered by the front door, only to see that the two were walking toward him from the kitchen.

"Vartella," said Jessyla warmly, "this is my consort, Beltur."

"You're the one who killed all the Hydlenese hogs, aren't you?" Vartella's brown hair was short, well above shoulder length, only because she'd likely needed to cut it that much to remove the singed and fire-damaged longer locks. There were still faint traces of yellow across her cheekbones from the bruising she'd taken, and a new dressing covered most of her forearm.

"Many of them," Beltur admitted. "I'm sorry we couldn't stop all the Hydlenese soon enough."

She looked at Beltur, taking in his face. "You at least tried. For all your trying, your wounds will always be visible. Mine will not."

"I understand, I think," Beltur said. "In that respect, I'm sorry."

She just looked at him, almost incredulously.

"People will understand, looking at me. They'll never know what you've gone through, looking at you. That's good in some ways, not in others."

"What do you know?"

"I don't know what you went through. I do know that I couldn't save the man who earlier saved me, hard as I tried."

"How hard was that?" Vartella's voice was edged.

"Hard enough that I didn't know whether he'd live for days," replied Jessyla.

"Then you might have the smallest idea, Mage." With that, she stepped past Beltur and kept walking, to the front door and outside, closing the door surprisingly gently behind her.

Beltur looked to Jessyla. "I probably shouldn't have said anything."

"Sometimes there's no good answer, dear."

"What should I have said?"

"Perhaps just that you wished it could have been different."

Beltur nodded. That might have been better. After a moment, he asked, "Are you ready to go riding?"

"I am."

After securing the house, the two walked down to the barn, where they led their horses outside and mounted.

"Where are we headed first?" asked Jessyla.

"I thought we'd ride to the square and then south past Vortaan and Ennalee's stead to the road the raiders took." Beltur eased Slowpoke onto the street and then north.

Jessyla frowned as she joined him. "You think they'll come that way?"

"I think some of them will have to. That is, if they bring as many troopers as I think they will. The west road is too narrow, and if they bring several battalions they'll be strung out in a column more than a kay long. If we blocked the road, a single company could tie up their entire force and they'd take heavy casualties even without magery. Their commander has to know that. So they'll most likely attack in several places, not only to reduce their casualties but also to spread us out. They can get to that south road without coming that close to Haven."

"Unlike the back road to the north that runs from the Weevett road to somewhere east of Haven?"

"I tracked that down. It meets a side lane a half kay east of town."

"That's three ways. Are there more?"

"If they want to cross the rocky uneven grasslands west of the forest that's south of Vortaan's place, that would make four. Those are the most obvious." Beltur turned Slowpoke east on the main street.

"They were scouting even before we got here," Jessyla pointed out.

"That's true. But we likely killed most, if not all, of the officers who gathered that information. Even if we didn't, I suspect the commander of the next force is likely to do his own scouting."

"Then they won't attack immediately?"

"I'd be very surprised if they did, but that's always possible. So we'll have to be ready for that as well."

"What about shields?" asked Jessyla. "I think I might need to use shields the way you did."

"Can you just extend a thin part of your shields, close to chest-high?"

"I've practiced that."

"You shouldn't extend the edged shields more than a yard on each side."

"Yours were twice that."

"I'm a little stronger, and Slowpoke is a lot stronger than your mount. Also, even skirmishes with the Duke's forces may be longer."

"Longer than what you did before?"

"Possibly. That's why we'll both need to be more careful . . ." As they rode closer to the Brass Bowl, Beltur broke off his words and studied the inn, but it didn't look any different, and there wasn't a single sign of troopers. Obviously, Cheld had crammed all his men into the East Inn.

The main square was largely empty except for a girl filling a jug at the fountain and the front of the quarters building where two men in patroller uniforms stood talking—Therran and Dussef, Beltur thought, although he and Jessyla weren't close enough for him to be certain.

"I take it you don't want me to try what you did?" asked Jessyla.

"Not unless you don't have any other way to survive," replied Beltur, adding quickly, "That goes for me, too. I almost didn't make it after dealing with a few hundred troopers. I can't see the Duke sending less than several thousand."

"You have something else in mind, don't you?"

"I have many things in mind. Most of them won't be possible, but I'll keep them in mind just in case."

"Stop being so evasive, dear."

While Jessyla's voice was pleasant, Beltur could tell she was irritated.

"Look . . . I can redirect lightning a bit, but I can't create it. That means I might be able to do something if we have a storm, but we don't get many storms. If they have white mages who throw chaos bolts, I can probably throw some of them back—but only until they realize what I'm doing."

"Why would that—"

"Each chaos bolt could take out a score of men if not more, but I can't concentrate chaos like that. So if they stop throwing chaos bolts, they stop losing men. That means they'll lose some men to our blades, but not as many as to redirected chaos. Since we're outnumbered, they can afford to lose a lot more troopers than we can." As they left the square, Beltur's eyes focused on the charred cottage some fifty yards ahead, a structure that he didn't recall seeing before. *But then, you haven't traveled every single lane in Haven since the Hydlenese attack.*

"Will they see that?" asked Jessyla.

"I'd think so, but since they've not likely fought against black mages, they may not."

"Wouldn't they be more likely to think you're just a white throwing your own chaos bolts?"

"I can certainly hope so, but we can't count on it."

"Is there anything else you've been keeping hidden?" Her voice was wry.

"You know about using shields to slow a mounted charge. That might work at times. Other than that, at the moment, I can't think of anything else with questionable possibilities." After several moments, he asked, "Have you thought of any other possible uses of magery that would be to our advantage?"

"I know it sounds stupid," she said slowly, "but white mages throw chaos bolts. Why couldn't blacks throw order bolts . . . or spheres?"

Beltur thought about that for several moments, recalling how he'd first tried to throw chaos bolts. Finally, he said, "First, it would take much more effort. When a white throws a chaos bolt, part of the force propelling the chaos is the chaos itself. The chaos in the bolt is compacted, but some chaos at the back escapes and that pushes the bolt forward. Order doesn't provide that kind of force. The best I could ever do was to form a catapult out of order. It didn't ever work very well."

"You thought about throwing order?"

Beltur shook his head. "This was when I was in Analeria, just after we first met. Since I had trouble throwing chaos using chaos, I tried using order. It worked a little better than using chaos, but not all that well."

"You never mentioned that."

"I didn't think about it, until you asked about throwing order."

"Why not?"

"Well . . . because it didn't work. Using white mages' chaos against them worked much better."

"What was the other reason, besides taking more effort?"

"It wouldn't have that much effect on anyone besides the white, and I can get the same impact on the white either by linking order to a chaos bolt or using an order containment, without nearly as much effort."

Jessyla frowned. "In a way, you're doing the same thing."

"Pretty much. I guess what I should have said was that you had the right idea, but that there's an easier way to do it—except I hadn't thought it out that way."

"How do you throw chaos back?"

"Put a containment around it and push it back."

"But . . . how do you push?"

Beltur paused. "I don't know how to explain it. I sense where the white is and think about the containment being there. I made a lot of mistakes at first in Elparta."

"I might not try that . . . unless I have to." She gestured. "I can see Frydika walking toward Ennalee's place."

"I don't think she's terribly fond of me."

"She's looking for someone to blame. You couldn't have gotten there fast enough to save Samwyth, anyway."

By the time the two reached the lane leading up to Ennalee's stead house,

Frydika had already stepped inside. She'd never looked back, and that was fine with Beltur.

As they neared the point where the road from the steads ended just short of the rocky and rugged hills, Beltur did his best to sense whether there were any riders nearby, but all he could discern were large mountain cats and a few deer and smaller animals in the forest. He reined up just short of the narrow road that ran roughly parallel to the hills and studied the dirt and clay. The only tracks were those of a horse and cart, and they looked to be several days old.

"There's been no one riding here in a while," said Jessyla.

"That's good. Now all we have to do is to see whether there's a place farther west that would give us a good ambush—and whether there's an easy way to get there."

Jessyla looked at the uneven and rocky slopes dubiously. "The hills aren't that high, but they're uneven."

Beltur studied the hills more intently. They were more like the edge of an ancient and eroded mesa, rising almost vertically perhaps fifteen yards to a roughly flat top. The base of the escarpment rose from the gentle slope that extended down some thirty yards to edge of the path-like road, an uneven slope composed of reddish sandy soil. "No, they're not that high, not compared to Axalt, anyway. We'll keep riding and see if there's any place that looks better."

As they headed east, Beltur kept looking at the escarpment. While he saw what looked to be a narrow footpath, perhaps half a kay before they reached that stretch of the road that seemed squeezed between the forest and the hills, the footpath was steep and barely wide enough for a single person. He also kept studying the road, but the only tracks remained those of the single cart.

Once they reached the narrowest point between the forest and the low mesa, Beltur reined up and studied the terrain once more. There was less than forty yards between the trees and the base of the hills.

"This is awfully narrow," said Jessyla. "Do you really think they'll chance it?"

"If they have several thousand troopers, it's more than worth the risk to try to send a company or two, possibly even a battalion through here. Once they're past here, there's no easy way for us to stop them."

He pointed. "Behind that outcrop up there. That would be perfect for an ambush. We could also put archers in the trees . . . except that I don't see any way that a mounted squad could get up there, let alone get down quickly."

"What about archers on foot," asked Jessyla, "along that narrow path we saw?"

"That would be anything but quick."

"It doesn't have to be quick for them to get up there, not if we know they're coming this way."

"That's true," agreed Beltur. "We'll need to see if there's a path or way up on top on this side, though."

"I'd wager there's not. There are more people on the east side of the forest."

Beltur laughed. "You just might be right. Let's go see."

From what either of them could see, there didn't seem to be any path up to the top of the mesa. There were places where rock climbing might be possible, but it would have been tortuous and dangerous. After scouting that out, rather than retrace their route, Beltur and Jessyla only went back to the rocky grasslands he'd crossed before, then rode north until they reached the old lane leading into Haven, taking that only partway to a side street that ran due north into the main street.

Three quints later, they were riding west past the junction with the Weevett road toward the junction with the Hydolar road. Again, there were few tracks on the east-west road, and no recent prints at all on the Hydolar road, suggesting to Beltur that the Duke's army was still likely on its way to Haven.

The hills on the east side of the Hydolar road were much lower than those south of Haven, rising at the most only fifteen yards or so above the road bed, and were largely grass-covered, offering little cover.

"We could hide troopers behind them, but anyone on top would be visible, unless they were under a concealment," Jessyla pointed out.

"What if we kept the troopers farther away and waited until the bulk of the Hydlenese passed, then attacked their rear?"

"Wouldn't they just turn and encircle us?"

"A big army can't turn that quickly. I was thinking of just using a company, inflicting as many casualties as possible, and withdrawing across those fields to the lane where the first Hydlenese posted their scouts."

"Do you think you could move fast enough?"

"I don't know. That's something we'd have to discuss with Raelf. But let's ride that way, to see if it's even practical."

The fields were more uneven than they looked, but the lane was where Beltur had remembered it. Still, he had his doubts about how practical the idea was. But it couldn't hurt to talk it over with Raelf.

It was three quints before fourth glass by the time they dismounted at the barn.

"I'm glad you took me," said Jessyla. "I have a much better idea where things are and how to get there."

"If you come up with any ideas, I'd like to hear them."

"Let me think about them later. We need to do the horses and wash up. We're having dinner at Tulya's, remember?"

Beltur vaguely remembered that, but he only nodded. "I can do the horses while you're washing up."

"Thank you."

"Oh . . . after we eat, we should work with Tulya and Lhadoraak to draw up a map showing the area around Haven, with the possible approaches and potential places for attacks. Tulya's got a good hand."

"I was wondering about that. When you tell people, they tend to forget."

Especially officers like Cheld. Beltur knew he should have thought of the map sooner. *But better late than never.*

He took the reins to her mount. "You go get washed up."

"Don't be too long." She smiled.

L

Cheld had scouts out early on oneday, including those positioned on the low hills east of the Hydolar road, but even by midday, there were no reports on any troopers—or travelers—coming from the direction of Hydolar, or from Certis. By second glass, the scout watching the Weevett road reported that Raelf's forces were on the way, and a messenger conveyed that to the four councilors, who were at Lhadoraak and Tulya's house.

Once the messenger left, Lhadoraak was the first to speak. "We should meet with Raelf immediately. All of us."

"Do we send word that we'll meet with him at the East Inn upon his arrival, since the Hydlenese burned down the Council House?" asked Beltur.

Lhadoraak nodded. "That would be best."

"Which patroller?" Tulya looked to her consort.

"Therran. He's the youngest, and he also has a blue uniform. It should be a written invitation," added Lhadoraak.

"Not an invitation," suggested Beltur. "Just a statement that, since it would be in the interest of all parties to exchange information as soon as possible, we will be awaiting him at the East Inn."

"I'll write it," announced Tulya. "You two get a mount and Therran ready."

Beltur knew exactly which two she meant. "I'll get the horses ready."

"I'll walk to the quarters," said Lhadoraak, "but we'll need mounts for later."

"I'll have them ready," replied Beltur.

In less than two quints, Therran was on his way.

Little more than a quint after that, Beltur sensed the arriving force close to two kays west of Haven. All five, including Taelya, mounted up and rode to the East Inn, where they tied their horses and made their way to the public room.

Cheld was already there, and a momentary frown crossed his forehead as he saw the five enter. "The majers haven't arrived yet."

"We know," replied Beltur. "They'll be here in less than a quint. We thought an immediate meeting would be useful."

"Oh?"

"It's likely that it won't be that long before the Hydlenese arrive."

"What makes you think that?"

"There have been no travelers on the Hydolar road for almost an eightday. That suggests that traders and others know that there's going to be some sort of conflict very soon—"

"Everyone in Hydolar knows that by now," declared Cheld.

"But traders like to make silvers, and, like the spice merchant, they'll move ahead of the armies. Since we haven't seen any traders at all, that suggests it's too dangerous for traders, and the only way that could be is if the army is already moving toward Haven," returned Beltur.

"You're counting a great deal on traders," said Cheld sardonically.

"Only on their greed," interjected Lhadoraak, his tone bitingly sarcastic. "It's a better indication of how they'll act than honor . . . or even promises to those who've saved them."

"Yet you come from Spidlar."

"Who else would know better?" said Tulya.

Cheld looked askance at her, as if she had no part in the conversation.

"I think I hear riders outside," offered Beltur. "We can continue once the majers arrive."

Cheld immediately rose.

"I'll come with you," Beltur said quickly, not wanting to let Cheld out of his sight.

Cheld headed for the front entry to the inn, but Beltur stayed right beside him, and the two were outside just as the first riders neared the inn.

"I thought you said you heard riders?" Cheld's tone was accusing.

"I sensed them. I've gotten into the habit of saying I've heard what I've sensed because some people don't believe me." While that was partly true, Beltur hadn't wanted Cheld to say something about Tulya that couldn't have helped matters. But then, Beltur was beginning to feel that nothing was going to be that helpful with the undercaptain. *You could be wrong.* He hoped he was, but he wasn't that optimistic. He turned to greet Raelf.

"Cheld! Mage!" offered the dusty and balding majer as he reined up. "Are the others here as well?"

"The other three councilors are waiting in the public room," replied Beltur.

"Excellent. I'll get Majer Rojak, and we'll join all of you and Cheld shortly."

"We're glad you're here, and we'll be waiting," said Beltur, managing not to smile at Raelf's indirect order to the undercaptain not to accompany him.

"Yes, ser," replied Cheld.

"Shall we go?" said Beltur.

Cheld just nodded.

Once back in the public room, Beltur announced, "Majer Raelf and Lydian Majer Rojak will be joining us shortly."

The six seated themselves around the circular table. They waited for almost half a quint, but even Taelya remained quiet. Beltur couldn't help but recall that Raelf hadn't shown any surprise at Beltur's black forehead. Had Therran told him? Or was Raelf that schooled and polite? Or both?

Then Raelf and another officer entered the public room.

Since Cheld immediately rose to his feet, so did the five others.

"Councilors, this is Majer Rojak, in command of the three Lydian companies that have joined our forces." Raelf gestured to the tall blond officer in Lydian maroon. "Majer, these are the councilors of Haven, except for the young woman, who is a beginning white mage. The taller mage is Lhadoraak; the other mage is Beltur, who is also a healer; and the healer is his consort, Jessyla, and she is also a mage. The last councilor is Tulya, who is the town justicer, and also Lhadoraak's consort."

That statement definitely impressed Beltur because it meant Raelf had made considerable inquiries, especially since the statement about Tulya wasn't something that had been determined until after the four had come to Haven.

On the other hand, Majer Rojak looked anything but impressed, although he did frown slightly as his eyes settled momentarily on Beltur, and his smile was polite, but little more. Beltur doubted that Rojak was more than ten years older than Beltur himself, and he couldn't but wonder whether Rojak had been promoted to majer just for the assignment.

"You had some matters to discuss, I believe," Raelf said.

"We do," said Beltur, gesturing to the table, and then pulling another chair from an adjoining table.

Once everyone was seated, Beltur turned to Raelf, seated on his left, with Rojak on Raelf's other side. "You read the dispatches we sent to Weevett, I take it. Has Majer Rojak been briefed on those attacks, including the one by Hydlenese troopers wearing Lydian uniforms?"

"I've read all of the reports." Rojak's tone was almost bored. "I have to admit that I'm slightly puzzled as to why these supposed Hydlenese troopers have been attacking a small town that is close to nothing of great import and offers no particular resources or riches. And then, the report that a full battalion attacked and that with no real forces, you managed to kill hundreds . . . that seems rather . . . odd."

Lhadoraak, surprisingly to Beltur, immediately spoke up. "Majer . . . given your obvious doubts, I think you should see the sabres we took from the slain Hydlenese . . ."

"What would a few sabres show?"

"There are more than a few. More like four hundred."

"Four hundred . . . isn't that a bit far-fetched?"

"Since it appears far-fetched to you," said Lhadoraak evenly, "that would indicate a certain skepticism. That skepticism might carry over into your view of other matters. That's why it might be best to put matters of doubt to rest immediately. So there won't be any claims of . . . misunderstanding."

"I think we should take the suggestion," said Raelf cheerfully.

"Since the Hydlenese burned the Council House, we had to put them in our root cellar," said Beltur.

Majer Rojak frowned.

"It's a short ride," said Jessyla, "and it might just settle your mind about what we tell you."

"I'll call your bluff," declared Rojak.

Raelf couldn't quite hide the momentary wince that crossed his face. He quickly managed a smile. "Remember, Rojak, black mages don't bluff."

Rojak stood. "I have my doubts, Majer."

Raelf shrugged. "Then by all means we should see the sabres." When Rojak headed for the archway from the public room, he murmured to Lhadoraak, "He might as well find out now."

Just over a quint later, the eight, including Cheld and Taelya, filed down into the root cellar under Beltur and Jessyla's dwelling.

Lhadoraak pointed. "There they are."

Rojak just looked at the rows of neatly stacked sabres. Then he actually began to count one stack.

"There are three hundred and sixty-three here," said Lhadoraak. "We think the townspeople kept quite a few. We counted over four hundred bodies. We burned them, of course."

"But . . . if you could do this . . ." The Lydian majer shook his head.

"The battle against one battalion almost killed Jessyla and Beltur," said Tulya from the back of the group. "They'll send an army next."

"Most likely with mages," added Jessyla.

"But why . . . Haven's not . . . I beg your pardon, but it's not the most prosperous of towns. To lose an entire battalion, and then risk losing even more . . ."

"We thought the same thing," said Lhadoraak, "until we realized that it's not about Haven. It's about who controls the road that leads to Lydiar."

"You honestly think . . . ?"

"What else can we think?" asked Beltur. "You just pointed out that

Haven doesn't have enough of worth to merit losing a full company, let alone a battalion."

Rojak shook his head. "Commander Heissyl . . . he said that was a possibility, but a distant one. That's why . . ."

"He only sent three companies?" asked Lhadoraak.

"Then, too," said Raelf, in a musing tone that he didn't feel, Beltur could tell, "it might be that Commander Heissyl couldn't believe that the most honorable Duke Massyngal would actually break his word and try to take over this part of Montgren."

"The commander didn't mention that," replied Rojak.

"I'm sure that was just an oversight," said Raelf ironically.

Rojak frowned.

"If Haven falls to Massyngal," replied Raelf, "he'll control the road and access to Lydiar itself. He could muster an army here and march directly there." The majer shrugged. "Of course, if we lose Haven, then Montgren would have no further reason to take on Hydlen. But, I'm sure someone in Lydiar must have thought of that. I can't imagine why that wasn't discussed with you. The dispatch from the Duchess to Duke Halacut pointed that out."

Rojak tried not to swallow.

"There is one other matter," said Jessyla coolly, turning to Rojak. "Black mages don't lie. Ever. They may be mistaken, and at times they may not tell everything they know, but they never intentionally lie. I don't know how you got to be a majer without learning that, but it's something you need to keep in mind."

Beltur could sense immediate anger from the younger majer.

"Who are you—"

Rojak's words were choked off by the shields Jessyla had slapped around him.

"I'm also a black mage who could kill you in a few instants. We demonnear died protecting the road to your duchy, and you come in here as an arrogant bastard who knows nothing about the military situation or about mages and presumes to tell *us* what happens to be going on?" She held the shields until Rojak started to turn blue before releasing them.

"I'll take my men—"

"That would be most unwise," said Raelf. "If you do not support us, I am empowered to negotiate a safe passage for all Hydlenese forces through

Montgren to Lydiar, provided, of course, that Haven is spared. Do you really want to be responsible for that?"

Rojak stared. "You wouldn't."

"I most certainly would. And don't bother to threaten anyone. Three mages destroyed a battalion, without any troop support. I have three companies here . . . and the mages."

Beltur managed not to show surprise at Raelf's absolute firmness. Just why did he seem so in control? He couldn't have wanted a fight with a supposed ally.

Raelf smiled. "What will it be, Rojak?"

The Lydian majer looked from face to face, then swallowed. "Perhaps . . . I was hasty. Of course I'll support you."

Raelf offered an inquiring look to Lhadoraak.

The older mage nodded, then said pleasantly, "One other thing. Black mages can tell when you're being deceptive. Like now. What did you plan to do? Agree . . . and then ride off as soon as you could manage it?"

Rojak opened his mouth, then shut it.

"It gets a little hard to talk your way out of something when someone can tell if you're lying, doesn't it?" asked Tulya.

Rojak looked to Raelf, then said, "This is totally unacceptable. Totally."

Raelf smiled sadly. "You're absolutely right, Rojak. Absolutely. Your attitude and behavior are totally unacceptable." He turned to Cheld. "Undercaptain, I'd appreciate your gathering all the company officers, both from Montgren and from Lydiar, and bringing them here for a meeting. Majer Rojak will remain here with me and the mages."

Rojak looked to Raelf. "You can't do this."

"I haven't done anything. Not yet. Neither have you. We have a problem. Both our lands are threatened. We obviously disagree about what needs to be done. So a conference of all the officers is definitely in order." Raelf gestured to Cheld. "Go ahead."

Cheld hurried up the narrow steps and into the kitchen, as if glad to escape the confrontation between superiors.

Rojak glared at the Montgren majer. "I'm the senior officer of the Lydian force."

"Even your duke placed you under my command," replied Raelf. "Now, I think we should repair upstairs, but leave the cellar door open. Healer-Mage, if you'd go first, and then make certain that Majer Rojak, who will be next, continues to enjoy our company while the rest of us follow."

Jessyla smiled pleasantly. "I can do that."

Once Jessyla and Rojak were up the steps, Lhadoraak turned to Raelf and asked, his voice barely above a murmur, "Might I ask how you're going to get the Lydian company officers to follow you?"

Raelf offered a tired smile, then replied quietly, "I already have. I was once a Lydian undercaptain. I worked with two of the three captains. I've been quietly talking with all three of them on and off ever since they arrived in Weevett. I delayed our departure for two days to obtain additional supplies . . . and to talk to them."

For Beltur, that explained more than a few matters, but he immediately asked, "What do you want us to do at this officers' conference?"

"Just answer questions."

"I have just one more question. Where is Captain Karch?"

"He remains in Montgren, with an understrength company to provide some protection for the Duchess. He delayed taking his stipend to take that duty. He's not so well as he appears, nor as young."

Beltur nodded, recalling what Jessyla had observed.

"We'll need to bring over more chairs," said Tulya.

Raelf nodded, then gestured for Lhadoraak to take the steps. "If you would, please." When everyone was standing in the parlor, Rojak turned to Raelf. "Once this is over, I'll have your head. I will."

"No, you won't. Either the Hydlenese will, or we will have defeated them, and you can return in glory to Lydiar. You really wouldn't want to cause trouble between Lydiar and Montgren. That's the last thing Duke Halacut would want from you. You know that better than anyone . . . don't you?"

Rojak offered a crooked smile. "You don't have any sense of loyalty at all, Raelf. Your so-called loyalty only serves your ambition."

"If that belief comforts you, then hold fast to it."

"Without loyalty, nothing holds together," declared the Lydian majer.

"We agree on that."

"Tulya and I are going to get more chairs," declared Jessyla, looking to Beltur.

"I'll watch things here."

Once the two women and Taelya left, Raelf said to Beltur, "I understand that you were able to take out most of the Hydlenese officers. Was that by coincidence or by plan?"

"By plan. From what I'd learned, the Hydlenese punish troopers and even officers severely for failing to obey orders blindly and instantly. I thought removing officers and squad leaders would disarray them. It did to some extent, enough that it allowed us to pick off the scattered squads over time. That would have been more difficult otherwise."

"Could you do that again?"

"If I had a squad to support me, it might be possible. It would depend on where the senior officers were."

"That's . . . dishonorable," said Rojak. "What if all armies fought like that?"

"There might be a bit more reluctance to attack other lands," replied Beltur dryly. "And younger sons from wealthy families might not be quite so eager to become junior officers."

"What do you know—"

"Former Undercaptain Beltur has fought in more battles than you'll likely ever see," interrupted Raelf. "He's killed more men than most companies ever will, and he's likely seen more broken bodies than either of us, both as a mage and as a healer. You really don't think that the Duchess put these three mages here on a whim, do you?"

Again, Beltur had to admire Korsaen. Clearly, the lord had made sure Raelf knew everything. But that also raised other, much more disturbing questions, such as whether Korsaen and the Duchess had anticipated what had come to pass. The fact that Raelf had brought the bulk of Montgren's forces, as well as the fact that Raelf was the particular officer chosen to command them, suggested a long-thought-out strategy. *But why hadn't she sent all her forces?*

Rojak's almost stunned reaction to Raelf's questions reinforced Beltur's concerns that he and the other councilors were just plaques to be played in an elaborate and high-stakes game. Fleetingly, he thought of the gambler whose hands he'd mostly healed, who had asked Beltur if he'd ever gambled for something of great value. Beltur smiled. *You only thought the stakes were high.*

"What are you smiling at?" asked Rojak.

"The gambles people choose to take . . . or not take," replied Beltur.

Again . . . Rojak looked as though he might say something, but decided against it. Abruptly, he moved to the settee and seated himself.

Within half a quint there were eight chairs and a stool arranged beside and behind the settee, not enough for everyone who would be there, but all that they had.

"That will do," said Raelf. "You councilors and I will be standing anyway, and the young woman should take the stool but be beside you." He gestured to Tulya.

In another half quint, the six captains, Rojak, and Cheld were seated, and Raelf stood before the empty hearth facing them. To his left were the councilors and Taelya.

"Captains," began Raelf, "I'd like to introduce you to the councilors of Haven and you to them. As some of you may know, three of the four councilors are mages, and two of those mages are also healers. Two of them also fought as mage-officers in Elparta against the Gallosians . . ." Raelf went on with an even more detailed introduction than the one he'd given earlier, including the results of the skirmishes already fought over and around Haven. Then he began naming the officers. "From Lydiar, we have Captain Naajuk, who successfully destroyed a pirate enclave set in the cliffs northeast of Renklaar, using unconventional tactics. Captain Deminaar, who has successfully turned brigands into useful soldiers, albeit with means not always endorsed by his superiors . . ."

At that, Beltur saw that Rojak's mouth opened, then quickly shut.

". . . and Captain Zekkarat, who escaped from an Analerian slaver as a boy, stowed away on a Lydian merchanter, survived the docks of Lydiar until he could join the Lydian guard, and then worked his long way up to captain over more than twenty years." Raelf was far more perfunctory in introducing the two Montgren captains, Reynaard and Knutwyl, just mentioning their names and where they'd been posted.

Naajuk was burly, broad-shouldered, and blond, with a narrow white scar across his forehead. Deminaar was a good head shorter than Beltur, but wiry, with an easy smile and short-cut auburn hair, while Zekkarat had skin the color of light amber, and black hair and eyes. Reynaard had sandy-red hair and deep-set pale blue eyes, and faded freckles sprinkled across his face. Knutwyl was blocky, but not fat, square-faced, with brown hair, and deep brown eyes that never stopped moving.

"The reason why I've gathered you all together so soon after our arrival,"

Raelf went on, "is because I've heard a number of misconceptions about the task facing us and about the four councilors. I'd like to clear some of those up, and I also thought you should meet the councilors and offer any questions you have to them. While I've done my best to answer your questions so far, your arrival in Haven may have raised others, and it's best we address them before the Hydlenese arrive.

"First off, there seems to be an idea that the Hydlenese will be sending a massive army against us, and that we'll be overrun immediately. That's not only wrong, but it's nonsense. As you should have heard by now, the four councilors here effectively destroyed an entire battalion. Less than fifty troopers survived. Duke Massyngal will react by sending as large a force as he can, but . . ." Raelf stopped for emphasis. "Without relying on levies, he only had six full battalions. He is trying to raise another two battalions, but they are nowhere close to ready. He already lost one entire battalion, as well as most of the company that was posted here earlier. Since he can't raise levies quickly, he can't afford to send all of the five remaining battalions against us. I know some of you will say that Massyngal has twice that many troopers. You're right, but those other six battalions are in Worrak, and it would take a season to get them here. Not only that, but if he did, he'd likely end up losing half his land to the pirate lords, because those battalions are all that keep them in line.

"The most we're likely to face is four battalions, and almost certainly less. He will also send white mages, but he is also limited there, and he won't send all of them here, not when they're needed to maintain his power in Hydolar. Our mages should be able to overcome his mages, or at least, keep them from reducing our numbers. Also, we have certain weapons, based on what the mages learned in their battle against Gallos, that will help reduce the power of the white mages. Given that our men are better trained, we have an advantage there, but it won't be easy. Now, what questions do you have?"

The smiling Deminaar said, "If this is so, why is he attacking? And why do we need to fight here?"

"He's attacking for several reasons. First, Haven will only get stronger with the mages here. Second, he wants an easy and direct path to Lydiar because that will give him a better port than Renklaar and one that the pirates can't easily raid. Third, he hates being denied anything, and the councilors have done that. We're fighting now, because when we defeat his forces here, that will reduce his power enough that he won't be able to attack again for years, if ever. Also, it will be easier now than if he has two more battalions by autumn."

"Why are you so confident?" replied Deminaar, still smiling. "At best, we'll still be outnumbered, almost three to one."

"Three mages destroyed a battalion. That's a hundred and fifty to one." Raelf smiled back at Deminaar. "Two black mages and a healer-mage. I'm only asking each of your troopers to take out two or three men who aren't trained as well."

"He's got a point, Deminaar," said Zekkarat. "Besides, my gutter rats'll take out three apiece to make it easier for your boys."

"Promises, promises . . ." But Deminaar's smile briefly became a grin.

"There's one other thing," said the burly, blond Naajuk. "Duke Halacut only has two mages, and neither's worth sowshit. And there are only four more decent companies in Lydiar. One way or another, we'll fight. I'd rather fight here and now."

"If this is so important," Deminaar asked Raelf, "why aren't all your companies here?"

"Because Fourth Company can't get here any time soon. The squads have been dealing with hill brigands west of Lavah. And Fifth Company is an understrength training company from which we took the best armsmen."

As the comments and questions progressed, and it became clear that the three Lydian captains, for various reasons, supported Raelf, Beltur watched Rojak, with both eyes and senses. He thought Rojak was resigned to the situation, but that could change at any time.

Then, out of nowhere, Rojak addressed Jessyla. "Healer-Mage, how many did you kill in that battalion?"

Jessyla looked momentarily surprised, then smiled. "I couldn't say. At the beginning, I kept a rough count, but then there was too much going on. After a score or so, I stopped."

Beltur suspected that Jessyla really hadn't wanted to know. He certainly hadn't kept track.

"Isn't killing somewhat . . . opposed to healing?"

"I can't very well keep healing if I'm not around to do it and if there's no one left to heal," replied Jessyla, not quite tartly.

Beltur noticed that almost all the captains looked amused at her reply. Rojak must have noticed as well, because he didn't venture more.

"Are there any more questions?" asked Raelf, looking across the group.

"I do have one," said Deminaar. "To the young woman on the stool. Why are you here?"

Taelya looked surprised.

Tulya said gently, "Taelya . . . tell the captain what you are and why you're here."

"Ser . . . I'm a beginning white mage. No one in Elparta wanted me there. No one in Axalt wanted me there. This is the only place I can be. I'm here to protect my mother."

"How will you do that?" asked Deminaar.

"My shields will protect us both for a little while. I'm not strong enough to hold them for more than a quint."

Deminaar nodded politely to Taelya, then said, "Thank you." He turned to Raelf. "When a child is willing to put her life on the line, how can I do otherwise?" After a pause, he added sardonically, "Especially when I'd still have to fight later under less advantageous circumstances."

Rojak looked to Raelf. "You've made the situation very clear, Majer. We fight."

Beltur could sense both agreement . . . and reluctance, suggesting that Rojak still needed to be watched closely.

"Undercaptain Cheld's scouts have seen no sign of the Hydlenese so far, but since the road from Hydolar has been clear of travelers for several days, it's likely that it won't be long."

Beltur cleared his throat. "As some of you know, I was an undercaptain in a Spidlarian recon company when the Gallosians attacked Elparta. For the last few eightdays, I've been reconnoitering the terrain around Haven. There are four possible approaches and several places where we might be able to use our talents to facilitate ambushes that would reduce the numbers of attackers with less risk to our men." He looked to Raelf.

"Go on."

Beltur quickly summarized what he had seen and concluded by saying, "These are only my observations. I would suggest the first thing tomorrow that I conduct you to each of these possible sites and that you decide, based on what we can do, and what you feel is practical and possible."

"That makes sense," replied Raelf. "Such an overview may also reveal either weaknesses or additional possibilities. We'll begin early. Sixth glass at the East Inn."

The way Raelf handled that suggested that the meeting was over, and in less than a quint, he was the only officer left with Beltur and the other councilors and Taelya.

"You knew something like this would happen?" asked Tulya.

"Sooner or later. Lord Korsaen told me that we'd get a barely competent officer and the worst companies Lydiar could spare. The companies are much better than I'd hoped. Rojak is what we expected."

"How did that happen?" asked Tulya.

"Competent officers can't be blindly loyal, not and get their men to follow them. We were given the companies headed by officers who were considered less loyal to Duke Halacut. He saw that as a way of weeding them out. Lord Korsaen had thought that a possibility. I was less hopeful. He was right."

"Or perhaps Maeyora?" asked Jessyla.

"There's no difference between those two names," replied Raelf wryly. "They act as one, and they're seldom wrong."

"I'm sorry for creating a confrontation so soon," began Jessyla, "but practically every word Rojak said was either deceptive or condescending."

"It's likely better this way," replied Raelf. "At least we know where we stand . . . and so do the Lydian captains. As does Rojak."

"He's not the most trustworthy," said Jessyla.

"He won't go against his captains. Not now."

Or not until and unless we've obviously lost. Beltur kept that thought to himself.

"In time, that could change." Raelf offered a lopsided smile.

"I have one other question," said Beltur. "You mentioned weapons based on what we told you."

"Iron arrows and crossbow bolts. It crossed my mind after our meeting in Weevett that developing such weapons might be a good idea. Montgren has very few mages and none as capable as you. I decided on the crossbow quarrels because iron arrows, even with thin shafts, don't have that great a range. We do have almost two hundred iron arrow shafts and fifty crossbow bolts."

Once again, Beltur found himself impressed with Raelf, far more than with Rojak. "Those could prove very useful."

Raelf nodded, then said, "I do need to go. There are more than a few logistics to deal with."

"We won't keep you," said Lhadoraak, smiling as he added, "Not any longer."

Once Raelf had departed, Beltur looked to the others, and then, because he didn't want to be the first to hazard an opinion, he asked, "What do you all think?"

"Besides the fact that we've been set up, you mean?" asked Lhadoraak.

"We're not the only ones who've been set up," said Jessyla. "Raelf's been set up as well. I think Maeyora must have a druid's foresight. I don't like that. Foresight shows what is, but it's colored by the desires of the seer."

"They must think we can win," suggested Tulya.

"No," countered Jessyla. "They must think they can win. That doesn't mean that it will end all that well for us."

"But they never lied to us," said Beltur.

"That might be because we didn't ask the right questions," said Lhadoraak. "We weren't looking far enough ahead."

"There is one other thing to consider," Beltur pointed out. "If we don't survive, it's unlikely they can win."

"There's also another," said Tulya. "What if there's no foresight, and they're just doing the best that they can, just like we are? What if Korsaen and Maeyora have just been trying to get the best people that they can?"

"That's possible, I suppose," said Lhadoraak, his tone slightly dubious.

"Maybe Maeyora has a vision, but it's not complete . . . or what it means is unclear?" asked Jessyla.

"That sounds more likely to me," suggested Lhadoraak.

"Does it really matter, right now?" asked Beltur. "One way or another we need to figure out a way to win . . . and survive."

"The troopers need to take the brunt of the attacks, and then we need to find ways to whittle the Hydlenese down," said Lhadoraak.

Although the three other adults all nodded at what Lhadoraak said, Beltur knew that, even if they won the coming battles, and there would likely be more than one, that wouldn't necessarily end the matter, but there was little point in saying that because, unless they prevailed, they wouldn't face that problem.

LI

As Jessyla and Beltur hurriedly ate oat porridge, cheese hunks, and bread for breakfast on twoday, Beltur said, "You should come with us."

"Who said I wasn't?" asked Jessyla.

Beltur managed not to wince.

"I can do a concealment big enough for a company." She paused, then added, "If it's not too spread out. And the captains should know from the beginning that I'll be accompanying one of their companies. It's one thing to hear that; it's another to see it."

Beltur was well aware of that. He was also aware that some of the captains might be more than a little reluctant.

Possibly reading his expression, Jessyla went on. "Since there are only three mages and six companies, Raelf can see from the captains' reactions where we might be most effective and most appreciated."

"That definitely would be for the best," said Beltur as he finished the last of his ale. "We also need to fill our water bottles with ale. It's likely to be a very long day." *In more ways than one.*

Even after dealing with horses and water bottles, the two arrived at the East Inn a little less than a quint before sixth glass.

Cheld was waiting for them as they dismounted and tied their mounts to the hitching rail. "The majer's in the public room. He wants to talk to you before he gathers the captains."

"We thought he might," said Jessyla cheerfully.

"Healer-Mage . . ." began Cheld carefully, "I had no idea . . . you also fought so effectively."

That statement, Beltur suspected, was about as close to an apology as the undercaptain could bring himself to utter.

Jessyla laughed, a laugh both gentle and slightly bitter. "Until I had to, I had no idea that I could, either. I had no choice. With the number of Hydlenese we'll face, I still don't. None of us do."

"You're all mages, though."

"We've had our lives threatened and disrupted in four lands," replied

Beltur, making sure he had the map that he and the others had worked on. "It would seem that wouldn't change for the better if we moved on. Certainly not in Certis or Hydolar. Nor in Westwind or Sarronnyn. So . . . the only real choice is not whether we fight, but where we fight . . . and for what." He offered a pleasant smile. "We'd best not keep the majer waiting."

"Oh . . . of course, sers." Cheld turned toward the door into the inn and gestured for them to precede him.

Raelf was indeed in the public room, seated at the circular table, perusing several maps, but he immediately stood as the two mages approached.

"How are matters going?" asked Beltur.

"As expected. I'd forgotten how poor the ale is, though." Raelf shook his head.

"Bythalt used to have a keg of the better ale," ventured Beltur.

"That's what I'm talking about," replied the majer. "The other stuff's barely drinkable."

Both Beltur and Jessyla laughed, as much at Raelf's near-plaintive tone as at his actual words.

"There is that," said Beltur. Then, gesturing at the table and the maps upon it, he went on. "Jessyla and I have scouted out the various approaches that the Hydlenese have used, and some others that they could use. We've also noted where we might be able to attack. To make it a little easier for you, we also put together this map." Beltur handed Raelf the rough map that he, Jessyla, and Tulya had drawn up earlier.

Raelf unrolled it and laid it upon the table, studying it for several moments before saying, "You've given this some thought."

"After what we've already been through, we've tried. We're showing what we know, but we're deferring to your experience, especially if you see problems or better opportunities."

"I can't tell you how much I appreciate this and how valuable it will be. Do you mind if I bring it with me?"

"Not at all," replied Beltur, "but be careful. We didn't have time to make a second copy."

"I'll be very careful." Raelf turned to Cheld. "If you'd tell the captains that we'll be riding out shortly."

"Yes, ser." Cheld turned and headed out of the public room.

"Just the two of you are riding with us?"

"We're the ones who've done all the scouting. Lhadoraak's skills are better suited to providing concealments and limited shields."

Raelf looked to Jessyla. "Some may question your riding with troopers. Not because you aren't a warrior, but because you're a healer."

"If we don't win, there won't be any need for healers."

The majer smiled. "Some may need to be reminded of that."

"Will Rojak be accompanying us this morning?" asked Beltur.

"He wouldn't have it any other way. Neither would I."

Despite Raelf's hopes of a departure close to sixth glass, it was two quints past the glass when the party rode away from the East Inn, a party consisting of both majers, Beltur and Jessyla, the five company captains, and Cheld, accompanied by a squad of Montgren troopers, just in case they happened to encounter any Hydlenese scouts.

The tour of Haven and its environs began with a ride east on the main street, with Beltur pointing out where the false Lydians had attacked, and then where the Hydlenese had fired dwellings and other structures. From there, they proceeded south and west to the lane that led to Samwyth's stead, past Ennalee and Vortaan's stead.

When the group halted where the lane intersected the narrow east-west road bordered on the south by the rugged hills that led west past the overgrown forest, Beltur turned to Raelf and Rojak. "The first time, they brought just a squad this way. The second time, they brought a full company . . ." He went on to explain what lay ahead and how he and Jessyla had thought a small groups of archers might inflict serious damage, especially if supported by a company on the narrow road.

Then the group rode west, and Beltur and Jessyla pointed out the foot trail up the hills and the narrowness between the hills and the forest.

"I don't know that I'd count on the Hydlenese to come this way," said Rojak.

"They might not," agreed Beltur. "But they did twice before, and we thought you should know that."

Raelf just offered a noncommittal nod and said, "It's good to see all the possible approaches. That way, when scouts tell us where they're headed, we'll be at least somewhat familiar with the possibilities."

After the forest ended on the north side of the road, Beltur pointed out the uneven rocky grassland and said, "That extends north for nearly three kays, and the narrow lane you'll see ahead on your right winds through it and eventually joins a lane that leads to the main square of Haven. That's also marked on the map. The Hydlenese have never gone that way, possibly because it's narrow, uneven, and some of the turns are sharp."

Beltur then led them to the deserted encampment the Hydlenese had used for their raid on Samwyth's stead, then along the better road to the second stead where the Hydlenese had established themselves. It was also deserted. Beltur did note that the entire barn where he'd set the fire had burned to ashes.

From there, they proceeded to the Hydolar road and to the low hills on the eastern side before it joined the road that led west to Certis and east back to Haven.

"We could conceal troopers on the back sides of those hills," Beltur pointed out.

"The western side isn't much steeper than the east side," observed Captain Deminaar.

"We could charge at one side and be on the road," replied Naajuk.

"If they followed, we could attack their flank from that rise ahead," added Reynaard.

"We'll keep that in mind, Captains," said Raelf.

Rojak said nothing.

By the time the group reached the east-west road, it was past second glass, and Beltur had drunk all the ale in the first of his water bottles. He reined up and pointed west. "A little more than a kay west of here, there's a narrow road that leads to a hamlet. Several days before the battalion attacked, a squad of Hydlenese attacked the hamlet. We scattered the squad and killed several of them before they did too much damage." He didn't mention that some in the hamlet hadn't been all that pleased. "That road might link to the Weevett road, but we didn't have a chance to follow it."

"Didn't have a chance or didn't choose to?" asked Rojak.

"There are three of us who can do that," replied Beltur. "We're training several patrollers, but we've been stretched rather thin."

"I've also been required to do quite a bit more healing," added Jessyla.

Rojak didn't quite snort.

"We were brought here to be councilors," said Beltur mildly, "not war mages. Councilors do have to deal with other duties." *Such as putting the town back together and protecting the people from overbearing bravos and greedy traders.*

"War mages are all that Massyngal will heed," replied Rojak.

"The mages are certainly aware of that," interjected Raelf. "They've acquitted themselves well in that regard. I'm also quite certain Duke Massyngal and his commander will heed what we and our troopers do." He turned to Beltur and Jessyla. "Is there anything else we should see?"

"Just what we'll see on the return to Haven."

Raelf nodded, then urged his mount eastward toward Haven.

On the way, Beltur pointed out the hill overlooking the junction between the Weevett road and the east-west road as well as where he, Jessyla, and Lhadoraak had engaged the Hydlenese battalion.

When Beltur and Jessyla reined up outside the East Inn, it was nearly fourth glass, and Beltur was sweating profusely. Obviously, the officers were more accustomed to the damp heat, because they didn't look nearly as wilted as Beltur felt.

Rojak rode straight to the stables, but Raelf reined up beside the two mages.

"That was extremely helpful," said the majer. "Your experience with a reconnaissance company shows."

"Rojak didn't seem very pleased," observed Jessyla.

"His captains were," replied Raelf. "That's important, because they're the ones leading their troopers."

"Has Rojak ever been in a real battle?" asked Jessyla.

Raelf laughed, then said, "Very few of us have. I have, when I was a junior undercaptain. Naajuk might as well as have been. Reynaard fought Sligan marauders, as did Knutwyl. I don't know about Deminaar. Most likely, your consort has more time in fighting than anyone. You, just by fighting against that battalion, have endured more intense fighting than most of our forces. Fortunately, the Hydlenese have only a few companies with any fighting experience at all. From what Lord Korsaen has been able to discover, in the few times they've fought, they've often just outnumbered those they fought and taken tremendous losses. Then they hired more blade fodder. That might be why your strategy of removing officers and squad leaders was so effective."

"They'll definitely have many more troopers than we will," said Beltur, "and that will make it much harder."

"Not necessarily. There are a number of approaches to Haven. All of them have points where the number of riders that can pass is limited. If the Hydlenese mass their troopers, they can't advance quickly. We can use archers to shoot into the middle of their men. If they split their forces, then it will be easier to target individual officers. There's also one other fact. I doubt they know that's what you did."

Jessyla frowned. "How could they not know? Not many officers survived. Maybe not any."

"Exactly," replied Raelf. "How could they tell? Few if any officers survived to report that. Almost eight out of ten men died. With casualties that high . . ." A sterner expression appeared on his face. "We're still facing a considerable challenge. I will say, since we're alone, the last thing we need is any sacrifices by any of you. In short, stay alive. Make them sacrifice themselves. They aren't going to attack full-out immediately. We need to be ready for that, in case they're that stupid, but they'll likely have orders to destroy us and Haven, and to do that takes more than a blind rush." He shrugged and smiled ruefully. "I could be wrong. Very wrong. We'll have to see."

"Tomorrow morning, then?" asked Beltur.

"Every morning at sixth glass, starting tomorrow. While I think it will be several more days before their advance units appear, we can't count on that. Now, if you'll excuse me, I need to talk to Majer Rojak."

After Raelf turned his mount toward the stables, Jessyla looked to Beltur. "We'll need to tell all of this to Lhadoraak and Tulya at dinner."

Beltur nodded, then gestured in the general direction of their house. "I could use a cooler ale."

"So could I."

Without another word, they turned their mounts back west.

LII

Early on twoday night, well after dinner and after Taelya had been put to bed, the four councilors sat around the kitchen table in the older couple's house as Jessyla and Beltur described their day and their observations about the two majers and their captains.

After they finished, Tulya said, "The more I hear about Rojak, the less I like it . . . and I didn't like him from the moment he arrived."

"He's a younger majer who's likely related to someone important in Lydiar and thinks he knows more than he does," said Lhadoraak.

"I don't like him," said Jessyla, "but, in a way, I feel sorry for him."

"How can you feel sorry for an arrogant bastard like him?" replied Tulya.

"No matter what happens, it won't go well for him, and he doesn't even see it. That's one reason."

This time Lhadoraak looked puzzled.

"If we win, and he survives, he'll go back to Lydiar even more full of himself, and overconfident. That won't turn out well. If we lose and he survives, Duke Halacut will blame Rojak. And if he doesn't survive . . ."

"I still don't think he deserves even pity," declared Tulya.

"Why do you think it won't turn out well if we win and if Rojak survives?" asked Lhadoraak.

"Because it will be obvious that he had nothing to do with it, and he won't accept that," replied Jessyla.

Beltur was about to say that he doubted that, thinking about Waensyn and how he'd taken credit for things he had nothing to do with . . . except, in the end Waensyn had overplayed his plaques, because he'd believed he was more than he'd actually been. "It might be a while before matters catch up with Rojak, but, one way or another, they will."

"Good," declared Tulya.

"Why do you dislike him that much?" asked Jessyla.

"Besides being overbearing and full of himself? I could stand that. But the way he leered when he looked at Taelya. That was too much."

Beltur hadn't seen that, but since Tulya clearly believed it, and she hadn't been someone to overreact, he could definitely understand her feelings. "Did Taelya say anything?"

"She said she didn't like him, that he pushed feelings at her."

Beltur couldn't help wincing, but was glad that Taelya wasn't old enough to fully understand what those feelings really meant. That also meant that Jessyla needed to talk to Taelya about untoward "pushy feelings" and a few others things. Beltur wasn't totally surprised, though, because Taelya had sensed that Naerkaal, the black mage on the Council of Axalt, had been sad when no one but Beltur had sensed Naerkaal's feelings.

"She's reading what people feel," said Jessyla. "She's awfully young for that."

"She's been awfully young for everything," said Lhadoraak, looking toward Beltur, as if the younger mage had had something to do with that.

"It could be that all children are naturally blocked from sensing order, and that only those who will be mages or healers lose that blocking as they grow. In healing her, I might have released some of those blocks early."

"We didn't have any choice," said Tulya. "She would have died. She was already almost dying." She gave a long hard look at Lhadoraak.

Lhadoraak took a deep breath. "It's just that . . . I worry."

"You don't think everyone in this room doesn't worry about her?" asked Tulya.

Beltur was glad that Tulya had been the one to make that point, although he certainly worried about Taelya, and about how much to teach her and in what fashion.

"What do you two think about how Raelf felt?" asked Lhadoraak, as if he didn't want to say more about Taelya. "Especially about Rojak."

"He's worried about Rojak," replied Jessyla. "But the way Raelf's dealt with the Lydian captains . . . it's almost as if Rojak was sent as a figurehead and told not to get in the way . . . and he doesn't like it."

"He wasn't very politic," added Tulya.

"Maybe he had been until they got here and knew where we stood," suggested Jessyla.

"Or maybe Rojak behaved himself until he met us," said Lhadoraak, "and he wanted to prove he had some power."

"We'll just have to see," returned Beltur. "But Raelf made the point that Rojak had never been in a real battle, and that all of us had. It won't hurt to watch him, at least as much as we can."

"Along with everything else?" asked Lhadoraak.

"As we can," repeated Beltur.

"Do you think Raelf really meant that statement about us not sacrificing ourselves?" Lhadoraak's words carried some doubt.

"He definitely meant that," declared Jessyla. "He as much as said that the chances of winning without all of us were slight."

"That's as much a burden as a relief," said Lhadoraak dourly. "He did say he didn't think the Hydlenese would show up for another few days. Is that right?"

"He did, but he said we couldn't count on it," replied Beltur. "That's why he wants us to meet early every morning."

For several long moments, no one said anything.

"You realize, don't you," Lhadoraak finally said, "that we made the Prefect even more of a problem?"

Tulya offered a puzzled frown.

Jessyla started to speak, then stopped and nodded to Beltur.

"Because we gave his troopers and mages extensive battle experience, and no one else besides Spidlar has that right now?"

"Experience counts," replied Lhadoraak. "The Spidlarian naval marines were one of the reasons why we won that last battle." He smiled ruefully. "I should say the combination of Beltur and the marines . . . but the point remains."

"Gustaan's company seemed to have at least some experience," Jessyla pointed out.

"Except half of them were killed, and the rest were forced out," replied Beltur. "That ties in with what Raelf said about the Hydlenese using up troopers." He paused, then added, "It also means that we'll likely have to kill quite a few of them." He didn't voice the other thought he had . . . the question of what they could do so that they weren't fighting the Hydlenese continually. That wouldn't be a problem unless and until they dealt with the oncoming force.

"Why can't they just leave us alone?" asked Tulya.

"Because Lydiar and Haven are both seen as weak, and Duke Massyngal wants to take over Lydiar. We're just a troublesome inconvenience in the way." With those words, Beltur still wondered how much Korlyssa, Korsaen, and Maeyora really had known. He had the feeling that they'd felt Massyngal might be a problem in the future, but not if he were headed off by a strong set of councilors in Haven. He still wished he'd known enough to ask more pointed questions about Hydlen and Massyngal. But that was water long gone downstream.

Tulya tried to cover a yawn. "I'm sorry."

"It's getting late," said Jessyla, "and more talking won't change anything." She stood, glancing to Beltur, who also rose from the table. "We'll see you in the morning."

"In the morning," agreed the older mage.

Within moments, Beltur and Jessyla had left the house.

"Lhadoraak's worried," said Jessyla quietly as they walked through the too-warm night and across the narrow street toward their own house. "I've never seen him like this."

"As the gambler in Axalt—"

"Klaznyt?"

Beltur nodded. "As he might have said, the stakes are higher now. For all of us personally. It's different when you put yourself in a position where there aren't any ways out, only through."

"You're saying, in a way, that we've had fewer ways out, and Lhadoraak's never before been quite where we've been."

"Do you think I'm wrong?"

She shook her head.

"You also need to talk to Taelya about those 'pushy feelings,' with Tulya there . . . the three of you women."

"I know. That can wait a little, but not long. She senses too much for her age."

Far too much. And that bothered Beltur, too.

LIII

Twoday night wasn't that much cooler than the day, and when Beltur rose slightly before fifth glass, he had no doubts that threeday would likely be the hottest day of the year, at least so far, and that would likely make it the warmest and dampest day he'd ever experienced . . . and that didn't count whatever might occur with the Hydlenese.

"It's going to be hot today," he told Jessyla.

"Tulya's enjoying the warmth."

"I'm glad someone is."

"You'll get used to it."

Beltur wondered about that, but only briefly because he and Jessyla had to hurry to wash up, dress, and eat. As they quickly finished eating, Jessyla asked, "Should we saddle the horses or just walk?"

Beltur thought for a moment. "Just walk. I'd rather not have them waiting out in the heat when there's no sign of the Hydlenese. We'll need them rested later. If I need to scout, I can always saddle Slowpoke later."

"I'll clean up here, then, and I'll tell the others that we're walking," said Jessyla. "You water the horses and check their feed."

Beltur nodded, then rose and hurried down to the barn, where he quickly dealt with the horses, or as quickly as he could. When he secured the barn, he saw Jessyla talking to Lhadoraak outside the older mage's house, and he made his way there.

"Tulya and Taelya will be out in a moment," said Lhadoraak. "She's not happy about Rojak. I told her that Taelya could stay with Gustaan and the patrollers, but she said that she wasn't about to have Taelya separated from us right now."

"Definitely not now," declared Tulya as she and Taelya left the house. She glanced around, then said, "At least we're not freezing all the time here."

"It is a bit warm," offered Beltur.

"I can deal with warmth," replied Tulya, "not cold that seeps deep inside your bones."

Beltur caught the glance from Jessyla and nodded, then said, "We'll walk. We don't need to tire the horses yet. We'll likely be asking a lot of them before long."

"We'll be asking a lot of everyone before it's over," murmured Lhadoraak.

Beltur could agree with that.

Although threeday was market day, it was too early for anyone to be setting up in the square when the five crossed it on the way to the East Inn, and when they reached the public room, only Raelf and Rojak awaited them.

"The captains are dealing with their companies," said Raelf, gesturing for the five to join them at the larger round table.

Rojak just nodded.

"I take it that nothing's changed," said Beltur as he and the others seated themselves.

"So far there's no sign of troopers or even scouts," declared Raelf.

"I still question whether they're even coming," said Rojak.

"I'd like to think they weren't," countered Raelf mildly. "That's unlikely. Duke Massyngal has never ignored any challenge to his power. Both your duke and my duchess don't believe he'll start ignoring a challenge now—

even if the councilors here were only defending their town against his attacking troopers."

"Also, some traders came through here before you arrived headed for Lydiar," said Beltur. "They said that Duke Massyngal was readying an army."

"Traders? Do you trust them?"

"Only to act in their own self-interest, but when their self-interest shows itself in their fleeing, it's at least suggestive."

Raelf offered an amused laugh. "I tend to agree with the mage on that, Rojak."

"What do you have in mind for dealing with the Hydlenese scouts when they appear?" asked Lhadoraak.

"If the circumstances permit, we'll harass them and eliminate them immediately where we can. That's if our men can do it without taking casualties. Right now, that is. That will make it harder for them to learn anything about us. It also will reduce their numbers."

"Of course, that will make them even angrier," said Rojak.

Raelf raised his eyebrows. "I doubt that anything we do will make their officers any angrier than they'll already be. Their troopers will be like all troopers. Most of them, anyway. They'll just want to do their job and stay alive." His eyes went from Lhadoraak to Beltur. "You've had experience with scouting. What would you do?"

"Just what you've suggested. I'd like to be notified immediately once you discover any sign of the Hydlenese forces. I might be able to discover more."

"We can do that." Raelf paused. "You're not thinking of acting alone, are you?"

"I might scout, but I'm more interested in finding as soon as possible if they have mages. Also, how many and what kind."

"Why?" asked Rojak.

"Because that will tell me what those mages can do against our forces and how we should be used to be the most effective. The numbers and types of mages they bring also will allow you to know what tactics are likely to be more effective."

"How so?" Raelf's question was curious, not pointed.

"Black mages are more likely to be able to sense concealments at a distance. Whites aren't very good at that until they're close, but up close their chaos bolts are more effective, unless one of us is there to shield against chaos-fire."

"What else can you do?" asked Rojak.

"Each of us is a bit different. What Lhadoraak does best is concealments and then shields. My shields are stronger, and I can also break through a line, enough for troopers to take advantage of it. Jessyla's not quite as strong, but she can shield and conceal squad-sized units."

"You didn't mention how effectively you can strike down attackers," said Rojak. "Why didn't you mention that?"

"Either Jessyla or I can take out attackers if they get close to us. Given the way our skills work, the more space we have, the more effective we can be. But that's only for short periods of time."

"That seems at odds with what you did to that greencoat battalion," pressed Rojak.

Beltur shook his head. "It took me most of a day. It wouldn't have been possible if the Hydlenese hadn't scattered so much."

"Wasn't that in part because you'd removed much of their command structure?" interjected Raelf.

"It definitely was," said Jessyla. "What Beltur did wouldn't have been possible against a force twice that size."

"What we do works better when we support troopers, not act independently of them," said Beltur. "That was how Spidlar was able to defeat the much larger forces of Gallos at Elparta."

"You're suggesting that each of you be with a different force element, then," said Raelf.

"That's right," said Lhadoraak, "with a commander who will listen, especially to Beltur."

"Why Beltur?" asked Raelf. "Why not you? You're older and presumably more experienced."

Lhadoraak shook his head. "I'm older. He's more experienced. He also can sense the battlefield as a whole—where troop concentrations are, where there are weak spots."

Beltur was glad Lhadoraak didn't elaborate on that, especially about how he and the naval marines had been able to break the Gallosian line and target the command companies to create the disruptions that had fragmented the Gallosian army. He doubted that any of the companies were anywhere close to as good as Captain Toeraan's naval marines had been, and he certainly didn't want Raelf to have unrealistic expectations.

"You didn't mention that," Raelf said to Beltur.

"I told you I could sense troopers from a distance," replied Beltur.

"Doing that in the middle of a battle is different. Was that one reason why you were able to kill so many Hydlenese troopers? That you knew where they were, even when you couldn't see them?"

"That helped."

Raelf turned to Rojak. "Is there anything else you'd like to know?"

"Did you have to kill all those Hydlenese troopers?" Rojak asked Beltur.

"Yes. Otherwise we'd have to face them once more when Duke Massyngal attacked again."

"Didn't you think that was a judgment better left to the Duchess?"

"No. She granted us the authority to do what we thought necessary. Also, she wasn't here, and the opportunity was."

"So you thought—"

"Majer," declared Raelf forcefully, "what the councilor said is true. When Massyngal attacks, neither of us will be able to consult the Duchess or Duke. The councilor had the same problem." He cleared his throat and asked, "Do you have any questions of us?"

Beltur looked to Lhadoraak, then Jessyla, and finally Taelya. Seeing only headshakes, he replied, "Only the request that you continue to keep us immediately informed."

"Then we should meet tomorrow morning, unless we receive information. Thank you."

Rojak did not appear especially pleased, but he did not speak as the five rose and left the public room.

Once they were outside and walking toward the public square, Lhadoraak spoke. "It doesn't look like we'll have that much to do today."

"That makes it a good day for more instruction in magery," said Beltur. "I haven't spent as much time with Taelya—or Jessyla—as I should have in the last few days." What he wasn't saying was that even a slight improvement in Jessyla's skills, and possibly even Taelya's, might just be the difference between winning and losing the upcoming battles, since Beltur doubted that there would be just one massive battle.

More likely skirmishes trying to get advantages leading up to a decisive encounter. But even that was speculation.

He blotted his forehead as he kept walking across the still-empty square.

LIV

The four councilors, accompanied by Taelya, met with Raelf and Rojak again on fourday morning, but there were no signs of any travelers at all on any roads heading to Haven, which, regardless of what Rojak thought, suggested to Beltur that merchants and others knew an army was riding toward the small town.

Beltur once again spent most of the morning working with Taelya and Jessyla on improving their shields, and then later with Jessyla on handling shields and containments simultaneously. Somewhat to Beltur's surprise, and also to his relief, a light breeze blew out of the northeast, and that made the morning and early afternoon much more bearable than threeday had been.

Just before noon, when Jessyla and Beltur were seated on the settee in the front room, each enjoying an ale, they both sensed a rider approaching the two houses from the east—most likely from the East Inn.

Beltur was at the door before the trooper was.

"Ser, the scouts have sighted troopers from Hydlen. Majer Raelf awaits you and the other councilors at the East Inn."

"Thank you. You can inform the majer that we'll be right there."

"Are we walking or riding?" asked Jessyla.

"Walking, but it may lead to riding before long."

"You are not attacking them."

"I'd thought more about just sensing what I could."

"Then we'll do that together."

Less than a quint later, the five were once more in the public room of the East Inn with Raelf and Rojak.

The Lydian majer looked anything but pleased, but said nothing. His eyes lingered on the blue Spidlarian uniforms that both Lhadoraak and Beltur wore.

"They're Spidlarian arms-mage uniforms," Beltur finally said. "We'd rather not be singled out too obviously as mages."

"I see." Raelf cleared his throat and then said, "The scouts watching the

Hydolar road have reported two reconnaissance companies. They're five kays southwest of where that road meets the road to Certis. They're making no secret of their presence. They're carrying the green ensign of Hydlen prominently. So far, there's no sign of wagons or other units. We don't plan to engage them." He looked to Beltur.

"I'd suggest that Mage Jessyla and I ride south to see if there are other companies moving in away from the main road."

"The scouts haven't seen anyone yet."

"We can sense farther than they can see. Also, we need to know if there are mages with the advance companies. You need to know that as well."

"That would be for the best." Raelf frowned for just an instant. "I'd feel better if you were accompanied."

Beltur wasn't about to argue. "Half a squad will be enough. We're not planning on getting very close at all. We'll do our best not even to be seen."

This time Rojak was the one to frown. "Does it matter? They must know that you are mages."

"That may be," replied Beltur, "but there's likely no one left alive who's actually seen us. The more unknown we seem, the better it will be for your troopers. Is there anything else we should know?"

"Not so far," replied Raelf.

"Then we'll saddle up and meet your troopers here in about a quint."

"They'll be waiting."

Rojak nodded at Raelf's words.

Slightly more than a quint later, partly because filling the water bottles with ale had added time that Beltur hadn't counted in, he and Jessyla rode toward the eleven troopers who waited on the west side of the inn, almost on the square itself. They reined up short of the squad leader.

"Squad Leader Khaamyn, sers." The squad leader was clearly a good ten years older than Beltur or Jessyla. His eyes barely lingered on Beltur, unlike those of some of his rankers. His glance did linger slightly on Jessyla.

"It's good to see you, Squad Leader. I assume Majer Raelf told you that this is strictly a recon patrol."

"Yes, ser. That's why I'm here."

"You're one of his senior squad leaders, and he thought it would be useful for you to have a better view of the terrain?"

"Just so, ser."

"We'll go through the square and head south. After we get out of town, we'll pass two steads . . ." Beltur gave a quick summary of their planned route, then added, "There aren't that many places with sources of water south and west of here, and since the ways that approach Haven from the south and west can be narrow in places, I have the feeling that there will be troopers bivouacked in some of the places they used before. Knowing that . . . and how many will be useful."

Khaamyn nodded. "Any time you're ready, sers."

"We're ready." Beltur urged Slowpoke forward.

From the inn, Beltur and Jessyla led the way through the square and then onto the lane that carried them to and past Samwyth's stead. As they left Vortaan and Ennalee's stead behind, Beltur stretched his senses as far as he could, but could discern nothing for almost three kays but those in the few dwellings north-northwest of them and various animals, largely within the overgrown wood to the west.

"So far, there's no one close," Beltur announced, largely for the benefit of Khaamyn.

Less than a quint later, they neared the road that flanked the rocky and rugged hills to the south, and Beltur said, "This is the road that they used on the first raids of the outlying steads. We'll follow it between the hills and that overgrown wood ahead. There's still no one within two kays."

"You can tell that, ser?" asked Khaamyn.

"Unless there's a heavy rain or thunderstorm. Then we can't sense nearly that far."

They had passed the wood and most of the rocky grassland on the north side of the narrow road when Beltur began to get a feeling that there might be riders farther to the southwest. He looked to Jessyla.

"There's something."

"It's beyond the burned-out stead ahead. They might be headed from the main Hydolar road to the larger stead with the burned barn." Beltur adjusted his visor cap, then blotted his forehead before uncorking his water bottle and taking a long swallow of ale. Then he turned in the saddle. "Have any of your men ever ridden under a concealment?"

"Under a concealment, ser?"

"We're going to disappear for a moment." With that Beltur put a concealment around himself and Jessyla.

"Are you there, sers?" asked the squad leader.

"We are. You can see that a concealment doesn't stop sounds, and if you look at the road, you can see that we still leave tracks. But if a company or squad waits quietly, they can't be seen—except by a black mage at a distance or a white mage fairly close." Beltur lifted the concealment.

"That could be very useful, sers."

"It could. Now . . . I'm going to put a concealment around you. You'll only see blackness. Just keep riding. The road ahead is straight. Your horse might stop suddenly or he might not. If he does, I'll lift the concealment immediately. We don't want your men running into you."

When Beltur put the concealment around the squad leader, he immediately sensed that Khaamyn's mount slowed, and after several moments, he raised the concealment.

The squad leader shook his head, then said, "You can ride and not run into things?"

"We can sense where we're going."

"How big a force can you hide?"

"That depends on how strong the mage is and how long the mage has to hold the concealment. I could conceal a company for possibly a glass. Jessyla could likely only conceal a squad for that long, but possibly a company for a quint."

"You are most definite about what you can do, but not so about her. Why?"

"I've already done what I've said I could do. She's concealed small groups, but not an entire company."

"There aren't many female mages," added Jessyla. "I might be the first to have been in battle since Saryn of the black blades. It's not something that a healer plans for."

"It seems . . . strange," replied Khaamyn.

"I know. Healers are supposed patch up all those wounded by men and not say or do anything else. I'd rather have a say in who gets wounded and who doesn't."

After a moment, Khaamyn shook his head, but, somehow, the gesture was respectful. "The Duke of Hydlen, I fear, will not appreciate your words. He will appreciate them less after the fighting is over."

"He doesn't have to appreciate anything," said Jessyla. "One way or another, he'll have to accept those words."

As they neared the burned-out stead, Beltur could tell that no one was near. They rode through the charred ruins and out the lane that led to the somewhat better road and the larger stead previously used by the Hydlenese.

When they were about two kays from that stead, the one where Beltur had burned the barn used as a stable, Beltur reined up. Not only were there troopers ahead, but there was at least one white mage, possibly two. "This is as far as we're going on this road."

Khaamyn frowned. "I don't see anyone ahead."

"Just beyond that wooded hill is a stead. At the moment, several companies of troopers are riding into the stead I mentioned earlier. There might be a full battalion and likely two white mages. We'll retrace our way and take the narrower path along the north side of those hills heading west—at least until we run into more Hydlenese."

"You don't need to go closer?"

"No . . . and it's better if we don't." Sensing that Khaamyn was puzzled, Beltur went on. "We can sense white mages from farther than they can sense us. Right now, we know there are two whites with that battalion. They know nothing. If we come closer, they'll know about us, and we won't know any more than we already do." Beltur turned Slowpoke. He thought the squad leader understood.

"Khaamyn," added Jessyla, "it's very important that the white mages don't know how many of us there are and where we are."

"That way," continued Beltur, "they won't change their tactics. The way most commanders use white mages works to our advantage." *At least it did in Spidlar.*

"The majer said you had been an undercaptain in Spidlar."

"He was," said Jessyla. "He spent much of that time with an advance recon company."

"Is it true you killed hundreds?"

"I didn't keep count," replied Beltur.

"He did," added Jessyla.

Beltur could tell that the squad leader still didn't know quite what to make of him and Jessyla.

Before that long, the small party was back on the narrow road on the north side of the hills, hills that got smaller the farther west the group rode. In the distance ahead, to his left Beltur could see where the hills ended, just east of the Hydolar road. That was where he'd thought of mounting a concealed attack.

As he and the others neared the hills and the Hydolar road, Beltur began to sense riders, but not on the road. Rather there was at least a company of troopers on the highest of the hills and the one with the best view of both the Hydolar road and the east-west road from Haven to Certis . . . and where the Hydolar road joined it. There were already troopers there, setting up some sort of post or encampment.

There goes that idea. He frowned. Perhaps not. The advance company didn't have a mage. While the narrow road they had followed turned left a half kay ahead of where they had halted and eventually joined the east-west road, most of the ground between where the road turned and the hill was fairly flat, with only grass and scattered bushes. *Just possibly* . . .

He reined up.

So did the others.

"Ser mage?" asked Khaamyn.

"I just learned something else. You see that taller rise ahead? Not the one at the end on the left, but the taller one just to the right of it?"

"Yes, ser."

"That's where the Hydlenese are setting up an armed post. From there they can watch the road from Haven and the Hydolar road. They have a company up there at the moment. At some point, when they're not expecting anything, it might be worth attacking." As he sensed Jessyla tensing up, he quickly added, "If they don't reinforce that company and if we can take them totally by surprise."

For a time, Beltur just sat in the saddle, concentrating on where the Hydlenese troopers were. He couldn't sense anyone closer to Haven than those troopers on the top of the hill, and, at the moment, there weren't any other troopers within a kay of the hill.

If no other troopers are around . . .

He continued to study the hill, especially the area to the east and slightly to the south, where the slope was slightly steeper, but still seemed even.

Finally, he turned. "I think we need to head back. We've seen what we need to see for today."

"Is that all, ser?"

"For now."

Jessyla didn't say anything until the small column had turned and headed back toward Haven. "I know what you're thinking," she murmured.

"Am I wrong to think it? Do you think it's unwise?"

"If you try it, you're not to attack if you don't have complete surprise on your side."

"We can't afford anything else."

"Ser?" questioned Khaamyn from where he rode behind them.

"We're discussing what we should do next."

"Someone said black mages seldom attack, that you're better at defending."

"That's true," replied Beltur, "but there are times when attacking makes sense, even for a black."

"Unfortunately," added Jessyla in a low voice.

Or as the gambler might have said, you have to play the plaques you're dealt. Knowing that didn't make Beltur feel any better.

LV

Raelf must have heard the horses returning, or he'd posted a trooper to inform him, because he appeared next to the stable hitching rail as Beltur and Jessyla were dismounting at roughly two quints past third glass.

His first words were, "We should talk inside."

After tying the horses, the two mages and Khaamyn followed the majer to the public room. Obviously, the majer had taken over the chamber, except possibly at meal times, because there was no one else there.

Once they were seated, Raelf asked, "What did you find besides what the scouts already reported?"

"We discovered that a full battalion is taking over the stead with the burned barn . . ." Beltur went on to fill in the details before finishing with a description of the recon company on the low hill.

"That takes away one point of attack, then."

"Not necessarily. That's a single company, without mages. They're far enough from the battalion that those mages won't sense a company attacking them. They may bring up mages later. That's why I think an attack there now might be worthwhile."

"You're sure there are not any supporting companies there?"

"Not right now. If more show up before we get there, we turn around and come back."

"Since there's no cover, one of you would have to conceal our troopers." Raelf raised his eyebrows. "I thought you felt defenses would be a better use for mages."

"Mostly, but I can't resist the idea of inflicting massive casualties on a recon company. I'm not sure we'll have many opportunities like that."

"Could they be setting us up?"

"That's always possible, but there weren't any other riders or troopers, either mounted or on foot, anywhere near. If there turn out to be other companies nearby, we'll just slip away. I have no interest in losing significant numbers of troopers in a skirmish. Losing a few men to destroy a company seems to be an acceptable trade-off. Am I mistaken?" Beltur looked directly at Raelf.

"So long as one of you is the one accompanying the company, I see the possible reward worth the risk." Raelf's eyes went from Beltur to Jessyla and back to Beltur.

No one else could do it. "I'll be the one."

Raelf looked to Jessyla.

"He's done that many more times than I have."

"When would you propose such an attack?"

"We should be in position by sunset."

"Why then?"

"Your uniforms will be harder to see when I drop the concealment. Also, no one attacks at sunset. Dawn, yes, but I've never seen nor heard of a sunset attack."

For several moments, Raelf did not speak. Then he said dryly, "It might be because the advantages appear to belong to the defenders."

"Only if they can see the attackers."

"Just how are you going to get a company in position when you're the only one who can see?"

Raelf's question showed just how much the majer had looked into Beltur's capabilities, because Beltur didn't recall mentioning to Raelf anything about troopers being unable to see under a concealment. He'd said it to Khaamyn, but the squad leader hadn't had the time to talk to Raelf. "That will depend on how the Hydlenese are positioned on the top of the hill and how the troopers' mounts react to being under a concealment . . ." Beltur went on to explain.

"That could work. Will you assure me that you won't attempt the attack if you cannot set it up properly?"

"I will. The last thing I want to do is to lose troopers."

Raelf paused again before speaking. "Then I'll assign the Weevett company under Cheld to you and this mission. When do you think you should leave here?"

"Fifth glass. The last two kays will take a while to cover. You'll take care of the rope?"

"Rope we can supply."

"Now . . . there's one other thing. No, it's not another attack," Beltur added as he saw Raelf stiffen. "What about a concealed line of pikes or sharpened stakes?"

"With so many approaches to Haven, choosing where to put something like that would require a great deal of effort and would likely be useless."

"Not necessarily," replied Beltur. "I was thinking about frames that could be placed in less than half a quint and then be moved where they would be effective." He went on to sketch out what he had in mind, a framework with long sharpened poles attached to a heavy timber, and lighter cross-members that could be placed in a shallow trench and then raised into position and covered with a concealment.

"How would you propose to make that work?"

"Have our forces make a quick attack, not even make contact, but fire shafts into their force, then withdraw back along the road in a space where it's clear that our riders follow the road. When the last rider passes, our troopers pull the framework into the trench, brace it with stones, and then withdraw a few more yards. One of us holds a concealment over the troopers and the pike frame. If the Hydlenese come at a walk, our archers stand in the road and loose shafts, prompting the Hydlenese to charge into hidden pikes."

"What if they don't charge?" asked Rojak.

"Then your archers will kill quite a few greencoats. It will also back up their advance. If you have archers placed where they can loose shafts from the side, you might cause significant casualties."

Once more Raelf frowned. "For someone devoted to preserving Haven, you seem willing to fight in the town itself."

"If we destroy the Hydlenese, we can rebuild whatever they burn or damage. If they don't want to enter the town, we can whittle down their forces until they don't have any."

"If you're successful in taking out most of a company, I don't see Duke Massyngal's officers waiting for us to come to them."

"Then you could use something like those pike frames."

"I have some men who might be able to do that, but not enough, especially if they have to be ready to fight."

Beltur turned to Jessyla. "Do you think you could persuade Gorlaak and Jaegyr to build a few like that while I'm dealing with the patrol? It would be in their interest."

"I might have to talk to Julli as well, but I'll see what I can do."

Beltur looked back to Raelf. "Are we set?"

Raelf looked to Khaamyn. "Do you have any questions, Squad Leader?"

"Can we practice riding under a concealment on the way out of Haven?"

"I'd thought we would."

Khaamyn nodded. "I don't have any other questions now."

Beltur understood that. Khaamyn had questions for Raelf that he didn't want to ask around Beltur and Jessyla. "Then we'll make our preparations." He stood, as did Jessyla, and the two made their way from the public room back to the rear of the inn.

Once they were outside, Jessyla turned to her consort. "You need to promise *me* that you won't do the attack if you're facing other mages and if you have any doubts."

"How about serious doubts? I always worry and have doubts." Beltur's smile was wry.

Once Jessyla had mounted and headed in the direction of Julli's house, Beltur took his water bottles from their saddle holders and went to the kitchen through the back door.

Claerk looked up from where he was wiping up something from one of the tables. "Ser mage?"

"I need to refill these with ale." He laid three coppers on the table. "The regular ale will do, and in a bit, I'll also need a bite to eat. Whatever's available that you don't have to cook."

"Yes, ser."

After Claerk refilled the water bottles, Beltur said, "Just leave them there. I'll be back in less than a quint for the fare."

Then he used a concealment and eased into the public room, where Cheld had just appeared with Khaamyn, who had apparently been sent to request the undercaptain's presence.

"You're taking the company this afternoon. You'll accompany Mage Beltur and attack a Hydlenese recon company on the low hill to the east and overlooking the Hydolar road. The mage has assured me that he will not require you to carry out this attack unless the circumstances are favorable. You are in command, but you are to regard the mage as a senior captain of an allied force."

"Ser?"

"Cheld, he has more recent combat experience than any of us. The last thing he wants is to lose any men unnecessarily. Even with his ability to shield himself, he's risking his life as much as any of us. You may point out anything that you think he may not have seen or considered. You may ask polite questions."

"Might I ask why you agreed to this attack?"

"Because Captain Beltur happens to be right. If you're successful either in killing a significant number of Hydlenese or effectively destroying an entire company, at the least, it will reduce their numbers. At the most, it will also require them to use additional troopers to protect that outpost. That will reduce even more those troopers you'll have to face in the field. If they choose not to reinforce that post, then their ability to scout our positions and deployment will be less effective. Is that clear?"

"Yes, ser."

Beltur could tell that Cheld wasn't entirely pleased, and also that Raelf ignored Cheld's unease.

"Now . . . tell me which squads should be in what positions, and why . . ."

As the two began to discuss more company matters, Beltur eased back into the inn's kitchen, where, after again checking with Claerk, he took some bread, cheese, and a slice of mutton as an afternoon repast of sorts, not that the inn's fare was anything other than solid and only slightly better than barely acceptable, something he realized after having eaten Tulya's cooking for the past half season.

After eating, he went back to the stables and led Slowpoke inside, where he fed and watered the big gelding, talking to him as he did. He doubted that Slowpoke understood or cared what he was saying, but Slowpoke definitely appreciated the attention.

Before he knew it, Cheld was mustering the company, and Beltur led Slowpoke out and mounted.

The undercaptain looked for a moment or two longer than necessary at Slowpoke, then said to Beltur, "Company Three is ready to ride, ser. They've been briefed on the attack and its need."

"Thank you, Undercaptain. As Squad Leader Khaamyn suggested, we'll need to give your men some limited experience in riding under a concealment. Before we begin, I'd like to place a concealment over the entire company, while no one is moving, just so that no one is surprised when we're riding and begin practicing riding under a concealment. If you would have your squad leaders pass the word."

Beltur waited until he was certain all the troopers had been informed, then turned to Cheld. "Your company will appear to vanish." Then he placed the concealment over the entire company. At that moment, the only figures that appeared to be in the stable yard were Cheld and Beltur.

Beltur immediately called out, "Squad Leader Khaamyn! What do you see?"

"Nothing but blackness, ser."

Beltur lifted the concealment, then said to Cheld, "I'm going to conceal you so that the troopers can see that concealments work and that I wasn't blinding them to no effect."

Cheld appeared to vanish.

"Are you still here, Undercaptain Cheld?"

"I'm here."

Beltur waited a moment, then lifted the concealment.

Cheld blinked several times, then said, "That's why you wanted the rope, then—to guide everyone."

"Exactly. We can practice squad by squad on the way. We'll start immediately. That's so the troopers can get used to it on a level surface. Does each squad have its ropes?"

"They do," replied Cheld.

"We'd better get started," suggested Beltur.

"Company! Forward!" ordered Cheld.

From the square, Beltur led the company south on the narrow streets, finally taking the one that led to the solitary dwelling and outbuildings on the hilly and rocky grasslands. In turn, he cast concealments over the first squad, then the second squad. Doing so definitely slowed their progress, but not so much as trying to approach the hill holding the Hydlenese troopers would without any practice. He stopped using the concealments on the narrow winding path through the grasslands, where he did use his senses to see if whoever lived there happened to be present, but he could detect no one. Either people were absent, or they were hiding in a root cellar or the like. Once the company was on the narrow road paralleling the hills, Beltur resumed having the squads practice riding under a concealment, cautioning the squad leaders that the concealment didn't stop sounds from carrying.

Once they passed the side lane leading to the burned-out stead, Beltur kept sensing both ahead and to the south. He thought he could sense mages, possibly more than two, at the larger stead that the Hydlenese were using, but that was farther away than he could discern anything clearly. He also had to keep blotting his forehead and eyes in the damp heat of the afternoon, and he couldn't help but notice that the heat and dampness didn't seem to bother Cheld.

When they reached the last part of the road not visible from the hilltop, Beltur had Cheld call a halt, to both rest men and mounts, and also so that he could devote his full attention to the hill and the surrounding area. Beltur couldn't discern any sign of mages near the recon outpost, but there was what appeared to be a loose picket line or line of sentries roughly circling the hill, possibly about a hundred yards below the roughly flat area at the top. Then he looked to the sun, still well above the tops of the scattered trees along the sides of the east-west road.

After studying the southeast side of the hill for a time, he turned to Cheld. "There aren't any mages here now."

"How can you tell?"

Beltur managed not to frown. Surely, Cheld should have known that. "By the increased amount of chaos around them. Or, if they're blacks, the increased amount of order." After a moment, he went on. "Once you think everyone is rested enough, we'll proceed. From here on, until we begin the attack, everyone will be under a concealment. We'll proceed at a slow walk. That will make it easier for the squads to keep in position. It will also keep the road dust down enough that it shouldn't be noticed. Once we move off the road and through the grass and bushes, dust won't be a problem."

The calf-high grass might pose some difficulty if the sentries saw it moving, especially at the moment, in the still air, but around sunset, there was sometimes a light breeze, and the lower light level would make it harder to see. And if the Hydlenese noticed the approaching force, then Beltur would just have to drop the concealment and withdraw. But he wasn't about to mention that at the moment.

While Beltur waited and took several long swallows of ale, Cheld rode down the column, informing the squad leaders, then returned.

"Everyone's ready, Captain. Ropes are in place."

"Then we'll begin." Beltur was counting on the slow ride of more than a kay to take a good glass, if not longer. He checked the rope tied to the fan buckle, then eased Slowpoke forward at a slow walk. He set the concealment so that the troopers only entered it just before they might have become visible to a sharp-eyed lookout or sentry.

Since, for a time, whispered instructions would be possible, Beltur was ready to issue them, but for the first quint, it wasn't necessary, since, once around the gentle curve, the narrow road was relatively straight until it neared the next turn, where it headed almost due north. Just short of the turn there was a gap in the scattered bushes, and the ground was more level than it was immediately west of the center of the curve in the road.

As they neared the point where they needed to leave the road, Beltur said in a low voice, "I'm turning off the road. There are bushes on each side. Keep between them. Pass it back."

He'd gone not more than twenty yards when he sensed one of the troopers veering into a bush, but somehow, between the others and the horse, he recovered. Although Beltur couldn't "see" the sun, from the angle at which its heat struck him, he could tell that it was nearing the horizon.

Then he heard a muffled sneeze, but there was no reaction from the sentries much farther up the hill. There shouldn't have been, given that they were almost half a kay away, but Beltur still worried.

Perhaps half a quint later, the air felt just a trace cooler. For a moment, he wondered, then realized that they were in the shade of the hill itself. From what he could sense, the squads behind him remained in a rough order, although he kept having to widen the concealment as the troopers' mounts slowly picked their way up the hillside, most likely following Slowpoke's scent or aura.

By the time another quint passed, Beltur sensed a trooper, most likely posted as a sentry, little more than fifty yards ahead, partly shielded by the large protruding rock ledge beside which he stood, positioned so that he appeared to be looking to the east, both north and south of his post as well. The trooper was posted a good two hundred yards from the apparent perimeter of the recon post, not that the Hydlenese had yet thrown up any earthworks, at least not on the south or southeast sides of the hilltop. The next-nearest sentry was a good fifty yards to the south, but that was still far too close.

Frig! There's no way we'll get around either of them. Even if they don't see us, they'll hear us. And that left Beltur no choices in dealing with them. *Hydlenese troopers are enemy troopers, whether sentries or not.*

As Beltur continued to ease Slowpoke up the gentle slope, he kept some of his attention on the two sentries.

Then, he heard voices.

"Karkyl! Do you hear horses?" Those heavy accented words came from the nearer sentry.

"Don't hear a thing. Don't see anything, either." The reply was in the same accented dialect, except Beltur couldn't help thinking that he probably spoke a dialect to them.

At that point, although it was a definite strain, Beltur put a containment around the nearer sentry. Because he didn't want to strain himself any more than necessary, he just covered the man's upper body and held it until the black mist of death appeared. Then he did the same to the second sentry, feeling both sad and relieved to let go of the containment.

They were little more than fifty yards from the edge of the encampment when Beltur heard more voices, lots of them. "I'm dropping the concealment. Dress your men and charge behind me."

For a moment, all Beltur could do was blink. Even though the sun had set, it was early twilight, with more light than he'd anticipated. *It's too late to worry about that.*

Then, thirty yards ahead, he saw three men in green uniforms, just staring, possibly because of the surprise or possibly because Beltur wore an unfamiliar uniform and carried no visible weapons.

Urging Slowpoke forward, he formed his shields into the killing blades, but making them somewhat narrower, knowing he had to take advantage of what little surprise was left but that he also couldn't afford to exhaust himself the way he had before. The greencoats seemed frozen, or perhaps it was that time seemed to stand still as Slowpoke's hooves dug into the mix of sand and grass and propelled Beltur toward the three.

He was less than ten yards away when two of the troopers suddenly unsheathed their blades and the third planted a long spear in the ground.

"Bluecoats attacking! Bluecoats attacking!" someone somewhere to Beltur's left yelled. "From the southeast."

Slowpoke stumbled on loose sand and rock for an instant, then regained his footing and charged toward the three troopers.

"To the southeast!" came a command.

"Second Squad! On me!"

Beltur turned Slowpoke just slightly and cut through the three hapless troopers. Beyond them he saw another group of troopers, perhaps half a squad, running toward the oncoming Montgren company.

"Let's go, big fellow."

As Slowpoke charged toward the oncoming troopers, a Hydlenese with a pike dropped to the ground in front of the gelding, seemingly out of nowhere, and braced the pike. The impact on Beltur's shields nearly stopped Slowpoke and Beltur, if but for a moment before the pike snapped, possibly weakened by the knife edge of the shields. With that impact, the pikeman was thrown to the side, already dead before his body slammed into the side of a tent.

Slowpoke kept going, but, feeling shaken, Beltur narrowed his shields a bit more just before riding through the half squad of troopers. Even so, three died instantly, sliced by Beltur's shields, and several others were wounded or flung aside.

After that, Beltur just kept moving, trying to pick off unsuspecting Hydlenese, while keeping an eye out for pikes or anything that might deliver that kind of blow to his shields. In less than a quint, most of the fighting was over. It was clear that the attack had in fact been a total surprise and that the defenders had been unable to organize into an effective force.

Because they were tired from the ride from Hydolar . . . or because they expected us just to defend? Tired as Beltur was, he decided to think about that later.

At that point, he just reined up and took several long swallows of ale, as Cheld's troopers finished off the last of the Hydlenese who had not fled, although Beltur hadn't seen that many leaving. Not wanting to have Cheld's company surprised in return, Beltur kept trying to sense other troopers, but so far as he could tell, there weren't any, except for a handful of fleeing riders. The other thing he wondered about was why a recon post had pikemen, or had there just been a few pikes and he and Slowpoke had been unfortunate enough to run into a trooper who had one?

As he drank, he noticed that one of the squad leaders was throwing items onto a cookfire, clearly to burn whatever they could that they couldn't carry off. He hadn't thought of that, but he was glad that Cheld or his squad leaders had.

After he finished a last swallow of ale, he corked the water bottle. As he replaced it in the holder, Beltur sensed someone riding toward him, and he turned to see that it was Cheld.

"You knew I was coming, didn't you?"

"I could sense you."

"Have you sensed any others?" asked Cheld.

"Some riders headed in the direction of the stead where those two battalions are based. I don't know that they'll try to mount an immediate attack, but it might not be a bad idea to take everything we can and return to Haven."

"I've got the men doing that already. We have over sixty mounts, some packhorses, and several days' provisions for a company."

"What were our casualties? Do you know?" asked Beltur.

"We lost four men, and seven more suffered wounds. Most of the wounded will likely recover."

"And theirs?"

"Over seventy dead. It could be more. It likely is." Cheld paused. "Your initial charges . . . they destroyed any chance they had to get organized." The undercaptain looked closely at Beltur, then said, "All you did . . . and there's not a mark on you."

Beltur laughed sardonically. "I'll have bruises in more than a few places. That's because my shields distribute the force of attacks. Slowpoke and I couldn't avoid a pikeman. My shields spread the force of the pike. Even so, I have some large bruises. Some of them will likely turn brilliant purple and yellow. Too many bruises can also kill."

Cheld frowned.

"Today, we took out about a company and a half," explained Beltur, taking off his visor cap and pointing to his forehead. "You've seen this. Before the battle against the Hydlenese battalion, my skin was like yours. Afterward, I was so badly bruised that all the blood turned my skin black." That wasn't precisely how it had happened, but it was close enough, and it was something Beltur hoped the undercaptain would understand. He readjusted the cap and looked to the west, where the glow of the now-set sun had vanished.

"Your unseen shields . . . they're like armor, but if you get hit time and time again . . ."

"That's right," said Beltur. "I have to choose how much I can take. Otherwise . . ." He paused. "There were five mages who died in fighting the Gallosians when their shields took too much punishment." He actually didn't know the number, but just saying "mages" without a number didn't have an impact. "We'd better move out as soon as we can."

"Yes, ser." Cheld inclined his head, then called out, "Form up! On the double! We're heading out."

Beltur took a deep breath. He could already feel the soreness in his chest and shoulders.

In less than a quint, the company was off the hill and headed down the part of the narrow road east of the hill that led directly to the east-west road that would take Beltur and the others back into Haven.

LVI

Jessyla, Lhadoraak, Tulya, and even Taelya were waiting with Raelf at the East Inn in the last glow of twilight when Beltur and Cheld reined up outside the stable.

"You didn't lose many, I see," said Raelf, looking at Cheld.

"No, ser. Four dead, seven wounded. We also brought back supplies and nearly sixty mounts. They might be useful, and there was no point in leaving them."

"We should all meet inside." Raelf sounded neither pleased nor displeased, but he turned and reentered the inn.

Jessyla looked to Beltur. "Are you all right?"

"Other than a few bruises, I think so." Beltur tried not to wince as he dismounted.

Jessyla stepped forward and touched his face, then raised her eyebrows. "A few bruises?"

"Just a few."

"Beltur . . ."

"I tried to avoid too much contact, but Slowpoke and I couldn't move fast enough to stop a pike, except with my shields. That was the only time anything like that happened. I did my best to avoid doing things that would strain me or my shields or Slowpoke."

Jessyla sighed softly. "You're being honest, but you need to look farther ahead."

Beltur had thought that himself, but he still didn't know what a pike had been doing on the hilltop when there hadn't been any other pikemen.

With Jessyla's help, Beltur did make sure Slowpoke had a place in the stable to himself, as well as water and feed, before they made their way toward the public room.

"I'll need to see the wounded," she said. "The majer said that they'd be bringing them all here to the inn. I may leave the meeting if it lasts very long."

Beltur could understand that. "I could help."

"You've used too much order today already."

"I can use free order some, and sensing takes little effort." Unless it was raining or snowing, but that wasn't a problem at the moment.

The two entered the public room just after Cheld.

Raelf had made certain that there were beakers and pitchers of ale on the table, and Beltur filled his beaker as soon as he sat down at the big table, then took a long swallow. Cheld did the same.

"If it's agreeable to you, Captain Beltur," said Raelf, "I'd like to make this as quick as possible. I'd thought Undercaptain Cheld would report first. Then we'll hear anything you have to add after he finishes."

"That's fine with me," agreed Beltur.

Cheld took another swallow of ale, then began. "Captain Beltur led the company from the inn south from the town square, then southwest over a narrow and winding lane. While we rode, he had each squad practice riding under a concealment . . ."

Beltur listened carefully. He had to admit that the undercaptain's description of the ride to the hill, as well as the approach to the Hydlenese position, was unbiased and accurate, but he did wonder how Cheld would describe the actual attack.

". . . The captain maneuvered us within forty yards of the southeast perimeter before the Hydlenese sentries started to shout about an attack. He dropped the concealment and led the initial charge, breaking through the few defenders immediately present and killing most of them. Then he smashed through the first organized squad that approached. Most of those troopers were killed or badly wounded. Then he continued to attack and take out scattered elements of the Hydlenese company while we subdued the others. We quickly counted the Hydlenese dead and came up with more than seventy. I would estimate that almost half were the result of the captain's actions . . ." After that, Cheld described the gathering of mounts and supplies and the ride back to Haven.

When Cheld finished, Raelf turned to Beltur. "Would you care to add anything, Captain?"

"A few clarifications. First, the Weevett company had no experience in riding under the blackness of a concealment, except for short intervals on the ride to the attack. Despite that, Undercaptain Cheld and his squad leaders managed them so well that they did not give the enemy any indication that we were there, even when we reached a point within fifty yards of their perimeter. That speaks highly of their training. Second, the undercaptain credits me with too great an effectiveness in dealing with the Hydlenese after the initial charge and my attack on a small squad of organized enemy troopers. I helped where I could, but, frankly, I was trying to avoid too much hand-to-hand combat."

"Why was that, Captain?"

"Right after the initial attack, a clearly experienced pikeman expertly almost spitted Slowpoke and me, and we took a heavy blow to my shields. I had no idea if there were others, but too many impacts like that would have left me unable to help the company, and would have limited my effectiveness for days."

Raelf frowned, then turned back to Cheld. "You didn't mention pikemen."

"Apparently one squad of the Hydlenese was equipped with pikes, but the suddenness of our attack meant that they couldn't form up as a unit. We found fourteen pikes, but decided they were too long and unwieldy to carry back with horses."

"You left them there?"

"We started a fire and burned the ones we found. That may not have totally destroyed them, but it will have damaged them enough not to be usable. We also burned everything else that we could."

"Excellent."

Beltur thought so as well. He'd seen the fire and approved of it as a way to deny the Hydlenese anything that the Montgren troopers hadn't been able to carry off, but hadn't noticed the pikes.

Raelf looked to Lhadoraak. "To your knowledge, could any other mage have done what Beltur did?"

"I could likely manage to conceal a company, but I would be hard-pressed to do so under the conditions described by the undercaptain. I cannot kill in the way that Beltur does. I don't know of anyone else who can. Jessyla can conceal small groups and kill individuals, but not great numbers."

Raelf nodded, seemingly more to himself than to anyone. Then he turned back to Beltur.

"You realize how the Duke's commander will feel when he discovers that you—or we—massacred almost an entire company, don't you?" The majer's tone was almost genial.

"They'll be angry."

"They'll be furious . . . and so will the Duke."

Beltur shrugged, trying not to wince as he did. "If we play the plaques by his rules, we'll lose."

"We both know that," replied Raelf, "but our winning in that fashion is going to kill quite a large number of Hydlenese officers and rankers who'd claim that all they did was follow orders."

"What's the difference between their following orders and our following orders?" returned Beltur.

"You don't have to follow orders. I do, and so do the Duke's officers."

"No, you don't. All officers choose to follow orders. They do so because they believe in their ruler or they believe in what they do, sometimes both. Those of us who are councilors choose to do what we're doing because following other rulers' orders would have resulted in our death or eventual exile. The argument you're advancing suggests that following orders is a justification, but self-preservation as individuals or as a smaller group is not."

Raelf smiled. "I happen to agree with your point. Most rulers and most officers in other lands will not. I just wanted to make that clear." After the slightest pause, he said, "That's all I needed from both of you this evening. I doubt that the Hydlenese will attack tomorrow, but if the scouts find out to the contrary, I'll let you know. With what you've been through and accomplished today, I thought we might meet at eighth glass tomorrow morning, unless the Hydlenese appear to be massing for an attack."

Beltur didn't think that likely, but then, if he were the Hydlenese commander, he might have considered that.

"Also," continued Raelf, "it will be a while before Healer Jessyla is finished here, since I already requested that she take a look at the wounded this evening."

Beltur was about to mention that he'd help as well—until Jessyla shot him a glance that kept him from opening his mouth.

Then she said, "If you accompany me, all you can do is let me know if there's deep chaos."

"I can do that . . . and help with splints."

"We'll see what's necessary." She rose. "I'd like to see to them immediately."

Beltur rose with her, half wondering why she'd been so firm publicly, when he'd already agreed not to overstrain himself.

Not until they were out of the room did she say, "I wanted to make certain that Raelf knew what that attack cost you." Then she added, "It cost you more than you think."

As you'll likely find out tomorrow morning when you wake up. It was also a reminder that he'd better avoid pike lines, no matter what.

Jessyla had obviously been busy while Beltur had been gone, because the tack room that had confined Gustaan and the others "recruited" by the white mage had been turned into a surgery of sorts, with two pallet tables and some simple wall shelves that held what healing tools Jessyla had brought or found in Haven.

"You did all this?" asked Beltur.

"Julli, Jaegyr, and I all worked together."

"Jaegyr? I thought . . ."

"He and Gorlaak and some of the majer's men will be working on the pike frames tomorrow. Gorlaak said it would take the rest of the afternoon to get and load the timbers."

"Healer?"

They both turned to see a squad leader standing there.

"Are you ready to see the wounded?"

"We're ready," said Jessyla.

In moments, two troopers carried in another and set him on one of the pallet tables. Beltur could immediately sense the broken leg beneath the blood-soaked dressing that covered a long gash. Surprisingly, the end of the bone had not broken through the skin, but there was already a great deal of chaos in the wound.

Beltur watched as Jessyla removed the deeper chaos and then used a small containment across the wound that was part cut and part bruised and compressed muscle so that she could remove the old dressing and clean the area around the wound without further damaging the leg.

"You're not going to take my leg, are you?" asked the trooper.

"You should be able to keep it, but you're going to have to be very careful. Either I or Beltur will have to see you briefly every day. Now, first we'll finish dressing it before we put a splint on it. I can't put a full splint on it. That's why you'll have to be careful . . ."

Beltur mostly watched as Jessyla finished with the first trooper, although he did help with positioning the splint and remove a few bits of nasty wound chaos with free order.

The second trooper had a long slash across the back of his left shoulder, to the bone in places, and Beltur couldn't help but ask how it happened.

"Was turned to deal with a pair of greenies, and another one threw an ax. Grimstad took care of him, and bound me up."

"Battle-axes? I didn't see any of those."

The trooper frowned, then looked closer at Beltur. "Captain, ser . . ."

"I'm also a healer, but not as good as she is. I'm just here in case there's something that takes two. About the axes . . . do a lot of the Hydlenese use them?"

"We saw three or four, ser. Couldn't tell if they had a squad that all used them."

"Thank you. That's good to know."

After the trooper with the shoulder wound left, Jessyla said, "He's more fortunate. Unless they're wounded in the neck or spine, the upper back wounds usually aren't as dangerous, awful as they look. He will have quite a scar."

Although Cheld had said that there were only seven wounded, by the time Jessyla and Beltur left, she had actually dealt with ten, but with four the wounds were relatively minor, and, if needed, three of the four could likely fight. Still, that meant that the extremely "successful" attack had effectively reduced the fighting strength of the Weevett company by a tenth. *And matters won't be that favorable again, most likely.*

As the two rode through the darkness toward their home, Beltur considered the question that Raelf hadn't asked, although his questions had certainly suggested it: Did the end justify the means? Self-preservation was a good reason for almost any means, but did trying to obtain control of one's life justify any means?

"You're awfully quiet," offered Jessyla. "Are you all right?"

"Just thinking. So many people are going to die because a duke wants to take over another land and because we're stubborn enough to want to stop him."

"Beltur, we didn't start this. Besides, Montgren's a much better land than Hydlen. At least from what everyone says. When people like Gustaan and Graalur aren't happy with their own land . . . even Raelf left there, you know."

"I know."

"Unless someone stops people like the Duke, it just gets worse."

"I still wonder. I stopped Cohndar and Waensyn, and it appears that Caradyn just took over where they left off."

"That's because we couldn't stay to stop him. Here we can."

But how many battles will we have to fight for how many years? Or is there another way . . .

Beltur had the feeling that there was, but that it too would exact a high price.

LVII

When Beltur woke on fiveday morning, it was later than usual. That he could immediately tell because he was alone in the bed and because the light was too bright for it to be anything but full morning. He gingerly levered himself into a sitting position, then looked down at his chest and shoulders. The now-purpled bruises weren't as large as he'd feared, but even the movement of sitting up had let him know that he was sore in a few other places as well.

Jessyla immediately appeared in the bedroom doorway. "How do you feel this morning?"

"I'm a bit sore."

"You're in better shape than I thought. You had me worried last night."

"Part of that might have been that concealing a whole company for almost a glass did take a little more effort than I'd anticipated. Have we heard anything from Raelf?"

"He sent a messenger a glass ago. So far, the Hydlenese aren't moving. They sent some scouts to look at the hill you attacked, but they didn't stay. He doesn't expect any more greencoats until this afternoon at the earliest. So you can get washed up, and I'll get you something to eat."

After washing up, Beltur debated what to wear—the blues or his old blacks—and decided on the old blacks. If he had to do a patrol, or something, he could always change, but especially after the message from Raelf, he doubted that he would be riding out. At least, he hoped that wouldn't be necessary.

When he sat down at the kitchen table, on his platter were some cheesed eggs, mutton strips, and a fresh pearapple, with part of a loaf of bread on the side. "Thank you."

"You're welcome. The bread's not bad. Tulya said that the starter yeast you worked out is the best so far."

Beltur smiled. "That's a polite way of saying that it's barely edible and that I need to come up with something better."

"I had some. The bread's better than that."

After eating most of the eggs and mutton, Beltur took a bite of the bread, then said, "It's better than edible, but it's a long way from what Meldryn baked."

"It might take a while for you to get to that," said Jessyla, "since we're in the middle of a war."

Beltur frowned. "A war? Not just battles over Haven?"

"After we—mostly you—destroyed that battalion, I think it became a war. Things were heading that way, but we hurried it up."

"Do you think we could have done it differently? Better?"

"We could have done it differently. I don't think, in the end, we could have avoided fighting Hydlen. Not when they sent a battalion."

As Beltur took the last bite to finish the pearapple, there was a knock at the door.

"I'll get it." Jessyla rose and left the kitchen.

Moments later, she reappeared, carrying what appeared to be a Spidlarian uniform tunic and trousers, except the tunic was like his with black bands on the ends of the sleeves.

"You had my uniform repaired overnight? By Julli?"

Jessyla shook her head, offering a mischievous smile. "Yours is fine. I washed it, and it's drying outside."

"Then . . . ?"

"It's mine. I realized something almost an eightday ago. Healer greens are close in color to Hydlenese uniforms. If I'm to be riding with Lydian or Montgren troopers . . ."

Beltur wanted to shake his head. He'd never even thought of that.

"You've had a lot on your mind. I just had Julli make up one for me. Since I'm also a mage . . ."

"You not only need it. You also deserve it. I should have thought about it." Beltur couldn't help but wonder how many other obvious things he'd overlooked.

"That's why we work better together." Jessyla was about to say more when there was another knock on the door. "I'll get it." Still carrying her uniform, she hurried back to the front door, returning quickly, accompanied by Lhadoraak.

Beltur studied the older mage as he stopped just inside the kitchen. Lhadoraak looked not only worried, but slightly haggard. "What is it that's bothering you? Is there something I don't know?"

Lhadoraak shook his head, then offered what seemed an apologetic smile. "I can't help but worry where it all will end."

"We're all worried. No one with any sense wouldn't be."

Jessyla nodded, but looked intently at her consort.

Beltur managed not to frown, even as he was trying to decipher the message she was clearly trying to send. After a momentary hesitation, he motioned to the chair at the end of the table. "Why don't you take a seat, and we can talk about it."

As Lhadoraak sat down, Jessyla laid her uniform over the back of the chair at the end of the table before taking Beltur's platter and putting it on the side table. Then she took a beaker and filled it with ale, setting it before the older mage.

"Thank you," said Lhadoraak.

"You're welcome." Jessyla reclaimed her uniform and said, "I need to ask Tulya about something. I'll be back in a bit." Then she slipped out of the kitchen, heading toward the bedroom.

Lhadoraak took a sip of the ale, then smiled faintly. "It's much better than Bythalt's best."

"Much," agreed Beltur. "In the future, the widow might do very well."

"In the future . . ." mused Lhadoraak. "That sounds so promising. You make it sound that way. It's one of your many talents, you know?"

"I try. You can't make things better unless you believe it's possible."

Lhadoraak laughed softly. "There you go again."

Beltur smiled apologetically. "I'm afraid it's one of my faults."

"One of my faults . . ." Lhadoraak paused, lifting the beaker, then setting it back on the table without drinking. "One of mine . . . I worry more about the worst that can happen." He shook his head. "You know . . . if Taelya had taken after me, or Tulya . . . we'd still be in Elparta, and I'd be doing whatever Caradyn wanted. I wouldn't have liked it, but I would have done it."

"Do you really think so?" asked Beltur, trying to project doubt in his voice.

"You're being kind, Beltur. That's one of the many things I like about you. You want the best for everyone, and you've risked your life to try to make it so." He paused again, then took a small swallow from the beaker. "I've never been that brave."

"You've never been as foolish as I've been. I've dragged person after person into places that they never wanted to be. My uncle might well have lived if he hadn't been burdened with me. You and Tulya wouldn't have been pushed out of Elparta except for your friendship with me. Barrynt would still be alive if Jorhan and I hadn't been so determined to create a magnificent mirror for Halhana. We wouldn't be facing an army if I hadn't been so insistent on finding a place where people wouldn't bother me. How much of that's because I'm proud and don't want to bend my neck to others?"

Lhadoraak smiled again. "You are proud. Maybe too proud. I'll grant you that. But I think your uncle would have died anyway. The Prefect was after him and all the blacks. Athaal would have been forced to do just what he did, and both he and I would have died without you. Taelya would be dead by now. And sooner or later, even without the mirror, Barrynt would have run afoul of Emlyn and Sarysta, and without you, Sarysta would have destroyed Johlana, Halhana, and ruined Eshult."

"You knew about Sarysta?"

"Knowing how strongly you feel and what you can do, it was the only way she could have died in that fashion. Naerkaal figured it out, didn't he? You didn't think I could?"

"I hoped you wouldn't."

"Beltur . . . I don't think any less of you for that. I think more of you for having the courage to do it. I don't have that kind of courage."

"And it's gotten us all just in a deeper hole."

"I'll grant you that, too," agreed the older mage. "But should you get us all out of this hole, then Taelya will have a future she never could have had. I won't ever have to worry about not being courageous enough, and Tulya can live somewhere that she won't find cold and miserable." He smiled sardonically. "Of course, I am counting on you to do what I can't, and that's hardly fair. I'm being honest, though."

Beltur wasn't quite sure how to respond. Finally, he said, "You've worried about this for a while, haven't you?"

"Haven't you?" Lhadoraak's tone was gentle.

"Not as much as you have, I think. Perhaps not as much as I should have."

"It's time to stop worrying about how we got here and concentrate our worrying on how we get out of where we are."

Beltur smiled wryly. "I agree. Would you like more ale?"

"I would. Jessyla won't be back any time soon. Not if Tulya has anything to say about it."

They both laughed.

LVIII

On fiveday afternoon, another Hydlenese battalion arrived and set up camp at a stead two kays west of the low hill where Beltur and the Weevett company had defeated the enemy recon company. Raelf's scouts reported that none of the Hydlenese troopers or scouts had actually ventured into Montgren.

Late that afternoon, accompanied by a squad of troopers from Captain

Knutwyl's company, Beltur and Jessyla rode out far enough on the old east-west road that they could sense the new encampment that had grown up around the small stead. Neither could sense any mages. Then they took the narrow back road past the hill where the recon company had been and got close enough to the other stead, but there were only the same two mages there, unless there were others who could manage a total concealment of the type Beltur could, and, given the effort required, that was unlikely in a non-battle situation.

As they rode back toward Haven, Jessyla said to Beltur, quietly, "That makes something close to three battalions so far. Raelf thought that the Duke couldn't afford to send more than four."

"I'm wagering that he'll send enough to give the impression of five, or close enough," replied Beltur. "When other mages arrive will be when we know they'll be close to ready to start fighting."

"Why? Because they want to use the mages to deal with the three of us?"

"Partly. Also because word's likely gotten out that our mages wiped out an entire battalion. Their commanders want to assure the officers and men that their mages are here so it won't happen again."

"Would the rankers even know that?"

Beltur laughed. "I found that the rankers often knew more than the undercaptains."

"Gustaan knew more than his undercaptain. You told me that. But they punished him."

"That's one of the differences between Montgren and Hydlen. Raelf talks to his men. It's one of the reasons his troopers are better." Beltur could only hope that they were enough better, although the attack on the recon company had been a hopeful sign.

It was well past fifth glass when Beltur and Jessyla returned to the East Inn and met around the big table with the two majers in the public room, not that anyone else was in it.

"What did you find out?" asked Raelf.

"So far, we haven't found any sign of more mages at either encampment," said Beltur. "Just the first two."

"Do you think they'll attack without more mages?" asked Jessyla.

"I have my doubts," replied Raelf, "but it's possible. We'll continue to keep a very close watch on them. With so many companies, they'll have to coordinate their attacks, and that means we'll have some time to think about how to counter anything we haven't already considered."

"We'll also need to find out where they place their mages," added Beltur. "And where the strongest and weakest are."

Rojak frowned. "Won't they just send their strongest?"

"No two mages are exactly alike. Even among the Prefect's mages, and he likely had more than any ruler in Candar, there was quite a variation in their abilities and strength."

"Can you be as effective as you were the other day?" Rojak asked Beltur. "That's the real question."

"I can do what I can do, but I'd likely be unable to continue long before dealing with more than a few companies."

Rojak turned to Raelf. "How can we entice or force the Hydlenese to split their forces?"

"We don't have to do anything for that to happen. It they insist on massing their forces, we'll loose arrows into those in the middle until they do split. There are also a few other ways we're working on to slow or stop their advance in a way that will make them more vulnerable. If we can do that and continue to reduce their numbers, in time, we can destroy them."

"They won't give us that time," snapped Rojak.

"They already have, and they've lost a company."

"One out of possibly twenty-five. We have six."

"I doubt that they can bring that many companies, but we'll see," said Raelf.

"That we will. Now . . . if you'll excuse me." Rojak pushed back his chair and stood, then turned and walked from the public room.

Once Rojak was gone, Raelf smiled and said pleasantly, "Don't mind Rojak. He's begun to understand that he's not here to deal with a band of barely organized brigands and that the mere appearance of companies of troopers from Lydiar isn't going to make Duke Massyngal back off. Now . . . where were we?"

Beltur didn't know whether to laugh or shake his head, and it was a moment before he replied. "Talking about whether the Hydlenese would split their forces and in what fashion, and where they might put their mages."

"You know more about that than I do," replied Raelf. "Where do you think they'll place them?"

"I'd think they'd want them close enough to protect their frontline troopers, but far enough back so that they could move elsewhere as needed. Part of that depends on how many mages are accompanying their troopers. I don't see how they can have enough to put a mage with every company. If they sent ten, they might have enough to put one with every other company, but I wouldn't do that. That would spread them out too much, and if they know we even have one strong mage, that mage could take out the weaker white mages. I'd probably have two or three with the main attacking force, close enough together that they could reinforce each other. That way, if we don't have a mage opposing that force, they'll use chaos bolts to break our defenses without our being able to take out their troopers."

"You're saying that they'll limit the number of separate forces making an attack to what they can cover with at least two mages."

"That's what I'd do. I don't know what they'll do."

"You figured it out. So will they." Raelf's smile was grim. "How do we stop them without losing men and without spreading you three too thin?"

"Earthworks would help. Chaos bolts can't do much to rock and dirt. That's another reason why we thought that putting archers in the hills opposite that patch of forest would help. You could put some in the trees as well. Most chaos bolts can't burn through a really big and thick trunk."

"Couldn't they start a fire?"

"They could, but it would take a while to catch. It's summer, and everything here is pretty damp."

"Say that they attack from three separate points at the same time. How would you recommend we deploy you three mages?"

"That would depend on where they place their strongest mages."

"And you can tell from a distance which mages are stronger?"

"Comparatively. That's why Jessyla and I need to keep scouting their forces."

Raelf nodded. "Thank you. You've given me more to work with. We'll definitely keep you informed. In the meantime, please take care of yourselves . . . and let me know if you think of something else that might help."

"We definitely will," replied Beltur.

Neither said much until they had recovered their mounts and were riding back past the square toward their home.

"What else can we do?" asked Jessyla.

"Get their mages angry and flustered and get them to think we have whites as well by redirecting their chaos bolts . . . and keep their mages alive for a while."

Jessyla frowned . . . then abruptly smiled. "You didn't mention that to Raelf."

"No. I don't know if it will work, but there's no reason it shouldn't, especially if the whites aren't near the front lines."

"Lhadoraak can't do that," Jessyla pointed out. "I *might* be able to do it. I've never tried it, though."

"You'll likely have the chance to see," Beltur replied sardonically. *More chances than I'd ever want you to have.*

"Do you think I can? Lhadoraak can't."

"I don't see why not. You can use containments effectively."

"To kill people, you mean."

"I was being polite, but you've been working on holding and using multiple containments. I don't think Lhadoraak's ever been able to handle more than two. Several patrollers told me that most mages never got beyond two. You have."

"Only for a very short time."

"Chaos bolts don't last very long, one way or the other," Beltur said dryly. He glanced to his left, at the Brass Bowl, outside of which a squad of Lydian troopers was mounting up. *Scouting, training . . . or something else?*

"Do you think the rest of the Hydlenese will arrive tomorrow?"

"I'd be very surprised if they didn't come soon. Whether that's tomorrow or eightday, or even oneday, I couldn't say."

"Tomorrow," declared Jessyla. "And they'll attack on oneday or twoday."

"You're rather certain about that."

"I might as well be." She smiled mischievously.

"Then, I'll match that. They'll attack on twoday."

"That gives you three days to teach me something about redirecting chaos bolts."

"We'll start when we get home." *Another thing you should have thought about earlier.*

LIX

Sevenday dawned hot, and Beltur and Jessyla were awake soon after dawn.

"We might as well get up," said Beltur, immediately sitting up and blotting his forehead with the back of his forearm. "I'll sweat more lying here."

"In the summer, you sweat whatever you're doing," replied Jessyla as she sat up in bed. Then she grinned at him and added, "Even in bed."

Beltur flushed, then shook his head ruefully, stood, and walked to the washroom, where he took the pitcher and made his way to the kitchen cistern. There he filled the pitcher and headed back to the washroom.

After washing and eating a breakfast of porridge, bread, a little cheese, and a pearapple, Beltur then walked to the barn and dealt with his chores there, talking to Slowpoke and the other horses as he did, trying not to sneeze too much as he added hay to all the mangers, even though he liked its faint clean smell, if not the continual outlays for good hay and grain.

By the time he finished and returned to the house, Jessyla had cleaned up the kitchen and bedroom and was ready to go.

"We need to talk to Gustaan and the others, but we'll walk to the square," said Beltur. "We might need the horses later, and I'd like to keep them as fresh as possible." He smiled fondly at her. "When do you think the Hydlenese and their mages will arrive?"

Without the slightest hesitation, she replied, "Between third and fourth glass."

He grinned. "Still certain about that?"

She offered an amused smile in return. "I never said anything about the time, but since you wanted certainty, I'm happy to oblige. We should go. Julli said she might have some burnet and possibly even more brinn."

"You think they'll have a market day?"

"Of course. It might be the last chance for an eightday or longer. They all know that the Hydlenese won't arrive until later in the day, if they come today. So everyone will be there early."

The two set out, Beltur still wearing his older blacks.

When they reached the square, despite what Jessyla had said, Beltur found that he was still surprised to see Julli and her cart in the market square so early, along with Ennalee. "You two are here early."

"It just might be the last time to have a market for a time," replied Ennalee tartly. "I do hope you and the troopers can put those greencoat ruffians in their place."

"That's our aim," replied Beltur with a cheerful tone he didn't feel.

"After that," added Ennalee, "you need to go and put Duke Massyngal in his place. The very idea that any part of Montgren would ever want to be under his fat greasy thumb!" She shook her head for emphasis.

"We'll do what we have to." *And what we can.* Beltur nodded to the older woman.

"Do you have any more brinn?" Jessyla asked Julli.

"Some. I put it and the burnet in this old basket. You can keep it."

Beltur glanced at the sturdy reed basket as Jessyla took it. It didn't look all that old to him, but that was between the two women.

"Thank you."

"My pleasure. We all hope you won't need it."

That was definitely a vain hope, Beltur knew as he nodded once more.

The two turned and walked to the quarters building, whose front room now also served as the muster room for the small town patrol of Haven.

Gustaan stood on the narrow front porch, waiting as the two mages approached.

"Good morning," offered Beltur.

"The same to you, Councilors. You think the rest of the Hydlenese are going to show up today?"

Beltur waited.

"More than likely sometime this afternoon," replied Jessyla.

"It was bound to happen," replied the former squad leader.

"Why do you say that?" asked Jessyla.

"From what I heard and saw, no one can tell the Duke what he doesn't want to hear. Not if they value their life and family. Graalur said it got even worse after we were forced out." Gustaan turned to Beltur. "That's why the only thing that stopped that last battalion was killing most of them. They were more afraid of the Duke than death."

Beltur had felt that all along, but hearing it from Gustaan just confirmed his fears. "You make it sound like we'll have to do something like that again."

"You might not have to go as far, ser, but you'll have to beat them so decisively that they'll break and flee. No one will want to return from a defeat."

Make them break and flee? Slightly more promising than having to slaughter thousands of men who had put themselves in a position where they had little choice. "That's something to think about. Thank you."

"The others are inside." Gustaan gestured, then opened the door.

The other four—Therran, Turlow, Dussef, and Graalur, also in patroller blues—jumped to their feet.

"You can all sit down," said Beltur. "This won't take long. There are now three battalions of Hydlenese troopers southwest of Haven. Since we haven't discerned any mages, it's likely that the last contingent, a battalion or so, will arrive this afternoon, and no later than tomorrow. It's unlikely that any major fighting will happen until oneday or twoday. Your job is to keep order here in Haven as best you can. You are not to join the fighting unless you're attacked. Is that clear?" Beltur looked at each patroller, one at a time.

"Ser?" offered Gustaan.

"Yes?"

"Even with the Lydian troopers you're outnumbered."

"That's true. But once all the fighting's over, they'll all vanish, and if you all get yourselves wounded or killed, who'll be left to keep the peace? I know none of you would shrink from fighting, but you've all barely recovered from the last time you fought, and we'll need you after the fighting's done." Beltur paused, then added, "Part of this mess is because the Lydians let it get this far. Let them be the ones to do the sacrificing this time." He managed a lopsided grin.

"You're sure about that, ser?" pressed Gustaan.

"If I change my mind, you'll be the first to know. Also, once it's over I just might need you all for something special. But we'll talk about that when the time comes." Beltur gestured toward the square. "Market day is starting early today, and it might be good to have two of you out there."

"I'd thought that, ser," replied Gustaan. "Is there anything else?"

"Not right now. We'll keep you informed about what we know."

"Thank you, ser."

Once Beltur and Jessyla were out in the square, she looked at him. "Something special? Just what else do you have in mind?"

"Whatever might be necessary to make sure we don't have to fight again any time soon. I'm still thinking about what exactly that might be."

"You've already thought about it, haven't you?"

"I can't keep much from you, can I?"

"No, and I'm afraid I know what you're thinking, but we'll leave it at that because it doesn't matter unless we win."

"Until after we win," said Beltur firmly.

"Then we'll discuss it."

"I promise."

"Good."

"Since we're here," said Beltur, glad to change the subject, although he knew it wouldn't be forgotten, only postponed, "we might as well go see the majer before we head back to the house."

They found Raelf outside the stables, talking to several dusty troopers, but waited until he finished before approaching him.

"Is there anything new?" asked Beltur.

"Nothing's changed. Their scouts are staying on their side of the border."

"That doesn't make sense," said Jessyla. "They were the ones who started the attacks."

"It does if their strategy is to wait until they're all ready and they attack and wipe us out entirely. That way there's no one left to contest their version of the story, and that would be that we attacked a helpless recon company, and that they felt that Montgren had to be taught a lesson." Raelf's tone became increasingly sarcastic as he finished.

"What about the reports we sent?"

"There wouldn't be anyone left alive to corroborate them, and the Duke could claim that you councilors lied to cover up your misdeeds, and even that you misled me and the Duchess."

Beltur could see that happening all too easily, and, from the expression on Jessyla's face, it was clear that she did as well.

"Then, we'd better make certain that the only version of the story that is heard is our version," replied Jessyla, "the correct one."

"As soon as your scouts sight any new Hydlenese force," said Beltur, "we'd like to ride out and see if we can find out whether they have mages and where they are posted."

"You'll know immediately, and I'll be accompanying you. That will save time and give me a better feel of their disposition."

Beltur nodded, then said, "We'll be at the house."

"I'll send word."

"Until then."

Raelf turned and headed in the direction of the public room, and Beltur and Jessyla walked toward the square.

"Why are so many rulers like Duke Massyngal or the Prefect and so few like the Duchess?" asked Jessyla tiredly.

"You mean, men?" said Beltur lightly.

"Well . . . that could be a good part of it," she countered with a hint of a smile. "So far, I haven't seen as much arrogant stupidity . . . I take that back. Sarysta was just as arrogant and stupid as the Prefect and Duke Massyngal. Maybe there just aren't enough women in power for there to be as many stupid women rulers as men."

"That could be," replied Beltur, "but Sarronnyn and Westwind are both ruled by women, and I've yet to hear anything stupid from any of those women, and the Duchess definitely isn't stupid or arrogant. It could be that women rulers are more cautious because they feel every move they make is watched . . . and any weakness or failure is seized upon. It might be different if women had as much power as men."

"That could be. Sarysta thought she could do whatever she wanted." Jessyla shook her head.

"That's one reason why I've tried to be really careful with Taelya."

"Because you think she'll be a powerful white?"

Beltur nodded. "Everyone will be watching everything she does." Then he added, "People are starting to watch everything you do, now." *And they'll watch even more if we can put the Duke in his place.*

"Only Rojak so far," she replied dryly.

"And most of the town."

Jessyla just shook her head and kept walking.

Beltur smiled to himself.

Once back at the house, Beltur stopped short of the front door. "We really didn't get that much done last night with your sliding or moving chaos."

"I know. It bothers me." After a moment, she said, "You're right, though. Trying to practice it in the middle of a battle wouldn't be a good idea."

"It's my fault. I should have pushed you to do more earlier, but . . . we've had a lot to deal with."

"You also weren't in the best of shape."

That was unfortunately true, but Beltur didn't want to deal with that. Instead, he said, "Now . . . I'm going to concentrate some free chaos and surround it with order. Put a containment around it and try to move it."

The small ball of chaos-fire sparkled in the air. Beltur was vaguely surprised at how little effort it had taken, especially given how he'd struggled in trying the same thing for his uncle.

"I've never seen you use that much chaos," she said as she placed a containment around the order-bounded chaos.

"I'd prefer not to. This is an exception . . . for very good reasons. Now . . . move it."

The containment holding the chaos moved away from both of them, then stopped.

"Now what?" asked Jessyla.

"Move it as quickly as you can and then release containment as you're moving it."

Beltur watched as Jessyla did just that. The ball of chaos arced downward and struck the ground some five yards away, where the chaos immediately turned a clump of grass into a momentary flame . . . and then ashes.

"Oh . . ." Then Jessyla frowned. "It didn't go very far."

"You've got the basic idea right, but you either have to push the containment farther and higher or use some order to keep pushing and guiding the chaos. Why don't you try it again?"

Jessyla frowned. "You're sure you want to gather more chaos?"

"Small bits like that, especially surrounded by order, aren't a problem." In fact, Beltur was surprised at how little strain it was. *Because of all the work you did in healing with free order and chaos? Or just because your control is better?* With that, Beltur created another small ball of free chaos, still surrounded by order.

The second time, Jessyla propelled the small chaos ball into the street.

"You're getting better, but you might be better not aiming it directly at Tulya's house, just in case you suddenly improve a whole lot."

"You think I can?"

"It's clear you have the skill. Now, it's a matter of practice—"

"And your creating the chaos so that I can practice."

"I'm not creating it. I am gathering it."

"That doesn't hurt?"

"Not so long as I'm using order." Beltur created another chaos ball. "See how far you can throw this."

After almost two quints of helping Jessyla, Beltur was sweating heavily, and he could tell that she was tiring, although she was lofting the small chaos balls into the north-south street almost sixty yards away.

"One last time," Beltur said, "or maybe two. Except this time there won't be any order around the chaos. I'll gather it with order, but you aren't to put the containment around it until I remove the confining order. You need to sense the difference."

Jessyla winced. "I know it's necessary . . ."

"That's what it will take if you want to be as effective as you can be."

She took a deep breath. "Go ahead."

Beltur created the chaos ball, then stripped away the order.

Jessyla had the containment around it and flung the chaos ball. It flew a good twenty yards beyond her previous efforts. "Why did it go farther?"

"I don't know . . . exactly. I think it's because when we use order it's like a thin cord holding it back. It's a trade-off, though. I have greater control the longer I guide it with order, but it doesn't go as far."

Jessyla shuddered. "It still feels . . . wrong, in a way."

"As I told you before, it's just chaotic, and that goes against order. It's uncomfortable."

"Is it for you?"

"Not as much as for you, but that's likely because I was raised by a white mage."

"I wouldn't want to do this often, I mean, handling the chaos without the protection of order."

"It's not a good idea, but you needed to feel how it is that way." Beltur smiled. "I'm ready for an ale. How about you?"

"That makes two of us." She paused. "Thank you for working with me."

"I should have done it earlier." *Much earlier.*

"I'm not sure I would have been ready much earlier."

Beltur had the feeling that her words were mostly true, but that a little bit might have been to make him feel better—which made him feel a little guiltier.

Not unexpectedly, a messenger appeared at the house at two quints past fourth glass, with the news that another Hydlenese force had arrived, most likely somewhat larger than a battalion, and a request that Raelf join them on an immediate reconnaissance of the enemy positions and emplacements.

"We'll be ready in about a quint," Beltur said.

"The majer said that he'd join you here, sers."

"We'll be waiting."

Once the trooper rode off, Beltur turned to Jessyla. "You were right."

"I like the way you said that."

"The way I said it?"

"You weren't angry, chagrined, or irritated. You just stated it. Many men couldn't."

A year earlier, Beltur knew, he would have been one of those men, but Jessyla knew that, and there wasn't any point in stating it. "If you'd fill the water bottles with ale, I'll start on saddling the horses. Do you want the mare again?"

Jessyla frowned. "No. One of the others. I'd like her when we might have to fight."

"I'll still take Slowpoke. He told me he was restless this morning. Besides, you said twoday."

"I said oneday or twoday. *You* said twoday."

Beltur grinned sheepishly. "I guess I did."

"You're likely right. Since they arrived late today, they probably won't attack tomorrow."

"Let's hope we're not that surprised," Beltur said as he headed for the kitchen door.

Majer Raelf was as good as his word. Jessyla and Beltur had just led the horses out of the barn when Beltur saw a squad in the pale blue tunics of Montgren riding toward them.

The two of them immediately mounted and rode to join the two majers, since Rojak rode beside Raelf.

"Good afternoon," said Raelf as Beltur and Jessyla eased their mounts into the column behind the two officers.

"The same to you," returned Beltur. "Were your scouts able to discover how many companies are in this latest group?"

"Not precisely. It's more than a battalion by probably two companies, but it could be three."

"That was what you thought it would be," said Jessyla.

"Lord Korsaen's sources are usually accurate. I'd guess that several of those companies are here just to guard the encampments. That would free all the better-trained companies to fight."

"That still means four battalions," Rojak pointed out.

"I'd like to see what you two can sense," said Raelf. "All the recent arrivals went to the encampment to the west of the Hydolar road. I thought we'd take the east-west road past the turnoff for Hydolar, and if you need concealments to get better information, the scouts have briefed me on a set of back lanes. I've got a rough map, but it's not precisely to scale."

"It's likely close enough," said Beltur.

"There's also one other interesting thing," said Raelf almost offhandedly. "They only have something like fifteen supply wagons."

For a moment, Beltur didn't grasp the implications. Then he said, "If they don't have more on the way, they can't stay too long, unless they attempt to raid every stead in twenty kays, and that would make them more vulnerable."

"It also means that the Duke and his marshal didn't expect the first two attempts to take Haven to fail. Further, I suspect that the Duke insisted on the attack taking place now, rather than waiting for more supplies. I'd like to wait them out, but I doubt we'll be given that choice. They won't attack tomorrow, probably not on oneday. Twoday's most likely, and if not then, they'll strike on threeday."

"So we need to find out as much as we can in the next few days," suggested Jessyla.

"Precisely," said Raelf.

"Why would they put their two encampments so far apart?" asked Rojak. "There's almost two kays between them."

Raelf looked back at Beltur.

"I can think of two reasons. First, there aren't any large streams nearby. The only one of any size is the one that runs through Haven from the north, but it meanders southeast into Lydiar. Both those steads likely have springs with clean water. Second, there's a decent back road that connects the two, and they can reach the Hydolar road easily from both, even if we get heavy rain. Oh, and it's much harder for us to attack them undetected. That's likely why they didn't put a company on top of the hill where we attacked. They'll have a few troopers there all the time, I'm sure."

"They already do," said Raelf. "They also have some farther west on the road from Certis, a good five kays west, but on the south side."

"I can't believe the Viscount would come to our aid," said Beltur.

"He won't. He might attack Massyngal if it benefitted Certis." Raelf snorted. "That won't happen until after we fight, but if Massyngal's commanders want to keep a squad out of the fighting, I'm not one to complain."

The majers and the mages continued riding east from Haven, but Beltur didn't see or sense any Hydlenese near the road, although he did sense and later saw mounted sentries from Montgren posted at intervals along the road.

When they neared the still-defaced kaystone, Beltur began to gather in a sense of concentrated chaos to the west-southwest. He looked to Jessyla and murmured, "What do you sense?"

"There's something chaotic out there," she replied quietly.

By the time they had ridden another kay, Beltur was fairly certain. "They've definitely got white mages at the west encampment, and one is fairly strong. There's no sign so far of any black mages." Beltur would have been astounded if there were any, given Massyngal's reputation, but it was certainly possible. "We'll have to get closer before we can determine more."

"Do you know how many?" pressed Rojak.

"Not yet."

About half a kay past the junction with the Weevett road, Beltur began to be able to sense the different chaos concentrations within the western Hydlenese encampment, and by the time they were due north of the encampment, he was certain. "We can rein up."

"Squad! Halt!" ordered Raelf.

As everyone reined up, Rojak asked, "Why now? We're nowhere near the encampment, and there's no side road in sight."

"We don't need to be closer," returned Beltur. "There are four white mages. One's very strong, two are moderately strong, and one is much weaker."

"That doesn't seem like enough," said Raelf. "Do you need to get closer? Couldn't you find out more?"

"I don't know that I'd find out any more, and they might discover that we're here."

"Can't they already?" asked Rojak. "You know about them."

"It doesn't work that way. All the chaos around most whites means that they can't sense as far as blacks can."

Raelf frowned. "I don't believe I've ever heard that before."

"There's a rough balance," returned Beltur. "They can muster more destruction at a greater distance, but they can't sense as far. We can sense farther, but we can't do as much destructive. Some blacks can't at all, and some whites can't sense more than a hundred yards, if that."

"How close will you need to get to the eastern encampment?"

"If we take the side road east of the Hydolar road, the one that gets near the hill we attacked, we can likely get to a point north of the first encampment."

"What about the troopers on the hill?" asked Rojak.

"There were only a score." Raelf turned to Beltur. "Can you sense if there are more there before we get too close?"

"I can tell you at a distance of somewhere between two and three kays. That's about as far as where the side road meets the main road."

"Then we'll know before they'd even think about making an attack."

In moments, Beltur and Jessyla were leading the squad back east along the road.

Some two quints later, they reined up at the side road.

Beltur looked at Jessyla. "What do you sense?"

"There's no concentration of either order or chaos on the hill or near it. Beyond that, it's a little far for me."

Beltur focused his senses on the hill, but could only discern ten men and their mounts. He reported that to Raelf.

"The same as this morning. We should take the side road."

Another quint passed before the squad reached the wide curve in the road where it shifted from heading north and south to heading east.

"There are still only ten men there," said Beltur. "Five of them are watching us. At least, they've moved to the east side of the hilltop. There are also some scouts on the hilltops on those hills to our right. They're less than a kay away."

"That makes sense," said Raelf. "Their commanders would want to know if anyone is using this road. If we want to use it without them knowing, we'll have to take the back lanes south out of the center of town."

"We can't move as quickly that way," said Rojak.

"We also won't get attacked as soon."

After another quint, Beltur reined up and asked Jessyla, "What do you sense?"

"It's fuzzy. There is one small concentration of chaos, and one larger one."

"Good! You're getting better." Beltur turned in the saddle and pointed south. "The second encampment is a kay beyond the hills there. There are two whites at that encampment. One's moderately strong, and one is weaker."

"Six in all, then," said Raelf. "Twice your number."

"We're outnumbered four to one in troopers," said Rojak.

"More like three to one," countered Raelf.

"We've faced worse odds," replied Beltur, "but it would be better if we can keep the mages somewhat apart."

"We'll have to keep close watch on where they move companies, but we likely have a day, possibly two or three, because the latest troopers to arrive have been on the road almost an eightday."

"So have the mages," said Beltur, "and most mages aren't used to that much riding."

"That's a good point, but will their commanders consider that?" asked Raelf wryly.

"They might not," agreed Beltur. "The three of us have done more riding and fighting than any mages we know."

"Is there anything else out here we need to see?" asked Rojak.

Raelf glanced at Beltur.

"Nothing else we need to see here, but it might not hurt to follow this road east and into Haven. That way we can see if they've put more scouts in the hills farther east of here."

"I'd thought that might be a possibility," said Raelf.

Once they resumed riding east, Beltur and Jessyla kept sensing for scouts, but after they'd covered another half kay, there weren't any more scouts to the east.

When they reached the winding lane that ran through the rocky grassland south of the western part of Haven, Raelf stopped the squad and turned in the saddle to survey the road they had just taken. After several moments, he said, "The Hydlenese in the eastern encampment just might send a few companies along that road just to probe our defenses, possibly tomorrow or on oneday. We need to be ready for that possibility."

"What do you have in mind?" asked Rojak skeptically.

"Attack them either here or just south of those two steads."

"Not when they're between the forest and the hills?" questioned Jessyla.

"Not if they don't send a substantial force. I'd rather save the hills and forest for a time when they've got so many troopers that they can't move that easily. The area there doesn't look as confined as it is. That's because the ten yards closest to the bottom of the hills are much rougher than they look with that soft sand and small boulders. A company or two could more easily reverse and retreat, but that wouldn't be near as easy with a larger force."

Beltur hadn't thought of it that way, but what Raelf said definitely made sense.

"That does mean," added the majer, "that we might need one of you on very short notice."

"You know where to find us," returned Beltur.

"We'll take this winding lane back," said Raelf. "I'd like to get a better feel for it. We might be able to use the ground to our advantage."

Beltur didn't see how, but if the majer could that was all for the best. He uncorked his water bottle and drank some of the ale. He was not only thirsty but hungry . . . and until they returned to Haven, and dealt with the horses, ale would just have to do.

LX

Just after Jessyla and Beltur reined up outside the barn on sevenday evening, Taelya came running across the street. Beltur couldn't help but notice that the order and chaos around her were almost perfectly separated, and that both were stronger than he recalled.

"Aunt Jessyla, Uncle Beltur . . . Mother says that you're to come to dinner as soon as you finish with the horses."

"That's very kind—" began Jessyla.

"She also said you can't say no."

Beltur grinned.

Jessyla shook her head. "Then we won't."

"Can I help?"

"You can fill each of the buckets half full with oats," said Beltur.

"All six of them?"

"All six."

A little more than a quint later, the three left the barn, which Beltur secured with both locks and order, and crossed the street to Lhadoraak and Tulya's house. Taelya walked beside Jessyla.

A smiling Lhadoraak had the door open before they reached it. "Your timing is good. Dinner's just about ready. Tulya said I'm to escort you straight to the table."

"Whatever it is smells wonderful," said Jessyla as she entered the front room.

"It certainly does," added Beltur.

"Tulya's always had a way of making the simplest dinners taste wonderful," said Lhadoraak.

She had to, given how little most mages in Elparta were paid. But Beltur just nodded and followed the others.

"It's really kind of you to fix dinner," said Jessyla the moment she stepped into the kitchen.

"I enjoy cooking," replied Tulya from where she stood beside the stove. "This is simple enough, just a fowl burhka with a few additions and bread."

"What you cook is never 'just' something," replied Jessyla.

"It's easier here, especially now. I've never had a stove and an oven, or a kitchen cistern. This is the largest house I've ever lived in, and we own it. Now, do sit down."

"You and Lhadoraak are paying for it in other ways," said Beltur wryly as he seated Jessyla and then sat beside her.

"We paid as much in Elparta, and we got less," replied Lhadoraak, carrying a basket of bread to the table and seating himself. "Enough of that. What did you find out on your ride?"

"The Hydlenese brought in another battalion and four more mages. Only one is strong. Three are moderately strong, and three aren't all that strong."

"Compared to you, or compared to the rest of us?"

"Compared to you," replied Jessyla.

"They're all whites," added Beltur. "I think your shields are strong enough to withstand any chaos any of them could throw at you. Taelya could likely take one chaos bolt from the weakest mage."

"I could?"

"You *probably* could," said Jessyla.

"The problem is that he'd throw a second one at you," Beltur said. "That wouldn't be good. Shields have to hold against more than one chaos bolt, but that shows you're getting better. When you started . . ."

"It takes so long to get better," said Taelya almost despairingly.

Still standing beside the stove, Tulya looked hard at her daughter.

"I know, Mother. Everything takes time if you want to be good. But Father and Uncle Beltur need more mages. If I were better, I could help."

"You'll be more help later," said Beltur, "when you're still young and strong, and your father and I are old and feeble."

"That's a long time from now," declared Tulya firmly. "Taelya, you can carry the bowls to the table." She ladled the burhka into the first bowl. "This one's for Aunt Jessyla."

Taelya took the bowl and set it carefully before Jessyla.

In instants, or so it seemed to Beltur, everyone was served, and Tulya settled herself beside Lhadoraak.

"Where did you get the fowl?" asked Jessyla.

"Ennalee had two. I got the second one. She said they were the nervous type that stirred up the other hens, and there were bound to be things stirring them up enough in the next eightday."

"I can't imagine that," said Lhadoraak dryly.

"Will they try to raid people again?" asked Taelya.

"Not if the majer can help it," replied Tulya, "but we're not talking about that at dinner." She turned to Beltur. "Taelya's been a help in starting the fire in the oven. I don't have to spend so much time with kindling and shavings and muttering at the striker."

"I have to put the free chaos in just the right place, too."

"She had a tendency to overdo it at first," said Lhadoraak, "but she's gotten to where it's just the right amount."

"I have to say," added Beltur, "that you've kept your natural chaos, natural order, and free chaos very cleanly separated lately."

"She's made that part of beginning every day," said Lhadoraak.

"It shows." Beltur smiled at Taelya, then took a small mouthful of the burhka, not certain how spicy-hot it would be. He was relieved that, while it was definitely spiced, the heat was moderate. "This is very good."

"Thank you. I tried to make it not too spicy for you and Taelya, and not too bland for Jessyla and Lhadoraak."

While Tulya was talking Beltur quietly sensed her, noting that there was no untoward chaos around her and the child that she carried. Then he ate a mouthful of bread, thinking that, once everything was settled in Haven, he really needed to develop a better bread yeast. *If indeed everything here will ever be finally settled.*

"Did Rojak go with you this afternoon?" asked Lhadoraak.

"He did," replied Beltur.

"It was a good thing he did," added Jessyla. "There's a lot he didn't know."

"That seems strange for a majer," said Lhadoraak evenly.

"There's a great deal about Lydiar that must be strange," declared Tulya, "but we can talk about that some other time."

"How did you get the quilla in the burhka not to be so bitter?" asked Jessyla.

"You told me about how that trader's cook did it in Rytel, and I soaked it in ale overnight. That helped a lot."

Beltur smiled faintly. There would be no more talk of fighting or the events that might occur in the days ahead. Not for the evening, anyway.

Much later, as Beltur and Jessyla walked through the darkness toward their house, Jessyla said quietly, "You made that comment about when you and Lhadoraak get old and feeble. I wonder about that."

"Everyone gets old and feeble."

"Not if they try to do too much when they're young and strong." Her words verged on the tart side.

"You're really worried . . ."

"After the number of times you've almost died, how can I not be worried?"

And that's a good and very fair question. "I'll try to be more careful."

"Don't try. Just be more careful."

"I'll definitely be more careful."

"And listen to Slowpoke."

Listen to Slowpoke?

Jessyla went on. "If he doesn't want to go somewhere or do something, try something else."

Beltur couldn't help but wonder what lay behind those words, but since Slowpoke had seldom balked at anything, if he did balk . . . He nodded.

"Now," she continued as she unlocked the door and opened it, "we need to get to bed."

Beltur hoped her words meant what he thought they implied.

LXI

Although Beltur slept well after he and Jessyla finally got to sleep, he woke abruptly just after dawn, only to find that Jessyla had awakened almost as suddenly.

"Did something wake you?" he asked. "Besides me, that is?"

"No. I just felt that I had to get up."

"Then we'd better get ready." If they were worried for no reason, they might lose a little sleep, but if there was a reason . . .

That thought was lost as he watched Jessyla get out of bed.

"That was last night," she said with a warm smile. "We do need to get ready."

The two washed and dressed, Jessyla having donned her arms-mage blues, then ate quickly, and filled the water bottles with ale. The sun hadn't even peeked over the horizon by the time they were readying Slowpoke and the mare. That was when a trooper rode up to the house.

"We're down at the barn!" Beltur called.

The trooper immediately turned his mount, and in moments, he reined up short of the two. "Sers, the majer requests you join him immediately."

"Just us, or all three mages?"

"Those who are ready immediately. The others as soon as possible."

"Then we'll ride across the street and tell Lhadoraak to join us as he can." Beltur then mounted, as did Jessyla.

For a moment, the trooper looked confused; then he said, "Yes, ser."

Even before the three reached the walk leading to Lhadoraak's door, the older mage was standing there, albeit in smallshirt and trousers. "They're attacking on an eightday morning?"

"Apparently, they're doing something," said Beltur. "We're headed to the East Inn. Once you're ready, saddle a mount and join us. Don't take the chestnut. Jessyla rode him yesterday. We'll see you there."

"I'll get there as soon as I can."

"Oh . . . and if you'd secure the stable."

"I can do that."

Then the three turned their horses toward the inn.

As they rode past the Brass Bowl, Beltur saw a company turning out, confirming that at least some Hydlenese forces were moving.

After dismounting and tying Slowpoke and the mare just outside the stable, Beltur and Jessyla hurried to the public room.

For a moment, Raelf frowned as he looked up from the maps on the table at Beltur and Jessyla. Then he said, "I didn't recognize you in the blues for a moment, Healer."

"Today, I'm an arms-mage. Besides, it struck me that wearing greens in a possible skirmish could lead to some misunderstandings."

Raelf nodded. "Good thought."

"Lhadoraak will be here shortly," said Beltur. "We were almost ready when your messenger arrived."

"Oh? Some sort of magely foresight?"

"Hardly. We were just worried," said Beltur. "How many companies are moving and where are they headed?"

"The scouts report that a company or more is saddling up at the eastern encampment, but they hadn't left and likely wouldn't for a quint more at the time the scout sent the report. That suggests that they're coming eastward, either to set up east of town, or just to feel out how we'll react. I have my own ideas, but I'd like to hear yours."

"There are several possibilities," suggested Beltur. "One might be to ride toward Haven and do nothing, just to see how we react."

"I'd thought of that. What else?"

"They could be trying an attack from the south with the goal of reducing our forces, since they have to know they outnumber us . . . or they might be trying to sneak forces out east of town over the next day or so. That way, they could attack from three directions at once."

"You're as cynical as I am," replied Raelf, his words ending with a short sardonic bark of laughter. "What would you suggest?"

"If they're only sending one or two companies, I'd suggest waiting just north of the two steads on the southern outskirts of town. That way, if they come toward the steads we can engage them there. But . . . if they're trying to sneak companies east of Haven by that southern road, we could swing in behind them . . . and another company could be waiting and concealed where that back road joins the road to Lydiar east of town."

"That way, we'd have them trapped." Raelf paused. "That could be as much a danger to us as to them. Cornered rats have to fight. They can't flee."

"You'd be a better judge of how they'll react than I would." Beltur had to admit that he'd never considered that an enemy might not fight. "What if the company waiting didn't attack, but held at a distance, then gave the impression of withdrawing, and the pursuing company then attacked, followed by the waiting company?" Beltur hesitated. "That might be hard to work out in practice, though."

"It might be better to just have a squad in sight, and then have the balance of the company attack from the flank."

Beltur nodded. He could see how that might be more practical. "Either Lhadoraak or I could conceal the balance of the company so that the Hydlenese could only see the one squad."

"I've already ordered two companies to muster, with another in immediate reserve. If the scouts report that the Hydlenese are heading east we'll follow your suggestion. Where Mage Lhadoraak will be depends on where the Hydlenese are heading."

Before Raelf could say more, Beltur spoke. "For this first skirmish, Jessyla will accompany me. After that, we'll decide what is the best deployment of the three of us."

"You're more likely to understand that aspect of the fighting." Raelf's tone was cool but pleasant.

"We need to work out to what degree she can use certain new techniques. She's been in skirmishes before, but she'll be trying some additional uses of order. Also, with the two of us in one company, that may allow us to take a more active role."

Raelf raised his eyebrows.

"We have to protect your troopers as much as possible because we're outnumbered so much. It's difficult for one mage to both protect and attack. My ability to attack is going to be very limited in large battles."

"You're thinking of trying to inflict large losses before any major encounters?"

"Only if I can do it without weakening my abilities later."

From the corner of his eye, Beltur saw Jessyla's slight but definite nod to his words.

"We don't have that many iron arrows and crossbow bolts," said Raelf. "I'm inclined to save those for a larger attack, but I'd like your thoughts."

Beltur didn't even have to think twice about that. "We'll need them far more in dealing with a larger attack."

Before Raelf could say more, a trooper hurried into the public room, stopping at the side of the table. "Ser. Trooper Scout Massaat reporting. The Hydlenese have dispatched three companies. All three are heading east on the narrow road just north of the hills. They're proceeding at a walk."

"Is that all, trooper?"

"Yes, ser."

"Then stand by for a return message." Raelf turned to Beltur and Jessyla.

"You two are to join and support Reynaard and his company. You'll go to the two steads to block any advance there. Knutwyl and I will take his company and head out east to keep them from establishing another position. Mage Lhadoraak will be with us. Cheld will have the Weevett company in reserve, to head wherever he's most needed."

"Where is Captain Reynaard?"

"His company is mustering at the south end of the stable yard."

"Then we'll join them immediately."

At that moment, Lhadoraak appeared. "I got here as quickly as I could."

"You're just in time," said Raelf cheerfully before turning back to the other two. "Tell Reynaard I'll be there to brief him in a few moments."

"We can do that."

As Jessyla and Beltur walked toward the stables, he asked, "Do you think I was right about the iron arrows?"

"Yes. We should make it clear to Raelf that Lhadoraak will need those when we have to fight more companies at the same time."

"We need to talk to him about how to use them," said Beltur.

"*You* need to talk to him."

"I will."

After reclaiming their mounts and walking them through the companies forming up, Beltur saw Raelf striding swiftly toward Reynaard, already mounted and talking to his mounted squad leaders. "We'd better mount up."

Both did so, and when they reached the captain, Raelf looked up, then said to Reynaard, "Here are the mages. You three can talk on the ride out of town."

In moments, or so it seemed, although it was closer to a third of a quint,

Beltur judged, he and Jessyla were riding beside Reynaard as the company rode south from the square.

"They're only sending three companies. That sounds more like a feint or a ploy to see how we'll respond," said Reynaard, adjusting his visor cap over his reddish sandy hair as he studied the lane ahead.

"That's possible," agreed Beltur. "They also could be under orders to advance as far as they can. They know they have us outnumbered, and they might figure we're more likely to engage them on a company-to-company basis. That way, they could send companies until we've been bled dry. That's one reason why we're here."

"To keep us from being bled dry?" asked Reynaard cynically.

"No. To make sure they're the ones being bled dry. We should be able to shield you from arrows, if they try that, and from chaos bolts. We can also conceal your company if it would give you an advantage."

"I heard that was how you wiped out the recon outpost."

"They didn't notice us until we were within fifty yards."

"There are more trees near the town. They'll expect us to attack from hidden points."

"They won't expect you to be on an open road where they see nothing."

Reynaard paused. "They might find that unsettling. For a few moments, anyway."

"There's also one other thing we can do. We can blind them just before we attack, but only until we're about to reach them."

"That's . . . rather unusual."

"When we put a concealment around someone, it shuts off the light. So they can't see. We can sense what's happening, but only mages and healers can do that under a concealment. But I've realized that if I put a concealment around the enemy, they can't see. The problem for our troopers is that they can't see who's concealed, but doing so just before an attack can be very confusing. So if the Hydlenese seem to vanish . . . they haven't. I'm just blinding them momentarily."

"I think I'd better pass that on to the squad leaders, just so that they know."

While Reynaard turned and talked to the First Squad leader, including telling him to brief the other squad leaders, Beltur concentrated on trying to sense the Hydlenese, but he only had a vague sense of a large number of men and mounts, and possibly a mage or more, somewhere to the south-southwest.

"If you're going to insist on attacking personally," murmured Jessyla, "please keep it brief. Break their line and let the troopers clean up."

"You can break their line?" added Reynaard.

"Sometimes," replied Beltur. "That's if we don't have to spend too much order dealing with a mage."

"Do they have one?"

"I'll know shortly. Well before they see us."

Once they neared the southern edge of Haven, Beltur began to get a far better sense of the Hydlenese forces. "There's definitely a force headed this way."

"I don't see anyone on the road," said Reynaard. "No dust, either."

"There's a force somewhere over two kays away, just north of where this lane meets the back road that leads east. It's a little far to sense exactly how big it is."

"Are you sure?"

"If Beltur says it's there, Captain," said Jessyla pleasantly, "it's there."

"I apologize, but I haven't worked with mages before, and it's . . . strange to have someone tell you something you cannot see."

By the time Beltur could see the two steads clearly, he also had a solid sense of what they faced. "Captain," he said pleasantly, "there's only a company coming this way. The other two are continuing east toward the road to Lydiar. This company only has one mage, and there's one with the other two."

"Courier!" called out the captain.

A trooper rode up, matching his mount to Reynaard's. "Ser!"

"You're to find Majer Raelf. Tell him that two green companies are riding the back way to the Lydiar road. They have a mage with them. On the double!"

"Yes, ser."

Reynaard turned to Beltur. "What do you suggest we do now?"

"Let them come almost to the steads. We'll need separation between the two Hydlenese forces. Let the company coming up the south road seem to attack us. Once they're committed, we'll counterattack."

"It would seem to me that we'd have the advantage if you concealed us, and we attacked."

Beltur almost felt like hitting his head. He'd demonstrated so many times in the past year and talked so much about concealments that it had totally skipped his mind that Reynaard had no idea about the limitations of concealments. "That won't work as well. I'll show you. First, I'll conceal Jessyla. Just watch." Beltur placed the concealment around his consort.

Reynaard nodded. "She's gone."

"No," said Jessyla, "I'm here. I just can't be seen."

"I don't see the problem."

"Now, I'm going to put a concealment around you. You won't be able to see anything."

Beltur did so.

"It's . . . pitch black."

Beltur turned in the saddle and gestured. "Squad Leader, can you see the captain anywhere?"

"No, ser."

Beltur removed the concealment. "Because troopers under a concealment can't see, moving at any speed is dangerous. It took the Weevett company almost a glass to cover a kay under a concealment, and I had to guide them with ropes. I apologize for not making the problem clear. But you see why dropping a concealment over the Hydlenese for a few moments could disconcert them, and why I don't recommend an attack or a charge under a concealment."

Reynaard removed his visor cap and blotted his brow, then replaced the cap. "That does make matters clearer. Much clearer." He paused, then said, "You plan to conceal us until they get closer, then reveal us and let them attack?"

"I think it would be better to conceal all the squads except First Squad. If they see a whole company appear . . ."

Reynaard nodded. "I can see that. You'll let them attack . . . What if they don't? What if they turn?"

"Then we'll need to follow them because they might go east, and that would mean that the majer would be outnumbered. I'd thought that, if they did attack, once we finished with them we'd continue to the back road and move to cut off the other companies."

"You don't lack confidence, Mage."

"Let just see how it goes."

Beltur studied the road ahead. Samwyth's stead, more properly Frydika's now, was only a few hundred yards away. "It will be another quint before they reach the steads. Perhaps the company could move under those trees just ahead for a time. The concealment doesn't stop the heat of the sun, and for them to wait in the hot darkness . . ."

"We can do that."

"Company! Halt. Squad leaders forward!"

Beltur eased Slowpoke into the shade of a tree he thought was a maple, then uncorked his water bottle and took several swallows. Then he blotted the sweat off his forehead. Even at around seventh glass in the morning, he was sweating. *Seventh glass on an eightday, no less.*

He hoped that it wasn't a foreshadowing of the entire conflict over Haven.

"What do you want me to do?" asked Jessyla in a low voice.

"This mage doesn't seem that strong. If he starts throwing firebolts, I'll take care of the first one, and you try the second one. We'll work it out from there. I'm going to try not to take out the mage as long as he's throwing chaos."

"You're . . . oh . . . because you can . . ."

"Exactly."

Reynaard rode over to join them. "I've briefed the squad leaders. Now . . . what do you think will happen if they attack?"

"Once they're committed, we move toward them, but only at a fast walk. They'll likely be charging, and their mage will fling firebolts—chaos bolts—at our first ranks. We should be able to divert them. Jessyla and I should be forward, but on the side, so that we can see and sense clearly. Then I'll charge and smash through their front ranks at an angle. At that point, your men need to speed up and follow me."

"I thought you were only defending," said Reynaard.

"I can do this on a company level. It's far more dangerous and far less successful in a huge pitched battle with lots of white mages. That's why I want to destroy as many as we can before we get to a mass battle."

"What if they have a mage as strong as you?"

"This company doesn't. That's why I'm willing to risk a charge like that here."

"You can tell that? How?"

"By sensing the chaos around the other mage." *And by how well it's marshaled and controlled.* But Beltur wasn't getting into explaining that, not at the moment.

After perhaps half a quint, Beltur could sense that the Hydlenese company was about to come into sight coming over a low rise a little more than a half kay away. "It's time to get into position. I'd leave the four other squads under the trees. We can conceal them there as well."

"First Squad! Form up!"

"We should move forward to the open space in front of the stead on the right," said Beltur. "Your other squads will have time to move up that hundred yards once we drop the concealment."

Reynaard raised his eyebrows. "If you weren't as experienced as you are, I'd be concerned."

Beltur smiled. "You still are. But I'm trying to put as little strain and wear on your men as possible. We'll need every last one of them before the battles for Haven are over."

"You sound more like Commander Pastyn than a mage captain."

Beltur just nodded, concentrating on the road, where he could now see dust.

"There's dust . . . They're moving at a walk."

For the next half quint, Beltur just waited and watched as the green-uniformed troopers moved toward and then past Vortaan and Ennalee's stead.

When the first rank of the Hydlenese company was a little less than a hundred yards from the apparently single Montgren squad, a trumpet sounded, and the greencoats urged their horses into a charge.

A chaos bolt arced from the rear of the attacking company and angled down toward the first ranks of Reynaard's first squad. Beltur dropped the concealment from around the rest of the Montgren company and said, "I'll take this one. You get ready for the next one." He immediately used a small containment to divert the chaos bolt into the riders leading the attack, creating a splotch of flame that consumed two horses and riders and set the three riders following aflame.

A second chaos bolt followed the first.

Beltur watched and sensed as Jessyla caught and confined the chaos, then turned it back toward the attackers . . . but released it too soon, so that the chaos dropped a good ten yards in front of the attackers.

"Frig . . ." muttered Jessyla.

"I'll take the next one."

The third chaos bolt was slightly weaker than the first two, but Beltur managed to spread it across several more riders.

The fourth was much weaker, and Jessyla barely managed to lob it back onto the riders behind those now leading the charge.

"You've got the firebolts for now. Put them on the right side of the attackers, if you can," Beltur told Jessyla, then turned to Reynaard. "I'm going to cut across their leading riders. When I seem to disappear, your men should charge." With that, he extended his shields into cutting blades, if not so wide as he'd used before, and urged Slowpoke forward, simultaneously dropping a concealment over the first squad or so of the attacking troopers.

A firebolt arced over him toward the first squad. Beltur sensed Jessyla redirecting it into the middle of the last squad of the attackers, then aimed the big gelding slightly to the right of the middle of the attacking force. He kept low in the saddle, reducing unnecessary shield exposure, and lifted the concealment from the attackers just before he and Slowpoke slashed through the front rank. They plowed through four more ranks; Beltur turned the gelding and cut through two more ranks, then pulled up on the west side of the road and concealed himself as death mists chilled him in a way that wasn't in the slightest cooling.

A very wobbly firebolt arced in his direction, and because Jessyla would have to wait for it and because the white was running out of chaos, this time he redirected it back at the Hydlenese mage, encircling it with a mass of free order. The resulting fireball destroyed the remainder of the last squad of Hydlenese.

In a few more moments, the Hydlenese were turning their mounts, trying to flee, but the charred forms of mounts and men slowed many of them.

Beltur just removed the concealment, not wanting to use any more effort than necessary.

More than two quints passed before Reynaard rode up and reined in his mount. "That was rather effective. I'd guess that less than a squad escaped."

Jessyla joined them as the captain finished speaking.

"We need to move on," said Beltur. "Lhadoraak can shield better than Jessyla, but he can't redirect firebolts, and I'd wager that the mage with the other companies is stronger than the one here."

"What happened to him?"

"I used him to incinerate their fifth squad."

Reynaard swallowed.

"There wasn't any sense in wasting all that free chaos. Form up the squads. We need to get moving."

"Yes, ser."

As Reynaard moved away, Jessyla said, "You upset him."

"I know. He doesn't like to see troopers who were just following orders destroyed so wantonly. I don't, either, but if we don't . . ."

"I know." Her voice was sad.

"You did well with the chaos bolts."

"Except for the first one. I managed better with the next one he threw while you were cutting through their troopers."

"Do you think you could handle stronger chaos bolts?"

"I can certainly block them. I can likely divert most of them. How well and how far . . . I don't know. Certainly far enough so that they won't hurt our troopers."

"Good. You may have to."

By the end of the third of a quint it took Reynaard to get the company back in order and riding south toward the hills, Beltur was internally chafing at the delay, worrying about what might be happening with the other companies, and whether they had already engaged with the Hydlenese, as well as wishing that he'd sent Jessyla with Lhadoraak.

But you didn't know what she could do.

True as that was, it didn't allay his worries.

Once they were well away from the steads and the carnage, Beltur asked Reynaard, "What were our casualties? Do you know?"

"Three dead, four wounded, one seriously."

Beltur nodded slowly. That wasn't as bad as he feared, but the losses were bound to be greater in the next skirmish—the one to which they were headed.

"Do you mages ever get wounded?" asked Reynaard.

"Not until we're killed," replied Beltur.

"Or until a mage uses so much order that he dies," added Jessyla. "All of the mages who died in the war between Spidlar and Gallos were unwounded until the moment of their death."

Reynaard frowned and was silent for several moments before speaking.

"Is that because a mage cannot be wounded except when he faces a greater mage or when he has so exhausted his order that he can no longer defend himself?"

"Mostly," said Beltur. "A few mages have died without being physically wounded when they no longer had enough order in their bodies to survive."

"Beltur has been close to that point three times," added Jessyla.

"For just that reason, I wouldn't have survived the last battle here without Jessyla."

"Is that why—"

"No," replied Jessyla coolly. "Since the last battle, Beltur has been teaching me how to return firebolts. But I've never done it before. If I failed in trying to do it, you'd have lost half a squad, possibly a full squad. Beltur felt we couldn't risk that kind of loss, and Lhadoraak couldn't have helped me or caught a firebolt if I failed."

Seeing the puzzled expression on Reynaard's face, Beltur added, "Jessyla's always been a healer, but until we were consorted and I began to teach her, she didn't know she was a mage as well. She's only had shields for less than two seasons. She's had to learn a great deal in a short time."

This time Reynaard was the one to nod. "I apologize for my lack of understanding. That explains a great deal." He paused. "I take it that there aren't many blacks who can return firebolts."

"There aren't and we'd prefer that the Hydlenese don't know we can. The longer the Hydlenese mages think we're just whites like them, the better."

"I can see that."

Almost a quint passed before the company turned east on the road bordering the rugged hills. While there were definite hoofprints in the road dust created by the Hydlenese troopers, Beltur could only vaguely sense the companies. What puzzled him was that they didn't seem to be moving.

Another quint passed, and Beltur could not only sense the Hydlenese, but also the two other companies, those under the majer. "We're nearing the Hydlenese rear, about a kay ahead. The majer's forces are there, too, several hundred farther northeast, most likely at the junction with the Lydiar road." He frowned. "There's a rider headed our way. He just got on the road."

"How far out?"

"In the middle of the curve ahead, where the road turns to the northeast. The rear guard of the Hydlenese is about half a kay beyond that. He probably stayed off the road until he was out of sight of the greencoats."

"How large a rear guard?"

"Two squads, I'd say."

"Coming out of the trees and fields and onto the road and before a battle, the rider has to be one of ours."

Beltur nodded. He'd felt that, but hadn't realized why.

As soon as the rider came around the corner, his pale blue uniform confirmed Reynaard's assessment. The courier made his way to the captain and reined up. "The Hydlenese are about to attack. The majer's kept them guessing for more than a glass, but he needs to know if you can attack from the rear."

"We can. How far do we have to go?"

"Around that curve. It's about half a kay to their rear guard, and less than a few hundred yards after that to the main force."

"Tell the majer we're on the way."

"Yes, ser."

Reynaard turned. "Forward! Fast walk!" He looked back to Beltur. "Please keep me informed on what's happening."

"So far, neither side is moving."

"The longer they don't move, the better."

"When we come around the corner," asked Beltur, "do you want a concealment?"

"I think not. If they see us, they won't throw all their forces against the majer."

Beltur kept sensing the Hydlenese and the majer's forces, and less than half a quint later, as the first ranks entered the relatively straight part of the road where they could see the rear guard ahead, he sensed that the right half of Raelf's forces was withdrawing, but not the left, suggesting that the left half was under concealment. Then the Hydlenese began to move forward.

"The Hydlenese are beginning their attack, ser."

"Are they charging all-out?"

"No, ser. Right now, it's a measured advance. The majer's withdrawing part of his force, leaving one company on the side concealed."

Reynaard just nodded. After several moments, he asked, "Can you smash through that rear guard the way you did before? Even just the first few ranks?"

"We can do the first few ranks."

"Just that," added Jessyla. "You'll need him to do more later."

Reynaard merely nodded, although Beltur felt that Jessyla's words had irritated the captain.

The time seemed to stretch out forever and yet it felt like only a few moments before Beltur and the first rank of the company were less than fifty yards from the Hydlenese rear guard.

Beltur studied the mounted group, formed up five abreast, noticing immediately that about half of them—every other trooper—carried a lance. He immediately said to Reynaard, "I'm going to charge them under a concealment. That way I can strike from the side without their turning and that will make their lances less effective." *And keep me from taking too many unnecessary impacts.*

"However you can be most effective. That's up to you."

At that moment, the Hydlenese spurred their mounts forward.

Beltur concealed himself and moved Slowpoke to the right side of the road, then urged him on a full speed, waiting until he was roughly ten yards from the lancers before extending the knife-edge shields and angling Slowpoke between the two center riders.

Slamming through two ranks of mounts and men, even at a slight angle, left Beltur feeling several hard impacts, but the second line carried only sabres and small round shields, and the big gelding went through them with comparative ease, taking out two and possibly three troopers. But Beltur sensed another double rank following the first, and he turned Slowpoke to minimize impacts as they tore a similar gap through the next two lines.

Even though the second squad was scrambling into position, Beltur eased Slowpoke off the road and onto the shoulder, where he remained under a concealment and scouted for the white mage, who was almost half a kay farther away and throwing firebolts toward Raelf's command.

From what Beltur could tell, Lhadoraak was successful in blocking those chaos bolts, which was good because Beltur was too far away to try to do so without overstraining himself.

Still . . . you need to get closer to the white.

He returned his attention to what was happening around him. The first Hydlenese rearguard squad had broken apart, and the survivors were fighting the advancing Montgren troopers hand-to-hand, trying to stave them off while the second squad was heading to join battle.

Beltur took a deep breath, dropped the concealment, widened his shields, and angled across the back side of the greencoats still fighting, leaving a line of downed and slashed troopers and mounts. Then he turned Slowpoke toward the center of the second squad and went straight back through all four ranks, leaving carnage behind him. That effort left Slowpoke moving at little more than a fast walk by the time Beltur and the gelding had cleared the last rank. Then Beltur guided Slowpoke to the right side of the road and slowed him to a walk. While he needed to get closer to the main body of the Hydlenese, exhausting Slowpoke would serve neither of them. As he rode, Beltur pulled out his first water bottle and finished off the ale in it, hoping that would refresh him some.

The rear of the main body of the Hydlenese was still some three hundred yards away, but appeared not to be moving.

Not yet.

Beltur sensed the pattern of order that had to be Jessyla, closing the gap between them, and he turned as she rode up beside him.

"I think Lhadoraak's beginning to have trouble with that mage," she said. "We need to get closer. I told Reynaard we had to deal with the white mage."

"I know, but I didn't want to push Slowpoke." Beltur let his senses range over the gelding. "We can move faster now."

Before that long, the two were within fifty yards of the rear of the Hydlenese force, and within perhaps a hundred yards of the mage who had stopped throwing firebolts, at least for a time. From what Beltur could sense, Lhadoraak was holding out, although Beltur wondered how long the older mage would be able to block more chaos bolts.

"Attack from the rear!" called out a voice, likely that of a Hydlenese officer or squad leader. For a moment, all that happened was that some of the Hydlenese troopers turned in their saddles. Then another string of commands followed, and the last two squads or so began to turn to their rear.

Beltur glanced over his shoulder to see that Reynaard's men had broken through and likely dispatched most of the rear guard and were moving at a fast trot toward the Hydlenese who were still turning their mounts to face south in order to confront the unexpected attack.

A chaos bolt arced out of the Hydlenese force toward Reynaard. Beltur caught it and redirected it back into the troopers just behind the first rank of the Hydlenese who had just dressed their line, creating a blast of flame that turned more than a handful of troopers into ashes and charred forms and leaving a gap between ranks.

A second firebolt flared toward Beltur, who directed it back into the main body of the Hydlenese troopers, careful to keep it away from the white mage.

Beltur knew he and Jessyla had to get closer to the white mage, and quickly, and that wouldn't happen on the road, not with all the troopers massed there. "This way!" he said, guiding Slowpoke off the road and across a depression that might once have been an irrigation ditch and then through what seemed to be an orchard, although he had no idea what the fruit might be. He could sense Jessyla behind him, as well as the renewed fighting as Reynaard's troopers reached the weakened ranks of the Hydlenese rear.

Going through the trees allowed some progress, as opposed to almost none, but Beltur felt like it took forever to cover the perhaps hundred yards that brought them abreast of where he sensed the white mage to be, a mage who was clearly as strong as some of the Gallosians Beltur had faced.

He turned Slowpoke through a gap in the trees and then over a section of a collapsed rail fence before he and Jessyla could again reach the shoulder of the road. Two troopers gaped as the two mages appeared.

Three others turned their mounts toward Beltur, then backed off as the white called out, "Get out of the way! Now!"

For the first time, Beltur saw the other mage, less than ten yards away, and surrounded by a swirling flux of free and natural chaos. "Stay behind me," he said tersely to Jessyla.

The other formed a massive chaos bolt, but before he could hurl it, Beltur clamped an order-line confinement around the white, with secondary shields angled to both sides.

Everything around Beltur went brilliant, eye-searing white, and then black for a moment, as he felt lifted out of his saddle and almost ripped off Slowpoke, only to drop back into the saddle with a bruising thump.

His eyes were watering so much that for several moments he could see nothing. Surprisingly, he still had some personal shields, but little else.

He turned immediately, but Jessyla was still there.

"I'm fine. Your shields took most of the blast."

His eyes went back to the road, only to discover that he and Slowpoke stood at the edge of a blackened circular space some fifteen yards in every direction, containing only gray ash. Beyond that, for several yards, all that remained were scattered ashes and the charred forms of men and mounts.

He looked down the road to the northeast, where blue-clad troopers were cutting through the remnants of the Hydlenese. Then he looked back to the southwest, where the same thing was occurring.

Beltur's legs were shaking. He decided he needed some ale. So he drank some, as did Jessyla, and the two of them waited until Reynaard and Raelf rode toward them. Beltur kept watching and sensing, but he could find no trace of any other Hydlenese or mages.

The captain arrived first, looking from Beltur to Jessyla. His eyes widened as he looked at her.

Beltur took another look at his consort. He managed not to swallow or gulp as he took in her shimmering silver hair. "Are you sure you're all right?" As he spoke, he sensed her, but could find nothing wrong, although her natural order seemed slightly stronger.

"I'm fine." She frowned. "Your natural order . . . there's more, and your hair . . ."

"What about it?"

"It's turned silver. Not old. Silver like a druid's."

Beltur swallowed and said, "So has yours."

For a moment, Jessyla said nothing. Finally, she shrugged, a gesture Beltur knew she didn't totally feel. "It could be worse."

"At least your forehead didn't turn black." Beltur tried to keep his voice light. He looked back to Reynaard. "I hope you didn't lose too many men."

"Mage Jessyla followed you. The Hydlenese were so disorganized after the two of you that they were easy pickings. Then, when that chaos flare killed half or more of the Hydlenese, those few who could scattered. We lost one man, and had two wounded."

As Reynaard finished speaking, Raelf reined up. "It looks like we lost eleven men out of both companies, and there are a score of wounded, about half seriously. If you hadn't come when you did, it would have been much worse. Lhadoraak did keep the firebolts from burning anyone."

"How is he?"

"He's pretty shaky right now. He likely couldn't have done much more, but he did enough. That mage could have wiped out half our men."

"We were afraid we couldn't get here in time," admitted Beltur.

"When I got word that you were only facing one company, and two were headed east, I decided to change our plans. It seemed prudent. I had scouts circle around the road and sent the courier to inform you. We feinted, and then withdrew, so that the mage was the only one who could attack . . . well, until we couldn't afford to withdraw any longer." After a pause, Raelf asked, "How did you manage to burn up an entire company? I thought ordermages . . ."

"We can't," replied Beltur. "We got close enough to the white mage that he felt threatened and tried to throw the largest chaos bolt I've ever sensed. I put a containment lined with order around it for just a moment or so before he was going to release it. The combination of order and chaos caused the explosion. It also killed him."

Raelf smiled wryly. "All told, we've eliminated close to one battalion. That only leaves three more or so."

What the majer wasn't saying was that matters were only going to get more difficult.

Beltur just nodded. Belatedly, he realized that not only was his smallshirt soaked, but so were parts of his tunic.

LXII

Almost two glasses passed before Beltur, Jessyla, and Lhadoraak finally rode back to the East Inn, where Raelf insisted that Bythalt feed them before they all discussed what might happen next and how to counter it.

The best that could be said for the dish, which resembled a fowl stew spread over noodles, was that it was filling, and that, after he ate it, most of Beltur's headache subsided. Then too, the second beaker of ale might have helped. "Are you feeling better?" he asked Jessyla.

"I still have a bit of a headache. What about you?"

"The same."

"How many of their troopers escaped?" asked Jessyla.

"Perhaps a hundred," replied Raelf. "We didn't try to take prisoners, but we didn't chase down those who fled, either. I doubt that any of those who escaped will be of any use to the Hydlenese. Many of them won't return immediately, either. The scouts have reported a few stragglers making their way back to the eastern encampment. Not as many as you'd expect."

"Gustaan could explain that," said Jessyla. "It's never the fault of the officers."

Tulya, sitting beside Lhadoraak, kept looking at him worriedly, and her eyes kept straying to Jessyla and then Beltur, as if she couldn't quite believe what had happened to their hair. But she nodded at Jessyla's words. Taelya watched Raelf.

"That should work in our favor, then," said Rojak.

"A bit," said Raelf. "They still have three full battalions and most likely two additional companies."

"Have the scouts reported any other companies or movement?" asked Lhadoraak, still pale, although Beltur sensed that his natural order levels were only a trace lower than they should have been.

"There have been riders traveling between the two separate encampments and some going to the recon hill," replied Raelf.

"What will they do next?" asked Tulya.

"If I were their commander," replied Raelf, "I'd attack with everything tomorrow. I don't think they will. Most commanders will try to find out what went wrong before making another attack. I'm guessing that they won't do anything tomorrow, but that they will on twoday. Then they'll make either another attack like today, except from the western encampment, and try to strike from the west or northwest . . . or they'll make a massive attack, most likely in three or four places at the same time."

"Are they as smart as you?" pressed Tulya.

Raelf laughed softly. "That presumes that I am, and that I know something about their commander. I'm moderately intelligent, but I know nothing about who might be commanding."

Beltur shifted his weight on the chair, reaching back and trying futilely to separate the damp smallshirt from his skin while trying to concentrate on what was being said.

"He's not as smart as you are," said Jessyla. "After losing an entire battalion, would you have sent just three companies out, even with mages, and then split them up?"

"If I'd lost a battalion to a town without any troopers or armsmen, I would have cautioned the Duke against any military action."

"And if the Duke had insisted?"

"I'd have done intensive scouting and then attacked with everything." Raelf smiled sadly. "They will get around to that sooner or later. They've already seen that if they send comparable forces against us, they'll lose. Whether they understand that enough not to repeat the mistake remains to be seen. It might take one more lesson, but I wouldn't wager on it."

"We lost almost a hundred men, between the dead and wounded," pointed out Rojak. "They might think they can wear us down that way."

Raelf cocked his head, as if mentally calculating, then said, "At those rates, we'd both end up destroying each other. No commander will want to report that he spent four full battalions to the last man over a single town. Not when it will leave Hydolar defenseless on its border with Certis."

"Then why are they continuing?" asked Tulya.

"You mean," asked Raelf with an ironic smile, "why are they going to pursue a battle that, even if they win, will leave Hydolar vulnerable to Certis, and unable to attack Lydiar for years?" He paused, then answered his own question. "Because their commander has been ordered to take Haven and the surrounding lands. If he doesn't do that, he'll lose his command and likely his life. If he did make the decision to disobey the Duke, most likely his majers would kill him for disobeying the Duke's orders, because they'd likely be killed as well if they went along with the decision not to fight. That's why we have to find a way to kill most of them."

"But won't it just happen again in another few years?" protested Tulya.

"It might, unless we defeat them so convincingly that the Duke accepts the fact that he can't win." Raelf shrugged. "That's our hope and strategy. If the Duchess gives up Haven and these lands, then what will Duke Massyngal want next year . . . or the year after?"

"Then why didn't she send all her troopers?" demanded Tulya.

"She summoned all of them, but as I mentioned when I arrived, Fourth Company's squads were dispersed across the northern hills. Whether they could even be assembled into a full company wasn't certain. When I left Vergren, the Duchess had not even received a return message from Captain Byquaast. I only received the message that Fourth Company is on the way from the north last night. The fifth company is a training company. Given the seriousness of the situation, it will accompany Fourth Company. The odds are that we'll have fought before Fourth Company even reaches Vergren."

"This morning, you didn't mention any of this," said Lhadoraak.

"That was my decision. It's unlikely that Fourth Company will arrive before next eightday at the earliest, and I didn't want anyone thinking that they didn't have to do their best."

Beltur could see that. He also had a question, one he should have asked earlier. "What about those pike fences?"

"That was a good suggestion, and the carpenters and I figured out a way to use them without relying on you mages. That will allow you to do what you do best. If you don't have any other questions, I suggest you get some rest. I'll send messengers the moment I know anything." Raelf pushed his chair back from the round table and stood.

So did the others.

Then the two majers left the public room.

"I still think he should have said something about the fourth company earlier," murmured Tulya.

"He was telling the truth, Mother," said Taelya.

"Sometimes the truth isn't enough, Taelya," replied Tulya. Then she turned to Jessyla. "We're all having dinner at our house tonight."

"Are you sure?"

"I'm very sure."

"That's very kind," added Beltur.

"If you're all well-fed, you'll be in better shape to deal with the Hydlenese, and I cook better than Bythalt's cook."

"Much better," agreed Beltur. "We'll see you later. I want to talk to Gustaan. I'm hoping he can give us some insights."

As Beltur and Jessyla walked toward the stable, she said, "You shouldn't spend too much time with Gustaan. You need rest."

"So do you. That's why it won't be long." The others who needed rest and food were Slowpoke and the mare, as Beltur well knew, and Lhadoraak, especially Lhadoraak.

The former squad leader was standing in the small amount of shade afforded by the narrow front porch of the quarters building by the time that Beltur and Jessyla dismounted and tied their mounts. "What do you need, Councilors?"

"A few moments of your time and your thoughts," replied Beltur. "The Hydlenese are likely to attack in full force before long. You've mentioned that the Hydlenese officers aren't . . . well, that they tend to follow orders to the word."

"Most of them do. There are a few who ask what the objective is, but they get disciplined or leave."

"Because the Duke expects complete obedience and that gets carried down the chain of command?"

"What else? I've told you my story. Every man who's survived being a trooper in Hydlen can tell you the same sort of tale."

"Are the squad leaders any better than the officers?"

"Most are a little better," said Gustaan. "The few good officers cut their squad leaders some slack. As much as they dare."

"So . . . leave the undercaptains and take out the squad leaders?" asked Beltur.

Gustaan winced. "If you have to. But take out the majers first. Most of them are bastards, but they usually know what they're doing. The captains just carry out orders, and the undercaptains don't know sowshit."

"What else?"

"The second company in a formation is usually better than the first. The first company's often blade fodder. Not always, but it's a decent wager."

"In a large formation, how far back are the mages?"

"I don't know, ser. I never fought with mage support. They save the mages for really large battles."

"Would you say that's true for most troopers?"

"Yes, ser."

Beltur asked another handful of questions before nodding. "Thank you."

"Are you sure you can't use us?"

"I may have a special need for you, Gustaan, before this is all over, and you might not be there if you get involved in an all-out battle with the Duke's forces. And you're the only one I could trust to get it right. So do us a favor, and keep yourself in one piece."

"You're not just saying that, ser?"

"I'm definitely not."

"Thank you, ser."

Beltur nodded, then looked at Jessyla. "Do you have any questions?"

"Do you ever regret being here?"

"No. Even if this goes badly, I won't."

Jessyla nodded, then turned to Beltur. "We need to go."

Beltur agreed. He was more than ready to ride back to the house and rest—after they made sure the horses were groomed, watered, and fed. He also knew that dinner would be good, and that Tulya would insist that they not talk about the coming battle.

That was fine, too.

LXIII

Dinner on eightday evening was roast lamb, with new potatoes and baby beans, which had to have cost Lhadoraak and Tulya more than a little, but no one spoke about what they'd paid for such a comparatively lavish meal . . . or why. Beltur enjoyed it as much as he could, and tried not to think too much about what might happen in the days ahead.

Taelya did ask why Beltur's and Jessyla's hair had turned silver.

Jessyla's answer was simple. "We don't really know, except that it happened when there was a large explosion of order and chaos. Just like we don't know why Uncle Beltur's forehead and scalp turned black."

Beltur did sleep soundly that night, most likely because it was slightly cooler, because his stomach was full, and because he was exhausted.

He and Jessyla woke up just after dawn on oneday.

"Not today," she said.

"I think you mentioned that before," he said with a cheerful smile. While he was fairly certain she was right, he still worried. *What if they attack later in the day, hoping to catch us off-guard?*

Even by eighth glass that morning, after they were both dressed and had eaten, there were no messengers from Raelf, and Beltur could not sense any large groups of troopers outside the town. Everything felt unnaturally calm.

"How did you know so soon?" he finally asked Jessyla after he returned from dealing with the horses and talking to Slowpoke for a short time.

"I don't know. I just knew."

"Do you know what we should do tomorrow?" he asked wryly.

"Whatever we can to stop them and stay alive. I can't be more specific. What do you have in mind?"

"They've got four mages left. That is, if we counted correctly. We took out one weak mage and one moderately strong mage. That means they have one very strong mage, two strong mages, and weak mages left. They'll put the strong one and a weak one with the largest force and the other three either together or with separate forces, depending on how they attack."

"Raelf suggested that they'd attack in a mass."

"He didn't quite say that. He said that they'd attack with everything they have. If they mass their forces, that favors us. If they split their forces, though . . ."

Jessyla nodded slowly. "Lhadoraak may end up with more than he can handle."

"Hopefully not if he can use archers with iron shafts. But if we don't have a mage opposite each force, then their mages will be unopposed and destroy scores and scores of our troopers."

"You're saying that you need to be with the troopers opposing the strongest force, and Lhadoraak and I need to be together if they only attack on two fronts." She paused. "Are you saying that I'm stronger than Lhadoraak now?"

"I don't know that your shields are any stronger, but you can do more things with them, and that reduces your vulnerability. You can redirect chaos, and that means it doesn't get as close or strike as hard. You can move better because you can use your mount and shields as a weapon. Also, the fact that you can redirect chaos will make an opposing mage more cautious."

"Don't you think Lhadoraak knows that?" asked Jessyla.

"He may suspect it, but he hasn't been in battle with you."

"Is it fair . . . to make him fight?"

"In some ways, no, but, without him, we're more likely to lose. I just hope the iron shafts will help. He seemed to think they would when I reminded him about them last night. Also, if he doesn't fight, and we don't prevail, what happens to Taelya?"

They both knew the answer to that question.

Finally, Jessyla said, "We've put him in a terrible place."

Beltur wanted to point out that they were all in a terrible place. *But it's all your doing. You didn't think you could stand up against the blacks in Elparta. So you fled. You didn't want to deal with the lingering and growing unpleasantness in Axalt. So you left. It's come down to the fact that you'll have to fight somewhere.*

What couldn't be avoided was that each "flight" had resulted in a larger potential conflict.

"No . . . I've put him—and you—in a terrible place." *And I can only hope that we can get out of it without paying too dearly.*

LXIV

On twoday morning Beltur and Jessyla were up, dressed, and fed before dawn. Lhadoraak joined them as they were about to enter the barn, all three carrying two water bottles filled with ale.

"I see you didn't sleep late, either," offered Beltur.

"Taelya woke us," Lhadoraak said. "There wasn't much point in going back to sleep, and I saw you two were up and headed here."

Beltur had the feeling that there was more the older mage hadn't said, but he didn't press as the three readied the horses.

In less than a quint, they led the horses out, mounted, and rode away from the two houses. They'd barely turned onto the main street when a courier rode toward them.

"The majer is expecting you at the inn, Mages."

"That's where we're headed," declared Lhadoraak.

"Thank you, sers. I'll tell him you're on the way." The courier turned his mount and galloped back in the direction of the East Inn.

When the three passed the Brass Bowl, troopers were already out, and the courtyard was a swarm of activity. The area around the East Inn was less crowded, but when Beltur looked east, he saw why. At least one company, possibly two, were already formed up and moving, presumably to where they could meet an attack from either the east or the south.

Even so, the troopers around the inn moved away from the three mages as they made their way to the stable, where they quickly tied the horses and hurried inside.

Raelf motioned them to the table where he and Rojak sat, then immediately began to speak. "They're split into three forces. One battalion is headed east, likely to the Lydiar road, because they started early. I've already moved archers to the hills opposite the small overgrown forest. They'll be relatively safe from firebolts, and you three are going to be needed closer to Haven."

"Did I see two companies headed that way?" asked Beltur.

"You did. Two of the companies from Lydiar—Deminaar's and Naajuk's. Majer Rojak will be in command there. He'll be leaving as soon as we finish here."

"What about in the forest?" asked Beltur.

"There are some archers there, too," answered Raelf. "The other battalion at the eastern encampment was just getting ready to move out. They're far enough back that they'll likely make a separate attack. I'd guess that they're going to attack from the south, either the way they did earlier or possibly along the winding lane through the rocky grassland. The largest force is coming from the eastern encampment. Two battalions are moving toward the Hydolar road."

"Which one will be in position first?" asked Jessyla.

"It looks like they're going to try to make a simultaneous attack. The middle force, the one that looks likely to come from the south, may be in position the soonest."

"If we can engage the middle battalion before they get in position . . ." began Beltur.

Rojak frowned but didn't speak.

"What do you have in mind?" asked Raelf.

Rojak leaned forward slightly, his eyes on Beltur.

"Jessyla and I could see what we could do about weakening them, enough so that she could handle the magery there, and then I could still get to our forces on the west side of town before the Hydlenese attack. Lhadoraak would need to be with the forces in the east because they'll be farther away." Beltur had no intention of revealing entirely what he had in mind, largely because it might not work. *But if it does . . .* "But Lhadoraak's going to need some archers or crossbowmen with iron shafts."

"I've already thought about that. I'm sending half a squad from the Weevett company with him, and I've told Naajuk and Deminaar that the squad is completely under your control," Raelf said to Lhadoraak. "That way you can direct their shafts when and where necessary."

Lhadoraak nodded.

"As for your suggestion, Beltur, that will work into what I'd planned," said Raelf. "We've set up a line of concealed earthworks more than a kay west of town flanking the road, and a squad is out there finishing earthworks across the road. We'll use the earthworks to slow them down. We've also got more than a few dummies stuffed with brush there, to give an impression of more men than we have."

"Won't they just go around them?" asked Lhadoraak.

"That's harder than it looks. There's a swampy marsh to the south and some orchards and woodlots to the north. If they try to circle around, they'll expose more of their troopers to our archers. If they try the marsh, they'll get slowed in the muck, and that will cost them a few troopers. Just when they're close enough to charge the earthworks, our troopers will withdraw quickly past our second line of defense. Those are the pike-like fences you suggested. They're flat now and smeared with dirt and clay, except for the points. That will make them harder to see since there are quite a few trees there." Raelf laughed ironically. "Of course, something will go wrong, but that's the plan."

"You didn't use any pike fences to the east?" asked Jessyla.

"We couldn't make enough. They'd also be less useful there because there are more ways to avoid them on the east road."

"If the Hydlenese are already moving east," said Lhadoraak, "shouldn't Majer Rojak and I be on our way?"

"Is there anything else you need to know?" asked Raelf.

"Nothing that will change anything." Lhadoraak smiled wryly, then looked to Beltur as he stood. "Once this is over, we need to deal with a certain Duke."

"First things first," replied Beltur. "But, yes, we do."

Rojak stood as well, and the mage and the majer walked swiftly from the public room.

"I'd thought to split the remaining archers with the iron shafts," said Raelf, "between the two other forces. That is, unless you have other thoughts."

"If . . . if we can remove the mage from the force coming from the south, I'd like that group of archers to move with us to the main force."

"I'd already considered that. There is a half squad of archers with each force. They're yours to employ in the manner you see as most effective against the Hydlenese white mages." Raelf looked to Jessyla. "*Either* of you. I've made that very clear."

"You're posting two companies to the east, two to the south then?" asked Beltur. "And the last two to the west."

"That's where we'll start. Reynaard and Zekkarat's companies will comprise the south force. Reynaard's in command, but he's under orders to listen to you."

Beltur understood the assignments perfectly. Both of the companies facing the two battalions were from Montgren. And the companies closest to Lydiar were Lydian. "You're planning on getting support from Reynaard and Zekkarat, then."

"Not planning, but I'm hopeful. That's why I like your idea of seeing what you can do to break the southern attack first. Between various impediments, the pike fences, and a few other tactics, we'll be trying to delay the two battalions. Some of that will be their own doing, I suspect. But we should get moving. The archers will be with Reynaard and with me until you arrive."

In what seemed like moments, but was more like a third of a quint, Beltur and Jessyla were riding south from the square, flanked by Reynaard and Zekkarat, with ten archers riding immediately behind them.

Reynaard glanced back over his shoulder, then said, "The scouts report that the archers in the hills and forest took out as many as a hundred Hydlenese before they had to withdraw. That was both dead and wounded. The second Hydlenese battalion appears to be heading for the rocky grassland and that lane. It's winding, but there's not much cover, except in the forest to the east, and the lane's not that close to the forest, or to the marsh to the west. They won't be able to advance that quickly because the ground on either side of the lane is uneven. I thought we'd engage them just before they get to that stone cottage. The ground is mostly level, but the land south of there is more rugged, and that would allow us better footing while they'd be struggling to get into position." After a brief hesitation, the captain asked, "Can you do what you did last time?"

"We're likely to be able to do less because their troopers will be packed deeper, but that will depend on how they advance. We'll also have to see what their mage does."

"Will they have one?"

"If we counted correctly, they have four remaining. We'll just have to see."

Zekkarat cleared his throat, then said, inclining his head to Jessyla,

"Might I ask you, Mage, is it true that you gagged Majer Rojak with order and said that he was an arrogant bastard?"

Jessyla did not reply for a moment, then said evenly, "Only after he suggested that we didn't know what we were talking about and that we'd lied to him. Oh . . . and that we exaggerated and were bluffing."

The honey-skinned captain grinned. "First time I've ever heard a mage say anything that blunt. Don't be polite. Just tell us anything we can do that will help kill greencoats." Then he looked to Reynaard. "Where can we do the most damage?"

"From what you've told me, you do better with some room to maneuver. On the flanks, two squads to the east, three to the west."

"We'll move there when we near the more open ground," replied the Lydian captain. Reynaard turned to Beltur. "What do you have in mind for your archers?"

"I'd prefer them not to loose shafts immediately, then regular shafts on our orders. I'd like to avoid the iron shafts and crossbow bolts as long as possible, if we can. We'll need them more later."

Reynaard turned in the saddle. "Wystaan! Did you hear that?"

"Yes, ser. Hold shafts until ordered. Then use regular shafts. Iron shafts and crossbow bolts later on the mages' orders."

Reynaard turned back to Beltur. "Can you tell where the Hydlenese are? Those we're supposed to deal with?"

"Not that clearly. They're to the south, but we're not within three kays yet," replied Beltur.

"Could they be on that winding lane yet? Or somewhere else?"

"They'd have to be near the beginning if they are. I don't think they've gone more eastward the way that one company did yesterday." Beltur kept trying to sense exactly where the battalion happened to be, but a good half quint passed, and he and the leading troopers were within a hundred yards of where Haven proper ended, before he began to get a much better sense of where the Hydlenese were. "They've stopped at the edge of the uneven grasslands. It feels like they're re-forming. They do have one strong mage with them." Beltur had hoped for that, if only so that there weren't more mages in the forces facing Lhadoraak and Raelf. *But if you can't deal with this force quickly, you'll have to leave Jessyla to handle it and get back to Raelf's companies.*

"Let me know when they start to move."

"I will." From what Beltur recalled, the distance from the narrow east-west road on the south side of the uneven grasslands to the stone cottage was about a kay and a half, but the Hydlenese would have to be within half a kay to see the defenders. "It's only a little more than a half kay to the cottage from here. We'll easily be in position before they arrive."

A half a quint later, Beltur reined up and looked out at the boulder-strewn grassy hillocks and the narrow lane winding southward from the flat graveled space around the cottage and the barn. There was no way he was going to be able to make a sustained charge, not without risking being unhorsed or breaking Slowpoke's legs. He patted the big gelding's neck. "We'll have to find another way of disrupting them." Had the Hydlenese picked the grassland approach for just that reason? Most likely.

He glanced to his right. The cottage was shuttered, but, according to his senses, not empty of people. Two figures were within, but had not ventured forth, and would likely not be seen or heard. Not knowing when he might have another chance, he took out his water bottle, uncorked it, and took a long swallow before replacing it.

Jessyla looked at him, then followed his example.

"Where are they now?" asked Reynaard.

"The lead riders are a kay away," answered Jessyla. "The mage is farther back."

Beltur was concentrating on the mage, who was definitely strong and surrounded by a large swirl of free chaos, almost as if he'd been collecting it. *Which he probably has.*

"I'm going to move my men up somewhat from yours," Zekkarat declared. "That will give us an angle on them. We've got more than enough shafts to spare."

"There's one thing," said Beltur. "Their mage may be able to block your shafts. If he does at first, don't loose more shafts. Save them for later when he's occupied with me and Jessyla."

"We'll keep that in mind, ser," replied the Lydian captain.

"Companies! Re-form!" ordered Reynaard.

The re-formation created two columns, five abreast, flanking Reynaard, the two mages, and the archers.

Less than a quint passed before the Hydlenese riders appeared. Their advance immediately slowed, and they re-formed into a broad front, fifteen men across, suggesting that the formation was some thirty ranks deep.

Beltur studied the formation, wondering what the reason for it might be and watching as the Hydlenese moved forward.

When the leading greencoats were only slightly more than a hundred yards away, Zekkarat's archers loosed a volley of shafts, but a curtain of chaos-fire sparkled before the oncoming Hydlenese, and the Lydian arrowheads tumbled down out of the air and hit the ground and grass well before the attackers. A second volley met the same fate.

Then two quick volleys of arrows soared from the Hydlenese, aimed primarily at the center of the defenders.

"I'll take those," said Beltur, momentarily extending his shields to block the shafts and drop them to the ground.

Two more volleys followed, but Beltur stopped those as well.

Neither side loosed any arrows as the distance between the two forces narrowed, nor did the Hydlenese mage launch any more chaos bolts.

Beltur studied the ground, judging how close the Hydlenese would have to be before he could use Slowpoke and his shields to best effect. When the distance was less than fifty yards, he said to Reynaard, "Sometime shortly, just before they get ready to charge, I'm going to try to break their front. They'll likely throw a barrage of shafts at the same time. Jessyla will have to handle those shafts."

"After that?" asked Reynaard.

"After that, we do what we can to kill as many of them as we can."

Beltur kept watching and waiting, until the Hydlenese reached the less uneven ground closer to the defenders and the stone cottage and barn. The moment Beltur could sense there was enough near-level ground behind the first few ranks of the attackers, he urged Slowpoke forward.

The big gelding was at full speed within a few yards.

Almost immediately, a chaos bolt flew from the rear of the lead company, a bolt that Beltur lofted toward the rear of the battalion, letting it spread as it splattered across a squad of riders, possibly more. A second chaos bolt followed the first, this one clearly aimed at Jessyla, showing that the mage could definitely sense both of the Montgren mages. This one Beltur also intercepted and flung to the middle of the Hydlenese formation, before concentrating on his shields angling toward the most even ground beyond the first riders, all of whom had lifted lances.

A third chaos bolt followed, but when Beltur redirected it, the white mage turned it back toward Beltur, who could barely keep it away from the troopers near the other mage, but managed to sear Hydlenese troopers to the west of the white.

When he was less than ten yards from the leading riders, Beltur dropped a concealment over the first three ranks. The riders behind gaped, possibly thinking that Beltur had actually destroyed their comrades. Then Beltur, using his senses, turned Slowpoke almost perpendicular to the advancing Hydlenese and extended the knife-edge shields.

At the last moment before his shields were about to cut into the right leading rank, he dropped the concealment. With that slight angle and Slowpoke's power and speed, Beltur's extended shields sliced through men and mounts.

The following riders tried to avoid the carnage by reining up. The mounts of those who didn't went down, and the riders behind jammed up behind those who had stopped or fallen. Then Zekkarat's archers loosed shafts at close to point-blank range, and low enough that the white mage couldn't use a chaos curtain.

Beltur turned Slowpoke back to the north and reined up at the eastern edge of Reynaard's company, watching what was happening and keeping his senses focused on the white mage.

The Hydlenese tried to adjust to the carnage and congestion along their front ranks by lofting arrows from the rear, but Beltur could sense that Jessyla was able to block the center of the volley. In moments the Hydlenese had lost almost fifty troopers in the front ranks, and possibly also as many from the redirected chaos bolts.

So now we're only outnumbered by two to one.

Then the Hydlenese riders behind the front ranks surged out to the side and around the mass of trapped and fallen mounts and troopers—and into a hail of arrows from Zekkarat's archers.

The white mage immediately flung two chaos bolts, one toward each flank of the Montgren force, in an effort to turn the archers into flame and ash, but Beltur caught one and flung it back into the mass of mounts and men, while Jessyla did the same with the second.

For several moments, the mage did nothing, as the shafts from Zekkarat's troopers continued to slash into the Hydlenese force.

Then a truly enormous chaos-firebolt shot barely over the heads of the Hydlenese troops, directly toward Beltur, who barely had time to contain it and hurl it back toward the opposing white. But the white was clearly ready for the return, because he added more chaos and redirected the chaos bolt back toward Beltur.

In turn, Beltur had prepared for the white's second effort, and clapped a containment around the chaos bolt, and a second containment outside the first, the second filled with free order, redirecting the twin containment back to the white, and releasing the outer containment just as the white reached out with his senses to re-redirect the chaos bolt.

Recalling what had happened before, Beltur closed his eyes.

Even with his eyes closed, he could see and feel the searing wave of white flame that consumed the white and the middle of the Hydlenese battalion.

Beltur still couldn't see when he opened his eyes, because they were watering so much.

For several moments, it appeared that all the troopers on both sides, those hundred or so remaining greencoats, and most of the Montgren force, had been frozen in place.

Then Reynaard shouted out, "Montgren! Forward!"

Accompanying his order was a bugle call.

For several moments Beltur watched as the lead squads of Montgren troopers began to cut their way through about half of the remaining Hydlenese, the other half having turned and fled as fast as their mounts could carry them. He immediately tried to sense what was happening to the east, where Rojak and Lhadoraak faced another Hydlenese battalion, but where, so far as he could tell, little or no fighting was occurring. He shifted his sensing efforts to the west. There, it was clear that Raelf was being pushed back or withdrawing, if slowly.

Then he urged Slowpoke toward Reynaard, reining up beside the red-haired captain. "Rojak hasn't engaged the Hydlenese yet, but the two battalions to the west are moving toward the edge of Haven. They're less than a kay from the west edge of town. The majer's either withdrawing or being forced back. We're needed there as soon as possible."

Reynaard surveyed the uneven battlefield for several moments, then said, "It will be a fraction of a quint before we can disengage."

What Reynaard meant, Beltur thought, was that recalling the Montgren company wasn't going to be effective until they'd finished killing or routing what was left of the Hydlen battalion.

The captain turned to the courier posted a yard back. "Find Majer Raelf and tell him that we're on the way. Tell him we've routed the Hydlen battalion, and that we're close to full strength. Tell him we plan to make a flank attack. Ride as fast as you safely can."

"Yes, ser!"

As the courier departed, Reynaard returned his attention to Beltur and asked, in a tone that seemed almost matter-of-fact, "Did you turn that mage's chaos against him, or something like that?"

"Yes . . . with a little extra order."

"You were using his chaos to destroy his own troopers as well, then?"

"Until he realized what I was doing, but I'm hoping that the survivors will report that two white mages battled it out."

"I can see where that would be useful." Reynaard turned to the bugler beside him. "Sound the recall. Now!"

In less than a quint Reynaard had the two companies, largely intact, moving on the back streets of Haven toward the northwest and the outskirts of the town, where Beltur could sense that Raelf was slowly withdrawing.

"How do you feel?" Beltur asked Jessyla, who was riding beside him. He could sense that she seemed fine, but he still worried.

"I'm more worried about how you're doing . . . and Lhadoraak."

"We've ridden far enough west that I can't sense clearly what's going on east of town, but Lhadoraak's still there. The fighting hadn't started when we left the stone cottage. I don't like leaving him there, but . . ."

"The Hydlenese will crush Raelf if we don't get there soon. He's withdrawing and delaying to give us time to reinforce him."

"Where are Raelf's forces now?" asked Reynaard.

"Those closest to the Hydlenese are about half a kay west from the edge of town," replied Beltur.

"There's a lane that curves away from town and joins the main road a hundred yards or so outside of town, but the lane never connects with any lanes or streets. Do you recall it?" Reynaard asked Beltur.

"Yes, ser."

"One of the southern back streets is close to that lane. It's only separated from the lane by about fifty yard and a shallow creek," said the captain. "We're going to take the back street and ford the creek. That's if there aren't any Hydlenese troopers there. Can you tell me if there are?"

Beltur had to concentrate, because there were so many people on and around the main road and close to the west end of the town, but finally he said, "There's a squad, possibly two, posted in the middle of the curve. If I understand what you have in mind, that's a little more than two hundred yards northwest from where you want to cross the creek." What he didn't mention were the powerful swirls of chaos surrounding the white mage who seemed to be roughly in the middle of the main body of the Hydlenese force.

"That will have to do. We need to hit them where they're not expecting it. Can you do another charge like the last one?"

"It might be best if we both did," interjected Jessyla, "moving away from each other. I won't make as big an impact, but they'll notice it." She turned in the saddle and fixed Beltur with her eyes, as if telling him not to say a word.

He didn't.

"Good," declared Reynaard as the lead company turned west on the back street paralleling the one on which the mages all lived, some five blocks north.

Less than a third of a quint later, Beltur saw the end of the street ahead, as well as the thornbushes that grew on the low rise beyond which flowed the creek.

"I'll use my shields to clear the bushes," declared Jessyla, adding in a murmur to Beltur, "I can already sense that white mage. You're going to need every bit of order you have."

Beltur had to agree. He watched as Jessyla eased the mare forward, then extended thin and sharp edges to her shields at close to ankle level, but leaving those shields a little wider than normal higher up. The mare had to struggle a little, it seemed to Beltur, to cut through the bushes. When Jessyla reached the bank of the creek, she turned the mare, and the two came back, leaving a path wide enough for two mounts abreast.

Beltur moved Slowpoke up beside Jessyla, and the two of them walked their mounts through the shallow creek, little more than ankle deep, and then out into the field beyond, which appeared to be planted in wheat. He couldn't help but feel a little sorry for the grower, who was going to lose part of his crop come harvest, but if they didn't stop the Hydlenese, the grower would likely lose a great deal more. Beyond the creek, on the west side, was only grass, for which Beltur was grateful.

While the others crossed the creek and re-formed, Beltur took another swallow of ale, then blotted his forehead. Despite the warm dampness of the air, and the comparative stillness of the late-morning air, Beltur could smell dust, although he couldn't see it anywhere.

Before long, both companies were across the field and riding along the lane toward the main road.

Beltur turned to Reynaard. "The lead companies are past where the lane joins the main road, but they've almost slowed to a stop. I can sense some deaths among their first riders. It might be that they ran into the pike fences that Raelf set up."

"That will make the Hydlenese even angrier."

"Because they think that's an unfair way of fighting?" asked Jessyla.

"Anything you don't anticipate that kills your men is unfair," replied Reynaard sardonically.

"Then this will be recorded by the surviving Hydlenese as the most unfair war ever," rejoined Jessyla.

"We're about to where the greencoats can see us." Reynaard gestured, and the riders behind re-formed into a three-abreast column, since only three mounts would fit side by side on the narrow lane, intermittently bordered by trees of assorted types and sizes. He looked to Beltur. "Are you willing to charge the squad around the curve? I'd like to get through them quickly, if possible."

"Then let me go ahead under a concealment, and have your men charge once you hear the yelling."

"We'll both go," declared Jessyla. "Just in case there's a mage closer than we think."

Reynaard cocked his head for an instant, then nodded. "How much farther can we go before they'll see us?"

"Another fifty yards, I'd judge—about where that dead stump on the right is."

"We'll stop short of there and wait for you to engage."

For you to engage . . . that sounds so much cleaner than charging into unsuspecting troopers and doing your best to slaughter them before they can really do anything. Rather than say anything, Beltur just nodded.

The company rode quietly, but as they neared the stump, Reynaard raised his arm and dropped it. The troopers halted.

Beltur raised a concealment, and he and Jessyla kept riding.

"I'll go first," said Beltur, once they were a good ten yards farther around the curve and away from Reynaard. "You follow and try to cut down the ones I miss."

Jessyla nodded, then said, "Don't do any more than you have to. Not a single trooper."

"I'll do my best."

"Stop short rather than do too many," she insisted. "The troopers can clean up the strays. That white ahead is stronger than any I've ever sensed."

While Beltur already knew that, he understood that her words were both a warning and a reminder. Because he could also sense that the Hydlenese were again beginning to press Raelf's command, he forced himself to keep Slowpoke at a fast walk, fearing that he'd need the gelding's full speed and strength all too much once they were through the road-guard squad.

"I'm not going to lift the concealment until we're about ten yards away, or sooner if they somehow notice us. Charge as soon as you can see."

"I will." Jessyla's voice was low and tense.

As they neared the road guards, Beltur caught traces of conversation.

". . . aren't so tough . . ."

". . . not when we outnumber 'em . . ."

". . . any good-looking women here . . ."

"Dohlan! You hear riders over there?"

"Now!" snapped Beltur, dropping the concealment, and urging Slowpoke to full speed, then shaping his shields to suit the lane. Two of the riders had barely turned their mounts before Beltur and Slowpoke were on them.

The yells and screams were thankfully short.

Of the twenty-trooper squad, most were down when Jessyla reined up beside Beltur. Of the four who had escaped the attack and were riding through the green stalks of wheat toward the main road, just one glanced back over his shoulder.

Beltur looked at Jessyla. She looked pale. "You need some ale."

"In a moment." She swallowed, hard, then said, "So do you."

Beltur followed his own advice.

Jessyla took out her water bottle, but just held it for a time. Finally, she took a small swallow, then another, before corking and replacing it in the leather saddle holder. "This is the first time . . . I really saw . . ."

Beltur wasn't quite sure what to say. He nodded and waited.

"I'm upset . . . and angry. I'm angry that we have to kill so frigging many men, especially the young ones, because a spoiled duke wants to conquer people who don't even like him." She might have said more, but closed her mouth as Reynaard reined up beside them.

"You didn't leave any for us."

"They only had a squad here," replied Beltur. "We need to move on. Raelf's being pressed hard."

Reynaard gestured, and the companies resumed the fast walk toward the main road, a good two hundred yards away, the first hundred of which were curved.

After a moment, the captain said, "When we get within a hundred yards, past the end of the curve, we'll re-form. The lane's too narrow for that before then."

"What if they see us and attack first?"

"Then that should take some of the pressure off Raelf," replied Reynaard. "We'll fight through them toward the road. You two do your best to protect us from their wizard."

"There are two," said Jessyla. "The strong one is only a few hundred yards to the west of where the lane meets the road. The weak one is with the rear guard."

"Most likely to fend off a possible attack from the rear," suggested Beltur.

"Where do you want your archers?" asked Reynaard.

"Not in the van, but later. On the east side of the lane just off the main road. That's if we can get to the main road." As they rode, Beltur kept checking the position of the stronger white mage, but he still appeared to be over a hundred yards west of the lane.

At about the same time that Reynaard ordered the company to re-form, a mass of greencoats moved onto the lane and rode toward the Montgren force.

"Good thing that there's only room for one company on the road," said Reynaard cheerfully.

"One at a time, anyway," murmured Beltur.

"Forward!" A bugle call followed the captain's order. After the last few notes died away, Reynaard asked, "How do you want to handle the company ahead?"

"We'll try to break through the first rank or so and then move to the east side of the lane in order to deal with the mage."

"You think he'll throw firebolts immediately?"

"I don't know. He hasn't been throwing them against Raelf. Not since we've been close enough to sense them, anyway."

"That seems strange," replied Reynaard.

"He's saving himself in order to deal with Beltur," said Jessyla. "He likely sensed the chaos/order explosion. He knows that Beltur is heading toward him."

"How strong is he?" asked Reynaard.

"Stronger than any mage I've run across in years." *At least since I left Gallos.*

"Stronger than you?"

"We'll find out."

By now the distance between Beltur and Jessyla and the approaching Hydlenese was little more than fifty yards.

"What do you need me to do?" she asked.

Beltur understood what she wasn't saying. "I'm going to split the middle of the first rank, then angle through the next rank or two and move to the left and off the road, and let our troopers fight the Hydlenese. You follow me closely, but slightly to the left so that the left front of their column is smashed in."

"Good. You don't need to try any more until we know more about their mage."

"I'd thought that."

When Beltur reached a distance of just over ten yards, he urged Slowpoke into a gallop, then adjusted the sharp-edged shields, noting with a certain relief that the Hydlenese troopers ahead had neither lances nor spears, but only circular shields and sabres. In moments, he and Slowpoke had ripped through three ranks of troopers and he was slowing the big gelding to a stop in the wheat field with a scrubby-looking tree between him and the lane.

Jessyla eased the mare up behind him.

Before she could say a word, a large chaos bolt arced between the scrubby tree and a taller oak toward Beltur.

Beltur redirected the firebolt into the Hydlenese force on the main road, spreading it slightly so as to take out at least several ranks.

Even before Beltur finished the redirection, a second and narrower firebolt flew toward Jessyla, who, caught partly unaware, still managed to fling it into the Hydlenese troopers somewhat farther north on the lane.

"Mages! They've got fire-mages . . ."

Beltur frowned at that for a moment, thinking that it was strange that no one had told the troopers. *But then, the Hydlenese don't seem to talk to or listen to their rankers.*

He didn't have much time to think about that before another large firebolt arced toward him, a firebolt that he redirected back to the main road, into troopers farther east, hoping that the fiery impact would slow the advance and help Raelf and his troopers.

The white then arced another firebolt, not at either Beltur or Jessyla, but straight east on the road, clearly directed at Raelf's front lines.

Beltur had to stretch some, but managed to bring that one down just behind the leading Hydlenese troopers.

The moments turned into much longer than that, but there were no more firebolts, only the sounds of battle, the clash of blades, occasional muttered epithets, and the slow advance of Reynaard's troops toward the main road. Beltur could still sense both white mages, but neither threw any more chaos bolts.

Belatedly, Beltur realized that the half squad of archers had drawn up behind him and Jessyla, and he looked at the squad leader.

"Ser?"

"In a moment . . ." *What do you do now? The whites have figured out that you're using their chaos against their troopers, and they're not about to throw more of it, not when they have the advantage in numbers.*

"We need to go hunting," he said to Jessyla.

"The whites?"

Beltur nodded. "We have to make them use chaos against us." Then he turned back to the squad leader and was about to say something when a handful of Hydlenese troopers burst off the road, heading between the two trees toward Beltur and Jessyla.

Beltur swung Slowpoke around and started him toward the five while spreading the knife-edged shields. The attackers' momentum was going to have to do some of the damage, but any movement forward by Slowpoke would definitely help. At the last moment, Beltur angled Slowpoke between two riders.

Four of the five went down. Even before Beltur could halt Slowpoke, the fifth, who was at the end of the line the five had formed, gaped and then turned his mount, spurring it back through the wheat in the direction of the main road.

Beltur immediately rejoined the others and said to the archers' squad leader, "Jessyla and I will cut the way across the lane. You stay close behind us. Once we're on the other side, we'll go through the field toward the main road. I think we can get within fifty yards or so of the stronger white. You'll use iron shafts, and I'll tell you where to aim. All that iron coming at the white will force him to act."

At a retching sound, barely heard over the clamor from the lane to the west and the main road to the north, Beltur glanced toward a younger archer at the edge of the group who wiped his mouth with a rag. He smiled wryly and said, "I've felt that way more than once. We need to go!"

He looked through the gap between the trees, but could only see pale blue uniforms.

He turned Slowpoke to the north and motioned for Jessyla to move alongside him, then looked over his shoulder. "Close it up tight! On the double!"

Once the archers were in position, he gave the command. "Forward!"

The two rode north through the green stalks of the wheat, until the uniforms on the lane were all green. Then Beltur found another gap in the trees and turned Slowpoke, making sure Jessyla was beside him, before urging Slowpoke forward at a pace more than a fast walk, but all that he dared on the uneven ground between the field and the shoulder of the road.

"Cutting shields," he said, turning his head toward Jessyla.

The two plowed through the riders on the road, slicing some men and mounts and shoving the others aside. Once they were on the west side of the lane, Beltur glanced back. He didn't see the young archer who'd been at the end, but he couldn't wait to see if the young man could make his way clear. He guided Slowpoke northwest at a fast walk toward a point on the main road that was possibly seventy yards west of where the lane met the road.

To Beltur, crossing those hundred or so yards to a point some twenty yards off the road seemed to take a glass, rather than the fifth of a quint that probably passed. Where he reined up was behind an irregular line of waist-high bushes marking the edge of the field. Between the bushes and the road was a shallow depression. Trees at irregular intervals rose from the southern edge of the depression. Immediately, Beltur ordered, "Ready bows! Nock shafts."

He concentrated on locating the mage, then said to the squad leader, "Do you see that dead branch on the short tree on the other side of the road, roughly north-northwest?"

After a moment, the squad leader said, "Yes, ser."

"Drop your shafts into the middle of the road there. Loose shafts!"

As the iron arrows left the bows of the archers, a squad of troopers immediately swung off the main road and rode toward the group. One of the mounts stumbled and went down, most likely because of a rodent burrow or a small sinkhole. The others continued toward Beltur, Jessyla, and the archers.

Beltur took a deep breath and turned to Jessyla. "Shield the archers if anyone gets close to them. Tell them to stop loosing shafts if you have to raise a shield."

Then he readied his own shields, watching as the troopers tried to force their mounts through the bushes. When most of them were slowed and close together along the bushes, Beltur extended the knife shields far enough on one side that they stretched several yards north beyond the bushes, and raised them to roughly neck-height. Then he turned Slowpoke west and urged him at what Beltur thought was a slow canter along the south edge of the bushes. The extended shields slashed or severed necks and shoulders of about half the squad, whose fallen forms and dead or riderless mounts created even more of a barrier.

Beltur immediately turned his attention back to the white mage, who had created a sparkling shield that was blocking the iron arrows and dropping them on the Hydlenese troopers around him. At least some of the deflected and largely spent shafts were red-hot and burned anyone they touched on their fall toward the road. The white mage's shield turned a few into drops of molten iron. While the Hydlenese troopers in front of the mage tried to flee that rain of hot iron, many were too hemmed in by their compatriots to avoid it.

"Another volley!" Beltur called out.

The archers were so quick to nock and release their shafts that Beltur only managed to add a coating of order to a handful, but those shafts exploded violently when they struck the sparkling shield.

"Again!" shouted Beltur. With that volley he was much more prepared, and a half score of those shafts exploded, raining even more hot metal on the troopers beneath.

Unhappily, by then another squad or so of Hydlenese riders had broken through the bushes farther to the west of Beltur, Jessyla, and the archers, and were riding through the wheat—with no one but Beltur and Jessyla between them and the archers.

"You take the ones next to the bushes! I'll get the others!" Beltur told Jessyla, then urged Slowpoke forward.

Just as Beltur's shields were about to cut into the leading Hydlenese, a firebolt seared barely above the heads of the greencoats on the road and slammed into Beltur's shields with enough force to jar him, but the shields held and sprayed chaos-fire across the nearest and now hapless attackers. While the fire momentarily blinded Beltur, he could sense well enough to keep Slowpoke moving between falling riders, rather than into them. The would-be attackers farther back were also partly blinded. A few turned away. Slowpoke and Beltur slashed through the rest.

Then Beltur turned Slowpoke, and while the gelding walked around the fallen and back toward the archers, he returned his concentration to the white mage, who seemed to be rebuilding his shields. "Another volley!" A brief sensing reassured him that Jessyla had turned her mare and was closing on him.

As the shafts flew, Beltur added more order to a half score. The resulting explosions pelted more hot metal into the troopers on the road. Beltur thought that he could sense some wavering in the white's shields. "Fire again!"

This time, he managed adding order to eleven shafts, and the explosions as they struck the white's shields were far less spectacular, but the shields held, although the wavering increased.

By now, the Hydlenese troopers on the road had moved away somewhat from the mage.

"On my command!" Beltur called out, guiding Slowpoke some ten yards farther west to a point where the bushes were markedly thinner—and where he was even closer to the white. Then he issued the order. "Loose shafts!"

Beltur added even larger amounts of free order to a half score of the iron shafts, then formed his shields into a narrow wedge and urged Slowpoke through the bushes and the low depression and toward the small gap that had opened between the troopers and the white.

A massive firebolt arrowed directly at Beltur so fast and low that it was all Beltur could do to throw it back at the white, but he immediately followed it with what he could only have called an order bolt. Then Beltur anchored his shields to the ground, hoping that would be enough to protect him as the order bolt merged with the firebolt—just after the iron arrows impacted the white's shields.

He closed his eyes, but not quite quickly enough to escape the sight-searing flare of intense whiteness that washed over him. His shields reverberated with a high whining sound and pain more intense than scores of needles ripping through his body and skull. Although his shields held, Beltur felt as though he'd been shaken within them.

He opened his eyes, but could see nothing. Nor could he sense anything.

Then, slowly, he began to discern fuzzy shapes. When Beltur could see, he found Slowpoke and himself at the edge of a blackened area, almost fifty yards across, filled with gray ash in the center, and the charred forms of men and mounts farther out . . . and charred trees on both sides of the main road. He could also discern the order focus that was Jessyla, and he let out a breath that he didn't know that he'd even been holding.

Beyond the circle of destruction to the west, Beltur could sense at least two companies of troopers . . . and one much weaker white mage. To the southeast, the fighting on the lane and the road had largely died away, but farther east, the increasing number of black death mists showed that the battle between the lead Hydlenese companies and Raelf's outnumbered forces had been joined in full.

An officer rode up, not Reynaard, but Zekkarat. With him was Jessyla, and the archers followed her, moving east into the charred area.

"Ser! The green bastards took down Reynaard. What are your orders?"

"Send two squads with me. We need to finish off the troopers to the west. There's one more mage. Take all the other squads and assault the rear of the forces attacking Raelf. There aren't any mages there, and he needs support." *Especially so that they can turn and reinforce Rojak and Lhadoraak.*

"Yes, ser!" Zekkarat nodded and turned his horse. "First and Second Squads! On the mages. Mage-Captain Beltur's in command!"

Jessyla moved the mare closer to Beltur. "What are you going to do?"

"Get a swallow of ale," he said as he pulled out his second water bottle and uncorked it. After taking a long swallow and recorking and replacing the bottle, he added, "We need to start ripping into the troopers ahead. Try to get the last mage to use chaos bolts. If he doesn't, we'll have to cut into the greencoats and then back off and let the troopers do some of it."

"Then we should alternate."

"To begin with." That was all Beltur was about to agree to. More than that depended on how they and their shields held up, particularly Jessyla and her shields.

In moments, the two squads rode into the ashen area. Beltur quickly briefed the squad leaders on what they planned, then ended by saying, "In short, we'll rip a hole in the Hydlenese and you alternate squads in following up."

"Yes, ser."

Beltur turned Slowpoke eastward, vaguely surprised that the greencoats had neither advanced nor retreated. *Waiting for orders?*

In a way, he felt sorry for the Hydlenese troopers, but he pushed the feeling away. *Gustaan stood up to bad officers and orders.* And he ended up being disgraced and working for a renegade white. *Thinking that through has to wait.* With that, he extended his shields and urged Slowpoke into almost a gallop.

As he neared the center of the Hydlenese troopers, several moved forward, raising shields and sabres. One trooper on the end bolted, spurring his mount toward the trees and bushes on the south side of the road, clearly aiming for the field beyond. Then Beltur was through the first two lines, angling to the north side of the road, where he knew the shoulder to be firmer and without a muddy depression, such as on the south side.

Then the first squad followed, and for a time, sabres flashed, since about a third of the Hydlenese put up a fight, but their efforts were hampered by those who were more interested in finding a way out and those who fled.

Suddenly, a good fifty yards of the road east of Beltur's small force was empty of troopers. Beltur blinked, then realized that whoever commanded the Hydlenese had left a single company to hold the road, or at least clog it, while pulling back the remaining force and re-forming it.

Almost before Beltur realized it, a triple line of lancers, with a well-dressed front, was charging toward the somewhat disarrayed first squad.

Frig!

Beltur did the only thing he thought might even work, based on the hope that the Hydlenese commander hadn't actually seen Beltur's previous charge. From where he'd reined up Slowpoke on the north side of the road, he put a concealment around himself and the gelding, extended the knife shields, and brought Slowpoke to a full gallop, using his senses to guide the gelding on an angled path that he hoped would not only take out a number of lancers, but also create consternation and confusion among the attackers.

As Slowpoke cut through the lancers, Beltur sensed that Jessyla was doing the same thing right behind him, except she'd started from the south side of the road and moved to the north.

He pulled up to the south side of the road and dropped the concealment so that he could see better, as well as shrank his shields close enough just to protect himself and Slowpoke.

Immediately, a trooper charged at him and slashed with a sabre—except when the sabre struck Beltur's shields, the force of his slash against the unyielding shield ripped the weapon from his hand. Then another greencoat attacked . . . with the same result. At that moment, the Montgren troopers from First Squad arrived, and began to cut into the disarrayed Hydlenese company.

Beltur concentrated on trying to sense what the rest of the Hydlenese to the west were doing, but from what he could tell, the other two companies were doing nothing, but just waiting. There were also no chaos bolts.

Frig!

The Hydlenese strategy was more than clear—to make the fight one of arms against arms so that Beltur couldn't use the whites' chaos against their troopers.

As the Montgren troopers pushed forward, if slowly, Beltur eased back and crossed the road to where Jessyla was.

"We were supposed to alternate attacks," were her first words.

"You're right, but we need to find the archers and use concealments or whatever to move though the fields and orchards to get to that last white . . ."

Before he could say more, Jessyla said almost crossly, "I understand. The archers are with Second Squad. We need to move quickly, or we'll lose all the Montgren troopers."

Beltur immediately turned Slowpoke, as did Jessyla.

After reaching the archers, they ended up going back to the section of bushes they had broken through earlier in order to get into the field. There were no troopers in green farther west in the field, and Beltur couldn't help wondering about that. Admittedly, it was a small field, not much more than a hundred yards paralleling the road, and less than fifty yards deep. Possibly the bushes had deterred the Hydlenese from using it or perhaps their commander had already decided that staying on the road would be the best way to whittle down the outnumbered Montgren forces.

That would fit with what they've done. Even so, Beltur kept sensing, knowing that they needed to deal with the last mage as quickly as possible.

At the west end of the field, Beltur could sense that they still needed to move farther west, since they were roughly abreast of the middle of the remaining Hydlenese force, and that required riding through an overgrown, and possibly abandoned, orchard. Beltur thought the orchard held apple trees—at least the green globes looked like apples. Just before they neared the western end of the orchard they crossed a narrow grassy track wider than the spacing between trees.

"We'll head back to the road here." Beltur gestured.

As he rode north, he could sense that the mage was less than a hundred yards to the northwest, with roughly a company behind him. There were also several troopers posted at the end of the track that had likely once been a lane.

Beltur turned in the saddle. "When we reach a point just off the road, we need you to loft iron shafts at another mage. We'll block any troopers from coming at you."

"We have less than ten shafts a man, ser."

"We'll use them all, if need be." He didn't say that their chances of prevailing were getting slight indeed without using the white's chaos against his own troopers. "You just put them where I tell you."

"Yes, ser."

With the overhanging and protruding branches, Beltur thought that trying to proceed under a concealment would be unwise, and using shields would take more strength than he wanted to use. He was already feeling the effort.

That thought reminded him to drink more of the ale in his water bottle, but there were only two swallows left—and that was in the second bottle. He didn't remember drinking that much, but he must have. He replaced the water bottle and then thought about the troopers ahead.

Then he smiled and kept riding. He'd let the troopers guarding the lane make the first move.

It wasn't that long before one of them called out, "Who goes there?"

Beltur's response was to drop a concealment around the lane guards.

"I can't see!"

"I can't either . . ."

Beltur eased Slowpoke into a fast walk and extended his shields just slightly, enough so that he could press against the concealment-blinded guards.

"Stop pushing!"

"I'm not . . ."

The three guards, disconcerted by the concealment, ended up colliding with the troopers on the road, who, as the guards under the concealment neared them, also found themselves unable to see. The shouts and epithets from unseen troopers added to the disarray of the nearby Hydlenese troopers.

Beltur turned to the squad leader. "Can you see that taller trooper who's about opposite that tall oak?"

After a moment, the archer answered. "No, ser."

"Do you see the oak, maybe ten yards west of the gap in the trees on the north side of the road?"

"Yes, ser."

"When I give the order, put your shafts in the middle of the road just forward of the oak."

Beltur shifted his shields so that the archers could loose their shafts, hoping that any Hydlenese archers wouldn't notice.

"We're ready, ser."

"Loose shafts."

Beltur only added order to a few of the shafts.

The weaker white's shield appeared only a yard or so above the heads of the Hydlenese troopers, invisible to the sight, although Beltur could sense it. When the ordered iron shafts struck the shield, they stopped and then dropped, but they weren't fragmented by the shield, and they didn't fragment and burn the troopers underneath, as had happened with the stronger white.

Frig! Now what?

"Another volley!" ordered Beltur, adding order to several more shafts.

Just then, a Hydlenese officer or squad leader called out, "Troopers! If you can see, hold your position. If you can't see, follow the road east. If you run into others, you're riding the wrong way. Now! Move!"

All that meant Beltur didn't have much time before the momentarily disorganized Hydlenese nearby would regroup. Beltur also had the feeling he was on the edge of getting light-headed, and that was anything but good.

The iron arrows slammed into the mage's shield, pushing it down, and Beltur could feel the wavering of the chaos behind it.

"Another volley!" This time Beltur added more order to the shafts, especially to one of them.

The iron shafts came down, and a line of fire flared across the road, just above the troopers, enough to stop the arrows. Beltur strained and wrapped order around that chaos-fire, hurling it at the white mage, who blocked it, added more chaos, and flung it all, not directly at Beltur but toward the unshielded archers.

Beltur smiled grimly, jamming two containments around that chaos. Then he redirected it all back at the white, closing his eyes as he did. He barely had them closed when the searing white of the explosion hammered on his shields, which, since he was between the mage and the archers, largely shielded them as well.

When he opened his eyes, the first thing he saw was sparkles of light wherever he looked. The second thing he realized was that he had almost no shields. He immediately reduced those he had to barely cover himself and Slowpoke.

"Beltur!" Jessyla's voice was low and intense as she moved her mare up beside him.

He turned, and even that motion left him a little dizzy.

"You can't use any more order or chaos. You can't."

Before answering, he took in the damage. The order/chaos explosion wasn't as large as the previous one, but because the troopers were more closely formed up, almost an entire company of Hydlenese troopers and their mounts were turned either to ashes or charred husks of what they had been.

Still, there had to be almost another company behind those destroyed.

"We're not finished," he replied quietly.

She handed him a water bottle. "There's some ale left. Drink it. It's up to me now."

"Archers! On the mages! Forward!" Beltur ordered. He hoped that the sight of Montgren uniforms emerging from the swirling ashes and charred forms would unnerve the remaining Hydlenese troopers. Then he turned in the saddle and looked to the lead archer.

"Form three ranks. Do you have enough shafts left for several volleys?"

"Four, maybe five, full volleys, ser."

"After Mage Jessyla cuts through the lead lines of the Hydlenese, I'll order a volley, maybe two. Half into the front lines, half farther back."

"There are only eleven of us, ser."

"Then you'll have to be very accurate," replied Beltur, uncorking the water bottle and drinking the remainder of it. He hoped the ale would lessen the light-headedness and the sparkles in front of his eyes.

When the two of them, followed by three ranks of archers in Montgren blue, reached the western edge of where the order/chaos conflagration ended, another Hydlenese company was drawn up, seemingly waiting.

Waiting for what?

"I'm charging them, before they have time to think about it." Jessyla immediately urged the mare into a canter, aiming toward the north side of the middle of the Hydlenese troopers. The leading troopers raised shields and sabres, but barely had time to move before she slashed at an angle through two ranks, leaving a trail of blood and dead, dying, or wounded troopers.

Then she reversed the mare and rode across the front of the third rank of troopers, momentarily reining up on the south shoulder of the road, leaving a second line of blood and death among the green-coated troopers.

"Loose shafts!" ordered Beltur as loudly as he could. "Volley one!"

After a long moment, Beltur repeated the command.

Jessyla didn't have to make another charge. The remaining greencoats turned their mounts and withdrew, except in moments, it was a wild flight.

"Ser?" called the archers' squad leader.

"We're riding back east! Now!" Even as he spoke, Beltur wondered what he and Jessyla and eleven archers could do, given that he was close to exhausted and Jessyla, from what he sensed, was only in a little better shape.

After a few moments, the small force was riding back through the charred and ashen area, toward Haven and whatever was happening there. Beltur had another confirmation of his unsteady state when he realized he was only able to sense a few hundred yards. He looked to Jessyla. "Can you sense what's happening ahead?"

"Not any farther than I can see, and all I can see are a few wounded men, lots of bodies, unattended horses—" At that moment, she sneezed, twice, before finishing, "and a few riders in green trying to sneak away through the wheat field over there." She gestured.

Beltur counted six riders, and a man walking toward a riderless mount, then squinted as he looked eastward, trying to see what might be waiting ahead in the streets of Haven. The number of bodies increased as they neared the lane from which they'd begun their attack, then vanished as they rode through the second part of the road that was little more than ashes and charred forms. Beyond that, there were so many bodies that it was impossible to count them all. While most of the fallen wore green uniforms, there were far more than a few bodies wearing blue and maroon.

Just ahead, Beltur saw several youths, clearly bent on looting bodies, look up and then scurry away from the road, vanishing behind trees and bushes and into the afternoon shadows. Beltur found he was too tired to care . . . and too worried about what he might find or encounter on the east side of Haven.

Once they were several hundred yards past the posts marking the west end of the town proper, there were no more bodies, only scores of hoofprints in the street suggesting that the combined forces of Zekkarat and Raelf had prevailed and had hurried eastward to reinforce Rojak and Lhadoraak.

Beltur hoped that they had been in time for Lhadoraak, but he had his doubts. "It's looking like we prevailed here in the west."

"They might still be fighting on the east end of town," said Jessyla.

"Can you sense that far?"

"I can only sense about to Julli's house. There's no one on the main street there."

As they neared the Brass Bowl, a figure hurried out to the edge of the street, a man Beltur belatedly recognized as Phaelgren. "What happened west of town?"

"The remaining Hydlenese troopers fled," said Beltur, not halting Slowpoke. "What happened here?"

"We don't know." The innkeeper had to walk fast, almost trot to keep abreast of Beltur. "A company or so of troopers in blue and maroon rode past here, a glass or so ago. No one rode back."

"They might still be fighting," said Jessyla. "The Hydlenese sent a battalion to attack from the east."

Phaelgren looked as though he didn't understand.

"They sent three and a half battalions," said Beltur tiredly. "Something like two thousand men. We're headed to see if we can help." *Hoping it's not necessary.*

"You caused all this!"

"No," snapped Beltur. "You did. You wouldn't support your councilors, and you pandered to the traders and smugglers. I don't want to hear another frigging complaint from you as long as you live."

Phaelgren stopped in his tracks, opened his mouth, and then shut it.

Beltur looked ahead, but all he saw was the empty main street.

No one came out as they rode past the square and then past the East Inn, which was shuttered and eerily silent.

When they were a few hundred yards west of the eastern edge of town, Beltur saw a squad of troopers riding swiftly toward them, then let out a breath he hadn't realized that he'd held when he recognized the pale blue uniforms.

The two forces reined up on the street just opposite Julli's small house.

"What happened west of town?" asked Raelf.

"There's maybe a company of Hydlenese left," said Beltur. "They're scattered, and the last we saw, they were fleeing. We didn't know if you needed more help. What happened here?"

"There might have been fifty Hydlenese survivors, and less than that from Naajuk's and Deminaar's companies. Deminaar's wounded. He might survive."

"What about Lhadoraak?" asked Beltur.

"What he did likely saved us. The initial assault by the Hydlenese killed almost half of the Lydian companies. Lhadoraak must have seen that. He rode with his archers into the middle of the Hydlenese battalion. He said that way any chaos bolts thrown at them would be deflected into the Hydlenese troopers. He had the archers firing iron shafts at their white mage. I don't know exactly what happened, because it occurred before we could get there. Whatever he did created an explosion around himself that gutted the middle of the Hydlenese force . . ."

Around him? Beltur had an immediate sinking feeling.

". . . The white mage didn't survive the explosion, but neither did Lhadoraak. After that, it was hand-to-hand for almost two glasses, and the remainder of the Lydian forces were on the verge of breaking when we arrived. Without your efforts, and without Zekkarat's company, we wouldn't have been in time or able to destroy them. All three Montgren companies are little more than a third full strength. Zekkarat's company is around half strength." Raelf shook his head. "I wouldn't call it a victory. More like survival."

"Did you expect anything less?" Jessyla's voice held more than a tinge of bitterness.

"No." Raelf's tone was surprisingly gentle as he went on. "I didn't. You might recall that I did recommend putting an armed post here over a year ago."

"I recall your mentioning that," replied Beltur.

"I would suggest that you councilors claim all the horses, blades, and everything you can. That might fund your own company, and that would not require the agreement of the Duchess."

Beltur understood what Raelf wasn't saying—that golds would likely govern what the Duchess could and would do. "We make that claim, and we request that you and your men honor and support it."

"That's the very least we can do. All weapons and valuables possible will be placed in your storeroom. We'll make arrangements for the horses."

"Also," Beltur added, "I'd like to request twenty greencoat uniforms, as undamaged as possible. We might need them in the future, and it would be much easier to procure them now."

"We can do that as well."

"Thank you. What about Rojak?" asked Beltur.

"Deminaar was in command for most of the battle, until he was wounded. Then Naajuk took over, until he was killed, and I arrived and took command."

"And Rojak?" pressed Jessyla.

"Naajuk reported that Majer Rojak's command group was attacked, and his neck was slashed in the fight. He bled to death before anyone could help." Raelf's tone was level.

Beltur had a feeling that he knew what that meant.

"Of course, we'll report that he died heroically in supporting Mage Lhadoraak's charge to kill the Hydlenese mage and destroy the center of the Hydlenese battalion."

"I see."

"With your experience, Mage-Captain, I'm certain you do." There was an underlying feeling of regret and sadness in the words.

"Mage-Captain?" asked Jessyla.

"Both of you," replied Raelf. "Zekkarat was most astounded at what both of you accomplished. Conferring the rank of captain is within my purview. It might prove helpful. You also seem to have an ability to recruit former enemies to your side."

Beltur also understood what went beyond Raelf's words, but all he said was, "For the moment, is there any immediate need for us?"

"Not at the moment."

"Then we need to inform Tulya."

"Convey my appreciation and regrets as well. I will do that in person as soon as possible." Raelf's tone was anything but perfunctory.

"We will," replied Jessyla.

"Also, I'll have four of my men escort you. I have the feeling that neither of you is in much condition to fight further . . . or am I mistaken?"

"I'm not," replied Beltur. "Jessyla is in very slightly better condition."

"Then, you'd best get some rest and food. I'll talk to you later."

Beltur nodded, then turned Slowpoke.

In moments, they were riding back toward the center of Haven.

Beltur would have liked to have asked, "Why Lhadoraak?" but he knew all too well the reasons why . . . and most of them were his doing.

LXV

Beltur said little until they had ridden past the square and then the Brass Bowl, without any sign of Phaelgren. "It's my fault. Lhadoraak, I mean."

"Partly," agreed Jessyla. "But he made his choices as well. He chose Taelya's life over staying in Elparta. He chose Tulya's not wanting to be unhappy over staying in Axalt. He chose to take on the white mage in hopes that would make Tulya and Taelya safer for the rest of their lives. I think he also knew that no matter what happened, he'd likely die because the white mage was stronger. He wanted his death to make a difference. It did. Otherwise, that battalion would have overrun the Lydians long before Raelf could reinforce them, and the Hydlenese would have had a company that he cost them. Those were his choices, not yours."

"Still—"

"Beltur . . . we both made mistakes. We did what we thought best. We didn't decide to leave Elparta. That was Waensyn's doing. Barrynt's killing Emlyn was Sarysta's fault as much as Barrynt's, and you can't blame that on your making a beautiful mirror."

That was all true, but there was more there, and Beltur didn't feel as though he was thinking clearly. "I need to think about it . . . when I can think."

"We both do."

They rode to Lhadoraak and Tulya's house, dismounting at the foot of the path leading to the front door. Beltur handed Slowpoke's reins to the nearest trooper. "We'll be a little while."

"Yes, ser. We'll be here as long as you need us."

"Thank you."

The two walked up to the door.

Taelya opened it. "Mother says you should come into the kitchen."

"Thank you, Taelya," said Jessyla.

Once they entered the front room, Beltur could smell something cooking, and he had another sinking feeling.

Tulya stood by the stove, on top of which was a large pot.

Burhka. Beltur could feel his eyes burning even before he looked to Tulya.

"You don't have to tell me," Tulya said. "I felt it the moment it happened."

Beltur could see that her eyes were red. "He saved us all. He took on one of their strongest whites . . . The Lydian companies had already almost been destroyed . . ."

"You don't have to make him more than he was—"

"Don't make him less," said Jessyla quietly, but firmly. "What Beltur said was true. Lhadoraak not only took out the white, but he kept the Hydlenese from overrunning the Lydians. If that had happened, they would have trapped Raelf before we finished dealing with the other force, and we wouldn't have been able to do anything. Beltur was on the edge, and I'm not much better."

"You survived. I knew you would," Tulya said to Beltur, "because Jessyla was with you. Without her . . ." She shook her head. "I couldn't do that for Lhadoraak. I would . . . if I could . . . have . . . he tried . . . so hard . . . to . . . give us . . ."

Jessyla stepped forward and put her arms around the sobbing Tulya.

Beltur looked to Taelya. "We need to go into the front room for a little bit."

"Yes, Uncle Beltur."

He took her hand, and they walked from the kitchen. Beltur could still smell the aroma of the burhka as he settled Taelya on the padded bench and sat down on the other end facing her.

LXVI

In the end, on twoday evening, Jessyla served Tulya's burhka, and stayed at Tulya's house, in Taelya's room, while Taelya slept with her mother. Beltur took care of the horses and the stable, and slept alone in his and Jessyla's house. Tired as he was, he did not sleep well and woke early on threeday morning still thinking about how else he could have dealt with the Hydlenese in a way that would not have forced Lhadoraak into sacrificing himself to save others.

Except Lhadoraak had taken on the white to save Taelya. And possibly to atone for Athaal's sacrifice? Beltur doubted he'd ever know. What he did know was that, without Lhadoraak's efforts, matters would have turned out very differently . . . and very much worse. *But if you hadn't offered for him and Tulya to come to Haven?*

There seemed to be no end to the thoughts and counterthoughts with which he struggled, and he finally got out of bed, discovering from sight and soreness that he again had bruises on his arms, shoulders, and chest . . . and possibly elsewhere that he couldn't see.

By the time the white sun crept above the horizon, Beltur had washed up and changed into a pair of blacks, cleaned the stable, cleaned the tack he'd been too tired to do the day before, groomed the horses, and then fed and watered them.

He washed up again, after partly refilling the kitchen cistern, and then walked across the street.

Jessyla opened the door before he could knock, saying immediately, "You're better, but your order levels are still too low."

"So are yours," he replied dryly.

"Not so low as yours."

Beltur couldn't argue that, not when he still couldn't sense much farther than half a kay. He lowered his voice. "How's Tulya?"

"What do you think?" Jessyla replied softly.

"Devastated."

"That's about right, but she's determined not to show it."

"Tell Beltur to come in," called Tulya from the kitchen. "He can say what he has to say here. I hate whispering."

Beltur winced at the despairing hardness in Tulya's voice.

"Just keep it in mind," murmured Jessyla before saying more loudly, "We're coming."

The two moved quickly into the kitchen, where Tulya and Taelya sat at the table. Beltur noted that a place had already been set for him. Beltur studied Tulya with his senses, but her order/chaos levels were close to where they should have been, and, equally important, so were those of the child she carried.

Jessyla returned to the stove. "Breakfast is just egg, potato, and mutton hash, with bread."

"And ale, Aunt Jessyla."

"And ale," added Jessyla, as she took the platters and began to serve the hash, beginning with Tulya.

Beltur sat down at the table beside Taelya, who still sat at the end on the stool, which left the place beside Tulya empty. He filled his beaker from the pitcher of ale on the table.

"How are the horses?" asked Jessyla when she served Beltur.

"They look to be in better shape than we are."

"Both of you have bruises on your face," said Tulya. "Elsewhere, also, I suspect, from the way you're moving."

"Aunt Jessyla, your order levels aren't that strong," observed Taelya. "Uncle Beltur's are really low."

We'll get better. Your father won't. "That happens when people attack you." Beltur took a swallow of ale, and then a bite of the hash. He chewed it slowly, not really tasting it at all, trying not to look too often at Tulya.

"I'm not delicate porcelain, Beltur," said Tulya, a wryness covering swirling feelings beneath.

"No, you're not." *You're iron re-forged by sorrow and anger.* "But you have its refinement."

"Hardly." Before Beltur or Jessyla could say more, Tulya went on. "What are you doing today?"

"We'll need to meet with Raelf . . ." began Beltur.

"Taelya and I are coming," declared Tulya.

"You should," agreed Beltur. "You're a councilor and our justicer." *And you've paid a higher price than any of us.*

There was little more to be said about that, and Beltur didn't feel inclined in the slightest to talk about the weather, hot and damp as it already was, unsurprisingly, since it was almost midsummer, nor did he want to talk about anything else that meant nothing just in order to be saying something.

When Jessyla finished eating, she said, "I really do need to clean up."

"Taelya and I will finish up here," said Tulya.

"I'll get the horses ready," said Beltur.

"Not Slowpoke and the mare," said Jessyla.

"I could ride Slowpoke," Beltur pointed out. "We're only going to the East Inn and back today. If we do a little healing, it will be there."

Both women looked at him.

"There are extra mounts in the barn," Jessyla said, adding firmly, "If *I* do a little healing, it will be there."

At Jessyla's words, the hint of a smile flitted across Tulya's face and vanished even more swiftly.

"I'd forgotten. I wasn't thinking," admitted Beltur.

More than two quints passed before Jessyla walked down to the stable wearing her greens, and carrying a small duffel that contained healing supplies.

"You really think you should be healing?" asked Beltur.

"Sense me. What do you think?"

Beltur did. "You could do a little."

"You come with me. You can tell me when I've done enough."

Just like you warned me yesterday. "I'll do that."

"Good."

A half quint later, Tulya and Taelya joined them, and the four rode away from the stable toward the square and the East Inn. Beltur studied the main street, but nothing appeared that much different between their houses and the square, but then no fighting had occurred along that stretch. When they passed the Brass Bowl, he did see that a makeshift corral had been built which was filled with mounts, but whose mounts they had been was another question.

When the four rode up to the stable at the East Inn, several troopers immediately turned and stepped forward.

"We can stable your mounts, Councilors," offered the first man to step up.

"We'd appreciate that," said Beltur as he dismounted. "Thank you."

Jessyla also dismounted and quickly unfastened the duffel with the supplies.

Once they were inside the inn and walking toward the public room, Taelya said, "They were frightened."

"They should be," murmured Jessyla to Beltur.

Someone had obviously hurried ahead to alert Raelf, because the public room was empty, except for the majer, who stood waiting beside the circular table. "Councilors . . . I was hoping to see you."

"We're here." Tulya stopped short of the table.

"At times such as these," said Raelf, looking directly at Tulya, "I cannot imagine your loss. I can only say that we would not have prevailed without your consort and what he did. He changed the course of the entire battle by removing a white mage at a time when the Lydian forces had been almost destroyed. In the end, only about fifty of them survived, and half of those were wounded. Some still may not live. Lhadoraak not only annihilated more than a company, but he brought that part of the battle to a halt. That allowed the companies freed by Jessyla and Beltur the time to turn and take on the remaining Hydlenese. If you don't already know, neither Beltur nor Jessyla could have done any more by that time."

"It took all three of them," replied Tulya quietly, her voice hardening and turning cold as she continued. "This battle killed Lhadoraak, almost killed Beltur, and could easily have killed Jessyla. It never should have happened. We—and you and your men—paid for the mistakes made by the Duchess or for her unwillingness to purchase the armsmen necessary to protect her land. That . . . that I will neither forget nor forgive. We have kept our word, and we will continue to do so. Order and chaos help her if she ever makes that mistake again."

Beltur thought Raelf paled slightly at Tulya's words.

"As you know," the majer replied, "I had recommended putting a post here. I was not heeded. You are right. Still . . . despite any failings the Duchess may have, I would still prefer her to any other ruler in Candar."

"So do we," said Tulya, "but I trust you will emphasize to her that we strongly suggest she not make the same mistake twice."

"With your permission, I will suggest that she support your establishment of your own company of armsmen here in Haven. You will have enough mounts and tack to support them, and you will likely have more than a few volunteers after what you accomplished this past eightday."

Tulya looked to Beltur, who nodded.

"Thank you, Majer." Tulya inclined her head.

"You mentioned a few volunteers," said Beltur. "That suggests prisoners."

"We have thirty-some who were unharmed. We've found over a hundred wounded Hydlenese. Some have already died. There may be others who fled and who will not wish to return to Hydlen."

"What about your wounded?" asked Beltur.

"There are fifty or so."

"How many did you lose?"

"A hundred and fifty-one dead out of the three Montgren companies. A hundred eighty-three dead from the three Lydian companies."

Beltur managed not to swallow. Usually, the wounded far outnumbered the dead. He also realized he'd heard nothing about Cheld, and he hadn't seen the undercaptain. "Cheld?"

"He led the initial charge once we reached the collapsing Lydian forces. He blunted their advance. He went too deeply into the Hydlenese forces." After a pause, Raelf went on, "We don't know exactly how many Hydlenese died, but we've found over a thousand bodies. We're burying them. There's not enough time or wood to burn them. That doesn't count those who were turned to ash."

"I'd judge there were over four hundred turned to ash," said Beltur. "About a hundred fled back toward Hydolar."

"If they have any sense, they'll head elsewhere. The Duke doesn't tolerate failure, even from rankers."

Belatedly, Beltur remembered that Raelf had started his career as an armsman in Hydlen. "So I've heard."

Raelf turned to Jessyla and said cautiously, "I see you're wearing greens today."

"I can do a little healing today," Jessyla offered. "Beltur can't. If we're careful, we can do a bit more tomorrow. I hope you have more dressings. The Hydlenese burned many of my supplies."

"Dressings we have, and some clear spirits, as well as some splints and some brinn. Some of those who could benefit are in the tack room," said Raelf. "There are others in rooms in the inn."

"I'll start in the tack room."

"Taelya and I will wait here," said Tulya, gesturing to a small table set against the wall. "You shouldn't be that long."

Even before Beltur followed Jessyla into the tack room, the feel of wound chaos was almost overpowering. *Because you have only the slightest of shields?*

Once inside, Jessyla stopped by each man and sensed him briefly. Beltur did, too. Just from small signs he could tell that there was one trooper who would definitely not live, and that was a bearded Lydian veteran with wound chaos throughout his chest. Beltur suspected that he'd breathed hot chaos ash. Each breath was a shuddering effort. Even if Beltur and Jessyla had been at full strength, there would have been little they could have done.

The injuries of the others were primarily deep slash wounds or broken bones, if not both, often with more chaos beneath the dressings than Beltur would have liked to see. Some of the wounds required more cleaning and better dressing, and all could have used some free order to reduce the chaos. *Free order that you can't provide because it would tariff your natural order to make even that effort.*

Neither spoke much as Beltur assisted Jessyla. But after almost a glass, he looked at Jessyla. "You can't do any more."

"You're sure?"

"I'm more than sure."

The two slipped away and walked back to the public room, empty except for Tulya and Taelya.

By the time they had recovered the horses and returned to Tulya's house, and Beltur had stabled and groomed the horses and then walked to join the others, it was close to midday.

Jessyla, Tulya, and Taelya were sitting at the kitchen table when Beltur entered and joined them.

"I'm glad you didn't overdo it." Tulya paused, then said, "Yet I also wish you could have done more. Those troopers didn't deserve to be wounded or die because of the weakness of the Duchess or the greed of Duke Massyngal." She turned to Jessyla. "You said it before, but I need to say it as well. What will keep him from doing it again once he builds up his forces?"

"We will," said Beltur quietly. "Before he gets that chance."

Jessyla nodded.

Tulya offered a puzzled frown.

"He has no armsmen to speak of left in this part of Hydlen," explained Beltur. "We're going to pay him a visit. Once we're recovered, of course." He knew that it was something he'd have to do, and not Jessyla, but he wasn't about to mention that at the moment. Not until he had a chance to talk with her about what needed to be done.

"Why?" asked Taelya. "He's evil."

"To give his successor a message," replied Beltur.

Tulya nodded slowly. "That might work."

"If it appears that it doesn't," said Beltur, "then we'll pay another visit. As many times as necessary until someone gets the message."

LXVII

When Beltur and Jessyla left for the East Inn on fourday morning, her order/chaos levels were better . . . if still low . . . but, as she pointed out, "There's lots of healing I can do without order, and I'm physically stronger today."

So was Beltur, but Jessyla had made it clear that his order/chaos levels were still likely lower than hers had been on threeday.

After leaving Jessyla to her healing, Beltur rode Slowpoke over to the quarters building, noticing that Dussef was posted by the fountain and Therran near the chandlery, not all that far from the quarters building.

Gustaan came out to meet Beltur almost as soon as he had dismounted.

"I heard about Lhadoraak, ser. I can't tell you . . ." The former squad leader shook his head.

"We wouldn't have prevailed without him."

"They said . . . you weren't much better, ser." Gustaan looked at Beltur. "Your hair . . . they say Councilor Jessyla turned silver, too."

"She did. I likely would have ended up like Lhadoraak, except she stopped me from doing more. She had to do the last magery in the west, and we also wouldn't likely be here without her. How have you managed with the town patrol?"

"We haven't had any problems with the troopers. Not so far, anyway."

"A number of the Hydlenese scattered at the end, and Majer Raelf said he had some prisoners."

"He came to see me yesterday. He said he didn't want to bother you. He wanted to know if we had anywhere that we could lock up prisoners. I told him we didn't. We talked for a time. He wanted to know how I came to be here. I told him. Then he said that perhaps, if you approved, we might be able to use some of the prisoners in rebuilding some of the places that got burned down. I told him that was up to the Council. That's right, isn't it?"

"It is. We're getting most of the captured Hydlenese mounts and pretty much all the tack and gear they left here. The majer suggested that perhaps we should use all that to create our own company."

"Might be a good idea, but it would take a lot of doing, ser."

"Think about it."

"Was that what you were talking about before, ser?"

"No . . . that was something else. I might need some men who know their way around Hydlen and especially Hydolar."

Gustaan frowned.

"If I do, when the time comes, you'll be among the first to know. What about you and your men?"

"I know some of Hydolar. Not that much except the Duke's palace and the troopers' post there. Turlow'd know more. He's from Hydolar. Dussef's from Sunta, and Therran comes from a little town near Telsen. Never asked Graalur."

"I'll keep that in mind, and I'll let you know once things settle." *And I get my strength back.* "One way or another we're going to need some more good men."

"I was thinking that. Maybe I could ask the majer if I could talk to some of those prisoners. Wouldn't promise anything, though. Not until you tell me."

"That's a good idea. I'll mention it to the majer."

As Beltur rode across the square, his thoughts went to where might be the best location for a fort or post. Then he shook his head. He didn't even know how they'd pay for running an entire company.

Still . . . what about two squads?

He was still smiling wryly when he dismounted outside the inn's stables.

"The healer's in the back there with the other wounded, ser," offered a trooper sitting on a bench, his right arm in a sling and splint that looked to be recently applied.

"How's the arm?"

"I've still got it, and that's better 'n a lot, ser."

"Carry on, trooper."

"Thank you, ser."

Beltur decided to see Raelf before looking for Jessyla and seeing how she was doing. He found the majer in the front room of the inn, talking to Bythalt. Since it sounded like the two were finishing, he just waited in the archway until Raelf turned.

"You're looking better this morning."

"I am feeling better," Beltur admitted. "I was just talking to the town's chief patroller. He said you mentioned something about prisoners . . . that we might be able to use some for rebuilding."

"I did."

"If it's acceptable to you, I'd like to have him talk to some of them and see if they might work out."

"That's fine with me. The fewer we have to deal with the better." Raelf cleared his throat. "It looks like we've recovered all the mounts from Montgren and Lydiar that went riderless, and all the tack from our mounts that were killed. I would also request that you allow us to take twenty captured horses as pack animals. We're leaving the remaining Hydlenese horses for you. There are close to a hundred. They should prove useful. So will the tack. And gear. We're working on getting those Hydlenese uniforms, but finding enough that are usable . . ." Raelf paused, then went on. "From what they tell me about the greencoat uniforms, I'm just as glad I wasn't there to see up close what you and Jessyla did to those poor bastards."

"We weren't happy to do it, but unless we killed a lot of them the Duke would be back with more before long."

"He will be. Not this year, but next year or the year after. That's what I'm reporting to Lord Korsaen and the Duchess."

"Why do you think that?" Beltur agreed with Raelf, but wanted to know the majer's reasons.

"Zekkarat's company was the only Lydian company worth even a demon's ashes. Sooner or later, Massyngal will find that out. He'll want to take over Lydiar even more, and the only roads are through Haven. I've also heard that he doesn't like anyone who denies him."

"I've heard both of those reasons. Are there any others?"

"From what I've heard, Massyngal doesn't need any others." Raelf's words were wry.

"That's why you think we should have our own troopers?"

"You'd still need help from the Duchess and Duke Halacut against an army. Having your own troopers, especially with your talents as mages, would stop harassment. It might also give Duke Massyngal some pause for thought. Over time, that is."

"There's the 'small' problem of having enough golds."

"The troopers handling the bodies decided that they'd keep the coins of their spoils, but forgo the jewelry and rings and turn them over to you mages."

Beltur smiled crookedly. "Was it hard to persuade them?"

"Not really. I just pointed out that, without what you two did, and without what Lhadoraak did, most likely all of them would be dead. I also said doing that might keep them from being called back here any time soon. There's already a partial chest of silver and gold jewelry. Most of it's small, but silver and gold are still silver and gold."

It was more than clear to Beltur that Raelf never wanted another battle like the last one, and neither did Beltur. "Thank you."

"Montgren owes a great deal to you. Whether anyone else will say it I don't know. But I know it, and I want you to understand that I do."

And he's doing everything he can to show it. "We appreciate it."

"It's to Montgren's advantage." Raelf grinned. "And Korlyssa might complain about what I've granted, but what's done is done, and it's a lot easier for you to keep what you rightly won, than to ask for it back from her."

"Thank you."

"You all paid for it. Dearly. None of us want to pay again."

"That's true." Beltur paused. "If there's nothing else . . ."

"Not at the moment. Go get some rest. You could use it."

From the front foyer, Beltur walked back to the stable and to the other room, whose previous use he could not discern, where wounded troopers were laid out on pallets barely above the rough plank floor.

He'd hardly stepped inside the door when Jessyla motioned to him. He walked carefully along the narrow space between the first two rows of wounded until he stood beside Jessyla, who knelt beside an unconscious trooper.

"If you'd see what you can sense?"

Beltur nodded and let his senses range over the man. He didn't sense more than minor wound chaos in the trooper's body, likely from bruises or cuts, but in the area behind his right temple was a large dull red area, at the edge of which were scores of tiny reddish-orange chaos points.

"He must have taken a blow to the head. I'd say it was with the flat of a sabre, because there's bruising there, but no cut, and I don't sense a break in the bones underneath."

"Could you do anything?"

Beltur shook his head. "There are too many chaos points."

"He's bleeding inside his skull, then." Jessyla rose. "I thought so, but . . . I wondered if you . . ."

"It's not the same as the boy I healed." Beltur looked down at the dying man, wishing he could do something.

For the next glass, he followed Jessyla, occasionally supplying a tiny bit of free order where it just might make the difference . . . or provide a touch of comfort.

Once they rode away from the inn, Jessyla said nothing until they rode past the Brass Bowl.

"So many dead. So many wounded and maimed. For what?"

"Do you think we were wrong to fight?" asked Beltur evenly.

"No. It wouldn't have made any difference. Hundreds or thousands of men would have died, just not here. Most likely in Lydiar, and the deaths among the people there would have been greater." She took a deep breath, then let it out slowly.

"Lhadoraak would still be alive," Beltur said.

"He would have lived longer," replied Jessyla. "But what would have happened after Massyngal conquered Lydiar? A year later, we would have been surrounded on three sides by unfriendly rulers, and the Duchess wouldn't have been able to stop an invasion of Montgren."

Beltur considered that, and the fact that, if Massyngal had taken Lydiar, their situation would have been far, far worse. "I still wonder if we could have done things differently."

"We could have. Tell me how all the rest of us would be better off, especially Taelya."

Especially thinking about Taelya, Beltur couldn't. *Why can't you? Because she's right? Or because you weren't smart enough to see far enough ahead?*

He was still mulling over those thoughts when Jessyla said, "We're having dinner at Tulya's."

"Shouldn't we have her at our house?"

"Later. Right now, she needs something to do. We need to be warm and pleasant, but not falsely cheery."

"We could talk about Taelya and what she's learned and what she needs to learn."

"Some, but not too much. She's the reason why Lhadoraak did what he did, and she shouldn't know that now. Not at her age."

Not the only reason. But there was little point in discussing that, either.

LXVIII

On fiveday morning, Beltur felt considerably better, and he could sense well over a kay, although his various bruises remained yellow and purple, if somewhat faded from the previous day. He had just finished cleaning the stable and dealing with the horses when a wagon, escorted by four troopers, rolled to a stop in front of the house. Curious to see what might be in the wagon, he walked over to the lead trooper.

"Mage-Captain, ser . . . where do you want us to put all these Hydlenese blades, lances, and axes?"

During the battle, Beltur hadn't even noticed that some of the Hydlenese troopers besides those in the recon company had carried axes. "I'd better look at what you have first."

"They're all wiped clean, ser."

"We appreciate that." Beltur peered into the wagon bed.

The troopers had separated the weapons by type. Directly behind the driver were straight-swords, mostly in scabbards. Farther back were sabres, which filled the middle of the wagon, almost overtopping the wagon sideboards. The score or so of battle-axes were against the tailboard, almost lost behind the hundreds of sabres. *Lances?* Then Beltur realized that they were on the far side of the wagon, set lengthwise and protruding over the tailboard.

"This is just the first wagonload, ser," added the trooper. "Might take two more, maybe three."

"Let's start with the axes, then the straight-swords . . ."

Two quints later all the swords, sabres, and axes were stacked, at least roughly, in Beltur and Jessyla's cellar, where there wasn't that much room left, not without filling the part that was the root cellar proper. The lances had gone on one side of the barn's hayloft.

Beltur was blotting his forehead from all the carrying in the summer heat and about to see Jessyla off on her way to the Brass Bowl and the wounded there . . . when the second wagon arrived.

She looked at Beltur and smiled. "I'll ride over to Tulya's and tell her that you'll be storing more weapons in her cellar."

"At least until we can build an armory . . . or rebuild something."

"That's going to take a while."

Beltur was afraid she was right.

Another glass and a half and a third wagonload later, Beltur and the troopers had stowed all the weapons so far collected and wiped off. While they certainly represented a great deal in silvers and golds, there was the question of who would ever buy them. Even if the Council could raise and pay a few squads of troopers, Haven would likely never need that many weapons.

A good smith could use all that iron. But a good smith was something else that Haven didn't have at the moment.

When the third wagon left, Beltur washed his hands and face, again, saddled Slowpoke, and then rode to the East Inn. He finally found Raelf outside the far south end of the stable, watching a handful of troopers trying to replace an axle.

The majer turned. "You got the weapons, I take it?"

"Three wagons' worth."

"There will be another in a day or so. We should have those uniforms by then."

"What did you report to the Duchess? Or Korsaen?" That was something that he should have asked earlier, but he hadn't been thinking all that clearly.

"They each got the same report. I reported what happened."

That could mean anything.

Raelf smiled wryly, obviously in response to Beltur's skeptical expression, then said, "I made it simple. We were outnumbered four to one. You three mages managed to destroy over half their force and cripple more than that. Together we killed or wounded, mostly killed, more than fifteen hundred Hydlenese, not counting the battalion you destroyed earlier. Lhadoraak was killed in destroying more than a company. The Lydians lost close to two-thirds of their men, one captain, and Majer Rojak. We lost more than half. We're doing our best to clean up the bodies and other carnage."

"That's all?"

"I wrote it almost that bluntly. Except for suggesting a letter to the Duke praising Rojak for his heroic and gallant efforts."

"How long do you plan to stay in Haven?" asked Beltur.

"I'd thought at least another eightday for the Weevett company. What's left of Reynaard's company will be leaving for Woolsey the day after tomorrow. Knutwyl has squads patrolling the border south and west of Haven. That's to deal with any Hydlenese stragglers. It's going to take another few days. The Lydian companies will be leaving on eightday. That's to allow some of the riding wounded a little more time. Zekkarat's senior. He isn't looking forward to reporting to Duke Halacut. I wouldn't be, either."

"Couldn't he find a place in Montgren? He was very effective."

"I mentioned the possibility . . . if things go poorly for him. The Weevett company will need a new captain. I think Lord Korsaen would find him acceptable, but I can only recommend."

"He'd make a better majer than Rojak did."

"That's why Duke Halacut won't promote him."

"Is Halacut as incompetent as he seems?"

"More. He's also losing, disgracing, or driving away advisors who try to counsel him honestly and wisely."

"And the Duchess was willing to lose all those men to help him?"

"Helping Montgren. Would you want to turn over Lydiar to Massyngal?"

Beltur shook his head. Left unsaid was the fact that the Duchess didn't have either the troopers or the desire to conquer and hold Lydiar. *Especially now.*

"Why else would Korlyssa essentially turn over a part of Montgren to you?" asked Raelf.

"Because all the alternatives were worse." *And because she wanted us to pay enough for it that we'd guard Montgren's southern border, if only to save ourselves.* "She and Korsaen planned it well." He couldn't quite keep all the bitterness out of his voice.

"They planned it the only way they could. While your costs were high, it also wasn't exactly without cost for Montgren, either. You saw that." Raelf offered a sad smile. "Is there anything else you need at the moment?"

Since Beltur didn't, and since the question was almost a polite dismissal, Beltur returned the smile. "Not now. We appreciate all you've done, and we'll look forward to receiving those uniforms whenever you have them."

"It shouldn't be long. Now . . . if you'll excuse me . . ."

"Of course." Beltur turned and walked back to where he'd tied Slowpoke, wondering slightly about the majer's reserve. *Because you didn't acknowledge enough the costs to Montgren?*

After mounting, he rode out of the yard and turned Slowpoke west on the main street, toward the Brass Bowl. There was something about Raelf's last words about costs . . . something . . .

Beltur stiffened. Raelf had said that the battle and the defeat of the Hydlenese hadn't been "exactly without cost for Montgren" . . . as if Haven were no longer part of Montgren, but something separate.

Another message from the majer, and all of them saying the same thing—that Haven was and needed to be independent . . . and that Raelf wasn't completely happy about it, as if it were a bitter necessity.

But making that happen was going to be quite a challenge.

LXIX

On fiveday evening, Jessyla and Beltur fixed dinner. Beltur did wonder where Jessyla had found the duck that went into the cassoulet along with the white beans.

As Tulya set down her spoon after finishing the last bean in her bowl, or perhaps the last scrap of duck, she looked to Jessyla. "This was good."

"It was excellent," added Beltur. "I've never had anything like it before."

"How did you come up with it?" asked Tulya.

"We stopped by Julli's. She had a scrawny drake that was being difficult. She said she was ready to wring his neck, and that she'd rather sell him to me." Jessyla looked a trace sheepish. "I had to ask her how best to cook the duck."

"I never would have known," replied Tulya.

"I had her wring his neck as well," confessed Jessyla, adding before Tulya could say anything, "I couldn't do it. After . . . everything . . . I couldn't kill a duck for dinner. Somehow . . . that seems . . ." She shrugged helplessly. "Ridiculous . . . stupid . . . I don't know what . . ."

Beltur understood how she felt. He wasn't sure that he could have killed the drake, either, not at the moment.

"Maybe you just couldn't kill anything else," said Tulya.

"It didn't even look helpless. It looked as mean as Julli said it was. We needed something for dinner. Yet I just couldn't. It doesn't make any sense."

"It makes sense," declared Tulya. "I can't tell you why, but it does."

"It tasted good," said Taelya. "Aren't ducks meant to eat?"

"It tasted very good," added Beltur, trying to suggest that enough had been said about the unfortunate but tasty drake.

Jessyla refilled the beakers at the table with ale from the chipped pitcher, then said, "You might be interested in what Raelf told Beltur today."

"It's more like he revealed it," Beltur explained.

"He doesn't seem the type to disclose what he doesn't wish to," replied Tulya, not quite tartly. "So . . . what was it?"

Beltur smiled crookedly. "That the Duchess is either accepting or resigned to the fact that we'll become independent from Montgren."

"He actually said that?"

"Of course not," replied Beltur, "but every time I've talked to him since the battle, he's made a comment that either hints at or suggests it. He can't do more than that. Sooner or later, if we do become independent—"

"No," said Tulya coldly. "We pretend to be her councilors and press for every gold we can find while we do our best to make Haven as independent as possible. She owes us more than we'll ever get. But we should take everything we can."

Beltur definitely understood Tulya's feelings.

"In time," added Jessyla, "we should change the town's name."

"To what?" asked Tulya.

"To Fairhaven. We'll offer a fair haven to anyone who comes here and obeys the laws and pays the tariffs."

"We'll get riffraff and worse," said Tulya.

"Not if we make them promise to behave and throw them out or execute them if they go back on their word. And we won't accept them if they lie to us in the beginning."

"We'll need our own code of laws," said Beltur.

"Who's going to write them?" asked Tulya.

"Well . . ." began Beltur with a smile, "we do have a justicer who's studied the Montgren laws more than anyone else . . ."

"You think I should . . ." She stopped. Then she nodded. "You're right. We've seen enough bad laws."

"We're going to need them fairly soon," added Beltur. "Gustaan is talking to some of the Hydlenese wounded and prisoners."

"You and Jessyla will talk to those he thinks are suitable, I assume." Tulya's words were anything but a question.

"We will, but I think you and Taelya should be there as well."

"Taelya?"

"She has a good sense for feelings," Beltur said.

"I need to think about that."

"That's fine. We won't be doing that for a day or two." Beltur paused, then ventured something he worried about, but felt was necessary. "We also need to get back to teaching Taelya more about handling order and chaos."

"Can we? Tonight?" asked Taelya.

"Yes, you can." Tulya smiled.

While the smile was real, Beltur also sensed something beneath, a certain . . . something.

Not anger, not sadness . . . determination.

"Father said that I needed to work very hard at being a strong mage."

"When did he say that?" asked Tulya, clear curiosity in her words.

"Before the big battle . . . before he left."

Beltur saw Tulya look away, unable to look at her daughter.

"He was right," Jessyla said quickly. "He worked hard at being a good mage."

"Will I be as good?"

Beltur managed not to swallow, then said carefully, "You'll have to work very hard to be as good a person as your father. You're a different kind of mage. So there's no way to compare what you might be to him, but you could be a very, very strong mage if you work at it."

While Taelya was looking at Beltur, Tulya quickly blotted her eyes with her sleeve, then said, "It's getting late. If you want a lesson from Uncle Beltur, you two need to go into the front room and work there while Aunt Jessyla and I clean up dinner."

"Are you sure, Mother? I could help first."

"No. You need your lesson, and we'll be fine in the kitchen."

Beltur stood. "You've been keeping your order and chaos where they should be very well, and that means you just might be able to try a stronger kind of shield." He gestured toward the front room.

Taelya slipped out of her chair and hurried from the kitchen.

Turning back to Tulya, Beltur asked, "How long before you'd like to go?"

"Not until Taelya's done as much as she can for the evening."

Although Tulya's words were even, Beltur sensed the cold iron beneath them. He felt like shivering, despite the warmth of the summer evening. Then he nodded and followed Taelya into the front room.

LXX

On sixday morning, Beltur and Jessyla slept late, or late for Beltur, since he didn't get out of bed until after seventh glass. He still felt tired, even though Jessyla assured him that his order/chaos levels were much better, and in the late morning they made the rounds of the wounded of both sides. The rest of sixday was relatively quiet, and Tulya and Taelya joined them to finish off the duck cassoulet, along with some bread Beltur had baked.

Sevenday morning, both Beltur and Jessyla were up earlier, not early enough to see Reynaard's company riding out, but early enough that they finished their rounds of checking the wounded before ninth glass. As they were about to leave the East Inn, Bythalt edged toward them.

"Mages . . ."

"Yes?" Beltur managed to keep his voice level, despite the feeling he had that Bythalt was about to complain about something.

"I would not wish to seem ungrateful . . ."

"Then you shouldn't," replied Jessyla even before Beltur could say a word. "What problem do you have now?"

"The Lydian majer . . . he paid for the fare of the Lydian troopers . . ."

"And no one is paying you now?" asked Beltur.

"No, ser."

"Did you talk to Majer Raelf about it?"

"He is from Montgren."

"Talk to him. He's in command of the entire force." *What's left of it.*

"I had hoped . . ."

"That we'd do the dirty work for you?" interjected Jessyla.

Before Jessyla could say more, Beltur immediately said, "Talk to the majer. If you still have problems, then let us know."

"Yes, ser," replied the innkeeper, dejectedly.

"You come to the Council as the last resort, Bythalt," added Beltur, "not as the first step."

"Yes, ser," replied Bythalt, no less dejectedly than before.

Beltur just nodded, then turned away.

"How has he even survived as an innkeeper?" asked Jessyla once they had left the innkeeper and were walking out of the inn.

"That's how. By being subservient and apologetic to anyone with power . . . and pleading with them to solve any problems he has. Once we get Haven back together, he'll have to change his approach. It took me a while to realize that." Beltur laughed ruefully. "It's taken me a while to realize a lot of things."

"Later's better than never." She smiled and added, "And it's not that much later. We're still young."

"At the moment, I don't feel that young, and I don't feel that much wiser, either. I wish I did."

"Auntie once said that anyone who had any brains never felt wise. The more they knew, the more they understood how much they didn't know."

"Your aunt said that?"

"Beltur . . . she may be sharp-tongued, but she's seen a lot."

After a moment, Beltur nodded. "That's fair."

"You're headed to the stables. I thought you said we had to see Gustaan."

"I thought we'd ride over. It's market day, and you told me that the larder was bare, or almost so. I assume that the baskets you put in your saddlebags were for a purpose. So . . . if we ride over, we wouldn't have to lug everything back to the horses."

"Do you think there will even be anything for sale? Anything we can use, I mean."

"There will be. The Hydlenese didn't have a chance to raid the steads this time. Also, there will be some troopers with coins that they got from the dead greencoats. Those with anything to sell will know that."

As soon as the two stepped out of the inn, Beltur looked west. While the square wasn't exactly thronged, especially not in comparison even to Axalt, there were more carts and wagons than he'd ever seen in Haven, and several score troopers walking between them.

"I hadn't thought about the looted coins," said Jessyla. "Or wanted to forget."

"They haven't," said Beltur, untying Slowpoke.

"Did you ever . . . back in Spidlar?"

Beltur laughed. "You might recall how I ended up after almost every skirmish or fight. I never even had the chance to be tempted. The one time I did have a share of spoils was from arms captured from Analerian brigands, and we never even had a chance to collect the coins from their sale because the next day Uncle was dead and I was hiding in your house."

"I wouldn't say you were hiding."

"Looking for refuge, then."

"It's a good thing you were. I don't think either Mother or Athaal realized how dangerous Gallos was getting for blacks."

"I hadn't thought of it that way."

Jessyla smiled. "I didn't either. Not until later."

They mounted and then, because the square was relatively crowded, they rode around the south side, past the charred ruins of the Council House and the healing house and then up the west side to the quarters building. Even so, several of the troopers in the square gestured toward them, and one young trooper hurried away, although he wasn't close to being in their way. Beltur saw that Gustaan had three men posted around the square—Dussef, Turlow, and Graalur.

As they approached the quarters building, Beltur saw Zekkarat standing there talking to Gustaan.

As they reined up and dismounted, the Lydian captain turned. "Mage-Captains . . . I didn't want to intrude on your healing, but I'd thought you might come here or to the square after you finished."

Beltur and Jessyla tied their mounts and joined the Lydian officer on the narrow porch.

Gustaan eased away, walking to the end of the porch, suggesting that he realized Beltur and Jessyla needed to talk to him, but clearly understanding that Zekkarat wanted a few moments with the two.

"You're heading back to Lydiar tomorrow, I heard," said Beltur.

"I am. Not without . . . certain concerns."

"Such as Duke Halacut not understanding how successful you were against terrible odds? Or how you likely saved Lydiar from being invaded?"

"The Duke only understands losses," said Zekkarat. "Not the cost of avoiding far greater losses."

"That's unfortunately true of other rulers as well," replied Beltur. "Without you and what you did to support Majer Raelf, we all would have lost far more."

"What my men did was only possible because of what you mages did. Without you, we'd have been slaughtered to the last man. I know that. The Duke will likely not accept that in his heart, no matter what his words say."

"If matters go badly . . . I suspect Lord Korsaen might look upon you with great favor," Beltur said quietly.

"I appreciate your words. The majer has hinted at that as well. I would prefer it not come to that." Zekkarat paused, then said, "Whatever may happen, I know that without you three mages, all of us would have perished. I have talked to some of the captives and wounded. All of them say that they were under orders to give no quarter and to leave no one alive in Haven."

Beltur tried not to shiver. To believe that had been the case was one thing. To have Zekkarat confirm it was another, since absolute conviction was in both his words and feelings.

"No one has mentioned that to us," Jessyla said evenly.

"Have you asked them? Do you think any of the wounded would dare offer such words to those healing them?"

"We didn't think of it," replied Jessyla.

"That is because you are a healer at heart and a captain and warrior only from need."

Beltur couldn't have agreed more—about Jessyla. *But you should have thought about it.*

"And you, Mage-Captain Beltur, already understood Duke Massyngal. You had no need to question what you knew. I can only hope that Duke Halacut has a fifth of your understanding." Zekkarat smiled. "I have nothing else to say. I only wished to convey my appreciation."

"You have ours," replied Beltur. "You and your men made what we did possible. We wish you well."

"*You* will always be welcome here in Haven," added Jessyla.

"I hope I do not have to accept that welcome, but I appreciate it. Thank you. Again." Zekkarat paused. "I need to attend to some details."

After Zekkarat strode off across the square, Gustaan approached the two. "Councilors, he wished a word with you."

"We're glad he did before he left," said Beltur. "He's a very good officer."

"I got that feeling."

Not wanting to dwell on Zekkarat's departure, Beltur gestured toward the carts and wagons and the troopers around them. "What do you think about that?"

"It looks like a real market square," observed Gustaan.

"It does," agreed Beltur.

"I don't think that's why you're here, though, ser."

"No. I wanted to know how you're coming in finding possible recruits among the Hydlenese prisoners and wounded."

Gustaan offered a wry and lopsided smile. "There are forty wounded who look to recover. Some of those"—he looked to Jessyla—"you've healed. I'd guess that thirty-five of them want to stay here. Twenty-three of the prisoners feel the same way."

"Good," replied Beltur. "It's possible we can use them all."

Gustaan frowned. "I thought you only needed ten or so."

"Ten as town patrollers. Majer Raelf suggested that it might be a good idea for Haven to have a company of troopers. There's no way we can afford a company. A squad or two, though, we just might be able to work out."

"Can the Council afford that?"

"We do have something like a hundred horses, over a thousand blades of various sorts, and other assorted goods that we might be able to convert into coins."

Gustaan raised his eyebrows. "The Duchess and Duke Halacut aren't . . ."

"No. They aren't. Now . . . there's one other matter. I need you to be in charge of a recon squad I need to take into Hydlen, possibly into Hydolar itself. We'll be wearing greencoat uniforms."

"A recon squad into Hydlen? After all . . . this?"

"I'm not looking for a fight. Between the uniforms and my being able to conceal the squad, we should be able to avoid using arms. You'd mentioned that Turlow knows Hydolar and the area around it. Did you find out about Graalur?"

"He's from Asula. A recon squad?" asked Gustaan once more.

"That's as good a name for it as any," replied Beltur. "Can you get together another nine men who would be suitable and who you'd trust in the next day or so?"

"Might be better if I got a few more and had you meet them."

"Oneday morning, then." Beltur had hoped that Gustaan would suggest something along those lines, and had wanted to see if the former squad leader would do that.

"Yes, ser. How soon would this squad be leaving?"

"Not for another few days at the soonest." *Not until most of the troopers and Raelf leave.* "It might be longer. It will happen, but the timing depends on a few other matters."

"You don't want Dussef or Therran in the squad?"

"Councilor Jessyla will need some experienced patrollers with you and Turlow gone." Beltur paused. "On oneday, maybe we should also meet two or three men who you think would be better as town patrollers."

"I can do that."

"Good. Now . . . we're going to see if we can find some things out there in the square. If you, or someone, would keep an eye on the horses? It won't be long."

"We'll watch. I need to be here anyway."

"Thank you."

Beltur waited a moment, while Jessyla retrieved two baskets from her saddlebags. Then, once they were well away from the quarters building, he asked, "What did you sense?"

"He was a little worried about the recon squad, but he seemed pleased to hear about more troopers here."

"That was my feeling, but I wanted your view because I might have been sensing what I wanted him to feel." Beltur kept walking. He didn't recognize the holder who stood beside the first cart that they approached.

"Ser mage, lady healer, the best cherries you'll find anywhere in Montgren."

Beltur suspected that they were the only cherries in Haven. "How much?"

"Two coppers for a quint stone."

Beltur looked to Jessyla. "Do you think . . . some for us, and some for Tulya?"

Jessyla nodded, then handed over four coppers.

When they moved on, she murmured, "That's a lot for cherries, but he didn't have that many left. They're good for a woman carrying."

Not to mention that they taste good.

In the next quint, they bought some new potatoes and a block of white cheese, ignoring the cage full of coneys for sale and a smaller cage filled with tree rats, before they came to Julli's wagon.

"I thought I might see you two." Julli smiled, then frowned as she looked at Beltur. "You, too? The silver hair, I mean. You two look like druids. They're supposed to have that silver hair."

"I don't feel like a druid. It just happened to us both at the same time in the battle."

"Well," replied Julli, "you won't have to worry about going gray."

"I suppose not," replied Beltur, glancing past Julli. "Those beans look good."

"They're good," agreed Julli. "I would have had more, but those greencoats who wore maroon trampled a good part of that garden."

"We'll take some," said Jessyla, "and the banty rooster. If you'll wring his neck."

"Now?"

"Now," replied Jessyla.

"Speaking of greencoats," said Beltur. "We might have some tailoring for you. We have some uniforms . . ."

Julli frowned.

"I thought it might be useful for some of the town patrol to have green uniforms when they're scouting on the other side of the border. Do you have time to do that in the next eightday or so?"

"If you're paying, I've got the time."

"Perhaps on twoday or threeday?"

"I'll be at the house." Julli turned to Jessyla. "Why don't you come back when you've finished looking around."

"We're done now. We just need the beans and the rooster."

Beltur didn't look away as Julli casually wrung the rooster's neck, but it did make him a little uncomfortable.

He was still wondering why when they rode back to their house.

LXXI

On eightday, Jessyla and Tulya collaborated on turning the banty rooster, which Jessyla had plucked and marinated in ale and various spices overnight, into a flavorful stew for diner. Beltur suspected that, without the marinating and Tulya's touches, the rooster would have been tough indeed.

While they were collaborating, Beltur spent several glasses with Taelya, both working on her shields and helping her to move chaos in a precise and targeted fashion, as well as answering, as well as he could, the questions she asked about why the Duke of Hydlen was such a cruel ruler that he wanted to kill people in Haven.

By seventh glass on oneday, after stabling Slowpoke and the mare at the East Inn, Beltur and Jessyla were at the quarters building, where Gustaan had gathered four Hydlenese captives—two recovering from sabre slashes and two who had been captured. Even the two who had been captured sported cuts, scrapes, and bruises.

Jessyla and Beltur sat on straight-backed chairs in the main-floor chamber that served not only as the patrol duty room, but also as the off-duty gathering place.

"Before we start," Beltur said, "there's one other thing I'm going to need."

"Yes, ser?"

"I need a rough map of the way to Hydolar, with the names of all the towns or large hamlets we'll pass through."

Gustaan frowned.

"I know you don't need it, but I do. How can I ask an intelligent question or know what someone's talking about . . ."

A brief smile appeared on Gustaan's face. "Hadn't thought about that, ser. Between us, we can put something together. Might take a day or so."

"Thank you. Now . . ."

Gustaan went to the rear door, opened it, and ushered the first man in, a black-haired stocky man with a splint on his left forearm. "This is Laussag. He's from Renklaar."

Laussag's eyes focused first on Beltur, narrowing, presumably at his black forehead and silver hair, and then turning to Jessyla. He frowned, then said to her in an accent Beltur didn't recognize, "You wore blue to fight, didn't you?"

"Yes. How did you know that?"

"I saw you appear after you'd smashed a line. Except your hair was red, then. You were also the one who set the bone in my arm, weren't you?"

"I set it. Beltur later removed some of the chaos that was there because it hadn't been set earlier."

"Gustaan said you are looking for men who would like to be town patrollers here."

"We are," replied Jessyla.

"How do you know you could trust me?"

"We don't. We can tell if you're lying or if you're upset, or calm. Would you be interested in being a patroller here?"

"I might be. There's no point in going back to Hydlen."

"What might be keeping you from being interested?" asked Beltur.

Laussag moistened his lips. "Who really controls the town patrol?"

"We do," replied Jessyla. "The two of us and the other councilor."

"No merchants or traders?" Laussag's tone was skeptical.

"No. The Duchess chartered us as the Council. There aren't any wealthy traders here. There's no one from the Duchess's family, either," said Jessyla.

"That's why we can't pay as well as some towns can." Beltur smiled. "We do have quite a few blades and other weapons that we can turn into coins in time. Also, some horses."

"What do you expect from patrollers?"

"To keep the peace. To be honest. Not to steal from the people they're protecting or from anyone else. To be a good person on-duty and off-duty."

Beltur paused, then asked, "What would *you* expect from a good patroller?"

Laussag shifted his injured arm, wincing slightly. "Everything you said. Also, to know weapons well enough not to have to use them and to use only as much force as necessary."

"That's a good point," agreed Beltur. "We feel that way, but hadn't mentioned it."

By the time Beltur and Jessyla had talked to the four men Gustaan had selected, it was past ninth glass, and the three were alone in the duty room.

"What do you think?" asked Gustaan.

"You chose well," said Jessyla. "Do you have a preference?"

Gustaan shook his head. "Each has different strengths, but I'd be happy with any of them."

"Then offer a position to each of them. They know we can't pay that much? And that they'll sometimes have to help with building and other things?"

"They know. That's not a problem."

"Good. Now . . . what about troopers? Especially nine who'd be willing to reenter Hydlen for an eightday or two. With me and you, of course."

"You, ser?"

"I've always wanted to see Hydolar, and since there's a need for me to go there, I thought wearing green uniforms would make it . . . less adventuresome. A half squad is large enough to forestall questions, especially since I'll be wearing a captain's uniform, and big enough to deal with local . . . authorities. It's also small enough for me to easily conceal everyone for as long as necessary."

"You're not looking to fight then?"

"I absolutely don't want you and the men to fight if there's any way possible to avoid it."

"Might I ask why . . . ?"

"I have to deliver a message to the Duke. Personally, and in a way that he, and those around him, understand that I could do so again, especially if I ever heard that he was amassing troops again."

Gustaan's mouth opened, then closed.

"I'm trying to make it clear that he will pay a personal price if he tries something like this again."

"Do you think he'll listen . . . if you can even get to him?"

"If you can put me close to the palace, I can get to him. The rest is up to the Duke."

"That might be harder than you think."

Beltur nodded. "Everything has been harder than we thought. We still have to try. Can you have the trooper candidates here at first glass?"

"Yes, ser."

"Then we'll go over to the inn and have an ale while you get them ready."

"Ah . . . ser . . . when will this . . . evolution take place?"

"Soon. I'll know more in a day or two. We're not talking even as long as late summer."

"That soon?"

"Right now, there are troopers scattered all over the north of Hydlen, I'd wager. The sooner we can leave the less anyone will think about it."

Gustaan nodded at that.

Beltur and Jessyla walked back across the square, empty in the midday heat, unlike on sevenday, and made their way into the public room. There, Raelf was seated at a table with Knutwyl. He motioned for the two mages to join him. Set before him was a chest a half yard wide and half that high and deep. "I was hoping to see you two." He nodded to the chest. "This is for the Council."

Beltur knew instantly what was in the chest. "The Council is most grateful."

"It might help some with your rebuilding."

"At this point, we can use that." Beltur seated himself.

"I've thought as much." Raelf eased the chest in front of Beltur.

Beltur noted that Knutwyl maintained an even expression, but there was a certain chaotic uneasiness behind that pleasant demeanor. "This will help us build a stronger Haven, so that there won't be a repetition of what happened."

"That's my hope," replied Raelf. "I'd hate to have lost men for nothing."

"We understand," said Jessyla. "We do."

They'd only been seated for a few uneasy moments more before Claerk appeared with two more beakers of ale. "This is the better brew, Mages."

"Thank you."

Claerk hurried off.

"I saw you headed to the town patrol building," Raelf said.

"We were talking to Hydlenese troopers who might make good town patrollers."

"Hydlenese?" asked Knutwyl.

"Almost none of the captives or the wounded feel safe in returning to Hydlen. Apparently, the Duke isn't especially welcoming to those he feels failed him. They need a new home, and we need patrollers. In time, we'll likely need at least a squad of our own troopers. Where else would we get men as good?"

Knutwyl looked to the majer, who nodded.

"We also healed some who might not have lived," added Jessyla. "By the time they fully recover, we might be able to use them."

"Does the Duchess . . ." Knutwyl let his words trail off.

"We couldn't have fought off Massyngal without help," said Beltur. "We couldn't in the future, either. But a squad and a mage can handle up to a company of Hydlenese . . . and any trader brigands. That's why the Duchess made us councilors."

"She's aware of what the mages can do . . . and what they can't," added Raelf, looking at Knutwyl, then turning back to Beltur and Jessyla. "We've decided that Knutwyl and I will be leaving on fourday. His patrols haven't seen traces of stragglers lately, but I'd like to make sure over the next few days. I've received word to leave a full squad from Weevett here under Daaskin for another two eightdays, or a little longer, if you think it necessary, along with the last supply wagon."

"Thank you," said Jessyla. "That will make matters much easier when we deal with the Hydlenese captives and wounded."

"How are you going to handle that?" asked Knutwyl.

"If they want to leave, we'll escort them to the border." She smiled sweetly. "If they want to stay, we'll find something for them to do. We need structures and houses rebuilt. Who knows, they might even have some skills we're lacking."

"Given the way Massyngal's behaved," added Beltur, "we might even attract a few traders once we've put things to rights." He took a sip from the beaker. The brew he and Jessyla had gotten from the widow was definitely better.

"You might at that," agreed Raelf. "Haven won't ever be the same, and it will be good not to have to worry about it. We're likely to have enough trouble dealing with the Viscount."

"Have you heard anything about what's happened near Passera?" asked Beltur.

"There have been skirmishes, but no major battles. Not as of an eightday ago. Neither the Prefect nor the Viscount wants to back down, but neither wants a battle that he might lose."

Raelf laughed softly. "Once they learn what happened to Duke Massyngal, they might be even less eager to fight."

"The Viscount might be less eager to fight," said Knutwyl. "I have doubts about the Prefect."

"I'd agree with your view of the Prefect," said Beltur. "He lost something like six mages in the battle for Elparta, and he immediately started picking a fight with Certis."

"Duke Massyngal's fortunate the Prefect doesn't have an easy way to Hydlen," returned Knutwyl. "Otherwise . . ." He shook his head.

"Massyngal's also fortunate that Lydiar's weak right now," added Raelf. "If Lydiar had a strong duke, like Heldry or Heldacar, after a battle like this, Massyngal would be fleeing for his life." He shrugged. "But we live in the times we live in, not in other times. Our times are interesting enough."

Too interesting. Beltur just smiled and took another swallow of ale.

A little more than a glass later, Beltur carried the chest with him across the square to the quarters building. He hadn't looked into it and wouldn't until they and Gustaan finished with talking to various troopers and they rode back to the house, where Tulya and Taelya could see as well.

When they reached the duty room, Gustaan looked at the chest that Beltur set on the side table.

"Ah . . . ser?"

"A gift from the Hydlenese to us, courtesy of Majer Raelf. It might pay for some more patrollers and troopers."

"The majer gave it to you?"

"To the Council. The majer doesn't ever want to fight a battle like the one here again. He believes that if Haven is strong enough to discourage the Hydlenese he won't have to. I'd appreciate your keeping that to yourself. There are those in Vergren who might not approve, and we need every ally we can keep."

"Yes, ser."

"We might as well get started." Beltur took off his visor cap and set it on the table, then seated himself.

Jessyla sat down on his right.

Gustaan walked back to the rear door and opened it. "Khraas, you're first."

The trooper who entered wore a green Hydlenese uniform, with dark splotches in places, splotches that were likely what remained of blood that Khraas had tried to remove. He stopped short of the table, standing erect. "Sers, Trooper Khraas." His eyes widened slightly as he took in Beltur, but they lingered only a moment before he quickly studied Jessyla, then waited.

"Khraas, how did you come to be captured?" asked Beltur.

"When your other mage took on our mage, the whole middle of the company was wiped out. Maybe more. Outside of that weapons, shields, all sorts of stuff got blown everywhere. Something hit me in the head. When I woke up, there were some angry Lydians looking at me. They decided not to cut my throat."

Beltur nodded slightly. So far Khraas was telling the truth.

"Do you know why we wanted to talk to you and the others?"

"The word is . . . Ser, your squad leader said that you wanted volunteers. After this mess, my life wouldn't be worth a bent copper in Hydlen."

"We're looking for both town patrollers and troopers to form the beginning of a Haven company. Would you rather be a town patroller or a Haven trooper?"

"Ser . . . if it's all the same to you, I'm a good trooper. I wouldn't be a good patroller. I get mad too quick when people are stupid."

"Some squad leaders and undercaptains are stupid."

"Ser, begging your pardon, you don't strike me as keeping stupid squad leaders."

Beltur could sense the amusement behind Gustaan's pleasant expression.

The trooper went on. "Most stupid squad leaders don't last, and the good ones can keep most dumb officers from really stupid stuff. Ser."

"Usually, but not always," replied Beltur.

"Yes, ser. That's why some of us are here. That is, the Duke, Duke Massyngal, he doesn't like really smart officers. Smart officers wouldn't have even tried to attack Haven. Not after what happened to the first battalion."

"I need troopers to wear Hydlen uniforms and accompany me on a recon mission deep into Hydlen. Would you be interested in being a trooper if that were a requirement?"

"So long as you're leading the mission in person, ser."

"You wouldn't regard it as a way to get home safely and to avoid the Duke's men?"

"Ser . . . if any of us tried to go home, we'd be killed on the spot."

The absolute certainty behind the trooper's words chilled Beltur.

After perhaps another half quint, Beltur dismissed Khraas, thinking that the trooper was a likely prospect.

The next five men, while they had been captured under differing circumstances, had much the same attitude and honesty as Khraas. The seventh trooper to enter had managed to largely clean up his uniform. His brown beard and hair were short and trimmed, and he looked openly at Beltur and then Jessyla.

"Caaldyn, trooper, ser mages."

This time, Jessyla repeated the opening question.

"Ser mages . . . I was in the second rank of Fifth Company when one of you charged and broke the line. My mount was pushed sideways. He stumbled over something and went down. I recall nothing after feeling myself pitch forward. I must have hit my head. The next thing I clearly remember was two mounted Montgren troopers, one with a bow drawn and a shaft pointed at me, and the other ordering me to my feet."

Beltur could sense that Caaldyn was evading something. "How long do you think you lay there on the road?"

"I couldn't say, ser. Like I said, the next thing I knew, there were these troopers checking the fallen."

The part about troopers checking the fallen was certainly truthful, but Beltur extended his senses to the trooper, and could find no trace of wound chaos or bruises anywhere on Caaldyn's head.

When asked about whether he'd rather be a trooper or a patroller, Caaldyn replied, "I didn't have any choice in becoming a trooper. All the young men on my street were conscripted."

At that point, Gustaan said, "Might I?"

Beltur and Jessyla both nodded.

"What street was that, Caaldyn? Was it in Hydolar?"

"Yes, Squad Leader. It was Clapton Close."

That statement was completely true, Beltur sensed.

"Thank you," said Gustaan.

"About being a patroller or trooper," Beltur prompted.

"Yes, ser. If I have a choice, I'd rather be a patroller. I've never liked the killing part of being a trooper."

"Why else would you rather be a patroller?" asked Jessyla.

"I like staying in one place."

Again, that was true, but there was a chaotic overtone, and the rest of Caaldyn's responses during the brief talk were similar.

Once Caaldyn had left, Jessyla turned to Gustaan. "Not him. Not for anything. He presents an honest and open appearance, but everything underneath is calculating. Much of what he said was only partly true."

"I would agree," said Gustaan. "Also, Clapton Close is one of the worst streets in Hydolar. Even when I was stationed at the palace post, I'd heard of it."

"Then we need to keep him with those who aren't considered for either," said Beltur.

"What do we do with them?" asked Jessyla. "Sending them back to Hydlen might get them killed."

"Give them a choice to find work here as a laborer, or to go elsewhere as they wish," said Beltur. "We'll need to make it clear that, if they stay here, any attack or assault on anyone will merit execution or banishment."

By fourth glass, the three had decided on twelve men who might be possible troopers, and left it up to Gustaan to choose the nine to accompany him and Beltur.

Once Beltur and Jessyla had left the quarters building, reclaimed Slowpoke and the mare, and were riding back toward their house, Jessyla turned to Beltur. "I don't like the idea of your going to Hydolar alone."

"We both can't go. There has to be a mage here to keep things under control," Beltur pointed out, balancing the chest in front of him, since it was too big to fit in the saddlebags. "I'm back to strength, and I can sense even a bit farther than I could before. I won't be alone. I'll have Gustaan and the others. And we won't be looking for a fight, but to avoid one."

"Somehow, that doesn't reassure me. You haven't been looking for a fight since I've known you. Did that matter? You've fought Analerian brigands, a Gallosian army, three different brigand groups, a battalion of Hydlenese, and then the biggest force Duke Massyngal could send."

"It's safer now than it would be later," Beltur pointed out. "If we don't deal with Massyngal now, we'll have to face another army, and I don't think either the Duchess or Duke Halacut will be nearly so supportive a second time. Massyngal hasn't had time to rebuild his forces or even to move some of those from Worrak to Hydolar, but it won't be that long. Also, there will still be some troopers straggling back to Hydlen."

"Not many, from what the ones we talked to were saying."

"There will be some. More important, the local people won't think it's unusual right now."

"You're probably right about that," Jessyla said glumly. "I don't have to like it."

"Do you think I do?" asked Beltur wryly.

LXXII

Early on twoday, Beltur and Jessyla rode to Julli's house, each carrying a stack of Hydlenese uniforms, including one that had been a captain's and two that had belonged to squad leaders.

Julli was working in the rear garden when the two reined up. Still carrying the short spade that Beltur remembered all too well, she walked swiftly toward them. "I see you've got some uniforms for me to alter. What? One for each of you? Who else?"

Jessyla dismounted, tied the mare to the hitching post at the rear of the house, and said, "Just for Beltur. The others are for two of our patrollers and nine other men that Gustaan will bring over later today. Some of them are former Hydlenese troopers, but some only have portions of their uniforms left."

"You're trusting them?"

"They're also trusting us," replied Beltur as he dismounted. "If they get captured in Hydlen, they'll likely be killed. If they carry out this mission, they'll have a place, and we'll have the beginning of our own company of armsmen." He paused, then added, "To which you'll be able to sell quite a few things."

Julli turned back to Jessyla. "You're not going with him?"

"One mage has to stay here and take care of matters."

"Humph. I suppose that makes sense. Come on inside. I can take Beltur's measurements now."

Beltur turned and lifted his stack of uniforms off Slowpoke, while Jessyla took hers from the mare.

"Quite a load you've got there."

"There should be enough to fit everyone," replied Beltur. "You'll have to alter the two captain's uniforms, the ones with the higher collar, to fit me, and a squad leader's to fit Gustaan."

"You need two?"

Beltur nodded. He wasn't about to explain why. The fewer who knew the better.

"When do you need them?"

"As soon as you can finish them. You'll be paid immediately when they're ready."

"That will depend on how much alteration I have to do." Julli opened the door and stepped back. "It sounds like you're headed to do something dangerous." Once they were inside the kitchen, she headed for a room to the side.

"We're just going to deliver a message."

"It's not my business . . . but, if you think I believe that, I've got some ancient cupridium I'd be happy to sell you."

Beltur just smiled behind Julli's back at Jessyla, who shook her head.

Julli used a cloth tape quickly, writing down Beltur's measurements on a small scrap of paper with a grease stick. "You're broader than you look." She shook her head. "You're also more dangerous. Both of you. The greencoats found that out."

"We've just been trying to find a place that will be home," Jessyla said.

"Well . . . you've found it. You just have to protect it now."

"There is that," Beltur said dryly.

"So far, you're doing fine. Now . . . off with you. I need to finish the gardening so I can get to work on those first two uniforms."

"Is it all right if Gustaan brings the others over in a glass or so?"

"A glass, but no sooner."

"We can do that."

Once the two were mounted and riding back, Jessyla said, "Things would have been even harder without her and Jaegyr."

"I know. She'll get some extra." Beltur didn't mention that without the four councilors life would have gotten much worse for the couple.

Their next stop, at the quarters/patrol building, was brief, just to give

Gustaan the directions and times for him to take his men to Julli's so that they could be measured for alterations to whatever they needed to have complete uniforms for the "recon mission."

After that came a stop at the widow's to arrange for new kegs of ale for the two houses. Beltur had thought about supplying one to the quarters building, but decided against that for the moment, fearing it might be too great a temptation for some of the new patrollers.

Then they returned to their house, and Beltur took out the chest that Raelf had presented them. Earlier he'd looked into it, and done a quick estimate. This time they counted. When they finished, Beltur looked at the figures on the paper—four hundred seventeen silver rings, twenty-three gold rings, seventy silver chains, and five gold chains, plus another thirty-five pieces of silver jewelry, including thirteen silver buttons.

"That's somewhere close to a hundred golds' worth of jewelry." Beltur looked to Jessyla. "I'd wager the gold rings and chains came from officers and senior squad leaders."

"We won't get that much for it," she pointed out.

"We will if we turn it into coins."

"How do you propose that?"

"Make molds for golds and silvers. Have Taelya use chaos to melt the metal, and I'll use order containments to get it in the molds."

"Can you do that?"

"We did the glazes that way, and she's better now than she was then." Beltur shrugged. "We'll have to see. Maybe we'll have to get a silversmith, but even that would be better than taking a loss." He didn't mention that sooner or later, having their own coinage would be a step toward eventual independence from Montgren, but before that the molds could simply be duplicates of other coinages.

Somehow, with one chore or another, it was time for dinner at Tulya's, and Beltur was wondering where the rest of twoday had gone.

When Beltur and Jessyla entered the kitchen, escorted by Taelya, Tulya looked up from the small side table where she'd set the beakers for the ale. "If you'd fill the beakers, Taelya, and put one at each place. Only water in your beaker. You can have some ale after you've eaten a little."

"Yes, Mother." She hurried over to Tulya and gave her a hug, then took one of the beakers to the keg and began to fill it.

"Taelya's been quite a help," said Tulya.

That's because she senses how much you need her. But Beltur just smiled and said, "She's always been helpful . . . and something smells wonderful."

"Roast lamb. Lamb, not mutton. Frydika asked me if I'd like some. How could I refuse? Especially with early apples and new potatoes."

"My mouth is already watering," said Jessyla. "Can I do anything?"

"Just sit down with your ale and talk to me. There's not that much to do. You two were out and gone early today."

"We had to take the Hydlenese uniforms to Julli, and then we had to let Gustaan know about where to take the new troopers to make sure they had complete uniforms. We also stopped by the widow's and arranged for more ale. She'll have Jaegyr deliver it in the next few days. If you run out before then—I think we have more because we've been eating here more—just send Taelya with a pitcher."

"I think we're fine, but that's good to keep in mind."

The conversation from there on was light, and the lamb was every bit as good as it smelled, as were the fried apples and cheesed new potatoes that accompanied it.

Then, while Jessyla and Tulya cleaned up after the meal, Beltur took Taelya into the front room, as he had most nights since the battle.

"Tonight, you're going to work on focusing chaos to a point while holding the strongest shield that you can."

"I can already focus chaos."

Beltur looked at her.

"Mostly."

"Mostly isn't good enough, and if you want to be a strong mage, you need to be able to focus chaos at the same time. Can you tell me why?"

Taelya frowned. "Because . . . because I might have to hurt someone to stop them from hurting me, and they might be attacking me."

"That's true," Beltur agreed. "You're also the one closest to your mother."

After a long moment, Taelya said, "I didn't think about that. I might have to protect her, and I can't hold my shield that long yet." Her jaw set. "What do you want me to do first?"

Beltur hadn't liked playing that plaque, but the plain fact was that Taelya just might have to protect her mother, and she needed to know that. "Remember. You only focus chaos on people or animals that are attacking you or your mother. Bad words don't count. Just acts."

"Yes, Uncle Beltur. Where do I start?"

A glass later, when Taelya was exhausted from her session with Beltur and had gone to her room, where she was almost asleep before she climbed into bed, the three adults returned to the kitchen, sitting around the battered table.

"What you're doing isn't just a recon mission . . . or even a messaging mission," said Tulya, her tone worried.

"It's a very specific messaging mission," replied Beltur. "One that's absolutely necessary, because, without it, we'll be faced with another army in a year or so."

"I know, but will it ever end?" Tulya sighed.

"We'll always have to be on our guard," Beltur admitted.

"I worry about you," Tulya went on, "especially now."

"I can't afford not to do it," replied Beltur. "You two can't afford for me not to do it. It took all three of us to stop this last force. If we don't send a message that the Duke of Hydlen can understand personally and clearly, the next army will be even bigger."

"Don't get yourself killed to deliver the message," said Tulya. "That would be even worse."

"And don't tell us you have no intention of getting killed," added Jessyla tartly. "Intentions don't count. We need you. Haven needs you. If you can't do what you have in mind without getting killed, don't do it!"

Beltur smiled wryly. "You both have made that very clear." He stood. "I understand. I also agree. But I have to see if it's possible. Would you like another ale?"

"I would," said Jessyla, "but don't dismiss us. Think of it this way. If you don't think I could do it, then you're not to do it. That just *might* make you cautious enough."

That just might make you cautious enough. The love and concern underlying those words tore at Beltur. Yet he *knew* that Massyngal was mad enough to attack until he was stopped.

LXXIII

Much of threeday, Beltur and Jessyla spent with Tulya while the three of them went over what Tulya had drafted as the possible laws for Haven—Fairhaven to be at some time in the future, once the three were convinced that the time was right. Later in the afternoon, Raelf brought Squad Leader Daaskin to the house to go over the duties and responsibilities of the squad remaining in Haven.

On fourday, Beltur, Jessyla, Tulya, and Taelya were up very early and rode to the East Inn to see the departing companies off on their return to their home posts . . . and to see Raelf off to report to the Duchess and Korsaen in Vergren.

As Beltur dismounted and tied Slowpoke outside the stable, since none of them planned to remain there long, Daaskin appeared.

"Ser, the morning scouts report no sign of Hydlenese anywhere."

"Thank you, Squad Leader. The longer it stays that way, the better."

"I'd be surprised if any of them want to come near Haven again, ser."

"The ones who were here may feel that way. Those who haven't likely won't believe those who have." *Which is another reason why you have to deal with the Duke.*

"That may be, ser."

"You say that because you've been here, Daaskin. Tell some of your friends or people who aren't troopers once you get back to Weevett and see how much they believe. And, by the way, the more senior an officer, the less likely they are to believe. At least, that's what I've seen." Beltur laughed ironically.

Daaskin tried, and failed, to hide a grin. "Might be, ser."

"Keep up the patrols. We both might be wrong."

"Yes, ser. Besides, it's better than garrison duty."

"And it will give us time to train some troopers and town patrollers."

"You're going to use Hydlenese?"

"Those who don't want to return to Hydlen and whom we can trust. One advantage of being a black mage is that we can usually tell when someone is lying. That makes it a little easier."

"Oh . . . I can't say that I knew that."

"We've already determined that some of the wounded and captives aren't suitable. That means, if they don't want to go back to Hydlen, they'll have to go to Certis or Lydiar."

"Don't know as the Viscount or Duke Halacut would like that."

"They may not, but Haven's too small to keep possible troublemakers here, and there just might be better places for them. If not, we at least give them a chance."

Daaskin nodded slowly. "I can see that, ser."

"I don't like it any better than you do, but they were the ones who attacked us, not the other way around. I know most of those troopers likely didn't want to fight, but we're giving the honest and hardworking ones a chance. If they'd won, their orders were to kill everyone they could."

"I'd heard that." The squad leader shook his head, then looked past Beltur. "Here comes the majer, ser. I'd best be back to the squad."

"Thank you."

Jessyla, Tulya, and Taelya moved closer to Beltur as Raelf approached.

"Good morning," said Beltur. "We thought we'd come to see you off."

"I'm glad you did," replied the majer. "Otherwise I'd have had to seek you out."

"We came because no one else could have handled the battle and everything else as well as you did," said Jessyla.

"I wish I could have handled it better," replied Raelf, looking directly at Tulya. "If I could have, I would have."

"I know that," said Tulya. "You did the best you could. It was more than anyone could have expected."

"We wouldn't have prevailed without your sacrifices. It was that close."

"I know." Tulya's voice was low.

Raelf handed a heavy-looking leather bag to Jessyla. "I was given a supply of golds for our time here. This is most of what remains. You'll need them."

"Won't the Duchess . . . ?" began Jessyla.

"I was told to spend them carefully and as necessary. I see supporting Haven as very necessary. I've also seen enough to know that none of you will waste anything. Daaskin has enough to pay for his men and their lodging and what food they need."

"We thank you," said Tulya. "You've been very thoughtful."

"I'd like to think I would have been anyway, but Lord Korsaen also instructed me to leave you all with every resource possible."

"Thank him for us," said Beltur. "Personally, if you would."

"He did ask me to report to him first on my return." There was what might have been a twinkle in the majer's eye when he replied. "Is there anything else you need from me?"

"I think you've given everything possible," said Jessyla.

Raelf grinned. "I do hope so."

Even Tulya smiled in return, if faintly.

The majer nodded, then turned and walked to where a Montgren trooper held his mount.

"If there were more like him, we wouldn't have had to fight," said Tulya.

"Most of the officers in Montgren were good," replied Beltur. "It's just that neither Massyngal nor most other rulers favor thoughtful and fair-minded officers."

"Or even sensible ones," added Jessyla acidly.

"That's usually because they'd have to listen to what they don't want to hear," Beltur pointed out.

Within half a quint, the last wagon, which looked almost empty, had rolled westward on the main street, and the four untied their horses and walked them over to the patrol/quarters building.

As usual, Gustaan came out to meet them. "It looks like we're more on our own."

"There's one squad left. A full squad," said Beltur. "They'll stay for two eightdays, possibly a little longer. Did Julli tell you when the uniforms would be ready?"

"She said to tell you that yours are ready. Some of the others are done. They'll all be finished by sixday afternoon."

"And those maps I asked for?"

"I've got them inside. They're rough, ser, but between all of us, we got most of the names and places on them, leastwise those on the way or close to it."

"Thank you. I thought a Hydlenese captain ought to know some of them, at least so I don't look surprised when someone mentions a place."

Gustaan nodded.

"How much time do you need with the half squad you have before you're comfortable with them?"

"They're all veterans. A few days at most. I can work with them on the road as well. I doubt there will be any Hydlenese troopers around for the next few days." Gustaan paused. "What do you intend to tell the people in Hydlen? What we're doing?"

"I'd thought to say that we'd been dispatched to look for stragglers."

Gustaan snorted. "I don't know that the Duke cares, but it's the sort of thing folks would believe."

"Isn't that what counts?"

The squad leader nodded, then said, "There is one thing, ser."

"Yes?"

"Your forehead. More than a few Hydlenese troopers had to have seen you. It might be better if you had a dressing across it, like you'd taken a cut there."

"You're likely right, especially once we get close to Hydolar."

"I can make up some dressings," said Jessyla. "You'd better wear them."

"I will."

Beltur turned back to Gustaan. "We should leave early on sevenday."

"We'll be ready, ser."

Jessyla swallowed.

"The sooner we leave, the less they'll expect anything . . . and the sooner we'll be back."

From Jessyla's expression, Beltur knew exactly what she was thinking and would not voice. *If you come back.*

LXXIV

Late on fourday evening, well after Jessyla and Beltur had counted the nearly two hundred golds that had been in the leather bag and placed them in the hidden and order-protected iron box, the two sat across the table in the darkness of an unlighted kitchen. "Nearly two hundred more golds." Jessyla shook her head. "Two hundred golds, but the Duchess wouldn't put a post and troopers here."

"Raelf calculated it out, remember. It would have cost her five to seven hundred golds a year, and probably more than that."

"She's likely spent more than that by now."

"It's close," agreed Beltur, "but without us, she would have lost Haven, and all of Montgren would have been threatened. By giving us Haven, even if she has to help us in the future, it will likely cost her less. She and Korsaen are wagering that we'll make Haven prosperous again."

"It might not be a wager. Maeyora may have foreseen a prosperous Haven."

"That's still a gamble of sorts. The dead white wizard had a vision, too. His vision of a great white city rising from Haven might well be accurate many years from now, but . . . his interpretation of what he saw didn't include us." *Or his death.* That was something Beltur wasn't about to mention at the moment.

"I still worry about your going to Hydolar."

"So do I, but I feel strongly that it's absolutely necessary."

"Didn't the white wizard feel the same way?"

"He was convinced that he'd overcome everything. I just want to sneak into Hydolar, deliver a forceful message, and sneak out. I'll avoid any direct armed confrontations. I have no interest in being a hero."

"That's one thing I love about you," Jessyla said softly. "You do what's necessary, not what makes you look good. When others are better at something, you let them do it, and help them if you can."

"That only makes sense."

"To you, and sometimes to me, but not to people like Duke Massyngal or Sarysta or most of the blacks still in Elparta."

"Sometimes to you?"

"I like to be recognized when I do something good. I'm not proud of wanting that, but I know I do. I think I want that more than you do."

Beltur had to think about that for a moment. "I like it recognized when I do something well. I think everyone does. I also want to make a place where everyone can do good things . . . where Jorhan and I can make beautiful objects out of cupridium and not worry."

"You miss him, don't you?"

"Some. If I'm honest, I miss more what we could create together. Except he did the creating. I just made it possible."

"Maybe that's what you do best . . . make things possible."

"Like making possible a huge battle that killed thousands?"

"And saved thousands of others from being killed and conquered."

Neither spoke for several long moments.

Finally, Jessyla said, "Sevenday . . . that's . . . so soon." She swallowed. "You're just now getting back to full strength, and not all the bruises are even gone."

"If we don't act soon, while the Duke isn't expecting it . . . there won't be a good time again. Also . . . with Daaskin here, you'll have more support than if we wait." Not wanting to dwell on that obvious worry, Beltur said, "You'll do fine dealing with the patrollers and Daaskin. They all know what you can do."

"That's true . . . but it's hard not to worry about you. I can't not worry about you." She reached across the table and took his hands in hers.

"Then I'll just have to make sure that you don't have anything to worry about."

"You'd better," she said firmly. A ragged laugh followed her words.

Beltur squeezed her hands, then released them and stood. "We'd better get some sleep."

She stood and wrapped her arms around him. "In time."

LXXV

Beltur didn't sleep that well and woke up early on sevenday, stunned at how quickly the previous two days had passed, what with preparing for the "recon mission" and watching closely on each day as Gustaan drilled the ten men who would be accompanying them. The squad leader had been right about the troopers. They were definitely veterans, and Beltur couldn't help wondering at the outcome of the battle—even given what he, Jessyla, and Lhadoraak had done.

He was still wondering on sevenday morning as he pulled on the uniform of a Hydlenese captain, but he pushed those thoughts to the back of his mind in the deep gray light before dawn.

"You look every digit a distinguished greencoat captain," said Jessyla. "I almost hate to put this dressing on."

He stood still while she adjusted the cloth dressing. "It's not too bad, and it might help keep the sweat from my eyes."

"Be careful when you take off your cap. It might stick to it if it gets really damp."

"I'll try to remember that."

"You need to eat. Gustaan and the others will be here soon."

Beltur nodded. The squad leader had pointed out the afternoon before that there was no need for Beltur to ride east to the patrol building, only to turn around and ride back west.

Breakfast was oat porridge, bread, ale, and fried apples and eggs, and Beltur ate every bit that Jessyla had ready for him . . . after he had saddled Slowpoke and fastened his gear behind the gelding's saddle, which included the better captain's uniform. His saddlebags held a fair amount of travel food, and both water bottles were filled with ale.

Beltur had barely finished eating and had just downed the last of the ale in the beaker when Jessyla said, "I can sense them turning off the main street."

He immediately stood and wrapped his arms around her.

"Remember. You're to be careful."

"How could I forget?" *You've made it very clear over the past eightday.*

"Just don't. I need you. We need you."

His lips found hers, and he held her tightly for several more moments before he let go.

Then the two of them left by the rear door and walked down to the barn. Jessyla stood waiting while he led Slowpoke out. Then he embraced her once more before mounting and riding toward Gustaan. Behind the squad leader were the ten rankers in double file, with the last rider leading a spare mount loaded with packs largely containing travel rations.

"Good morning, Captain."

"The same to you, Squad Leader. I take it that we're ready."

"Yes, ser."

Without another word, they turned and headed back to the main street under a sky that was still gray. One of the reasons for leaving early was so that no one would notice the color of the uniforms they all wore and another was to travel well into Hydlen before anyone watching might ask what greencoats were doing coming from Montgren so long after the fighting had ended.

Once they were back on the main street, Beltur asked, "Is Dussef comfortable as acting head patroller?"

"He'll do fine. He's heard plenty about what the mage-healer did in battle, and he knows he can call on her if there's something he can't handle."

"What about the new patrollers?"

Gustaan laughed. "Ser . . . every one of them saw what at least one of you did. None of them want to disappoint any of you. The only reassurance any of the troopers behind you needed is your presence."

Beltur felt almost as though massive weights had been dropped on his shoulders, and he didn't quite know why. It wasn't as though the same thing hadn't been true before the battle. *But no one said it quite so bluntly.* He not only had to be careful of himself, but also of the men who followed him, believing that he'd keep them from harm as well. He was still thinking about that after they rode past the defaced kaystone and approached the Weevett road, which, early as it was, happened to be empty.

The sun peered over the eastern horizon, or the low hills above it, about the time the half squad rode past the hill where the fighting had started when Beltur and the Weevett company had ambushed the Hydlenese scouts. It was hard to believe that first skirmish had been more than three eightdays earlier, or that the battle that had finished off the Hydlenese had been more than an eightday ago.

Beltur shook his head, then looked to Gustaan, still riding beside him. "Vaarlaan is the first town on the map you made. Are there any hamlets before then?"

"There are some groups of houses you can see from the road. One place had to be abandoned. All the roofs were missing. The others? Elshon—the white wizard—he only had us stop where there were inns. He got a room, and so did the other mage. We got haylofts, just like when I was last a squad leader." Gustaan shook his head. "Never thought I'd wear a green coat again. Even as a disguise."

"Let's both hope it's the last time." Beltur looked at the hills to the east and then at the long road ahead curving slowly in a more westerly direction. Another five days, at least, just to get to Hydolar, and who knew how long to deliver the message.

He took a deep breath, and looked at the map he held in one hand, trying to fix names and places in his mind, even though he thought he knew most of them after several days of studying them.

Two glasses later, Beltur could make out a scattering of houses that didn't look much more numerous than those in the unnamed Montgren hamlet where he had captured Graalur.

A quint later, they reined up at the small inn in Vaarlaan. Beltur paid for ale and some bread for the squad and himself. After watering the horses, they continued.

Outside of the small town, the road turned almost due west, and the ground flattened, and there were far fewer trees, most of which looked stunted in some fashion. By early afternoon, knee-high bushes flanked the road for at least a kay on each side.

"Bitterbush," declared Gustaan. "Grows in salty ground. Even the goats won't eat it."

"How far to Eskaad?"

"We should make it before sunset."

Fourth glass came and went, and there was no sign of anything except bitterbush, hills to the north, and more bitterbush to the south, but the ground began to rise so slowly that Beltur didn't realize it until he looked back east.

"Beyond that low ridge ahead, everything changes," Gustaan said quietly. "You'll see."

What Beltur realized before they reached the top of the rise in the road was just why the Hydlenese force had arrived in stages. Then, from the top of the rise—Beltur wouldn't have called it a ridge, not after riding through the Easthorns—he saw an irregular patchwork of fields, orchards, woodlots, and even places that glinted in the afternoon sun and were likely lakes and ponds.

"Another glass until we reach Eskaad. It's even got two inns." Gustaan paused. "You can't do what you did in Vaarlaan, ser. Greencoat officers don't do that. We'll have to take the stable, and you get a chamber and eat in the public room."

Beltur grimaced. "I thought that might be the case. Can I arrange for a second ale for everyone?"

Gustaan grinned. "The good captains in Hydlen do that."

"Do they pay the innkeepers?"

"They do, but they complain and try to bargain. Usually it doesn't work."

As in towns in Montgren, there were cots set in the middle of fields, or occasionally orchards, on the outskirts of the town proper. All of them were of wood, and many were ramshackle, but none looked to be abandoned.

The main square held two inns—the Yellow Dog and the Black Horse.

"The Yellow Dog is better, and they cost the same," murmured Gustaan as they rode into the square, where close to twenty carts or wagons were set up.

For a moment, Beltur wondered why, before realizing that it was sevenday afternoon, usually a market afternoon in most small towns in Candar, unlike in the cities, where there were vendors in the square every day but eightday.

For a few moments, many of those in the square immediately looked at the riders, took in the green uniforms, and then resumed what they had been doing. When Beltur reined up in the side yard of the Yellow Dog and dismounted, Turlow rode forward and took Slowpoke's reins.

Beltur walked into the inn and paused to look into the public room, where perhaps a third of the tables were taken. Immediately, a thin man with sparse sandy hair and a narrow face moved from where he had been talking with a server toward Beltur.

An expression of both surprise and puzzlement crossed his face as he neared Beltur and stopped. "Ser . . ."

"I need a room and space for my squad—half squad. We'll just be here tonight . . . and for breakfast."

The innkeeper nodded. "We can do that. Four coppers for the room, and three coppers for each man in the empty hayloft. That includes supper for them with one ale. Breakfast with ale is another copper. Hay, cup of grain, and stalls are a copper a horse." The innkeeper paused. "In advance."

"Not the breakfast. I'll pay for that in the morning."

"Before they're fed."

"Seems like it was less before."

"All of you say that. It never has been."

"That's thirty-seven coppers for the men and thirteen coppers for the mounts." Beltur reached for his belt wallet, took out five silvers, and handed them over.

"Didn't expect to see any more of you. True that the blueboys . . . got the better of you?"

Beltur had the feeling that the innkeeper had meant to be more direct in his description of what had happened. He managed to glare at the man. "Not me. We were sent later." That was accurate, if misleading.

"Is it true?"

"They had better mages. They weren't supposed to have whites who could throw chaos bolts. They hid their troopers under some sort of mage concealment. We got one of their mages. They got all of ours."

"That's what I heard."

"From the deserters who came through here? When?"

"Must have been two eightdays back. That's why . . ."

"Why you didn't expect us?"

"Ah . . . well, yes."

"It took a while for us to get there. Now we're headed back."

The innkeeper gestured toward the foyer. "I need to get you a key for your room, Captain."

Beltur followed the innkeeper.

After he received the key, he and the innkeeper headed out to the stable, but Beltur let Gustaan deal with the innkeeper so far as lodgings went, while he went to find the ostler and make sure that the horses were properly stabled. Then he unsaddled and groomed Slowpoke.

As he was finishing, a stableboy appeared, his eyes darting from Beltur to Slowpoke and back. Finally, he said, "He's a real warhorse, isn't he."

"He is."

"Why do you groom him? Most officers don't."

"He's saved my life more than once. I want to make sure he's taken care of."

"The grain Carsos has isn't that good."

Beltur refrained from smiling and produced two coppers. "I imagine you can find better grain for all our horses."

"Might be able to."

Beltur added two more coppers, holding them up. "After I see the grain."

"Yes, ser."

Once the stableboy had returned with two large buckets of oats for Beltur to inspect, he handed over the coins and then accompanied the boy to each of the stalls that held the squad's mounts—beginning with Slowpoke, who got a larger share.

Then Beltur checked with Gustaan, who assured him that all was well, and gave him three silvers to pay for a second ale for everyone before carrying his gear up to his chamber, where he washed up before returning to the public room and taking a small table at one side, next to an open window. That didn't mean the table was cool, only that it was as warm as the air outside, rather than warmer, the way most of the rest of the public room was.

The single server was a dark-haired woman who looked fifteen years older than Beltur and likely wasn't nearly that much older. She approached him with resignation. "Captain, we only have mutton hash, shepherd's pie, or mutton cutlets with brown sauce."

"How is the sauce?"

For a moment, she looked surprised, then said in a lower voice, "Sauce is fair to middling. The cutlets aren't."

"What about the shepherd's pie with the brown sauce?"

"That might be best, ser." The faintest hint of a smile, and the lack of chaos in her words, suggested she meant it.

"And the ale?"

"Pale and dark."

"The less bitter one."

"That'll be four coppers when I bring it."

Beltur nodded, then studied the room after she left. The three men at the nearest table tried to avoid looking at him as they talked about dray horses and wagons, suggesting that they might be teamsters. Farther away were two white-bearded men who sipped occasionally from their beakers, but didn't seem to be talking to each other. Then there were five young men in a corner throwing dice, one of whom kept looking covertly but worriedly at Beltur, in a way that made Beltur wonder if the man was a deserter.

He waited less than a third of a quint before the server returned with a pale ale and his platter, which contained a heathy chunk of shepherd's pie, most of which looked to be a thick brown crust and potatoes and root vegetables. Looking at it, Beltur was very glad he'd asked for the brown sauce. He handed over four coppers, then slipped her a fifth.

She looked surprised.

He shook his head, and she nodded in response, then said, "Let me know if you'd like another pale ale."

He sipped the ale, gingerly, but, while not great, it wasn't bitter, and it was definitely better than anything Bythalt served. Then he took a bite of the shepherd's pie, the crust of which was heavy and a little dry. The brown sauce mitigated that.

He ate slowly, studying the public room, but it seemed as though no one had that much interest in him, possibly because no one wanted to call attention to themselves. As he was nearing the end of the heavy and filling meal, he saw a woman with long blond hair tied back, and with an instrument that was likely a lutar, since it wasn't a guitar and he didn't recognize it, step up onto the cold hearth and begin to sing.

"When I set out for Lydiar
A thousand kays away . . .
That spring, it scarcely seemed that far,
a season and a day . . ."

Beltur had the feeling that the song was somehow familiar, but he didn't recall hearing it. *Are you sure?*

"When I reached my end in Lydiar
A thousand kays away,
A journey not so very far,
My hair, I found, was gray."

One of the white-bearded men smiled at the last words.

As Beltur looked at the singer, for a long moment, another image appeared before him, and his eyes burned, long after the image faded. He swallowed, then took a last sip of the pale ale. *You did hear it.*

Without his really sensing her, the server returned and said quietly, "Bhreta's good."

"She is."

"Would you like another ale?"

Beltur hadn't intended to take another, but he found himself nodding, even as he listened to the next song, one he realized he had once known, and almost forgotten.

"When masons strive to break their bricks
And joiners craft their best with sticks . . .
When rich men find their golds a curse,
And Westwind's marshal fills your purse,
Then sea-hags will dance upon their hands
And dolphins swim through silver sands.
Hollicum-hoarem, billicum-borem . . ."

When the singer finished and was about to leave, Beltur stood and walked toward her. She was older than she'd seemed, closer to the age someone else might have been, and that was right, too.

Her eyes widened in alarm.

He smiled sadly. "Thank you. If anyone asks, tell them I paid you a family debt." He slipped her a gold, then turned and left, heading for his room.

Once there, he barred the door. He just hoped he'd sleep well.

LXXVI

The next four days were a variation on sevenday—ride until midday; take a break for men and mounts; ride some more; take another break; ride some more and find an inn—except for oneday, when they had to stop for the night at an excuse for a way station.

By late morning on fourday, it was more than clear that they were nearing Hydolar. The road that they had followed ended at the main road along the north side of the Ohyde River, and the main road was actually stone-paved, even if there were often gaps in the paving stones. Beltur did notice that the carts and riders that they passed barely looked at them as they rode westward along the river.

While he'd studied the rough maps that Gustaan and Turlow had given him, he still had questions, some of which he should have thought out before. "Is there a section of barracks in the main trooper post that we could just take, instead of the marshaling post?" asked Beltur, worrying that the kay or so between the marshaling post and the main post might prove a problem.

"No, ser. You have to have written orders, or have a majer or commander personally order the billeting officer to assign barracks or officers' quarters in the main post. That's why we decided on the marshaling post. We say we're recovered wounded awaiting reassignment to another company. They don't have good records on the wounded who make it, and not many would pretend to be a trooper when they could get sent anywhere. It'll take a few days for them to assign us."

Beltur paused. "Then I'll have to stay at an inn, like we planned. You said most of the inns weren't near the palace."

"The ones a captain could afford aren't."

"What if I pretend that I'm the son of a rich merchant that doesn't like captains' quarters? Is there an expensive inn close to the palace?"

Gustaan grinned. "If you're willing to spend a lot of silvers, and a gold or two. The Palace Inn is right across the Duke's Square from the palace."

Beltur smiled in return. "If you billet yourself at the marshaling post, can you get out of there quickly if someone decides to assign you somewhere? And let me know?"

"We can do both. I can just send Turlow to you as a courier. I got the seamstress to make up some courier armbands. There are always rankers carrying messages."

"Should one of the men ride to the inn with me?"

Gustaan frowned, then shook his head. "You'd be outside the rules. That would make the ranker breaking rules as well. If you're rich no one would say anything so long as you met your duty assignments, but that wouldn't protect the ranker, and even a spoiled rich captain would know that."

"That undercaptain that caused you all the problems was like that?"

"He wasn't that smart," said Gustaan flatly.

Beltur nodded and turned his attention back to the road and the river to his left, its water grayish rather than blue and slow-moving. Several flatboats stacked high with goods seemed to drift with the current. The seemingly haphazard cargo stowage suggested that there were no rapids or stretches of rough water between Hydolar and Renklaar.

After riding another glass, the twelve were definitely on the outskirts of Hydolar, with small buildings and piers jutting into the murky water on the left, and run-down cots and cottages on the higher ground to the right of the road. Less than a kay ahead, Beltur could see red stone walls rising over the lower buildings, and he realized that Hydolar was a city within a city, the inner, and likely older, city being walled and on a low bluff. Within those walls was the palace. Gustaan and Turlow had mentioned the walls, but he hadn't pictured them as quite so tall, or how many houses and buildings were along the river on the east side of the walls.

He looked to the south side of the river opposite the walls, but could only see scattered huts on platforms rising out of the reeds.

"Why did they build Hydolar on the north side of the river?"

"Because so much of the south side is marshland and swamp."

Beltur couldn't help but wonder why one side of the river was marshy and the other side wasn't. *But that's not your problem.*

"The river gate's ahead, ser," said Gustaan quietly. "We shouldn't take it, but follow the wall road around the north side of the city. It's faster and all troopers posted here know that."

The gate guards barely looked at Beltur and the others as they followed the wall road away from the river gate. In the meantime, Beltur thought over all the possibilities that he and Gustaan had discussed on the ride from Haven, and what he should say in each case. He just hoped he could remember them all.

The farther they got from the river, though, the fewer houses and shops there were, until when they reached the redstone tower that marked the northeast corner of the walls enclosing the old city, there were only fields and scattered cots in the lower land to the north of the walls.

"There aren't any houses here," Beltur said as he turned Slowpoke onto the west-heading section of the wall road.

"That's because this part of the land floods most springs, and even sometimes in the late fall. Up ahead, where you see the road, that's the way to Jellico. It runs right into the north gate. That's the one you want to take on the way back. Just follow the gate avenue south until you come to the square. The palace is on the south side. Farther east, beyond its walls, you can see the headquarters post."

When the twelve rode past the gate, none of the guards gave them more than a glance, nor did the two troopers riding eastward shortly after that. West of the walls of the city proper there was a low swell where wheat grew. Looking at the lands surrounding the city, Beltur had to wonder if it once had been surrounded by water, or if those lands could still be flooded to thwart an attacking force. Beyond the swell through which the road dipped was another rise, on which was located a number of buildings surrounded by a brick wall little more than two yards high.

"That's the marshaling post?"

"That's it, ser."

Two guards stood outside the open iron gates, not quite blocking entry.

"Ser?"

"Headquarters detailed me to make sure these men reached the marshaling post."

"The first building on the left. Have them wait outside."

Beltur nodded and rode toward the one-story oblong structure. Once there, he dismounted and tied Slowpoke to the old iron rail, then made his way inside.

Seated at a table stacked with papers was a graying squad leader. "Ser?"

"I have a half squad of recovered wounded, with a squad leader."

"Where's the marshaling order for them?"

Beltur launched into what Gustaan had briefed him to say. "The majer said it had already been sent and not to worry."

"Not to worry? You bring in half a squad, ser, and I'm not to worry?"

"I just got here from Telsen, and I'm supposed to question a majer?"

"If you could, ser, the next time Majer Kellth tells you to do this, at least ask for one."

That suggested, as Gustaan had said was possible, that even headquarters occasionally lost orders. "I'll do that, Squad Leader. I'd like to ask a favor in return. These men fought hard, and they have good records. Can you make sure that they get in a good company?"

"We don't have control over that, ser."

"What's your name, Squad Leader?"

"Quaid, ser."

"Quaid, I'd very much appreciate it if you'd make an effort."

"I'll see what I can do, ser."

"Thank you."

"Now . . . let's go see these troopers. You say they're all recovered?" The squad leader heaved himself out of the chair.

"They are." Beltur followed the older trooper outside.

The marshaling squad leader looked to Gustaan. "You're in charge?"

"Until relieved, Squad Leader. Gustaan."

"You all look healthy." The older squad leader looked to Beltur. "There's nothing more for you to do, Captain. Remember about the marshaling orders next time . . . if you would."

"I appreciate the reminder." Beltur untied Slowpoke and mounted, then rode out of the marshaling post. The guards' nods as he left were perfunctory.

It took Beltur half a glass to ride back to the west gates of the inner city. The pair of guards there glanced at him, seemingly saw the captain's insignia on his collars, and just nodded as he rode past, heading due south on the avenue toward the Duke's palace. Near the gate, the houses stood wall-to-wall, but most were one or two stories, almost all built of stone or brick or some combination, with tile roofs. Closer to the square, the houses gave way to shops in three-story structures, with what appeared to be living quarters on the upper levels.

Even in Fenard, Beltur had never seen so many shops so close together, and the concentration of both fragrances and odors was almost overpowering in the damp still air of late midafternoon. He touched the dressing across his forehead—moist, but not soaking.

Just before he reached the north side of the square, he sensed the presence of two white mages in the west wing of the palace, the chaos swirling around them so strongly that he doubted either would be aware of his presence until he was closer, but certainly they'd sense him once he entered the palace unless he fully shielded himself.

The avenue seemed to end at the north side of the square, but then Beltur realized that it formed an oblong border around the paved space, in the center of which was a large fountain. Directly opposite Beltur, on the far side of the square, were the iron gates to the palace, set in a brick wall some four yards high. A bronze crest ornamented each gate, but Beltur couldn't tell what the crests represented because the gates were swung open. He turned Slowpoke to the right and began to ride around the square. The orderly array of carts and wagons reminded him more of Elparta than Fenard, as did the two patrollers he saw in green-and-gray uniforms.

He was almost abreast of the Palace Inn, which was to his right, before he noticed it, simply because he had been looking more in the direction of the square and the Duke's palace. Rather than a side yard and a stable, there was a paved lane leading to an arched entryway. Beltur could sense people in the inn and horses to the rear, and he guided Slowpoke up the lane, noting that the archway was high enough that he didn't even have to duck, an indication that coaches were expected more than infrequently.

He had just passed the archway when an older man liveried in blue trimmed with cream stepped out on the side porch.

"Captain . . . this is not a livery stable."

Beltur reined up Slowpoke. "I was under the impression that it is the Palace Inn. Am I mistaken?" His words were cool and formal.

"Are you here to see a guest or to deliver a message?"

"No. I'm here to stay for a few days, until I'm posted. I don't relish . . . my current accommodations."

"There are a few chambers on the third level that run two silvers a night. Those on the second level are five."

"What are the beds like on the third?"

"They are more than . . . adequate."

Beltur looked hard at the functionary and said, "I'd heard that your establishment was known for courtesy and respect. Perhaps I was mistaken. Or perhaps you take me for an ordinary travel-weary captain." Beltur extended order around the man, not enough to restrain him, but to create a feeling of presence.

The functionary swallowed. "I apologize, ser. How may we be of service?"

"A chamber with a washroom, and I'll need this uniform taken care of, and, of course, a stall with plenty of grain for my mount."

"Ah . . . the stall and feed are five coppers a night."

"Excellent."

The functionary rang a bell. In moments, a stableboy in blue appeared. Beltur followed him into the stable, which had well-swept stone floors. The stall given over to Slowpoke was not only clean but had fresh straw on the floor.

"Is there anything special about grooming him, ser?" asked the stableboy.

"You'd better let me unsaddle him. Don't push him. Talk to him, that's all." Beltur handed him a pair of coppers.

Before he could think of lifting the duffel, a blue-liveried porter appeared and took it.

Beltur followed him to an ornately carved counter of goldenwood at one side of the front foyer.

The clerk behind it looked at Beltur, his eyes taking in the dressing across Beltur's forehead below the visor cap. "Ahaarf tells me you'll be staying for several days, Captain . . ."

"Beltur, out of Telsen. That's correct."

"A third-floor chamber with a private washroom will be three silvers a night, and the stall is, as Ahaarf may have told you, five coppers—"

Beltur put two golds on the counter, both of them the recently minted ones from Hydlen that had been in the white mage's strongbox. "I'll be here for at least three days, but I won't know how much longer for a day or two."

"Thank you, Captain Beltur. I am Faarkad. If you need anything else, you only have to let me know."

"I will indeed. I trust there will be some warm water in the washroom. And can you clean this uniform?"

"Yes, ser. If you leave it with the hall porter in the morning, we can take care of that."

"Thank you."

Beltur followed the porter up the wide stairs to the third level. The chamber was certainly not as large as the one he and Jessyla had shared at Johlana's, but the bed was as wide, and the coverlet and the upholstery were all in blue and cream.

"Will that be all, ser?" asked the porter, a strapping young man.

"Yes, thank you." Beltur handed him two coppers as well.

Once he was alone in the chamber, he walked to the window, which, unsurprisingly, opened overlooking the rear stable. While waiting for the porter or a maid with the hot water, he unpacked the duffel and smoothed out the second uniform.

In less than two quints, he'd spent more than two golds, but he couldn't think of a better way to get within walking distance of the palace. He just hoped he could carry off the act as the wealthy provincial second son forced into service as an officer, at least for as long as necessary.

The hot water arrived, two kettles carried by a muscular older maid, who left with another pair of coppers. Then Beltur washed up, shaved, and then used a damp cloth to get the worst of the dust and grime off the uniform he'd been wearing. He put on another dressing and re-donned the uniform. Waiting until he sensed no one else was outside in the upper hall, he eased out of his chambers under a concealment and made his way down the stairs to the first level, exploring with his senses the two small, and currently empty, private dining salons, the public room, the covered and railed front porch where a single man—older, judging from his lower chaos/order balance—sat in the shade, apparently reading.

Then he sensed someone approaching the front counter, behind which stood the clerk.

"You actually let a mere captain in, Faarkad?"

"Ser . . . you said that, in the summer, if someone had golds and looked acceptable . . . He asked for a washroom and paid with two good minted golds, and he tipped the porters and the maid. He's up on the third level. He has to be the second or third son of a wealthy provincial. He has a trace of an accent, but he's well-spoken . . . and he pays. He's awaiting a posting, and he'll likely be gone in less than an eightday. We've had to deal with far worse. You remember that Gallosian merchant . . ."

"Don't remind me. Just don't make it a habit."

Beltur smiled. Faarkad had noticed the dressing on his forehead, but had said nothing to his superior about it. With that thought, he slipped away from the counter and into the back hall, where he dropped the concealment and walked toward the public room. It was almost late enough for an early dinner.

He couldn't help feeling a little guilty about his quarters and the meal he'd likely get, compared to what Gustaan and the others were doubtless getting, but there hadn't seemed any other way to get them close enough and comparatively safe while he did what was necessary. And he had promised them a healthy reward when they returned to Haven.

LXXVII

Fiveday morning, Beltur was up early, since he needed to eat and leave the inn before sixth glass. He turned his duty uniform over to the hall porter for cleaning, and then walked down to breakfast—cheesed eggs and ham rashers, with sweet dark bread and an ale. Like everything else at the Palace Inn, it was expensive—six coppers. He ate quickly.

The sole server in the public room looked at him as he finished the last morsel of bread and rose. "You'll have to hurry."

Beltur smiled and adjusted his cap. "I know."

"They really made you go back on duty while you're still wounded?"

"It's almost healed."

"Did the fighting turn your hair silver-white?"

"Actually, it did. It happens." He handed her a pair of coppers. "I'll likely see you tomorrow morning." Then he hurried out of the inn and in the direction of headquarters.

Once he was out of sight of anyone who might have been watching from the inn, he stepped into an alley off the avenue, and raised a concealment, but not a full one. That was tiring if he had to hold it for too long, and could wait until he neared the palace and the two white mages.

He walked carefully back toward the palace, noting that the main gates were closed, most likely because it was early, at least for everyone but troopers and their officers, and let his senses range over the building and its two wings. It didn't take him long to discover an entrance at the river end of the east wall surrounding the palace, where there was a great deal of activity.

The entrance used by tradesmen and teamsters, of course. Walking carefully so that no one ran into him, Beltur continued eastward past the main gates and then along the east palace wall. Even before he neared the side gate, he could sense the guards posted there, but there were no mages. From what else he could sense, the guards were inspecting every wagon that went through the gate into the bailey.

That made his entrance relatively simple. He just walked in close beside a large wagon, hidden by his concealment, and then eased toward one of the loading doors, moving inside the building. His progress from the serving and storage areas up into the administrative and function room was slow, partly because the corridors on the lower level were narrow, and he often had to wait for someone to leave a passageway before he could enter it.

While he wasn't totally sure, he suspected almost a glass had passed before he emerged from a service stairway into a wider corridor on the second level, the one he would have entered if he had come through the main gates. Two guards stood just inside the closed doorway that led to the front courtyard. Neither spoke, although the corridor was empty except for them and Beltur. He waited a time, but no one spoke. So Beltur turned and headed back in the direction of the river, passing several small chambers, one of which contained a fair amount of free chaos, although Beltur could sense no one in the room. *A study for one of the whites?*

He moved on, past empty chamber after empty chamber, before taking another narrow staircase up a level. The third level he judged to be the one devoted to the Duke and various functionaries, although, again, most of the chambers were empty. In the center of that level, he located a chamber with double doors, and with a pair of guards posted there, one on each side. Thinking that the space beyond might be an audience chamber, he eased closer to the guards, who he thought might be murmuring back and forth.

". . . won't be long now . . ."

". . . can't wait . . . all in a foul humor . . ."

Then, abruptly, bells pealed, and Beltur sensed people moving into the level where he stood from staircases, corridors, and who knew where. He pressed himself into a recessed alcove that held some sort of statue that he couldn't identify merely by sensing, and tried to keep track of what was happening.

You just got here earlier than all the functionaries did.

A man walked toward the pair of guards, then stopped and said, "The Duke won't be holding any audiences until first glass of the afternoon, today or tomorrow. He'll be in his study."

Whoever that functionary was turned and headed down the corridor. Beltur decided to follow him. Then, he sensed a growing presence of chaos and immediately put himself behind full shields. As he followed the man who'd informed the guards, he tried to discern where the white mage might be, then decided that he was a level below, and, for the moment, that suited Beltur.

The functionary turned left at the next side hallway, one much narrower, which ended at a doorway with an open door. Beyond the door was an open space, where two men sat at table desks.

"No audiences until this afternoon. You should be able to catch up by then. You can take the first audience, Bhaarkhan."

"The Montgren mess, ser?" asked one of the men.

"Don't mention it. Especially if one of the Duke's ears is around."

"No one knows—"

"Exactly. All you need to know is that Commander Vashkyt is acting marshal and that the Duke and the heir will be conferring with him when he arrives."

"That must be tomorrow."

"It hasn't been announced." The functionary walked into the small chamber behind the larger one and closed the door.

"You shouldn't have said anything," offered the man at the other table desk, who had not spoken before.

"Everyone knows—"

"Then don't say it. He's right. You know what it's like when the Duke's in one of his moods."

Neither man spoke, and both returned to what they were doing, which appeared to be copying, but what that might be Beltur couldn't tell under a concealment. He eased out of the chamber carefully because, while he was unseen, loud footsteps could certainly be heard.

He took a side corridor and headed farther west. It ended in the middle of a larger corridor. While the right side was unguarded, the left side was guarded by two troopers, which suggested to Beltur that it just might be where he needed to go. There was enough space between the troopers for Beltur to slowly make his way past without either being the wiser.

Farther down the corridor, there was another pair of guards posted outside another doorway. Beltur carefully made his way there, edging along the wall, then stopped a yard or so away, just to wait and listen to see what happened, since guards posted inside a guarded corridor suggested that the Duke just might be inside that chamber, or, if not the Duke, someone fairly highly placed.

"Straighten up," murmured one guard. "Seneschal Paaltrun's headed this way."

A man neared, clearly older from the fainter order/chaos around him.

After the door opened, Beltur heard just a few words before it closed.

"Honored heir, your sire . . ."

Those words suggested that the heir was alone in the chamber, possibly a small audience room, standing in for the Duke.

In a fraction of a quint, the door opened, and the seneschal stepped out, carefully closing it behind himself, if firmly, almost, Beltur thought, as if the man wanted to slam it shut and dared not.

Both guards relaxed slightly, but neither spoke.

Beltur waited, hoping someone else might arrive who would provide more information, or that the two troopers would. Neither happened. A good quint went by, and no one neared the small audience chamber, although Beltur sensed a number of people moving in and out of chambers on the unguarded end of the corridor.

Then he sensed a palpable and powerful chaotic presence headed in his direction. He stiffened, waiting to see if the white mage sensed him, even though he was fully and completely shielded, but the mage turned down the unguarded section of the corridor. Beltur slowly and quietly let out his breath.

"Did you sigh?" said one of the guards.

"Not me."

"Must be hearing things. Last thing I need now."

"Better here than some other places. Uh-oh." The trooper stiffened.

After a moment, so did the other one.

Beltur sensed three men striding down the corridor in his direction. Their steps suggested officers in a hurry. He tried to sense more, but all he could discern was a faint swirl of order and chaos, slightly more chaotic than orderly, surrounding the officer in the middle, who stopped short of the guards and said, "Commander Haarkyn to see the heir. At his request."

"Yes, ser." The shorter guard turned, rapped on the door, and announced, "Commander Haarkyn."

There was a muffled response that Beltur could not make out, and the guard opened the door.

The commander entered and closed the door.

Since neither the guards nor the two newcomers spoke, and since a commander wouldn't likely be accompanied by rankers, and since Beltur couldn't sense rank insignia, he deduced that the two who had accompanied the commander were officers, likely majers, possibly captains, but definitely not undercaptains.

The uneasy silence continued for half a quint. Then the commander left the audience chamber, closing the door firmly, just short of slamming it. He said nothing, just strode back down the corridor, the other two officers flanking him.

"Think he's going to Montgren?" murmured one guard.

The other shook his head. "With what? Not even a battalion left north of Worrak. Might be two companies in Renklaar. Wager old iron-ass had to tell the heir that."

The two lapsed into silence.

Beltur waited another quint.

Then the chamber door opened, and two men stepped out. One was another trooper, and that meant the other was likely the heir.

The heir announced, "We're done. We'll need this audience chamber tomorrow morning, with double the guards."

Then all four walked down the corridor.

Beltur followed them to a narrow doorway, where two more guards were posted. The door was iron-banded. That he could sense even as one of the guards opened it. The staircase beyond was also narrow. None of the guards accompanied the heir, and the door guard closed it behind him.

Beltur stepped back, thinking.

Delivering his message without having guards everywhere might be harder than he thought.

Meanwhile, you'd better scout out everything you can in the palace.

LXXVIII

By late afternoon, Beltur was more than tired. He'd scouted out all of the chambers on the second level of the palace while under a full concealment. He'd discovered three staircases up to the third level of the palace, all of which were heavily guarded and all of which had iron-bound thick doors, and that meant that any successful effort to get to the Duke would require some sort of brute order-and-chaos force . . . or subterfuge that would take days.

His best opportunity appeared to be to try to take advantage of either the small audience chamber or the audience hall, and, either way, those opportunities would have to wait until sixday. He'd also managed to stay far enough from the one white mage he'd sensed in the morning, as well as a second white who appeared to be somewhere on the third level, possibly as a protector of the Duke.

As he slipped out through the main gates, walking concealed behind a coach somewhere after third glass, his head pounding from the strain of holding full shields for so many glasses, Beltur began to wonder whether he could do what he had in mind.

You have to do something.

Once he was in the square, he dropped the part of his shields that concealed his order/chaos flows, and eased through the scattered afternoon shoppers until it was close to fourth glass, when he made his way to the inn stables and the stall where Slowpoke was.

The big gelding nuzzled him even before he dropped the concealment.

Beltur patted him in return. "It's good to see you, too. I hope you enjoyed your day of rest."

Slowpoke whuffed, almost skeptically, Beltur thought.

"I know. You like doing things. We all do, but right now, we both have to be patient, even though it's not in our natures."

Beltur turned as he sensed someone approaching and relaxed as he saw it was only one of the stableboys.

"Ser . . . I didn't see you come in."

"I just wanted to check on my horse."

"He's doing fine. You came from fighting, didn't you?"

"An eightday or so ago," Beltur admitted. "Did you grow up here in Hydolar?"

"Yes, ser. My da's the head ostler here. I want to be a trooper. He says it's better to be an ostler."

"You'll likely live longer as an ostler." Beltur doubtless wasn't saying anything the youth hadn't heard, but he couldn't encourage him to be a trooper, especially in Hydlen.

"That's what he says," the boy replied glumly. "Can I do anything for you . . . or your horse?"

Not bothering to hide a smile, Beltur handed him a pair of coppers. "He's a big gelding. He could use a few more oats."

"Yes, ser."

After making certain that Slowpoke got his oats, Beltur made his way back to the inn proper and to his chamber.

His gear had been looked through and replaced in close to the same order as he'd left it. Beltur nodded. There was nothing in it to indicate that he was anything except a trooper captain, and all his coins were secreted in what he wore. He washed up, then made his way down to the public room, where only a third of the tables were occupied, most likely because it was summer and because it was comparatively early.

Beltur had just ordered a pale ale and had taken a single swallow when, out of the corner of his eye, he caught sight of a green uniform. He forced himself to turn slowly as if casually studying the room. He wasn't totally surprised to see Turlow moving toward him. The ranker wore a white-edged green armband Beltur hadn't seen before, but that meant that Turlow was a messenger or courier, or impersonating one.

"A message from the majer, Captain," said Turlow, just loud enough to be overheard.

Beltur motioned to the server. "I'll be back in a moment." Then, leaving his ale on the table, he followed Turlow out to the front porch.

"How did you find me?"

"I just asked for a Captain Beltur. The fellow at the desk said you were in the public room."

That meant that Faarkad was keeping a close eye on him.

"Things are fine now, ser. We've got about three days before we'll be assigned. We're now in the reassignment barracks. That's two buildings back from where you left us."

"I'm hoping I can do what I need to tomorrow morning. If I can, we'll need to leave as soon as possible. I'll find my way there. If I can't get it done tomorrow, it may take until oneday."

"Tomorrow would be better, ser. Squad Leader thinks there will be problems if we stay much longer."

"I have the same feeling, but I've run into a few difficulties."

"Anything we can help with, ser?"

"I don't think so, but I'll find you all if I need you."

"Yes, ser." Turlow stepped back, inclined his head, then turned sharply and left.

As Beltur headed back to the public room, Faarkad stepped from behind the counter. "How are you finding the Palace Inn, Captain?"

"Comfortable enough, and better than the cramped quarters where I'd otherwise be sleeping."

"Your other uniform will be in your room early tomorrow morning."

"Most likely after I've left for duty," replied Beltur. "But I do appreciate it."

"Might I ask . . . ?"

"You could, but if I said too much, Commander Haarkyn wouldn't like it." Beltur smiled politely, then continued on to the public room. He could tell that the commander's name had startled Faarkad. He was gambling that the clerk and greeter didn't have any direct contact with Haarkyn.

Just a few moments after he returned to his table, and sensed the ale he'd left behind, finding no traces of chaos, the server returned with his meal, a fowl breast with a cream sauce, filigreed lace potatoes, and green beans almandine. Beltur took a bite, enjoying the taste, even as he tried to listen to other conversations around him.

". . . say that the Duke . . . still furious . . ."

". . . wore red shimmersilk . . . absolute nerve of her . . ."

". . . his white wizard turned Marshal Raxnyr into ashes . . ."

". . . hate having to stay here . . . summer . . ."

". . . Duke would have left for the summer palace . . . except . . ."

". . . young captain there, dressing on his forehead . . . think he came back . . . ?"

". . . too young to be important . . . merchant's younger brat . . ."

Beltur lingered over the meal, but didn't hear anything more interesting, and finally finished his second ale, then left the public room, another two silvers poorer, absently wondering who had the coins to stay at places like the Palace Inn often or for any length of time.

LXXIX

Although Beltur fell asleep early, most likely because he was tired from carrying full shields for much of fiveday, he slept uneasily and woke early on sixday. He was still pondering how to get into the audience room, when he suddenly smiled.

There's more than one way to deliver a message.

He washed up, shaved, and dressed in the darkness just before dawn, then eased out of his chamber under a simple concealment and made his way down to the main level, where after quietly searching, he found an inkwell, a pen, and some paper. After returning to his rooms, he wrote out what was necessary, let the words dry, and then, again using the concealment, returned the inkwell and pen, after which he visited the kitchen and made off with a loaf of bread and some cheese. He ate both in the stable after checking on Slowpoke.

After dawn, unconcealed, he walked from the stable out across the almost empty square, noticing that the main gates were both closed and guarded, and then around toward the bailey gate. As he half expected, it was closed as he walked past it in the direction of the river. Then, roughly fifty yards farther south, he turned in to a narrow lane and ducked into the doorway of a cooperage that had not yet opened. There he raised a concealment. Then he walked back to the bailey gate and waited.

A quint or so later, two guards appeared and opened the gate. Under his concealment, Beltur simply walked between them and made his way to the door which they had used to enter the bailey from the palace. He opened it quietly and stepped inside. There was no one in the empty hallway. From there, quiet step by step, he made his way up to the second level, which, as he suspected might be the case, was almost totally empty except for a bevy of women scrubbing and polishing the floors. He was careful to give them—and the sections of the floor that seemed damp—a wide berth, not wanting boot tracks to appear before the eyes of any of the women.

As Beltur had hoped, not only was the small audience chamber where the heir had been seeing officers the morning before unguarded and empty, but the door was not locked . . . because there was no lock, just a sliding bolt on the inside. He had to wait almost a quint until the scrub women and the polishers were farther down the wide hall before he dared to open the door and slip inside.

Once there, he dropped the concealment so that he could see exactly how the chamber was set up and where he could be out of the way and where even his breathing could not be heard. At the end of the chamber opposite the door was a dais, raised not quite half a yard, floored in goldenwood, on which was a large and ornate goldenwood armchair, upholstered in dark green velvet, trimmed with gold. The rest of the dais was empty, but the two yards on each side of the chair could accommodate other functionaries or guards, if standing. Below the dais on each side were narrow table desks, possibly for scriveners to record proceedings, although Beltur had sensed no scriveners leaving the audience chamber the day before. The polished green marble floor below the dais stretched some five yards from door to dais and contained no chairs except for the backed stools tucked mostly under each table desk.

Definitely no place to hide . . . except with a concealment. The only spots where Beltur could likely stand without too much risk of having someone bump into him were the corners on the wall holding the doorway.

He walked to the corner to the left of the door and sat down to wait, easing just a visual concealment around himself. He knew he'd sense any of the whites long before they could sense him. In the meantime, he most likely had a lengthy wait.

More than a glass passed before the cleaning women vanished, and several more quints passed before the interior palace guards appeared. Shortly, a trooper opened the audience room and stepped inside, looking around.

"It's empty, like always. You look, now."

So they both have to look.

From what Beltur had already seen and overheard, Duke Massyngal worried a great deal about his personal safety.

I can't imagine why. He smiled at the sarcastic thought and settled back to wait some more, hoping that events would go the way he had overheard them being described the day before, and knowing that they might not.

Then, around eighth glass, or so Beltur judged, he sensed quite a few people seemingly headed toward the audience chamber, including one of the strong white mages. He immediately shielded himself completely, waiting.

A third of a quint passed, and the door opened again. This time the white mage peered in, obviously sensing something. Beltur forced himself to remain perfectly still.

"There's more order around here than there should be." The words were to someone standing outside the chamber and between the two troopers standing guard.

"The heir was the last one here, ser."

"The current heir doesn't have that kind of order."

"The healer has been visiting him every day. For that boil."

"That might be it. Still . . ." The white stepped inside the chamber and walked to the dais, then to the two table desks.

With all the chaos swirling around the mage, Beltur wondered how he could sense any order at all.

Finally, the white turned and stepped out, saying, "The chamber's empty. You stay here. Right there." Before the white closed the door, Beltur realized that the other figure was younger and also was a chaos mage, if so much weaker that he'd been initially masked by the chaos of the stronger mage.

Another quint passed.

Then Beltur sensed what could only be called an entourage approaching. He stood and pressed himself into the corner, waiting.

Once more, the strong white was the one who entered the chamber, but instead of looking around he moved to the dais and stood beside the audience chair, on the left facing the door. Then another man entered, and he took a position on the right of the chair.

Neither spoke as a third figure entered and made his way to the chair, settling into place.

The chamber door closed, with the weaker white guarding the door from outside.

"Galmaas . . ." rasped the man in the chair, "why did you suggest that we formally invest Vashkyt as marshal?"

"If you leave him as acting marshal, that weakens his authority."

"I could just issue a proclamation naming him and be done with it."

"Sire . . . this isn't a full investiture. It's enough that Marshal Vashkyt can announce he was invested by you. That will be useful in the seasons to come."

"That's a stoat-like way of saying that he needs everything he can use to send another army against those blue bastards."

"He'll need that authority even to raise and conscript the necessary forces, Sire."

"As my heir, you need to remind him . . ." Massyngal shook his head. "All of you are useless. Fear is all any of you understand. Fear and power." He turned his head toward the white. "Isn't that so, Erhlyn?"

"As you have said, Your Grace, power must engender respect and even fear."

"Respect and fear. Exactly," added Galmaas. "We must obliterate Haven and devastate Montgren."

"We?" asked Massyngal acidly.

"You are 'We,'" replied the heir. "You act and speak for all of Hydlen."

"Your brother had difficulty remembering that. I trust you will not."

"I understand absolutely, Sire. Your word is and must always be the law."

Beltur could sense the untruth, and the fawning deception, as doubtless could Erhlyn, and he wanted to shake his head. Before he had actually been inside Massyngal's palace, Beltur had thought to deliver a message by killing Massyngal and making it clear that the same could happen to the heir. Standing there and listening, he was actually glad he hadn't tried that approach. It would have been more dangerous and gained him—and Haven—even less than what he now planned. *If you can make it work.*

He swallowed silently, forcing himself to wait.

It seemed like glasses, but it was less than a third of a quint before a knock on the door was followed by the words, "Acting Marshal Vashkyt is here at your request, Your Grace."

"Have him enter," declared Massyngal, the volume of his voice only making its raspiness more cutting.

The door opened, and Vashkyt stepped inside, immediately taking one step and bowing deeply. "Your Grace and Mightiness, you summoned me?"

"Step forward. I don't like shouting." Massyngal gestured to a point a yard from the edge of the dais.

Vashkyt stepped forward and stopped where the Duke had gestured, inclining his head respectfully.

"In view of the tasks before you, Vashkyt, I have decided to name you as full marshal of Hydlen, with all the rights and powers of that position. I will so proclaim after this audience. That should quiet any rumors that I lack confidence in you or that you will soon be gone."

"I greatly appreciate your confidence in me, Your Mightiness."

"I'll also expect a written plan for the destruction of Haven and the subjugation of Montgren in no less than an eightday."

"Knowing your concerns, Your Grace, I have already begun working on such a plan."

"Excellent. I don't ever want another miserable effort like that of your predecessor."

"You have made that quite clear, Your Mightiness."

"Do you have any questions, Vashkyt?" asked Massyngal.

At that moment, Beltur realized that the audience was going to be short, very short, possibly lasting only a few more moments.

He immediately clamped a full order containment around Erhlyn, adding as much free order as he could draw from nearby, and compressing the white's shields back against his skin and garments. Then Beltur flattened himself against the floor and concentrated on holding that containment.

The white tried to lash out with such force that Beltur could feel the containment weakening. *You . . . will . . . not . . . break . . . out!*

For a moment, none of the non-mages in the room moved, as if they knew something was happening, but not what. That moment seemed to stretch.

Beltur felt as though his head was splitting, with iron bands constricting against it, but knew that was because of the effort that Erhlyn was making to break the skintight containment. Another wave of chaos pressed against the containment.

"Guards!" shouted someone.

As that word died away, Beltur sensed two things—a black mist of death and an explosion of order and chaos.

In that instant, he added another layer of shields, dropping the full concealment . . . and hoped they'd hold against the conflagration racing from the exploding chaos-fireball that had been Erhlyn. At the same moment, the door opened.

A wall of white rushed over Beltur, followed by a momentary blackness.

At least, he thought it was momentary, but there was silence as he struggled to his feet in a chamber that held only ashes . . . and him.

He could sense that the wave of exploding order and chaos had overwhelmed the white who'd stood in the open doorway, and thrown the troopers away from the door. He managed to throw a concealment around himself, knowing he couldn't hold both shields and concealment, and judging that, if he weren't seen, he wouldn't need the shields.

Then he laid the single sheet of paper in the doorway and stepped away from the troopers who were running toward the audience chamber, keeping himself against the wall as, slow step by step, he made his way to the service stairway he'd used to get to the second level. Once inside the stairway, he sensed no one near and dropped the concealment, knowing that he didn't have the strength to hold it long and that he'd need it more later. And every moment he wasn't carrying shields would allow him some additional time to recover. Even if he were to be seen, he doubted any servants behind the walls would actually confront him.

Once on the first level, he used the concealment to leave through the bailey gates, then dropped it as soon as he found an alcove to step into. From there he walked through the square, carrying the lightest of personal shields, simply because he didn't feel like getting robbed, then used the side entrance to the inn and reached his chamber undetected, where he quickly packed everything into his duffel.

A glance in the mirror showed that his face and hands were reddened, as if he'd taken far too much sun, but there wasn't much he could do about that.

Unfortunately he ran into the hall porter just outside his chamber as he was leaving, duffel in hand.

"What happened to you?" asked the porter.

"There was a fire in the palace. I was too close. I've been told to take quarters at the post. Immediately."

"That doesn't sound good."

"It's not." Beltur pressed a silver on the porter. "Thank you for taking care of my uniform."

"My pleasure, Captain."

Beltur hurried down the staircase carrying his duffel, wondering if he should have let himself be seen. *But you'll need the concealment later.*

In less than half a quint, he'd saddled Slowpoke and was riding out of the Palace Inn. He glanced across the square at the palace, but nothing seemed changed, nothing at all.

He couldn't help but wonder at why there weren't more people scurrying around. *Are they all so stunned that no one is quite sure what to do?* That could be, Beltur reflected. He'd just removed the Duke, his heir, and the top military officer. *But that quiet won't last all that long.*

Another half quint passed before he was through the north gates and riding west toward the marshaling post. When he did reach the post, the guards barely glanced at him as he rode through and headed in the direction of the barracks that Turlow had described.

He had just reined up outside what he thought was the right building when a trooper in greens gestured from across the street that ran through the center of the low-walled post. After a moment, Beltur recognized Turlow and rode over to meet the trooper.

"Ser. Everyone but me is in the big barn here. The squad leader has had one of us watching since noon," said Turlow. "He managed to get us on stable duty. No one likes that so it wasn't hard to make the switch. Everyone else in the squad is there."

"Good. We need to leave immediately."

"All the gear is in the stable. Gustaan thought that might be what happened."

"He did?"

"Ah . . . yes, ser. Something like that."

Meaning you're not about to tell me. "Just lead the way to where he is."

"Yes, ser."

Beltur followed Turlow into the east side of the spacious barn, less than half of which seemed to contain horses, and toward what appeared to be a tack room. Inside it, several troopers looked to be cleaning saddles. Presumably they were Beltur's men, although he couldn't see them clearly enough to determine that.

"Squad Leader," called Turlow, with a grin.

Gustaan stepped out of the tack room, then smiled broadly. "Ser! It's good to see you." He frowned. "Your face looks burned, or you got too much sun."

"It's even better to see you, but we need to get out of here now. I'll explain later."

"We'll be ready to go in less than a quint."

"Will the guards protest if we just ride out?"

"No, but the captain in charge of the stable will. He's been watching us closely. We managed to get the gear here from the barracks early this morning, but he keeps checking on what we're doing. He'll likely be here in a few moments."

"Then we'll need to tie him up and stash him somewhere he won't be found for a glass or so." Beltur paused. "There's one thing. I really could use some ale, or something to eat. It's been a very long day already . . . and I can't do much magery."

"Then you've done a lot already today."

"More than I planned."

Gustaan looked past Beltur and asked casually, "Can you put a containment around the captain. He's coming to see why you're here, interrupting the work."

Beltur turned in the saddle and waited for the graying captain to reach him and Slowpoke.

"Might I ask what you're doing here, Captain?"

"I came to say goodbye to my old squad leader before I left Hydolar." Beltur smiled. "Is that a problem?"

"Couldn't you have waited until after duty hours?"

"By then, I'll be long gone, Captain," replied Beltur.

The older captain frowned. "It's most irregular."

"I know. The entire day has been irregular, what with the fire in the palace."

"A fire in the palace?" The captain looked shocked.

Gustaan looked only surprised.

"Haven't you heard? No one knows who did it. Some say it was a Certan mage, and others think it was a Montgren mage that set it. You might want to check and see if you've gotten a dispatch about it. There was something about the marshal, but no one would tell me. They just told me to proceed."

"I suppose I should. You'll be gone, I gather, when I return."

"I'll be gone in a small fraction of a quint," agreed Beltur.

Once the captain was out of sight, Gustaan gestured. Seemingly, from nowhere, the rest of Beltur's half squad appeared, leading out mounts already loaded.

Beltur couldn't quite believe that the older captain didn't even run into the street as the twelve riders and the spare mount headed toward the main gates, but he didn't.

Nor did the gate guards even ask anything as Beltur led his men out of the marshaling post. Once they were well away from the gates, Gustaan handed Beltur a chunk of bread and a water bottle.

"It's got ale. Not much better than Bythalt's, but it's ale."

"That sounds wonderful." Beltur uncorked the water bottle and took a long swallow. The ale even tasted good.

LXXX

Although Beltur half expected Hydlenese pursuit of some kind, nothing of the sort ensued, but that didn't keep him from looking over his shoulder and sensing back toward Hydolar continually for the next five days, as he and his half squad rode back toward Haven along the way that they had come almost two eightdays before. None of the innkeepers or locals in the towns in which they stopped showed any more interest in them than they had on the trip to Hydolar. All were polite and took Beltur's silvers and golds, but evinced no obvious interest in the apparent Hydlenese troopers, almost as if they wished them to depart without any fuss. And that was fine with Beltur, although he was very aware of the fact that they well might be riding just ahead of the news about the Duke.

It might be hard to connect twelve troopers and an apparently wounded captain with a mage-fire in the palace, but Beltur didn't intend to stay in Hydlen any longer than necessary. So it was a relief when in the early afternoon on threeday he and the others turned east off the road to Hydolar and onto the road to Haven that eventually led on to Lydiar.

Part of that relief was his sense of a strong ordered presence ahead, confirmed when he finally saw a silver-haired figure in Haven blue, accompanied by two men, also in the same blue. For a moment, he blinked, because he'd been looking for Jessyla as if she still had red hair.

"We've got a welcoming group, it seems," declared Gustaan.

"I'm glad to see them."

"Not as glad as she is to see you, I'd wager," returned the squad leader.

Beltur wasn't about to take that wager, and he couldn't stop smiling as he rode toward Jessyla, Therran, and Dussef. The three swung their mounts so that Therran and Dussef rode beside Gustaan, who had slowed his horse to allow Jessyla to ease the mare in beside Slowpoke.

Jessyla's eyes went to Beltur's face. "You got your skin burned. Is that all?"

"You can sense that's all that happened to me." In turn, he ran his senses over her, but could discern nothing amiss. "You're out here to meet us?" He grinned. "We haven't been gone that long."

"Long enough, but I also didn't want people in Haven shocked by a squad in Hydlenese green riding into town, especially since I knew that none of you took other uniforms."

"That would have been too dangerous. Are Daaskin and his squad still here? How is the town patrol working out? And Tulya and Taelya?"

She smiled. "So many questions. Dussef here has done quite nicely running the patrol. He and Graalur have also been training the new patrollers. Tulya and Taelya are fine. And Daaskin and his squad are still here. He said he wouldn't leave until you came back. I think he really meant until he knew whether you'd been successful."

"Successful . . . yes . . . after a fashion. Things didn't work out quite the way I'd planned."

"And?" Her voice was anxious.

"Duke Massyngal is dead. So is his heir, and so is the current marshal, well, the man who was marshal when he perished. Also, one very strong white mage and one weak white mage. And I left a message outside the audience room full of ashes and little else that said a similar fate would await any ruler of Hydlen who again attempted an attack against either Haven or Montgren. Then we sneaked away, and no one even chased us."

From behind them, Gustaan added, "That's because they never even knew how it happened. We didn't, either, until he told us."

For a moment, Jessyla said nothing.

"You told me to be careful, and not to do anything that I couldn't safely carry off. Delivering a message in person would have been much more dangerous."

Abruptly, she laughed. "Only you . . . only you would find a way to deliver such a message."

"I did my best to follow your directions," Beltur said. "Five deaths are much to be preferred to another battle like the last."

"Very much. I'd think that would give the Duke's successor pause."

"I think it will, but," Beltur shrugged tiredly, "at the very least, it will buy us more time. Quite a bit more, I think. The death of the ruler, the heir, and the marshal should have gotten the attention of their successors. And I also realized that there's likely only one white mage left in Hydolar, and possibly in all of northern Hydlen. If that doesn't send a message," he grinned raggedly, "we could do something like that again."

"I doubt that will be necessary," she said dryly, "especially if they couldn't even figure out how you did it." Then she added, her voice even, "I . . . we . . . got a letter. Yesterday."

"Is that good or bad?"

"It's from Johlana." Abruptly, she broke into a wide smile. "She and Jorhan are leaving Axalt. They're coming here . . . to stay, and to open a factorage. They're bringing Mother . . ."

"And?"

"Auntie's coming, too."

Beltur shook his head, with an expression between ruefulness and amusement. "They'll need houses."

"I know. I've already talked to Jaegyr."

"You seem to have everything well in hand."

"Everything but you."

"Oh . . . you have me very well in hand." Beltur couldn't help smiling, once again.

She returned the smile. "Now . . . we need to get you all back into town and out of those awful green uniforms."

Beltur could agree to that . . . and to being home.

LXXXI

Much, much later, as Jessyla and Beltur lay side by side in the bed that Jaegyr had made for them, Jessyla asked quietly, "Are you awake?"

"I am. Why?"

"I was thinking. Everything—the defeat of the Prefect in Spidlar, the corruption of the blacks in Spidlar, the deaths of Barrynt, Emlyn, Sarysta, massacres, the death of Massyngal . . . all of it happened because the Prefect killed your uncle. Haven will become Fairhaven, and the entire history of Candar will be changed. Yet a hundred years from now, no one will know that the murder of a white mage in Fenard led to the destruction of an entire Hydlenese army and the beginning of a city that may change Candar even more."

"Most people don't know that now, and no one will recall anything more than the Duke died in ten years," replied Beltur.

"In ten years?" Jessyla laughed warmly. "More like ten eightdays. That doesn't alter the fact that you changed history, just so we could find a place where we could live and be accepted."

"Whatever the future brings, I didn't do it. We did. You, me, Lhadoraak, Tulya, and Taelya, maybe even Korsaen, Maeyora, and the Duchess. And don't forget the lesson of Elshon."

"Elshon?"

"The renegade white mage, the one who had the vision of the white city rising from Haven. His dream wasn't what he thought it would be . . . and ours likely won't be, either."

She eased her arms back around him. "That's for the future to judge. We can only do what we can." Then she drew him to her again.